OF LOVE AND LIFE

OF LOVE AND LIFE

Three novels selected and condensed
by Reader's Digest

CONDENSED BOOKS DIVISION
The Reader's Digest Association Limited, London

With the exception of actual personages identified as such, the characters and incidents in the fictional selections in this volume are entirely the product of the authors' imaginations and have no relation to any person or event in real life.

The Reader's Digest Association Limited
11 Westferry Circus, Canary Wharf, London E14 4HE

www.readersdigest.co.uk

ISBN 0-276-42494-8

For information as to ownership of copyright in the material of this book, and acknowledgments, see last page.

CONTENTS

anna maxted

GETTING OVER IT

From the moment her father dies, Helen Bradshaw's life is never the same. But why? They weren't that close. Helen is not even sure if her father loved her—he nicknamed her the Grinch, didn't he? As she helps her mother come to terms with her loss, Helen tries to carry on her life as usual but finds she can no longer drown her sorrows in a bottle of tequila or cheer herself up with a new man. Reluctantly, she realises that the time has come to confront her past and to resolve, once and for all, her relationship with her father.

Chapter 1

WHEN IT HAPPENED, I wasn't ready for it. I expected it about as much as I expect to win Miss World and be flown around the planet and forced to work with screaming children. Which is to say, it was a preposterous notion and I never even considered it. And, being so unprepared I reacted like Scooby Doo chancing upon a ghost. I followed my instinct, which turned out to be hopelessly lost and rubbish at map-reading.

Maybe I was too confused to do the right thing. After all, the right thing rarely involves fun and mostly means making the least exciting choice, like waiting for the ready-cook pizza you've torn from the oven to cool to under 200 degrees before biting into it. Or deciding not to buy those sexy tower-heeled boots because they'll savage your shins, squeeze your toes white, lend you the posture of Early Man, and a vast chunk of your salary will moulder away at the back of your wardrobe.

That said, the day it all began, I came close to making a very smart choice. Here it is, bravely scrawled in black ink, in my blue Letts diary:

I am dumping Jasper, tomorrow.

Words that whisk me back to another time. Barely one year ago but it seems like an age. Yet July 16 remains as sharp in my mind as if it was today. Maybe it is today. And this is how today begins:

I am dumping Jasper, tomorrow.

He deserves it for being called Jasper, for a start. And for a finish, he falls several thousand feet below acceptable boyfriend standard.

Unfortunately, Jasper is beautiful. Tall, which I like. I'm five foot one, but I wear five-inch heels so he doesn't notice the discrepancy. He has floppy brown hair, paradise-blue eyes, and, my favourite, good bone structure. And, despite being the most selfish man I've ever met—quite a feat—he's a tiger in the sack.

I'm on my way there now. Sackbound. For one last bout. Except I'm stuck in traffic on Park Road. There appear to be roadworks with no one doing any work. I'm trapped in my elderly grey Toyota Corolla (a cast-off from my mother who was thrilled to be rid of it), and trying to stay calm. In the last twenty minutes I've rolled forward a total of five inches. It's 2.54. I'm due at Jasper's at 3.30. Great. My mobile is out of batteries. I pick the skin on my lip. Right. I'm phoning him.

I assess the gridlock—yes, it's gridlocked—leap out of the car, dash across the road to the phone box, and dial Jasper's number. *Brrrt brrt. Brrrt brrt.* Where *is* he? He can't have forgotten. Shit, the traffic's moving. I ring his mobile—joy! he answers. 'Jasper Sanderson.' He sounds suspiciously out of breath.

'Why are you out of breath?' I say sharply.

'Who's this?' he says. Jesus!

'Your girlfriend. Helen, remember?' I say. 'Listen, I'm going to be late, I'm stuck in traffic. Why are you out of breath?'

'I'm playing tennis. Bugger, I forgot you were coming over. It'll take me a while to get home. Spare key's under the mat.'

He beeps off. 'You're such an original,' I say sourly, and look up to see the gridlock has cleared and swarms of furious drivers are hooting venomously at the Toyota as they swerve round it.

Forty minutes later I arrive at Jasper's Fulham flat. I kick the mat to scare off spiders, gingerly lift a corner with two fingers, and retrieve the key. Ingenious, Jasper! The place is a replica of his parents' house. There's even a silver-framed picture of his mother on the hall table—happily, he's never introduced me. His most heinous interior crime, however, is a set of ugly nautical paintings that dominate the pale walls. I poke the scatter of post to check for correspondence from other women, and see the green light of his answering machine flashing for attention. Jasper calling to announce a further delay. I press PLAY.

As the machine whirrs, the key turns in the lock. Jasper flings open the door and I turn, smiling, to face him. Oof he's gorgeous. I'll dump him next week. This week, he's mine to have and to hold and to feel and to feel bad about. He's like eating chocolate for breakfast—makes you feel sluttish, you know you shouldn't, you ought to stick to what's wholesome, but Weetabix is depressing even with raisins in it. Jasper is un-nutritious and delicious. He opens his eminently kissable mouth to say 'Hiya, babe!' but is beaten to it by a high silvery voice that echoes chirpily from one eggshell wall to the other.

'Hiya, babe!' trills the voice. 'It's me! Call me! Kiss! Kiss!'

Jasper and I both stare at the answering machine which, having imparted its treachery, is now primly silent. Knowing the answer, I croak, à la Quentin Tarantino, 'Who the fucking fuck was that?'

Jasper is not amused. If this were Hollywood there would be a muscle twitching in his jaw and his chiselled face would turn pale under its caramel tan. As it is, he carefully places his sports bag on the floor, and rests his tennis racket neatly on top of it. At least he *was* playing tennis, although he's so damn sneaky I wouldn't be surprised if it was an elaborate cover. He gazes at my red fear-ruffled face and says smoothly, 'My ex. She likes to keep in touch.'

I'll bet she does. 'When did you last see her?' I snarl.

'A week ago,' he replies. 'We just talked.' Ho really.

I'm like Fox Mulder. I want to believe. And Jasper wants me to believe too. He's tilted his face to a penitent angle. Cute, but from what I know of Jasper, plus the gut-crunching phrase 'it's me', induces scepticism. 'It's *me*' is as proprietorial as a Doberman guarding a chocolate biscuit. A woman does not ring an ex-boyfriend and say 'It's me', because for all she knows—and *she* obviously doesn't—there is now another me. *Me*.

'Did you have sex with her?' I roar.

Jasper looks hurt. 'Of course I didn't, Helen,' he purrs. 'Louisa calls everyone "babe".'

Names ending in *ah*. Argh! I narrow my eyes and give him my best shot at a cold stare. The big brave words 'You're sacked' are warm, ready to roll, but they stick, feeble and reluctant, in my throat. Now, I tell myself, is not the moment. Why, he'll think I'm in love with him! The only decent thing to do is to walk. 'I'm going home,' I say huffily. The rat steps gratefully aside. I intend to sweep out in a *Gone with the Wind* flourish and it's going to plan until I reach the doorstep and trip. I stumble, and I'm unsure if the snorty-gasp I hear is Jasper not quite trying to suppress mirth, but I don't look back to find out. Face clenched, I stomp down his concrete garden path, plonk into the Toyota, lurch hurtle a three-point turn and rattle off into the fading afternoon.

I wrestle my mobile out of my bag in case he calls, grovelling, then remember it's dead. Piece of crap. You wanker. I have no intention of gracefully erasing myself from the picture so Louis-*ah* can steal the scene. She's reared her smugly head before. A month into our relationship, as I like to call it. Jasper called to say he couldn't meet as he was staying with his friend Daniel in Notting Hill. Beyond my surprise that

Jasper *had* a friend in Notting Hill, I didn't question it. I trusted him. The next afternoon, he suddenly said, 'I told you a pack of lies last night.' *What?* 'I . . . I stayed with my ex.' Turned out he'd missed the last tube home (he doesn't drive, his most unfanciable trait) and so he'd walked to Kensington and rung on the ex's doorbell. 'She was really good about it.' Good about it! I'm sure she was great about it! Further interrogation revealed that she'd fed him Cornflakes with brown sugar for breakfast. The sly witch—she was trying to nurture him! Happily, she was too needy to appeal and so a large bowl of cereal was wasted. But maybe she's sharpened up. And maybe *my* appeal is blunted. Oops, my personality is showing.

The first weeks were glossy enough. I met Jasper at a book launch—for a paperback sex manual. I'd gone from work with Lizzy and Tina. Partly because Laetitia, our misnomered features editor, didn't want to go, and it is my job as features skivvy on *Girltime* magazine to pick up her slack. And also because Tina, the fashion assistant, and I are hardcore champagne tarts—anything for a free chug of Krug (or Asti, let's face it). And although Lizzy is health and beauty assistant in professional and personal life and her drink of choice is soya milk, she can be persuaded.

The launch was in a smelly Soho backstreet. I'd glammed up for the occasion—black trousers, black boots (five inches), black top. The celebrity funeral look. I'd also smeared a blop of metallic silver glitter on my cheekbones. It looked scarily Abba-ish.

Usually I don't talk to people at parties. I survey the hordes of glamorous best friends all gabbling, laughing, bonding in impenetrable cliques and I want to run away home. But the Jasper party was different. I was one of a sparkly three-girl group, I glugged two glasses of sparkly wine in the first twenty minutes, and I was smeared in more sparkly glitter than a Christmas fairy. I sparkled! So it was only natural that Jasper appeared before me and offered me a fag.

'I don't smoke,' I said primly. In a flash of brilliance I added coyly, 'I'm a good girl.'

He didn't miss a beat. He replied, 'Well, you look filthy.'

It was the best compliment I've ever had. What could I do but shag him out of gratitude?

Jasper was 'in publishing', which turned out to mean he wrote press releases for a pipsqueak company based in Hounslow. I, therefore, terrier-torso assistant on *Girltime* magazine based in Covent Garden, was a great contact. Not that we review many books on Elizabethan sanitation or the indigenous insects of Guatemala but, roughly at the point I looked on his ravishing face and he gazed at my sparkly one, we decided to do business together. For a few weeks I upheld my airbrushed image. I exaggerated the importance of my job. And I edited all trace of squareness from my conversation and pumped up the wacky free-spirit factor. Of course, I realised after three days that we had bugger all in common—he called orange juice 'OJ' and was stockpiling to put his son through Eton (a tad premature as he didn't yet have one)—but I don't like sameyness so it was fine by me.

But sometimes, more recently, I've been sure the bubble is at bursting point. We spent an afternoon in the park last Saturday and I swear we had nothing to say to each other. I brooded all the way home.

So, as the silences grow, I slowly blow my sassy cover. He doesn't seem to have twigged, but I feel increasingly uncomfortable. He doesn't get my jokes and I feel wrong and not right. I am so not right for Jasper and he is so not right for me but he still seems amused by me. Breaking up is hard to do. Louis*ah* does not make it easi*ah*.

I swing into Swiss Cottage and begin the three-hour search for a parking space. You'd think no one ever went out around here. Some time the next day I manage to squeeze the Toyota between a Saab and a Mini an hour's walk from the flat. I'm scrabbling for my keys when the door is wrenched open. My flatmate Luke looks, if possible, even scruffier and wild-eyed than normal.

'What!' I sing, to his loud silence. He is regarding me oddly. 'Jasper's rung!' I suggest. 'I've won the lottery! You want a bike and a house! And a trip to Bali—we'll fly Concorde!'

He shakes his head. Then he reaches out and grasps my upper arm.

'No, Helen,' he says. 'Your mum rang. Your dad. Your dad's dead.'

When I was fifteen and never been kissed, I fed the hunger on a gluttonous diet of Mills & Boons. The willowy innocence of these paperback heroines was as far removed from my fat chastity as a diamond from a lump of coal, but nonetheless gave me hope that one day *I'd* swoon at the sight of—ooh, let's say a gunfight, and a powerful, masterful man would gather up my flaccid form and spirit me away to a life of love, happiness, and endless passion.

At least, when Luke informs me of my father's demise, he keeps hold of my arm, so when the words penetrate my skull and whirl around my head and make me dizzy, I sway slightly but remain on my feet.

'Your dad is dead.' All that came before this moment hurtles into it. My dad is dead. My father is dead. Daddy is dead. But he isn't dead! He wasn't dead yesterday, or the day before that. He's been alive ever since I've known him. A minute ago, he wasn't dead. And now he's dead?

How can my father be dead? Dead is old other people like Frank Sinatra. It doesn't happen to me. Or my parents. *Death*. Don't be mad.

'Wha-what? When?' My mouth is a gob of jelly, it's wobbling all over the place. Poor old Luke looks terrible. Breaking anything to anybody is purgatory for Luke. When he broke it to me that he'd just popped into our landlord's room to borrow a razor and that my kitten, Fatboy, appeared to have done a large poo in the middle of Marcus's white duvet, he was puce and stuttery with the stress of prior knowledge.

This is different. The words pour from him in a torrent. 'He just collapsed massive heart attack your mother rang about an hour ago your mobile's off I didn't know where you were she's at the hospital she's really upset you've got to call her but they keep saying she's got to turn off her mobile so if—' Luke is very worked up and a large fleck of spit lands on my cheek. I surreptitiously try to wipe it off without him noticing. My hand is trembling. It's too late. Too late to decide not to come home just yet and to drive to Tina to moan about Jasper in blissful not-knowing. Too late. Luke has said the words. They can't be unsaid. Saying it makes it real. Luke insists on driving me to the hospital.

Both my parents are alive. No, I mean it. My dad is nearly dead. Luke, the berk, got it wrong although—seeing as he spoke to my mother—I can guess how the misunderstanding occurred. Luke swerved into the car park and I ran dippety skippet into Casualty and started babbling at the first uniformed person I saw. She directs me to the relatives' room next to 'Resuss'. *Resuscitation*. Shit. I run down a corridor, past a man stripping sheets off stained mattresses. Then I hear the sound of my mother's voice and bolt towards it. Oh no, Nana Flo.

'Helen!' chokes my mother, and bursts into tears. Nana Flo, who thinks extreme emotion is vulgar, looks on disapprovingly. My mother clings to me as if snapping me in half will make it all go away.

Although I am gasping for breath, I wheeze, 'Wa, when did he die?'

At this, my mother flings me from her like a flamenco dancer. 'He's not dead yet!' she shrieks. 'Oh, Maurice! My poor Maurice!'

My mistake. My father is, as we speak, being fiddled with by experts after an almighty heart attack during lunch. As his lunch tends to involve four scrambled eggs—when I know, from Lizzy, that the recommended intake is two per week—this doesn't greatly surprise me. Also, he smokes like industrial Manchester. My mother, who was upstairs, found him slumped into his plate, egg on face. Being my mother, she wiped the egg off his face with Clarins and—I kid you not—*cleaned his teeth*, before calling the ambulance.

There is nothing for us to do, according to some busybody calling herself the A & E sister, until the doctors have finished working on my father. She talks about drips, monitors, oxygen and blood tests, and drops the bombshell that he's 'very unwell'. So we sit in the drab peely-walled cafeteria. At least the coffee is filtered. My mother keeps bursting out crying and jumping up to ring everyone she knows. Then she decides she can't cope with anyone fussing so I have to ring back and dissuade everyone from descending on the hospital.

I gaze at Nana Flo. Shock has drawn her thin mouth even tighter, like a purse string. Her skin is as washed out as her beige nylon dress and her eyes are saggy like a salamander's. I feel a twist of pity but know better than to voice it. As ever, she converts all anguish into aggression, and today Luke is on the receiving end of it. Nana assumes he's my boyfriend and is grilling him. Her swollen hands are clasped on her lap but not tightly enough to disguise the tremor. And she doesn't look at me, not once, and I know it's because she won't let me see her pain.

I allow Luke to flounder and ignore his pleading glances for assistance. I stare unseeing at the peely walls, and my grandmother's gravelly voice, usually so penetrating, floats disembodied around me. Everything feels unreal. I feel hollow. What am I doing here, sitting in a hard orange chair? I should be shagging Jasper. My father should be sitting in his study smoking a cigar and reading the *Sunday Times*. Parents are just there, a constant, in the background. Wallpaper. Peely walls.

Imminent death—the ultimate in suspense. An excuse to call Jasper and make him feel guilty. For both reasons, my heart is whapping along at 140 beats per minute. At least it *is* beating. First though, I ask Luke if he'd be sweet enough to go home and feed Fatboy.

He leaps up and cries happily, 'I'd love to!' before glancing fearfully at Nana Flo and adding sombrely, 'Anything I can do to help.'

Nana Flo sniffs. 'Cats,' she says. 'Vermin.'

I feel sorry for Nana Flo. She finds very little in life to smile about. She's not at all what you want in a grandmother. No jolly fat legs and a bun, no five-pound notes on birthdays and buying you sweets behind your parents' back. She's the Anti-Grandmother and I suspect she speaks highly of me too. I run to the payphone.

My conversation with Jasper is infuriating. He starts off with a wry 'Oh hi, it's you,' and I derive brief satisfaction from telling him the news and jerking him out of his indifference. I can't really believe it myself, can't believe I'm saying the alien words aloud. So, maybe not that amazingly, Jasper refuses to believe me! He keeps repeating, like a posh Dalek, 'I'm sure it will be OK.'

I say firmly, 'No, Jasper, he *is* actually seriously ill,' but to no avail.

His last offer is 'Call me tomorrow and tell me how he is.' After Jasper's disappointing response I don't want to speak to anyone else.

Another hour of wall-staring and we return to the relatives' room next to Resuss. It's drab, poky, stinks of smoke and is a dead ringer for my sixth-form classroom. Finally, a red-eyed adolescent approaches and informs us that my father has been moved to the coronary care unit, and to follow him. The teenager has a stethoscope hanging round his neck. Minutes later, the house officer, as he claims to be, stops in front of a wizened old man flat on a bed and it's a moment before I recognise him.

My father, senior partner. My father, the quiet but respected king of every golf club soirée. My father, who only ever wears tailored suits. My father, who deems nudity on a par with Satanism. My father, who only last week told me—via my mother, of course—that he thought it was time I moved into a flat of my own and would I like him to advise me on location. This shrunken, helpless creature who lies motionless, bare-chested, attached to a spaghetti of wires, smelling faintly sickly sweetly, pale and hollow-cheeked, rasping, unseeing, in an ugly metal bed. This is my father. He looks fucking dreadful.

While I am mute with shock—although I can't help thinking this is a week off work at *least*—my mother is loudly inconsolable. Nana Flo says nothing, but her hooded eyes glisten. I reluctantly place a hand on her bony shoulder. To my surprise, she pats it. Then I hug my mother, murmur useless words into her ear, and watch her hold my father's still hand and wail into his sheet. Nana Flo has blinked away the tears and sits silently beside her, like a grouchy angel of death. The adolescent quietly suggests that if we go to the relatives' room he'll fetch the medical registrar. Five minutes later, he returns with a bloke who I am sure is twenty-two, max. He introduces himself as Simon, and he tells us that 'Dad's very sick.' Surprise! Then he explains, in kindergarten language, what a heart attack is. He tells us they're doing all they can. Very powerful drugs. But so much heart muscle affected. No blood pressure. Kidneys failing. Fluid collecting on lungs. Hard to make a precise estimation. Got to take it an hour at a time. Judging by the woeful look on Simon's face, my father hasn't got long to live.

Nana, me and my mother sit helplessly by my father's bed until the sky turns black and we're ushered into another dingy relatives' room. We spend the night sitting, pacing, staring, sighing. Hilary, a soft-voiced specialist cardiac nurse, keeps popping in to update us. Twice, thanks to my mother's wailing and gnashing, we're allowed into the unit for a brief vigil. Every time my father rasps I have to restrain her from pressing the red emergency button. During vigil two, Hilary asks her to keep her voice down as other people in the unit are trying to sleep. My mother gives a shriek of rage at the audacity and runs into the corridor. I make an apologetic cringe to Hilary and scamper after her. It's a long night.

Shortly after dawn, my mother goes to 'stretch her legs' and Nana Flo goes to the Ladies'—which happily takes her twenty minutes. Hilary leans round the door and says, 'Would you like to see him?' I nod. My heart thuds. A second later I am alone with my father. A rash of dirt-grey stubble covers his chin and the shock hits me like a slap. I gently rest my hand on his. I ought to say something. But it's embarrassing. The most embarrassing thing, the thing my father would be most embarrassed by, is the large square transparent plastic wee bag which hangs from a tube that thankfully disappears under his bedcover. The other patients' bags are full of orange urine. My father's, I am relieved to see, is empty.

I hate to sound like someone who works for a women's magazine but you'd think they'd try for a more stylish wee bag. I am idly wondering if Prada would agree to an NHS catheter commission, when my father emits a loud rasp. Shit! Say it, say it, now, now, say it! But I am dumb. I clutch my father's hand and think, stiffly, I love you, in my head. Dad, I love you. Dad, did I tell you, Dad, I hope you know, Dad, I know we weren't, we didn't . . . Just say it. Can't. The words are glue.

The hours pass, and I still don't say it. My mother bustles in with a copy of the *Daily Mail* and marches off to bother Hilary. So, instead of saying 'I love you, Daddy,' and crying daughterly tears all over my father's frail dying body, I read him extracts from the *Daily Mail* financial section. And then, suddenly, the quiet murmur of the ward becomes chaos, with screams of 'He's arresting!' and 'Put out an arrest call!', and swarms of people in blue and white run towards me shouting, pushing trolleys, yanking curtains, and in the blur as I am dragged away I see the orange reading on the black heart monitor screen is a wild scribble. So I am with my father when he dies, but each of us is alone.

My father is dead. He dies at 7.48pm. He dies during the golden hour—when the setting sun cloaks the world in a warm yellow blanket of enchanted light. No more golden hours for Maurice. It is a beautiful day and my father is dead.

Cinderella's glass slippers were made of fur. But when the French interpreted the original text, they translated fur-lined as *verre*. My mother's voice warms as she tells me this and I know she is reassessing Cinderella as a more homely, snuggly girl than the brash madam who click-clacked around the royal ballroom in hard shoes of glass. She loves stuff like this, which is why, as an infant school teacher, my mother kicks butt. The children adore her.

At home, my mother reverts to a fairytale of her own. She is a north-west London princess, with a handsome prince called Maurice to look after her. You'd never guess she was an intelligent, educated woman. She wants everything to be nice and if it isn't she stamps her feet until it is.

This is partly why my father's death—my father's death!—is a problem. She doesn't want to get involved. She didn't want to 'view' his body (although to be fair, neither did I), she refused to see the hospital's bereavement services officer—'Don't say that word!'—and she wanted nothing to do with the funeral arrangements. So it's been left to me and Nana Flo who, amazingly, has become a whirr of efficiency.

Work have been great. I called Laetitia on Monday morning. She was sympathetic but pressured and suggested that I come into work 'to take your mind off things'. I said, 'Er, I think he's on the brink, actually.' Anyhow I've got a week off, free, compassionate leave. If I'm still off next week, I get half-pay. Feeling mad and light-headed, I ring in to confirm what's happened to my dad on Tuesday morning. Immediately, the editor's secretary sends a huge bunch of orange flowers to my parents' house. Luke's agreed to nanny Fatboy and my mother's a wreck, so I'm staying there. One thing I'll say about *Girltime*, they do a good bouquet.

Lizzy calls me, says how sorry she is, and asks if I'm OK.

'I'm fine,' I say quickly, before I can think about it.

She says, 'Are you sure?'

Really, I tell her, in a brittle pantomime voice, I'm fine, I'm busy, my mother's freaking because she can't believe the Passport Office are 'cruel' enough to demand back my dad's passport. Lizzy wants details and when I tell her about collecting my dad's clothes and his watch in a plastic bag and my mother not wanting to leave the hospital, she starts sobbing. Unfairly, I am annoyed by this. How dare she cry!

Then Lizzy says something no one else would dream of saying. 'Helen,' she says solemnly, 'I'm sure you were a wonderful daughter. I'm sure your father was very proud of you.' Jesus! That is *horrible*.

'Lizzy, please don't say things like that,' I whisper, and hurriedly put the phone down. I'm trembling. My head feels leaden and unstable. I breathe in quick short sniffs until the comfort blanket of numbness resettles. Only then do I trust myself to speak. 'This house is pitch-dark and freezing cold,' I say crossly to Nana Flo. I stamp around turning on radiators and switching on lights. I remain chilly but feel calmer.

My mother is sitting on their—her—bedroom floor sniffing my father's jumpers. I leave her a cup of decaffeinated tea as I fear the real thing would send her into a drug-crazed frenzy. I've also hidden the Nurofen. Meanwhile, Nana Flo and I have divided the death duties, of which there are roughly a million. Lawyers, notices, certificates, application forms, wills, probates, pensions, policies, insurance, tax. Jesus. If I think about how much I have to do I will scream and go mad, so I am trying not to think. Ideally I'd like to slump on my bed and stare into space, but my heart is still pounding so it's impossible to relax. It's doing wonders for my metabolism and I now know why bereaved people get so thin. Also, I never thought I'd say this, but thank heaven for Nana Flo. She managed to shake my mother out of her stupor for long enough to show us where Dad keeps his paperwork. She's phoned all our ghastly relatives and told them not to come round just yet *and* she's insisted on registering Dad—which involved an exhausting trek to Camden Town Hall. She returned triumphantly with the death certificate and several copies. She also got the infamous green form everyone's wittering on about. It allows you to bury the body and dead people wouldn't be seen dead without it. Ah, ha, ha, ha.

When I phone the local funeral home—home! are they kidding?—I say, 'I'm ringing on behalf of my father.' Like I'm booking him into a hotel!

Despite the laughable horror of the situation, the funeral guy is very sweet. He looks, as I expect, like Uriah Heep (or what I imagine Uriah Heep to look like having never got further than the first page of any Dickens novel). He is tall, bony, with watery blue eyes, and grey hair in a critical stage of combover. His handshake is creepily limp. I brace myself for a grasping parasite but he turns out to be kind. He ushers me into a room, offers me a coffee and talks me through the options. We flick through a coffin brochure. Uriah says that if a client chooses a cremation, 'We recommend what I call a plain, dignified coffin.' He adds tactfully, 'It's not top-quality wood, but you know what happens in a cremation.' I nod and smile as if I discuss cremating my father most days.

The cost of a grave is unbelievable and Uriah is suitably disparaging about London prices. 'A plot of land that would eventually cater for three people'—excuse me?—'would cost a thousand pounds.' He sees my shocked face—although I'm less shocked by the rip-off cost than the prospect of a threesome—and adds, 'London land is very expensive. A plot in Highgate cemetery can cost fifty thousand! Whereas, not so long ago, I had cause to bury my mother in Cornwall. The plot was five pounds!' At the punch line I raise my eyebrows and say that, despite the cost, I think my family want a burial.

My father's burial grave death body—a new vocabulary of ugly, alien, disgusting words. It's grotesque and I can't believe I'm here. I sit frozen in my seat, feet neatly together, and all the while my brain is screaming *this is ridiculous it can't be real* and I want to run and run until it's not. Uriah, meanwhile, is keen to stress that he'd liaise with the hospital, the minister, provide the hearse, the cars, remove all the hassle from my girlish head, and until the funeral, 'Dad would stay here with us.' I smile and nod although I can't imagine anything Dad would like less. Uriah suggests that I go home, discuss the finer details with my mother, and ring him tomorrow. He sees me off with another weak handshake and I run to the Toyota.

I walk in the door and, do I believe my eyes! (I love that phrase—the Wizard of Oz says it). Who do I see sitting at the kitchen table charming the bloomers off Nana Flo—who is old enough to know better—*and* my mother—who has magically applied full dramatic widow's make-up plus long black dress—but Jasper.

'Jasper?' I say in a shrill squeak.

'Heeelen!' bleats my mother, sweeping out of her chair and crushing me in a long, sorrowful hug. 'You've been gone so long! I was terrified! I thought you'd had an accident!' Oh, please! Like she ever hugs me!

'Mum, don't be silly,' I say. 'I was sorting out Da—, the funeral. I'll tell you about it later.' I wriggle out of her steely arms and kiss Jasper chastely on the cheek. Foolishly, stupidly, I am delighted he's here. Nana Flo and my mother show no sign of wanting to give us any privacy, so I suggest to Jasper that we go upstairs. We plod up to Dad's study, which is in fact my old bedroom.

Jasper has got something to say. His face is very serious. 'Helen,' he begins. 'I am so sorry for your loss. Poor you. At least he didn't suffer. And he had a good innings. And, I promise, time does heal.' He stops. I am furious. Mealy-mouthed twit!

'That's very comforting,' I say, not bothering to hide the sarcasm, 'although, Jasper, I'd actually prefer it if he was still alive.' This throws him. In Jasper's world of Victorian etiquette women don't snap back.

He falters, and adds, 'Quite. It must be very difficult for you. And it must be even worse for your mother, she's known him for longer than you.' Jesus Christ! It must be worse for all of us, you stupid prat!

'Look, Jasper,' I say. I am so angry I can barely speak. 'My father has just died and I have a lot to do. And you, saying things . . . saying stuff like . . . like what you were saying, it just isn't helping.' For the first time since this fiasco started I am close to tears. 'Now, Jasper. Do you have anything else to say to me?'

He looks at the floor. Then, to my surprise, his face turns slowly crimson. 'Sunday,' he announces. 'I lied. I saw Louisa last week. And we boffed. I—I didn't mean to. It just happened.' He looks straight at me. I stare back. 'I felt bad,' he explains. 'And, seeing as your father passed away, I thought I owed you the truth.' What a fine courageous upstanding citizen you are.

'Well!' I say. 'Some good came of my father's death after all!'

Jasper doesn't get it. He looks pleased, and says, 'Yeah.'

'Jasper,' I say, clenching my fists. 'You are a wanker. Please leave. It's over.' His head jerks in surprise.

'But,' he stammers, 'but, babe, it was an error of judgment.'

I glare at him. 'It certainly was,' I say.

Jasper pushes his hand through his hair and in a patronising tone says, 'Helen, you're—'

I interrupt. In a harsh voice I say, 'Jasper, you're dumped.'

The paradise-blue eyes harden and he shrugs.

Then he leaves. He shuts the door quietly behind him.

Jesus. What have I done. The dizziness is back. Angry tears start falling, fast, uncontrollably. Furious, I sniff aggressively and smear them away. I walk into the kitchen in a daze. I feel ill, headachy, exhausted.

My mother looks up. 'Helen! What a nice boy! I can't believe you never introduced us. He bought me lilies.' Pause. She sees my blotchy face and adds gently, 'Darling. Did you know that during the war they grew vegetables in the Tower of London moat?'

For my fourth birthday, my father took me to see *The Nutcracker* and I shamed him by roaring, 'I want to be a fairy too!' I have since revised this ambition, for the sad single reason that fairies wear skirts. I don't wear skirts. I refuse to wear skirts. I haven't worn a skirt for approximately five years because my legs are short and stocky and if I wear a skirt I tend to look like a dressed-up bulldog.

Incredibly, my mother refuses to accept my 'no skirt' rule. 'You can't wear trousers to a funeral!' she squawks.

'Why not?' I snap. 'I'm sure Dad wouldn't mind.'

When I say this, she stamps her foot. She's fifty-five years old! 'Yes, but I mind!' she screeches.

'But—'

Her voice starts to crack. 'Just *do* it, Helen! Don't argue with me, I can't take it!' My mother could teach Elton John a few things about being a drama queen and my patience is wearing so thin it's anorexic.

Did I mention my father deemed nudity on a par with Satanism?

Well, he also deemed religion on a par with Satanism. Consequently, his funeral is to be—as I commanded Uriah—spiritual-lite. No hymns, no house of worship. And no yellow because my father hated yellow. Just a simple graveside ceremony.

'Performed by whom?' asked Uriah.

'A minister, of course!' I said. This puzzled Uriah until I explained that I couldn't think who else could perform it (although Cousin Stephen offered) so a minister would have to do. But he's to keep it brisk and, if possible, avoid yellow and God references.

My mother is well aware of all this, yet blows up the skirt issue to intergalactic proportions. Suddenly, the thought of spending one more minute in her shrieky, flailing company is unbearable. 'Fine,' I say. 'You win. I'll wear a skirt but I've decided'—and I decide this as I say it—'I want to drive to the funeral myself. I don't want to go in the procession thing. I think it's grim. I refuse.' Cue, world war three.

I employ a ruse gleaned from one of the many psychologists I interview at *Girltime*. The Broken Record Technique. Whatever my mother throws at me—accusations, threats, pleas, the crumpled-up *Guardian* Education section—I calmly repeat the same intensely irritating statement: 'Yes, I realise that, but I've decided to drive to the funeral myself.' On the fifth repetition, she gives a deep yowl, screams, 'Shut up shut *up* I can't stand it!' and runs upstairs. I take this to indicate surrender and drive back to the flat triumphant. I don't feel guilty, why should I?

The morning of the funeral dawns. I lurch into consciousness and feel the nauseating grip of fear without knowing why. Then I remember. The sky is blue but it is a cold, blustery, vicious day. The kind of day that ruins your hair even if you've moussed it to a brittle crisp. To make matters worse, Tina has been in New York on a fashion shoot and so unavailable for consultation, and the only cheap skirt I could find on my lone shopping trip was long, black and stretchy with a non-detachable material bow at the waist. I put it on and immediately look like Alison Moyet. I am looking for my earrings when I glance at the clock and realise that it is twenty-five past ten and the funeral starts at eleven.

Six road-raging minutes later I am crawling through Golders Green, trying to apply lipstick in the rearview mirror. At least twenty-five Volvos are double-parked in the middle of the road. I'm wishing I'd taken a different route when I sense a familiar movement in the blurry distance. I focus on it and I see my father walking along the pavement. My stomach flips as I watch his striding march, the broad square of his shoulders, and then he glances behind him and he isn't my father at all and there is an enormously loud tinny bang and I jolt forward and stop abruptly, having veered—slowly but with conviction—into a parked orange Volkswagen Beetle. 'Oh, nooooo!' I shout.

My first thought is to ring Dad. I could burst out crying but I'm wearing non-waterproof mascara. Instead, I leap out and run to inspect the damage. Then I hear the sound of screaming.

'You've totalled Nancy!' screams the voice. The voice belongs to a tiny blonde woman wearing emphatic lipliner and a white coat. Her face is pinchy with rage as she runs towards me.

'N-n-nancy?' I stammer in horror. Oh God, I've killed someone.

'Nancy, my car, you stupid cow!'

The whoosh of relief as I realise I won't go to prison plus the slow-brain processing of the fact a twee car-christening stranger is calling me a stupid cow fuse into a rush of adrenaline and I roar, 'For fuck's sake stop screaming, it's a crappy little coke can car!' She looks shocked—probably didn't think someone wearing a skirt like this would use the word 'fuck'. She opens her over-made-up mouth to answer back but I am *not* in the mood. I bellow, 'I'm sorry! But I am on the way to my father's funeral and—'

I stop mid bellow. I stop because a tall, dark-haired guy, also wearing a white coat, has jogged up to us and seemingly expects to be included in the conversation. 'Yes?' I say icily.

Instantly, the blonde turns coy. 'Tom!' she simpers. 'Look what she's done to Nancy!'

We both regard Nancy's crumpled backside. Then we look at Tom. She looks adoringly. I look snootily, do a double take. Tom is gorgeous. Or rather, he's got—and I know this doesn't sound terribly complimentary but you'll excuse it as a personal fetish—eyes like a husky dog. A cool, pale, piercing blue. Woof. And his teeth. Wolf teeth. I know this, because he flashes me a surprise smile. Pointy canines do it for me.

'Celine, it's mainly the bumper. Stop yelling,' says Tom. Then he turns to me and says, 'Are you OK? Do you want to sit down?'

I shake my head. 'I'm late,' I say shrilly. 'I'm late for my father's funeral, and now this!' My voice chokes up.

'What about Nancy?' says Celine sulkily.

'I'll deal with the car,' says Tom. 'You go inside.' Celine flounces off. Tom winces. 'Sorry about her,' he says. 'You look a bit wonky to drive. Can I call you a cab?'

I shake my head. 'It starts in ten minutes,' I wail. I feel weak and feeble, not to mention a great big frump.

'*I'll* drive you,' announces Tom. 'I've got the van.'

'The van?' I say gormlessly.

'The vet's van,' he says.

'You're a vet!' I say.

'Yes!' he grins.

'That explains the white coat,' I say. Then I decide to shut up. I stand there, gormlessly, while Tom moves the Toyota 'round the back'. Three seconds later, he reappears at the wheel of a dirty white van with the word MEGAVET emblazoned on its side. Classy. He toots, and I clamber in. Because of my clingy student skirt it's a gawky, knock-kneed manoeuvre.

'Don't you have loads of animals waiting to see you?' I ask, confirming my already stunning reputation for eloquent repartee and dagger wit.

'Nah,' he shakes his head, 'Wednesday's always quiet. Monday and Friday are the killers. Right. Where are we going?' Of course, I can't remember, so Tom scrabbles under his seat and retrieves a ragged *A to Z*. Once we escape from Golders Green, Tom speeds up. I know we're in a rush but it feels like he's trying to take off.

'All right, Wing Commander?' I mutter edgily.

He glances at me. 'This isn't fast!' he says. 'You don't want to be late!'

'No,' I say. 'But I don't want to be dead either.'

He slows down. 'I'm sorry about your dad,' he says.

'It's OK,' I reply.

'How did he die?'

I pick the skin on my lip. 'Heart attack,' I gasp, as the van squeals round a corner. Tom, rather sweetly, gives a loud tut. I want to change the subject. I need to change the subject. I rack my fuzzy brain for information that may be of interest to a good-looking vet who I have known for not very long and produce the conversational corker: 'I've got a kitten called Fatboy.' Jesus, what's wrong with me? Suddenly I possess the vocabulary and articulation of a three-year-old.

Thankfully, Tom says politely, 'Oh yes? Any particular sort?'

Here at last is my chance to prove that, despite all evidence to the contrary, I do actually own an IQ. And what do I say? 'He's orange.'

I am considering an emergency operation to have my voice box removed, when Tom says kindly, 'Orange. Good sort of cat.' This inspires me to silence.

Seven excruciating minutes later, we screech up to the cemetery gates. 'Thank you it's so kind of you, thank you,' I say awkwardly, trying to inject some bouncy gratitude into the flat monotone. 'What shall I do about the Toyota?'

Tom waves me away. 'You'd better rush. Just stop by when you have a moment. You can sort the insurance with Celine whenever.' He nods at the mass of cars jamming the cemetery entrance. 'Will you be OK?'

I nod stiffly, give a silly bye-bye-baby wave, and turn away. My eyes are watering. It's ridiculous. Being shouted at I can take. But *gentleness*. Spare me. Even the word makes me cringe. It's almost as bad as 'tenderly'. Blue eyes and pointy teeth notwithstanding, I go right off him. I see Luke in a too-tight navy suit hovering just inside the iron gates with an impeccable Tina and a sleek Lizzy and run gratefully towards them. Tom roars away in his dirty white van, and I don't even look back.

Luke is a nicotine addict. He says he could give up any time but refuses to chew gum as 'it gives you stomach ulcers'. He smokes in the bath ('for me as a bloke it's the equivalent of a scented candle'), and he smokes while he eats his thick crust pepperoni pizza in front of *A Question of Sport* ('it's a stressful programme, you wouldn't understand'). Did I mention that as well as smoking his insides to soot, Luke says what he thinks without thinking? So it's no great surprise that when I burst through the cemetery gates he grinds his toe agitatedly on one of five smouldering fag butts and shouts, 'Helen! You, mate, are *dead*!'

'I'm *what*?' I say.

He has the grace to blush. 'I mean,' he stutters, 'your mum is going mental. She's murderous. Everyone's waiting in their cars.'

I look at Tina and Lizzy. Tina flicks her fingernails and mutters, 'Bloody hell!' Lizzy pulls a woeful face and wails, 'Oh, poor Helen!'

I take their discomfort as corroboration. 'Hang on,' I mutter, and weave my way through what looks like a staged motorway pile-up—studiously avoiding eye contact with the goggling faces inside the cars—to the big shiny black Jaguar parked behind the big shiny black hearse.

As I approach, the window shoots down. 'Where. Have. You. Been?' spits my mother from under a great black saucer of a hat.

I'm surprised at her courteous restraint, then I realise the chauffeur is listening agog. I bend down, wave guiltily at Nana Flo who is clutching a lace handkerchief so tightly her knuckles are white, and say I got held up. 'What's going on?' I ask, to distract my mother from her fury.

'They're in the cemetery office,' says my mother in a high, hysterical voice, 'they're doing all the paperwork and [sniff] we're not allowed to get out of our cars until it's done, and—oh I've had enough! I'm getting out! I can't just sit here! Mind out!' I hop to one side as my mother leaps from the car. Immediately, hordes of car doors click open and swarms of po-faced, droopily dressed people start plodding slowly towards us. I stiffen in fright. No offence to our family friends and relatives, but it's like *Night of the Living Dead*.

I spend the next ten minutes suffocating in a blur of powdery, lavendery, lipsticky kisses, awkward hugs, warm breathy murmurs of 'I'm so sorry!' and 'So sudden!', a sharp assertion of 'You must be relieved he went so quickly' (oh, delighted), and 'You *are* taking care of your poor mother, aren't you—such a shock for her!' I glance at my mother who is lapping it up like Fatboy having stumbled on an illegal bowl of ice cream.

'Yes,' I say grimly. 'She needs a lot of looking after.'

I spot Uriah—done up like a dog's dinner—emerging from the cemetery office with the minister. Who, I recall in a stab of panic, left two rambling messages on my answering machine which I ignored then forgot. As I approach, Uriah's lips twitch in a careful smile. 'Miss Bradshaw,' he says. 'We're ready to embark on your father's last journey. Do you wish the arrangement to stay on the coffin, or shall we remove it?'

I'm stumped. 'Er, what do people normally do?' I say.

'Most folk prefer to take it off,' he says. 'They often like to donate it to an appropriate hospital ward—in this case, the cardiac unit,' he adds helpfully. How jolly for the patients.

'Oh fine, do that then,' I blurt. I turn and my heart thuds as I see that the dark draculaesque coffin has been rolled out of its hearse and six sober-suited men are slowly hefting it onto their shoulders. I stare at it in horror. This solid, ugly, stark token of death. Jesus! My father is in there. Dead. Cold. Stiff. Starting to rot. How long before the rigor mortis is softened with the stink of decay and . . . I am wrenched from my rotten thoughts by my mother who storms right up to Uriah and shouts in his face: 'Morrie's Cousin Stephen wants to carry the coffin!'

Not by himself, surely, I say in my head. Cousin Stephen is about ninety-three and the height of a Munchkin. 'Mum,' I begin, glancing nervously at Uriah, 'we were supposed to sort—'

Uriah stops me with a light touch on my shoulder. 'It's not a problem,' he says grandly. After a short flurry—and when I say short I mean short—Cousin Stephen is promoted to a pallbearer. Uriah somehow organises everyone into a long straggly line and takes his place in front of the coffin, with the minister.

My mother, Nana Flo and I stand behind it. I glance at Nana to see if she might faint, but she has a strong, angry look about her, like she's preparing for battle. My mother is trembling and her face is swollen with tears. I hug her and nearly collapse as she promptly relaxes her entire weight onto me. She clings with one arm, and uses the other to keep her hat from whizzing off her head and spinning across the white sea of gravestones. I feel as if I'm acting a part in a film. It's ridiculous! Today is a chill, blustery Wednesday morning. I should be sitting at my desk in an overheated office, slurping a double espresso and leafing through the *Sun* on the pretext of doing research. Instead, here am I, with a great troop of people, stumbling over the muddy earth behind a big brash coffin containing my dad, towards a freshly dug grave to bury him deep in the ground.

For the first five steps of the funeral march, the coffin is—thanks to squat Cousin Stephen—wobbly and uneven. Thankfully, Uriah's men hoick it up and off Cousin Stephen's short shoulder until he is actually standing underneath it. He is forced to be content with placing a nominal hand of support on its polished surface and our bizarre procession shuffles on. I glide forward like a zombie. Everyone is hushed and the only sound is a plane droning overhead and the wind whipping the soft, feathery branches of the elderly yew trees.

We make it to the graveside. I try to steer my mother's attention towards the garish floral tributes propped around the hole and away from the fresh pile of earth heaped beside it and the two scruffy men standing not quite far away enough, each one casually leaning on a great big sodding dirt-encrusted shovel.

The pallbearers and a relieved Cousin Stephen lower the coffin to the ground. No one is quite sure where to stand. The minister approaches us and asks if there is anything we'd like him to say.

'Like what?' my mother says.

'Well, er, any particular tribute to the deceased,' he replies.

'No one told me about tributes!' she exclaims rudely. 'Helen, you should have said! I'd have written something down!'

'*Me!*' I cry. I have just about had it with her flouncing. 'How should I know! Why is it my fault?' A small worm of guilt niggles its way into my consciousness because possibly vaguely maybe I sort of recall the minister's message might have mentioned the wisdom of writing a short note for him to include in his address, but, I'm sorry, I can't be responsible for every piddling detail!

'He was a loving, attentive father,' I lie, reading off a nearby gravestone, 'and a wonderful, kind, adoring husband,' I add in a rush to appease my mother. She sniffs approval.

'He was good at golf,' she says. 'Say that.' The minister nods, backs away, clears his throat, trots out a thin service and the speediest, tritest, most anodyne accolade I have ever heard bar the one my headmistress made at my school leaving ceremony.

The coffin is then lowered into the grave. I note Uriah nodding surreptitiously to the fourth pallbearer, who grabs a rope before Cousin Stephen can wimp, sorry—muscle in and make a hash of it.

We sprinkle dirt on the coffin—Luke manages to hurl a large clod of earth containing a stone at 110mph that goes *pank!* as it hits the casket and makes a slight dent. I keep my arm around my mother on the pretext of lending her loving support, but really to prevent her throwing herself into the grave. I doubt she will, as her black Jaeger dress cost—according to Tina's informed guess—approximately £250. But I'm taking no chances.

Uriah waits a decent while before slinking up to me and saying, 'Whenever you're ready we'll take the cards off the flowers for you.'

'One second', I say. I move over to Nana Flo, who is standing tensely over the grave staring blindly at the mud-splattered coffin. I touch her shoulder softly, and say, 'The funeral director asked if you would like him to take the cards off the flowers yet.'

My grandmother seems to drag herself back from somewhere far away. Her head turns slowly like a tortoise. She says in a bright hard voice, 'Yes, thank you, that would be lovely.' I tell Uriah to go ahead.

Uriah's men go to work and I stand as inanimate as a maypole, while a sweep of blurry faces whirl and chatter around me. Eventually, a gentle hand on my arm forces me to snap into focus. 'Helen,' says Lizzy softly, 'everyone's going back to your mother's house. Do you want me to stay here with you for a little longer?'

I blink, and see that most of our guests are revving up their cars, the cards are gone from the flowers, and the gravediggers are inching towards the abandoned grave. Uriah, in the distance, is helping Nana Flo into the black limousine. 'Let's go,' I say to Lizzy. She takes my arm and we walk in silence through the mass of past lives to the cemetery gates where Luke and Tina are waiting. My mother is snug in the plush car and content to meet me at the house. I squeeze into the back of Tina's yellow Ford Escort—a secret obsessively kept from her fashiony friends—and we roar off. And that is the end of my father.

'All this way for a sausage roll,' is one indiscreet but apt verdict on the after-show party. Our Canadian relatives—having secured free bed, breakfast, lunch, dinner, entertainment, electricity, fluffy towels and hot water from my mother—have repaid her by dragging their slothful selves to Asda and spending roughly three quid on a few loaves of white bread (economy), foul-tasting margarine (economy), potted shrimp paste (which until I tasted the disgusting evidence, I assumed was a spiteful myth devised by Enid Blyton to dissuade children from going on picnics) and four packs of crisps (Asda own brand).

My mother narrowly saves the day by picking the lock on my father's drinks cabinet. Everyone falls upon the alcohol like alcoholics. My mother—who has a history of embarrassing my father at parties by demanding a cup of tea—swallows four double Baileys in ten seconds.

I wish that everyone would leave. I don't want to talk. Not even to my friends. It's effort. I don't want to hear how my father and Cousin Stephen went camping together when they were boys. I don't give a shit. I don't want to be sociable. I want my father to walk into the kitchen and say, 'Helen, make me a cup of coffee, will you.'

The doorbell rings, and I sag, dramatically, like a sullen teenager and plod grumpily towards it. As I approach I can make out a familiar figure through the frosted glass. Surely not. I ping out of my slouch and curse myself for not changing my student skirt the second I returned to the house. Marcus. As if on cue, Luke wanders out from the lounge. 'Marcus said he might turn up later,' he says brightly.

'Thanks for warning me,' I say as I smooth my hair and open the door.

'Hell-*ie*,' says Marcus in a soothing tone. 'You poor love. I am *so* sorry I missed your old man's send-off. I so wanted to be there but some doll from this new girl group Second Edition needed showing round the gym. I tried to get out of it but it was no go.'

'I'm sure you were desperate to escape from the glamorous star,' I say.

'Oh, Hellie, don't be like that,' he grins. 'I'd prefer to spend time with you any day.' I do a token-feminist tut to disguise a large smirk. Incidentally, Marcus is the only person in the world I would ever allow to call me Hellie.

I have had an unrequited crush on Marcus for approximately nine years, ever since I spied him in the dinner queue at college. We had Luke's friendship in common, but as Marcus spent every waking hour at the gym I only got to know him at close range three years ago—when he bought his flat in Swiss Cottage and needed someone, preferably more reliable than Luke, to rent a room. (Fortunately there wasn't anyone, so Luke suggested me.)

Marcus is undeniably vain and an unrepentant philanderer, but alluring even so. His job—assistant manager and personal trainer at an exclusive London health club, pardon me, health spa—suits him down to the ground and, not infrequently, into the bedroom. He knows that I fancy him, am humbly resigned to his romantic indifference, and that my lust is lying fallow. He therefore deduces—correctly—that I am delighted to be his friend and lodger even if he does charge slightly more than I can comfortably afford (there's a surcharge for Fatboy). And he is fun to be with. If I were ever to think about it—not that I do of course—I'd say that Marcus is fond of me.

Marcus kisses me on both cheeks, lightly resting a warm hand on the back of my neck. A *zing!* of lust shoots down my back and my sunshiny temperament is magically restored. 'Would you like a drink?' I purr.

'G and T would hit the spot, low-cal tonic if poss,' he replies immediately. I nod, direct him to where Lizzy, Luke and Tina are sitting, and obediently trot off. 'Nice skirt, Alison,' he calls.

'Piss off,' I shout, as I bump into Great-Aunt Molly, Nana Flo's sister over from Canada. She looks straight at me and bursts into tears. I grit my teeth. 'I didn't mean you, Auntie Molly,' I say in a saccharine voice.

'Oh, no, dear, I know you didn't. It's all got on top of me—*sob!*—talking to Florence. Such a tragedy, losing her baby, her baby boy. I know it's hard for you too, dear, but losing a child, a child—no parent should ever have to bury a child—' Great-Aunt Molly is revving up for a big, bosomy, tear-stained rant, breezily innocent of the fact that I am itching to slap her. I squeeze past her, snatch the gin bottle from a comatose Cousin Stephen, pour Marcus's drink (full-fat tonic, I'm afraid), and speed back to him and the others.

Luke and Tina are deep in conversation and Marcus is baiting sweet, courteous, well-mannered Lizzy about precisely why she ditched her last boyfriend. 'Was he a marshmallow in bed?' he demands.

'No! No, I mean, I'd really rather not—'

Marcus nods knowingly: 'He had a matchstick dick!'

Lizzy nearly spills her glass of Perrier. 'Really! Really, I don't think—'

I shove the G & T at Marcus without making eye contact, march out of the lounge, up the stairs and into the bathroom. I sit on the side of the avocado-green bath, and laugh and laugh and laugh. I refuse to cry.

Chapter 2

ALMOST EVERY NIGHT, from ever since I can remember to the age of thirteen, I dreamed one of two dreams. Like most of the young female population I'd attend school wearing no knickers—an omission I'd discover as we queued for assembly. Most frequently, though, I'd walk alone into our local wood, in the terrible knowledge that a family of wolves lurked in the bushes. I'd start running, and they'd chase me. The dream never varied. Recently, however, my dreams have taken on a more urgent note. I dream I am hiding from a group of nameless baddies, in a huge empty house. I know they will hunt me down and the dream always ends as they yank me out of the attic cupboard. I try to relate it to Marcus, but he yawns loudly, blips on the TV and says, 'There's nothing more boring than other people's dreams.'

The bastard's right, so I ring Lizzy and tell her about it instead. Lizzy immediately consults a book she has, entitled *Definitive Meanings Of Dreams Dreamed By People We've Never Met But Whose Unconscious We're Experts On*. Or something like that. 'Your ambition is pursuing you and pushing you towards success,' she declares.

'Are you sure?' I say doubtfully. Lizzy recommends that tonight, before I go to sleep, I imagine confronting the baddies and demanding to know what they want from me. 'Mm, OK,' I say, knowing full well I will do nothing of the sort. Anyhow, I know what my dream signifies: that I am tired of being hassled by relatives who I can't escape.

Last night—after the hoi polloi finally left and the beneficiaries sobered up—our family solicitor, Mr Alex Simpkinson, read out my father's will. Maybe I drank more than I thought, because all I remember is my mother sobbing, Cousin Stephen whining, and Nana Flo shouting: 'Silence!' I'm sick of the lot of them. I have two more days of compassionate leave and my mother is badgering me to 'pop round'. In other words, to share the burden of familial duty. Joyously, I have a valid excuse: my car is at the vet.

'You mean the garage,' she says.

'Yeah,' I reply, because I can't be bothered to explain.

'Get a taxi, then,' she says quickly.

I tell her I'm broke and furthermore, this week I'm on half-pay. 'I'll pay,' she growls. I tell her thank you, but I'm urgently busy. This isn't, funnily enough, a lie. I have to locate my car insurance details, and I haven't the least idea where they are.

Luke discovers me, thirty minutes later, hyperventilating on the bed. I whine out the tale of the horrid, spiteful car insurance papers and he gives a cursory glance around my bombsite bedroom, pokes aside a rogue pair of greying knickers with his toe, picks up a few sheets of paper festering underneath them, and says, 'Isn't this it?' I am too relieved to be embarrassed. Anyway, it's only Luke.

'Thank you,' I say stiffly.

'No problem,' he replies. 'What are you going to do now?'

'I'm going to put on a ton of mascara and get my car back.'

Luke nods approvingly. 'Say hi to Tom,' he says.

Tom, it turns out, used to play football against Luke when Luke—fighting fit on a mere twenty a day—was a goalie in the Sunday league. I know this because as we motor home from the funeral Luke demands, 'How do you know Tom?' Not, you'll note, 'Why did you arrive at your dad's funeral in a vet's van?' But then, that's Luke. I assume Tina didn't notice and Lizzy was too polite to ask.

An hour later I am standing in the reception of Megavet, attempting to be civil to Celine. Who is, pleasingly, on her hands and knees wiping up a yellow puddle of labrador wee. But it's impossible. We exchange details in the same manner as, I imagine, Batman and the Joker after a prang in the Batmobile. I employ my snootiest, shop assistantest expression throughout, then realise I need to ask her a favour. I decide to be brazen. 'Is Tom around?' I say in a bored tone.

She looks down her ski-jump nose and drawls, 'He's busy.'

I am on the verge of leaping over the reception desk and throttling her when the surgery door clicks open, a large dough-faced woman carrying a tiny Yorkshire terrier waddles out, and Tom appears—a happy medium—behind her. I rearrange my expression to saintly.

'*Hello*,' he says, when he sees me. He jerks his head towards the surgery door. 'Come in—I'll be one second.' Tom then turns his attention to totting up the bill, so I cross my eyes at Celine, smile nastily, and sashay into the surgery. I sit down, and am suddenly overcome with the irrational fear that I have spinach in my teeth (unlikely as I don't eat spinach) so I dig through my bag, extract a make-up mirror, bare my teeth and peer into it. So when Tom walks in I am making a face like an aggressive baboon. I shut my mouth and the mirror about as fast as the speed of light. I *think* he didn't notice.

'How was it?' says Tom. 'If that's not a stupid question.'

I look at him blankly. 'How was what?'

'The funeral,' he says.

'Ohhhh! Oh, that. Terrible, actually.'

He wants to know why so I tell him, at length. Then I wonder if he *really* wanted to know or if he was just being polite. 'Anyway,' I say quickly, 'it's over now. I really just came by to get my car and say thanks again for the lift.'

Tom's face breaks into a smile and he says, 'Any time,' like he means it. There is a short silence, then we both speak at once.

'I think you know my flatma—' I say.

'I wondered if you—' he says. He stops, quickly.

'You say,' he says.

I giggle nervously, and say, 'I was only going to say, I think you know my flatmate Luke Randall. Or at least, he knows you.'

Tom wrinkles his nose. 'Luke, tactless Luke?' he says.

'Yeeees!' I say, in a disproportionate squeal of pleasure.

Tom laughs. He then tells me about the time a bunch of them went on a boys' night out to a rough East End nightclub and the screw on Luke's glasses came loose. 'So he goes up to the barman and says, "Have you got a knife?"!'

We are sniggering fondly when there's a sharp rap on the door as it is hurled open. Celine, in a voice of doom, declares: 'Mrs Jackson and Natascha Tiddlums The Third have been waiting to see you for twenty minutes and if you keep her waiting any longer she's going to be late for her charity lunch.'

Tom mutters under his breath, 'Who, Mrs Jackson or Natascha Tiddlums?' Then he smiles at me and says, 'I'd better get on.'

He looks as if he wants to add something so I hesitate. But he doesn't, so I say awkwardly, 'OK, see you, then. Bye.' As I walk towards the surgery exit I am aware of Celine's beady eye burning a hole in my back, so I turn round and sing in a sarcastically gay tone, 'Byee!'

I drive home in the dented Toyota, smiling.

I sent flowers to Tom yesterday. I discussed my intention with Tina and Lizzy first, in case it was a blatant gaffe. But Lizzy thought he sounded 'angelic' and agreed he deserved flowers for chauffeuring me to the funeral. Tina thought he sounded 'suspiciously nice, probably married', but agreed he deserved flowers for helping me to irritate Celine. He hasn't called, though, to say thank you. Oh well. See if I care. I'm far too busy lying on my bed staring at the ceiling to worry about men. And I've taken next week off as holiday. Inexplicably I've started waking up—head buzzing, blood jangling—at 5.00am. *Me*, who usually has trouble rolling out of bed at 8.15.

Lizzy suggested it might be to do with my father—she insists on relating everything to my father, she's obsessed. Finally, I told her coldly, 'I don't think about him at all. I did on the day of the funeral but now I don't. There's no point.' It's not quite a lie. The death of my father is a constant, like tinnitus. It's just *there*. My edginess is probably the dread of returning to work. I'm exhausted, and I don't feel strong enough to spend nine hours, five days a week, sweating and toiling under Laetitia's manicured thumb. Or maybe I'm just lazy. Trouble was, I knew the feeble excuse 'my father just died so I'm knackered' would cut no ice.

I have also been screening my calls. My mother has rung about fifty times and I know I should be with her in her hour of need, I know it's bad of me to be avoiding her, but just the sound of her petulant voice . . . it's suffocating, it hems me in, and I want to scream at her to go away, leave me alone, stop *wanting*, I can't stand it.

Jasper and Tom, however, haven't rung at all. Meanwhile, Marcus—Luke tells me—has been giving the doll from Second Edition a series of intensive personal training sessions which, it would appear, involve him staying at her Hampstead pad five nights in a row. All I can say is, her inner thigh muscles must have been extraordinarily out of shape. Lizzy has also been calling but I'm not up to facing her good intentions.

Finally, on Tuesday evening, Tina broke the lethargy spell. She marched round to the flat (I only opened the door because I thought she was from Domino's), barged in, and bellowed, 'You old slag! Donchou look a state! You've got a day—one day—to get yourself decent! Tomorrow night we're going out and we are going to party!'

She was so forceful that Fatboy puffed up his tail in fright and helter-skeltered down the hallway. 'If you say so,' I replied meekly. The party is at a hip new bar in town and Tina is picking me up at eight, on the premise that if we arrive unheard-of-ly early, we can stake out the best table—and the best men. Before she leaves, she shoves a silver carrier bag at my chest. I open the bag to find she's pinched a hot pink camisole top from the fashion cupboard, the one I was drooling after last month when these things mattered.

Wednesday lunchtime and I am wandering around the flat, peeling apart my split ends and prising the flaky bits off my fingernails, when the phone rings. I brace myself, but it isn't my mother, it's a man, it's *Tom*. 'Hi, this is Tom, calling for Helen, to say thank you again for the brilliant flowers, called on Friday and spoke to your landlord, he said he'd pass on the message but—'

I snatch up the receiver. 'Hello, Tom?'

'Helen?'

'Hang on, let me switch off the answering machine. OK. Hi!' I am garbly with pleasure and indignation: 'Marcus never told me you rang!'

Tom says, 'Yeah, well, he sounded like he was in a rush, so I thought I'd ring again to make sure. Those flowers were wild! Thank you so much, you didn't need to! So how come you're at home, anyway?'

I am unable to think of a funky excuse so I say, in an attempt to sound attractively rebellious, 'Oh, you know, can't be arsed to go back to work.' Realising this could easily be interpreted as unattractively loser-ish, I add (may God forgive me), 'Also I've been looking after my mother.' Hmm, too spinstery. 'And seeing friends. I'm seeing my friend Tina tonight, we're going to this new bar.'

My *fwend*! I curse myself, but Tom says warmly, 'Sounds good. Where is it?'

I am seized by a burst of recklessness, 'Just off Piccadilly Circus. It's supposed to be cool. Do you want to come?' So as not to appear too keen, I add, 'Bring someone if you like.'

Pause. Tom says, 'Great! I'd be on for that. Although it'll probably just be me. I'm on call tonight, but it shouldn't be a problem.'

So I arrange that Tom will meet Tina and me inside the bar at 9.00pm. I put down the phone, and ring Tina immediately in a panic. 'Do you fancy him?' she demands.

'Not sure,' I say.

'That means yes,' she replies and tells me what to wear.

Ten past nine. Squidgy red leather sofas. Dim lighting. Retro music. Beautiful women with hair clipped up in that messy, sexy, just-got-out-of-bed-wanna-go-back? style, sleek men in slim-fit shirts and dark trousers. Feeling smug. Looking good, for me. Slinky top. Black trousers. Killer boots. Subtle slap. Girly talk with Tina. Sips of champagne. Half past nine. More champagne. Bigger sips. Golden tequila. Thick golden tequila. Ten past ten. Don't care. Gimme a straw. Chunky glass after glass of Cuervo Gold tequila. Screechy, slurry, blurry talk with Tina. Twenty to eleven. Staggering, giggling, swaying, to the loo. Dazed, smudgy mascara, jerky check in mirror, puffing up limp hair. Lurching, dizzy, teary, back to Tina. Eleven thirty. Feel ill. More tequila my purse take it what who lemme alone tired wanna lie down tom tom Tom *Tom!* flucking buddy late you tossing tosser tissing posspot . . .

I wake up. I feel sharply awake. I am lying in my bed. The ceiling is in clear focus. But something isn't right. 'Helen?' says a male voice. I emit an involuntary whimper and stare in terror at Tom who is sitting, scruffy, fully clothed, on a chair in the middle of my bedroom debris. He looks as if he is trying to stifle a grin. 'How are you?' he drawls.

I realise several things at once. I am wearing a T-shirt and nothing else. I can't recall what happened last night. There is a curious absence of head pain. But I think it was bad. 'Wa, what? How?' I croak. As I use my voice for the first time I realise my throat is sandpaper.

Tom coughs. I suspect he's playing for time. 'Tina undressed you—you had sick on your top. She's asleep in the lounge.' He stops.

'What happened?' I whisper.

Tom looks sheepish. 'I was on my way and there was an emergency. It was bad timing. I called the flat to say I'd be late but you'd already left. I'm so sorry. It's kind of my fault.'

What is his fault. He's talking in code. He sees my fearful expression and grins again. 'You were impressively plastered.' I manage a nod.

Tom shifts to his feet. 'I've got to go to work, but I'll call you later.' He strides over, kisses me once, on the forehead, then walks out, softly shutting the door behind him. I wait until I hear the front door shut, leap out of bed, scrabble for my track-suit bottoms, yank them on, run into the lounge, shake Tina awake, and wheeze in a—painful but aurally pleasing—husk, 'Shit shit shit what happened now now now!'

Tina struggles upright, groans, screws up her face, growls, 'Get me Nurofen out of my bag,' and swallows two Nurofen dry. Then, she tells me.

'Helen, you big tit. You made a right prat of yourself. He was late but it wasn't his fault. He'd tried to ring but he didn't have your mobile. I think he might've even called the bar but they're too arsey to take messages. He came straight from doing the op. I think it was an Alsatian. This Alsatian escaped from its owner and ran into the road, and this car, I think it was a BMW, a green one, three series, fuel injection, and—what? OK, OK. Well, he got there just before twelve and we were both wasted, but you, you were something special. You'd been on the tequilas, neat tequila all night. You were storming! Anyway. So Tom turns up and excuse me but that man is fit. And you're about comatose. You were rude to him actually. Called him a tosspot except you said it teapot, so maybe he didn't realise. You were jawing on and on and on about how you're sick of gittish men and you can't stand it and this always happens to you and you just want a bloke who doesn't let you down. Then you tried to stand up to, I think, slap him, and you fell over. He caught you and then the bar staff were getting narky so we dragged you outside but none of the cabbies would let you get into their cabs. So I used the *Girltime* account. Then you started crying because you felt sick and then you were sick and then the cab came and it had to stop to let you be sick again and maybe that's why you don't feel so bad today but you will darling because we got back to your flat and we tried to find your keys and then you wet— I mean then we rang the bell and woke up Luke and—what? No, nothing. Helen, I'm telling you you don't want to know. All right, then. You asked. You wet yourself. Easy, tiger, my head's killing me. Look, you asked, what can I tell you? Yes, of course he saw. What? He gave you a fireman's lift. *I* don't know if any went on him! I was wasted! Look on the bright side, the geezer works with animals, he's used to being pissed on! What? Ow! Take it easy, I was trying to help! So he put you on your bed and I said I'd undress you which I did, and I said I thought you were OK, but he said he'd sit with you in case, and so I crashed on the couch and Luke went to bed and yeah, that's it. That's the end of it.'

Shall I kill myself now or later?

I've lived in this red-brick mansion block for three years and every springtime, as soon as the trees blush pink with blossom and the air turns hazy with warmth, they appear. They sit together, he and she, on the lawn. They have a favourite spot, a few metres from the brook that runs behind our communal gardens. He's gorgeous, flamboyant, very striking. She's plump-chested, plainer, yet quietly beautiful. Sometimes, the sight of their constant love makes me smile. Other times, I hurl a few hunks of bread onto the grass and think, 'Helen. You're twenty-six and you have a less fulfilling relationship than a pair of puddle ducks!'

And today, I don't have any relationship at all. In fact, even daring to compare the state of our love lives is grossly insulting to mallards. I make the mistake of telling this to Tina on the phone who says, 'Stop it, you're freaking me out.' Tina makes a huge show of her cynicism towards men to disguise the embarrassing fact that she has never lost in the mating game.

Blessedly untouched by the Jaspers of this world, she therefore sees male–female relations in prewar black and white. Her attitude is—if you like him, you date. If he gives you trouble, you don't. So, she cannot understand why I don't want to speak to Tom. Even when I tell her the man has wormed his way into my life, messed me around (Alsatian or no Alsatian), and frankly, I don't like to make a great galumphing fool of myself in front of people I barely know.

'You mean pee your pants in front of ravishing men,' says Tina.

'Will you stop going on about that!' I shout. Having played the urination scenario over and over in my head a million mortifying times I don't need reminding of it. 'Anyway,' I add sulkily, 'I am never going to drink tequila ever again ever, and I do not wish to see or speak to this man ever again, or at least, for a very long while!'

Oddly, this seems to pacify her. All she says is, 'Ring us if you want to go out this week. Laters!' and puts the phone down.

A picosecond later, the phone rings again. I snatch it up and bark, 'Now what!'

There is a pause then a voice says uncertainly, 'Helen?' It isn't Tina.

'Yes,' I reply shortly. 'Who is this?' In fact, I know damn well who it is and I am nursing a grudge of watermelon size.

'It's Michelle, honey!'

Oh, I say in my head. Would that be the same Michelle who professes to be a close friend yet doesn't turn up to my father's funeral, explain her absence, or bother to send her condolences? Sadly I am the Terminator in theory and Stan Laurel in practice, as pathetic at confronting friends as I am at confronting spiders. So all I say is an unenthusiastic, 'Hi.'

Michelle is oblivious. She rushes on, 'Gotta make it quick. The reason I rang is—and I guess you forgot, but never mind—it's my birthday tomorrow, and we're going for drinks at the U-Bar in Soho.'

She's got a nerve. I say frostily, 'Unfortunately, my father died two weeks ago, as you may recall, so I'm not really doing much socialising.'

I have known Michelle for over twenty years and in all that time I've never heard her say the word sorry. She doesn't break with habit now. There is a hammy gasp down the phone. 'I know that! That's why I haven't called—I thought you'd want to be left alone! That's why I didn't mention it! I didn't want to remind you!'

A likely story. 'I'm hardly likely to forget, am I?' I say sharply.

'I realise that,' she says, equally sharply, 'but apart from anything else, it's a tradition in my family. Women don't go to funerals.' Really, I think. That will cause a dilemma when one of them snuffs it.

'So will you come?' she demands. I give in. There is little point making a principled stand because as well as being as thick-skinned as a rhino, Michelle is a hard-core grooming addict and will actually believe me if I say I'm devoting all of tomorrow night to washing my hair.

'Yes, OK,' I sigh, 'I'll be there.'

'Honey, you're the best!' says Michelle, who has read Jackie Collins's *Hollywood Wives* four times and adapted her speech patterns accordingly. I replace the receiver, slump onto the sofa and exhale crossly through my nose. Michelle and I were thrown together aged five because our mothers were determined to share the school run. As my discriminatory powers were yet to kick in, her impressive collection of Walt Disney stickers sealed our friendship. Twenty-one years later, I curse Bambi and Thumper and all their twittering companions.

I call Tina to request back-up. She is looking for a reason to avoid staying in tomorrow tonight as she is trying to wean herself off *Coronation Street* and is delighted to accept.

I expected the U-Bend—sorry—the U-Bar, to be tacky, but it way exceeds my expectations. Michelle is resplendent in a fake leopardskin crop top and tight white jeans and appears to have modelled her hairstyle on Monica Lewinsky's.

I am dressed in bog-standard black trousers and a crumpled silver shirt I retrieved from the depths of my linen basket. When Tina saw it she asked in a carefully neutral tone, 'Where did you get that?'

I replied, also in a carefully neutral tone, 'From the linen basket.'

She gave me a reproving look and murmured, 'I'll say no more.'

I glared at her and said, 'Good.'

My mood does not improve when—after ignoring us for an hour in favour of a stocky ginger guy whose back is shaped like a Dairy Lea triangle—Michelle sashays over for a 'quick chat'. Tina immediately excuses herself and speeds to the Ladies'. I clink the ice in my Coke. Michelle glances at my drink. 'Jack Daniel's and Diet Coke?' she says.

'No,' I say evenly, 'just Coke.' I know what's coming.

'Aren't you dieting?'

I slam the Coke on the table and squeak, 'No, I am not! Are you?'

Michelle laughs and pats her pancake-flat stomach. 'Sweetheart, are you kidding! Born lucky, I guess.'

Born going to the gym seven days a week and eating one meal a day like a Weimaraner, more like. I am speechless with indignation, which gives Michelle enough time to summon an oily-faced man with a concave chest, press him down beside me, say, 'Helen, sweetheart, this is my cousin Alan, I know you'll just mesh,' and swan off.

Heart pounding, I scan the room for Tina and, to my dismay, spot her propped against the bar practically rubbing noses with a handsome blond man in a dark suit. She flicks back her hair and cups his hand as he gallantly strikes a match to light her cigarette. The brazen hussy. I'll get her for this. If Alan doesn't get me first.

I'm cornered. He asks me a question about *me*—as all the self-help books for social lepers recommend—but as soon as I've rapped out a sentence he—as I very much doubt the self-help books recommend—ricochets it back to the glorious subject of *him*. For instance, where did I last go on holiday? I went to Spain. What a coincidence! He went to Spain when he was three, yes, he went to Madrid and saw a bullfight and decided he wanted to be a matador but, ha ha, he's settled for being an intellectual property lawyer, and drone drone drone.

I've sunk into a trance which I snap out of when Alan's woolly-jumper-clad arm snakes round my shoulder. I shake it off and snarl, 'I've got a boyfriend.'

Although this is a lie he looks greasily insulted. 'And I've got a girlfriend!' he says preeningly. 'But I presume we can still be friends.'

I shoot him a killer look and hope he dies—or at least goes away, but no. Alan's type never do. He prattles on about himself for approximately eternity. Then, praise the Lord, a swig of his lager and lime goes down the wrong way and he stops bragging to choke for a minute. I take this fortuitous opportunity to stand up and say, 'Bye, I'm going now.'

I elbow my way through the U-Bar's brightly attired clientele—heaven knows where Tina got to—and leg it to the tube.

Even the train journey is incensing. I don't mind the hordes of raucous, rowdy, shouty, drunken louts—after all, any other Friday night they're me and Tina. It's the pair of canoodling pensioners who sit directly opposite me holding hands and smiling soppily who make me want to scream and scream.

It's disgusting at their age. Why aren't you dead? I think. You should be dead. My father's dead, why aren't you? By the time the train pulls into Finchley Road tube station I am buzzing with a hatred so vivid I feel physically ill. I stamp home in the dark, daring any mugger, rapist or murderer to attack—just try it, matey, and you'll wish you hadn't.

I arrive home, unscathed, ten minutes later. It's only 10.50. I quietly shut the door, take a deep, slow breath, glide to the kitchen table and sit down. Then I rest my head in my hands and think, 'Help me, someone, please help me,' over and over and over. I don't know what to do. I'm going mad. 'Oh God, please help me.' I think I say this aloud, because suddenly Marcus is beside me stroking my hair and saying softly, 'Hey, Hellie, my all-time favourite girl, what's up?' and I burst into tears.

Ten minutes later, I'm snogging Marcus.

I'm not entirely sure how this happened. One minute I am bawling like a red-faced baby with wind, the next, Marcus has hauled me out of my seat and into his strong (yes!) firm (oh my!) muscle-bound (bonus point!) arms. I cried and snotted onto his linen shirt, leaving a wet, greenish slime mark which, fortunately, escaped his notice. He stroked my hair some more and whispered, 'Poor Hellie, poor little chicken, hush now, don't you cry.' Then he started kissing my head. Marcus J. Bogush! Kissing *me*. After all these barren years!

Pensioners forgotten, I clamp my mouth to his. He pulls my head back by grabbing my hair, which is painful, but I don't dare ruin the moment by saying 'ouch'. We kiss long and hard, but—horror of horrors—his snogging style isn't quite as blissful as his reputation with the ladies suggests. To be miserably honest, I'm disappointed. This man produces an inordinate amount of saliva, I'm thinking ungratefully, when the phone rings. It clicks to the answering machine.

'Hi, Helen, Tom here! Calling to see if you fancied a tequila some time.'

I freeze. Tom's timing is very, bad, indeed. Marcus lets go of me as if

I'm radioactive, the lustful bleariness vanishing from his clean-cut face as if he's torn off a mask. 'So I've got competition,' he remarks airily.

'Not really,' I stammer.

'*Yes*, really,' says Marcus pleasantly. 'Perhaps I should leave you to it.'

I say, 'It's just that he's been—' I stop as I look at Marcus who stares back unblinkingly.

'Your choice, Helen,' he says.

I pick up the phone. 'Hi, Tom?' I say.

'Oh!' he says, 'screening your calls. And I made it!'

This—despite all my recent protestations to Tina—is going to be difficult. I glance nervously at Marcus, who crosses his arms Gladiator-fashion and yawns. 'Tom,' I say sadly, hesitantly.

He interrupts. His voice is somewhat cooler. 'This isn't going to be good, is it?'

I bite my lip. 'Tom,' I sigh, 'I like you and everything but I'm really busy right now, at work and stuff, but I'll, why don't I give you a ring some time.' I glance again at Marcus. He looks unimpressed. So I add, 'But, huh, don't hold your breath.'

There is a short pause. Then, in a cold, contemptuous voice, Tom says, 'Message received and understood.' The line goes dead.

'Ker-bam!' says Marcus loudly as he smoothly removes the receiver from my hand and spins me round to face him. 'So,' he continues—kiss kiss on my neck—'what'—kiss kiss on my throat—'shall'—unbutton nibble—'we'—unbutton kiss—'do'—unbutton slurp—'now?'

I cling on to Marcus's broad shoulders and close my eyes in a parody of desire, but inwardly I feel about as turned on as a dead bunny rabbit. I have humiliated Tom, but *I* feel humiliated. Those four words—message received and understood—fill my head and shame me.

I am roused from my non-lecherous thoughts by the unwelcome realisation that Marcus is giving me a love bite. Pardon me but I grew out of teenage territorial marking behaviour *at least* three months ago. My lack of enthusiasm is maybe obvious, because Marcus abruptly ceases his suction pump impression and says in a solemn tone, 'Hellie, we can stop right now or we can take this further.'

I snap out of it. This is Marcus, my nine-year lust object, for heaven's sake! 'Let's rock!' I say in what I hope is a sex-kittenish growl.

He smiles a triumphant smile, says, 'That's my girl!' then picks me up, grunting slightly with the effort, and lugs me into his bedroom.

Six and a half unerotic minutes later, Marcus and I are lying side by side under his white duvet and I am trying to think of something to say. 'That was nice,' I lie. Amazingly, considering his cut-price performance, he believes me. He props himself on one elbow and idly twiddles a finger—I never noticed before how little his hands are—round my right breast. I glance up and, with a shock, see he has an amused expression on his face. 'What?' I say suspiciously.

Marcus wrinkles his nose. 'Nothing,' he grins, 'they're cute.'

The impudence! For the record, my bosoms happen to be size 36A, and for the record again—seeing as we're being so free and easy and judgmental about other people's body parts—Marcus's dick happens to be size AA, as in pocket-camera battery size. Only it doesn't last as long. I am bristling with pique, when Marcus throws aside the duvet, announces, 'I'm going to shower,' and springs out of bed.

'Fine by me,' I murmur, drawing the duvet up to my chin.

'So,' he continues, a little brusquely, 'aren't you going to shower?'

I prop myself on my elbows and purr, 'Is that an invitation?'

Marcus looks embarrassed. He scratches the back of his left calf with his right foot and says, 'Hellie, I have this thing about showering? It's kooky but I like to shower alone. But you can go and use *your* shower.'

'What, and come back here afterwards?' I blurt.

Marcus hesitates and says, 'If you like, although it might be awkward if Luke spots you, that's the only thing.'

I will the hurt not to show on my face. 'You're so right,' I say slowly. 'Would you mind passing me my shirt.'

He passes me my shirt. 'You know, Hellie, I'd love to spend the night with you. But this way you'll get your beauty sleep! Another time, eh?' He delivers this cliché like it's a Perrier-Award-winning joke.

'Ha,' I say. He's all right. He's *Marcus*. Marcus is Marcus. With an entire body pointlessly pumped up except for that one crucial part. My resentment dissipates. 'Go and have your shower,' I say in a kindly tone, 'and I'll see you tomorrow.'

This elicits a showcase beam. 'Night, night,' he says.

He turns away (phew he's hairy!) and walks, starkers, towards his en suite bathroom and I feel a pang. 'Marcus!' I blurt.

'Yes?' he says, only a tad tersely.

As I speak I am wriggling into my worst-ever knickers. 'I'll make you dinner tomorrow night, if you like.'

I can't quite decipher his expression but he replies cheerily, 'Great, see you then,' disappears into the bathroom and shuts the door.

I heave myself out of his bed, collect my clothes, plod to my bedroom, remove my shirt and fall into bed. I haven't removed my make-up, washed my face, cleaned my teeth or flossed. 'Big fat hairy deal,' I say sarcastically to the ceiling. Then I lie stark staring awake till 4.00am.

I open my eyes at, according to my under-used alarm clock, 2.18pm, and for the second time that week think—without yet knowing why—'Oh no.' My memory allows me half a second's grace before it all comes trickling back. Oh no. I churn over last night's events. The U-Bar. Alan. The pensioners. Marcus. The cocktail sausage. The shower. The dinner offer. The *acceptance*.

Maybe not so oh no after all. Then I run through what I can cook and am back to oh no again. I march to the untouched clutch of cookery books on Marcus's highest kitchen shelf and pull down a few.

The Italian one falls at the first chapter because I don't know what a trevise is. The English one devotes 100 pages to stodgy main meals and 425 pages to full-fat desserts. As Marcus would rather boil himself in oil than eat anything cooked in it, I'm left with the American one which lists recipes for mashed potatoes (I can do that!) and chicken pot pie. Easy! Oh bugger. It expects you to make your own pastry. Get real. I abandon the books and decide to improvise.

I'll make mashed potato (peel potatoes, boil potatoes, mash them, stir in tub of margarine) and the fish dish (chop leeks, wok them, put them in baking dish, plonk block of frozen fish on top, plonk Greek yoghurt on top of fish, grate Cheddar on top of yoghurt, cover and stick in oven for as long as it takes to seduce your guest). Lizzy told me how to make the fish dish and it's delicious. And, more importantly, it requires four ingredients as opposed to ninety. I check the fridge. My section (Marcus has partitioned it to cut down on pilfering) is empty except for a cracked yellow rock of Cheddar, and a crumb-encrusted pat of butter. I could trim the butter but the cheese is on its deathbed.

Which reminds me. I really should call my mother. As of Wednesday she's stopped phoning which is brilliant but curious. I'll ring her tomorrow. I'll just ring Tina before schlepping to Waitrose.

She simpers, 'Oh, Helen! Bloody hell!' Her voice oozes woozy post-orgasmic wonder.

I say accusingly, 'It's that blond bloke!'

She sighs blissfully, 'Oh, Helen, it certainly is!'

At this point I'll interrupt to say, this is peculiar. Not normal. Usually when Tina meets a man the most you'll get out of her is a grudging 'he's OK'. I am rapt. 'Tell me. Now.'

She sighs down the phone, 'We-e-ell, his name's Adrian—'

'*Adrian!*' I squeal.

'Yes, Adrian!' she says sharply. 'What's wrong with Adrian?'

I gulp, 'Nothing, nothing, it's a lovely name. Yes, so carry on.'

Adrian, apparently, is perfect. He is perfect from the tips of his perfect toes to the top of his perfect head and he is particularly perfect around the groin area. He has a perfect job as an architect, he owns a perfect bijou flat just outside Maida Vale, and, most perfectly of all—he thinks Tina is perfect.

'What, already?' I say. 'But you've only known him eight minutes.'

Tina cackles down the phone, 'I'm telling you, girl,' she says, 'this is the big one. I feel it in my . . . pants!'

I am not entirely delighted about this. I rely on Tina's eternal disenchantment with men—despite the fact it's a sham—as a reassuring romantic barometer. Her reaction to my news about Marcus doesn't make me feel any better.

'But he wears tanga briefs!' she shrieks.

This stumps me for a second, so all I say is, 'How do you know?'

'I can see them through his chinos!' she shouts.

I speedily recover composure. 'So what!' I snap. 'We can't all be members of the fashion police!'

Tina chooses to ignore this jibe. 'Helen,' she says in a more serious tone, 'I don't want to rain on your parade, I know you've fancied him for years, but we're all agreed, he's even worse than Jasper. He's an enormous great plonking plonker.' If only. 'So,' she continues blithely, 'how big was his todger?' I admit it is bonsai and we honk with laughter. 'So why bother with him?' she gasps.

I shrug down the phone. 'It's just . . . I can't explain it. I *like* him. I feel—don't laugh—drawn to him. And he was so sweet when I was upset. Maybe he was nervous. Maybe it was cold in the room—'

'Maybe,' Tina interrupts, 'he has a needle dick!'

We chortle some more—although her chortling is rather more hearty than mine—then I excuse myself and plod to Waitrose.

Five exhausting hours later, the lair is painstakingly prepared. I've banished an incredulous Luke to the pub (he didn't take too much persuading) and tidied the kitchen. The mash is mashed, the fish is cooking, the table is laid, the candles are lit, the wine is chilled, the butter is trimmed, and *I*—aka dessert—am washed, brushed, dressed and tarted to the max. The only missing ingredient is Marcus.

I wait until ten to ten, eat the entire fish dish myself and let Fatboy feast on the mash.

It's days like today I wish I'd invented Tetra Pak. Billions of quid for one minute of basic origami. To add insult to jealousy, yesterday I tried to squeeze open a Tetra Pak carton of mushroom soup and instead of neatly transforming into a controlled, soup-pouring lip it became a raggedy mess and the soup glooped all over the floor.

Luke suggested I was attacking it from the wrong side but I snarled, 'Since when are *you* the expert? You only ever eat out of boxes and tins.'

He looked hurt and about to argue, then noticed my rabid expression and kept quiet. Luke has been tiptoeing around me ever since Marcus went AWOL. Admittedly, on Sunday morning he did exclaim, in a voice of epiphany, 'He must be staying with that pop star from Second Edition!' This must be Marcus's inimitable way of telling me he doesn't want a relationship. That apart, Luke's been a model of sensitivity and tact. I, meanwhile, have been a model of sourness and temper. Partly because of Marcus, partly because of Tom, mainly because—thanks to my non-innovative mind—I have to return to work today.

I slink into the office, trying to avoid attracting attention. There is a barely perceptible hush as I walk in, almost as if I'm wearing last season's trainers. Which I am. Tina breaks the silence by shouting, 'Bradshaw! Welcome back!' Lizzy rushes over to give me a fierce hug. 'Helen,' she says bossily, 'take it easy today. If it gets too much go for a walk. And here, take this. It'll help you sleep better.'

She presses a small object into my hand before running back to her desk. It is a bottle of aromatherapy oil. LAVENDER GREEN ABSOLUTE, it reads—and in smaller letters for the more intellectual users—*Lavandula officinalis*. I'm touched.

Some colleagues—after wary observation of my apparently stable exchange with Lizzy—trundle up to say they're sorry about my dad. Others send me kindly emails, and a few look shifty and treat me as if I have Ebola. Laetitia doesn't know *what* to do and murmurs, 'Stiff upper lip, stiff upper lip.' Then she dispatches me to fetch her breakfast (one slice of wholemeal toast with peanut butter, *no* butter, and a cappuccino with cinnamon, *no* chocolate). I buy a double espresso and a blueberry muffin for myself, which I eat guiltily while Lizzy's back is turned.

The day isn't too bad. I spend it transcribing readers' letters and other yawnsome copy onto the computer system. I ring freelance writers to remind them of the impending features meeting (the layabouts never send in ideas otherwise). And I collect Laetitia's trouser-suit from the dry-cleaner's. The one advantage of being back at work is that I have less time to brood about Marcus. Or Jasper who, I realise, hasn't rung me for over two and a half weeks. The one disadvantage of being back at work is that when Lizzy, Tina and I go out for lunch I am forced to listen to the wonder of Adrian for sixty minutes. Even Lizzy stifles a delicate yawn. It looks like being an uneventful week.

On Thursday morning I notice that Fatboy is, for the first time in his well-fed life, off his food. He opens his pink triangle mouth and meows loudly, slinks around my ankles—leaving a fine dusting of orange fur on my black trousers—leaps onto the kitchen surface (Marcus would freak) and butts my arm affectionately with his head. But when I open a tin and empty the gunk into his blue china bowl, he sticks his tail in the air like a mast, and swaggers off. Then he starts howling. This is a truly terrible noise. I feel I have failed as a mother. 'What?' I say in exasperation.

'*Ma-uuaaaaaaaa-w!*'

'I'm sorry, I don't understand,' I say crossly before realising I'm late for work and running out of the door.

I brood all Thursday morning about Marcus and Fatboy until the afternoon when I call my mother. There's no reply. So I start brooding about her. Since the funeral, I haven't been very attentive to my mother. That is, I haven't seen or spoken to her. I should have. But I didn't want to. I'd have been no good to her anyway. I won't feel bad, I refuse. Why can't I cut off for two, three weeks without it being a bloody great issue? I call her mobile. It's switched off. Please try again later. Where *is* she? I call the house again and let it ring until finally it clicks onto the answering machine. I almost drop the receiver as a voice intones, 'You have reached the home of Maurice and Cecelia Bradshaw. We are not available to take your call. Kindly leave a message after the long tone.'

My heart is hammering at such a rate I expect it to explode out of my chest—*my father's voice*. I replace the receiver and dial again. Then I hunch over my desk, close my eyes and relish my father's deep, powerful voice. 'We are not available . . .' Mesmerised, I listen to his message again.

Finally, I leave a message. 'Hello, Mum, it's me. Hope you're OK. Sorry I haven't called. I've just been mad at work. Give me a ring. OK. Bye, then.' Maybe she's out shopping with her friend Vivienne. Or gone swimming. This is what I tell myself. But I don't believe it. I am sitting at my desk and Laetitia is ordering me to ring the book critic to remind her that her copy is a week late and all I can think is that my mother is dead and it's my fault. She's had a stroke and is rotting away at the bottom of the stairs. I am choked with dread and I just *know*. My mother is dead. I need air.

'I'm sorry,' I gasp to an amazed Laetitia and rush out of the office and into the street. I look about wildly, having no clue what I'm doing or where I'm going, run across the road, flop on a wooden bench—*In fond memory of Anthony Bayer, who loved London*—oh God, and try to breathe. I feel hot and cold and sick and faint. Five seconds later, Laetitia appears.

'Helen,' she says twitchily. 'Whatever's the matter? Did you have a tiff with whatshisname, Jason?'

'My mother is dead!' I whisper.

'You mean your father,' she says.

'My mother. I know it.'

Laetitia clears her throat. 'Helen,' she says, 'your mother just rang. She asked me to take a message.'

Shit. Laetitia never takes messages. Ever. I breathe slowly, deeply, and sit up straight. 'Thank you, Laetitia, very much,' I say hurriedly.

'She said, if you're free, you could visit her this evening.' If I'm free? My mother, thinking of someone other than herself? Amazing. I nod and, panic over, meekly follow Laetitia back inside and spend the rest of the afternoon trying to keep up with her unstoppable flow of 'little tasks'. I leave work at six on the dot and go straight to my mother's.

I ring the doorbell. No reply. I ring again. Most unusual. I ring again. Finally! A figure glides slowly down the stairs and approaches the frosted glass. Clank! Clank! and the front door is heaved open. 'Since when have you bolted the—' I begin as I step inside. Then I look at her, I *see* my mother. And I am frozen with shock. She looks like death.

She has always been slight (I take after my father), but in the three weeks I haven't seen her she has shed at least a stone in weight. Her hair hangs in clumps, filthy and lank, her wan face is devoid of make-up and her skin is dry and papery. This! A woman who cleanses, tones and moisturises religiously, flosses after every meal and showers once in the morning and again before bedtime. And what is she wearing? A knitted brown jumper five sizes too big for her and saggy black leggings.

'Oh, my God!' I say, when I recover the power of speech. 'Oh, my God, look at you! Mum, you look terrible, *terrible*! You're a skeleton! And that horrible jumper! It's summer! You look like a tramp!'

She stares back at me dully. Her eyes are blank. Then she says, 'It belonged to your father,' and starts to weep. Huge, gulping, hiccupping, gut-wrenching sobs. I grab her and, in an awkward half-hug, carry her to a chair. Jesus! She's lighter than Fatboy!

'Oh, Mum,' I whisper, 'what have you done to yourself? When did you last eat, for Christ's sake! The state of you! Shit! Why didn't you call me?'

She is sobbing so hard the words are swallowed almost as she says them. But while they are indistinct I hear them and her answer is like a knife slashing at my heart: 'I did.'

She starts to cry again. I crouch and rock her and stroke her flat greasy hair and the sobs become more savage until she is yowling like an animal in pain. 'Owww,' she howls, 'I can't re-mem-berrrr . . .'

I gulp. 'What can't you remember, Mummy?' I'm terrified.

'I—I can't remember him, just the hospital. I want to remember him alive but'—now screaming—'I can't! I can't! Why can't I? I can only remember him dying.'

I close my eyes. I have goose pimples and a hard painful lump in my throat. 'Oh, Mum,' I whisper. The tears are pricking at my eyes, but not out of grief—out of guilt. I picture myself necking tequila, rolling around naked with Ape Boy instead of calling my mother, and the pain is acute—I shudder and shrink from my thoughts as if they are blows.

And yet. I feel a fraud. Separate. Untouched. The feeling is like an out-of-body experience—as if I'm watching my mother and myself, dispassionately, from another place. The yowling continues until my mother exhausts herself, then it subsides to a whimper. I keep stroking her hair and its greasiness is sticky on my hands. I also notice that she smells. Unwashed. Stale. 'Mummy!' I say in a stern voice as if she were a small child. 'Listen to me! I am going to run you a bath and if you like, I will help you wash your hair. I'll even wash between your legs if you can't manage it yourself. What do you reckon?'

My mother stiffens in horror. 'Certainly not!' she squeaks in a voice so high and loud it would deafen a bat.

Thought that'd snap her out of it. All the same, I escort her to the bathroom, turn on the taps, pour in a litre of bubble bath, and alert her to the whereabouts of the shampoo. 'I want you to stay in there for half an hour and get your hair squeaky clean,' I say. 'I am also going to put some clean clothes on your bed for you to change into.' My mother hovers uncertainly on the bathmat. Wafty as she is, I give her a gentle hug. 'I'll get you a clean towel from the airing cupboard.'

I leave my mother to undress, dig out a towel, and march to her wardrobe. I select white knickers and matching bra, a light blue cotton blouse, a beige belt, and a navy pair of what I believe elderly people call slacks. Sunny, tasteful, but not too garish in the face of death. I am laying this outfit on her bed when I catch a whiff of the sheets, and even I recognise that it is high (and I mean high) time for a spin in the Zanussi. I strip the bed of its sheets and pillowcases—an old nightshirt flies out so I grab that too—punch the whole lot into the washing machine, pour in a generous slug of Persil, and twist the dial to boil wash.

My priority is to force my mother to eat. I open the fridge—the fridge that I always make a beeline for whenever I visit my parents in the secure knowledge that it will contain: A, chocolate mousse, B, smoked salmon, C, exotic fruit, D, expensive cheese, E, homemade vegetable lasagne. In other words everything my own deprived Third World fridge never contains. Today, however, my parents' corporate fat-cat fridge is bereft of its bounty. Its contents: A, one tub of peach yoghurt (a week past its sell-by date), B, one wrinkly tomato, C, a micro-portion of Edam cheese, D, a small bar of Dairy Milk chocolate, E, a packet of Cornflakes, F, a copy of *The Firm* by John Grisham. Jesus. (I don't mean Jesus is *in* there, I mean . . . goodness me.)

I place the Cornflakes in the larder and *The Firm* on the bookshelf. I don't know what to do first. Should I run to the twenty-four-hour Tesco for supplies? Or should I vacuum the lounge? I reason, if my mother has starved herself thus far, she can go hungry for a few more hours. I'll tidy up the hallway and work my way through the house. I am, to be honest, fearful of what I'll find. And my fear is justified.

I peer into a plastic bag minding its own business by the umbrella stand and discover that it is stuffed full of envelopes—all unopened.

Frantically, I tip the plastic bag upside-down and shake its contents onto the floor. Gas bills, telephone bills, credit card bills, electricity bills. There is also a letter from our solicitor Alex Simpkinson—dated fifteen days ago—stating that my father's assets, debts and liabilities need to be ascertained in order to complete the probate papers, that my mother should forward any demands on to him, that he'll be in touch as soon as he is in possession of all the relevant details, but in the meantime, should she require any advice she shouldn't hesitate to get in contact. I am trembling with—I don't know what—stress? shock? sadness? But I grimly, methodically, open every envelope and place each communication in one of three piles according to status. I don't have the strength to tackle my mother on this subject right now. And right now, I don't think she has the strength to be tackled.

The rest of the downstairs is, thankfully, reasonably tidy. It is in the lounge that I make my next shock-discovery: a crisp pink pristine stack of the *Financial Times* neatly stowed behind my father's easy chair. His reading glasses and a heavy wood humidor of Cohiba cigars are on the side table, his red velvety slippers underneath it. I feel like Hercule Poirot. And my mother has mutated into Miss Havisham. This gloomy suspicion is confirmed by an earsplitting shriek from upstairs.

I gallop up to the master bedroom, two stairs at a time. What now? My mother, wrapped in a towel, hair dripping, screeches, 'You stupid girl, what have you done?'

What I have done is to commit the most heinous, mindless, criminal act of vandalism in the history of the world. I have washed my mother's bedclothes and my father's nightshirt in a Zanussi washing machine with lashings of Persil at the extremely high temperature of ninety-five degrees, thus exterminating the immeasurably treasured lingering scent of Maurice Bradshaw for ever.

I spend the rest of the evening apologising, tidying, cajoling, consoling and force-feeding. I make an emergency dash to Tesco and buy spinach soup, strawberries, avocados, cottage cheese, bananas, wholemeal bread, butter, fresh pasta, ready-prepared fresh tomato sauce, salad in a pack, fresh salmon, and a packet of brazil nuts. Most of this is on Lizzy's advice—I call her on my mobile while overtaking a truck on the A1. Apparently, my mother needs oodles of vitamin B6 which, says Lizzy, will 'cheer her up'—which I doubt.

I am less than thrilled when my mother manages half a carton of spinach soup, one slice of buttered toast, then announces she's 'full up'.

I growl, 'At least you ate something' and vow to work on her tomorrow. I make her eat a vitamin pill, send her to her freshly laundered bed, and tell her I'll return to check on her first thing in the morning.

The trouble with death is, there isn't an end to it. It goes on and on and on. Sometimes, I'll forget it's happened. Or I won't believe it. But then I'll remember. And I will not believe it as much as I like, but it won't go away. My mother pores over photo albums obsessively. As if—because the image of my father is evident in glorious Fuji technicolour—he can't be dead. I, meanwhile, am at a loss. I don't know if my mother is in such a state because she loved my father or because she is on her own.

I spend the entire week fussing and fretting and decide that from now on, I shall devote every Sunday *plus* Monday and Wednesday evenings to fattening up my mother and distracting her from widowhood. Unfortunately, this plan necessitates me forfeiting my social life and learning to cook.

I also ring a few of my mother's friends. According to my mother, they have 'abandoned her'. From what I can gather, this is not strictly true. I play back the string of ignored messages on her answering machine and discover that her old pal Vivienne has called nine times. Nana Flo has called fourteen times. I cringe as I listen to her cracked, splintery voice. She sounds lost. 'Cecelia, are you there? Hello? Hello? Is this machine broken? Hello?'

I'd forgotten about Nana Flo. Oh, all right, I'd forgotten about her in the way that you forget about a dental appointment. I'll ring Vivienne first. Vivienne's early messages are along the lines of 'Cessy, it's Viv. I do hope you're bearing up, give me a tinkle when you have a moment. Call any time, day or night.' Her later messages are along the lines of 'Cecelia! Vivienne here. I'm very concerned. Why haven't you called? Have I done something to offend you? Do call. I'm dying to—I'm desperate to see you. We should do lunch.'

It emerges, when I quiz my mother, that Vivienne *did* visit her, three weeks ago. She popped round to invite my mother 'for a casual bite, Monday lunch' and to disinvite my mother to a dinner party, Saturday night, arranged five days before my father selfishly popped his brown Church's lace-ups and put out Vivienne's table plan.

I tell my mother that while Vivienne has done ill, she means well, and to give her another chance. Meanwhile, I tell Vivienne—I catch her on her mobile between Harley Street and the hair salon—that my mother has no intention of pinching anyone else's husband yet and on that basis, I trust her dinner invitation is reinstated with immediate effect.

Vivienne is flustered and blustering. 'Helen, she's more than welcome, you know that,' she trills. 'But you have to know I was, first and foremost, thinking of *her*. We're going to be five couples! Us, the Elworthys, the Williamses, the Schnecks and the Strutherses! The last thing I wanted was to rub salt into the wound.' I overlook the glaring fact that at least three of these guests are having affairs and explain, while it will certainly be painful for my mother to sit amid these shiny prototypes of married bliss, she would doubtless prefer it to sitting at home on her own eating a piece of Edam cheese in front of *Casualty*. The upshot? My mother—dressed in black from obstinate head to defiant toe—goes to the ball.

I, meanwhile, sit at home on my own eating a piece of Edam cheese in front of *Casualty*. It is a joy and a pleasure. The only bluebottle in the ointment is Fatboy who picks at his food like a sixth-form girl on a diet and remains on hunger strike throughout Sunday. On Monday morning I ring work, explain to a frosty Laetitia that I have 'toothache', and take my cat to the vet. Megavet. I am jittery with anticipation and fear. I wince as I recall my recent shameful exchange with Tom. Maybe another vet will be on duty. And yet . . .

Tom waves me into the surgery without a glimmer of recognition or warmth. 'What's the problem?' he says as I empty Fatboy from his Pet Voyager—he clings frantically to its vertical side like a passenger on the sinking *Titanic*—onto the surgery table. 'Well,' I say nervously, 'he's lost his appetite. He's also had diarrhoea.'

Tom's expression turns even more disapproving. 'How long has this been going on?' he says coldly. Isn't that a line in a song? I think, but don't dare say. I am desperate to beg Tom's forgiveness but too certain of being rejected.

'Well, I'm not entirely sure,' I say, squirming with guilt, 'but [*gulp*] maybe a week, two weeks.'

Tom glares at me. Then he says, 'In a young cat, symptoms like these can be the first signs of leukaemia, feline AIDS, or FIP—a horrible disease which starts with diarrhoea and snottiness about food and ends with respiratory problems. I'm going to have to run some bloods.'

I gasp, 'Oh no!' and, in a small piteous voice, add, 'Fatboy won't die, will he?' I am near tears and about to report myself to the RSPCA.

The side of Tom's mouth twitches and he says, 'We'll get the lab results tomorrow.'

I am weak with remorse and shame and terror. I watch in silence as Tom feels Fatboy's lardy abdomen, prises open his jaw and peers down his throat, and pushes his lip into a sneer (Fatboy's, I mean—Tom's own lip is already in a sneer). Then he gently presses Fatboy into a crouch, restrains him in a firm hug and—to loud, hissy indignation—slides a greased thermometer up Fatboy's bottom. 'All right, big chap,' he murmurs in a soft, low voice.

My heart flips. Eventually, he removes the thermometer and says sharply, 'He has a slight temperature.' I nod sadly. He then summons the vile pouting Celine, trims a tiny square of fur on each of Fatboy's front legs, swabs each shaven patch and, while Celine holds down Fatboy who I will to bite her, takes a squiddle of blood from each vein. He then squirts it into two transparent tubes, one pink topped, the other orange.

Considering his roller-coaster ordeal, Fatboy isn't as outraged as he should be. He emits a deep, angry growl, but allows Tom to weigh him while I, the evil abuser, choke back my tardy tears of penitence. Tom leans down, strokes Fatboy's head, and plops him back into his Pet Voyager.

He glances at me, seems to hesitate, then says, in a firm, but not *terribly* hateful, tone: 'That cat is taking on the proportions of a boudoir madam. I want you to starve him for today, and I'm going to give you a supply of special bland cat food. I'm putting Fatboy on a weight-reducing diet. And I'll let you know when we get the lab results. But if he pukes or squits again, bring him in immediately.'

I nod meekly and whisper, 'So there's a sliver of hope for Fatboy?'

Tom turns away—I think, to cough—then says sternly, 'More than a sliver. You want to know his real problem? He's a mummy's boy!' With that, he tots up the (extortionate) bill, hands over the 'recovery pack' and nods in his next client. He says, 'Bye,' but looks a fraction past my ear as he says it. I go home, groom Fatboy, and feel ashamed of myself.

I award myself compassionate leave for the rest of the day and stay awake all of Monday night praying. Tom rings me at work on Tuesday at 11.39am to inform me, in a brisk tone, that Fatboy is fine apart from a small increase in his red blood cells indicating he may have worms. I rush to Megavet straight from work. Tom briefly appears to hand me a worming tablet and a quarter (because Fatboy is so fat) in a blue and white envelope. 'If he pukes within half an hour it hasn't been digested,' he says, sounding about as warm as a deep-frozen polar bear. 'If he pukes any later it's worked, it's just upset his tummy.'

I spend a good forty minutes before managing to poke the pill down Fatboy's throat. Then I spend twenty minutes dabbing my wounds with antiseptic. I am angry and upset. I call Tina. She's out. I call Lizzy. She's out. So I call Michelle. Who has run up an almighty overdraft whinging about her boyfriend Sammy, so she owes me.

I rant and rave about Tom. I am not quite sure how I want Michelle to react, but she puts on a satisfying show. Boy, does he sound like a piece of work! Messing with your head like that! He should lighten up! He's way intense! Etc!

I am inflamed and inspired to consult her on a matter that has been niggling for some time. I miss Jasper. I keep thinking about him. I want to call him. Again, Michelle obliges. He's a cool guy and I should go for it. Encouragement and permission! So I do.

To my disbelief and delight, Jasper is 'chuffed' to hear from me. It would be 'ace' to meet up some time. 'How are you fixed for tomorrow night?' I say (an hour of listening to Michelle and even Luke would start talking like a Hollywood Wife). 'I'm around,' drawls Jasper. 'Why don't you stop by?'

I squirm with coquettish pleasure and purr into the phone, 'I could do that . . .' I replace the receiver, head swirling. Jasper Sanderson & Helen Bradshaw. The return of! To borrow a favourite Jasperian phrase: Michelle—you played a blinder. I make a beeline for my underwear drawer and start choosing knickers.

Chapter 3

If ever Tina and I want to irritate Lizzy, which we frequently do, we call her Mogadon Girl. This is because Pure Unadulterated Elizabeth is petrified of flying and before she'll set even her littlest toe in a Boeing she has to pop a great fat horsepill of a Nitrazepam. Of course she tried hypnotherapy, acupuncture and peppermint tea first but, to our private glee, they didn't make the tiniest dent of difference and the Wholesome One was forced to resort to legalised drugs.

Until four months ago, when my father died, I couldn't comprehend Lizzy's fears. Before my father died I was invincible. I'd read about a honeymoon couple whose plane erupted in flames over a turquoise sea, a woman stabbed as she walked home from work, friends blown up as they sat in a pub drinking on a warm summer's night, a young man shot at a bus-stop, and I'd feel pity and turn the page. I knew that kind of thing happened to other people.

Now, I read about other people and they are me. I am tearful, angry, and obsessed. I imagine their last carefree minutes before the end. I wonder if they comprehended the actual moment of death. I ache for their poor, bewildered families, the stricken mother saying, 'Why him? Why do they always take the best?' The fiancé, face pale, eyes red, whispering, 'She was my life. I can't believe this has happened.' I feast sorrowfully on their pain with the self-loathing and monomaniacal compulsion of a bulimic devouring chocolate cake.

These days, my mouth is dry with fear. I get out of bed in the morning and I think, 'This could be the day I die.' I feel my heart beating and I think, 'This could stop at any moment.' Of course, I reason to myself, 'Get a grip, you silly, silly cow.' But then people do just drop down dead. People who, might I add, eat fewer Dime bars than I do and exercise more regularly than once a month. There's no guarantee. I'm jittery. Snappy. Tense. Unless I'm engaged in a specific and enjoyable task—namely, watching *Xena: Warrior Princess*, reading murder books, or sleeping—I feel hollow and detached from the world and in the absence of anything better, my default emotion is terror.

As I struggle in my neurotic pyschotic phase, my mother graduates from What Ifs. Possibly, the What Ifs are infectious and I've caught hers. Because, in the weeks following my discovery of the pink paper mountain and literary fridge, she became obsessed. What if she'd forced my father to economise on his egg intake? What if she'd ordered him out for a brisk walk after dinner? What if she'd bought him Allen Carr's *Easy Way To Stop Smoking*?

To which I could only reply, in my head, 'What if my father was another person—specifically, one who didn't come from a family riddled with heart disease?' To her face, I said, 'Mum, please don't torture yourself. You did everything you could. If it was going to happen, it was going to happen. And anyway, you know Dad wouldn't have listened.' As these lumbering platitudes were as novel and astonishing as a model dating a rock star—what can I say that isn't a cliché?—my mother sped on with the verbal self-flagellation.

What if she'd postponed plucking her eyebrows and was watching my father eat lunch? What if she'd made him a salad (no dressing, obviously)? 'Mum!' I shouted. 'Now stop it! If you'd made him a salad he'd have thrown it in the bin. You were a brilliant partner. You made him very happy. You have nothing to feel guilty about.' This made her cry and I realised, with annoyance, that I had expressed to my mother practically the exact trite sentiments that, not so long ago, Lizzy had expressed to me.

However, after four cosseted cocoony months (you didn't want to be there) my mother has perked up and I've become such a social worker it's a constant surprise to me that I haven't started wearing a smock.

I started off by cooking for my mother. I made vegetable risotto from the recipe on the back of the risotto rice pack, Tina's coriander chicken recipe (chop and fry onion and garlic in olive oil, chop and add chicken, then coriander, white wine and half-fat crème fraîche—in deference to my father) and—because I can—potato wedges. After our fourth potato wedge dinner in a row my mother screeched, 'I'm sick of potato wedges! They're junk food!' and threw her plate across the room. At this point, I would have happily left her to starve.

Instead I hissed, 'All right, wise guy. You're so clever, you show me how it's done!'

This rashly thrown gauntlet heralded the start of phase two—an unenjoyable period in which I spent every Monday and Wednesday night in my mother's kitchen spoiling the broth and being shouted at. She had fun, though. I think she misses overfeeding my father.

As for me, three months after I renewed my biblical acquaintance with Jasper, he suggested we 'cool it'.

I was stunned. 'Why?' I said, gnawing at the skin on my lip. 'I thought we were getting on really well.' This, crazily, isn't a lie. We only met occasionally. And when we did, we had proper conversations. Jasper told me about going to boarding school and being unfavourably compared to his brilliant elder brother. I told Jasper about *wanting* to go to boarding school. Jasper told me about his parents moving to Singapore and seeing him once a year. I told Jasper about my parents living in Muswell Hill and seeing me once a quarter. I thought Jasper and I were having fun. Admittedly, the sex wasn't quite as fabulous as before, but that was mainly because I worried my father was watching.

'We *were* getting on well,' said Jasper, 'we *do*. Babe, I really like you, but, er, you remember my ex-girlfriend Louisa . . .' This is not a question.

'Yeeees,' I said, 'if she's the same Louisa you've been slagging off for the past twelve weeks. What about her?' The penny dropped like a wingless plane. 'Oh, my God,' I shouted, 'not again!'

Jasper waggled a finger to silence me. 'Helen, shussh, it's not what you think.'

'What then?'

Jasper coughed. 'I'm broke, the lease is up here, and Louisa's just bought a two-bedroom flat and needs a lodger.'

To which my witty riposte was: 'Bollocks.'

But Jasper widened his paradise-blue eyes and insisted. 'She's seeing someone, there's nothing between us, babe, hand on heart.'

You don't have one, I thought. Then I had another thought. 'So if you're not shagging Louisa,' I enquired cunningly, 'why should *we* cool it?'

His risible excuse? 'It's a single room.' He started to waffle about 'time out to reflect', but I held up a stiff hand in protest and he shut up.

My parting shot: 'Actually, Jasper, if you'd cared to ask you'd know that I'm also buying a flat. And *my* second bedroom will be a double.'

This morning, before work, I relate the outrage to Luke in florid detail. Luke's first bathetic comment is: 'But you had nothing in common.' Luke's second bathetic comment: 'So *are* you buying a flat?'

I roll my eyes in despair. Some men have truly no idea about how to talk to women. 'Luke,' I say patiently, 'I don't want you to make unhelpful comments and ask silly questions. I want you to say "oh dear", "what a bastard", and tut a lot.' He looks hurt so I add quickly, 'I'm sorry. I didn't mean to snap. But, no. I'm not buying a flat. Me and Fatboy are staying right here.'

What I don't tell Luke is that as of two days ago, I *could* buy a flat. That is, I could put down a deposit for a modest pad in a reasonably un-crime-ridden area. The reason for this is I have, to put it bluntly, profited from Dad's death. To cut a boring tale short, a month ago, our solicitor, Alex Simpkinson, informed my mother—as executrix and main beneficiary of my father's will—that the probate papers were ready to check and sign.

My mother rose to the occasion. She's progressed. After the first 'hear no evil, see no evil month', Mr Simpkinson *had*—in desperation—offered her the option of renouncing her legal responsibilities to another beneficiary, i.e. me or Nana Flo. My mother considered it. Then, as she declared to me over a TV dinner—brandishing her empty fork in emphasis—'I told myself, "Cecelia, if that's what Morrie wanted, you do it."' I think she needed an excuse to renew the FT subscription. And the kindly attention of tall men in tailored suits never went amiss.

But most importantly, my mother realises that Maurice Bradshaw entrusted the fruits of his working life to his special princess and, like a good royal, she takes her duties seriously. She scrutinises the share prices each morning and plagues my father's broker to ensure he's investing in the latest tip stock. Cecelia Bradshaw may have turned a corner. Her return to school last week—she spent the first half of the autumn term at home on sick leave on full pay—has also helped.

I think even she was impressed at the joy with which Mrs Armstrong, the head teacher, welcomed her back. Even if her boss's delight was financially related. Consequently, when probate was granted fourteen days ago, my mother shared a cab with Nana Flo to the freeze-dried offices of Messrs Pomp, Simpkinson & Circumstance and, as she told me proudly, 'Alex went through everything again and I understood every word.'

She'd suggested we meet afterwards for tea, but her offer clashed with a features meeting. Anyhow, I didn't dare ask Laetitia if I could leave work early, because I sense she is bored to death of the bereavement saga and approximately one millimetre away from firing me.

Anyway, it didn't matter. I got a cheque in the post. As I opened the envelope, details of the will being read aloud on my father's funeral day loomed into focus. Specifically the short paragraph, boomed out by Mr Simpkinson, beginning: 'I bequeath the sum of £20,000 to my daughter Helen Gayle'—(Dad *knows* I hate my middle name!)—'which I hope she will invest wisely, for instance, in property . . .'

I held the cheque in my hand and grimaced. 'Posthumous parental guidance!' Any other time I'd be straight down the shops but right now, I don't have the life in me to spend spend spend. Nor the strength to beat off estate agents. So, despite my words of bravado to Jasper, when I tell Luke I'm staying put, it's the truth.

Fatboy's next appointment with Tom is at the ungodly time of 9.45am on Saturday. As I do not wish to arise one moment earlier than 8.45—and even that's cutting it fine—I plan my wardrobe in advance. Towering black boots, black trousers, plain white scoop-neck T-shirt and black cardigan. Minimalist, classical, elegant. Especially as I intend to trowel on a good thick inch of subtle make-up. Tina would be proud. If, that is, she could stop dribbling and mooning over Adrian long enough to notice. She is *shameful*! A lesson to us all. Well, to me anyway. I pray I was never ever like that. Even with Jasper. She rarely sees us outside work and when Lizzy suggests a girls' night out she looks uncomfortable and makes a weak excuse such as 'I promised Adrian I'd make him dinner that night.'

To think I used to admire her untamable free spirit. Envy her level-headed approach to romance. Wish for a wisp of her immunity to infatuation. Initially I put it down to her growing up with three brothers. However, in regretful hindsight, I am forced to conclude that her brothers had diddly-squat to do with her bold invulnerability. I think the simple truth is, that until she met Adrian, she had never fallen in love. Not even for one mad minute, blissful hour, or whirlwind day. So my admiration is cancelled out.

I awake on Saturday at 8.45am feeling groggy. Is there no justice? I went to bed at ten! I bolt to the mirror and my worst fears are confirmed. I'm piggy-eyed. My peepers are as puffy and bloated as if the five Dime bars I ate this week (tiny little things, can't possibly be fattening) went straight to my eyelids.

I creep to the fridge and steal two slices of Marcus's cucumber, replacing it in an upright position to give him an inferiority complex. If I was him I'd stick with baby sweetcorn. Then I lie on my bed, with cucumber eyes, for five tedious minutes. When I can bear it no longer I jump up and rush to the mirror. As puffy as Puff the Magic Dragon after a birthday blowout. And my skin is as scaly. Bugger. I slap on about twenty quid's worth of moisturiser, use eyelash curlers to disguise the eyelid bloat, then spend a full fifteen minutes fluffing my hair in a vain attempt to stop it lying flat on my head. I end up looking like David Bowie *circa* 1972. Let's hope Tom is a fan of 'Space Oddity'.

I arrive at Megavet—Fatboy wailing and clawing inside his Pet Voyager—in bad humour. It is not improved when I see Celine. She blanks me. I return the compliment and pretend to be engrossed in *Dogs Today*. I am wading through a three-page feature on mange, when the surgery door swings open and a deep, resonant voice shouts 'Next!' I nearly faint with nervous tension and look hesitantly into those blue eyes. 'Hi,' says Tom, not quite smiling. 'Won't you come into my parlour?'

'Delighted,' I whisper, trundling into the surgery. I spend a full minute coaxing Fatboy out of his Voyager in order to compose myself. Then I lift my wriggling cat onto the table and mutter—in a pre-emptive strike—'He hasn't lost much weight, but he seems happy. It must be his metabolism. I don't want to give him a complex.'

Tom looks sceptical and declares, 'I'm going to have to pull you in on that one, madam!' But his tone is friendly.

'Tom,' I blurt before I can stop myself. 'I just wanted to say, I mean, I've been wanting to say for ages, I'—Fatboy chooses this delicate moment to emit a silent but poisonous fart—'I, that wasn't me by the way, I swear, he always does that when he's nervous, but the point is, well, I just wanted to say that I'm sorry that I was so rude to you on the phone and I still cringe about it.' As the words tumble out it hits me that they sound arrogant. As if I assume Tom has spent the past three months withering away because of my childish telephone snub.

So I blather on, 'Not that, I'm sure, you care or you've thought about it much or anything but'—I am about to explain I was under stress because of Marcus, my mother, my father, the Toyota, but realise they are all monstrous excuses so I finish with—'but I have thought about it and'—Jesus, I'm making a hash of this—'I wouldn't want you to think badly of me.' I dig my nails viciously into my palms to prevent myself bleating out even one more brain-dead syllable. Why doesn't Tom speak instead of gazing at me like that? Finally he grins.

'Apology accepted. And I don't think badly of you. Not *that* badly.' He grins again to indicate that this is a joke. Fatboy parps out another evil fart. I'll kill him, the spiteful orange git.

Tom gives the windbag the once-over, skims his medical notes, and says casually, 'And *I'm* sorry if I scared you about Fatboy's health. I went a bit over the top.'

I jump at the chance to be magnanimous. 'I deserved it,' I say.

'He's got a good colour and a nice shiny coat. He's still a podge but otherwise healthy. I'm just going to give him his worming pill. If you hold him like that, while I prise open his jaw. Good. All right, big chap'—*grraowwww*—'There! That wasn't too bad, was it?' As Tom strokes a glowering Fatboy I think to myself, No, it wasn't bad at all.

'Thank you,' I say, lifting Fatboy into the Voyager. I am reluctant to leave but I don't want to loiter foolishly like an infatuated schoolgirl. My thoughts bypass my brain and whirr into speech without permission. 'You probably won't but—' I begin.

'Don't if you—' Tom starts.

We both stop. I giggle. 'You first,' I say.

He rakes a hand through his dishmop hair. 'Do you want to go for a drink some time? Orange juice even?'

I beam as widely as it's possible to beam without straining a face muscle. I squeak joyfully, 'I'd love to.' Fatboy immediately farts again, but my delight is such that frankly, my dears, I don't give a damn.

Tom has asked me out on a date. Not a vague, hopeless 'we'll speak some time next week to arrange something' half-promise, but a real, solid, write-this-down-in-your-diary *date*—me, Helen Gayle Bradshaw, a stumpy, grumpy dogsbody who drives a Toyota and kills spiders without a twinge of regret. Here is my chance to make it right!

The second jolly surprise of the week is that Lizzy has finally pinned

Tina down to a girls' night out. 'Wot, no Adrian?' I joke to Tina.

'He's got a stag night,' she says curtly.

'Oh, right,' I say. In truth, I feel hurt. As if Lizzy and I are a stopgap. But I force myself not to take it personally. I don't own Tina. It's *her* life. She's not obliged to see me. It's not like we're related.

The evening in question is this Thursday. On Wednesday Lizzy informs us: 'Bring some loose-fitting clothes for tomorrow night.'

We stare at her suspiciously. 'What?' we chorus.

'We are,' says Lizzy—in a voice as pretty and munificent and autocratic as Glinda the white witch—'going to my health club to do a Tai chi class. It's booked and paid for. Afterwards, we're eating in the juice bar. Oh my! I'm late for my lunch appointment! See you tomorrow!' Of all the rotten low-down cheatin' tricks.

'Does the juice bar sell fermented grape juice?' I shout after Lizzy, as she speeds out of the door. The coward.

Tina and I regard each other in dismay. I say grumpily, 'Do you even know what Tai chi is?'

Tina makes a face. 'It's a martial art.'

At this I perk up. 'It's not aerobic?'

Tina shakes her head. 'Nah.'

I pause for a second, recall every James Bond film I've ever seen and decide that women who do martial arts really impress men and it's about time I became one of them. 'I'm quite looking forward to tomorrow,' I tell Tina.

'Me too,' she says vacantly.

I'm stunned. I feel like Little Red Riding Hood duped by a wolf disguised as a pink lacy grandmother. Lizzy deserves to be frog-marched to McDonald's and force-fed five Big Macs. I should have trusted my instinct and scarpered the minute I clapped eyes on Brian, our Tai chi instructor. He had long hair, wore purple trousers and his first word was 'basically'. Tina and I, loitering at the back of the studio, exchanged a snide look. For the 'newcomers'—here, a lingering smile at Lizzy and a meaningful glance at Tina and me—he began with a short introduction to Tai chi. Tai chi is an ancient Chinese art, a slow pattern of movements constructed thousands of years ago to promote vitality and inner harmony.

I nodded briskly, in the hope that he'd hurry up and show us a few karate chops. To my disbelief, he droned on for eight further minutes—during which I lost the will to live—then announced, 'I'm going to teach you how to walk.' As I learned how to walk a quarter of a century ago, I presumed this was a joke. Sadly, no. We spent eighty-five minutes walking in slow motion. To my delight, Tina looked like a junior clerk from the Ministry of Silly Walks, but it didn't compensate. I wanted to scream with boredom. It was sooooooo slooooooooooooow.

I stifled forty yawns and didn't dare look at Tina because I knew we'd both keel over laughing. Afterwards in the juice bar, Tina and I, hysterical with relief that the nightmare was over, mutated into a pair of fourteen-year-olds who found everything in the world rude and/or funny. When Lizzy politely enquired of the etiolated teenager behind the bar 'Is your juicer working?' we hooted and howled with raucous mirth. When I ranted about Brian's pointing foot—'The way he pointed his foot at stuff! His slowwwly pointing foot, pointing for what seemed like daaays . . . !'—we snorted and sniggered until our stomachs hurt.

Then Lizzy did a very unLizzylike thing. She swore. She snapped, 'Will you two bloody shut up!' Our mouths clamped shut in surprise. '*Bloody*' from the woman whose expletive of choice is 'Fiddlesticks!'

'Why?' said Tina, shocked.

'We were only joking,' I added, stifling a giggle. Lizzy looked murderous. 'It was lovely of you to arrange it, though,' I continued hastily. 'It just wasn't our thing.'

Lizzy glared at me. 'I'd prefer it if you didn't take the piss'—'the piss'? Good Lord, this is unprecedented!—'out of Brian.'

'Ah, come on, Lizzy, leave it out! Brian's an arse!' Tina squawked.

Lizzy's face tightened. She placed her fork neatly at the side of her bowl of walnut, avocado and leaf salad and said sharply, 'He is also, as of one week ago, my boyfriend. So'—and her next words were much more Jane Austeny, much more reassuringly Lizzy—'I'd thank you to keep your horrid opinions to yourselves.'

'He's forty-five if he's a day!' I screech to Michelle about Brian, who has ditched Sammy and couldn't give a rat's arse about other people's boyfriends.

'Some women like older men,' she says blandly, to stifle the line of conversation so she can bring it round to the more interesting subject of her. 'Sammy and me were about the same age,' she adds wistfully. (She's sixteen months older than he is.)

I make sympathetic noises and wish the doorbell would ring so I'd have an excuse to get off the phone. It's Friday night and Luke has got *Die Hard* out on video. Marcus and I are barely talking but as neither of us wants to gratify the other by retreating to our room, we are about to watch Bruce Willis be macho together.

'So how are you fixed for tonight?' says Michelle suddenly.

'I'm watching a video with Luke and Marcus,' I say, trying to make my company sound as unappealing as possible. There is no way I am driving to Crouch End to entertain Michelle.

'Sounds wild! I'll be round in thirty!' *Pank!* It takes me approximately twelve seconds to work out that Michelle is making the journey to Swiss Cottage because the long-hours, no-perks position of Michelle's Boyfriend is now vacant and she wishes to fill it. Will the victim be Luke or Marcus? She hasn't met either and I wonder who will appeal most.

Luke? He's not *my* type—too kind and easily intimidated—but Michelle thrives on bullying. And, if you aren't privy to Luke's odious, malodorous bathroom habits, he *is* beguiling. Messy blond hair, green eyes, winsome smile, clumsy manner. I dismiss the thought that I am concentrating on Luke's potential because I suspect Michelle and Marcus will get on—will get *it* on.

I do not want this to happen—I know Marcus would see it as a triumph against me—but I have a bad feeling about its inevitability. Michelle knows that my recent hate campaign against Marcus isn't born of indifference. As for Marcus, whatever else he is, he isn't choosy.

Consequently, when Michelle arrives fluttering under such a weight of mascara it's a miracle she can keep her eyes open, I brace myself. I march into the lounge where Luke and Marcus are slumped on the sofa. 'You two, this is Michelle,' I mumble, hoping her entrance will go unnoticed. Their necks jerk round like ventriloquist's dummies. Michelle wiggles her fingers in a cutie-pie wave and is treating Luke to an appreciative once-over when he emits a loud, involuntary belch. 'Pardon me,' he says politely, but he's blown it. I curse him as she transfers her predatory gaze to Marcus. He looks her straight in her come-hither eyes, and pings from the sofa and across the room.

'Charmed,' he says, taking her hand and gently pulling her towards him to kiss her cheek.

'Me too,' she replies silkily. I flare my nostrils in disgust. A millisecond in and they're like a pair of baboons flashing their arses. Except more blatant. I can hardly bear to watch.

The remainder of the film is ruined as Michelle pretends girly mystification at the plot—it's *Die Hard*, for God's sake!—and keeps whispering at Marcus to explain. Needless to say, the sleazebag is thrilled to oblige.

I walk to the kitchen and pour myself a mug of red wine. I knew this would happen. But I didn't know it would feel quite so bad. I try to feel good about bringing Ken and Barbie together. Michelle needs compensation after dumping Sammy. Meanwhile Marcus now hates me so it would be churlish—and pointless—to try to keep him to myself. Anyhow, he's soiled goods. This pep talk has no effect. I still feel like crying.

The tears are pricking at my eyelids when Michelle sings, 'Is that wine you're guzzling, you greedy girl? Are you gonna hog the whole bottle or can we guys have some?'

Self-pity is engulfed by violent rage. I casually rest one hand behind my back and tense it to a claw. This alleviates tension and allows me to reply in a fond tone, 'Ah, Michelle! I forgot—it takes more than a man to keep you off the booze! Help yourself!'

She darts me a look reminiscent of Nurse Ratched in *One Flew Over the Cuckoo's Nest*. I quake inwardly, keep the smile pinned to my face, and make a mental note to avoid ever being left alone with Michelle.

The rest of the evening is excruciating. I do my best to crush the sweet bloom of romance without success. My first bout of psychological warfare is to order four large pepperoni pizzas, 'On me!' Luke is thrilled beyond belief. Marcus and Michelle are—as planned—livid. Michelle faces a dilemma. She hates to eat in front of men—'it looks gross'—but loves to maintain that she gorges herself daily on chocolate and pizza as all self-respecting supermodels do. Ha ha ha.

Marcus is equally torn. Pizza and all its fatty cohorts—curry, kebabs, burgers—are purgatory to Marcus. He hails from a genetically obese family and is so afraid of nature taking its pudgy course, he observes the eating habits of an anorexic sparrow. He is painfully aware of the unmacho nature of his obsession and—as I've repeatedly witnessed—part of his seduction routine is to starve himself for two days to make room for a staged 'I'm a regular guy' blowout in front of his intended. Sadly, as Michelle is a surprise bonus, he's pitifully unprepared. He'll eat his pizza so as not to appear unmanly, but every bite will be poison. I chomp away happily and watch the lovebirds struggle.

'That was really kind of you, Helen,' says Luke with his mouth full.

'My pleasure,' I reply smugly, ruffling his hair.

Michelle pouts a small 'pouff!' indicating she's stuffed after just two slices. Yeah right.

Marcus gawks longingly at her cleavage. 'So don't you feel hungry?' he murmurs coyly. I nearly regurgitate my pizza on the spot. All further attempts at sabotage fail.

Towards the end of *Die Hard 2*, she snuggles closer and closer to Marcus until she is practically sitting in his lap. Their conversation becomes increasingly whispery and secretive. At midnight, Luke announces he's knackered and trundles off to his room. The deserter. I bid him a cold good night and remain stiffly, stubbornly in my chair. I'll stay up till dawn to foil their lustful plans!

At ten past twelve Marcus and Michelle start snogging in front of me. I concede defeat and go to bed.

Did you have a nickname when you were little? When I asked my friends this question, nearly everyone said yes. Luke's despairing parents dubbed him 'Trouble'. Lizzy's unofficial name was 'Jellytot'. Michelle's astute parents referred to their daughter as 'Madam'. Tina's mother rechristened her 'the Squeak'. And my father? His nickname for me was 'the Grinch'.

As I grew up, my father stopped calling me the Grinch and started calling me Helen. Only when scribbling my annual birthday card did he revert to the teasing familiarity of 'Dear Grinch'. As signs of affection were rare in our house, I accorded 'Dear Grinch' the same degree of symbolism that most patriotic citizens reserve for their national flag. And then I found out.

I was in the pub with Tina one Friday, a few months before my father died, indulging in a fond whinge about Jasper. He'd dismissed The Divine Comedy (my favourite band) as 'poncey shite' and had forced me to listen—on *my* car stereo, mark you—to Daryl Hall and John Oates. Secretly I admired his nerve, if not his taste in music. Tina exclaimed nastily, 'He's a grinch, that one!'

I started and said, 'A grinch? What do you mean by that?'

She gave me an odd look. 'You know! Mean. Petty! Fun crushing!'

I smiled weakly and said, 'Is that what grinch means?'

Tina hooted, 'Didn't you have Dr Seuss in north London? *The Cat In The Hat*? *How The Grinch Stole Christmas*? No?'

I shook my head, muttered 'No, no' and ran to the bar to buy the next round. The next day I sped to the library and asked the librarian to help me find a children's book. She smiled a collaborative smile.

And I discovered that a grinch was not—as I'd imagined—a cute, furry little love bundle but a spiteful, red-eyed, cave-dwelling creature with a heart 'two sizes too small'. Sure, he turns into a sweetie at the end. But right up to the penultimate page, the Grinch is a vicious, ugly slimeball with no friends.

I didn't want Tina to laugh at me again so I decided to share my life-shattering news with Lizzy. *She'd* give it the sober consideration it deserved. And she laughed at me! 'Helen,' she tinkled, 'it's a pet name! I'm sure he didn't mean anything by it! It's just a nice word, like . . . pumpkin! My dad still calls my sister Pumpkin—and she's thirty-one and as thin as a whippet!'

I staggered to bed tear-stained and woke up feeling foolish. Lizzy, the voice of reason, had spoken. My father dubbed me the Grinch because it was a nice word. Nothing sinister. In fact, I shoved this irksome nickname to the back of my mind, where it stayed. Only occasionally does it drift back into consciousness.

Such as this morning when I wake from a restless sleep and cringe at what a fool I made of myself last week, trying to stop Marcus shagging Michelle. At times like these, I *am* the Grinch. Mean-spirited. Petty. Fun crushing. My father was right. Meanwhile, I haven't seen bronzed hide nor coiffed hair of Michelle or Marcus. I presume he's staying at her place. He always disappears after scoring.

I wish them luck. I say this not because I'm nice suddenly but because I have a date with Tom tonight. (My mother, unwillingingly placated by the promise of a day at a health farm—has relinquished a Monday night.) Michelle is welcome to Marcus Microwilly. In all fairness, they're beautifully suited. Long foodless days pounding the treadmill, hours of mutual grooming, hot sizzling nights on twin sunbeds . . . It's midafternoon and I am wondering if I'll be invited to the wedding when the office phone rings. Please don't let it be Tom cancelling. 'Hello?' I say fearfully, snatching up the receiver.

'Helen,' says a quavering voice, 'it's Vivienne! And I'm afraid, I'm sorry to tell you, oh, it's shocking news—'

My voice is hoarse with terror: 'Tellmenow!'

Vivienne wobbles out five words before bursting into tears: 'Your mother's slit her wrists.'

Chapter 4

ONCE, AGED SIX, I was walloped and sent to bed at 5.30 for saying in front of Michelle's mother, 'Daddy, isn't it true we can't pay our mortgage?' Admittedly I didn't actually know what a mortgage was, but it was a phrase I'd overheard somewhere and was desperate to use.

Alas, Mrs Arnold's eyes lit up like Beelzebub's and my father blamed me for what he predicted as the certain ruin of his financial reputation. As I snivelled myself to sleep I prayed that my father and my mother, who hadn't dared tiptoe upstairs to console me, would die in a tornado.

At that moment I considered Orphan Annie the most glamorous creature in the world and wished fervently that I were her. Miss Hanigan was a pleasure compared to my evil parents! And I'd get to sing 'It's a Hard Knock Life!' in an American accent.

But twenty years later being an orphan patently doesn't appeal to me quite so much, because when Vivienne tells me that my mother has slit her wrists, my legs go numb and I sink to the floor with a moan that Lizzy later terms, in a whisper of hushed awe, 'feral, primeval, chilling, like a wild animal writhing in pain'.

As the most savage noise ever heard in the *Girltime* office is Laetitia snarling because the Dunkin' Donuts assistant put too much milk in her tea, my impression of a tiger with earache gets noticed. Lizzy and Laetitia leap towards me, crying, 'What's wrong?' Their faces are indistinct as if we're under water and it's hard to breathe and I gasp to the blurriness, oh please not my mother not my mum oh please God not her too, until the words form a seamless shroud that shields me from reality.

Meanwhile, the receiver dangles, faint hysterical squeaks emanating from it. Lizzy snatches up the phone while Laetitia takes this—perfect—opportunity to slap me hard and stingingly across the face. By the time I've said 'Ouch,' and glared at her, Lizzy is crouching and gripping my trembly, clammy hands.

'Helen,' she says in a clear, firm voice, looking straight into my dazed eyes. 'Your mother is OK. She's not dead. OK? She's fine.'

I stare helplessly at Lizzy. I don't understand. I feel like a five-year-old. 'She's slit her wrists,' I say doubtfully.

'Only superficial cuts,' insists Lizzy, in the kind of loud, emphatic voice my father used to use when addressing foreigners. 'Grazes. Vivienne was phoning from the hospital, they're in Casualty but it's not serious. Your mother is fine, she's fine, OK?'

I nod and say, 'OK.'

I am shaking like an elderly poodle in a cold bath. I don't know what to do. Happily, Lizzy makes an executive decision: 'I'll call you a cab to the hospital right now. Won't I, Laetitia?' she adds.

Laetitia, who doubtless relieved some long-pent-up tension with the slap, nods once and says, 'Absolutely.'

Lizzy helps me to a chair and sits me down. She rushes to the kitchen, returns with a cup of black coffee and a bag of brown sugar. She tips at least half the bag of sugar into the cup. 'Drink that,' she orders.

'*You* wouldn't,' I grumble, but take an obedient sip.

Fortunately the cab arrives within minutes and rescues me from Turkish coffee hell. Lizzy, who has packed my diary and other debris into my bag, helps me into the cab. 'Do you want me to come with you?' I shake my head. 'Be kind to yourself,' she says.

I sit in the cab. Kind. I'd like to be kind. Although, when I see my mother I am going to kill her. How dare she pull a stunt like this, the selfish cow! What possessed her?

When I run into A & E it's *déjà vu*, it's *Groundhog Day* meets *Amityville*, it's that vomitous, surreal whirl of impending doom all over again. I look wildly around and see, oh thank God, my mother and Vivienne huddled in a corner surrounded by people who look as if they've been there for years. Vivienne's bright orange fake fur coat (she bought it after being attacked in Islington while wearing her mink) shines out amid the drab defeatism like a bad-taste beacon.

I bound towards my mother and my anger dissipates as I see her weary, chalk-white face. She is wrapped in a grey blanket.

'Helen!' whimpers my mother. Her spindly wrists are wrapped in makeshift dressings. I bend and hug her tight. My mother sobs in my arms and I rock her like a baby.

'Oh Mummy, promise me, never never, terrible, Daddy would be furious, you know I'm here, what would I do? OK, looking after you.' While this isn't exactly a coherent sentence, it makes perfect sense to my mother who nods and sniffs and burrows closer to my chest. I glance past my mother at Vivienne who I can tell is gagging for a Marlboro Light. I indicate with my eyes to the exit. 'I'll join you in a sec,' I mouth. She draws her orange coat around her, smiles tensely, and teeters off.

My heart twists as my mother bawls silently, her fingers digging weakly into my lap. I wait and wait, hug and hug, until the crying subsides, and try not to think that I could have avoided this by meeting Tom on a Thursday. Then I say sensible things like, 'How long have you been here?' and 'Do you want a hot drink?' and 'Is the pain bearable?' She answers, respectively, 'Ages,' and 'Had one,' and 'Not too bad.' When I suspect she has no more tears left, I ask her if she minds if I see how Vivienne is. 'It must have been a shock for her too,' I say gravely.

My mother nods dumbly. 'I'll be back almost *immediately*,' I say, 'so stay right there and don't move. Promise promise?'

My mother recognises the phrase I'd squeak while bargaining for treats when I was five and we were a family. She manages a sad smile and replies, 'Promise promise.' I kiss her and run off to find Vivienne.

Vivienne sits on a wooden bench and lights what I suspect is her fortieth fag of the day. She breathes the smoke slowly, lovingly, out of her nostrils before speaking. 'She knew I was coming round at four thirty, after school and my Italian class. We were going out for coffee. Oh God, it was frightening. I think she'd only just done it.' Vivienne's scarlet mouth trembles.

'I rang the doorbell, and she didn't answer. I rang again. Still no answer. I thought she must have been held up at school. I was just turning away to go and wait in the Jag when she opened the door. She looked as weak as water and so pale. She held out her wrists, said, "Look what I've done," and burst into tears. It was horrific. She'd used a pretty blunt razor blade—she'd pushed it backwards and forwards, but not, thank God, deep.

'There were masses of scratches, and welts of blood. I was so shocked, Helen, I nearly fainted on the spot. She seemed fine on the surface—quiet, but fine. Back at work, busy with the children, on top of your father's finances—imagine! Cecelia! I, I never thought, not in a million years, that she'd do something like this. It's been, what, five, six months, I thought, surely, she should be over it by now . . .'

Vivienne, who has been talking more to herself than to me, glances at my face and stutters to a halt. I don't shout at her even though, at this precise moment, I'm busting for an excuse to shout at anyone.

But to Vivienne I keep my voice steady and say, 'Vivienne, I, I, you know, I, thank God you found her, you, I, no, I'm thinking, five months, it seems ages, maybe, to you, but to her, and, I mean, to me also, it's no time. No time at all. I, also, stupid, I thought she was, well, getting better, but she isn't. I don't know how long it'll take. Longer. Maybe she'll learn to live with it. But, sorry, I'm burbling, go on.'

Vivienne takes another drag on her cigarette. 'I brought her here, and they assessed her for suicidal intent, and from what she said they said it was probably a cry for help rather than a serious attempt to, you know, and they patched her up "for now" and, but, what gets me is, when they asked her why she did it she said, she said . . .'

Vivienne—who I thought would only ever cry if Gucci's flagship store in Sloane Street was wiped out in a freak thunderstorm—sniffs and dabs at the corner of each eye with her thumb pad.

'What?' I whisper.

Vivienne swallows hard and adds, 'Your mother said, "There's no point. Not without my Morrie." Oh, Helen. I didn't realise before, how much she loved him.'

I pat her trembling hand and suspect, meanly, that Vivienne is so overwrought because if *her* husband died she'd crack open the Bollinger, maintain he wouldn't have wanted her to mourn, and continue to prey on impressionable young men with even more gusto than she does already. But I shake my head and sigh, 'Neither did I.' Privately, I wonder to what extent today's dramatics relate to my mother's feelings for my father and to what extent they relate to her feelings for herself.

We go back inside. My mother has fallen asleep in her hard orange plastic chair. She looks about ten years old.

We sit and wait to be called and suddenly I realise. Tom! My date with Tom! Shit. A large notice forbids use of mobile phones inside the hospital so I grab mine and run outside again. It's 6.37pm. I ring Megavet and—a plague on my house or what—Celine answers. It's supper time and today's special is humble pie. 'Celine,' I say in my most winsome tone, 'it's Helen Bradshaw, the one who—'

'I know who you are,' she says in a sharp voice. Bugger.

'Is Tom there?' I say.

'He's busy,' she snaps. I refuse to freak out because I know that's what she wants. I decide to play it straight.

'Celine,' I say, 'I was supposed to be seeing Tom tonight but I can't because my mother has had to go into hospital suddenly. It's an emergency, very serious, and I've got to be with her. I'd be so grateful if you could pass on that message to Tom,' you sour bitch, I add silently.

I am amazed and grateful when Celine summons a shred of humanity from the air and says, in a serious tone, 'I'm sorry to hear that. Of course I'll tell Tom. Go and look after your mother and don't worry about it.'

I'm stunned. 'That's really kind of you, Celine,' I say.

'My pleasure,' she replies.

I beep off the phone. Wow. What did I do to deserve that? I hurry back to Casualty. My mother has woken up and is complaining that her 'wrists hurt'. You don't say.

Approximately three years later my mother's name is called and she, Vivienne and myself are ushered out of the godforsaken waiting room and into what seems to be a corridor separated into tiny cubicles. We can't all fit into the shoe-box cubicle, so Vivienne offers to wait outside.

In the shoe box my mother sits quietly on the cubicle chair and allows a nurse to dab a clear liquid on her wounds. I may need new glasses because I have to squint to see the cuts. 'This is saline solution so it's going to sting, but only a little,' says the nurse kindly. My mother nods. She is uncharacteristically docile while her wrists are wrapped in a thin bandage and a big sticky-tapey plaster, and remains silent even when she's given a tetanus injection. 'Just to be on the safe side,' says the nurse cheerfully. I smile gratefully at her. As soon as she leaves, Nasty Cop—alias Dr Nathan Collins, according to his badge—begins an interrogation.

How has she been sleeping? What's her appetite been like? Has she found it hard to concentrate? Has she had thoughts of wanting to join her loved one? Thoughts of wanting to go to sleep and never wake up? Why did she do it? Was it on the spur of the moment? Did she write a suicide note? Does she wish that she were dead? Did she want to be found?

I am agog at these bold, prying questions and half expect my mother to break down and run out of the shoe box. But she doesn't. The hot tears run down her face as she tells Dr Collins she's been sleeping a lot and eating a little—*A little!* I think, *we've chomped through Prue Leith's entire repertoire, twice!*—and found it impossible to concentrate and she's had no thoughts of joining her loved one but some thoughts about sleeping for ever and she did it because Morrie died and she misses him so much she can hardly breathe and no one understands and everyone thinks she should have bounced back and she hasn't and she thought it was getting better but it's getting worse. Yes it was spur of the moment, she just wanted everyone to 'sit up and take notice'. No she didn't write a note. She doesn't truly wish that she were dead; she wishes that Maurice was alive. Yes she wanted to be found.

He watches her closely then says, 'Mrs Bradshaw. You've suffered a terrible loss. The pain of bereavement is always far worse than you can possibly imagine. And you're right—people don't understand. It's hard for them to see you in pain. What they don't understand is that pain is part of the grieving process, and you have to go through it in order to heal. And five months is nothing!

'It can take twenty years to come to terms with the death of a loved one. Your reaction is not mad in the least, it's normal. It's very common for the pain to hit around now. In the early stages, you're in shock. And that's your body's way of taking care of you. You couldn't deal with all that grief at once. But now the penny's dropped because you know he isn't coming back. And that, Mrs Bradshaw, is the real bummer.'

My mother stares in awe at Dr Collins as if he's the Oracle, then wraps her skinny arms round my waist, and sobs piteously into my jumper. Dr Collins nods at me as if to say, 'She'll pull through.' I'm stunned. I don't know whether to hit him or hug him.

Vivienne drops us home. I thank her, tell her she's been wonderful, and wave her off. She departs at 90mph and I don't blame her. My mother is subdued so I keep talking. Dr Collins has given her Prozac and arranged for a 'CPN' to call her tomorrow. In the hospital my mother had been so mesmerised by her blue and white capsules, she forgot to ask what a CPN was. So, when she trotted off to show Vivienne her spoils, I asked. 'The community psychiatric nurse,' replied Dr Collins.

I stared at him in horror and shouted, 'But she's not mental!'

Dr Collins rubbed his bloodshot eyes and said in a scarily soft voice, 'My priority is to avert disaster.' To avert being struck off, more like.

'Dr Collins seems like a nice man,' I say brightly now, as I fuss aimlessly around the kitchen. 'So you'll probably go back to the hospital in a few weeks. Do you want me to take you?' I add, still brightly, hoping against hope that she'll say no.

'No,' says my mother, surprisingly.

'Are you sure?' I say suspiciously, wondering if she's planning a bunk.

'If I wanted to say yes, I'd have said yes,' snaps my mother.

I glance at her tired face and change the subject. I am trembling suddenly and feel an urge to grip my mother with both hands and prise a written guarantee out of her that she is going to remain alive and chipper for another sixty years. That's what I want, please. Because otherwise, otherwise . . .

'Mum,' I blurt, grasping her hands.

'Yes?' she says.

I want to say, I'm so afraid, so fucking afraid that it's killing me, but I can't. So I say, 'I wish you'd called.'

My mother replies shortly, 'You were busy.'

I feel clueless. I want to scream. I want my dad back. He'd shake some sense into her. I want control and I hate not having it. Should I make a 'to do' list? I'll make a 'to do' list. I make a 'to do' list.

To Do List

1. look after Mummy—indefinite—maybe Thursdays too?
2. go home and get clothes and toothbrush
3. phone Laetitia
4. phone Mrs Armstrong
5. ask Luke to feed Fatboy
6. phone Tom to apologise again
7. phone Lizzy for moral support

I don't dare leave my mother alone while I collect my stuff from the flat, so I ask her along. I am apprehensive about driving her silver Peugeot 206, never having driven a car I'm not ashamed of before, but I refuse to squander even one more penny on cabs.

'It'll be nice for you to see Luke, Mummy, won't it?' I say enticingly. I don't mention Fatboy as, both being loud, egotistical attention seekers, they can't stand each other.

The first noise I hear as we troop through the door is not Fatboy demanding dinner or Luke playing the Verve—and, no doubt, air guitar—in his room. The first noise I hear comes from Marcus's bedroom and it is 'uuuh! uuuh! uuuh!' and 'oh! oh! oh! my! *God!*' Oh my God indeed. I invite my mother to my flat for the first time in about a year—I thought it would depress her—and she discovers it's a bordello.

I start speaking loudly and incessantly to drown out the shrieks of Michelle faking orgasm. 'Mum, would you like a cup of tea I'll put on the kettle anyway or would you prefer to listen to the radio in the kitchen yes come into the kitchen and let's turn it on anyway oh look here's Luke, Luke you remember my mother don't you, yes Mum you remember Luke he was so helpful at the hospital last time and Luke would you mind terribly feeding Fatboy tomorrow morning as I'm staying at my mother's tonight and maybe for the rest of the week?'

I pause for breath. Luke and my mother look at me as if I'm a nutjob. 'Are you OK?' says Luke.

'Fine, fine,' I say, jerking my thumb towards Marcus's room and pulling an I'm-repulsed face.

'Oh yeah,' nods Luke, immediately. 'Marcus and your friend shagging. They've been at it like rabbits for, I dunno, ten minutes.'

Oh hooray. Luke the dufus goofs again. I glare at Luke, say, 'Sorry, Mum, Luke's just joking,' and wait for the cloudburst.

Instead, she starts giggling. 'Helen! Don't be such a priss! I do know what sex is! I have had it!' Said in a jovial patronising lilt and with a coy glance at Luke to indicate that she and he are the real grown-ups and I am the silly little girl. I'd forgotten how she mutates into a coquettish Judas in the presence of any man over twelve.

'Well I don't care if you don't,' I say sulkily, as Luke and my mother laugh at me. Traitors.

'So *will* you feed Fatboy?' I say to Luke, in an attempt to recover some dignity.

'Love to,' he replies. 'Fatboy's my mate.'

I smile and tease, 'That figures, what with your similar hygiene habits!' Fatboy, unlike normal cats, isn't overkeen on washing. As for Luke. He regards baths with the same affection as vampires regard garlic.

I expect Luke to laugh, but he doesn't. 'Thanks,' he says coldly.

'That was a joke!' I stutter.

'Well it wasn't a very nice one,' pipes up my mother who I will strangle if she offers one more unwanted opinion. I give up.

'Sorry, but I didn't mean it,' I say crossly. 'I'm going to make some calls,' I add as I stamp into the lounge. Luke and my mother are already gassing and ignore me. Unbloodybelievable!

The answering machine is blinking. Maybe Tom? I press PLAY. 'Helen, it's Laetitia. Calling to see if all is OK and to remind you there's a meeting about the Get Rich Quick supplement tomorrow at nine thirty sharp. I need oodles of ideas and I'm counting on you!' This is Laetitiaspeak for 'I don't give a damn if every member of your family has stiffed it because I am paying you (just) to be my maidservant, so be there or be unemployed!' Needless to say, I have *no* ideas for the supplement—I'm the poorest person in the office. What do I know about Getting Rich Quick?

Actually, here's a good one: Wait For Your Dad To Croak—Hey, It Worked For Me! Ooh, now Michelle would call that bitter. Calm down, Helen. I breathe deeply, and refer to my list. Phone Tom. I leaf through my diary to find his home number. I ring it and hold my breath.

'Hello?'

'Tom?' I squeak. 'It's Helen! I'm so sorry!' There is a pause.

'What's the excuse this time?' he says icily. *What?* I am horrified.

'You mean, you mean'—I am practically speechless with indignation, that sly lip-liner-abusing witch!—'You mean Celine didn't pass on my message?' Pause.

'So you bothered to leave one.'

Am I paranoid or does everybody hate me? 'Yes I did, actually. To tell you that my mother slit her wrists earlier today and had to be rushed to hospital.' Take that, Ice Boy! Pleasingly, my underhand strategy has the desired effect.

'Shit! Christ, Helen, that's terrible! God, I'm sorry! Is she, er, how is she? And how are *you*?'

I say, in an I've-got-the-moral-upper-hand tone, 'She's all right.' I feel like adding, 'But it was touch and go'. However, I restrain myself.

'And how are you?' says Tom again.

I nod down the phone before whispering a strangled, 'Fine.' I can't tell him the truth—that I am rigid with fear and seriously considering keeping my mother in a padded box at the end of my bed to avoid further fatalities. Instead I tell Tom an abridged version of the gory story and an elongated version of my phone call to Megavet. 'She's such a liar!' I shriek, adding, before I can bite off my tongue: 'She fancies you, you know!' The second I say it I regret it. Why don't I just shout 'I fancy you, you know!'? It's tantamount to the same thing.

'Oh yes?' says Tom coyly. 'Why do you say that?'

The bastard! 'I say it,' I reply in a cute, flirty singsong tone, 'because she guards you like a hyena guards an antelope carcass.'

Hm. That didn't come out the way I meant it to. But Tom's good humour is patently restored because he says drily, 'You flatter me.'

I giggle. 'I'm sorry about tonight,' I say. And I mean it. I am sorry. I'm also concerned that, this being the second time I've screwed up, a third offer won't be forthcoming. Do I dare ask him? Lizzy would ask a man out. Why am I the *Rules* girl?

'Would you, are you free some time later this week, or maybe next week?' I blurt, cleverly making it sound as if my life is a friendless void.

'Definitely,' says Tom, 'but maybe next week is better? Things might have calmed down a bit.' We fix on the Tuesday.

I put the phone down and straight away start analysing the conversation like a bad psychotherapist. By suggesting next week was he hinting that I was selfish? Neglectful of my poorly mother? And Tuesday—that's a worky, plodding, got to get up early tomorrow, good excuse to scarper at 10pm sort of day. Does that mean he . . .?

Enough. Enough already, you dork. I phone Lizzy. She picks up and in the background I hear what sounds suspiciously like monks chanting. So before I inform my friend that my sole remaining parent is at no immediate risk of death I address a more pressing issue: 'What the fuck's that you're listening to?'

She ignores the question and demands, 'How's your mum?' I tell her. And, eventually, she confesses that her CD is entitled *Gregorian Moods* and she'll tape it for me if I like.

'No, ta,' I say.

'Well, maybe for your mother then?'

I pause. It is a matter of principle that I automatically write off all Lizzy's spooky chanty health-freaky bean-munching willow pod worthiness as twaddle. That said, I want to help my mother in any way I can and I cannot see her yapping away with a shrink. I really can't. She has chosen *me* as her shrink. She doesn't want to speak to a stranger. My mother doesn't want people listening because they're paid to. She wants people to listen because they care about her. It's all highly inconvenient and I need all the help I can get.

'I'll pay you for the tape,' I tell Lizzy. I can't bring myself to speak the words 'Yes, I'd adore a copy of *Gregorian Moods*,' aloud.

I have rescued Luke from my mother and we are trotting down the hall towards the front door, when Marcus emerges from his room wearing a small white towel round his trim waist. His face falls when he sees a grown-up. 'Hi,' he stammers, 'I just, er, got out of the shower.' My mother ogles him, I'm ashamed to say, like a bird eyeing a plump worm.

'We heard,' I say chirpily as I push my gawking mother out of the flat. 'A fifteen-minute shower—must be a record!' The recall of his speechless fury keeps me smiling all the way to the Peugeot.

When I started work at *Girltime*, I suffered from an affliction known as Fone Fear. (OK, Phone Fear, but Fone Fear makes it sound less like an excuse and more like a syndrome.) Anyway, every time I had to make a call I'd put it off and put it off until it was 6pm and the person I needed to speak to had left the office. My illness lasted approximately three days before a verbal thrashing from Laetitia scared it out of me. Alas, the virus was cowed but not defeated. Because this morning I rang my mother's boss at the brisk hour of seven to tell her about her little relapse and it took me from 3.13 to 4.36am to perfect my lines, and another forty-five minutes to summon the courage to dial the number.

Mrs Armstrong's first *overt* concern was for my mother's health. 'Shocking news . . . best wishes for a speedy recovery . . . spring back to her old self.' Yet the undercurrent of strained patience and fretful guilt soon burst—gasping for atonement—to the surface.

Only last week, it emerged, Mrs Armstrong had 'had a quiet word' with Cecelia about 'organisation'. Not a reprimand, goodness no, just a reminder that the Christmas concert was fast bearing down upon us and the programme, rehearsals, costumes, scripts, timetable, ought to be under way. She hoped Cecelia hadn't taken this suggestion as a slight.

I reassured Mrs Armstrong that her 'quiet word' had in no way prompted my mother to slash her wrists, although privately I bloody well thought it had. I told Mrs Armstrong I'd report back on an approximate date for my mother's return to work (again) after consultation with the hospital. But from Mrs Armstrong's artful response—'It's easier for us to plan if we know someone is going to be absent for a while'—I suspected that Mrs Armstrong would prefer to rely on alternative cover until Christmas at least. For the sake of her own sanity, if not her budget.

At 8.30am—after a long hot shower that I'd have happily stood in for the rest of my life—I wake my mother with a cup of tea. She rubs her eyes, does a little double take on seeing her bandaged wrists, and slowly, gingerly, heaves herself upright. 'How are you feeling?' I say.

'I don't know,' she replies flatly. Damn.

'Mum,' I say, 'I've got to leave for work in three minutes or I'll be out of a job. But I've spoken to Mrs Armstrong, and she sends you her best and says don't hurry back until you're "right as rain". Now what are you going to do today? Shall I ring Vivienne and ask her to come round?'

My mother wrinkles her nose and says, 'Vivienne has her batik class on Tuesdays.' Inwardly, I'm starting to panic. I can't leave her alone already. She's got a great cavernous yawn of a day stretching endlessly before her. She might have another pop. An unwelcome idea begins to form in my head. I don't want to voice it. I'd rather ignore it until it retreats. Unfortunately it is now 8.33 and I have precisely no minutes to think of an alternative plan.

'Mum,' I blurt, 'I know you don't see each other that much, but what if I call Nana Flo?' The mere chattery sound of her name sends an ugly dart of remorse shooting to the pit of my stomach.

The truth is that since the funeral day I've spoken to her twice. Once, on discovering my mother had become Miss Havisham. It occurred to me that, for all I knew, my grandmother had turned into Darth Vader and it was my duty to investigate. When I explained that my mother hadn't returned any of her calls because she was—according to her GP—'suffering from grief, resulting in a depressive illness', Nana Flo said, 'Ah well, your mother always did like to play helpless.'

What could I say to that? After a stunned pause, I said, 'I'll get Mummy to call you when the doctor says she's strong enough.'

The second time I spoke to Nana Flo was when I actually saw her—the day probate was granted. After work I drove round to see my mother and my grandmother was sitting in the kitchen. We had a short, civil conversation about her blood pressure ('can't complain') and that was about it. Since then we haven't exchanged one word. And, not wishing to overdramatise my feelings on the situation, I'd rather jump off the top of the Empire State Building than speak to her now.

Although if I know my mother, I suspect she'll feel the same way and I won't have to. I am incredulous when my mother says, 'You go to work, I'll call her.'

At first, I don't believe her.

'Really?' I say shrilly. 'But you never call her!'

'And what do *you* know?' she says rudely.

'I know,' I say huffily, 'that you call Nana Flo about as often as I call Nana Flo.'

My mother regards me haughtily and replies, 'Then you obviously call her at least twice a week.' Do I believe my ears?

'Mummy, you're joking,' I say.

My mother looks as smug as it's possible to look when you've recently tried to unhand yourself with a razor blade. She says: 'We see each other every Thursday. She's good company—for a grouchy old crone!'

Needless to say, I skid into work ten minutes late for the supplement meeting.

When I slink out of the meeting exhausted but relieved (having winged it—or is it wung it?) there is an illegal copy of *Gregorian Moods* sitting on my desk and a note from Lizzy: 'Lunch?'

I accept, then ring my mother. She picks up and I rattle off about fifty questions: 'How are you? How are you feeling? Is Nana with you? What have you been doing?'

My mother, to my infinite relief, is calm. She's 'tired but feels better than yesterday'. Christ, I should think so with all those jollifying drugs inside you. My mother also tells me that Nana Flo came round although she only arrived at 11.30 because she took the bus. Nana Flo has been showing her pictures of Morrie as a small boy.

While I am impressed that Nana Flo is—for the first time in her life—doing the old person thing and hoicking about dreary aged photographs, I suspect my mother is keeping something from me. I can hear it in her voice. I ask a very stupid question: 'Mum, are you OK?'

She chirps, 'Fine! Nana Flo is moving in for a while.'

At first I don't believe her. I'd find it easier to believe that Santa Claus is shacking up with the Tooth Fairy. 'You're kidding!' I squeak. But she isn't. 'But why?' I say.

'Because Dr Collins said I need a support system,' she retorts.

'Well, that's great,' I say slowly. 'So you won't need me to stay over, then?'

My mother replies happily, 'No.'

This news should delight me, but it doesn't. It never in a trillion years occurred to me that my mother and Nana Flo might be driven to pal up, and that I'd feel spurned and jealous when they did. When we go out to lunch together on Friday, Lizzy, though, has more foresight than I do and has realised—in retrospect—that their friendship was a certainty.

'I suppose they have your father in common, if nothing else,' she says.

'Yes, but they've always had my father in common,' I say, with my mouth full of tuna mayonnaise, 'and it made bugger all difference.'

I pause, fascinated, as Lizzy daintily extracts the capers from her olive pasta sauce and lines them up at the side of her plate. 'Why didn't they get on?' she asks. I frown. 'Don't frown, you'll get wrinkles!' she cries.

'Sorry,' I say. I try to think without frowning. 'I get the impression Nana Flo disapproved of my mother.'

Lizzy gasps: 'Why? Your mother's lovely!'

I shrug. 'Well, although Nana worked herself, she doesn't really approve of married women working.' Lizzy rolls her eyes. I add: 'Less time to devote to my dad. And she was never a great housewife.'

Lizzy giggles. 'So that's where you get it from,' she says.

'I have other talents,' I grin. 'Talking of sex, how is Brian?' (I still think the man's a berk but for Lizzy's sake I'll feign interest. Anyway I am interested. In a repulsed sort of way.)

Lizzy blushes. 'Really well. We're getting on brilliantly.'

I widen my eyes and lean towards her: 'Specify.'

Lizzy beams. 'We were chatting recently and I happened to mention that I liked fresh figs but they're really expensive. And last night he came round to see me and he'd bought me a great big bagful! In November!' Not being a massive fruit fanatic I am unappreciative of the lengths one has to go to in order to obtain fresh figs in November. Don't you just walk into a shop?

Lizzy misreads the dim expression on my face and adds, humbly, 'He's not traditionally romantic, like Adrian is with Tina—all those bouquets—but I've never really cared about flowers. Not that it isn't lovely for Tina, of course. But the figs! It was such a thoughtful gesture.'

I jump to correct her: 'Oh no, I didn't think anything bad, it was a lovely thing for him to do . . . if you want your girlfriend parping away all night like a foghorn.'

Lizzy reddens again and giggles. Suddenly she stops laughing, and taps the table as if to redirect our attention to the business of the day. She says, 'So how come Nana Flo approves of your mother now?'

I have no idea. 'I have no idea,' I say. 'I think, she's never taken to my mother but she's always tried to be friendly.'

Lizzy nods. 'For your father's sake?'

I nod too. 'Yes, I suppose.'

Lizzy pauses. 'So maybe, now your father has . . . passed on, she's still being friendly for his sake.'

I wonder. 'Yeah, maybe.' I say, 'Maybe it's because he's no longer there to fight over. But I think it's down to my mum too. She never needed Nana Flo. And now, perhaps, she does.'

Lizzy looks excited: 'And maybe,' she exclaims in a breathy I-love-it-when-a-plan-comes-together whisper, 'now Nana Flo has lost a son, she needs a daughter! Now I think about it, it makes perfect sense!'

Blimey, I wouldn't go *that* far. I sigh and say, 'Yeah, she's not what you'd call sympathetic, but I suppose Nana Flo's better than nothing.' I think of my efforts to care for my mother and a small defensive voice inside me says, 'But *you* weren't nothing. Your cooking was vile but you weren't *nothing*.' Time to change the subject. The conversation has turned maudlin and, frankly, after Monday I've had maudlin up to my eyeballs.

'You know when you do that body brushing thing?' I ask slyly.

'Yes,' says Lizzy, sitting to attention.

'I always forget: you brush towards your hands and feet, don't you?'

Lizzy looks aghast: 'Oh heavens, no! You brush towards your heart! It's essential!' She embarks on a ten-minute lecture about exfoliation and friction and massage and on a deeper level improving microcirculation and removing toxins and excess fluid and—Nana Flo is forgotten.

Mission accomplished. I am relieved that when we next convene for lunch Tina deigns to join us and therefore serious conversation is banned. In fact, almost all conversation is banned. I start off on what I assume is a safe topic: Adrian.

Me: [*jokily*] 'So, Tina, how's lover boy?'

Tina: [*coldly*] 'What do you mean by that?'

Lizzy: [*diplomatically*] 'She, Helen, means Adrian—he seems mad about you. We wondered how he was.'

Tina: [*shiftily*] 'Well, thank you.'

Me: [*offended*] 'I don't see why you're so touchy about a simple question. It's not like I asked the size of his dick.' *[thinks]*: Anyway, back when this relationship wasn't such a holy relic you told me.

Tina: [*snappish*] 'Some things are private. We're not fucking fifteen.'

Me: [*goading*] 'What's wrong, are you premenstrual?'

Lizzy: [*hurriedly*] 'I'm sure Tina isn't but I've got some Evening Primrose Oil if she is. It's superb, really effective. I swear by it.'

Tina: [*furious*] 'I haven't got PMT! Bloody hell! And don't give me that flower oil crap! I swear by it too—it's fucking shite!'

Lizzy: [*shocked*] 'Tina, I'm sorry, I didn't mean to upset you.'

Me: [*sullen*] 'Me neither.'

We fall silent. Lizzy fiddles nervously with her steamed noodles, I prod sulkily at my baked potato, and Tina scowls at her baked beans on toast.

From then on, Lizzy and I restrict the conversation to *our* love lives. Or, in my case, lack of one.

Lizzy: [*shyly*] 'I'd love you both to meet Brian properly. Are either of you free tomorrow night?'

Tina: [*stiffly*] 'Ta for the offer, but I'm busy I'm afraid.'

Me: [*proudly*] 'Me too.'

Lizzy: [*after consideration*] 'Oh. What are you doing, Helen?'

Me: [*coy*] 'I'm seeing Tom actually. The vet. You remember Tom, Tina?'

Tina: [*more relaxed*] 'I certainly do, Tequila Girl!'

Me: [*suddenly keen to change subject*] 'Anyway, Lizzy, let's arrange to meet Brian another time.'

Lizzy: [*quickly*] 'Why don't we all go out later in the week? I'll bring Brian, and you two can bring whoever you like or it can just be the four of us? How about Friday?'

Me: [*subdued*] 'OK. But it'll probably be me on my own.'

Tina: [*rubbing it in*] 'I'll see if Adrian has any plans.'

Between the two of them I am relieved to get back to the office. Which is a first. Laetitia promptly sends me out again to buy her some non-perfumed deodorant. 'As you wish!' I chirrup and rush off. When I return, Laetitia asks me to call an expert for a quote on 'domestic violence' and I start ringing around immediately. Usually I faff around scrunching up bits of paper on my desk for at least half an hour in preparation. I know Laetitia is impressed by this afternoon's uncharacteristic enthusiasm because when I cry 'Done it!' ten minutes later, she replies, 'Good.'

I beam and reply, 'My pleasure.' I need every Brownie point I can scrape. I am also trying to distract myself from dwelling on the fact that on Thursday morning my mother has her first appointment with the Nut Nurse. (The nurse is coming to the house as my mother refused to go to the clinic.)

I decide that from now on I'm going to be ultra-efficient until Laetitia is forced to promote me. She won't want to, of course, but she'll have no choice. The thought of my imminent ascension to grandeur and the wealth and kudos it will bring cheers me.

By 5.00pm, I have been promoted (in my head) to editor in chief. I decide to take my mother out to dinner to celebrate. *Brrg brrrg!* 'Bradshaw residence!' croaks Nana Flo in her telephone voice.

I recover speedily enough to say in a friendly tone, 'Hello, Nana, it's Helen. How are you?'

She replies: 'Can't complain, Helen. What can I do for you?' Helen? She never addresses me by name! Could be the onset of senility. That or she's been watching *It's a Wonderful Life* and the euphoria hasn't yet worn off. Next thing she'll be calling me honeychil'.

Bemused, I ask to speak to my mother. 'How is she?' I ask quickly (best to be forewarned).

'Not so bad,' says Nana Flo briskly. 'We're keeping busy.' Oh?

'Like how?' I say, intrigued.

'Clearing out cupboards,' she replies tartly. I squeeze my nose to snuff the laughter. Let justice be done!

'Actually, Nana,' I say, when I regain composure, 'I er, don't have to speak to my mother, I can ask you.'

There is a pause. 'Yes?' she barks.

I clear my throat and say, 'I'd like to take you and Mum out for dinner this Thursday, if you're both free.' (That last bit was a courtesy.)

When Nana Flo replies her voice is as stern as ever: 'You sure you've got the money?' Of all the ungracious cheek!

'Yes,' I say (as I will have it when Barclaycard lend it to me).

'Then,' intones my grandmother plummily, 'I don't see why not.'

I grin down the phone and crow: 'Sorted!'

'What?' replies Nana Flo.

Chapter 5

Tom rings the doorbell at 8.10. His timing is suspiciously perfect and I wonder if he arrived early and waited in his car. I feel a twitch of irritation—not too early, not too late, but just right. Like Goldilocks and the porridge. And she was a little prig. I bet Tom is one of those men who asks for the bill with a squiggle flourish of one hand and a flat palm of the other. Like Marcus. Oh! Enough about Marcus. Jasper, as I recall, raises a languid hand and the waitress comes running.

I walk to the door and pinch my arm to exorcise my silly frilly killjoy thoughts. What's the matter with me? I hope Tom isn't wearing anything frightening, like a waistcoat. I yank open the door to face my doom. Tom grins at me, and I sigh with relief and grin back. He's wearing jeans, a khaki-green shirt, a white T-shirt under that, and brown loafery shoes. In the old days I'd have made a mental note of each item and reported back to Tina so she could assess if he was cool or if I should run for the hills. But as Tina has silently relinquished the position of my personal fashion adviser and Tom looks ravishing, I don't bother.

'You look nice,' says Tom, kissing me on the cheek. I should damn well hope so after one and a half hours of preening and primping.

'Thank you,' I say, 'so do you.' (Lizzy has briefed me in the importance of accepting compliments: 'If you don't it's insulting the person who gave it to you.')

However she obviously didn't brief Tom because he looks bashful, pulls at his shirt, and says jokily, 'What, this old thing?'

I giggle. Suddenly, I'm tongue-tied. I say, 'So, er, come in, um, do you want a coffee or'—I nearly say the immortal dolly-bird phrase 'something stronger' but manage to stop myself—'or a beer or something?'

Tom waves the plastic bag he's carrying and says, 'A client gave me a bottle of red this morning. We could open that if you like.'

I blurt, 'What, a hamster went and bought you some Pinotage?'

Tom says mock-huffily, 'No, actually. It was the hamster's Mummy.'

I beckon Tom towards the kitchen. There's a rattle as Fatboy beats it through the cat flap.

'So, how is your mum?' he says dutifully.

'She's OK, thanks,' I say, deciding that my mother is *not* going to hijack tonight.

'Yeah?' says Tom, encouragingly.

'My nan is looking after her,' I say shortly as I uncork the wine and glug glug at least half of it into two huge green goblets. Then, being me, I break my vow immediately and tell Tom the Curious Tale of the Secret Granny Meetings.

'I was seeing my mum three times a week. Why didn't she tell me?' I squeak, hating myself for caring.

Tom looks puzzled. 'It's a weird one,' he says. 'I might be wrong, but it sounds manipulative. A power thing.'

I am silent. I take a large slug of wine. Call me naive but to this second I've imagined that I've always done mostly as I pleased, despite my mother. But. Now Tom mentions it, the possibility dawns that I've always done as *she's* pleased—and if I haven't she's brought me sharply to book by, ooh I don't know, slicing her wrists.

I say slowly, 'She does love to be the centre of attention. But maybe she just didn't think. Or thought I wouldn't be interested.' Then I realise Tom and I have been sitting at the kitchen table discussing my attention-loving mother for a full twenty-eight minutes. Foiled again! 'Anyway, enough about her,' I say brightly. 'Tell me about your parents.'

So he does. In about three seconds flat. Tom's parents divorced when he was five. His mother remarried three years later and he regards his stepfather as his real father. He doesn't see 'Mum's first husband'. The way he says it, I know he doesn't want to discuss it further.

'Why?' I gasp.

He shrugs and tells me that they never got on.

'What!' I exclaim. 'Not even when you were four? What's not to like!' I see Tom's discomfort and add quickly, 'You don't have to tell me.'

Tom laughs and says, 'It's nothing sinister! He just wasn't too keen on kids. It wasn't just me. He was the same with my brother and sister. Mum was, has always been I suppose, liberal. You know, all for girls playing with tractors and boys crying, and her husband was the opposite. Girls should wear pink and dress their dolls and boys should wear blue and dress as cowboys.'

I pour myself another vat of red. Tom has hardly touched his, but I top up his goblet anyway to make myself seem less of a wino. 'So,' I say—desperate to know the answer but aware I'm treading on Jerry Springerish ground—'did you like to wear pink, then?'

I wince at my own crassness. Tom laughs. 'And what if I did?' he says, raising an eyebrow.

'Nothing, nothing. Nothing at all,' I blabber, thinking—I should have known. He's gay. The nice ones always are. If they're not married. Or both. I am so preoccupied with my train of thought that I don't hear Tom's next comment and have to ask him to repeat it. And it turns out that four-year-old Tom loved painting until the day his mother's first husband snapped his brush in half and smacked him round the face and then he went off painting and hasn't painted since.

'That's terrible!' I gasp, the gothic tragedy of the situation intensifying in direct proportion to my alcohol consumption.

'Not really,' grins Tom. 'My mother booted him out two days later, and we all lived happily ever after. Shall we go and get a pizza?'

I nod and say demurely: 'We could even splash out and get two.'

We hail a cab to Pizza Express because Tom reckons there's no way I can walk in those shoes and the conversation progresses to the certainty that Scooby Doo was much better off without that upstart Scrappy and that even if you can't do an accurate impression of Scooby Doo—or indeed any other cartoon or TV character—the fact that you've devoted the valuable time and painstaking effort makes you worthy of much respect. Tom does a superb Scooby Doo and he concedes that my Marge Simpson is second to none. My prowess wins me the last dough ball.

I notice that Tom doesn't talk with his mouth full and when it's time to pay (the staff start stacking chairs) he doesn't do an air-squiggle. We clatter noisily back to the flat and I know it's going to be a good night.

I've never believed that what goes around comes around. To judge from personal experience, the Wheel of Fortune has a flat tyre. So I don't entrust retribution to a medieval caprice. I implement it myself. This is why I recently tore a helpline number out of the *News of the World*'s problem page and pinned it to Marcus's noticeboard. As soon as he emerged from his room last Sunday morning, I scampered into the kitchen, drew up a chair, and feigned absorption in the *Spectator*. Marcus took one glance at my reading material and became instantly suspicious. Fifty seconds later he spotted the 'Manhood Too Small?' cutting, ripped it from the wall, and stuffed it in the bin.

I was hoping for histrionics but instead he leaned heavily against the sink, folded his brawny arms, and stared at me in menacing silence. Although I knew this was an intimidatory technique he'd filched from a Robert De Niro film, it worked. I was starting to squirm when Michelle marched in mewling for black coffee. I legged it, puffing with relief. But I puffed too soon. Because Marcus too is the live-and-let-die type. And he chose to wreak his grim revenge on Tuesday evening.

Tom and I had stumbled into the flat, squabbling over the relative merits of Cadbury's and Galaxy chocolate, when I clapped eyes on Marcus, sitting at his oak veneer table, flicking through the latest issue of *Musclebound* and sipping a banana milkshake. I stopped dead in shock, elation shrivelling. Tom veered to a halt behind me. Marcus smiled like a shark. 'Well, well, well,' he said in a portentous tone, 'so *this* is Tom.' I half expected him to cackle and add, 'Hello, my pretty!'

'Tom,' I said trying to sound calm, 'this is my landlord Marcus.'

Tom, the innocent, grinned and said, 'Hi!'

I—the guilty—twisted my hands and said, 'Marcus, you're up late.'

Marcus smiled another hammerhead smile. 'Couldn't sleep. But hey'—spreading his hands wide helplessly—'everything's for a purpose! Now I can chinwag with you two.' *Chinwag*. What is he, an eighty-year-old woman? He continued, 'I've heard all about you, Tom.'

What! No he hasn't! 'I don't think I've mentioned Tom to you,' I said. The edge in my voice made Tom glance at me.

Marcus laughed. 'Playing coy,' he chortled, nodding at Tom. 'She always does this with her men! Every week!'

This was serious. I blurted: 'Marcus, stop teasing. Please!'

The please hurt and Marcus knew it.

Tom began: 'I'm not sure I want to—' but I spoke loudest: 'Marcus, much as I'd love to stay and chat over your Tums And Bums magazine, I'm feeling exhausted and I've got to get up in, oh, five and a half hours' time, so, Tom's just about to leave so ah, say goodbye to Tom.'

I manhandled Tom out of the kitchen. What else could I do? Wrestle him into my bedroom? Although I'll admit that until Marcus made me sound like a slapper, that was the plan. 'My men' indeed! As I steered Tom into the hall I whispered, 'Sorry about him, he must have OD'd on the steroids. He pops them like Smarties.' This was—as far as I know—a lie, but I was desperate.

Tom replied solemnly, 'Must have.'

There was an awkward pause during which I cursed Marcus to hell.

I smiled at Tom and said, 'Well, thanks. It was really nice to see you.'

Tom smiled back. 'And you. I enjoyed it.' Pause two. 'I'd better go. I'll give you a ring, some time.'

Some time? That means never. 'Definitely,' I said, drooping.

Tom bent and kissed me swiftly on the cheek. Miles away from my mouth—practically on my ear. I kissed him back, feasting miserably on the scent of his aftershave, and waved him out of the door. Then I went straight to bed, pulling the duvet over my head to block out the sound of Marcus whistling the *Pretty Woman* theme tune.

Lizzy refuses to believe that anything is amiss. 'I'm sure Tom realised Marcus was joking,' she says, making me want to strangle her.

'He said I bring home a different man each week!' I shriek. 'That's not a joke! That's libel.'

Laetitia, who is listening, snaps, 'Slander! Unless it's true. Rah ha ha!'

I smile sweetly at her and curl my hands into claws under my desk. One day, when I am rich and successful, I will sponsor a tarantula at London Zoo and name it Laetitia Stokes.

The rest of Wednesday comes and goes and Tom doesn't call. I am tempted to call him on Thursday but can't as I am out of the office for most of the day accosting women in the street for an eight-page section Laetitia has commissioned entitled 'The Worst Way I Dumped Him'. I skid back into the office at 5.30. 'Did anyone ring?' I enquire hopefully.

'Your mother,' replies Laetitia shortly. 'How did it go?'

I nod. 'Fine, fine, I got some great quotes.' Laetitia ignores me. I trundle wearily to my desk and call my mother.

'I saw my *male* nurse from the clinic today,' are her first words. Heaven help him, so she did.

'How was it?' I ask warily, then add, 'Actually, don't tell me now, tell me later—I've booked a Thai restaurant for twenty past eight. Are you and Nana still up for it?'

My mother replies in her best teachery tone: 'Good, thank you, and if by "up for it" you mean are we still planning to join you for dinner, the answer is yes.'

I giggle and say, 'Don't be pompous, Mummy. I'm not one of your children. I'll see you later.'

I'm about to put the phone down when she squeaks, 'Is it smart? What shall I wear?'

'It's smart-casual,' I say evasively. 'See ya!' I sigh with relief and dig out my tape recorder.

I am looking for an excuse to postpone transcribing when—hallelujah—the phone rings. 'Hello!' I say, praying it isn't my mother again.

'Helen?' says Tom.

'*Hiiiiiiiii!*' I say. When he asks how I am I can tell from his voice that he's grinning. Wolf teeth. Rrrrr! 'Fine,' I say, wondering if calling a woman two days after a date classifies a man as wet. 'And you?'

He tells me he's well, and he wondered if I was free some time over the weekend. This is annoying. Can't he be more specific? I mean, if I say I'm free on Saturday night and then he says actually he meant Sunday, what kind of a loser does that make me? But, at the same time, he's so patently keen. It detracts from his allure. I can't help but find it off-putting. I am hit by a brilliant idea. 'Are you free tomorrow night?' I say. 'A bunch of us are going out for a drink. Tina will be there. You remember Tina, don't you?'

I can hear the smile again, as Tom replies: 'Tequila Night. How could I forget?'

For the second time in five minutes I replace the receiver, relieved. Safety in numbers. But I am also disappointed. Why didn't he have the decency to wait a few more days and make me sweat? It's highly unsettling and I brood about it until I realise it's 6.30 and way past going home time. I lock my tape recorder in my drawer. 'I'll start transcribing first thing tomorrow,' I shout to Laetitia on my way out. She ignores me.

I pull up to my mother's house bang on eight o'clock, and see Nana Flo nosing from behind the net curtain. I hoot and wave. A good ten minutes later she and my mother bustle out. Nana is wearing a faded purple coat that may well be made from thistles. Her grey hair is high and brittle under her thin headscarf. My mother is powdered and lipsticked and carrying a shiny black handbag. 'You both look nice!' I say, hoping to set the tone.

Nana grunts. My mother says, 'Do I?'

I tell them the place we're going to is called Nid Ting. 'What kind of name is that?' says Nana Flo.

'A Thai name,' I reply, wondering why I bother. I park the car and we plod in. To my relief, we are given a cosy table in the corner. Nana Flo looks at the red patterned carpet and the pink tablecloths and the windowsill buddhas and purses her lips. When the waitress offers to take her coat, Nana clutches it to her and snaps, 'No, thank you!' She sniffs suspiciously at the complimentary bowl of prawn crackers. 'They're Thai crisps, Nana,' I say, 'prawn cocktail flavour.'

My mother munches away happily and says, 'Do you know, I think I'll have a glass of wine!'

Nana surveys the other diners and tuts, specifically at a skinny man sporting a pierced chin and baggy jeans. 'Ruffian!' she hisses. 'It's a disgrace! Puts me in mind of that ragamuffin who showed up this morning.'

'What ragamuffin?' I say, addressing my mother.

'My nurse!' she replies.

'Ohhhh!' I say, which is all the encouragement she requires to embark on a monologue as long as the history of the world. My mother's nurse is not *at all* what one would expect. In fact, when he rang the doorbell she assumed he was 'a thug'. Only after inspecting his ID and ringing the clinic to check his authenticity did she let him in. (Luckily for him, when he arrived Nana Flo was at Asda.) But you could hardly blame her. A goatee and long sideburns! An earring in his ear! A rucksack! Army trousers! How was she to know! She'd expected a lady in a white uniform! And his name was Cliff!

Surprisingly, Cliff was 'charming'. Extremely chatty, very concerned, sorry to hear about the razor incident and interested to know what happened and how my mother feels now and to see the wound. Eager to be shown photographs of Morrie, intrigued at how they met (Cliff knows people who met at a dance too).

Cliff can't imagine how hard it is for my mother to cope on her own, tell him, how *did* she manage before she met Morrie? Captivated to hear about the tiny room she rented after leaving home and how she painted it herself—quite a thing in those days, although these days, absolutely, anything goes. He suspects she's being modest—she sounds so resourceful! Totally impressed to hear about her newfound financial prowess—what an achievement! But still, must feel resentful towards someone for dying—how does she feel? Asked to be shown around—

When my mother says Cliff asked to be shown around, Nana Flo—who has been quietly yumming down her steamed fish and plain rice while affecting huffy dislike—snaps, 'Casing the joint!'

My mouth drops open. 'I'm sorry?' I say.

'Florence watched *Starsky & Hutch* on satellite this afternoon,' explains my mother. 'You enjoyed it, didn't you, Florence?'

Nana Flo shrugs and says grudgingly, 'Not bad, compared to some of the modern rubbish.'

All of which keeps you pinned to the sofa, I say in my head. Aloud, I say, 'He does sound a bit nosy, Mum. Are you sure he's OK?'

My mother is most defensive. Cliff is a lovely boy.

So we hear more about Cliff. Keen to hear about you, Helen. He said it would be nice to have a chat with you so I gave him your number.

'What!' I shout, loudly enough for the couple at the next table to start eavesdropping. 'Why should this trendy wendy want to call *me*?'

My mother looks uncomfortable. She twiddles her noodles round her fork and says, 'To talk about *me*, probably.'

I sigh and say, 'Oh, OK,' although secretly I'm not convinced.

There is silence while my mother clears her plate. Then she says, 'He said he imagined that one reason I'd want to stay well was because you depend on me.'

I nearly spit out a prawn: 'That's a laugh—he doesn't even know me!'

My mother replies excitedly, 'Exactly! That's what I said! I said you were very independent.'

I nod, pleased.

Two hours later, I drop them off and heave a sigh as Nana's purple coat disappears into the house. In my grandmother's own words, the evening 'wasn't so bad, considering'. At one point I tempted fate by observing, 'I see you've eaten all your fish and rice, Nana.' To which she replied tartly, 'I don't like to see food go to waste.' She then gave me a look which said 'even if it is foreign muck', but I appreciated the effort it took to stifle the words. My father was mentioned once. My mother cried suddenly, 'Wouldn't it be nice if Morrie was here too—then we'd be a family!' I didn't like to say that if my father was here too, we'd all be out the door and up to the Savoy Grill in a shot. Or, more likely, we wouldn't be out together in the first place. So I said nothing.

Nana Flo said curtly, 'Please God he's looking down on us'—a curiously sentimental comment. No one mentioned him again. I am so surprised at having enjoyed myself—even if it was in a masochistic way—that when I return to the flat I slam the front door and wake up Marcus. I know this, because as I enter the bathroom, he bursts from his bedroom and storms down the hall to get a glass of water (I hear the furious whoosh of the tap). The perfect end to a not-so-bad-considering night.

Some days I think I may as well be fifty. I'm constantly tired. I haven't been to a club in about twenty years. And I've gone without sex for so long I wouldn't be surprised if it's closed up. I see Friday night as a chance to remedy two of these complaints.

The evening kicks off when Tina, Lizzy and I pile out of the office and into the loos to tart up at 6.01pm. 'Strictly speaking,' I say to Lizzy who feels guilty about quitting on time, 'we did an extra thirty-one minutes, so I'd feel good if I were you.'

Tina regards me smugly: 'The rabid ambition wore off, then,' she says.

I retort, 'It's not what you do, it's what you're seen to be doing. And when Laetitia left the office at 5.45 I was slaving over my desk.'

I smirk and dig my eyelash curlers out of my hotchpotch of a make-up bag (my eyelashes are unnaturally straight and if I don't curl them I look bald.) Lizzy opens a metal case that looks like it might contain a gun, retrieves a paintbrush from one of its compartments, and fluff-wuffs a waft of powder all over her face. Tina starts from scratch—carefully wiping off the day's shine with cotton-wool pads and cleanser. A mere touch-up isn't good enough for our lord and master Adrian, I think sourly. I know it's mean of me but she's so *precious* about him.

'I'm looking forward to meeting Adrian,' I say, in an attempt to combat my own nastiness.

'Good,' says Tina. 'Do try not to say anything offensive.'

I widen my eyes as far as they'll go and say, 'Cheeky cow! How about *you* try not to say anything offensive to Tom. No weeing jokes, OK?'

Tina smiles, says, 'Deal!' and turns back to the mirror.

'*You'll* like Tom,' I say, addressing Lizzy, 'I'm sure you will.'

Lizzy beams into the mirror and says earnestly, 'I can't wait to meet him, he sounds lovely.'

I smile my gratitude, finish my patch-up job and am instantly bored. 'How's the new flat?' I ask Lizzy, who has just bought an airy loft apartment in Limehouse.

'Oh,' she says, 'wonderful! The view of the Thames! I could look at it for ever. It's so beautiful.'

I was under the impression that the Thames was a stinky brown river, but I simper, 'How lovely.' Maybe it looks picturesque from a distance. 'Have you got much furniture?'

No, not yet. Lizzy wants to take it slowly. She'd rather build up a select number of 'signature pieces' (whatever they are) than a hoard of clutter. Last weekend, she tells us, she saw a brilliant 'Line chaise' (again, search me) for £650 from the Conran Shop.

'Six hundred and fifty squids!' shouts Tina. 'Are you mental?!'

Lizzy knows it's a tad indulgent but it is '*So* sleek.' And it would look sensational against the maple-wood flooring.

By the time Tina and I have stopped sniggering, we're at the pub.

Brian is the first man (if he qualifies) to arrive. He dutifully pecks Tina and me on the cheek and then turns to Lizzy. He gazes on her like an art-lover looks at a rare painting and lifts her hand to his lips and kisses it. Lizzy giggles and tucks her hair behind her ear. I can't help smiling, even though the gallant gentleman is wearing a patterned jumper and grey shoes. Tina obviously regrets the 'Brian's an ass!' remark because she leaps up and asks him, 'What can I get you?' But Brian insists on buying. He walks to the bar to purchase a still mineral water, a Beck's, and an orange juice ('Tina, aren't you feeling well?').

I look at Lizzy and she seems visibly to swell with pride. 'Aw!' says Tina—lighting her fifth cigarette in ten minutes—'young love!' I shoot her a fierce glance—Brian's knocking on eighty!—but neither she nor Lizzy notice the blunder. Brian returns from the bar and I am limbering up to despise him for being teetotal when I see he's bought himself a pint. I glance at Lizzy for signs of disapproval but there are none. She strokes his arm lovingly.

Brian settles down close to Lizzy and addresses the table in general: 'So, how's work?'

Happily, we are whisked from small talk-hell by the arrival of the Messiah, aka, Adrian. Tina jumps up to greet him.

'Everyone,' she announces formally as if she's introducing him at an AA meeting, 'This is my boyfriend Adrian. He's an architect.' Adrian smiles a shiny white smile and shakes everyone's hand.

'Hello,' I say, thinking, Wow. I take it all back. He *is* the Messiah.

Adrian is exceptionally easy on the eye. Exceptionally! He is wearing a tailored navy suit, crisp lilac shirt, and deep pink tie. His golden blond hair is as curly as a cherub's and you expect blue eyes but his are brown. 'Oh, Tina!' I say approvingly, 'I believe the hype!' Adrian laughs and so does Tina. She then speeds off to fetch him a red wine.

Lizzy nuzzles closer to Brian and chirrups, 'We've heard so much about you!'

Adrian smiles at her and says, 'All good, I hope?'

Lizzy giggles and says, 'Aha!'

Tina rushes back with Adrian's red wine which she places lovingly before him. Jesus, it's like *The King and I*.

'So,' jokes Adrian, slapping a hand on Tina's Miu Miu-clad thigh and giving it a fond shake, 'what have you been saying about me?'

Tina looks up startled and says, 'Nothing! Why?'

Adrian replies teasingly, 'Apparently, you've been telling your friends all manner of secrets—and I'd very much like to know what they are.' He lifts his hand from her lap and starts gently massaging the back of her neck and she shivers with pleasure. I don't wish to sound like Mother Superior but it's obscene. Flaunting themselves! Can't they wait? I decide to cut short the public foreplay session.

In a firm loud voice I say, 'She's told us you're handsome, successful, witty and all, but she's been most disappointing and hasn't revealed anything in the least bit private. So you're safe!'

I expect Tina to be irked at my grinchlike behaviour but she beams at me. So does Adrian. He rewards Tina with a kiss and murmurs, 'The truth will out!' Cultured too, it's sickening.

'All right,' I say, 'enough of that!'

When Tom turns up—soon after seven thirty as promised—I introduce him to everyone—'and you remember Tina, but we'll leave it there, shall we?'—he smiles, kisses, shakes hands and insists on getting the next round.

'You know Tom already, I take it,' says Adrian to Tina.

'I only met him once,' says Tina nervously—aware that I am monitoring every word and am willing to douse her in beer if she even dares to *hint* at a urine joke—'we went out with Helen for a quick drink.'

Adrian is intrigued. He narrows his gorgeous eyes and says, 'So why do we have to "leave it there"?'

I have no intention of allowing Tina to blurt out the hilarious tale of my alcohol-induced incontinence so I interrupt: 'Because I drank too much and got a bit tipsy.'

I stare at Tina in a way that I intend to appear benign to everyone else and threatening to her. It works. Instead of declaiming me as a drunken liar, she says meekly, 'Helen was embarrassed. She doesn't like to be reminded of it.' I beam at her.

Adrian suggests, 'Then it can't have been *that* quick a drink,' but Tina insists—as pokerfaced as a guard at Buckingham Palace—'Helen's like me, she doesn't drink much so her tolerance is low.' Frankly I am surprised her nose doesn't grow to Concorde size and smash through the pub window. I feel the rise of a giggle fit so I smirk gratefully at Tina and gabble that I'm going to the loo.

When I return, Tina and Adrian are deep in touchy-feely conversation, and Tom is chatting to Lizzy and Brian. My heart lurches in fear, *please* don't let Lizzy be ranting on about yurt weekends and Jungian psychoanalysis. Please let Tom like her, and please let her like Tom. (Brian is on his own.) Happily, they turn out to be discussing Cornwall. Brian was born in Morwenstow—right on the coast—and although he's lived in London for twenty years he misses the tranquillity.

'Doesn't Tai chi compensate?' I say wickedly.

He smiles and replies, 'A little. But above all I find Tai chi extremely useful if you suffer from pointy foot syndrome.' He bursts out laughing as that flap-mouthed ratbag Lizzy glides to the Ladies' and I cough-splutter into my drink.

In a very small voice I say, 'I am so, so sorry.'

Brian waves away my apology and says, 'Just teasing.'

I know Tom is about to cry 'What?' so I say quickly, 'Do you do, er, any sport, Tom?' It's a nerdy question but it's also an emergency.

'I run. And box,' he says obligingly, 'although I'm not that good.'

I exclaim, 'Rubbish, I'm sure you're brilliant!' mainly to sweep the conversation way and beyond the pointy foot episode.

'Oh?' says Tom, bestowing on me a sunshine smile, 'and why are you so sure?' He is looking at me in a way that would melt chocolate.

I jiggle my foot to stop myself blushing. Then I return the look, playfully squeeze his upper arm, and purr, 'You look quite hard—ooh you are hard!' To be honest, I'm useless at playing the vamp. I'm invariably thwarted by loose paving stones, dogs on heat, and stubborn revolving doors. But tonight I am shameless.

Tom puts his mouth to my ear and mutters casually, 'Try me.'

My heart does a massive thump—either there's a rabbit's foot lodged in my chest or I've got palpitations and need to see a doctor. I hold his ice-blue gaze and my cheeks burn and I murmur, 'Try and stop me.' By this point, Lizzy and Brian are tactfully talking among themselves.

I move closer to Tom until our thighs are brushing and my heart hammers. It *is* lust but not pure lust, there's something else in there too. I can't work it out. We sit in the pub and flirt disgracefully till chucking-out time, we go to a poky little club in Soho and shout above the music and touch hands and still I can't work it out. Tina and Adrian go home because they're exhausted and Adrian's working tomorrow, Lizzy announces she's got to be up early to do her Christmas shopping (only three weeks to go!) and I still can't work it out.

Tom and I roll into the street and hold hands and eat revolting kebabs and my heart is still racing and I still can't work it out. And then I spit my kebab into a bin and he pulls me to him and we kiss and kiss and clutch at each other and the rabbit foot is thumping at ninety miles an hour and we kiss and kiss and we're kissing and kissing and then I realise and I pull away for air. It's fear. I don't know why and I don't know if Tom knows but he doesn't say anything. He kisses me slowly and strokes my hair. Then he hails a taxi.

And then he hails another one for himself.

When I was at college and a stranger to grim reality, I briefly suffered from a surfeit of confidence. This had much to do with escaping my parents. Also, the majority of students were present to extend their sex education, so if you wanted action you could usually find it. Jabba the Hutt would have pulled. Indeed, I snogged him myself on several occasions.

So it was a shock when I went on the prowl with a girl named Beatrice who was as plain as a blank wall, and the guy I'd set my night on bought us both drinks but asked her to dance. The next morning Luke visited and—planting the seed of my misplaced passion—brought Marcus along. I decided to chew over the riddle in his presence. 'Do you think,' I said as I spooned peanut butter out of the jar, 'that he was playing hard to get? Using Beatrice to make me jealous?'

Marcus followed the spoon's progression towards my mouth with fascinated revulsion, and declared: 'Sweetheart, there's no mystery—he fancied Beatrice! If a bloke fancies you, he'll do you!'

I am reminded of these poetic words at 3.00am on Saturday as I pay the taxi driver and walk to the front door, alone. Yes, I pulled away from Tom first. I'm not sure about him anyway. But why did he have to follow *my* lead like a thick puppy? Hasn't he got a mind of his own? I flounce into the flat and am about to karate kick open my bedroom door when I see a note stuck to it: *Flat Meeting, lounge, Sat morning, 10.00am. Attendance compulsory.* And, I think, living with Marcus is like living under martial law. I scrumple up the note and set my alarm for 2.00pm.

I fall asleep and dream the empty-house dream. I am still being pursued by baddies, and still hiding in cupboards, but having been there forty times I am now used to it. I'm hunched in a wardrobe and someone, something, is banging on the wardrobe door, bang! bang! louder and louder. I wake up with a start, sweating, and hear bang! bang! Marcus is banging on my door and singing 'It's nine forty-five! This is your wake-up call!' I hurl a boot at the door and pull the pillow over my head. Marcus keeps banging, bang! bang!

'All *right*!' I scream, 'I'm coming to your meeting, leave me alone!'

I drag myself out of bed, pull on my dressing gown, plod to the kitchen, and make myself a coffee. There's no milk in my section of the fridge so I steal from Marcus's.

Luke has also been turfed out of bed to attend. He looks rumpled and tired. Fatboy is also up, stretching and yawning and prrrpling for breakfast. We're used to Marcus's Flat Meetings. He always hauls us in for a bollocking when our slobbiness rises in a crescendo and we always say that we're sorry and we won't do it again and continue as we were.

So it's a shock when Marcus tells me he wants me out of the flat by the end of the week.

'But I've got nowhere to go!' I bleat.

'Not my problem,' says Marcus coldly. I stare stonily at a black hair poking out of Marcus's nose—I refuse to cry or argue as nothing would please him more. Luke tries to stand up for me but I don't want him to be booted out too so I shush him.

'Marcus,' I lie, 'you're doing me a great favour. And you've got a black hair poking out of your nose. It's like a hamster's tooth.' And I stalk out of the lounge, into my room, and flop on the bed.

I don't believe it. I don't believe it but I should. Of course this was going to happen. How could it *not* happen? Marcus may be a grasping tightwad but he's also as proud as, well, as a man with a ripply back. I know this. And yet, ever since he rebuffed me I've been kicking him where it hurts. Although it does require careful aim with a target that small. See what I mean? Did I expect him *not* to retaliate? I suppose that I was so caught up in personally effecting his eternal punishment that the consequences didn't occur to me.

I look back and I don't think I could have stopped baiting him even if

I'd wanted to. I have this stagnating pool of hatred for him that kills rationality, and I don't know why. If I'm honest—something I'm not very good at—what did he do wrong apart from trying me for size and deciding I didn't fit? (And likewise.) Marcus's ego was bound to snap one day, and it has. I should be steeled for it, but I'm not. I'm scared.

I call Tom.

And the bastard isn't in!

I call my mother instead and tell her about my impending homelessness. 'You can come and stay with us!' she cries. I can just imagine it. Three witches and an orange cat. It would be like living in a tin drum. I tell her it's a sweet offer but no thanks. I spend from noon till five moping and grooming Fatboy—who is desperate to escape and claws at the door—and hoping that a passing fairy godmother will save me from being turfed onto the street or (worse) being forced into cohabitation with Psychomum and Nana Flo.

I must have fallen asleep because the next thing I know, Luke is shaking me awake and brandishing the phone in my face. 'Phone!' he shouts, unnecessarily.

'Who?' I mouth.

'Tom!' he shouts.

I snatch it from him. 'Thanks, Luke!'

Tom is friendly but says nothing about last night except he had a good time. Well what's *that* supposed to mean? He enjoyed his kebab? He asks how I am. I start off airy and defiant but the confusion and envy and self-pity merge and, to my absolute mortification, my voice cracks. 'Basically,' I sniffle—a word I usually veto on principle—'me and Fatboy have got nowhere to go!'

Tom is silent. Then he says, 'What are you and Fatboy doing tonight?' I consider spinning him a glamorous lie.

'Nothing!' I bleat.

'Do you want me to come round?' he says.

I know I should say no to, if nothing else, reclaim a sliver of dignity. But I hate the word should. 'Yes!' I say.

'Don't move,' he says, 'I'll be with you in a couple of hours.'

The doorbell rings and I freeze. He can't be early. That's cheating! I heave open the door. 'Surprise!' exclaims my mother, throwing her hands wide like the young Shirley Temple. Nana Flo lurks po-faced behind her. 'Aren't you going to invite us in?' cries my mother, blind to the fact that my face has fallen about ninety foot.

'Of course!' I say, recalling my promise to Dr Collins and forcing a smile. 'Come into the kitchen. Nana, would you like a cup of tea?'

(In times of doubt I resort to clichés. It gives me time to think. Although when I rack my brain for inspiration it's napping and won't be disturbed.) I have just poured a cup of PG Tips for Nana, a camomile tea for my mother, and retrieved half a packet of biscuits from my room, when the doorbell rings again. 'I wonder who that is!' chirps my mother, who is very obviously still taking the pills.

'I think it may be a friend of mine, Tom,' I mutter.

As I walk into the hall I can hear my mother squawking 'Tom! Tom? Do I know Tom?' and my grandmother growling, 'Tim, Tom, who knows any more?'

I squeeze the bridge of my nose between my fingertips, paste a smile to my face, and open the door. Tom is brandishing a wilting bunch of garish blue marigolds in what appears to be a doily. 'Garage flowers!' he declares. 'The finest and the best!'

I gasp and take them, exclaiming, 'The rare and priceless blue marigold! You shouldn't have!'

He grins and says, 'I pawned my Ferrari.'

I reply sweetly, 'Not your Ferrari *poster*?'

He nods, and says 'Don't be too sad, my 911's still on the wall!'

I feel an inexplicable surge of joy and—before I have time to reconsider—step towards him and kiss him on the mouth. I am about to pull away but he wraps his arms around me and kisses me and so I close my eyes and kiss him back and my heart does a delirious dance and 'Helloo-ooo! Anybody there-ere!'

My mother's brisk schoolmarm tone kills the moment stone dead and Tom and I spring guiltily apart. 'Surprise visit from my mum and grandma,' I explain hurriedly.

'What are you waiting for?' he murmurs. 'Introduce me!'

Dazed and grinning like the village idiot, I lead Tom into the kitchen and introduce him.

'You took your time,' says Nana, grouchily.

'What lovely blue flowers!' says my mother. I will her not to say anything akin to 'Is this your boyfriend?'

'Is this your boyfriend?' she asks, eyes wide.

'Tom and I are just good friends,' I say, trying not to sound panicked.

Tom says helpfully, 'I'm Fatboy's vet.'

My mother ogles him and says, 'I see.'

Nana Flo says snappishly, 'No need for it! In my day, a dog was a dog and that was that!'

Tom says politely, 'I see what you mean.'

I say under my breath, 'I'm glad someone does,' then louder, 'Tom, would you like a coffee and a biscuit?'

My mother, who keeps staring at Tom, says in a loud show-offy voice, 'Helen, haven't you got something more substantial to offer him?' I am tempted to say, 'My body?' to shut her up but she adds, 'You can't expect young men to survive on *biscuits*'—at which point Nana Flo joins the fray with—'A man needs a good solid meal inside him!'

Whereas a woman, I presume, can survive on sweetness and light. A plausible supposition slowly dawns in my head. And although my dearest wish is that the pair of them vanish in a whiff of sulphur (at least until tomorrow) I say casually, 'Mum, Nana. If I were to nip down to the corner shop to buy something nice for Tom to eat, would you like to join him, us, for supper?'

Nana Flo speaks up so fast her false teeth nearly fly out of her mouth: 'If you insist but don't go to any trouble!'

My mother says, 'I don't see why not. But no onions or red peppers. Onions and red peppers give me a migraine.'

More like the incessant yapping of your own voice gives you a migraine, I think but don't say. I turn to Tom who, to his credit, hasn't run away. 'Tom,' I say, hardly daring to meet his eyes, 'would you like to come to the shop with me?' There's no way I'm leaving him to the mercy of the Munsters.

Tom—and I can hear the mischief in his voice—says, 'No no no, *I'll* go to the shop, you stay here and keep your mother and grandmother company. It would be rude to leave them alone.'

Nana Flo nods at this and mutters, 'Quite right!'

'I'll see you to the door,' I say acidly. As soon as we're in the hall I try and whack him but he dodges me and, as he shuts the front door behind him, grins at me tauntingly, all teeth, like an ape.

'Well brought up!' remarks Nana Flo on my return, glancing at me dismissively as if to say 'unlike you'. Please, I reply in my head, don't put me off him.

'Where's that nice boy Luke?' trills my mother. She's insatiable!

'I think he's gone to work,' I say. 'He works in a pub.'

'I *do* like Luke,' purrs my mother, 'he's *so* charming.' In her hormonally charged state I suspect she'd find Frankenstein's monster charming and am wondering if I could bribe Luke to stick a bolt in his neck to test this theory, when Marcus sweeps into the kitchen.

He is wearing smart cream chinos, a yolk-yellow shirt, and his hair is as springy and bouffant as an expertly baked soufflé. His haughtiness turns to dismay on seeing my relatives. 'Hello,' he says awkwardly.

Nana Flo peers at him. 'Is this the one who's turning you out?'

I say quickly, 'He's not turning me out! I'm glad to be going!'

At this, my mother appears confused. 'Oh,' she says, 'but I thought—'

I interrupt her with the first piece of trivia I can think of: 'Marcus is going out with Michelle, Mummy. You know Michelle.'

My mother shrugs and in a flat voice says, 'Vaguely.' (As she has known Michelle for two decades this is intended as a slight.) She gives Marcus a cursory glance, starts, then stares. She is staring at him like a miser staring at a pot of gold.

Marcus pats his hair nervously and scratches his shin with the toe of his moccasin. 'Well, I'd better—' he begins, but my mother stops him.

'Sit down!' she orders. I stare at her in fury but she doesn't notice. Marcus sits, stony faced. She pulls her chair towards his, and says suddenly, 'Florence, doesn't he remind you of Maurice?'

'Nothing like!' bleats Nana. Her eyes bore into Marcus, and then she looks away and back again and says, quietly, 'Nonsense.' But she doesn't take her eyes off him.

'Don't talk rubbish!' shouts a voice, which turns out to be mine. The doorbell goes and I race to it.

Tom lifts a heavy plastic bag and says, 'I got some eggs. I was thinking of your Nan's teeth.'

I smile wanly and say, 'Brilliant.'

We troop into the kitchen where Marcus and his hair are still trapped.

My mother is grasping his wrist and exclaiming, 'The mouth and eyes are identical, identical! Helen! It's uncanny!'

I keep my temper with difficulty. 'No, it is *not* uncanny,' I say. 'Please.' My voice sounds shrill, panicked. She's mad. Everyone reminds her of my father. Next it'll be Fatboy.

I am about to command her to free Marcus when Ivana flounces in. 'Markee! Wher—Oh, hello, Mrs Bradshaw! And Mrs Bradshaw Senior!'

'Hello,' replies my mother dourly.

Nana actually recoils. 'Who are you? she says rudely.

'I'm Michelle!' says Michelle. 'You remember me!'

Nana scowls and says, 'All young women look the same to me.'

Michelle turns the full beam of her automated allure upon Tom. 'I don't think we've met,' she husks, lashes lowered.

'Tom,' he says briskly, extending a hand, 'I'm with Helen.'

The smile dies on her lips, to be briefly resurrected as she spies the blue marigolds. 'How sweet,' she croons, 'so the flowers must be from you! I'm always telling Markee that a gas station bouquet will do me fine but the angel insists on Paula Pryke!' and in the next breath: 'Markee darling, a black tea before we go out.' Tom glances, amused, at me. Marcus leaps up gratefully.

'Right,' I say. 'Mum, Nana, I'm making omelettes. It's that or nothing.'

My mother pouts.

I start yanking pans out of drawers and Tom says, 'Why don't you sit down and I'll make the omelettes.' He starts cracking eggs into a bowl.

Marcus says coolly, 'Not for us, we're eating at the Conran restaurant.' He hovers by Michelle, who has sat down at the table. 'Michelle, we ought to set off.'

'Five seconds, honey!'

I can see Nana gazing at Tom. 'Same height,' she says, 'I'll give her that.'

I grit my teeth and collapse into a chair. My neck is so tense it aches. By the time Tom starts placing omelettes in front of my mother and Nana, the tension has spread to my shoulders and jaw.

Marcus slumps unhappily into the chair next to Tom.

Tom winks at me. 'Ketchup, anyone?' he says.

'Yuck,' sings my mother.

Nana shakes her head. 'Not for me, dear.'

Pardon? I don't wish to be picky but I, her granddaughter, am rarely accorded the courtesy of being addressed by name, whereas Tom, a man she didn't know existed until an hour ago, is '*dear*'?

'Helen,' says Tom, 'ketchup?' I shake my head.

'Just me then,' he says cheerfully. He holds the bottle upside-down, gives it a hefty whack on its bottom, and a large red gloop shoots through the air and lands 'splat!' on Marcus's yellow shirt. 'I am sorry,' says Tom happily, as Marcus leaps up with a bellow of dismay, 'can't take me anywhere.'

I clamp a hand over my mouth and swallow a bit of omelette faster than I meant to. Michelle's mouth is a perfect scarlet O of dismay. My mother and grandmother gaze mesmerised at Marcus, as he shouts, 'You *idiot*!' at Tom.

Michelle escorts him to the bedroom to change. 'We are going to be *so* late!' she spits at Tom on her way out.

'My word, what a fuss about nothing!' Nana Flo snaps. I grin weakly at Tom. Much as his ketchup trick makes me want to hug him, I feel unable to rise from my chair. Because at the moment Marcus's mouth and eyes thinned in anger, a sickening jolt of perception hit. Why, how didn't I see it before? It's undeniable. Not so much the features as the posture, the temperament, the volatility. My father, the very image.

I run to the toilet and throw up the omelette. I've only eaten two bites but I can't stop retching.

Anyhow, soon after I spew up my omelette, Michelle and Marcus vroom off in his RAV 4 for a showcase meal, and my mother and Nana Flo depart in the Peugeot to catch a Clint Eastwood film on Channel Five. Before she leaves, my mother tells me, 'You needn't bother coming round tomorrow, I'm going shopping with Vivvy!' and my grandmother says, 'You're overexcited! You need an early night.'

I nod and say, 'OK, Mum,' and 'Yes, Nana.'

When they've gone I lean against the door and shudder at Tom. And the turncoat says, 'I'm with Nana Flo!' What is this, a conspiracy?

'There's nothing wrong with me,' I lie. I've got to be fine. Tonight, I am certain, we're seeing some action! Tom suggests I lie on the sofa for a few minutes while he stacks the dishwasher. 'All right,' I say, 'but only as a favour.'

I wake up four hours later when he carries me to bed.

Never in my life did I imagine that exhaustion would overpower my libido. I feel drugged. I can't even move a leg. 'Stay,' I murmur sleepily, as Tom lowers me onto the bed.

'Here?' he whispers.

'Mm,' I breathe.

I lie unfetchingly limp as Tom wrestles off my boots. A dilute fear washes over me—what if he sniffs them?—but I'm too comatose to care. He leans close and whispers, 'Can I undress you?'

I reply—and I swear I wouldn't have said this had I been conscious—'Yeah.' Which is how I wake up on Sunday morning at 10.22 squashed right up against Tom's naked—I'll say that again—n-a-k-e-d—chest.

My eyes ping open and I marvel at him sleeping. His hair is even more tousled than normal and his cheeks are flushed and he is breathing deeply. Broad shoulders. I lift the duvet a little to inspect his chest and whew, I've seen worse. Not too muscled but defined, *solid*. Nice nips. And not scarily hairy like Marcus. I wonder if he's naked all the way down and I am lifting the duvet higher so I can peer lower when a hand shoots out and grabs mine and he shouts 'Gotcha!' and I scream. He grabs my other hand and rolls on top of me—at this point I realise he's wearing boxer shorts—and pinions me to the bed. 'So!' he says, blue eyes boring into mine. 'Thought you'd sneak a preview!'

I am writhing and squealing—part shock, part horror—not least because my own chest is on full wobbly view and we haven't even slept together yet. In the rude sense, I mean. This is wrong!

'Do you mind!' I shout primly, trying to obscure my breasts with my shoulders (don't bother trying—it's physically impossible). 'I need to brush my teeth. They're filthy!'

Tom laughs and murmurs, 'But I like filthy,' and he bends and brushes his lips on my left nipple and a great whopping thud of desire whips through me and I arch against him and we're kissing and I say 'Woof!' to excuse my dog breath and he says, 'Helen, you're fucking gorgeous, God you're sexy' and I think, *me?*

And you know what, I do feel sexy, very sexy, the sexiest woman in the room, and suddenly I'm grabbing at him and kissing and sucking and licking and he's kissing and sucking and licking—I haven't been so delirious since I discovered that Dime bars occur in mini form and I'm attacking Tom in the same greedy passionate must-have way and he's grabby and ravenous and all over me too and when I pull at his hair and nibble at his neck he groans and runs his fingers down my back and over my stomach and down, and oh God that feels promising, 'get these off!' I hear myself saying—and he's yanking off my black knickers and I'm pulling at his boxers—navy but would I care if they were orange pantaloons, well maybe for a second but not—woho!

And it's wonderful and I hope my father isn't listening in and Tom and I are so desperate to—as I think I say—'Get it in!' his penis boinks against my inner thigh and we snigger and he says 'Ow!' and I giggle 'Nearly snapped!' and then, oh. my. God. it feels indescribably delicious and I'm oohing and aahing fit to burst and we're kissing and moving together and we're so together I don't want it to end and I never thought it could be like this.

So of course I have to ruin it.

I come first ('Ladies first!') jokes Tom before joining me five seconds later and the soaring rapture drowns in a fierce, inexplicable wave of sorrow. I bite my lip to stop the sobs. Tom flops out like a starfish, one arm flung warmly over my stomach, and says plaintively, 'Can we do it again?'—and I start laughing and say, 'It's like all my bones have been removed!' and he grins and rolls over and kisses the nearest bit of me—my chin—and says, 'Gorgeous Helen.'

He looks into my eyes and it's not the sweep of desire that's killing me, it's the ugh ugh I hate this word—*tenderness* of our connection—it's new and stupefying, it makes me recoil, so raw and exposed like an open wound. Then the weepiness is back with a vengeance and the tears start falling until they fall out of control and, stupid stupid girl, I'm blubbing and wailing like a great big baby and Tom looks horrified and says, 'It wasn't that bad, was it?' and I laugh but I'm still crying. He hugs me and rocks me and says, 'Tell me, Helen, please tell me what it is.'

Tom shouldn't have asked, he really shouldn't. It's nothing to do with him. But he does and it all pours out. Stuff I didn't even know was in there. And he lets it happen. He just listens while I rant.

'Hes gone hes not coming back, oh god i cant believe it and no one understands im so alone i don't know who i am any more who am i in the world and why is it like this we werent even close i never understood him he hardly knew me who i was and now its too late too late to make it right and i don't know why i feel like this and no one understands its all her its all about her and how she is and she never thinks about me and i thought i was over it i didnt cry at the funeral i was numb i felt nothing so i couldnt cry and i wasnt good enough and he died and i never said i loved him and he never said he loved me he said i was a grinch oh god i cant bear it i want to see him again i hate him i hate how he makes me feel i feel so bad adrift its the worst its worse than i ever imagined im a fraud im so angry the anger wont go i feel scared im so scared what if mummy dies too and nana shes on the way out and tina and lizzy and luke and fatboy and now you and im so scared they will and i cant say because they wont understand and oh god i cant believe it hes my dad its so not fair im so tired i cant even dream about him other people dream about dead people and they come back and hug them and smile and say its OK and be happy and i cant even do that he wont appear in a single dream he wont even tell me how hes doing its all too late its so fucking typical hes never there for me hes never been there so why do i miss him oh god help me its all my fault . . .'

Beat that for embarrassing.

Chapter 6

I'M SO MAD and distraught the horror of it doesn't dawn on me till later. When the words run out Tom rocks me and hugs me. He doesn't tell me to shush, he rubs my back and he listens. All he says is, 'Helen, don't you think, you've got um, stuff that needs sorting?'

I shake my head because I don't know. I feel ashamed. 'Please pass me my clothes,' I say stiffly. Tom leans down, grabs a baggy shirt lying on the floor, and helps me into it. I am sapped. 'Sorry,' I mumble, 'I don't know what happened.'

He replies, 'Doesn't matter. But, Helen—Lizzy, Tina, me, we're not going anywhere. And you mustn't think you're not good enough. I don't know what to say—you're great and'—at this point Tom's voice becomes fierce—'and your dad should have let you know that.'

This is kind of him. Although I'm not sure I appreciate him slagging off my father. I feel tired and teary again and I say, 'Do you mind if I have a quick nap?' Tom kisses me and then I curl up. Every time I think of what I said my heart bobs in my chest like a gull on a rough sea. I was nothing with my father and I am nothing without him. What is the point of me? I want to shrivel up and cease existing. I shrink into the smallest ball that I can and sink into a deadening sleep.

When I wake up it's twenty past two and I'm starving. I've also got a cracking headache. The craziness of the day seeps back into my consciousness and I cringe. I can't begin to think about the sex because I can't stop thinking about the blathering. I prefer to keep my basest instincts to myself. Deep dark Daddy emotions included. How *could* I let Tom tease them from me?

I wonder if Tom has gone, and I half hope he has. But no. I can hear a bark of laughter in the lounge. I tiptoe to the door, open it a crack, and realise he's talking to Luke. The conversation appears to be about the longest they've ever driven their cars with their eyes shut.

Tom managed three seconds before 'bottling out'. Luke trumps him with seven. I pull on some track-suit bottoms, tiptoe in, and say, 'How *could* you!' They both jump and start bleating 'It was the middle of the night' and 'There was no one on the road' until I hold up a hand and say crossly, 'I don't want to know. You could have killed someone!'

I can't bear to look Tom in the eye. Not because of his irresponsible driving but because, as of this morning, he knows me stripped bare in every sense and it's too awful to contemplate. So I focus on Luke instead. This is a mistake because he peers closely at me and says, 'Why are your eyes so puffy?'

I snap, 'No reason!' To deflect further interrogation I say, 'Is there anything to eat?'

Tom jumps up and says, 'Let's go out and get something!'

I look withering and say, 'What, with me like this?'

He lifts a hand, tilts my chin, and says, 'But Miss Bradshaw—you're beeoootiful!' And then, in a more serious tone, 'You are though.'

I wrinkle my nose and say, 'Hang on while I get some shoes and sunglasses.' Ten minutes later (after a detour to the bathroom to try and make myself look less like a gargoyle) I am ready.

'Can I come?' says Luke.

'No,' says Tom meanly, 'it's a boy–girl thing.'

Luke's eyes saucer. 'What!' he says. 'You and Helen!'

I'm not sure if I should be impressed or insulted that Tom hasn't told Luke about balling me. So I joke, 'Why are you so surprised, Luke? Is Tom out of my league?'

Luke shakes his head and says, 'No, mate—you're out of his.'

His delightful compliment is tempered by the appellation 'mate'. I don't wish to set feminism back but I'd rather be called 'darlin''. But I say gallantly, 'Luke, that is very sweet of you.'

Tom repeats cheerily, 'Luke, that is very sweet of you.' Luke gives him the finger. It's a relief when Tom says, 'Ready?'

It's a freezing winter's day but we speed to Golders Green, buy four cream cheese and smoked salmon bagels, and drive to the heath extension.

The heath extension is a higgledy assortment of green fields plonk in the middle of smart northwest London. I love it because it's mostly scruffy and overgrown and has a less commercial feel than Hampstead Heath. We walk to a wooden bench, clutching our bagels, and sit down to eat them.

'It's so peaceful,' I sigh.

'Mm,' says Tom with his mouth full of bagel. 'Gissa kiss.' I kiss him chastely on the cheek.

'Your nose has gone pink,' I say.

'It's so cold I can't feel it,' he replies.

I finish my bagel and he hugs me to him. We look at the view. Pale sky, bare trees, frosty ground, silence. Stillness. I sigh. A boxable moment of happiness. I begin to think that maybe I *did* need to tell someone about my dad and I am marvelling at how easy it is to be with Tom, how effortless, and what a bloody miracle he is in bed, when he spoils it by saying, 'Helen, about what you told me about your dad. I know it's hard for you to talk about your grief but you were, are, were so sad and I thought that maybe you were punishing yourself—for something that wasn't your fault and maybe it would help to—'

No no no no no no no. 'No, don't,' I snap, more sharply than I mean to. Tom stops. I hesitate. Then I say, 'It's kind of you but—'

This time Tom interrupts me. His tone is annoyed: 'Helen, this isn't me being *charitable*, this isn't some holy, po-faced exercise in making myself feel good—it may sound stupid and incredible to you but I like you and I'd like you to be OK but I don't think you'll ever be anything but miserable if you keep on denying what you feel about your father and how he was, and—'

I jump up from the bench and shout, 'Stop it! You don't know!'

Tom shuts up. He looks thunderous. I take a deep breath, sit down again, and pat his leg. 'I'm sorry,' I say. 'I don't know why I got so upset this morning, or rather, I do know'—and here I whip out my heart for a second and shove it on my sleeve to show the extent of my sincerity—'I got upset because my father died and it's weird, but it was mainly because, in fact, I'm sure it was because, well, I'm being turfed out and I've got nowhere to go. And it's just another stress on top of everything.'

This, I admit, is a bad habit of mine. I don't state what I want, bluntly, like Laetitia. I hint. Hinting is not, I know, the bravest way of asking. But at least if you hint and are rejected the rejection is blurrable rather than blistering. Whereas if you ask outright and are refused, the humiliation is as stark as a streaker on a football pitch. Anyhow, unless Tom is an imbecile he surely will take the hint and if he likes me as much as he claims, he will sweep to my assistance like a guardian angel and ask me and Fatboy to come and live in his flat. I pause. Tom says nothing. What is he, dumb? Then he says—and do I detect a hint of coldness—'Didn't your mum say you could live with her until you found somewhere?'

I reply crossly, 'Yeah, but you've met her—she's a nightmare! And I'm twenty-six! I can't live with my mum and my gran for chrissake!'

I expect Tom to understand but he plays obtuse. He snaps, 'It's better than being homeless. Can't you look for another place to rent?'

I lose my temper. 'Take me back to the flat!' I shout.

'Fine, if that's how it's going to be,' he growls. We stomp back to the car in silence. All that blarney and he can't even bail me out when I need him. He knew what I meant. We don't talk apart from once when Tom blurts out, 'If you ask me it'd do you good to shack up with your mother—you could tell her some of what you told me.'

I roar, 'I did not ask you!' He screeches to a halt outside Marcus's flat. I jump out, spit, 'Bye!' and slam the door. Tom clenches his jaw and roars off with as much haughtiness and speed as a Honda Civic EX F-reg can muster. Which, I am spitefully thrilled to note, isn't much.

I get in, shut the door, shout, 'Bugger!' and see Marcus storming towards me. He roars, 'That's *it*! That's it that's it that's it!'

I watch his tempestuous approach with detachment. This, I think to myself, is a truly remarkable day. I feel no emotion at all. I scream at the top of my voice (and in this respect I'm my mother's daughter), '*What's* it, you great big twittering ninny?'

Marcus's face turns purple. He bellows, 'You *dare* speak to me like that, you vicious little cow! Your fucking cat brought in a pigeon! A great big pigeon flapping round my kitchen, shitting on the surfaces!'

Even though I loathe Fatboy's bird-catching habit, I roar, 'Don't you know anything, you big fat fool, a pigeon from a cat is a present!'

Marcus is screeching so loudly his voice cracks: 'It took me two hours to catch it! Two hours! I was meant to be at the gym!'

I yelp: 'For what! To make your pecs bigger and your pecker even smaller?' This strikes me as funny and I start laughing.

Marcus shakes a hammy fist in my face and snarls, 'I want you out tonight! Do you hear me, tonight! And that fat slug of a cat!'

I march past him. Then I retrieve Fatboy from Luke's wardrobe—his favourite hiding place because it's full of warm, soft, dirty clothes—and carry him to my bedroom. 'Angel Baby,' I say, 'pack your things, we're moving out!'

I ring my mother and ask if she minds if I move in tonight. She says, 'Oh. OK. I don't know where you'll sleep though. There's no bed in the study and Florence is in the guest bedroom.'

I reply, 'I can sleep in the lounge on the sofa.'

She pauses. Then she says, 'But me and Florence are watching *The Horse Whisperer*.'

I sigh. 'Well I won't go to sleep until you're finished then, will I?'

What if my obituary states to the nation that I had a knack of failing at almost everything I did? I start fretting about this on reading about Mr Cane in the *Daily Express*. 'The prosecutor said Mr Cane, who had not been reported missing, was a shy, introverted loner who appeared to have a knack at failing at almost everything he did . . .' I sit on the train and I can't get the sentence out of my head. A knack at failing at almost everything. What a terrible legacy. It churns me up because I feel that I'm heading the same way.

I now live with my mother and grandmother, both of whom prefer Robert Redford to me. I'm too feeble to live on my own. And Tom hates me. We've destroyed the ozone layer. A forest fire somewhere hot has just decimated millions of trees. Which negates the fact I recycled all my newspapers last week. A meteorite is probably going to smash into Earth. Someone is poisoning dolphins. I have a fear of estate agents so am doomed to live with my mother for ever. My hair is as flat as if I'd pasted it to my head. And no one even noticed that Mr Cane was missing. By the time I get into work I'm feeling a bit low.

So it doesn't help that when I return from the toilet, Laetitia screams across the office in a voice as loud as Concorde taking flight, 'Helen—private call for you—it's your community psychiatric nurse!' I freeze and stare, as does the entire office. Laetitia trills sweetly, 'Shall I transfer him to you now?'

I stare at her in dismay and say, 'If you must.' She smirks.

I snatch up the phone. 'Yes?' I hiss, cupping the mouthpiece.

'Helen Bradshaw?' says a warm voice. 'Sorry to hassle you at work. Cliff Meacham—your mother's CPN. Hope she warned you I was going to call!' I swallow. I am bubbling with rage at his indiscretion when he adds, 'Your colleague wouldn't pass me on unless I identified myself.'

'What can I do for you?' I say politely.

Cliff tells me it's important for him to understand my mother's relationship with my father, and how she's changed since my father died.

'But I thought you asked her all that,' I say. He tells me it's useful for him to hear my impression of events as well as hers. I say, in the understatement of the year, 'She's been a bit up and down.' He doesn't say anything so I add, 'I've tried to look after her but she misses my dad.'

Then Cliff says casually, 'And how do you look after her?'

I tell him about the cooking and the listening and the forcing Vivienne to invite her to dinner.

Cliff says, 'Wow.' Then he asks, 'And what happens when you need looking after?' I'm stumped.

'I don't follow,' I say.

'Well, when *you* need mothering, what happens then?'

A question which would have been more appropriate when I was four. I say brusquely, 'It's not really like that.'

I hear Cliff take a deep drag on his homemade cigarette. 'I see,' he says in an indefinable tone, then he asks me how my life has changed since my father died. I think of my post-orgasm outburst and my insides float with panic. I itch to slam down the phone and bolt. After a full minute, Cliff says, 'I sense you're having difficulty in talking about how you feel.' He must have *The Ladybird Book of Psychiatry* open on his lap at page seven.

I reply tartly, 'I'm not feeling anything.' It's nearly true. Cliff is disbelievingly silent. I blurt, 'I've been too busy at work and looking after my mother. She's been very upset since, you know.'

'What?' he says.

'My father's death!' I snap. What did he think I was talking about? Her team's relegation?

'She cut her wrists!' I exclaim. Cliff seems to expect elaboration so I tell him what happened, even though I'm sure my mother has told him at rambling length. I make it plain to Cliff that the wrist-cutting night was the only Monday night I'd missed and of course, after that, I'd never ever miss one again. I don't want to be accused of parental neglect a second time.

But when I've finished Cliff says, 'You've been devoting a lot of your time to your mother.'

'Well, she needs me now,' I say. Cliff goes silent again. I joke, 'I turn my back for one minute and bam! She's whittling at her wrists!' It's not one of my best jokes and Cliff doesn't laugh. He says it sounds to him as if my mother was trying to punish me for not being there. 'Well you got that right,' I say sourly.

'But, Helen,' he says, 'what about *your* life?'

'What about it?' I say sharply.

'You can't be living it totally for your mother,' he replies. 'You are not responsible for your mother's behaviour. Only your own. The most helpful thing you can do for yourself and your mother—in that order—is to let her learn to manage her own grief.'

'And so I just ignore her, do I, until she leaps from a window?' I say sarcastically.

Cliff—who is turning out to be as charming as halitosis—admits that resisting my mother's demands is a gamble. But he also says if I'm always available to bail her out, neither of us will 'move on'.

'What do you mean by that?' I say haughtily.

Cliff coughs and says, 'If you can't deal with pain, the easiest thing to do is to put it back in its box. If a person spends all their time worrying about someone else's pain they distract themselves from their own.'

I feel uneasy so I say stiffly, 'I don't know what you're talking about.'

Cliff pauses. I suspect he's about to say something pompous. I'm not disappointed. 'Helen,' he says. 'When someone dies, a door opens into a room where there's grief. There may be more rooms. If you have the courage you can look further. Some people shut the door again.'

He then starts wittering about 'closing' and asks if there is anything else I want to say but there's nothing.

I stare into space for ten minutes then start calling estate agents.

I rounded up all my favourite memories this morning. They have one thing in common. Food. Being taken to a grown-up party and asking the hostess for fruit salad 'but only the cherries', and getting them. Michelle's grandma buying us comics and a Curly Wurly each. A peach in Spain as big as a ball, my skin smelling like toffee in the sun. All delicious.

But my best edible memories revolve around Christmas. Helping my mother make a currant-filled cake for her class and scraping out the bowl. Baking gingerbread men at school with cut-out shapes. Stuffing myself with Quality Street (except the purple ones) until I felt sick. Asking for six roast potatoes and leaving three and my father being too merry to boom, 'Your eyes are bigger than your stomach!'

My father was fun at Christmas. He'd creep into my bedroom late on Christmas Eve and plop a Terry's plain chocolate orange into my stocking. (I prefer milk chocolate but he wasn't to know.) We'd drive to the garden centre and choose a tree and I'd breathe in the smell of pine and and he'd say, 'Daylight robbery!' or 'Peculiar shape!' And he'd buy himself a cigar and me a pack of sugar cigarettes and we'd smoke them in the car on the way home. Naturally, this tradition came to an end when I turned seven, but I think of it today and I want to drag him out of his grave.

I am dreading Christmas without him and so is my mother, because at breakfast she declares, 'I'm not doing Christmas this year, I'm staying in bed. So don't expect any presents!'

I pause from feeding Fatboy his Turkey Pâté and exclaim, 'But, Mummy, we can't *not* do Christmas! Even Michelle does Christmas!'

My mother snaps, 'Michelle's father is still alive!'

I am about to say, 'Look, I know it's hard for you,' when I think of Cliff. I say calmly, 'I'm still alive. Nana's still alive. Just. What about the cake we made together?'

My mother slams down her teacup. 'I don't care about the stupid cake!' she whines. 'It's not the same without a man in the house!'

'Oh, Mum,' I say sadly, 'I know it isn't. But why can't we have a quiet Christmas, just the three of us?' She sticks out her lower lip. She must have learned it from one of her kids. It's so comical—a four-year-old's expression on a fifty-five-year-old face—I have to bite my tongue to stop myself laughing.

'I can't be bothered,' she says defiantly.

'Mum,' I say, 'is this because you're going to the clinic today?'

My mother snorts and says, 'No. It's because I want nothing to do with Christmas and I refuse to go Christmas shopping. I shun it!' Fine.

'All right, Scrooge,' I say sternly, 'then Nana and I will have to celebrate it ourselves. Won't we, Nana?'

Nana Flo, who has just shuffled in carrying her hot-water bottle, shrugs and mutters, 'Nothing to celebrate.'

I feel foolish for thinking that Nana would help me out. She doesn't go a bundle on helping people. Not even herself. I look at Nana Flo in her ugly black shoes and beige tights and drab frock and the opal brooch at her neck holding it all together and I wonder if she has ever been happy. And I'm not just saying that. Really, I wonder. 'Nana,' I say, 'when do you think you were, ah, when do you think you were happiest?'

Nana Flo's pinched face seems more colourless than usual. 'On my wedding day,' she says.

'Of course,' I mumble. 'Well, I'm going to work now, so I'll see you both later.'

I scurry out of the door, berating myself for my gabbering stupidity. Nana Flo married Grandpa Gerald on her eighteenth birthday, a fortnight before Hitler invaded Poland. A week after war was declared, Grandpa Gerald was conscripted. Two months after that Grandpa Gerald was blown to smithereens by a shell during training.

I think Nana Flo put her grief back in its box.

None of the four estate agents I called has got back to me. This isn't a huge surprise. When I rang J I & Sons in Kentish Town, Adam, the yob at the end of the line said, 'So what you looking up to?' I told him and he said, 'Have you tried our Surrey Quays office?' and the response from Wideboy Estates was: 'The cheapest we've got is two hundred thousand.'

So when Lizzy—who was on a shoot all day yesterday and is 'bursting' to hear my 'news'—suggests I join her for lunch, I grab the excuse to postpone flat-hunting. Only after accepting the invitation do I realise I don't feel like talking.

'Tell me everything!' demands Lizzy. 'No skipping!'

I pick at my lip. 'You're going to be disappointed,' I say.

Her face drops. 'Why?' she cries, brimming with genuine concern.

I wrinkle my nose and say, 'Tom and I had an argument and I shouted at him. Really shouted.' I cringe, remembering my frenzied rage.

Lizzy blurts, 'Oh no! Why? What about?'

I tell her. Or rather, I tell her the bits I want her to know. I don't tell her about the woe-splattered gunk that spewed from me like blood from a slashed artery. I'd prefer not to believe in it until it fades away. So I gut and dissect the truth and present Lizzy with the leftovers. Lizzy is torn. Partly, because she can't bear to speak ill of anyone. But also because I give Tom a lousy write-up.

Eventually, she says sorrowfully, 'What a terrible shame. He seemed so nice. Maybe he didn't mean to interfere. Although I must say, it's not nice to criticise someone else's parent.'

My conscience—which spends most of its life asleep—pokes me at this point and I mutter, 'It wasn't all Tom's fault. I did moan about Dad. Not very loyal of me, was it?'

Lizzy brushes away my gloom with an airy, 'Don't be so hard on yourself! Everyone complains about their parents occasionally—I know I do all the time!' (Lizzy only ever speaks of her mother and father in glorious glowing hyperbole.)

I sigh. 'You're right. 'You don't tell people what to do. It's intrusive.'

Lizzy, scrabbling desperately for a happy ending, says, 'Are you *sure* he wasn't just interested?'

I recall Tom's snub over the flat and I'm too mortified to confide in my close friend.

'Positive!' I growl.

She says dejectedly, 'Maybe it's best to leave it for a while then.'

I nod, keen to switch subject before Lizzy assails me with further questions. But every topic I consider is barred by a large 'DON'T GO THERE' sign. My head is one huge roadblock. I blurt, 'Liz, do you think I smother my mother?'

Instead of answering, Lizzy clutches my arm—I assume to show me my question is on hold—and cries, 'Tina! Tina!' I follow her gaze and see Tina ducking into a shoe shop. 'Let's ask her to have lunch with us!' exclaims Lizzy, skipping after her.

Seconds later she reappears with Tina in an armlock.

'Jesus! What happened to your nose?' I gasp.

Lizzy answers for Tina: 'She was getting a tin of baked beans off the top shelf and it fell on her. Poor thing!'

I say, 'Does it hurt?'

Tina shakes her head. I sense that she isn't overjoyed to be having lunch with us. Lizzy tries to lighten the mood by joking, 'Well, it just proves that tinned food is bad for you!'

No one laughs. And from this low point the mood goes into free fall. Tina appears to have taken a vow of silence, and I am nervous to ask Lizzy about her weekend in case she boomerangs it back to mine. So—foolishly—I whip a shred of beetroot from Lizzy's plate, stick it across the bridge of my nose, and say, 'Who's this!' Lizzy is quiet. Tina looks at me. I stare back and I'm shocked at the disgust in her eyes. I remove the beetroot from my nose and mutter, 'Bad joke, sorry.'

Tina says coldly, 'You always say that but you never change, do you? You're like a fucking broken record.'

My mouth drops open. 'Shit!' I squeak. 'I didn't mean anything by it, OK? What *is* it with you? You're so aggressive. I can't say anything any more without you leaping down my throat.' Tina's expression is molten rage but I rant on: 'Ever since darling Adrian came on the scene—Adrian! Adrian!—we're not good enough for you now!'

Tina bangs her fist down on the metal table making Lizzy and the plates jump. 'You, girl, are out of line!' she snarls. 'Vicious! What is it this time? Tom? Jasper? Marcus? Oh sorry, I lose track.'

I feel hot with anger and I spit, 'No, actually, it's not about a man. It's my father.' For once I am telling the absolute truth.

I expect it to silence her but she snarls, 'And the rest!' Then she jumps up and hisses, 'Don't use your dad as an emotional crowbar on *me*, Helen. You never liked him! You've strung it out long enough! Have some respect—let the bloke rest in peace!'

This is without doubt the nastiest thing anyone has ever said to me in my life. The fury is so fierce I want to hit Tina in the face. Luckily for her she flees the café before I've organised my fist. I'm so aghast I can't look at Lizzy. I sit trembling. I suck in huge gulps of air but find it impossible to catch my breath. Eventually, I feel a soft touch on my back and Lizzy says gently, 'Are you OK?' I nod and shake off her hand. She whispers, 'Tina didn't mean it.'

This rouses me from petrification and I snap, 'She did though. That's it with her and me.' The unwelcome thought occurs to me that I'm shedding friends and acquaintances at a rate of four a week—and there's Wednesday, Thursday, Friday and Saturday still to go.

Lizzy takes a breath. Then she says, 'I don't think Tina's happy. Despite Adrian. Or I can't believe she would have said those things.'

I shrug, 'Whatever.'

Lizzy perseveres: 'About what she said about your dad, well, firstly—it's your right to feel what you feel. Even if you weren't that close, which I can't believe.'

I mutter, 'I just said the dad thing to make Tina feel bad. She's right. I'm in a foul mood.'

Lizzy sighs and says, 'Why though? If it's not your dad, is it Tom?'

I knew this lunch was a bad idea. I throw my napkin on the table and say, 'Tom puts his hand up dogs' bottoms and his car is worse than mine. It isn't Tom.'

Lizzy says crossly: 'Helen, you don't give a fig about cars! And he gets *paid* to put his hand up dogs' bottoms!'

I mumble, 'What—and that's supposed to make me feel better?'

Lizzy purses her lips and says, 'Maybe it'll be good for you to be on your own for a bit.'

I tut loudly and say in a bored tone, 'Why?'

Lizzy dabs her mouth with her napkin (her perfect lipstick remains perfect) and like an archbishop delivering the punch line to a televised sermon declares: 'You've got to be happy alone before you can be happy with someone.'

I sit back, fold my arms and try to look agnostic. 'Liz,' I say, 'did you read that in *Girltime*?'

'I might have done,' says Lizzy airily. 'So?'

I reply sternly: 'I wrote it.'

As I slink in from work, my mother hijacks me in the hall. The first thing she says is 'Florence wants to move out!' and the second is 'I'm losing all my family!' and the third is 'I've made you tea!' I drop my bag on the floor and try not to look alarmed. I also try to respond fairly to all her statements.

'Is Nana moving out because of *me*?' I say.

My mother flaps her hands as if to ward off the idea. 'Sort of,' she says. 'It was the sardine pilfering!'

I squeak, 'What sardine pilfering?'

It emerges that this morning Nana placed her favourite lunch—three sardines and a slice of white bread—on the side to 'air'. Ten minutes later she discovered Fatboy, whose motto is 'Finders Keepers', chewing at his third sardine. This confirmed her every prejudice about living under the same roof as 'vermin' and as a direct result, Nana is returning to her string beans first thing tomorrow morning.

'Sorry,' I mutter, 'I'll try and stop her if you want.'

My mother shakes her head and says cheerfully, 'She's in her room, packing! Don't bother! You're here now! And I've made you tea!'

'But I don't drink t—' I begin as I walk into the kitchen. To my surprise and dismay the table is heaped, *heaped*, with sandwiches and little cakes—concoctions I didn't think existed any more like chocolate Wagon Wheels and pink and yellow Fondant Fancies. There is even a Battenberg cake.

'I made it for you!' she repeats, like a six-year-old who has fashioned a monstrous pompom at school with card and wool and expects her mother to attach it to her smartest hat.

'That's er, very kind of you,' I say as I sink into a chair.

She sits down excitedly and watches eagle-eyed as I reach for a Marmite sandwich. I hate Marmite. I take a small bite and wonder what the hell's going on. 'How are you?' asks my mother.

'Fine,' I say, trying to swallow the sandwich without retching.

She sighs pointedly as if this is the wrong answer and snaps, 'No, how are you *feeling*?'

I hear this sentence and it all becomes clear. The dastardly Cliff!

'Mummy,' I growl, 'what has Cliff been saying to you?'

She looks guilty and says sulkily, 'Nothing! Nothing at all!'

I point a finger. 'You never ask how I'm feeling! He must have said something! What did you discuss this morning?'

She wriggles crossly in her seat and says, 'He wasn't so nice this time. I didn't like him as much.'

I place my Marmite sandwich on my plate. 'Mum,' I say, 'the clinic is not a dating agency. You don't have to like him. So what did he say?'

But my mother is determined not to tell. 'It doesn't matter!' she insists. 'Just tell me how you feel! And don't stop eating!'

I grab a Fondant Fancy, peel away the pink icing, and lick a glob of cream off its top. If my mother is treating me like a toddler I might as well make the most of it. 'How I feel about what?'

'I don't know!' she cries. 'Everything!'

I take a sip of lemonade (she's bought that too) and try to think. What can I say that won't upset her? That I don't mind about Christmas? That the additives are delicious? That she shouldn't worry about Nana Flo? That I won't move out until she wants me to? That I'm glad she's returning to school in January? All these thoughts are anodyne, inoffensive and safe. Feelings are trickier. But feelings are what she wants. And if I don't tell her, she'll never learn. She has no imagination and if this silly tea is anything to go by, no common sense. Fine. She asked.

Finally I blurt, 'How I feel is that I miss Dad.'

My mother claps her hands and exclaims, 'That's how *I* feel!'

When the phone rings and I hear Luke's voice at the other end of it I practically deafen him, such is my joy at being whisked from Fondant Fancy & Feelings Prison. 'You sound pleased to hear from me,' he says delightedly.

'I *am*!' I squeal. 'How *are* you! I miss you!'

Luke says bashfully, 'I miss you too. It's not the same without you.'

I suggest, 'It's tidier?'

He laughs, 'Much.'

I beam. 'So what's up?' I say.

Luke pauses. 'Have you heard about Michelle and Marcus getting engaged?'

I reply, 'No! Really? I don't know who to feel more sorry for!'

Sounding surprised, Luke says, 'So you're not upset?'

My tone is shrill: 'God, no!' I squeal.

I can hear the smile in Luke's voice. 'Great! So, uh, how's Tom?'

It's my turn to pause. 'We're not seeing each other,' I say. 'We fell out.'

Luke replies, 'Oh. Well can you give us his number? I'm going out with the lads on Friday, thought I'd ask him along.'

'Hang on,' I say, plodding into the hall, emptying my bag onto the floor, and sifting through the rubble. Eventually I find my phone book. I read Luke out Tom's number and try not to sound miserable.

Then I trot back into the kitchen where my mother is staring forlornly at the Battenberg. 'Leave it, Mummy,' I say, 'I'll clear it.'

She replies crossly, 'You barely ate a thing! I'm going to wash my hair!'

I shout after her, 'I'm taking some up to Nana! It won't go to waste!' I listen to myself. I sound about ninety.

I knock timidly on Nana's door. 'Who is it?' she shrills.

'Fatboy!' I feel like shrilling back, but don't. 'Helen!' I bellow.

She shuffles to the door and pulls it open. 'Yes?' she demands.

I wave the cake plate at nose level. 'I brought you up some cake.'

She sticks out a hand and takes it. 'Thank you,' she says and tries to shut the door!

I stick my foot in the gap. 'Nana,' I say in a rush, 'I'm so sorry about my cat pilfering your lunch, and please forgive me for reminding you about Grandpa. I do hope you're not leaving because of it.'

Nana replies, not unkindly, 'Not a day goes by when I don't think of my Gerald. That's life and you have to face up to it. I make the best of things.' I don't answer, but I wonder about what she says. Do you? I think.

My way of making the best of things is to run away from them. And I don't care what anyone says—I stand by it as a basic human right. I wake up on Wednesday, become aware of a nasty sinking sensation inside, and remember that Tom and I aren't shagging and I wish we were. I get to work and confess to Lizzy who says, 'Call him, then.'

I have a better idea: 'Let's get wasted!' Lizzy pouts. 'On orange juice!' I add, knowing that the chance of getting Lizzy to put alcohol to lip is remote. Lizzy looks unconvinced so I say, 'Did I tell you Michelle and Marcus are engaged?'

'What? No! When? Ohmigod!' says Lizzy. 'All right,' she adds reluctantly, 'but don't think I don't know it's blackmail.'

The prospect of luring Lizzy to drink is so uplifting that I'm inspired to call an estate agent. To my surprise Adam has two properties to show me. They're both in Kentish Town and within my price range. One flat he describes as 'well located for all the local amenities'. The other is 'spacious and well positioned'. I tell him that I'm busy tonight but maybe tomorrow and he has a fit. 'There's lots of people viewing!' he screams. 'They'll disappear like that!' I hear a snapping of fingers. I agree to view the flats tonight.

I break the news to Lizzy at six and she doesn't mind at all. 'It'll be fun!' she says. We take the tube to Adam's office and announce ourselves. Adam is busy talking on the phone and gestures for us to sit down. Four minutes later he leaps up, manfully jangles a huge bunch of keys in our faces, and ogles Lizzy. I can tell he's impressed by her, and she and I are knocked out by him too—or rather by his foul industrial-strength aftershave.

'It's Joop!' whispers Lizzy, when Adam goes to pick up his Mondeo, 'but you're not meant to put that much on.'

I wipe my stinging eyes and murmur, 'You don't say.'

A second later, a white banger with a dented passenger door swerves to a halt in front of us. We jump back to avoid losing our toes. 'Lizzy, you can go in the front,' I say sweetly but she demurs. So *I* get to sit next to Adam. I say to Lizzy, 'I can't believe I'm doing this.'

She coos, 'Why not! It's brilliant living on your own! I love it! Imagine! Not having to share a bathroom!'

I nod and say, 'I suppose,' then the car lurches to a halt and Adam jumps out.

Fifty-nine seconds later we are all sulkily hunched in the car again. I glower at Adam's black leather shoes and squeak, 'Well located for all the local amenities? It's above a fish-and-chip shop!'

Adam can't see the problem. 'Sweetheart,' he says, 'for your money that's whatchure gonna get around here. And you'll never go hungry!'

I say suspiciously, 'Does that mean the other is next door to an all-night petrol station?'

Adam is impressed. 'Howge know?' he says.

'East Finchley's nice,' says Lizzy comfortingly, as Adam races off.

I wrinkle my nose. 'It's too near my mother,' I say. 'Let's find somewhere to sit.'

Fifteen minutes later we are perched at a table in front of a bottle of red. I am glugging and Lizzy—having been persuaded 'just this once'—is sipping. She is keen to hear the tale of Marcus and Michelle and we empty the wine bottle extremely fast. Or as Lizzy says—after two small glasses—'fasht'. I order a second bottle.

The conversation veers onto Christmas. I announce that I'm doing 'bugger all' and Lizzy says she's 'helping out at a koup sitchen'. We hoot with laughter. 'Wow. Good for you. But doesn't it make you sad?' I say when we calm down.

'No,' says Lizzy, 'ish uplifting! Ish what Christmas ish all about!'

I pour us each another glass. 'What—hassling the homeless so you feel smug *and* avoid your family?' I say. Lizzy looks dumbfounded so I add hastily, 'Only joking, but aren't you seeing Brian?'

Cue an hour-long ramble about Brian, during which *Lizzy* orders another bottle and I think 'but Brian's so old'. 'But Brian's so old!' I declare and I clap my hand over my mouth.

Lizzy smacks me playfully on the arm and yells, 'I heard you! He's not old! Well he's old*er* but sho what!'

I shriek, 'But it's like going out with your dad!'

Fortunately Lizzy whacks the table, peals with laughter, and squeals, 'He's nothing like my dad! You're funny! You're in denial! That's what my shycol, shycol, that's what my friend says!'

Lizzy is so busy flicking shiny hair and trying to pronounce the word 'psychologist', she doesn't notice my startled expression.

'About what?' I say, the laughter dying in my throat.

'I don't know!' she roars. 'Tom probly!' she sniggers.

I snigger too and shout 'Cak!' Then we snigger at the word 'cak'. I'm reluctant to stop laughing so I wheeze, 'But he, but he—' Lizzy gasps, 'puts his hand up'—we chorus together: 'dogs' bottoms!'

And then I say something that seems like a good idea when I say it. I suggest we go to Tom's favourite bar. 'It's just down the road!' I say.

'If ish just down the road,' says Lizzy, 'lesh go!' We pay and totter out. 'My legsh are like rubber!' sings Lizzy as we lurch along clutching each other for support.

'This is it!' I exclaim. 'Let's look in the windows.'

Lizzy is already jumping up and down. 'I can't shee!' she complains. 'Lesh go in!' and with that she boots open the door and yanks me in.

My life falls off a cliff and splinters in a second. We see Tom. Tom is grasping the hand of an elegant woman. Lizzy shouts, 'There he *ish*!' and falls over. Everyone in the pub, including Tom and the woman, stares at us. I become instantly sober and pull Lizzy off the floor. She uses one hand to stop wobbling, the other to point, and roars, 'Helen doeshn't like you any more Tom cosh you put your hand up dogs' bottomsh!'

It is small consolation that as I hurl Lizzy and myself out the door, everyone in Tom's local is staring at Tom.

Chapter 7

ONE OF MY MOST USEFUL habits is blaming other people. Giving yourself a hard time is *so* tedious and I'm sure it weakens your immune system. But sadly, there is no denying that the Dog's Bottom Disaster is entirely my fault. Alcohol and lunacy aside, what possessed me? What's it to me if Lizzy drinks cranberry juice? Aren't I big and bad and ugly enough to get drunk on my own? And what was I on to suggest we ferret around Tom's pub? What must he think of me? Why did I do it? Am I mad? Have I no shame?

Lizzy is keen to 'make amends' as she puts it. 'There are no amends to make, you idiot!' I say, as she hands me a large parcel. 'This is very unnecessary,' I add—you have to say that if someone gives you a present and you're over twenty-five—'but very sweet of you.'

Lizzy clasps her hands and whispers, 'I *do* hope you'll like it! I asked Brian went to Hong Kong on a trip, and I asked him to bring it back.' Lizzy watches, breathlessly, as I lift away the delicate wrapping and a heady waft of incense floats into the stale smell of my mother's kitchen.

Lizzy clutches my arm and says, 'It's, well, I—I thought it would be, well, it's more a present for your father than for you! But I thought it would be nice for both of you.' She shrugs. 'Open it and I'll explain.' I put the wrapping to one side and lift out the biggest item.

It is a cellophane-enclosed pack of confectionary—'Hichiload creamy milk choco bar with assorted flavour' it reads on the side. The pack is as light as air and purports to contain small boxes of chewing gum and biscuits too. I smile weakly and don't know what to say. Has Lizzy lost it? What does she expect me to do—sprinkle crumbs on my father's grave?

I seize a wad of what looks like toy money, also encased in cellophane. 'The Hell Bank Corporation promises to pay the bearer on demand at its Office here *One Million Dollars*!'

I turn to Lizzy who bursts out, 'It's a Chinese buddhist custom!' She grabs at another plastic pack and thrusts it at me. It looks like a child's toy set—a gold pair of glasses, a gold and silver watch with 'Rolex' printed on its face, a silver bracelet, a gold cigarette box, a pen, and a gold ring and a gold necklace, both with green bits stuck on them—all made of stiff paper and set against a bright red paper background.

'You burn it!' cries Lizzy. 'It's a man's gift set! A jade ring! And the money, see! And look, a box of paper cigarettes with paper lighter, and look! a paper Mercedes! I didn't know what car your dad drove so I told Brian to get a smart one!—you put it in a sack and address it to your father, see look, here's the sack'—she sifts through the pile and waves a grey paper bag printed with Chinese figures and burning joss sticks—'You put it all in the sack and you seal it with this yellow sash—it's a heavenly post office stamp—the spirit will know it's his parcel when he collects it and'—at this point she glances at me and falters—'you can glue on the sash with Pritt Stick, it's fine to do that, and you write the date you're burning everything on a Post-it note which you stick on the sack and, well, I thought it would be a comforting thing to do. Especially at Christmas.' She peers into my face. 'Are you OK?'

I nod, put my head in my hands and wail, 'It's such a wonderful it's such a boo hoo beautiful thing, Liz, it's so sweet of you! Oh God what an amazing thing!'

Lizzy runs to the side, rips off a square of kitchen roll and hands it to me. I dab my eyes and try not to think of how touched I am because I don't want to start blubbing again. I wipe my nose, scrunch up the kitchen roll, and say snufflingly, 'A candle on a wooden stick.'

Lizzy gasps and says, 'Oh yes! The red candles symbolise food! You burn the joss sticks first, three of them, and that gets your dad's attention.'

I say, 'Can't I just pretend I'm about to get a tattoo?'

Lizzy giggles and says, 'Well, if you want to be doubly sure.'

I wave a hand in front of my face to indicate that I'm shutting up, and gesture for her to continue. Then I notice something else in the pack—'What's this! It's beautiful. Look, sheafs of silver and gold leaf on funny thin paper!'

I look questioningly at Lizzy who sighs beatifically and says, 'It's traditional Chinese money—you burn it too. You fold it first, in the shape of a gold tael—the Chinese weight measurement thingy for a gold ingot. Look, like this, in the shape of a fortune cookie. There you go! Although I do think it looks too pretty to burn, but it's nice to think you're sending your father such pretty things!'

I nod. It seems a shame to say that my father never noticed pretty things when he was alive—not liking yellow ruled out sunflowers and cornfields and daffodils. Maybe death will have mellowed him.

'Where do you burn it all?' I say.

Lizzy pauses. 'Well,' she says, 'anywhere really. In Hong Kong you can burn it in your apartment block staircase if you want. You don't have to do it at the grave. You can do it at the roadside, although maybe in England it'd be better to do it in your garden. I thought the cigarettes would be nice for your dad—you said he smoked a lot.'

I say, 'But you hate smoking!'

Lizzy says awkwardly, 'Yes, but if he's already dead I suppose it's OK.'

I sigh and say, 'It's such a lovely thing, Lizzy.' Lizzy nods. She looks as if she wants to speak. 'What?' I say.

Lizzy bites her lip. Then she says, 'I'm not sure if I should tell you this bit but'—I raise my eyebrows—'OK,' she says. 'Well, people *do* do this mainly to look after the dead person, but it's also a bit selfish—it's to gain favour with the spirit. So he'll look after you and bring you luck. I just thought I should tell you, so you're aware of what you're doing.'

I squeeze Lizzy's hand. I don't want to reply in case my voice cracks. I pick up the packet of joss sticks and breathe in their rich scent, then jump up to make Lizzy a decaffeinated coffee. And I don't say this to Lizzy but I am already aware that if I do burn money from the Bank of Hell to send to my father it *will* be a selfish act. It will be selfish because it's not about my father. He doesn't care. He's dead. It's about me. Not wanting him to be dead. I want him to still be conscious, like me. I want him to be excited at getting a present through the post, like me.

When Lizzy leaves I gather up my death-kit and probably for the first time in my life, feel a girly burst of gratitude—towards who, I'm not sure—for my friends. I march to the phone and ring Tina. She answers immediately, in a small voice. 'Tina!' I breathe, lowering my pitch to match hers. 'How *are* you!' I am so delighted to speak to her that I forget I'm sulking. 'What are you up to tonight?'

'Nothing,' she says.

'I'll come round!' I cry.

'Oh no please don't,' she says quickly.

Something in her tone catches at my heart and I say, 'Tina, I'm sorry I said that stuff about Adrian, it was shit of me, and I *am* like a broken record sometimes—but I'm, hah, in the process of being mended.'

May I interrupt myself here to say this is possibly the noblest lie I've ever uttered—but I feel so warmed by the kindness of Lizzy that I want to be saintly and forgive. Tina says something not a million miles from 'Huf!' She adds quickly, 'Don't be sorry, Helen.'

I wait to see if there's more, but there isn't so I say, 'How about I bring round some *Blackadder* vids and smoky bacon crisps?'

Faster than the speed of sound Tina is saying no. 'Oh not tonight, no I don't think so, another time I—'

But my wish to forgive overrides Tina's wish that I leave her alone so I gabble, 'I'llbearoundinfortyminutesokbye!' and put the phone down. I leave a note for my mother and speed to the video shop.

Forty-eight minutes later—the traffic is preposterous—I'm ringing Tina's doorbell. I know she's there so I ring and ring and when she doesn't answer I sit on the doorstep and wait. After twelve minutes she slowly opens the door. 'What's wrong with you you nutt—' I begin the question but there is no need to end it. What is wrong with Tina is as plain as her cut lip and the ugly purple bruise on her chin. My eyes prickle and even as I deny reality I know the truth. I say, 'God, no. Tell me you had an accident. Why didn't you tell me. Tina, Tina, oh my poor Tina, I'll break his neck the fucker, the oh my God.'

The hate wells and I am afraid to touch her, this thin, broken shell of my bright, glamorous friend. I hold out my arms and she collapses into them and weeps on my shoulder and I hear myself mew with pity and anger as she begs, 'I want you to swear you won't tell anyone.' Only when I'd sworn on Fatboy's life would she speak.

She sat stiff on the edge of her yellow sofa and her eyes flicked about. She reminded me of a lizard trapped in a jar. She spoke in a whisper and directed her words to the floor and I had to strain to hear.

'I don't know if this counts, because it was just a row. And he was so sorry he cried. And I'm a right harpy when I get going. You can't blame him. It was the car. I should have had it serviced but I was trying to save money. We'd been to Adrian's boss's for dinner and I'd eaten a, a braised pea off my plate. With my fingers, before everyone was served. It was embarrassing for Adrian. Like he was going out with someone common.

'Anyway we got outside and he was distant. And cold. I didn't know what I'd done. It might've been OK except the car wouldn't start. I thought the battery was flat. And we hadn't brought our mobiles. Adrian didn't want to go and ring on his boss's door to call a cab. I'd ruined everything. He started screaming at me and kicking the car. I shouted back and so he pulled my hair to calm me down. I know he didn't mean to, but it hurt—a big clump came out—and my eyes watered. He says it was just a jokey tug.

'He was so sorry though, he cried too. He only did it because he hated to see me make a fool of myself in public. He was really really upset. He punched the dashboard and then the engine started and so he forgave me. The next day he brought me flowers and breakfast in bed. He's a doll like that. He hardly ever hits me. It's not continuous. Certainly not more than once every, hmm, six weeks. Most of the time it's great, you know—he's funny. He cracks me up. And so clever.

'I've never met anyone like him. He's under a lot of stress at work. It's tough for him. It's crucial he makes the right impression and I'd jeopardised that. So you can understand. We were fine after that. Fine. Until, until I did this stupid thing. I should have realised. We'd gone to the Dog and Duck up the road from me. We came back pissed and I forgot where I'd put the door key. Adrian was knackered. He had this meeting with a client the next day and it was imperative he got to sleep on time. I'd fucked up. He called me an ugly bitch and kicked me and banged my head into the door. I fainted and I woke up in bed. He'd found the key in his pocket. He was so sorry. He was so kind. Nursing me and putting ice and tissue on the cut. And saying it didn't need stitches, it was just a scratch. I still get headaches but it was a one-off. It wasn't like

I didn't deserve it. He only does it because I provoke him. I know it will get better. It will be OK so long as I cut back on my drinking. And learn a bit more about how to behave in public. So I'm sorry if I haven't seen you and Liz that much. It's that I'm trying to make it work with Adrian. So you mustn't tell anyone. It's my business, it isn't a big problem. It's him I feel sorry for, poor bloke. Stuck with me . . .'

She said other stuff but you get the drift. I look at Tina's determinedly blank face and gently suggest that Adrian is an evil, violent bully who should be banged up and she hasn't done anything wrong and furthermore there isn't anything she could do that warrants being hit. Ever. There is no excuse for it. None. Sorry and flowers don't make it better. And it won't get better. If she tolerates it, he'll keep doing it. Can't she see that? I say this in a quiet, casual way because I'm terrified she will block her ears and order me out. Tina is prisoner to the cult of Adrian and my words are blasphemy. She feels guilty for talking to me, she says. Disloyal. She jerkily folds her arms and mutters that she can't think any more, she's confused. She keeps repeating, 'It will get better,' like a chant.

With a shock, I realise she sees the world through *his* eyes. Her reality is an altered state. I can hardly believe I'm talking to Tina. I feel bereaved.

And she won't let me help her. I ask her, doesn't she feel angry with Adrian for what he's done and she hesitates and says maybe, once, but now she just feels angry with herself. My pulse throbs and I say sharply, does Adrian know she has three brothers, and more to the point, do her three brothers know about Adrian? Then I feel terrible because she is so scared and she tells me I have to promise again not to say a word because, because . . . She trails off and my gut clenches and I don't get how she can be like this but I hear her.

Tina tells me she's off work until the New Year now but I'm not to call her. She's fine, really she is, she's a bit run-down, she wants to rest and be quiet. When her face is better she's going to go home to her parents. Adrian is skiing in Val d'Isère with friends. He did ask Tina but kept warning her that it wasn't her scene, so she declined the invitation. My diplomacy bubble pops and I exclaim, 'Tina! Just listen to yourself! I can't believe you're letting him abuse you like this!'

I regret my outburst instantly, not least because Tina snaps, 'Excuse me? Jasper? Marcus? Hel-lo! I don't think you're in a position to preach, Helen, do you?'

I can't imagine what she means but I drive home fast at 3.00am, thinking fuck, fuck, fuck. I am stunned. It is as if Adrian was *my* boyfriend hitting *me*. I go straight to my mother's computer, log on to the Internet and scroll through a long list of books on abuse, which includes the corker *Domestic Violence For Beginners*.

I order four titles. Tina won't like this, but I've just bought her Christmas present. My heart is racing as I announce to the dark silence, 'Tina. You don't know it yet but you are going to leave that vicious bastard if it's the last thing I do.'

On Sunday morning I call the police and ask what they can do if a woman is being hit by her partner. The cold reply is that if the victim herself doesn't make an allegation, nothing. I call Tina on Sunday and Monday and Tuesday because I am determined that she see sense and dump Adrian this week but she doesn't answer and I don't want to leave a message and then it's Christmas.

On the morning of December 24 my mother and I receive a last-minute invitation to Christmas Day lunch from Vivienne. I reject it because I don't feel like being around a complete family. I'd feel like a spare part. Which—now I'm fatherless—maybe I am. My mother also rejects it then changes her mind because otherwise she'll 'just sit at home getting miserable'. This is an understatement considering that even the Grinch would walk in our door and start craving fairy lights. My mother is making a point to God. She hasn't even displayed the cards she's been sent—they lie in a scrappy pile on the kitchen table. I arrange the cards in a neat row before I go to work and suggest we light Chanukkah candles, sod it, *any* candles—frankly I'd set myself alight if I thought it would make the house less gloomy—but she's having none of it. She finds the beauty voucher I bought her hidden in the napkin drawer and sulks and says I've only bought it to make her feel bad. At this point my patience twangs and I reply sharply that the only person making Cecelia feel bad is Cecelia. And I'm right. She's vetoed joy. So yesterday I purchased a small turkey, a bag of potatoes, and a jar of cranberry sauce and dumped them in the fridge in defiance.

At 2.00pm on Christmas Eve I watch my colleagues twirl round the office in a haze of tinsel and mulled wine and goodwill and feel detached. I wonder what Tom's doing now and if I'll ever see him again. I think of us together and it feels like I imagined it. I knew it wouldn't last. I am staring into space when my mother rings to tell me in a grumpy voice that she's sorry for being grumpy and if I don't want her to go to Vivienne's tomorrow she won't go. She doesn't want me to spend Christmas in an empty house, she knows for a fact that Morrie wouldn't like it. (For a non-believer he was surprisingly fond of Christmas.) When she says this I feel like most normal mothers feel when their child takes its first step. 'Mum,' I say softly, 'that's very considerate of you, but I'd feel awful if I stopped you going to Vivienne's. I *want* you to go.' To which she replies 'Oh good!' and puts the phone down. I am wondering if it's possible to pinch oneself and awake in another dimension, when Lizzy bounces up and asks if I want to help her and Brian decorate her tree tonight. Although I'd love to, I feel she's asked out of compassion and I don't want compassion so I pretend I'm busy.

'But I'll come with you to the soup kitchen tomorrow!' I burst out, before I can stop myself.

Lizzy's hand flies to her throat and she exclaims, 'Oh, Helen! But you can't! I rang and they've already got more seasonal volunteers than they can cope with!'

I blush scarlet and mutter, 'Doesn't matter. I'd have depressed the tramps, anyway.'

Lizzy pauses then retreats, and with a heavy heart I ring my grandmother to see if she wants to join me for what I confidently predict will be the most depressing festive meal of my life.

To my relief Nana is spending the day at her friend Nora's, thank you, they've plotted their television schedule and they're playing bingo in the evening. And if—as Cecelia's mentioned—I've bought her a china ornament of Princess Diana's head, she doesn't want it because she's got five already and her mantelpiece is full up.

Owning a large gob and a short attention span, I remember very little of what I learned at school, which leaves me with not much. But I *do* recall a story we translated in our French class because, as they say in fairy tales, it smote my heart. It was about a factory worker who was so poor he couldn't afford to buy his little girl a Christmas tree. So he postponed Christmas. And when all the rich families threw out their Christmas trees in the New Year he crept to the rubbish dump and took one. And so his little girl got her Christmas tree and had the best Christmas day ever.

I don't have much in common with that little girl except that this year my Christmas comes late too. The day itself isn't bad either. Surprisingly peaceful. I act as wardrobe consultant to my mother, who is desperate to out-glam Vivienne. 'Are you sure you won't come too?' she says, in a rush of excitement. 'There'll be people your own age—some cousins, I think, and her son Jeremy and his friend Simon.'

I sigh and say, 'Jeremy and his *boy*friend Simon. Vivienne's in denial.'

I briefly consider going—Jeremy is warm, cuddly and irrepressibly cheerful, Prozac in human form—then decide that Vivienne is sulphuric acid in human form and I need to be alone. I give my mother the beauty voucher and she gives me a pair of blood-red silk pyjamas. 'You shouldn't sleep in a tatty old T-shirt,' she explains kindly, 'men don't like it.' Neither of us refer to my father. We tiptoe around his absence, which pollutes the air like smog. The effort is draining and I wave my overdressed mother out of the door with relief. Then I wrap myself in my duvet and read my present to me—*The Black Dahlia* by James Ellroy, with the television on mute.

I can't be bothered to cook the turkey so I make potato wedges and dip them in cranberry sauce. I break up the reading and eating with naps. I wonder what Tina's doing: I pray that Adrian skis into a tree. And I try but fail to interest Fatboy in his new clockwork mouse.

Boxing Day is quiet too. The real excitement starts ten days later.

My mother returns to work. I find a flat. Michelle forces Marcus to get his back waxed. It's all too much—where shall I begin? Actually that's a rhetorical question because if I keep Marcus's Discovery Of The Meaning Of Pain to myself for one moment longer my head will explode from pent-up gloating. I hear the tale from Lizzy, who heard it from Brian, who heard it from Sara, a beauty therapist at their health club.

Marcus was sent by his fiancée to get his back waxed and it took Sara forty-five minutes! And she was mortified because he was screaming the B-word and the F-word so loud when there were people in the other rooms having massages! And he was so hairy that afterwards he looked like he was wearing a tank top! She didn't know if she should carry on down his arms!

Lizzy rarely gossips but waives her morals on the grounds that this isn't hearsay, it's reportage. This peek at Marcus's new life in boot camp almost arouses my sympathy. But I manage to quash it and am recoiling at the thought of my one brief tussle with Gorilla Back and wondering what—apart from desperation—possessed me when the phone rings.

It's my mother. She is calling from the staffroom. Everyone has been *so* lovely. They all missed her. Her children have made her a Welcome Back banner out of coloured tissue paper. They're all on their best behaviour. She thinks Mrs Armstrong's had a word with them. She's so pleased to be back. And Mrs Armstrong has made her promise that if at any time she even begins to feel she can't cope she's to say so *instantly* and Mrs Armstrong will do all she can to assist. She has *heaps* to do, the schedule is crazy, but she doesn't care. Anyway she's got to go now, she's about to take a maths lesson.

It's 12.02 and I'm about to start work when the Joop!-drenched Adam calls to say that he's found the perfect property for me, it's right up my street, I gotta view it immediately, it's well cheap, no chain, cracking use of space, it's spot-on, it's in a much-sought-after location, handy for public transport, could do with updating, hundreds of people are interested, if I don't hurry it'll go, and there's sod all else around.

I decide I should see this (from what I can gather) bite-sized, ramshackle, prehistoric flat under a railway bridge. 'OK,' I say. 'How about six forty-five tonight?'

'Yeah?' says Adam, who doubtless expected me to put up a fight. 'Lovely jubbly! It's a date!'

'No it isn't,' I say.

Lizzy and I meet him in his office at 6.32. Adam ignores me and leers at Lizzy who is wearing a short skirt. I don't mind—partly because I've been shunned by men a lot higher up the food chain than Adam, and partly because if I was a bloke I'd choose Lizzy's tall tanned elegance over a pale-faced shortarse too. But mainly, my indifference stems from fretting over whether I should tell Lizzy about Tina. I know I promised to keep quiet and that Fatboy's corpulent life depends on it. But. I am convinced that if I *was* to tell Lizzy about Tina, for once I'd be divulging classified information for the right reason. Because when I rang Tina this afternoon she tentatively agreed to meet me tomorrow at my house on the condition that I 'don't have a go at' her. So I'm wondering quite how I am going to have a go at Tina without her noticing and as Lizzy is the diplomacy queen and I'm the diplomacy pauper, I need her advice. Yet however I justify it, the sharp stark words 'but you promised' peck at my brain. Eventually—just as Adam spies a parking space and swerves violently into the kerb—I settle on a compromise.

I say in a low voice, 'Lizzy. You know Adrian, Tina's bloke? Well, what would you say if I said that I'd spoken to a woman who went out with him a while ago, and who said that he'd, ah, roughed her up a bit?' Admittedly, this is a feak weeble adaptation of the truth and I'm aware that anyone else would decode it in a picosecond.

But Lizzy pulls an astonished face and says briskly, 'I can't believe it! Adrian's so nice! It can't be true!'

To be honest, I'm taken aback. I expected shock, horror, and flapping ears. I say, 'I don't think she made it up, Lizzy.'

But Lizzy says firmly, 'Adrian is so nice! She must have imagined it. And really, I don't think it's good of this person, to tell you nasty things like that.' With that, Lizzy clicks open the lock, slinks out of the car and slams the door. I feel like I've just tried to sell her double glazing.

Miserably, I glance at our surroundings. We are standing in front of a neat terraced row of wedding cake houses. They are all white, with beautiful bay windows and brightly painted doors. Adam opens the gate to the pebbledashed exception. 'Maybe you could get a builder to scrape off the pebbles,' whispers Lizzy, 'and remove the fridge from the front lawn.'

I nod and smile. I don't trust myself to speak to her, just yet.

Adam pushes open the shabby front door. The stairs are wonky, creaking and uncarpeted. The walls are covered in what I can only describe as a garish travesty of wallpaper and so, inexplicably, is the ceiling. Despite the breathtaking clash of orange and brown swirls, the effect is drab. Lizzy murmurs, 'How very, ah, unique!' I take a deep breath to stop myself suffocating.

'It's got a lot of potential,' says Adam brightly. I sigh and follow him into what masquerades as the kitchen.

'The owner obviously had a fetish for brown,' I say with a sour look at the stained mud-coloured lino. 'And an allergy to cleaning,' I add, on seeing the grimy sideboard.

'But the joy of this flat is that it's crying out for you to stamp your own personality on it!' replies Adam.

I huff and Adam shows us into the bathroom which is so small that only two of us can fit in it at once. Lizzy waits outside. 'Original tiling!' she whispers. 'Helen, you've *got* to have this!'

I glare at her and snap, 'It's a pit!' But then I see the bedroom and although the plaster is crumbling and the carpet is threadbare and the windows are filthy and cracked, something inside me tweaks.

I imagine ripping up the carpet and polishing the floorboards, repainting the walls yellow, and cleaning the large windows so that the sunlight streams in. 'Let's see the lounge,' I say.

'Original fireplace,' says Adam, as we enter the small, cobwebby room. 'And no chain. Once you've done the necessary you could move in in weeks!'

I say, 'Don't be ridiculous, it's uninhabitable!' but I don't say it with much conviction. My heart is thumping and I feel hot with trepidation. I don't know why but I want it.

The next morning I make an offer on the flat. Adam says coldly, 'I'll get back to ya.' Lizzy says soothingly that he's playing hard to get and gives me the number of her solicitor. And Tina rings to say she's sorry but 'something's come up' and she won't be meeting me tonight. I start to ask her how she is but she cuts off. Almost immediately the phone rings again and I grab it. 'Tina?' I gasp. But it's Adam relaying the joyful news that my offer on Flat 55b has been accepted. I relay my property news to Lizzy who bounces on the spot and suggests I line up a feng shui expert.

'I hate this,' I say, as I put down the phone to the dodgiest mortgage-broker in the land. 'I'm being stitched up.'

Lizzy does her best to look sympathetic and chirrups, 'But just think, it'll be worth it in the end!'

I sigh and say, 'Yeah. I'll be the proud owner of negative equity.' I gnaw at my lip and mutter to myself, 'Well, at least Tom will be pleased, the sanctimonious git.'

Tom is like a radio jingle—infuriating and unforgettable. Admittedly, I am desperate to distract myself from the hell of conveyancing and all the leechery that surrounds it. But the main reason is, Tom and I have unfinished business to attend to. And, while a bonk would be an enjoyable bonus, I'm not referring to sex. If I'm to get on with my life—a phrase which I *cannot* stand—I have to talk to Tom.

I don't want to but I need to. I keep backflashing to his astonished face on Dog's Bottom Night. The feeblest part of me wants to throw myself at his feet and explain but the bolshie rest of me wants to rant at him until he throws himself at my feet. How dare he preach to me about my wrongdoings when he was tarting around behind my back? How could he say the things he said and not mean them?

How could I be so naive as to think just because he said them he meant them? What did he think he was doing being so nice? Why wasn't he honest? Doesn't he realise I can deal with gittishness, so long as it isn't disguised as sincerity? These sly, maggoty questions burrow and squirm until I snatch up the phone, ring Megavet, announce that Fatboy is off his food, and make an urgent appointment for 6.45 tonight.

My mother is sulking because I haven't yet shown her the flat—the reason: I don't dare—so I am able to stuff Fatboy into his Voyager, and speed to the vet without being waylaid. As the Toyota chokes and shudders to a halt on Golders Green Road, I take a deep breath, check my hair in the mirror (as I thought, it's flat), retrieve Fatboy from the back, and plod towards Megavet's door. I lean my weight against it, push with my bottom, and stagger backwards into reception. This isn't a dignified entrance and I'm pleased to see that there are no animals and people waiting and Celine isn't standing behind the front desk. Sadly, Tom is.

He stares at me, as if he can't believe what the cat's brought in, and nods curtly. 'So,' I say sourly, 'we meet again.'

Tom throws down his pen, slams shut the appointment book and says flatly, 'You're next. You might as well come in.'

I heave Fatboy into the surgery and Tom shuts the door behind us and I feel frightened. I'm scared of what he might say so I speak before he does. 'Why didn't you tell me you had a girlfriend!'

Anger and shock vie for supremacy on his haggard face and he hisses, '*What?!*'

I am like Fatboy in that being hissed at is not my favourite thing and the fury and resentment fuse and I flare up like a lit match. '"What!"' I snarl, mimicking his surprise. '"*What!*" Don't give me "what" like you don't know what I'm talking about! Your girlfriend! You know, the one you were shagging while you were shagging me! Just about!'

Tom grits his teeth and growls, 'I don't know what you're talking about! What girlfriend?'

At this point I clutch my hair to stop myself shaking him, and scream, 'Don't lie to me, I'm sick of being lied to! The girlfriend we saw you with in the pub, you moron!'

Tom glowers at me and shouts, 'You stupid brat, that was my *sister*!'

This is absolutely impossible and I'm about to say so. But then I remember Tom telling me about his sister. And suddenly, the idea that the pub woman was Tom's sister is less impossible than it first appeared. If this is true my position is untenable.

Tom shakes his head in disbelief, then bellows, 'Why are you so selfish? Why don't you give anyone a break? There's no pleasing you is there?'

My voice is shaky with anger. 'Don't you shout at me, you pompous man, I won't have it!' Secretly I am mortified to the core about the girlfriend error, but I'll be damned if Tom's going to know about it. I screech, 'I can't believe I let you boss me about! You think you're so superior!'

Tom splutters, 'What are you on about?'

I stamp my foot and snap, 'Don't pretend you don't know! Preaching to me about what I should be doing, saying to my mum, feeling about my dad! Where I should be living! You knew I needed somewhere to stay! You never offered! You didn't care!'

Tom smacks himself on the forehead with the flat of his palm. This takes me by surprise and I bleat, 'Wh—what did you do that for?'

He sighs and says, 'Because you make me want to cry!'

I say sulkily, 'Why?'

He says in a slow, tired, heavy voice, 'I didn't offer, Helen, because I *do* care. Or did. I'm not a fucking emergency service. Now is there anything I can do for your irresponsibly overfed cat or did you cart him all the way here in a box as an excuse to yell at me?'

Like most petty criminals whose cover is blown, I am silent.

'I thought so,' says Tom, his blue eyes cold. He rips open the door. I snoot out. 'Your ca-at!' he shouts after me in a nasty singsong tone. I snoot back, snatch the Voyager, and snoot out again. I snoot around to say something horrid but Tom slams the door in my face. I look towards reception and see a Jack Russell and its owner staring at me in beetle-browed fascination, so I lean my bottom against the front door and snoot into the street.

Nana says that when something bad happens you know who your friends are. Lizzy says that when something good happens you know who your friends are. The upshot is I don't have a clue who my friends are, and I can't decide *what* has happened.

The only news is that after four knackering, nit-picking, hair-tearing weeks, my solicitor rings to say we're ready to exchange contracts on Flat 55b. I tell Lizzy that in less than a month I'll be a homeowner and collapse on my desk. She can't understand it. 'Aren't you thrilled? What's wrong? Oh my, it's so exciting! We'll have to go paint shopping!'

I'm not sure which is more upsetting—the fact I find paint shopping a happy prospect or that I am now committed to living alone by myself in a titchy derelict terraced box in a scruffy part of Kentish Town. At least the Toyota will feel at home. And the purgatory of argy-bargying with banks and brokers and wasting cash on surveys and searches and surveyors and being patronised and bullied is nearly at an end.

Lizzy's solicitor is called Dorothy Spence and Lizzy is forever praising Dorothy as 'thorough'. And thorough she is. Easily an hour thorough, reading through this clause and that clause and do I understand what this liability means and the import of this restrictive covenance and she's queried that and she's queried this but all her queries have now been satisfied and do I have any questions and if not she requires a deposit of £9,000.

I nearly fall off my swingaround chair. 'What, now?' I stammer.

'Yes, please,' says Dorothy briskly.

'But I, I didn't realise,' I bleat. 'I, I thought that was . . . just before completion . . . I misunderstood, I haven't done this before, so I thought . . .' Dorothy shoots me a look and I falter to a halt. I have made a foolish error. In my tizzy ignorance I assumed the 10 per cent deposit was payable on completion. Admittedly, Dorothy sent me a letter a week ago detailing what would be required of me, but, as I now recall, I glanced at it and forgot about it. As a result, the cash is breeding in a high interest account and I can't withdraw a penny without giving notice. I am a clueless fraud aping a dependable adult and the worst has happened. I've been exposed for what I am.

'Can I make a call?' I ask Dorothy in a small voice. She glances at her chrome clock, nods sharply and reclines in her plump leather chair. I call my mother's mobile and pray she answers. She doesn't. So I call the school and ask to be put through to the staffroom. 'Is Cecelia Bradshaw there?' I say breathlessly. 'It's her daughter.'

A distant voice replies, 'One moment.' Forty moments later, I'm still waiting and Dorothy Spence is tapping her foot.

Then the line goes dead. I bite my lip, smile weakly at Dorothy, and redial. 'I rang a minute ago and got cut off,' I say, keeping my voice hard and loud so it doesn't break. 'I need to speak to Cecelia Bradshaw. It's urgent.' Thirty seconds later, my mother is on the line. I feel weak with relief. I pinch my nose to stop myself crying and explain. The humiliation throbs through me in shock waves. When I finish declaiming my mother is silent.

Then she says in a wonder-of-you voice, 'It's not a *problem*, darling. I'll call the bank right now and get an electronic transfer to the relevent account. Let me speak to the lawyer woman.' I sink into a grateful trance and hand the receiver to Dorothy.

Fifteen torturous minutes later I am driving home in the Toyota. As any form of reflection is painful I spend the entire journey saying 'La la la' in a loud monotone to ward off thought. I slink into the office at 2.30. To my relief Lizzy isn't in the office—and as Laetitia wouldn't dream of asking how my morning went any more than she'd dream of buying shoes from C&A, I work undisturbed until 6.36.

Then I leave without speaking to anyone. As I sit on the tube I feel naked. I am convinced everyone is peering at me, talking about me, jeering at me. I feel claustrophobic and I want to scream.

By the time I'm home I am a gibbery quivery wreck. I intend to curl up in bed and sleep but as I tiptoe upstairs my mother appears like a shimmering genie in the hallway and exclaims, 'Helen! Come down here and talk to me!' Wordlessly, I swivel and descend. I feel as hunchy and evil as a tarantula. My mother, meanwhile, is as glowy and zingy and zesty as a teenage beauty queen. She beams and pats her hair and lifts her hands and says in a joyous voice, 'So?'

I stand before her and my lower lip starts to tremble. I scowl at the patterned carpet and clutch my arms behind my back. And I say fiercely, 'If Dad was here he'd have known what to do.'

I dig my nails into my palms and wait. I don't know what I expect. Huffing. Tutting. Not laughter. But my mother teehee hees and says, 'Yes, but I managed OK, didn't I?'

I nod and whisper, 'I miss my dad.'

My mother is quiet and I feel like a fart at a wedding. Then she looks at my face as if for the first time, and says softly, 'I know you do, darling, and I'm sure he misses you too.'

And suddenly, she takes a step forward and hugs me tightly and I am lost and found in a waft of Chanel. The range of sound effects available to me as a human seem inadequate and I wish I were a wolf so I could tilt my head and howl, owwooww owwwwwww, surrender my body and soul to the resonance of grief.

Instead I close my eyes and wail silently, absorb the warmth of my mother's purple jumper and feel her thin arms firm around me.

Chapter 8

I CLING TO MY MOTHER LIKE, I imagine, a rescued mountaineer clinging to a St Bernard. Oh God, I wail inside, *why* is it so bad, why? No one said it would be like *this*. I cling to my mother so heavily that her knees buckle and we gently crumple to the floor, where she strokes my hair and makes soothing noises. 'I don't know what to do,' I sob. 'I don't know what to doo-hoo hooo!' Even as I bleat the words I feel horrified at this pitiful collapse in front of the one person who needs me to be invincible.

But my mother rocks me and says, 'It's so hard, darling. And I know I haven't been much use. But you've been so brave,' and suddenly I am five years old again and being consoled after falling over and cutting my knee. I smile weakly and wipe my eyes.

My mother says softly, 'Come on, darling. I'll make you a hot drink.' I meekly allow her to drag me to my feet, and suddenly she bursts out angrily, 'Stupid hot drinks! Your father's dead and all we can do is have a bloody hot drink!'

I snivel-giggle and say, 'It's shit, isn't it?'

My mother makes a face and fills the kettle. We sit in silence, drinking hot chocolate and contemplating the fact that death is a monstrous affront to the living and shouldn't be allowed. After a long time my mother pats my hand and says softly, 'Remember, darling. Daddy may be gone but he'll always be with you.'

I look up, my mouth trembling, and see that she is crying too. And I realise that even amid the rubble, we've salvaged something.

I think my mother realises it, too, because in the weeks that follow my outburst, our relationship slips from fraught to placid like the stunned quiet after a flash thunderstorm. When she recounts a success she had at work and I tell her 'well done', I notice with surprise that she blushes. She's suddenly shy because what I think of her matters. I scramble upstairs, grinning to myself, and consider the inconceivable: that when I move into my flat tomorrow, I am going to miss her.

It's strange. After I completed on the flat, I expected my mother to shun me for at least a fortnight, but instead she offered to help me interview builders for quotes. I assumed this was for bicep-ogling purposes, but she turned out to be a shrewd, efficient ally. Her enthusiasm didn't fizzle out like it usually does. She dismissed Lizzy's recommendation (he wanted cash) and called the firm that Vivienne had employed to refurbish her kitchen and build a conservatory. 'Vivvy couldn't fault them!' explained my mother. Naturally I assumed they must be excellent—as most people employed by Vivienne are sued to within an inch of their livelihoods—and to my relief they *were* excellent.

After six backbreaking weeks, my builders have replastered, replumbed, rewired, and resuscitated my little flat. They have been masterminded by Terry who, in his own words, 'runs a tight ship'. And my mother and I have spent at least thirty hours trawling Greater London in search of—as she puts it—'fitments'. While I am as skilled in sourcing glass bricks as I am at completing *The Times* crossword—no, I won't lie—any crossword, my mother has been astounding. She's approached the flat refurbishment like a school project.

When I decided that multi-million-pound steel kitchen units were imperative or I'd be too embarrassed to invite people round, she consulted *Living Etc.* and suggested a visit to 'The London Metal Centre—look, darling! They sell stainless-steel sheeting from about five pounds per square foot! You stick it on top of that MFI cardboard stuff and it looks exactly the same!' I caught Terry chortling to himself, but I think he was secretly impressed.

I'm just thankful that she's fizzing with energy. I'm determined not to think about how long it may or may not last. Mostly, I'm succeeding. So maybe I have changed too. I feel calmer. And when I recall the incongruous sight of my mother in animated chat with Terry over architectural suppliers, I feel an airy flutter of delight.

I expect moving in to feel ceremonial, but though I carry Fatboy over the threshold, it doesn't. Possibly because I possess only seven large items: two chairs, a table, a television, a bed, a dartboard and a clothes rail, so it takes Luke and myself about seven minutes to hoick stuff up the creaky stairs and arrange it. Now the builders have gone the flat looks stark—in the same way that a pinhead looks stark. 'Helen,' says Luke, 'this is *so* tidy for you!'

After Luke leaves—he has an urgent date with a PlayStation—I walk around from room to room (it takes me nine seconds) touching the yellow walls, sniffing the chalky newness, stroking my craftily crafted steel and MDF kitchen units. Then I boil water in my shiny new kettle—courtesy of my mother—make myself a coffee, sit on a chair, and look at the polished wood floor. Silence.

Then, after three labour-intensive hours of arranging my duvet, moving four mugs and three plates from a high cupboard to a low cupboard, lining up my murder collection in a row on the bedroom floor with piles of bricks as book ends, scrubbing the bath, bleaching the toilet, sweeping the floor, placing my blue toothbrush next to the sink, and making a list of items I need but can't afford without a new credit card, I tire of homemaking and ring Lizzy to invite her round.

Lizzy is thrilled at my call and arrives clutching a bunch of daffodils and a sleek glass vase. The vase is beautiful—a warm burnished orange, like captured sunshine. 'It's gorgeous,' I squeak, 'it completes the room!'

Lizzy beams. 'It's my pleasure! Now show me round!' she exclaims. 'I can hardly believe it's the same flat. It's so dinky!' To my shame we spend the next two hours earnestly discussing glitter paint and sugar soap and sanding machines. I find myself gabbling desperately, incessantly, as if building a wall of words could prevent her from leaving. But at 6.00pm, Lizzy wrenches herself away (Brian's aunt is throwing a houseboat party) and Fatboy and I are alone. The evening looms ahead.

I switch on the TV, am confronted by *Songs Of Praise*, switch it off, wonder if the flat is bigger than a Wendy house, flop on the bed, stare at the ceiling, spot a money spider in the corner, run into the kitchen to find a broom to poke it with, realise I don't own a broom, run back, can't see the spider, know it's scuttling about the bedroom, suspect it's pregnant and laying spider eggs, and start panicking. I am about to ring my mother when I remember that Vivienne has taken her to an organic health farm for the weekend. I slump back on the bed and feel miserable. When the phone rings I almost swoon with gratitude. 'Hello?' I whisper, hoping it isn't a wrong number.

'Babe?' says a clipped voice.

'Jasper!' I squeal. 'How *are* you!'

Unbeknown to Jasper my delight is nothing personal as I'd have greeted a BT salesperson with the same shrieky degree of elation. But Jasper being Jasper, he takes it personally.

'Hey, steady there, Angelsweet!' he exclaims.

As I believe any man who says the words 'Hey, steady there, Angelsweet!' without irony should kill himself instantly to dispel the shame, I choke and pause before answering.

I say, 'Hey yourself, Smug One! Do you want to come and see my new flat?'

'Absolutely, babe! Where are you? I'll hop in a cab now.'

An hour later, Jasper and I are sitting at my table on my solid oak chairs, prodding at the remains of a Chinese takeaway. Jasper is wearing a blue-and-white baseball cap, but even so, he looks ravishing. I am explaining how laying tiles at a diagonal will give a feeling of space when I notice Jasper stifle a yawn. 'Sorry,' I say indignantly, 'am I boring you?'

Jasper's eyes widen and he drawls, 'Babe, I could listen to you for ever.' I tell him he's a liar. He sighs.

'What?' I say, surprised that I've made an impact.

'Oh nothing, Babe, *rien*.'

I snort. 'If you're resorting to French something is up. What is it?'

Jasper leans on his elbows and says slowly, 'I'd rather not say.'

Naturally, I am agog. 'Jasper,' I gasp, 'you *must* tell me!'

Jasper shifts in his chair and mutters, 'It's not fair.'

I clutch the sides of the table to stop myself flying at him and prising the secret out of his mouth manually. 'Is it your job?' I say.

'NO!' says Jasper in a loud voice. 'God, no! The job's A1!'

I try again. 'Is it, uh, Louisa?'

Jasper rakes his hand through his hair and leans back. I hold my breath. 'In a word,' he says.

At this point I realise a pool of saliva has collected in my mouth and if I don't swallow instantly I'm going to drool like a basset hound. I gulp and squeak, 'What happened?'

Jasper stretches his lips into a grimace. Then he says, 'She ah, wanted to get back together.'

My mouth drops. '*No!*' I say. 'What, what did you say?'

Jasper sighs again and says, 'I said, if I could, I would. But it wouldn't be fair on her.' He stops. Then adds, 'Because I'm keen on'—he sighs—'someone else.'

I gaze at him and he blushes. And immediately I know that Jasper has a belated crush on me. My eyes are like gobstoppers. I try to keep my voice level. 'Oh no!' I squeak. 'What did Louisa say to that?' Jasper looks uncomfortable. 'Well?' I demand.

He says quietly, 'Ah, I'd rather not say.'

I bang my fist on the table. 'Come *on*!' I bellow. 'You can't not tell me now!' I force the details out of him. Although he doesn't mention my name, he doesn't need to. I watch his mouth as he talks. And as he relates the woeful tale of his ex-girlfriend's unrequited love, and that a week before Christmas Louisa gave him three months to move out because she couldn't stand the agony of seeing his face and not being able to snog it, I exclaim, 'Jass! Jass! I've had a brilliant idea! Until you find somewhere—why not stay at *my* place for a few days?'

Jasper stares at me as if Fatboy has spoken. 'You can't mean that?' he says in an awed voice. I nod vigorously. Anything is better than living in poky isolation. His chiselled face breaks into a dimpled smile and he grabs my hand and kisses it. 'Angelsweet,' he murmurs, 'you're a shining star.' And then, 'Hey! I know! Why don't you drive me to Kensington and we can get my things now! It'll be fun!'

Though I cannot see how taxiing Jasper across London and lugging his gloomy ship paintings up my stairs will be fun, I can hardly refuse. As there is precisely nowhere to park in Kensington, I wait in the Toyota while Jasper fills it with his belongings. Clothes. Paintings. Stereo. And two hideous wicker chairs and a wicker coffee table. I blurt, 'I thought the crap furniture belonged to your landlord!'

Jasper laughs and says, 'Babe, these are original colonial pieces! Anyway I don't know what you're complaining about. They'll look ace in your lounge!' I am not so sure and my suspicion is confirmed when the chairs are in place. Even though it's great to have company, I feel cross.

I feel even crosser when Jasper snakes up behind me, grabs my hips, and whispers, 'Hey, babe, what say we christen the flat?'

I sternly imprison his hands in mine and say with forced sweetness, 'Sure, Jass. Only I should tell you I'm having a really heavy period. Honestly, it's like my uterus is being dragged out of me, so I'm warning you it'll be very messy, like having sex in an abattoir . . .'

Jasper sleeps on the lounge floor and doesn't bother me again.

The last four days have been interesting. My romantic notions of living—as Jasper might say—*à deux*—were shot to pieces within minutes. In the foolish seconds preceding my rash invitation I fantasised about a host of cosy things. Changing the message on my new answering machine to 'HelenanJasper aren't in right now'. Filling my supermarket basket with Jasperish items like smoked venison and freshly squeezed OJ as well as Dime bars and cat litter. Snuggling up on the floorboards in front of *Lethal Weapon*.

What was I thinking? The moment I saw those grubby wicker chairs polluting my territory I knew I'd made a mistake. I *liked* having an answering machine message all to myself. I didn't want a dead Bambi in my fridge. I preferred watching *Lethal Weapon* on my own, especially as—unlike some people—I would never exclaim loudly at a crucial point, 'This is preposterous, facile pap, let's watch a decent film like *Citizen Kane*.' What is it with me?

'But I can't tell him to leave,' I bleat to Lizzy over lunch. 'He's got nowhere to go.'

Lizzy, who is carefully inspecting her green salad for slugs, says, 'Really, Helen, I don't know why you asked him in the first place.'

I poke my lasagne with a fork and attempt to answer her question. Why did I ask Jasper to stay? 'I felt lonely after you'd swanned off to your boat party,' I say sulkily. 'And it was rainy and I was by myself.'

Lizzy shakes her curls and says, 'But that's my favourite thing! Being all cosy in a warm flat, watching the rain! And it was your first night in your own home. Weren't you excited?'

I sigh. Then I say in a grumpy voice, 'Yes, but I saw a huge spider. And I felt sorry for him. Jasper, I mean.'

Lizzy purses her lips. 'Why?' she says.

I feel hot and cross. I snap, 'Because Louisa turfed him out!'

Lizzy retorts, 'But couldn't he find his own flat?'

I growl, 'No.'

'Oh,' says Lizzy. 'Why not?'

I shrug and say, 'I think he's short of cash.'

Lizzy isn't convinced. She says, 'Well, he's lucky that he had you to fall back on. You're very kind, Helen, but I do think it's your right to tell Jasper to go if you've changed your mind about having him.'

Something Lizzy has just said chafes at my composure. I say huffily, 'We're fond of each other. And I feel sorry for him because I know what it's like to be living with someone you've been involved with and for it to go sour,' I say.

Lizzy emits a neat, ladylike snort and replies, 'Well, Helen, you certainly know now!' I tut and ignore her.

Lizzy is in a bad mood because she's twenty-eight tomorrow. Normally this wouldn't be an issue but she has booked a private room in a restaurant to celebrate with friends and yesterday afternoon Tina emailed her to say she would be unable to attend. She didn't give a reason. This shocked Lizzy and she rang Tina at home in the evening to ask why. Adrian answered. I can only assume that Lizzy charmed the bastard because he and Tina are now attending.

But Lizzy remains upset. She counts Tina as one of her ten closest pals and has made infinite excuses for the fact that recently she's been as friendly as a traffic warden with gout. According to Lizzy, Tina has been 'incredibly pressurised' because the deputy fashion editor has landed a job at *Cosmopolitan* and hasn't yet been replaced so Tina is 'snowed under with work'. Also, Tina is 'mad about Adrian' but 'they both work long hours' and so 'Tina wants to spend every precious minute with him.'

It has been easy for Lizzy to believe her own hype as she is one of those repulsively popular people who isn't possessive of her friends (they're two a penny and always ringing her). But while she's a liberal pal she is a birthday fascist. This is because Lizzy's family have always made a huge fuss of birthdays and Lizzy continues to regard birthdays as sacrosanct. So Tina's attempt to wriggle out of Lizzy's birthday dinner is an unpardonable sin. And that Tina's now been forced into attending doesn't erase the snub. I open my mouth to say 'How many people have you invited?' when Lizzy opens *her* mouth and says, 'Helen, do you mind awfully if I don't invite Jasper?'

I am astonished. Lizzy blushes and adds hurriedly, 'It's just that I don't think he'll enjoy it at all. Oh, I do hope you're not offended, it's just—'

I overcome my surprise and say, 'Liz, honestly, it's fine. In fact he can't make it, he's going out with the guys from his college cricket team tomorrow night. So don't worry.' Even as these words drop glibly from my lips, a thousand more rough and tumble inside my head. Do I believe my ears? So Jasper is blackballed but the wife-beater is cordially invited! This is heresy! It's tantamount to God telling Adam that Eve isn't invited to his Garden party but the Snake is.

I don't sleep well on Thursday night and wake up on Friday morning feeling groggy. I drag myself to work and try to wake up. But I can't. I drink two double espressos which make my body jangle but have no effect whatsoever on my dopiness. Lizzy bounds up and tinkles, 'Are you looking forward to tonight? What are you going to wear?'

My smile dissipates and I say, 'Er, this.'

Lizzy looks at my baggy, faded grey top and frowns. 'You can't wear *that* for my birthday! It's my *birthday*!'

Grow up, I want to say but don't. 'Well I haven't got anything else,' I growl. Lizzy peers under my desk. 'Oi!' I squeak.

'I wanted to see what shoes you were wearing,' she explains, 'and I have to say, those stack-heeled boots aren't my favourite.' To be frank, my stack-heeled boots aren't anyone's favourite. But *I* like them. 'I know!' sings Lizzy. 'I'll ask Tina to lend you something fabulous from the fashion cupboard. I'm sure she will when she—, I'm sure she will.'

Lizzy tootles off, consults with Tina and reappears at my desk brandishing a pair of strappy black stiletto sandals and a yellow wraparound top with mauve lace edging. '*Ay, caramba!*' I say crossly.

'Don't be silly!' snaps Lizzy. 'These will look gorgeous with your black trousers.'

I reply, 'Yes, but what about with me in them?'

Lizzy ignores my grumblings and forces me to try everything on. I stare dourly at my reflection in the Ladies' mirror while Lizzy skips around me like a demented pixie, pulling and tugging and brushing at the top. Then she says, 'Helen, you look divine!'

She allows me to put on my grey top for the remainder of the day but confiscates my boots 'because I don't trust you'.

As I don't wish to disappoint Lizzy—and because when she leaves the office I search frenziedly around her desk for my boots but can't find them—I walk into the restaurant bang on 7.30 wearing my black trousers, carnival top and strappy sandals. And the first person I see is Tom. He is standing in the far corner of the room, and is in conversation with Brian, who is wearing stonewashed dungarees. I'm so astonished (not at the stonewashed dungarees, they complement the green Day-Glo T-shirt perfectly) I double take and nearly drop Lizzy's present on the floor. The birthday girl skips over. 'Surprise!' she squeaks in my ear.

My face feels hot and red. 'Oh my God, you maniac! Keep it down!' I mutter, trying to keep the inane grin on my face under control.

Lizzy clamps a hand over her mouth to muffle a loud giggle. Luke appears at my side, digs an elbow into my ribs and winks.

'That was subtle,' I say.

'Tom came with Luke, so don't blame me!' exclaims Lizzy happily.

Luke chirrups, 'We went to loads of trouble so don't bugger it up.'

I murmur delightedly, 'You meddling kids!'

Luke takes this as a sign of approval and cries, 'I'll go and get him, shall I?'

He is only prevented from doing so when I grab his shirt, drag him backwards by the scruff, and hiss 'No!' But then Tom walks across the room, gazes at me for a second, and says boldly, 'Hello, you.' And I know he's being bold because when he says it he turns pink and his voice trembles slightly. I open my mouth and realise it's as dry as stale toast, so my 'hello, Tom,' emerges as a faint croak.

Luke nudges Tom and exclaims, 'Aren't you gonna kiss her, then?'

I freeze as the godawful words boi-oi-oing around our ears. Lizzy—

who I conclude didn't *quite* understand what she was dealing with when she went into cahoots with Luke—looks aghast. Tom's horrified expression cracks and he roars 'Arrrrrgh!' and pretends to throttle Luke.

'Come away now!' orders Lizzy sharply, like a nanny who is watching the rhinos with a five-year-old when they start rutting.

Tom and I are left to face each other. My hands dangle awkwardly by my sides and I don't know what to do with them. The rabbit foot is thumping away crazily in my chest, and I look at his face and all I can think of to say is 'How've you been?'

Tom tilts his head and nods and mutters, 'OK, thanks, and you?'

I nod too and say, 'Fine, thanks. Just fine.' Just fine! Who do I think I am? Dolly Parton? I bite my lip and wince and because I am starting to panic, blurt, 'Luke says funny things, doesn't he?'

Tom nods miserably and says, 'Yeah.'

Suddenly he looks as if he might cry and my insides squeeze and I take a deep breath and say, 'But sometimes he says things I think but don't dare say.'

I say this, can't believe I've said it, stare at the floor and screw up my face, thinking, fool, fool! When I dare to look at Tom again, he's looking at me like he's starving and I'm a large kebab, and we step forward at the same moment and he gently holds my face to his and we kiss. We kiss as soft and warm as velvet on velvet and I close my eyes and feel choked with joy and when I open them for a quick peek *his* eyes are shut, so I glance around the room to see if anyone has seen us—twenty people are ogling—so I close them again and sink deeper into the kiss.

'Everyone's looking,' I mumble.

'So what,' whispers Tom and holds me tighter, and I hug him back hard, and I gaze into his blue eyes and it seems madness that we've been apart—mad, stupid—and I think 'this must not happen again' and the warmth hits me like sunshine after rain. I love you.

It's not like anything else, ever. Everything that has gone before Tom is all very nice, but nothing. Tom is it. I look at him and I think of that old-fashioned phrase 'I love you with all my heart'—if I recall, it's what the handsome prince says to the flaxen-haired princess—and that is what I feel. He kisses my face, my hair, and says into it, 'Sorry for being a git.'

I rear back so fast I nearly knock out his teeth on my skull. '*You're* sorry!' I squeak. 'Don't be! You were right! *I'm* sorry.'

Tom shakes his head. Then he smiles. 'When you fell into the pub that time with Lizzy, even though, what she said'—at this point I nod hastily to encourage him to gloss over it—'I wanted to run after you and kiss you to death.'

I glow and say, 'Did you!'

He nods and kicks at the floor, like a small child, and says gruffly, 'It was shit without you. I hated it.'

I can barely believe it's Tom saying these things—not some balding, smelly-breathed goon, the sort that usually trap me in bars—but *Tom*. Tom who I lust after. Tom who fancies me. Oh God, please let it be real.

Dare I say it, I think Tom is thinking along similar lines, because we sit next to each other during dinner and he keeps beaming at me, and kissing me, and squeezing my hand, and he barely eats a thing. And, in an unprecedented scene, neither do I. We just talk.

Tom wants to know everything, like what I did for Christmas, and did I think of him at all, and how my job is, and how Laetitia is treating me right now (like a serf), and how Fatboy is doing (so spoilt that if I stroke him much more a genie will emerge from his arse), and Nana and my mother and how are things with me and her—although I don't have to tell him—and how I found my flat and how I did it up and did I miss him and how long it took and what I chose and how I feel and he keeps gazing at me as if I'm some unimaginable beauty and I want to know everything about what he's been doing, if Celine is still working at Megavet (no, she was sacked for gross incompetence after dropping a hamster then treading on it), if his sister is OK (great), if he's still doing his boxing (sort of, if you count watching *Rocky I*, *II* and *III*), how his family is (fine: his stepdad had a smallish win on the pools last week and is taking Tom's mum to the Lake District), and if he's got over his fear of painting (nice of me to remember), and if he's had sex with anyone since me (the cheek, and can he ask me the same question?), and can we go to the heath extension again in the Honda and eat bagels?

When I ask him about the heath extension, he stares at me and says, 'I'd do anything for you, Helen. I mean it.'

And I don't bleat 'Ah, but you didn't let me stay in your flat' because now I understand. I gulp and whisper, 'And me for you.'

I keep gazing at him and grinning and thinking he likes me, and what the hell was I doing rejecting his advances like a cat refusing cream. We smile at each other until our mouths ache. And until I catch Luke's eye across the table and he immediately opens *his* mouth wide (without bothering to swallow the chewed-up burger inside it) and sticks a finger into the gunk to communicate his repulsion at the fact his closest female friend and one of the lads have mutated from normal decent people into a nauseating pair of twittering lovebirds.

Tom sees Luke and tauntingly feeds me a chip, mouth to mouth. Luke puts his head in his hands as if in great sorrow. Tom sighs and says, 'You know he's going to blackmail me for ever?' and I nod and say, 'So, can we have sex later?' and he grins. I promptly stand up, scraping my chair. Tom looks at me, raises an eyebrow, and jumps to his feet—and a waiter brings in a huge pink birthday cake and we all have to sing happy birthday, dear Lizzy. Tom and I squawk it with gusto. We are exchanging sneaky 'shall we, now?' looks when I glance across the table to see if anyone has noticed and catch sight of Tina.

And the happiness drains away. She looks terrified. Cringing, servile, like a starving dog. She is sipping water and her hand is shaking. She won't look up. The person to her left has given up trying to engage her in conversation and is talking to the person on *his* left. The person to her right is to blame. Adrian is dapper in a pale green shirt and a beautifully cut dark grey suit and his blond hair is styled just so. He is in animated chat with the woman next to him.

'What's wrong?' says Tom, following my line of vision.

'Oh, er, nothing,' I say. 'I think Lizzy's onto us. We'd better, ah, save it for later.'

Tom glances at me and says, 'Something's wrong.'

I shake my head and say, 'I'm just going to talk to Liz for a sec, you'll be all right, won't you?' At this point, Luke appears behind Tom and tries to poke a bean in his ear, and Tom shouts with laughter, grabs his wrist and twists it so that Luke is forced to his knees.

I grab my chance and hurry over to Tina. I say 'Hi' and she looks horrified. She says feebly, 'I see you and Tom got it together.'

I smile and say 'Yeah!' and 'Why don't you come over and have a chat?'

Tina glares at me as Adrian swivels round, an ingratiating smile tacked to his face, and croons, 'Helen! How *excellent* to see you! You look terrific. And I love your top, it's so you.'

Much as I'd like to spit in his eye, I can see Tina quaking, so I force the corners of my mouth upwards and say, 'Yes, it's a nice top.'

I pause and add, 'Don't let me interrupt you—I was just about to drag Tina over my side of the table for a sec to see Tom and Luke.'

Adrian's smile remains fixed as he replies, 'We'd love to, but'—show glance at his Tag Heuer—'my lady's been nagging on all night about being exhausted, so I'm sweeping her home to beddybyes, right now. Rouse yourself, darling, the cab's waiting outside!'

Tina stands up like a robot and says in a strained voice, 'Good night, Helen.'

They kiss and hug Lizzy, then leave. I can't relax. Lizzy skips over and says that she and Brian and some others are going on to a club and would I like to come too. She adds quickly that she won't be offended if

I wouldn't. I start to apologise but she squeezes my shoulder, nods towards Tom, and whispers, 'Be happy.'

Tom sees that people are dispersing and he turns to me and says bashfully, 'Would you like to share a cab?'

I reply, 'Of course.'

Luke sticks his head between us and exclaims, 'Great! I'll cadge a lift!' Tom and I glare at him and Luke smiles and says, 'What?' then, 'Don't worry, you can drop me off first!'

Tom growls, 'You got that right!'

We tumble into the street and Tom hails a taxi. Luke puts his feet up and lights a fag, and Tom strokes my hand and says, 'You've gone quiet.'

I nod. I can't speak. There is nothing on this earth I want more than to drop Luke at Swiss Cottage then speed home with Tom and tear off his clothes and make mad passionate love on the hallway floor and then again on the lounge table. I *need* it. I need to make love to Tom, to feel that connection, like I need to breathe.

But how can I knowing that Tina's gone home with Adrian?

If this is a bright shiny new beginning, I want it to be perfect. I think of my friend's terror and the thought impedes my libido. What's he doing to her now? It pains me to consider it. There's no option. I tap Tom on the leg and tell him the truth about Tina and Adrian.

Then I divert the cab to Tooting and I pray we get there in time.

Although I look odd in a bikini and inevitably get burnt to a crisp, I love beaches. I like watching the sea and seeing the waves froth and fizzle on the shore. Or digging my feet into the warm sand and feeling it grainy between my toes. I love looking for shells—those curly ones like tiny unicorn horns—and smooth grey pebbles with white streaks of marble running through. I love closing my eyes and listening to the crashing waves and people's laughter. My favourite thing is to paddle in clear water, searching for gold. I'll see a glinting speck, and try to pinch it up. Of course it never *is* gold, just another grain of sand made shimmery by sun and water. But I don't mind because the joy is all in the seeking.

That's not how I feel when I lose Tom though. After all that searching I stumble on gold and let it slip through my fingers like sand.

Yet as we hurtle to Tina's defence like a squadron of black knights, there isn't a clue it will end like it does. I burble out the sorry tale and Tom says, 'Fuck!' and asks a thousand questions. Luke splutters and says, 'I don't get it.' They bristle and say poor poor Tina, and Adrian's got it coming to him.

'This isn't a boy's adventure game,' I say stonily, because I'm terrified of what I've started.

Tom says, 'Helen, we're only going to check she's OK. We won't do anything stupid.' He squeezes my hand.

Luke adds earnestly, 'You did the right thing.' I'm not sure I have.

I soon change my mind. When the taxi stops outside Tina's flat—'Adrian drives a Beamer!' squawks Luke, 'How *dare* he?'—and we tumble into the street, I can hear the screams. Luke wants to kick the door down, but Tom doesn't want to give Adrian warning. We sneak in the main door via the woman who lives downstairs. Curiously—or rather, uncuriously—she doesn't ask who we are. Then again, her neighbour is screaming like a pig, and that doesn't bother her.

We clump upstairs and Tom rings the doorbell. A whimper, a rustle, then silence. He rings again. He stands with his back to the door so if Adrian looks through the peephole he can't see who's there. 'Who is it?' barks a tense voice.

Tom barks back, 'Are you the owner of the black Z3 outside with slashed tyres—'

There is a loud exclamation and a clack-clack of bolts being drawn and Adrian rips open the door and as he does so Tom gives it a hefty boot and Adrian staggers backwards. Tom and I rush to Tina, who is cowering in the corner. Luke flings himself at Adrian in what I presume is a textbook rugby tackle—or maybe he just trips on the edge of the rug—and before I can say 'harder than that', is sprawled on top of him and shaking him so that Adrian's head makes a pleasing bonk-bonk-bonk sound on the floor.

When Tom sees the state of Tina his face goes taut. Adrian asks what the fuck's going on and bleats that we've misunderstood the situation and Tina and he were merely having a tiff and *yelp!* Adrian's rant ends swiftly as Tom squeezes an apparently sensitive point on his neck. 'Shut up,' says Tom in a hard voice. Adrian shuts up. I ring the police on my mobile as the phone has been ripped from the wall and Tom runs to fetch ice and a towel for Tina.

Tina has seven fresh cigarette burns on her stomach and is far from OK. Her head wound has reopened. Tom strokes her hair out of her face and gently dabs at the blood trickling down her forehead. He says, 'Christ, Tina, this is terrible. You don't have to put up with this.' In a quivering voice she jokes that she won't be wearing a crop top this summer then starts crying and clinging to me and Tom.

'Tina,' I say, trying not to cry myself, 'I had to, I couldn't leave it any longer, I'm sorry.'

When the police arrive Tina stops weeping and freezes. The police want to hear what happened from all of us, but especially from Tina.

'Please say,' I urge her. 'Be brave.' She quakes and glances at Adrian who stares ahead like he thinks he's the Maida Vale Terminator.

Silence. Tina says nothing and I hold my breath. Luke steps forward and Tina jumps but he only wants to offer her a scrumpled piece of toilet paper on which to blow her nose. 'I've only used it once,' he explains kindly.

Luke's gentleness steels her. After much snuffling and gulping, Tina points at her boyfriend and says, 'He—Adrian—he said cigs are bad for me, which they are. He, he st-stubbed them out on my belly.'

The male officer—whose stern expression is compensation for a faceful of freckles—writes this down in his notebook. Then Tina goes quiet so the female officer, a woman with bright yellow hair and a steel aura, ushers her into the next room. Freckles turns to Adrian. Adrian starts to say, in his plummiest, chummiest voice, that Tina has a drink problem. To my great joy, Freckles cuts in with, 'Right now I don't want to hear your explanation.'

I point out the ashtray full of stubs which, I assume, are riddled with Adrian's fingerprints, even though he doesn't smoke. Freckles obligingly pours the stubs into a plastic bag.

I then go into the kitchen because Tina wants me with her. I sit at the kitchen table while Blondie takes pictures of Tina's stomach and scalp with a Polaroid camera. She seems to understand that Tina is overwhelmed by her presence and its implications and says firmly, 'You're doing the right thing, love. You've done nothing wrong. This isn't what should happen in a normal relationship.'

I'm not sure if I'm allowed to talk, so I nod supportively behind Blondie's back, and try not to retch at the sight of Tina's injuries. Blondie then tells me to take Tina to hospital. I ring for a cab, then ask, 'Aren't you going to take a statement from Tina?'

She says she'll get a statement tomorrow morning. Tina, who's gone as quiet as a mouse in felt slippers, nods. As the cab arrives, Blondie marches downstairs to interview Tina's neighbour (which I am spitefully pleased about) and Freckles says to Adrian, 'I'm arresting you for assault occasioning actual bodily harm,' and handcuffs him.

'Careful of my cuff links!' Adrian snaps which, I am delighted to note, doesn't go down well. Freckles becomes, if anything, less careful of Adrian's cuff links. Adrian and his Savile Row suit are to spend the night in a police cell and tomorrow morning he'll be interviewed. Then he'll be up in court.

Tom wraps Tina in a blanket because she's shivering and carries her to the cab. All the way to the hospital we tell her well done and she's so brave and this is the end of Adrian. Tina doesn't seem to hear. She mutters into her hands, 'I'm so ashamed.' Tom and Luke and I chorus, 'Don't be!' and Tina smiles, then winces because her stomach hurts.

In Casualty, the baby-faced doctor says as if he can't quite believe what he's seeing, 'Your boyfriend did this?'

Tina replies, as if this explains everything, 'I smoke.'

The doctor looks suspiciously at Luke. Luke has appointed himself Tina's bodyguard and is standing beside her with folded arms.

'It wasn't *me*!' he blurts. 'I'm Luke! I'm looking after her!' Tina smiles at him tearily and Tom smiles at me. I glance at my watch and discover it's 3.23am, which means we waited in Dante's Hell—sorry, Casualty—for three hours. I feel a swell of exhaustion. I mutter that I'm going outside for a second.

I stumble towards the door. The thickly sweet smell of A & E is having an effect on my ability to breathe. And the swingy hospital doors, the bright glaring lights, and the shouty drunks, and the rushing staff in white and blue and sensible shoes, the whole lot converges and spins around my head like a small tornado and I am watching my father die again and the monitor is bleeping and curtains are being pulled and trolleys being pushed and I'm being yanked away and there are screams of 'He's arresting' and my mother is wailing and my father died and I sat there and missed it and I never told him I loved him because I couldn't say the words. The blood drains from my head and I feel nauseous and tottery. I need to sit down or be sick and I'm not sure which so I collapse on a bench—next to a ragged man swigging from a bottle—then I say 'Urgh' and vomit onto the pavement. Understandably, the man moves to another bench.

I clutch the side of the bench while the world sways. Then Tom is holding my hair off my face and rubbing my back while I retch and spit. I keep retching. Loudly. 'Romantic, this,' I mutter.

'Nah,' replies Tom cheerfully, 'this is nostalgic for me. It reminds me of our first date.'

I would look at him to laugh but I have dribble on my chin. I wipe it on my sleeve. 'How's Tina?' I say.

'Still in shock, I think,' says Tom. 'She said she felt bad about Adrian. But the doctor wasn't having any of it. He told her men like Adrian don't change. I hope he made some impact, poor Tina. Oh, and Luke's in love. He wants to stay and guard her.'

My eyes bulge. 'Luke's in love?' I squeak.

Tom grins and nods. 'Very,' he says. My brain is twisting in an attempt to absorb this when Tom adds, 'Has Tina got family? Do you think someone should phone her parents?'

I joke, 'What, to warn them about Luke?' Then I add, 'I suppose so. She needs all the support she can get. And I want her brothers to know. We should ask Tina though.'

Tom nods. 'Tom,' I say, 'I'm scared for Tina.'

I'm scared because I want this to be the end and I'm scared it won't be. 'I bet Adrian has a good lawyer,' I say miserably.

Tom replies, 'Yeah. I bet he does. But, we all know about him now. He can't isolate her any more. And I know this sounds weird, but Adrian strikes me as a man who cares very much about his reputation. And Tina has *three* brothers. *Three*. I reckon Adrian's in trouble. Fuck, if anyone did that to my sister—' Tom shakes his head. I shrug. I feel so despondent I no longer trust anyone to do the right thing.

'Listen, Helen,' says Tom, 'it's four in the morning. Luke's stuck to Tina like a lovestruck leech. They're not keeping her in, and Luke's going to stay with her, you can visit her at home, first thing. Why don't I take you home. I'll sleep on the floor.' I reluctantly agree. I run to see if Tina minds then sprint back to Tom. A small mercy in a mean world: I see Tom's found a black cab. He opens the door and I clamber in and sprawl like a rag doll on the back seat.

I close my eyes. There is a vague, elusive thought buzzing at my brain but I can't be bothered to identify and swat it. 'Wake me when we get there,' I whisper and fall asleep.

I awake as we pull into my road.

'Which one is it?' says Tom.

'Mm, it's too dark to tell,' I say, rubbing my eyes—and louder—'If you stop here, please, that'll be fine!'

We hop out and I spy pebbledash and realise my flat is the next one along. I am about to open the gate when Tom tenses and I stop instinctively. I peer into the shadows and see a figure slumped on my doorstep. And it is only as the figure jerks and stumbles to its feet that my vague buzzy thought pings into focus and hammers sharp and fast and deep into my still-fuzzy brain.

Jasper.

I stand as frozen as a particularly dim-witted pillar of salt while Jasper blinks at me. Then he blinks at Tom, and growls, 'Who the hell are you?'

Tom replies coolly, 'No, who are *you*?'

Jasper says, 'I'm her live-in boyfriend, you prick.'

Tom drops my hand from his grasp like a dead thing. To Jasper, he says icily, 'My mistake.' To me, he says nothing. He whistles at the departing taxi—which screams to a surprised halt—and steps in.

I watch him speed into the night and I know he's gone for ever.

Chapter 9

BEING THE LEAST ATTRACTIVE teenager in my class (so you can imagine) spectacles were not an option. I spent two years squinting, before my maths teacher—a spiteful man if there ever was one—cornered my mother at a parents' evening and told her I was as blind as a retired bat and rubbish at sums. The next day she dragged me to an optician, who asked me to read out 'the letters' on a blank white board then mysteriously declared that my eyesight was 'minus five and a half'.

When, soon after, I was presented with the monstrosity of an NHS pair of glasses I came close to tears. But when I put them on I felt like Dorothy entering Munchkinland. I could see! The world was crisp! It had sharp edges! Trees weren't fuzzy! They were precise! They had millions of individual leaves!

And, as Tom leaves my life, I relive that seminal moment where everything looms into focus. All that is blurred becomes clear. But this time it's as painful as if I were rubbing crushed glass into my eyes. Meanwhile Jasper shouts and shouts, but his words wash over me.

'Who the heck was that tosser i've been waiting here since 1.00am. i told you i lost the key i'm freezing my arse off here where the hell have you been it's a ridiculous hour how dare you leave me out here all night it's unacceptable i won't stand for it who was that git how dare he ask who i am who's he i want an answer i won't—'

I hardly hear him. I watch the taxi shrink and disappear, taking all my tomorrows with it. This can't be real. It's not allowed. It's not what I deserve. I stare at the horizon in the hope that Tom will do a Mills & Boon and come beetling back. He doesn't. Fuck. How can this happen. I take Jasper in out of kindness (mostly) and the toad repays me by scuppering my life. To lose Tom once, ouch. To lose him *twice more*. That's not carelessness, that's obscene.

How could I forget that I was sharing my bathroom with the worst flatmate since *me*? And Jasper. How could he? To describe himself as my live-in boyfriend is a large, malicious, havoc-wreaking lie.

I walk slowly to the front door—each step is like wading through glue—unlock it and look straight at Jasper.

'I'm so sorry,' I say calmly. 'There was an emergency. But wait there. I have a surprise for you.' Jasper opens his large mouth to object as I shut the door on him. I glide upstairs and walk into the lounge where his wicker chairs await. I walk to my pile of CDs and search for a suitable soundtrack. Ah yes. Then I heave open the bay window.

Jasper steps backwards, stumbles over a stray piece of wire embedded in the lawn, and shouts angrily, 'What the heck's going on?'

It's like someone's pressed a switch on my back marked 'insanity'. A fusion of shock from Tina's cigarette burns and Tom walking away. I sing, 'It's a surprise! You'll find out in a moment!' I survey the devastation that is my new lounge. Jasper's clothes are strewn over the floor. I press PLAY, pick up a pair of white Y-fronts and throw them out of the window. Surprisingly—I was reserve for the netball C team—they hit Jasper full in the face.

I lean from the window to watch what he does. And, as an anthropological exercise, it's worth it. Jasper rips the pants from his face and screams, 'What the heck was that for? You'—he pauses in disbelief as I retreat inside—'Let me in, for heaven's sake! What the heck are you playing at?' He soon finds out. I stagger to the window with his suitcase, position myself against the ledge so I'm stable, and sling it out onto the grass. Jasper leaps nimbly aside to save his head from being crushed.

'Stop it!' he bawls. 'What are you doing, you madwoman?'

He scrabbles frantically about the garden trying to stuff shoes, socks, trousers, vests, pants and shirts back into the case, and I laugh and sing 'Ja-spaar! Ready or not?'

He looks up and screeches '*Noooooo!*' as I fling the first of his nautical paintings into the road. It makes a pretty tinkle as the glass shatters.

Jasper runs into the road gibbering. He tenderly cradles the bits of gilt frame and I almost feel sorry for him. I drop the other two ship paintings so they land on a flowerbed.

Jasper's wicker chairs fall to their deaths to the tune of 'Let Your Love Flow'. He begs and pleads from the pavement but no deal. Jasper's wicker coffee table takes flight to a rousing 'Stand By Your Man'.

'Stop it!' sobs Jasper, nursing a detached piece of wicker. 'Turn it off! I'm sorry! Please!' Reluctantly I blip off the music.

'Thank fuck,' gasps Jasper (and everyone else in my street). I lean out of the window and smile. I am the Ice Queen and loving it. Jasper brandishes the snapped wicker leg and yells, 'Look what you've done! You, you . . . wicker killer!' I laugh nastily, which makes him stamp his foot. He bellows, 'Shut *up*! Oh heck, look at my stuff! Helen! Stop it! You're being weird! Please! Let me in! I've got nowhere to go!'

I stick my head out and bellow, 'I don't *care*! Goodbye, Jasper!' Then I slam the window and draw the blinds. I feel briefly elated—as if the albatross round my neck has eaten the chip on my shoulder and flown off—and blip on 'Sea of Heartbreak'. I am free. I snatch up Fatboy and whirl him around my de-wickered lounge, but he struggles, whines, claws me in the chest, and runs off. Story of my bloody life.

I switch off the stereo and walk into my bedroom in silence. Then I sit on my bed and think of Tom. Tom is gone. What have I done? What *have* I done? I am seized with dread—a dread of having made the most terrible mistake of my life. My head swirls with the irony of Tom and me in a taxi zooming away from Tina's doom towards mine. All I can think is that I was standing at the beginning of the rest of my life and I tripped over the starting line.

If I had an electrode attached to my toe which buzzed every time I did something stupid, maybe I'd be more efficient at learning from my mistakes. As it is, I make the same idiotic blunders again and again.

But Tom and Jasper's unscheduled meeting was in its own league. I didn't need a next time. My plans for the next six decades were botched, which piqued me sufficiently to draw up resolutions. Never again would I mismanage my life. Fatboy would eat at 8.15am and again at 7.30pm with a veterinary-approved snack before bedtime. From now on grazing would be outlawed (for both household members). I'd *budget*. I'd only get drunk on occasions. I'd visit museums and Nana Flo. I'd stop picking my lip and learn about car maintenance.

The list was long and imposing, but that week I was on time for work every day and forcibly courteous to Laetitia, even when she exclaimed, 'Not again! Your bladder must be the size of a thimble!' My flat was pristine to the point that I reached the Neolithic stratum in my linen basket. I stopped discussing other people's relationships apart from to tell Lizzy about Tina (with the heroine's permission). I listened to the forecast on Radio Four every night and was appropriately dressed for the weather. Although if I'd dressed to suit my mood I'd have worn sackcloth. Not even a visit to see *Grease* with my mother cheered me. Not even when she bought the soundtrack and said, 'Darling, do you think I'm too old to wear my hair in a ponytail?' Not even when we went for a pizza and I told her about Tina and she cried, 'And you used to be such a selfish girl!'

I even joined Lizzy at her gym and spent thirty-five minutes doing up my laces in the changing rooms, wondering if there was a tiny chance that Tom might listen if I called to explain but my head crushed all hope flat. From nowhere I recalled a rule of baseball—three strikes and you're out. I'd blown it. By Friday I was as miserable as sin and as dull as godliness. I tore up the list and threw it in the bin. But I still felt dead inside.

On Saturday though, I cheer up. The reason for this mood switch is that I hear from Luke.

Since last Saturday Luke hasn't budged from Tina's side. Whereas I haven't seen her since the hospital. I wanted to visit last Sunday but, Luke informed me, she was resting. When I rang back later, Luke told me that a plain-clothes officer had come round but then Tina had decided not to give a statement. 'But *why*?' I cried.

'She doesn't want to,' he replied.

'But she must!' I exclaimed.

'We can't make her,' said Luke.

'I suppose not,' I said sadly. 'Can I speak to her?'

Luke said, 'Only if you promise not to nag her.'

I promised and was passed on to Tina, although I was a little hurt by this. Tina informed me she was feeling better. And that the police were probably going to prosecute anyway. And that she had told her family. And that her parents were on their way over. Oh, and that she was *almost* sure she never wanted to see Adrian again.

Ideally, I'd have preferred Tina to drag Adrian through the courts, complete with screaming headlines and front-page mugshots, but I suppose I understand why Tina didn't want to pursue it. What I didn't understand is why Adrian pleaded not guilty and was instantly bailed as if his crime was forgetting to pay a parking ticket. 'But it's unbelievable!' I screeched, when Luke relayed the scandal. 'She'll never be safe! He'll probably come round tonight and blow up the house! Jesus! Don't you dare let her drive the Escort without testing the brakes.'

Although that last warning was applicable with or without Adrian's interference, Luke objected to my pessimism. One of Adrian's bail conditions was not to contact Tina. And maybe by the time the case came to trial in three or four months, Tina might have decided to testify. Meanwhile, he, Luke, was watching out for her now.

'Luke,' I snapped—more meanly than necessary—'As I'm sure you're aware, Tina has just been dragged out of a stifling, abusive relationship with a domineering tyrant. The last thing she needs is to be dragged into another one.'

Luke was, predictably, upset. 'Shhh!' he wailed. 'She'll hear! It's not like that! She doesn't think of me like that. She's fragile, Helen, she's nervous of being alone. She's scared. I'm *good* for her! I'm helping her to stay away from Adrian. I'm protecting her, I promise! She's still keen on the bastard! I'm distracting her! We talk. We've got a lot in common.'

I was tempted to reply, 'Don't make me laugh', but in keeping with my new 98 per cent spite-free personality I restrained myself. After all, if Luke was hardening Tina's heart against the Evil One, he was not a tactless, bumbling goof but a talented miracle worker.

This realisation didn't stop me being a teensy bit jealous of Luke's abrupt conversion from *my* ever-hopeful platonic friend to Tina's.

Excepting this emergency call, I don't hear from him. I don't ring Tina as—according to her new interpreter—'She's knackered and not up to chatting. But when you see Lizzy can you thank her for the fruit and the, the er, St John's wart stuff and the tea pee oil.'

I do as I'm told, sit tight, and pass on the message. When I tell Lizzy, she says, 'Oh I feel terrible, *terrible*! Adrian was so smiley! And all those flowers! And all the phone calls! Who would have thought it? Do you think I should send calendula too?'

I say it's a kind thought but Tina already has a diary. And anyway, I'm sure she'll get in touch if she needs anything. She doesn't. So when Luke rings on Saturday I am gagging for information. And my, do I get it. Although Luke is so hyper and gabbly it takes all my concentration to understand him.

'OK, Tina's brothers, Max, Sean and Andrew, were *spitting blood* when they heard about Adrian. They went mental, Max especially, he's the youngest, he was gonna go round and sort him *right* out. But Sean said no, they had to be clever about this, yeah, because Adrian sounded like the sort to press charges, so anyway, Tina doesn't know it, but Sean calls this mate of his, Ray. Ray runs a security firm, providing bouncers for clubs and you can pay him to warn people of the error of their ways, yeah, and he'll send somebody round, and so right, Sean tells Ray about Adrian and Ray hates wife beaters, it's his worst thing, and two of his men turn up at Adrian's door at two in the morning and they burst in and strap up Adrian's hands with his belt, and Adrian shouts that he'll go to the police and Ray says in a soft way that the police don't care about him, and then Adrian goes dead quiet and they rip up his living-room carpet, right, and they roll him up in his own carpet and stuff a hanky in his mouth and they *remove* him, OK, and they drive him off to this dungeon thing, like a cellar but worse, and they *warn* him, Sean'd said don't hurt him, just warn him, and Adrian was down with them for three hours and then they dumped him naked in the road outside his office and Ray spoke to Sean yesterday and said that he didn't think Adrian would be bothering his sister again.'

Dear me.

Unsurprisingly, I think about Tina for the rest of the afternoon. I will her to come through this. Maybe one day she'll look back and wonder at how it happened. Imagine. To be so blind to a person's true nature. To be so optimistic that when that person is killing you, you smile as they wield the knife. And then it strikes me. We're both mourning relationships we wanted but cannot have.

I can't understand why Tina loved Adrian but she did.

As for me, I am and will always be in love with Tom. But for the moment my thoughts aren't about him. I'm thinking of the other man, not in my life. And I think the same thing over and over, like a chant. I think, I never was a Daddy's girl and now I never will be.

The next day I ring my mother and invite her round for coffee. 'You don't need me now you've got your flat done,' are her first words.

'Now, Mummy, you know that can't be true,' I say sternly, 'or why would I be inviting you over?'

There is a sullen silence before she replies, 'I don't know. You want some more chairs?'

Her obstinacy should frustrate me, but it doesn't because I guess that right now she needs to do this. And our honeymoon was bound to end some time. I say in a gratingly jolly tone, 'Actually, I invited you for the pleasure of your company, but I'd hate it if you felt you *had* to come—'

'I'll be round at five,' snaps my mother.

She shows up, ready for battle. I offer her coffee ('only if it's decaff'—it isn't); I offer her tea ('only if it's Earl Grey'—it isn't); I offer her water ('only if it's mineral'—it isn't). Then I realise that tap water contains minerals so I shout 'OK!' and pour her a glass. When I present it she sniffs it and gives it a small push away from her.

'Aren't you going to offer me anything to eat?' she says.

'Yes, of course,' I say in an injured tone, trying to recall if I'd eaten a Dime bar that was in my handbag. 'Hang on a sec.'

I rush to the bedroom, tip the bag's contents onto the floor, and snatch the Dime bar from the smoking heap. I unwrap it (it looks nicer) arrange it centrally on my best plate (the best of two) and present it with a flourish. She inspects it from a distance, craning her neck slightly but otherwise not moving a muscle. I say briskly, 'This is a very superior confectionery, it—'

She rudely interrupts with, 'It's a Dime bar.' My discomfited expression makes her smile for the first time and she adds gruffly, 'Bernadette Dickenson always has one for lunch. She's got twelve fillings.'

I take this friendly snippet of information as a peace offering and say, 'You don't sound very happy, Mum.'

She reacts as if I've just sworn. 'Happy!' she spits. 'Happy! No I am not "happy"! I am extremely *un*-happy. My husband's dead as a dormouse! How can I be happy? I'm a widow! My whole life's unravelled!'

I wince and mutter, 'Sorry, bad choice of word.'

My mother glares. Then she blurts, 'It was your father's birthday and you didn't call me!'

I grit my teeth and say, 'I tried you, twice, and you were engaged both times. I thought if you wanted to speak to me you'd call. You know, like a grown-up?' My mother gasps as if I've slapped her. Immediately, I feel bad. I say gently, 'I'm sorry, Mum. I didn't want to upset you more than you were already upset. I know high days and holidays are tough.'

She replies wearily, 'It's not the high days and holidays. It's the every day.'

'Oh, Mum,' I say sadly. I lean across and touch her arm. She covers her eyes with both hands and weeps into them. I grimace, and wait. After approximately six minutes (an age in weeping terms) the weeping halts.

'Mum,' I say, searching for a grain of wisdom, 'you can talk to me.'

My mother squeezes my hand silently, and nods and sniffs. And we start talking about Dad. My mother tells me about their first date. He took her to a French restaurant where they ate snails and got food poisoning. 'It wiped me out for a week! Your father had to take me on three more dates to make up for it!' she cries, flushed at the memory. 'Of course, my mother didn't believe it was the food! She thought I had morning sickness. My own mother thought I was "fast"! She didn't say so to me, of course, but I crept to the banisters and heard her whispering to my father. Morrie used to say my mother had a whisper that could shatter eardrums! Oh, he made me laugh. Although'—she frowns, almost to herself, and I can tell she's immersed in her own little world—'I never could get him to put his teacup in the sink. Never! And God forbid I should speak to him when there was golf on television. "You don't need to *hear* golf, do you?" I'd say!'

My mother chuckles and I pitch in with, 'Mum, he wouldn't speak to us when *anything* was on the telly. He was worse than Nana! Remember when he took time off to watch Wimbledon and I ran in to show him a mug I'd made in pottery—what was I? Eight?—and I ran in front of the TV and he missed a match point and scowled at my mug and said, "That's sod-all use, it's the shape of a pine cone! How are you going to drink from it?" I threw it on the floor and ran upstairs!'

My mother tilts her head. 'I don't remember that,' she says. She pats my hand and says softly, 'Don't take it personally, darling. He could be very rude sometimes. I told him off for it.' She sighs. 'Oh, Helen, I miss him. The ache. It's always there. You understand. Some days it fades and then, I'll see his spectacle case in a drawer, and it'll be back with a vengeance.' I nod dumbly. What else can I do?

My mother sighs again. 'Oh well,' she says, snapping a large corner off the Dime bar, 'that's the price you pay for love.'

I feel *I'm* paying the price for love despite it bolting back to the shop before I could get any use out of it. I hesitate to tell her about Tom. I'm too delicate to cope with her booby-trapped reassurances. However, when I give in and confess, my mother is surprisingly optimistic.

'He'll come crawling back!' she says. 'They all do eventually!' She suggests we go shopping instead. 'You could do with wearing brighter clothes,' she says. 'No wonder you're such a mope.'

Her ability to ricochet from gushing to crushing never fails to astound me.

When I'm not being insulted by relatives, I sulk indoors. I have added a lamp to my living room and rude magnets to the fridge, and the flat feels more mine every day. I like to be in it. And I get every chance to be in it because I don't feel much like partying. If I do see my friends, we meet in the day. (They don't feel much like partying either.)

Talking of which, yesterday I saw Tina. She returned to work and while she looked fragile and on edge, the first thing she said when I bounded over was, 'All right, you big tart!' I beamed and replied joyfully, 'Hello, slapper!' Then we hugged.

Later on we snuck out for a coffee and Tina said she was feeling stronger. 'I take it Luke's still cooking for you, then,' I said teasingly, looking at her gaunt face.

To my surprise, Tina said fervently, 'That man is a gem. Everyone's been great, especially you. And the police were good. They gave me pamphlets. I'll never forget what you did, Helen. I, God knows, I needed the push. I—*ugh*—even to talk about it. I can't. It's too raw. Maybe later.

'But Luke. I don't know what I'd have done without him. He's been solid. Because this hasn't been easy, Helen. It's frightening, being out in the world again. It sounds mad but I felt safe with Adrian. And I, I haven't heard from him but I'm scared I will. He's got to be madder than hell. I'm almost resigned to it. Sometimes I think: I've survived this many beatings, what's one more? But Luke says I won't see Adrian again.

He's confident of that. I half believe him. I should feel happy, but I'm not sure how I feel. I don't know if I could have stuck it without Luke. Every woman deserves a Luke.'

Humbled, I said, 'No, Tina, *you* deserve a Luke.' Not wishing to sound soft I added, 'A Luke with good hygiene and some vestige of dress sense.'

But Tina said quietly, 'He's cool.'

Instantly, I felt mean. Trying to sound jokey—but wishing to procure serious information—I croaked, 'Oh! So it's like that, is it?'

Although Tina insisted that it wasn't like that and that she planned to remain single for a long while, I knew it was only a matter of time before it *was* like that. And this morning, as I hunch over my marmalade on toast, I think, Why can't it be like that for me? I would say I'm always the bridesmaid, never the bride, but I've never even *been* a bridesmaid. How dare bridesmaids complain! They don't know how lucky they are in their puffy lilac.

As I brood on the ungratefulness of some people, I hear a thud. Yet another crippling bill. I stomp downstairs to be financially damaged and see a large white envelope lying on the floor. I snatch it up, rip it open, and inspect its contents. A scrawled note: 'Darling, look what I found!' And a faded birthday card. The illustration is of a baby penguin wearing a woolly hat and scarf and carrying a flower (as they do). The message reads 'For You Daddy On Your Birthday'. I open it and my eyes prickle. 'To dear Daddy', a little girl has written in her neatest handwriting, 'With lots of love and kissis and hugs and best wishis lots of love forom Helen xxxxxxx oooooooo.'

I wait till 9.32 then ring Laetitia. 'Hello?' I whisper, forcing out a weak cough. 'Laetitia, it's Helen, I'm [*groan*] not well. I've [*wheeze*] got a cracking headache and I'm going to [*snuffle*] have to drag myself [*rasp*] to the doctor. I feel [*gasp*] terrible.'

I await the fearsome cry of 'Don't lie to me, you skiver, get in here this minute or you're out on your sodding ear!' But Laetitia merely says, 'Don't come in until it's officially not contagious.'

I agree, plonk down the receiver and crow, 'And the Academy Award for Best Actress goes to Miss Helen Bradshaw! For a staggering performance! Ta naaaaa!' Then I pack what I need, grab my metal bin from the bathroom, jump in the Toyota, and speed to the cemetery.

I'd forgotten how quiet it was. Quiet except for the insolent drone of aircraft every five minutes. I survey the desolate landscape of white stones and sigh. Who would have thought it. I hope no one sees me carrying this bin. Or wearing trousers.

I walk around, hugging the bin, until, finally, I stand and stare at the name. 'Maurice Bradshaw', etched in granite. And my first thought is, what the fuck is my father's name doing in this graveyard! I stare at 'Maurice Bradshaw' for a long time, and scowl. Slowly I reach out and touch the cold stone. I trace my finger along each solemn letter. Maurice Bradshaw. His row is nearly filled up, with people who have died since. Something about being here immobilises me. I feel I could stand here staring until dark.

I stare and stare. Then I kneel on the ground next to my father's grave, rummage through my bag for my notepad and my pen, and start scribbling. Pebbles dig into my knees through my trousers, but I don't mind. I like feeling the sharpness. When I've finished, my trousers are wet with mud and my knees hurt. I read what I've written.

Dear Dad,

I hope you're well. I'm not. I miss you and it has been awful. Of course, the family have been no help at all. I hate Cousin Stephen. He has disgraced himself. He was so greedy at the will reading that Nana had to tell him to shut up. He had egg mayonnaise at the corner of his mouth, it was disgusting. Nana Flo hasn't heard from Great-Aunt Molly for ages. But we've tried with Nana, and I think she's a bit better. She's a strong woman. Mummy is slightly less strong but I think you'd be proud of her (apart from the wrist business). She was brilliant when I moved into my flat. You'll be pleased to hear it's in a good location.

I lost confidence when you died. I didn't know who I was, suddenly. What to do. And if you must know, I don't feel too good at the moment. Maybe your death YOUR DEATH YOUR DEATH YOUR DEATH YOU ARE DEAD YOU ARE DEAD I CAN'T BELIEVE IT WHY CAN'T YOU COME BACK WHY WHY WHY WHY NEARLY A YEAR AND STILL NOT BETTER. Not many people understand. They decide how I feel, should feel, ought to feel, in relation to how bad Mum feels . . . I don't mean to complain. Mum and I are getting on better, which is good.

I wish we'd got on, Dad. I was hurt that you called me the Grinch. I tried hard with you, Dad. I loved you. I wanted you to love me back. If you don't mind me saying, it was like trying to force the Toyota up a steep hill. I meant to say I love you at the hospital, and I was saying it inside. I hope dying wasn't too bad, leaving us and sinking alone into the dark. I hope you play golf with Grandpa and get to know him. It must be nice for you both to meet at last.

I have wondered what I did to make you not care but now I see you did, in your way. Mum says you were rude in general so it's good to know it wasn't all me. No offence, but not all men are like you. Some try harder. Which makes me feel better about things.

Anyway, I hope you don't mind me saying this, but it was time. I still love you. And I feel better now. With lots of love and kissis and hugs and best wishis lots of love forom Helen xxxxxxx ooooooo

(Remember!?)

I don't want to over-romanticise the moment but I feel like I've just had an enema.

I sigh deeply and fold the letter. Then I turn to my death-kit. I open the grey paper sack and place the letter inside. I also put in the paper Mercedes (to ferry Dad to a heavenly golf club), the gold and silver watch with 'Rolex' printed on its face (he likes to be on time), the Chinese gold leaf, and the Bank of Hell notes (to buy a drink at the bar). And the five ripped-out end pages of *Single & Single* by John Le Carré (he hadn't finished it). I stick in the glasses, the pen and the cigarettes. Then I write my father's name on the sack, make a note of the date on a Post-it note and attach that too. Then I seal it.

I glance around to see if anyone is watching, but the place is deserted. Furtively, I light the three joss sticks—I crouch behind the headstone for shelter—and think 'Dad, Dad, Dad.' Then I realise, shit, I could be summoning *anyone*'s dad, so I quickly amend it to 'Maurice Bradshaw, Helen's Dad, Maurice Bradshaw, Helen's Dad.' After five fragrant minutes, I poke the joss sticks into the ground, and light the red candle. 'OK, Dad,' I whisper, feeling only slightly silly. 'I'm sending you cash, fags and a Merc, because I know that's what you'll appreciate, even if it isn't very zen. I've also sent you a John Le Carré but please read my letter first. OK, now I'm sending it.'

I jam the red candle in the earth, behind the headstone so it doesn't blow out. Then I wonder, do I torch the lot like a pyromaniac or do I play the control freak and burn it item by item? I might as well be organised. I tip everything out onto the ground. Then I set fire to the sack first, so that all I send has transport. I fold the Chinese money in the way that Lizzy showed me, plop it in the steel bin, and strike a match.

The money burns and curls, orange cinders squirming over it like bugs, devouring the paper until it is dust. I stare, bewitched. The smell is sweet, heady, almost sickly. I am nervous that the smoke will alert the gravekeepers (or whatever they're called) and keep peering over the headstone to see if any officials are thundering towards me shaking their fists. They aren't. Then I light the Hell notes. I watch and wait until they crumble to ash before lighting the cigarettes (I hope they're not stubs on arrival). Then I light the pen, the watch, the glasses, as I don't want a fire raging out of control. My father would be mortified. Then it's the turn of the Merc, which takes about three hours—not what I'd expect from a fast car. Then John Le Carré. And finally, my letter.

My eyes water from the smoke and other things and I wipe them with the back of my hand, before realising it's filthy. Then I glance down and see that so is the rest of me. I look like a charred potato. My face is hot and itchy from crouching over the bin, my throat stings, and my knees are damp and frozen. But I don't care.

My heart races as I watch the cinders fly.

I drive home in a trance, flames leaping before my eyes, my hands black with soot. I speed along, invincible. There are no tangible thoughts in my head, just an image of ash dancing in the air like a thousand white butterflies set free. I run upstairs to the mirror to see if I look different and a grubby urchin stares back at me. When I breathe deeply it is like I am encased in a steel corset. Slowly I place my hands on my chest and feel the frantic beat of my heart. I stand still. And the ache of loss, dragging on my insides like a devil tugging at my soul, seems fainter.

I phone Lizzy. 'I burnt your death-kit yesterday. It helped,' I squeak.

Lizzy nearly bursts through the earpiece with joy. 'That's *wonderful*!' she shrieks. 'Was it amazing? spiritual? intense? a release?' Lizzy—amid a host of other talents—is mistress of the superlative and I immediately fret that the posting ritual wasn't as emotionally extreme as specified.

'It was *quite* intense,' I say warily, 'but I was nervous about being caught by a grave warden.' I know Lizzy is about to reply 'A what?' and I can't be bothered to begin that conversation so I add swiftly, 'It was good. I feel much better *inside*, but also ill, if you see what I mean. Sore throat. Probably from the smoke. So I'm taking a few days off.'

The Blyton gene kicks in and Lizzy sighs, 'Oh, good for you! The pain is probably psychosomatic. Just relax and consolidate what you've achieved.'

I yawn and say, 'I plan to sleep.'

Lizzy, who's even more evangelical than usual, says, 'That's fine, but you mustn't sleep more than nine hours. If you do, and you're still lethargic, you could be lacking iron. And have you heard from Tom?'

I reply stiffly, 'No.' And then feel I should ask her, 'How's Brian?'

'We're no longer an item,' Lizzy says breezily, 'I ended it.'

'*What!*' I shout. 'Why? Was it something Brian did?'

'Sort of,' says Lizzy.

'Something offensive?' I suggest.

'Kind of,' says Lizzy.

My mind overruns with wild scenes of Tai chi orgies and punch-ups in the Gap over a last pair of dungarees. 'What on *earth* did he do?'

Lizzy pauses. 'You'll think I overreacted,' she says hesitantly.

'No, I won't,' I say. 'I promise.'

Lizzy falls for it and reveals that she dumped Brian—kind, generous, gentle Brian, who buys her figs and kisses her hand—because she was irritated by the sound of him eating. And I thought *I* was shallow.

Yesterday I returned to *Girltime*, paid my electricity bill, rang Nana Flo to check she was alive, took the work-experience girl for a coffee after Laetitia made her cry, asked the bank to extend my overdraft (it refused), bought bleach and Cling Film, attended a features meeting (suggested fifteen ideas to show up Laetitia), booked the Toyota in for a service (the garage was getting shirty), and thought, now I see why Dad always boomed, 'Schooldays are the happiest days of your life!'

I muse on how draining it is to be a grown-up, I take a large swig of espresso and feel calm. As if I've let something go.

Laetitia is safely engrossed in *Tatler* so I start fretting over the first-ever feature Laetitia has been coerced into commissioning me. She was most reluctant and reminded me of a spaniel I once saw being dragged into Tom's surgery on its bottom. Tina saw us exit the meeting and emailed me remarking that Morticia looked red in tooth and claw and was it because she'd missed her rabies injection? I replied, 'Rabies antidote rendered powerless by potency of subject's venom. Morticia irate because after years of meek submission the deodorant monitor has turned.'

Tina messaged back, 'Like it. But caged animals lash out, so go easy. Victim Support number here, if needed.'

Tina and I have a drink after work to, as she says, celebrate. I'm not so sure. Laetitia would rather publish a feature written by a spider monkey than anything composed by me, so my picture-byline is far from won. 'But since when did you care?' asks Tina.

I shrug. 'I need a raise. I'm sick of not being able to afford my lifestyle.'

Tina snorts, 'Well, one feature won't swing it!'

'Tina!' I squeak. 'I am being positive in the face of doom. You're not being helpful.'

Tina replies, 'Sorry. What I meant to say is, you go, girl! Keep at it and maybe in a year you'll get a raise that'll allow you to upgrade deodorant.'

I slump—bar stools are made for slumpers. 'How are you about

Adrian now?' I begin, but Tina shakes her head and crunches hard on an ice cube.

'Don't want to think about it,' she says.

I see the tension in her jaw and say hurriedly, 'Have you heard from Luke?'

This elicits a half-smile. 'I'm resisting,' she says. 'He's a doll but I need a break.'

I sigh and say, 'It must be great to be pursued, though.' Then I think about what I've just said and stammer, 'I mean, by a nice bloke.'

Tina gives me a playful kick which—from a steel-toed Prada shoe—feels about as playful as a kneecap.

'Ow,' I say, as Tina exclaims, '*You* were being pursued by a nice bloke. I don't get why you're not together. And you seem so laid back about it. Did you go off him?'

I think of Tom and feel a pang. I growl, 'No, I didn't go off him! I'm pining here! Haven't you noticed I'm off my Dime bars? The only reason I'm not whining on about it is that I've bored myself.'

'Bloody hell!' says Tina. 'I didn't realise! Why didn't you say?'

My bravado dissolves and I say sadly, 'There's no point. The look he gave me when Jasper said he was my live-in boyfriend. You wouldn't wish it on anyone, even Laetitia.'

Tina looks piqued. She says, 'But Jasper was only kipping on your floor! Have you rung Tom and explained?'

I sigh and say, 'I've agonised about calling him a million times. But there *is* no explanation.'

Tina clunks down her beer bottle so fast a small plop flies out. 'Yes, there is!' she cries.

'No, there *isn't*!' I exclaim. 'Whether we were shagging isn't the issue. It's that I'd invited Jass to stay at all.'

Tina frowns. 'But why?'

I say, 'It's to do with me needing Jasper there. It was stupid.'

Tina huffs, 'For Christ's sake!' she says. 'Tom's a sorted-out bloke. He'll forgive you one—'

I interrupt with, 'No, it's not that. It's not that. There were *multiple* mistakes. I know he's, ah, sorted out, but it's not that. It's to do with'—I pause to search for the correct word—'trust.' Tina falls silent. I say—feeling only a tad Mills & Boon—'It's not so much to do with him not being able to trust me. It's about me not being able to trust myself.'

Tina looks queasy and says, 'Stop it, you're churning me up.' But she means it kindly.

After she leaves I sit on the bar stool and wonder if I should phone

Tom. As a fantasy it's a kick. I imagine a tearful reunion, me flitting towards him across a buttercup field, my hair—blonde for the occasion?—streaming in the light breeze, the sun shining golden upon us, Tom lovestruck and smiling and tall, me not treading in a cow pat, and no ramblers. But if I made it reality the dream would crumble. Buttercups and breezes apart, I do not want to announce myself and be snubbed. But faint lady never won fair knight. Well, actually, she always won fair knight, but these days knights are lazier and ladies more proactive. At least, if I rang him, I'd know. I'll go home and phone him.

I sing 'La la!' to ensure my voice is working and flick to Tom's number in my address book. 'Come on!' I bleat to myself. I place the book on the sofa, and sit on its arm. Then I dial.

Brrrt-brrt! Brrrt-brrt! Brrrt-brrt! Brr—

'Hello?'

The phone is suddenly slidey in my hands.

'Hello, Tom?' I gasp.

'Who's this?'

I gulp and close my eyes. I've never sky-dived but this is what it must be like.

'Don't you remember?' I joke feebly. 'Me, Helen.'

Silence.

'Tom?' I whisper.

'Yes?' His voice is ice.

'It wasn't what you thought with Ja—' I begin. I can hear the sickening desperation in my own voice.

'I'm—' says Tom.

'*Please* listen!' I beg. Begging. Always works.

'Helen,' says Tom.

'Jasper and I weren't—' I say. He said my name. It's a start.

'*Helen*,' says Tom again.

'Yes?' I breathe, hoping.

'No,' says Tom.

'No, what?' I say in a small voice.

'Sorry,' says Tom.

'What?' I blurt. I think, he doesn't get it. I should be more specific.

'I—' begins Tom.

'I'd like to ask you out!' I exclaim.

Silence.

'Tom?' I whisper.

'Thanks,' says Tom. 'But you're too late.'

Clunk!

Ever since I emergency-baby-sat for the neighbours and their child bit me, I've firmly believed that no good deed goes unpunished. The sadistic truth is proven again and again.

And this afternoon I get my comeuppance for being civil to Vivienne. My mother rings me at work, as I polish my feature *How To Beat A Bully (When You're 24)*. Currently, it's 8,236 words long so it may need a slight edit. Laetitia is already muttering about lack of space in the issue.

'Darling?' says my mother in a voice I recognise as wheedling.

'Yes?' I say suspiciously.

'Darling, I have a favour to ask you. But it's a *fun* favour.'

My disbelief proves unwilling to suspend itself, but I say, 'Really?'

My mother launches into what is obviously a pre-prepared introduction: 'This Sunday Vivienne is having an afternoon tea.'

The words 'afternoon tea' explain my mother's tone. Vivienne's afternoon teas are legend. Vivienne adores giving afternoon teas. They provide her with an excuse to splurge on a new sequinned red dress. Her husband falls asleep in his salmon-pink leather armchair, presumably wiped out by the expense. Vivienne flirts with her current hunk of arm candy, thus providing every guest with sufficient gossip for the week. And she trawls the crowd for a young woman to marry her son.

This is where I and the afternoon tea connect. Not that Vivienne would dream in her worst nightmare of matching Jeremy with *me*—my mother once heard, via a friend of a mutual friend, that Vivienne considers me unsuitable for marriage as I'm too 'volatile'. This offended my mother but was fine by me, as I consider Jeremy unsuitable for marriage as he's too 'gay'. But Jeremy's mama refuses to twig, and I and the afternoon tea connect because even the volatile have friends.

'It's catered,' adds my mother, unnecessarily.

I sigh, 'Very nice. And what's the gimmick this time?'

Vivienne always insists on a superfluous element. Last year it was morris dancing and everyone under retirement age left early.

My mother says testily, 'It's not a gimmick. It's finger painting. *I* suggested it!' I am reflecting on what a sweetly typical and terrible idea this is when my mother gabbles, 'andshedloveitifyouandallyourfriendscamebecauseshelikeshavingyoungpeopleabout.'

This is such a brazen hussy of a lie I emit a derisive squeak before I can stop myself: 'Mum, you *know* that's not true! Vivienne loathes young people, they make her look old! Unless they're sleeping with her. The only reason we're invited is because she wants Jeremy off the shelf—even though he's having a perfectly nice time out of the closet.'

'Darling,' says my mother, 'Vivvy doesn't believe in all that. She has her heart set on a wedding. She was *very* helpful when you were looking for builders, wasn't she? And I was invaluable, you said so yourself!' Admittedly I did, and I belatedly realise that my praise will be held hostage until the seas run dry. 'And Vivvy has been very kind to me so it's the least we can do. And it'll be *nice* to go to a party, and I don't want to go by myself with all those married people saying "haven't you found anyone yet?" and I haven't seen Lizzy and Tina and Luke for ages and I don't want to be stuck with Nana Flo the *whole* time. So will you?'

I say, 'Yes, all right. It'll be nice to see Jeremy. I'll have to see what the others are doing though. I'll call you back.'

My mother says, 'It's OK, I'll call you.' When she says this I know that she wants us to attend Vivienne's afternoon tea very much indeed.

'Finger painting!' trills Lizzy. 'How creative! It sounds delightful! I *was* going to go have an extended session with my cranial osteopath but I can always reschedule.'

Tina says, 'Ooh, matron. *I* wouldn't.' Then Tina and I snigger at Lizzy's unamused face.

'Please come,' I say. 'I won't be forgiven if you don't.'

Lizzy chirps, 'I'm coming! I *love* this sort of thing!'

I reply, 'Actually I don't think you do,' but I say it in my head. Aloud, I exclaim, 'Lizzy, it'll be great. Tina?'

Tina wrinkles her nose.

'There's free food,' I say shamelessly.

'I'm not a student!' snaps Tina.

'Sorry,' I say quickly, then, 'Do it for me? For *meeeeee*? Oh go on, please? *Pleeeeeeze?* Pretty pleeee—'

'Oh bloody hell, all right!' shouts Tina. All that remains is for me to ask Luke. Here's how I predict the conversation will go:

Me: 'Hi, I'm calling to ask you to come to a tea party on Sunday hosted by a friend of my mother.'

Luke: 'Are you having a laugh?'

Me: 'Tina's coming.'

Luke: 'What's the address?'

When I do ring Luke, the conversation evolves as I expect. Which makes me all the more miserable that I didn't foresee Tom's new girlfriend before I rang *him*.

Naturally Tina and Lizzy have been supportive of me and dismissive of Tom. Not. Lizzy was 'disappointed' in him, but maybe he was going out with someone 'as a joke'. And Tina was even slower to condemn. I think she remembers how sweet Tom was after he'd booted in her door. She said, 'You broke his heart, Helen.' I was about to bristle when she added hurriedly, 'But he's still a prat.' The upshot is, I'm officially in mourning. This has one advantage—it entitles me to the fluffy treatment. I'm not that daft. If it wasn't for Tom, they wouldn't have accepted Vivienne's tea invitation in a million years.

Sunday dawns and Lizzy is the first to arrive, chic in a black cotton shift. 'It's washable in case I spill paint on myself,' she trills. 'It will be water-soluble, won't it?'

I say, 'Don't know, don't care.'

Tina turns up at 3.50, grizzling that north London is 'confusing'. At four o'clock, I ring Luke's mobile. He sounds flustered, and I can hear shrieky voices in the background. 'I got held up, I'm nearly with you!'

'And who's with *you*?' I reply.

Luke's voice soars proudly like an eagle in flight. 'Marcus and Michelle,' he sings. 'Michelle wanted to see you, she said you'd be pleased. I thought it would be a nice surpr—bollocks!'

I croak, 'Nice surprise! What, to see the landlord who turfed me out, and my ex-friend?'

Luke pauses then says, 'I can't say anything bad about them, they're with me.' At this, the shrieky voices get shriekier.

I shout, 'Serves you right!' and blip off the phone. Tina and Lizzy are consoling me when Luke's Fiesta judders to a halt outside the door.

Michelle spills from the Fiesta like a cloud of candy floss. 'Helen, honey, it's been yonks!' she cries, her hair and bosom bouncing in unison. 'Say, you're looking healthy, did you put on weight?'

I am trying to drum up a wittier riposte than 'possibly' when fast as a well-mannered bullet Lizzy blurts, 'Silly you—Helen's a slip of a thing!' and Tina chimes, 'But, Michelle, aren't you filling out! A bit of what you fancy and all that!'

Michelle's fluffy pink coat trembles as if it's about to explode and she snarls, 'I don't even *touch* what I fancy!'

Tina glances at Michelle's fiancé, who is standing behind his future wife as meek as a heavily sedated lamb, and croons, 'Poor Marcus!'

For the safety and sanity of all concerned, we proceed to Vivienne's in two cars. 'Oh, come *on*,' I shriek at the car in front, which is dawdling along at 40mph, 'it's like she's driving a hearse!'

'We're OK, aren't we?' says Tina.

'I said I'd meet my mother outside the house at four,' I bleat, 'she'll be incandescent.'

Sure enough, as we approach Arcadia I spy an irate leprechaun doing a war dance on the pavement. Closer up, the leprechaun morphs into my mother in dark green sweater and matching trousers. Nana Flo is sitting in the Peugeot chewing what appears to be the cud but is probably a mint. I wave and clamber out of the Toyota singing, 'Luke's fault!'

'Hurry *up*!' roars my mother, face flushed under a fierce layer of foundation. 'All the fishballs will be gone! Oh! Hello, Luke! Tina! Lizzy! And you two! Goody, everyone's here. Where's Tom?' My face and heart turn to stone and Michelle's ears flap like kippers in the breeze.

'He's cat-sitting Helen's cat,' says Tina.

'He's meditating,' says Lizzy.

'I ditched him,' I say.

'I thought he ditched *you*!' says Luke.

'He ditched you!' says Michelle. 'Gee, you must be devastated!'

The only dignified response is for me to laugh breezily, gesture towards Arcadia, pinch my nose and nasally intone, 'OK, guys, I'm going in.'

There is a collective gasp as Vivienne swings open the door, sausaged into a straining red dress.

'Wow, that dress looks tight,' says Luke in awe. Tina treads heavily on his foot.

'Your dress is to *die* for!' breathes Michelle. Vivienne recognises a kindred spirit and smiles broadly.

'Vivvy, there's lipstick on your teeth,' says my mother.

'Versace,' murmurs Tina. 'Six grand, easy.'

Nana Flo shuffles and says, 'Are we going to stand here all day? My legs are killing me.'

Chastened, Vivienne ushers us into her hallway where we are accosted by a pinafored waitress carrying a tray of champagne.

'Come into the garden, darlings'—gesturing to a bronzed creature with fluorescent teeth—'Zak will take your coats.'

'Do you have cranberry juice?' says Lizzy politely.

'Never,' replies Vivienne coolly.

'Vivienne is aiming to be the Raquel Welch of mothers-in-law,' I explain as we step into the garden, 'so you've just been ruled out as a potential wife for Jeremy. You're too picturesque.' I point out Jeremy, who is chatting to a waiter.

'Jeremy *is* dashing,' says Lizzy admiringly.

'Nice too,' I say glumly. Lizzy and I retreat to a shady corner and watch the spectacle.

Vivienne is brushing a piece of fluff off Zak's brawny arm—the piece of fluff totters angrily off on clicky heels to console herself with a vodka. Michelle and Marcus argue hissily by the trestle table. My mother flirts forcefully with Luke, who clings to Tina's sleeve like a nit clings to clean hair. Nana Flo eats a gargantuan wedge of lemon meringue then graduates to trifle.

'Shall we do some finger painting?' giggles Lizzy, after twenty minutes' captivating surveillance.

'Why not?' I sigh, and follow her to the huge blank canvas, propped towards the back of the garden at a safe distance from the conservatory.

Vivienne's party organiser has squirted a rainbow of paints into plastic basins and placed them in a neat row on the lawn. There is also a bucket of soapy water plus paper towels.

Lizzy gingerly dips a finger in red paint and, bang in the middle of the canvas, draws a heart. 'What fun!' she simpers. 'Go on, Helen! I can't be the only one!'

I look at Lizzy's heart and say, 'Tom used to paint.' Lizzy smiles sympathetically. I sigh deeply, dip a finger in the blue, and add a dagger to the heart.

'Oh, Helen!' says Lizzy crossly. 'Don't be destructive!'

I scowl and say, 'I thought being creative was about expressing your feelings.'

Lizzy dips both hands in the purple and prints an odd-looking butterfly above the heart.

'You two are crap!' says a cheerful voice. 'I'll show you how it's done.'

I roll my eyes at Luke—who is high with relief at escaping my mother—and say, 'Stand back for Leonardo, then.' Luke dips his right hand in the bowl of black and in huge sprawling letters, which cover at least half the canvas, writes 'Luke 4 Tina 4 Ever'.

I glance at Tina who covers her mouth with mock embarrassment. 'Luke,' she says, 'this isn't school.' But she smiles the luminous smile of a woman who knows she is adored. My throat constricts. And in a rush I think, 'Luke used to like *me*.' I look at Luke, who has swivelled round for applause. He has a black splodge of paint on his forehead. His shirt is rumpled and there is a dubious stain adjacent to his jean zip. I look at my favourite human labrador but he doesn't see me because he is blinking shyly at Tina. And the truth washes over me in an ice-cold ripple.

I love *Luke*.

Clasping my guilty secret and the *Daily Mail* to my chest, I shuffle into work on Monday hoping to avoid Tina. I'm not fit to breathe the same air. Happily, I learn that she's out of the office today, and that Lizzy is on a shoot. I sit at my desk like a Stepford employee and by lunchtime I've ruthlessly slashed my bullying feature to a miserly 1,200 words. That kind of thing is easier when you hate yourself.

I deposit a hard copy on Laetitia's desk and say tonelessly, 'I'll start my feature on *How To Get Ahead When Your Boss Hates You* this afternoon. Do you want anything from outside?'

Laetitia glowers at me and snaps, 'I'll get it myself, I'm not a cripple.'

I glance aghast at the editor, whose eight-year-old son has MS. Laetitia follows my gaze, sees the editor standing by the photocopier with folded arms, and blanches. *Hasta la vista*, baby, I think, wave at Laetitia, and walk out. She doesn't say a word. She's said enough already, I think coolly, as I step from the stuffy building into the cold air.

I wander around Covent Garden like—I fancy—a lost soul but more realistically, a lost tourist. After ten minutes of wandering I can no longer bear my own droopiness so I banish Luke from my head and walk briskly to Broadwick Street in Soho. I dash into the first art shop I see and start prowling. Aquamarine blue, deep violet and ivory black—the paint names are richly seductive but I know less than nothing about art and can't choose. Wistful watercolours or passionate oils? A vast expanse of canvas or a small sketchbook? I check the price of a large canvas and—forget passing out, I nearly pass on.

Less is more, I tell myself sternly—despite fervently believing that more is more—and reach for a small palette of paints and a square canvas. Then I race back to work. Laetitia is not at her desk, and doesn't reappear all afternoon, so I am excused from the usual errands and get a wodge of work done. At a conservative estimate, *How To Get Ahead When Your Boss Hates You* looks like romping home at 9,000 words. It is 6.02 and I'm wondering if I shouldn't stay late—6.10, perhaps?—to work on it, when the phone rings. 'Yes?' I say dully.

'Helen?' says my caller. 'You all right? You sound like an old woman.'

I feel joyful and irked all squashed into one big dizzy ball. 'Luke!' I exclaim. 'How are you?' Luke tells me he's fine. But he sounds as antsy as an ant in a pant. 'What is it?' I say.

'I need to see you,' says Luke. 'Urgently. Can we meet?'

The blood roars in my ears and I squeak, 'Yeah, sure, what, tonight?'

Luke says, 'I'll see you outside your office in fifteen.'

I tell him I'll see him then, and do a full three minutes of working late. Urgently. What does *that* mean? Luke has realised that I am The One and wants to profess his undying love? He wants to borrow a fiver? If his affections have reverted to me, he must feel dreadful about Tina.

Suddenly I remember I have a shiny face and unplucked eyebrows so I spend nine minutes performing emergency cosmetic surgery. At 6.17 I gallop into the street cursing and run smackbang into Luke. 'Whew!' he gasps. 'Check out the blusher! Wotcha Mr Punch!' Then he laughs (alone) at his hilarious joke. 'We'd better go to the Punch and Judy!' he continues. 'Ha ha!'

Am I really in love with this man? I wonder, confused. Tom wouldn't be so crass. Not that crass is *so* bad. And Tom does have the capacity to be crass. The ketchup trick wasn't exactly sophisticated. But then, Tom's crassness makes me laugh and want to kiss him whereas Luke's doesn't.

Luke and I descend into the bubbling Cityboy cauldron of Covent Garden's Punch & Judy and I am tongue-tied with confusion. Luke grins wickedly and says, 'I've got news for you that you're going to like.' Oh God. I *am* The One. He trots off to buy me a drink and there is a sick feeling in the pit of my throat.

I watch Luke jostling at the bar and picking at his backside (I assume his briefs have ridden up) and I think, no. I can't do this to Tina. Not now, not ever. There are some rules you don't break.

Luke waves a beer in front of my nose and sits down, still grinning like a maniac. You don't smile in London! As Luke sits, I leap up like a spring salmon whose bottom has just been groped by a trout and gabble, 'Luke, I know what you're going to say, but I think it's best I don't hear it. What you did for Tina at Vivienne's party was very sweet, if a little naff, and I'd hold out for her because I know she's keen, it's just that she needs time, all right, OK, bye!' As I flee the besuited crowds I glance back, once, at Luke and see he is still clutching the two beer bottles. The expression on his face is utter incomprehension.

But curiously, no trace of devastation.

I collapse into a cab, still clutching the box of paints I bought earlier. I hold the art-shop bag tightly and think, no Bud for me, thanks, just a bloody martyr on the rocks.

I've spurned Luke's advances about as elegantly as a ballerina in Wellington boots. I was an ego-shimmer away from betraying one of my closest friends. Well, at least everyone else will have a nice life. I feel a vicious urge to conpound my misery, so I redirect the cab driver.

'This is a surprise,' quavers Nana Flo, undoing the heavy chain on her flimsy door. 'And what can I do for you?' A rhetorical question.

'I didn't get a proper chance to talk to you at Vivienne's yesterday,' I shout over the television's volume, 'so I came to see you.' Nana Flo glances longingly at the screen and says she'll set the video. 'Shall I make tea?' I say, hoping she'll say no.

'The teapot's on the side,' says Nana. Her ankles click as she clutches the *TV Times* and kneels painfully on the carpet.

Five minutes on, Nana is sitting back in her recliner chair and I am perched like a paralysed parrot on the edge of her sofa.

But I know why I'm here. I want to talk to Nana about Grandpa and it can't wait. Maybe I'm a parasite who wants to soothe my pain by leeching off hers. Maybe understanding a fraction of her loss will diminish my own.

Understandably, Nana is surprised at my interest. She wants to know why I want to know. I tell her a vague but piquant tale about having lost the love of my life. (The tale is vague because I'm not sure if the love of my life is Tom or Luke but the cliché neatly covers both eventualities.) I suspect Nana doesn't believe me—the rolling snort is some indication—but at least it gets her talking.

Florence and Gerald met at a bus-stop. He told her he was a confirmed bachelor, then three days later gazed into her wide blue eyes and asked her to marry him. They were engaged for ten months as Florence's father wouldn't allow them to marry sooner—and went to Torquay for their honeymoon. 'There was barbed wire up, but I got through it and went in the water. I was so much in love, I was bouncing along,' says Nana, sipping her tea. The picture is so unlike her that I stare at her skinny, wizened face, trying to imagine my grandmother as a young woman so much in love that she was bouncing along. After Gerald died, she knew she'd never remarry.

I gulp. 'Why not, Nana?' I say, sniffling.

'He was such a wonderful husband, the short time I had him,' she replies. Then, dry-eyed, she looks straight at me, weeping on her sofa, and says softly, 'I couldn't replace him.'

Nana is sharper than I give her credit for. She knows I am crying half for me. 'So what's wrong with you?' she says, brusquely reverting to the Nana I know. Feeling ashamed in the presence of a woman who possesses the courage I lack, I tell her about Tom and I tell her about Luke. 'Luke?' she exclaims, her reedy voice so loud and incredulous that my china teacup clatters on its saucer. 'Nonsense! That long-haired fool! He's not for you! You're jealous, that's what you are! Oh, he's pleasant enough, but I know feckless when I see it!'

As a minicab ferries me home, I wonder why—even with a hundred and twenty quids' worth of new prescription lenses—I am always the last to see the obvious. Honestly. Talk about a prat.

There's a time in your life when you have to stop looking back and start looking forward, because otherwise you're going to walk down the road one day and bump into a lamppost. But it's not easy. When my father died I felt like the smooth carpet of my existence had been carefully positioned over a large hole. Until then I'd skipped carelessly around it, blind to its fateful presence. And one sly day I stepped on it and fell, down, down, like Alice in a merciless Wonderland, dragging precarious everything in my wake, all of it chaos, toppling, crashing, falling, wrecking all that I believed in and forcing me to start again at the beginning. How could I make sense of that lot if I *didn't* look back?

And when I looked I saw that grief is a murky pool of endless depth, and in a year of wallowing you might barely dip your toe in the water. Me, I was afraid of drowning. I learned to swim slowly and I'm still learning. Now I realise that sometimes it's only possible to go forward if you do look back. But not for ever. Talking to Nana Flo I realise how a person can be paralysed by their own past and stay bitter for a hundred years. So the evening after we speak, I decide to indulge in one last backward glance before plodding onwards like a little donkey. As opposed to a big ass.

I bolt home feeling sparky. Laetitia is still under a cloud and ostentatiously talking about opportunities elsewhere, and suddenly the office is less of a gulag. And tonight I have a date with Tom. Admittedly, he doesn't know about it but, as I don't want a bucket of scorn tipped on my head, I don't *want* him to know. I plan to come and go like the tooth fairy on a one-night stand. I wish him happiness and I need him to know it. But I can't quite bring myself to wish his girlfriend happiness. I try to be gracious in defeat but keep hoping she'll go bald.

I wait until dark. Then I tie my hair back, curl my eyelashes (he isn't going to see me, but I've made the 'I won't score tonight, I'll wear my grey period knickers' mistake once too often) and dress in black. I look like a young Italian widow. Not. Then I scamper to the car carrying the art bumf. I drive to Tom's road speedily enough to make all four tyres and one pedestrian squeal. As I approach I slow to a crawl and click off my headlights. (Which is such a thrill I decide that if I don't blossom at *Girltime* in the spring of Laetitia's inevitable resignation I shall retrain as a private investigator. I've read the books.)

I check that the street is deserted, then slide out of the car, shut the door gently, and tiptoe towards Tom's ground-floor flat. Warm yellow light spills from his windows although the curtains are tightly drawn. Holding my breath, I inch open the metal gate. It squeaks like a mouse at the mouse dentist. I wince, and creep up the garden path. The rabbit foot is hammering hard in my chest and I don't know if my face is damp with drizzle or sweat.

Softly, I prop the bag containing the paintbox and canvas against the side of Tom's green front door. I have stuck an envelope addressed to him on the bag. Should I ring his bell and do a runner? Leaving it for him to find by chance is risky—what if the postman's named Tom?

At this point, I wonder if I shouldn't have worn sensible shoes. A thought I dismiss instantly, as I regard sensible shoes on a par with bum bags. They mark you out as staid. I'm staid enough without advertising the fact. That said, sensible shoes are useful if and when you decide to climb on top of a metal bin to peer over the top of your ex-lover's curtains. I check the bin is stable, and clamber up, using the window frame as support. I crouch on the slippery surface and, wobbling like a jelly on a surfboard, attempt to stand.

The lid instantly collapses and I and the bin crash to the ground in a great cacophonous din that rings through Kentish Town loud enough for the neighbours to prosecute.

I lie stunned on the grass with a chicken carcass resting on my stomach and a stinky crush of eggshell in my hair for three dizzy seconds, before the front door swings open and Tom jumps out. I don't know what the protocol is when found trespassing and spying *and* coated in rubbish so I say 'Hi.' Tom stares at me like I'm naked and I am about to tell him it's rude to stare, when he exclaims, 'What *are* you doing?'

'A bin project, what does it look like?' I say crossly, moving my ankle to see if it's broken.

'Are you OK?' he says, stooping. He has a strange expression on his face and I can't tell if he's smiling. I nod. Tom removes the chicken carcass from my stomach and drop-kicks it across the lawn. It leaves a patch of grease and flecks of old skin on my black top. Well, thank heaven I curled my eyelashes. 'Why didn't you ring?' says Tom, crouching.

'I *did* ring,' I squeak indignantly. 'You told me to piss off!'

Tom looks embarrassed. He glances at his feet and stutters, 'No, I meant ring the door, just now.' My confusion must show because he blurts, 'Luke didn't tell you?'

'Tell me what?' I say, trying to wipe the rain off my glasses without smearing yolk in my eyes. I was hoping he'd notice the art bag but he's walked straight past it. Which means instead of him romantically discovering it and bursting into nostalgic tears, *I* am going to have to plonkily point it out to him and it'll be as awkward as sex in a bath.

'Tell me what?' I repeat, as Tom seems to have lost the power of speech.

He recovers it, abruptly, in a babble: 'I wanted to tell you, I was going to tell you but I didn't know how you'd react so I asked Luke yesterday and he said don't chance it, *he'd* tell you and then the fucker disappears and I didn't know if he'd told you and I couldn't get hold of him and I wanted to tell you myself and—'

'Tell me what?' I shout, screwing up my face and trying to recall Luke's exact words.

Tom picks a baked bean off my shoulder and says, 'So if you don't know, why are you here?' Here we go.

'I bought you a thing,' I mumble, 'it's by the door.'

Tom looks as startled as if I've just bopped him on the head with a wholemeal bap. He jumps up, sees the bag, and rips open the envelope containing the note. He reads aloud, '*It's about time you started painting again, love Helen.*' And to my dismay—although I knew this would happen and rue the day that Tom purchased a cheap bin—his mouth trembles and he blinks furiously. This makes me want to cry.

'Your nose is running,' I say sternly, trying to lighten the atmosphere, 'do you want to wipe it on my sleeve?' My binside manner obviously requires polish, because Tom covers his eyes with both hands and shakes his head. I look longingly at his square shoulders and tousled hair but decide it's best to wait this one out. Feeling like a gorilla, I pick chicken bits off my top and eggshell from my hair. Then I gently touch Tom on the arm and say, 'I didn't mean to upset you.'

Tom looks up and smiles in a way that thrills me. He says softly, 'You did a kind thing.' Even though the rest of me is as sodden as a British bank holiday, my throat feels parched suddenly. My God! You don't pick a baked bean off the shoulder of someone you despise *or* smile thrillingly at them (unless you roar past their Mini in your new Testarossa)—could it be that after months of banishment from the kingdom of love I am being ushered back to within its hallowed portals! I gulp and stare at Tom, willing him to speak. And he does.

He says: 'Helen, I wanted to talk to you about my girlfriend.'

The End.

The soppy grin taking shape on my face vanishes like a lemming off a cliff, and I scramble angrily to my feet. 'Thank you,' I hiss, 'but I don't want to know.'

Tom says, 'No, wait, Helen!' and tries to grab my arm but I shake him off and make for the gate and storm towards the Toyota. 'Helen, please!' shouts Tom, as I jiggle the key in the lock. Why do I bother? I *want* someone to steal this car, they'd be doing me a favour, I think miserably.

'Oh go *IN*!' I roar at the key. Tom catches up as I wrench open the door, which hits him on the knee. Good.

I slam the door.

'Helen!' he gasps, as I turn on the ignition. 'I made her up!'

What? I wind down the window.

'*What?*' I screech.

Tom assumes the expression of a puppy that has just weed on a sofa. He mumbles, 'I was going to tell you but I was embarrassed.'

'I would be,' I say sternly.

'Luke didn't blurt it out, then?' mumbles Tom.

'Certainly not,' I say, blushing.

Tom purses his lips and looks sorrowful. 'I was jealous,' he says, eyes lowered in penitence.

'Really,' I say primly.

'Of Jasper—' he says, wincing.

'Jasper—' I begin.

'I know that now,' says Tom.

I turn off the ignition.

'Thanks,' says Tom, 'I'm choking to death out here.'

I smile.

'I'm sorry,' says Tom.

I nod regally.

'Do you forgive me?' says Tom.

'Depends,' I say.

Tom squats so his face is level with mine.

'On what?' he whispers.

'On how many other lies you've told,' I say tartly.

'That's the only one!' he cries. 'I'm a very honest person!'

'Are you sure?' I say. 'This is important.'

Tom pauses. Then he says, 'When I was twenty, I um, used to tell women I was a navy diver. Does that count?'

'Should I stay or should I go,' I murmur.

Tom rests his arms on the Toyota's window frame.

Then he leans in and hugs me and drags me out through the window!

'The Dukes of Hazzard's lazy cousin,' I say, clinging on.

'You stink of old egg,' says Tom, tightening his grip.

'That's too honest,' I say, wriggling free.

I gaze at Tom, he gazes back, and we both blush.

In the silence that follows, I squeeze my hands into fists to give myself courage.

'Tom,' I say slowly, 'I never told you.'

'What did you never tell me?' he says softly.

'About my father,' I say. I smile tightly and nod, more to myself than Tom. 'You helped me,' I say. 'Really, you did.'

Tom looks stunned. 'What did *I* do?' he gasps. '*You* helped you.'

I bite my lip. 'All the same,' I say, 'you said things that helped.'

Tom says, 'I wanted to make it better. I knew I couldn't'—his voice cracks—'but I so wanted to. There was so much pain trying to get out.'

I wince. 'Better out than in,' I murmur.

'You,' says Tom, 'are stronger than you think.'

I shake my head. 'I couldn't face it,' I say falteringly. 'Not for a long time. Not brave at all.'

Tom looks straight at me and replies, 'Strong, I said. "Brave" is different. Overrated.'

He lifts a hand and strokes my face. Then he gestures to his front door. 'Helen, do you want to come in and, um, I'll make us some coffee?' he says finally.

'Yes. Yes, please,' I reply.

'How's your leg?' he asks.

'Not great,' I say.

'As a doctor,' says Tom suddenly, 'I don't think you should drive with a bad ankle.'

'Sorry, do I look like a Chinchilla?' I say.

But I smile as I say it.

ANNA MAXTED

Anna Maxted and I met in Bertorelli's, a favourite Italian haunt for many of London's writers and publishers. Over pasta and elegantly tossed green salad, we raised our glasses to toast the astounding success of Anna's first novel which has brought her instant fame and fortune. 'Getting it accepted in the first place was probably the greatest excitement of all,' she told me. 'I sent the first three chapters and a very in-depth plot synopsis to agent Jonny Geller and the next thing I knew I had a £350,000 two-book deal on the table. It was just incredible!'

The idea for the novel was sparked by the death of Anna's own father three years ago and she recalled how, when she wrote a feature for *Cosmopolitan*, it moved colleagues to tell her that 'You ought to write a novel about this!' 'Frankly, I never thought I was capable of writing a novel,' she told me. 'In a way it was cathartic, helping me to learn to live with my own father's death, but it was also a very emotional experience for me, as well as for my husband and my mother. What I've learned is that time does not heal. Time passes but you have to heal yourself, you have to be active in the process. You can't just bury the emotion or ignore it. Writing *Getting Over It* certainly helped me to heal.' Even though she was writing from personal experience, Anna still did plenty of research for the

novel. 'I interviewed bereavement counsellors and hospital doctors and psychologists and people who had also lost their fathers. I knew how I had felt but I wanted other people's viewpoints too.' Anna was determined that her heroine should grow and develop over the course of the novel. 'I didn't want the message of the book to be "Get a man and everything will be OK".' She also wanted to imbue her heroine with her own sense of humour, a great quality which became more and more apparent during our conversation.

Anna is currently writing her second novel, tentatively entitled *Silver Girl*. 'The heroine of *Silver Girl* works for a ballet company and so I have been hanging out with the English National Ballet Company on the pretext of research,' she told me. 'The truth is I love the ballet and like to go as often as I can!'

Anna is married to Phil, who is the creative director of an Internet TV station. 'We met, when we were both journalists, on a press trip to Milwaukee for Miller beer. Very romantic! I was particularly struck by him because he was so *rude* and I am—on the whole—*polite*. He was the antithesis of me, I guess.' They live in East Finchley, close to where Anna grew up. 'In fact, Phil is always teasing me saying, "you were born in Hampstead Garden Suburb, went to Cambridge for three years, then went back to Hampstead Garden Suburb. You've really travelled the world!"' While agreeing that she might not have travelled very far geographically, I reminded her that she had shot into the stratosphere as far as the publishing world was concerned. And, with great confidence, I once again raised my glass to her continued meteoric success.

Jane Eastgate

JOANNA TROLLOPE

MARRYING THE MISTRESS

'Your grandfather is proposing to leave your grandmother to whom he has been married for forty years and marry a woman with whom he has been having an affair for seven years,' Simon Stockdale tells his son Jack. What can this mean to a boy in the throes of his first love affair? And what of the mistress—a barrister who has fallen in love with a judge twice her age? And then, of course, there is the wife, cast aside, rejected but relentlessly manipulating her sons into taking her side against their father. Can this proposed marriage really go ahead in the face of all the conflicting expectations, obligations and duties?

CHAPTER ONE

'IT WOULD BE ADVISABLE,' the court official said to the security guard, 'just to keep the laddie up here for half an hour.'

They both looked along the courtroom waiting area at the defendant. He was smoking rapidly. He was also head and shoulders taller than the group of women clustered round him, like hens preening a cockerel, clucking and soothing and flattering.

The security guard rattled the bunch of keys chained to his belt. 'Trouble downstairs, then?'

'Not exactly trouble,' the court official said, 'but there's a few of the girl's friends and family waiting. Just waiting. Like they do.'

The security guard sighed. 'Wish he hadn't got bail. At least I'd know where he was then.'

The court official glanced again at the defendant. Good-looking chap, in a flashy, come-and-get-it-girls way. But not reliable-looking; not reliable, at least, where his stepdaughter had been concerned. 'He won't skip.'

'I'd still rather have him behind bars.'

A young woman went past, a briskly walking, black-clad young woman with reddish-brown hair tied back behind her head with a black ribbon. She nodded to the court official as she passed. 'Night,' she said.

The security guard watched her go. He'd been watching her all day in court, Miss Merrion Palmer, counsel for the prosecution, and admiring the way the tail of her wig sat so precisely above the tail of her natural hair. 'Nice legs,' he said.

The court official blew out a little breath and heaved at the slipping shoulders of his black gown. 'Oh,' he said, 'nice, all right.'

He glanced along the waiting area to right and left, then said, *sotto voce*, 'Know our judge?'

'Course I know the judge,' the security guard said.

The court official leaned closer. 'What's just gone past,' he said, his eyes fixed on the glazed door that led to the judges' corridor, 'is not just an advocate, any old lady advocate. What's gone past is His Honour's totty.'

Back in his room the other side of the glazed door, Judge Guy Stockdale took off his wig and hung it on its wooden stand. Both wig and stand had belonged to his father, as had the pocket watch in his waistcoat pocket, which he carried every day out of a superstitious apprehension that he might make a public fool of himself if he didn't.

He then took off his robe—purple, claret and black silk—and hung it on its hanger. Then he removed his black coat and put it over the back of a grey vinyl armchair and sat in the chair, leaning his head in his hands and putting the heels of his hands into his eye sockets.

'Would you like me to take off my wig?' he'd asked the girl-child witness over the courtroom's video link at ten thirty that morning. 'Would it be easier for you?'

She'd stared back at him, a clever little foxy face framed in a fake-fur coat collar. 'I don't mind,' she'd said. She hadn't seemed daunted. She hadn't seemed daunted by anything, all that day, except, occasionally, by the miserable intensity of remembering what she had felt, what had happened to her. 'You suit yourself.'

Oddly, he had rather wanted to take his wig off. He didn't usually. Usually, he was so conscious of being a representative of justice, rather than Guy Stockdale aged sixty-two, height six foot one, no need yet—impressively—for spectacles or false teeth, that he was happy to have his wig and gown remove him from the particular to the impersonal. But today had been different, because he had come, without particularly intending to, to a point when he had to implement a choice; he couldn't go on just looking at it and thinking about it and laying it carefully to one side to act upon some other day. This knowledge had made him look at the girl on the video link not just as an abused child—there were thirteen charges against her stepfather, six of indecent assault, five of unlawful sexual intercourse, two of rape—but as something of a fellow traveller in a world where things you wanted and needed began to conflict badly with the things you already, acceptably, had.

There was a light knock and the door opened. Penny Moss, a young clerk who had come to work at Stanborough Crown Court as a school-leaver, came in with a file. Guy took his hands away from his face and blinked at her. She took no notice of having found the Resident Judge with his head in his hands. She took no notice, ever, of anything except the immediate matter she had in hand at any given moment. She put the file down on the desk.

'It's Mr Weaverbrook of the animal sanctuary, Judge.'

Guy looked at the file. Mr Weaverbrook ran a so-called animal sanctuary as inadequate cover for dealing in stolen farm machinery. When required to come to court, he pleaded acute anxiety levels. His wife usually came instead and sat shaking in her seat, worn out with the effort of trying to divide her loyalty between Mr Weaverbrook and the need for law-abiding conduct. Guy felt pity and admiration for her.

'Do you want the case reserved to you, Judge?'

'Yes, Penny, I do.'

'And Mrs Mitchell and the order concerning her children?'

Guy shut his eyes again. Mrs Mitchell was a nymphomaniac with sado-masochistic tendencies, whose three children, all by different fathers, were being removed, with difficulty, from her nominal care.

'That, too, Penny. I'd like an earlier date for that case.'

'Judge—'

'Penny,' Guy said, 'I'm not delaying. I have the future of an eight-year-old to consider.'

Penny opened her mouth. She was going to say, as she always said when asked to do something she didn't want to do, 'Martin won't like it.' Martin was the court manager.

Guy stood up. 'Good night, Penny, and thank you.'

She picked up Mr Weaverbrook's file. He noticed that she wore, on her wedding finger, a band made of two little gold hands clasping one another. It looked vaguely Celtic.

'Night, Judge,' she said.

Outside, in the early spring dark, the court car park was bathed in a weird orange glow from the streetlights beyond its wall. Guy's car was one of only three left. The other two belonged to the two regular district judges who, like him, worked on until six most evenings, even though the courts rose at four thirty.

He opened one of the car's rear doors and put his work bag on the back seat. Then he climbed into the driving seat and turned the engine on. Then he turned it off again, and sat looking at the neat little red lights on the dashboard.

I do not, Guy thought, want to go home. I do not want to go home and confront the fact that I have finally decided and must now implement that decision. What I hate, he told himself, closing his eyes, is the inevitable infliction of pain. Whatever I do, I'll cause that, to myself as well as to everyone else. In fact I am already, have been for years. It's just that they haven't all known.

Merrion had looked at him—when she did infrequently look at him—very directly that day. She had never appeared in court before him until today, and he had thought, and said, that she never should. But she had accepted this case, and when it became plain that they two would be in public together professionally and for the first time, she'd said he wasn't to make anything of it. 'It's no big deal,' she said. 'A three-day trial and I won't even be staying in Stanborough. You know my feelings about Stanborough.'

He did. He knew her feelings about most things. It was one of the elements of her character that charmed him most, her directness, her candour, her capacity to see and describe things as they were, and not as she wished they were.

'You're married,' she'd said. 'You've been married for over thirty years. You've got two sons and you've got grandchildren. I'm young enough to be your daughter. I'm not married. I'm mad about you. *Mad*. We have a big, big problem and it's going to get bigger. No question.'

She'd been twenty-four when they met. That was almost seven years ago. He'd been taking an evening train up to London to have dinner with his son Simon, and there was a girl in his train compartment reading a book which was convulsing her with laughter. He could see that it was a battered old paperback of Lawrence Durrell's *Esprit de Corps*. He could also see that she had wonderful hair and long legs encased in narrow blue jeans. She wasn't pretty, in a conventional sense, but once he had started looking at her, he found he didn't much want to look anywhere else. So he stopped trying. He watched her steadily, smilingly, until she put the book upside-down on her knees and said, still laughing, 'I can't *help* it.'

He bought her a drink at Paddington Station. She'd been to see her mother in South Wales and was on her way back to London and work. She was pupil in a set of barrister's chambers specialising in family law.

He didn't tell her he was a judge. He didn't tell her anything much except his name, and roughly where he lived and why he was in London. Then he took her telephone number, put her in a taxi, and went to meet Simon. He ordered a bottle of champagne.

'What are we celebrating?' Simon demanded.

Guy raised his glass. 'It's purely medicinal.'

Almost seven years ago. Seven years of what the newspapers would call his double life—home with Laura and the house and the garden and the dogs, and away, with Merrion. Sometimes away was in London, sometimes in hotels, and sometimes abroad when he went to conferences, once—when they were desperate—it was a ten-minute meeting in the buffet on Reading Station.

'I'm your mistress,' she said.

'No,' he said, flinching a little, 'no, not that. My love—'

'Nope,' she said, 'sorry. Mistress it is. We sleep together, you pay for some things for me, I keep myself exclusively for you. That's a mistress.'

Guy turned the ignition key again. He'd heard that word again today in court. 'Did your stepfather,' the defending counsel asked the girl witness, 'ever refer to you as his mistress?'

'No,' she said. She licked her lips. 'He said, "We're lovers, we are." That's what he said. And then—' She paused.

'And then what, Carly?'

'He'd say, "You're better than your mum."'

'Better? In what way were you better?'

'At sex,' the girl said clearly.

Guy reversed his car out of its parking space, and drove slowly out into Stanborough's busy one-way system.

He'd glanced very briefly at the jury when the girl said that. They'd started the day, as most fresh juries did, looking reasonably alert and capable and then, as the time wore on, and the alleged facts of the case were spelt out in the baldest language imaginable, they had shrunk in their seats, their gazes fixing, their minds struggling to take in precisely what they were hearing.

'He liked it in the mornings before I went to school,' the girl said. 'When I had my uniform on. In the living room.'

'In the *living* room?'

'Yes. With the door open.'

'With the door *open*? While your mother and sister slept upstairs?'

'Oh yes, he liked the idea that Mum might catch us.'

A picture was emerging of an apparently commonplace three-bedroomed terraced house on an estate on the edge of Stanborough, in which a family lived, an equally apparently commonplace modern family of a woman and a man and the woman's two child daughters by a previous husband, where nothing was in fact what it seemed.

'He never touched Heather,' the girl said, sounding almost proud. 'She's younger than me, but he never touched her.'

'Why,' the defending counsel asked, 'did you let him touch you?'

She looked sulky, almost angry. 'He conned me.'

'Conned you?'

'He said, "You want periods, don't you? If you have sex, your periods will come." And they did. I wanted . . . wanted boys to like me. He said they would, if I let him. But they don't.'

The defending counsel leaned forward. 'If you knew you were being conned, why did you let him continue?'

There was a pause. The girl looked down and whispered something.

'Carly, the court cannot hear you.'

She took a breath and said tiredly but with a simultaneous small pride, 'He was like a god to me.'

A god. A forty-five-year-old man playing god to a besotted woman and her equally spellbound child. The terraced house, with its neat front garden and rather less neat back garden where the girls were allowed to keep pet rabbits in hutches, was, it seemed, less a family home than a cage for playing games in, improper, dangerous, cruel, degraded games. The jury had looked drained. Several of them looked as if they'd heard more than they'd bargained for, been faced with a raw reality they couldn't just switch off when they'd had enough. And this was only the first day.

But a god! That was what she had said, this fifteen-year-old child who had lived with her stepfather from the age of eight until a year ago, when she had finally told her mother what was happening. A god. You could, it seemed, go on about equality between the sexes until you were blue in the face, you could legislate, you could try to educate, but then along comes this bold, late-twentieth-century child talking quite simply and unselfconsciously about a man being like a god to her.

Guy wondered if he had ever seemed like a god to Laura, even in that first glory of love when the love object is truly something quite extraordinary. They had met at university, he reading law, she reading French and Spanish. They had both worked diligently—she because she was conscientious, he because he was ambitious—and had emerged with similar degrees. He had gone immediately to Bar School and she had applied to join the Foreign Office, failed, and taken a translating job with a firm of manufacturers who were developing their business in Europe. It was a dull job. Guy urged Laura not to take it.

'Try the BBC,' he said. 'Try the World Service. Try publishing.'

'I can't,' she said. 'If one of us doesn't make some money, we can't get married.'

'We *can*. We don't need money to get *married*. And if we do, I'll borrow it. I don't mind borrowing until I'm earning. But you can't do something your heart's not in.'

'I can,' she said. 'I don't mind.'

But she did. She didn't say anything, but her attitude, her moods, even her walk indicated that she felt she was drudging, that she wasn't allowing her brain to race ahead of her, as his was doing.

'Are you resentful?' he said, every so often.

And she'd look at him, with that clear hazel gaze that appeared to display such transparency of mind and heart. 'No,' she said.

He used to take her shoulders, give her a little shake. 'Can I believe you?'

'Yes,' she said.

So he did. Or, at least, he lived as if he did. He read as assiduously for the Bar as he had read for his law degree, and every so often he asked Laura to change her job, to find a more congenial one. 'I'm going to be earning soon. In two years' time, all things being equal, I'm going to be earning reasonably and I'll go on to earn well.'

'I can't believe anything,' Laura said, 'until it happens.'

That was not, he thought now, the sort of thing you said to a god. Laura's anxious practicality was not likely, ever, to find itself swept away by the presence of superhuman possibilities. Not as a young woman; certainly not now. Now! Well, how to think about that without a clutch of dread, of panic? Impossible. Laura was sixty-one. A nice-looking, well-kept, largely unassuming woman with the same clear hazel eyes but set, somehow, in a different context. Indeed, the way Laura's still-young eyes looked out of her much older face was a metaphor for the way things had changed place, moved round in the last seven years: since meeting Merrion the whole landscape in which Laura lived in relation to Guy seemed different. It was like walking very slowly away from something you knew very well, something you could visualise minutely when you were parted from it, and, as you moved away, that something shrank against its background and lost solidity, lost significance.

Guy cleared the last of Stanborough's raw, newish suburbs and turned down a minor road towards open country. Five miles, and then, across a curve in the road, he would see the lights glowing along the façade of his house and the twisted bare black outlines of the apple trees in the little orchard in front of it.

They'd bought the house thirty years ago, when Simon was eight and Alan was five. It had been three run-down cottages, sitting in a muddy welter of disused sheds and pigsties. But there was the orchard, and a village with a church and a pub, and there were good rail connections to London from Stanborough, ten miles away. And, in any case, Laura wanted it. She had finally given up her job when she became pregnant with Simon and, presumably because Guy was now earning, she didn't mention getting another one after he was born. She became a conscientious mother just as she had been a conscientious student. From the tiny terraced house in Battersea, Laura took him out to Battersea Park every day, and played with him. She cut out letters and taught him to read when he was four. She fed him bread she had baked herself and rationed his hours of television—he saw enough to enable him to fit in at school, but not enough to prevent him using his own imagination.

When Alan came along, three years later, he joined in this earnest and busy enterprise.

'Is this what you like?' Guy said to Laura, intending to be supportive whatever her reply. 'Is motherhood enough for you?'

'For now,' she said, not looking at him. She was pulling a tangle of coloured clothes out of the tumble drier. 'But will it always be like this?'

'Like what?' He crouched down on the little kitchen floor beside her.

'You working all the hours there are, most weekends, lever-arch files even in bed—'

'Not if I become a judge.'

'A judge!'

'I can't even think about it for fifteen or twenty years. But if that's what you'd like—'

She got to her feet. 'It's not my choice.'

'Laura, it is. It's as much your choice as it's mine.'

She'd looked down at him, holding the plastic laundry basket of clothes on her hip, biting slightly at her lower lip. 'I didn't quite visualise this.'

He stood, too. 'What?'

'Well, when I was working and you were still a student, I didn't think we'd—well, we'd get so *uneven*.'

'But we needn't be. You could go back to work.'

She rumpled some of the clothes in the basket with her free hand. 'Could we move to the country?' she said.

'Would that help?'

She gave him her clear, open look. 'Yes,' she said.

Even then, even temporarily relieved by a seeming solution, he began to be haunted by a feeling that it was possibly the worst thing they could do, that the hours he would have to travel would be added to the hours he would have to work, that a separateness would happen, that their priorities would cease to be united.

'Are you sure?' he said over and over.

'Yes,' she said, 'I want to be somewhere where I can make my own life. And I want the boys to have a garden.'

'You won't be lonely?'

She took a little breath, and he had an uneasy feeling that she'd been about to say, 'I'm lonely now,' but had decided against it.

'Look,' he'd said, with some energy, 'I can't give up the Bar because it's all I'm trained to do and I'm good at it, but I'll do anything else you want, anything. Move house, move to the country, have another baby, anything.'

She put her arms round his neck. 'I'd like to go to the country. To be somewhere where I'm visible. To myself as well as everyone else.'

'But if you wanted to work again—?'

'I won't,' she said.

But she had. Two years into the restoration of Hill Cottage, and she had. It was then that Guy had begun to see that Laura was feeling, however much she battled against it, that she had paid too high a personal price in marrying him.

And now. Now what was he about to do? He turned into the drive and felt the tyres crunch into the stones of the gravel.

'I feel like a slapper now,' the girl on the video link had said that day. 'I feel dirty. I feel naive and stupid.'

Guy let the car coast quietly to a halt outside the back door. That's how I feel, he thought. Dirty. Naive and stupid and dirty. He opened the driver's door and climbed out, a little stiffly, onto the gravel.

CHAPTER TWO

MERRION PALMER'S FATHER had died when she was three. He was an engineer, working for a construction company in South Wales, and had come home one day complaining of a violent headache and a curiously stiff neck. Within six days he was dead, of meningitis. Merrion was never sure whether she could really remember him, or whether she had absorbed all the photographs of him, and all the things her mother told her about him until they had combined to make something so close to memory she could hardly tell the difference.

She looked like him, that was for sure. He'd been tall, long-legged and square-shouldered, with thick dark hair and a face that relied upon personality rather than regularity for its charm. He had enough energy to fuel a rocket, her mother said. And he was funny, she'd said, he'd had a keen sense of the ridiculous. By her bed, when she was a child, Merrion kept a photograph of herself and her father. She was about two, dressed in a red sundress spotted in white, and she was sitting on his knee, very solemn, looking at the camera. Her father was looking at the camera solemnly, too, and he was wearing the tiny sunhat that matched Merrion's dress. It looked like a coin balanced on a grapefruit.

After he died, Merrion's mother married again, very quickly. She married her husband's best friend, who left his wife for the purpose, and took Merrion and her mother to live in France. He was a property dealer, in a small way, and he brokered deals between French farmers wanting to sell off cottages and barns, and English people wanting to buy them as second homes. Merrion remembered moving a lot, a succession of flats and small hotels and rooms in farmhouses where, more often than not, she slept in a bed in the same room as her mother and stepfather. She remembered the smell of French bathrooms and churches, black cherry jam and old men in caps playing boules on a sandy triangle under some pine trees in one of the little towns they ended up in. She also remembered the muttering. Her mother and stepfather muttered at each other all the time, in the car, in bed, across tables at meals. It grew louder, the muttering, as time went on, and then one day Merrion's mother announced that it was time for Merrion to go to school, and took her back to South Wales.

She only saw her stepfather once, after that. He came to the little house her mother was renting in Cowbridge and gave her a monster bar of Toblerone chocolate. Her mother took the chocolate away and sent Merrion out into the garden. When, after what seemed an eternity, she came out to find Merrion, she looked dazed, as if she'd been smacked in the face. She picked Merrion up. 'I should never have done it,' her mother said, and burst into tears.

It was quieter after that, but duller. Merrion's mother became a secretary at a solicitor's office in Cardiff, and Merrion's grandmother sold her house in Llanelli to come and live with them and help look after Merrion. For a few years, Merrion's mother talked nonstop about Merrion's father, as if by so doing she could somehow obliterate the episode in France, but then everything settled and Merrion allowed the memory of her stepfather—an eager, angular man—to be assimilated into the myth-memory of her father. Men were there, it seemed, and then they weren't, and when they weren't, you got on without them.

It wasn't until she was about twelve that she began to notice the men in her schoolfriends' lives. There were fathers and stepfathers and brothers—the latter mostly discountable on grounds of age, lack of hygiene, and gormlessness. They lent, Merrion noticed, a different flavour to home atmospheres; there was more energy and noise, more adventurousness, more food, more danger. A house with men in it had a definite excitement to it. Merrion watched girls at school who had men at home, and wondered if anyone could tell, by just looking at them, that they had something she didn't have. She put the sundress photograph away and found others of her father and herself, less goofy ones, and one taken of her father on his graduation day from college, with tidy hair and polished shoes. She spent a long time looking intently at this picture, as if something might emerge from it and influence her, affect the way she and her mother and her grandmother lived.

When her mother went out on infrequent dates, Merrion grew hopeful. 'Did you like him? Are you going out with him again?'

'Yes, but nothing'll come of it. Don't worry. I've learned my lesson.'

'Doesn't she want to get married again?' she asked her grandmother.

Her grandmother was doing the crossword. She'd done the same crossword in the same newspaper for forty years, at roughly the same time in the morning, and grew restive if something prevented her. 'No, I don't think so. The last episode wasn't very encouraging.'

'You mean with Ray in France?'

'Yes.'

'She could do better than Ray,' Merrion said. 'Ray was creepy.'

'Creeps put you off, though,' her grandmother said.

Merrion twiddled the ladybird clips that held her hair off her face. 'I'm the only one in the class with a dead father.'

'But not in the school.'

'There are twelve hundred people in the school. I don't know them. I know my class.'

Her grandmother concentrated for a moment and wrote something down in the newspaper. 'You'll feel better,' she said unhelpfully, 'when you're married.'

By fourteen, Merrion's father-preoccupation had become a marriage-preoccupation. She always looked at people's left hands, particularly women's, and if the gold band was absent would scan their faces to see if something else was missing, too, if singleness showed visibly, as she had once wondered if fatherlessness did. Just after her fifteenth birthday, Merrion's mother became engaged, to a local cabinet maker who had also lost his wife, and then disengaged herself almost immediately.

'But *why*?' Merrion said.

'I daren't risk it—'

'But you wouldn't have been risking anything! He's *OK*.'

'It wasn't him that was the risk,' her mother said. 'It was me.'

When Merrion was sixteen, her grandmother died, very trimly in her sleep, of a heart attack. She had left them everything she possessed, including the modest proceeds from the sale of the house in Llanelli, ten years previously, and Merrion had the idea, quite suddenly, that they should move from Cowbridge into Cardiff and buy a flat.

'But you'd have to change schools in the middle of your A levels—'

'I'll catch up.'

'And all your friends. And my friends—'

'We'll make new ones. You'll be nearer work. I can go wild.'

'Will you?'

'Probably not. But I'd like to have the opportunity. Mum, I can't just stay here always. I can't. I'm like a hamster on a wheel.'

They bought a two-bedroom flat—most reluctantly on Merrion's mother's part—in a seventies block with a view of a narrow public garden on one side and the back of an old industrial building on the other. Merrion discovered clothes shops, bookshops, music shops, boys, clubs, libraries and ice skating. Her mother crept to and from her office and wished herself hourly back in Cowbridge where the postman knew her by name and Saturday-night drunks didn't career under her window howling obscene rugger songs. They began to bicker. Merrion did better and better academically, grew her hair and had a butterfly tattooed on her ankle. Her mother could only see the wild hair and the butterfly. When Merrion's A-level results were published, and she was discovered to have gained three A grades, she went out to celebrate with schoolfriends and didn't come home until six in the morning.

They had the first violent row of their lives. They stood in the narrow kitchen and screamed abuse at each other, about loyalty and disloyalty, about courage and cowardice, about love and possessiveness, about Merrion's father and Ray and France, about lack of proper priorities. Merrion was exhausted from a night of revelling: her mother equally so from a night of anxiety. After an hour or so, Merrion flung herself out of the kitchen and into her chaotic bedroom, stuffed a few clothes into a rucksack and slammed out of the flat.

She had ninety-seven pounds in a Post Office savings account. She bought a train ticket to Bristol, and from Templemeads Station she called the brother of a schoolfriend who was at the university in Bristol, who offered her the use of a sofa in the student flat he shared with four others. For five nights, she slept in a chaos of old newspapers, unemptied ashtrays and smeared glasses, fighting off both the advances of two of the flat's inmates and the impulse to call home.

On the sixth day, she walked into a hairdresser on a whim and had all her hair cut off, and then she returned to the flat, emptied the ashtrays, washed up the glasses, stacked the newspapers and left two bottles of Chilean chardonnay in the kitchen with a note reading: *Thanks a million. All the best. M.* Then she went back to Templemeads Station and—not without a longing glance at the London timetable—bought a ticket to Cardiff. When her mother came in from work, Merrion was sitting at the table in the sitting room filling in a university acceptance form.

'I'm going to study law,' she said. 'I've got the right grades and they've said they'll have me.'

She waited for her mother to start screaming again. It was a long wait, minutes at least, and then her mother went past her into the kitchen, saying as she went, 'You are just *exactly* like your father,' and then, seconds later, 'pity about your hair.'

When Merrion went to university, her mother sold the Cardiff flat and went back to Cowbridge, buying a house in the street that ran parallel to the one Merrion had grown up in, and re-creating the interior of the first house as precisely as she could.

During Merrion's three years at university, a courteous gulf grew between the two of them. Her mother was proud of Merrion's academic prowess and resolute in her refusal to know anything of her wayward social life. Love affairs, bursts of intimacy with other girls, expeditions, adventures and experiments of one kind or another all had, Merrion discovered, to be compressed and edited into phrases incapable of causing anxiety or upset. Where had the woman of her childhood gone, the woman prepared to defy the respectability of her upbringing and the outrage consequent upon taking another woman's husband, and skip to France with her four-year-old child? Or had that woman taken a whole lifetime's supply of daring and enterprise and left no energy behind her, nothing but a husk of apprehensiveness and profound conformity? Whatever it was, and however much sympathy she might feel for it, Merrion knew that was not the way for her.

She obtained a good second-class degree at the end of her time at university, and moved to London, to enrol herself at Bar School. She shared a flat in Stockwell, financed by a loan from the bank—borrowing from her mother would have produced sleepless nights in Cowbridge—and, at the age of twenty-three, was called to the Bar in an august ceremony presided over by a judge. Her mother came up from Cowbridge for the occasion and seemed only anxious that she would somehow disgrace Merrion by saying or doing the wrong thing.

Only when Merrion was saying goodbye to her at the station did she suddenly relax and manage to say with real warmth. 'Oh, your father would have been so proud of you!'

And Merrion, standing looking at her mother, had found herself consumed with a fierce longing, a longing she had not felt for years and years, to have had him there.

She found herself a place as a pupil in a set of barrister's chambers specialising in family law. She worked extremely hard, started a relationship with another pupil in an adjoining set of chambers—he, too, had a widowed mother who only liked to count the sunny hours—and once every four or six weeks took the Friday-night train westwards to Wales, to see her mother.

It was on one of those journeys, a return journey to London, that she had met Guy. She had been rummaging, during the visit, in her mother's attic, and had come across a box of her father's possessions, a box of sports-team photographs, small silver-plated athletics cups and medals, a Swiss Army knife and some books with his name—Ed Palmer—written on the flyleaf. Ed Palmer, 1964. Ed Palmer, 1966. There were a couple of Raymond Chandler novels, and a motorbike manual, and a book by Len Deighton. Then there was a small, slender book in a stiff mauve paper cover. It was called *Esprit de Corps*, by Lawrence Durrell. It had a different look to the other books, and Merrion took it downstairs.

'Oh that,' her mother said, glancing at it. 'It always made him laugh. I could never see why. You take it. See if it makes you laugh, too.'

Merrion threw it in her bag and forgot it until she was on the train. When she remembered it, and retrieved it from under her sponge bag, she spent a long time looking at the flyleaf and the name written on it, and imagining her father's hand moving over the page, writing it. If he'd been alive, he'd have been fifty-four now. She looked round the carriage to see how many men of about fifty-four she could see. There were none.

She opened the book. It was stories, she discovered, absurd stories of imaginary diplomatic missions and episodes in the fifties. It was written in a stately and dignified manner and the accounts were ludicrous, farcical. The effect on Merrion was exactly as it had been on her father. She reached the description of two spinster sisters editing a newspaper in Cairo, and being compelled, owing to faulty typesetting machines, to write their copy on the Suez Crisis of 1956 omitting all 'c's including in the often-used phrase 'Canal Zone', and collapsed laughing.

Despite collapsing, she was very aware, at Stanborough Station, of Guy entering her compartment. The rest of the passengers were fairly nondescript and dressed with great attention to comfort. Guy was not only tall and personable, with a thick head of greying tawny hair, but he held himself well and was dressed in a dark blue, faintly chalk-striped suit that looked, in present company, as startling a contrast as a moonsuit.

Guy did not sit opposite her. He sat diagonally to her, across the aisle, and took out a newspaper. He read the newspaper with the sort of concentration Merrion had learned to associate with men who want to detach themselves from their surroundings. Round the cover of her book, held up close to her face, she examined his hair and his skin and his clothes and his hands and his shoes. It looked, as far as she could see, as if he might be in his fifties. Mid-fifties maybe. The age, perhaps, that Ed Palmer might have been if he hadn't caught meningitis. Then, with a huge effort, Merrion went back to her book.

When she glanced up again, he was watching her. He was watching her, quite openly, with interest and amusement. She returned to her book. She couldn't read it. She began to feel giggles surging up inside her, caused partly by the mood the book had induced and partly by excitement. When she glanced his way again, their eyes met. She felt obliged to say something. So she said, by way of explanation and gesturing at the book on her knee, 'I can't *help* it.'

'I know,' he said, 'I can see. That's what I like.'

He had what she would have called at school a posh voice. Hers was Welsh, not as Welsh as it had been when she was small, but it was still Welsh, particularly if she got agitated, when her voice rose dramatically at the end of sentences.

'Have you read his other books?' Guy said.

'Lord no,' she said, 'I've never even heard of him. I just found this in my mum's attic.'

When they reached Paddington, he lifted her bag down from the luggage rack and said, still holding it, 'Would you have a drink with me?'

She stared up at him, much surprised.

'Will you? Just fifteen minutes?'

She struggled to her feet, not very gracefully. 'Do you do this often?'

'No,' he said, 'I've never done it in my life before. In fact, I shouldn't think I've had a drink alone with a woman who wasn't a colleague for over thirty years.'

He bought her a glass of red wine in the station hotel.

She looked at his suit. 'Why weren't you in first class?'

'I'm not on business. Anyway, I prefer the company in standard class. Look at you.'

He drank whisky and water. She looked at the way his shirt collar sat, at the knot of his tie. She thought: I don't just want fifteen minutes.

He said, 'My name is Guy Stockdale.'

'Mine's Merrion,' she said. She sounded very Welsh to herself when she said it. 'Are you married?'

'Yes.'

'Silly question.'

'No. Necessary one. But you aren't.'

'No.'

He turned to look at her. He said with emphasis, 'I'm thankful for that.'

He insisted on getting her a taxi, and on giving the driver a ten-pound note.

'I don't want you to pay for me!'

'Give it back to me when we meet.' He was standing stooped in the doorway of the taxi cab so that he could see her.

'Are we going to?' she said.

'Yes. Very soon. If that's what you would like, too.'

She crossed the fingers of both hands and shoved them in her jacket pockets. 'OK,' she said.

It was almost two months before she went back to Wales. When she did she felt that she was, compared to the last visit, a completely different person, a person transformed, a person who had become—or was becoming—what she had always believed she could become, but had never known how. She wondered if her mother would notice.

'You look well,' her mother said. 'I like your hair tied back.'

'I have to do that,' Merrion said, 'in court. Sometimes I put it in a pigtail, one of those French plait things.' She sat down at the kitchen table. It was covered with a plastic cloth with neat bunches of flowers confined inside arithmetical squares.

'How's work going?'

'It's good,' Merrion said. 'I've got a chance of a tenancy in a set of chambers I really want to be in. They can't say so, but they've given me to understand that they want a girl. For abduction work, people taking their children across international frontiers against the wishes of another parent, that sort of thing.'

Her mother put a mug of coffee down in front of her. 'So sad. All those poor children.'

'Yes. But better to have someone like me trying to help sort out their lives than not.'

Merrion's mother sighed.

'Don't say things used to be easier, Mum,' Merrion said, 'because they weren't.'

Merrion's mother sat down opposite her. 'You look so well—'

'I am.'

Her mother took a spoonful of sugar and stirred it into her own mug. 'Can I guess?'

'I expect so.'

'A boyfriend?'

'A man,' Merrion said and her mother looked up.

'Why do you say that?'

'Mum, you're not going to like this—'

'He's married,' her mother said.

'Yes. And he's about your age, and he has sons a bit older than me, and three grandchildren, and he's a judge.'

Merrion's mother laid the spoon down on the plastic tablecloth with great precision. 'What are you *doing*, Merrion?'

'I'm in love,' she said.

'Where will it lead?' her mother said. She gestured wildly. 'What can possibly come of it?'

'I don't know,' Merrion said. 'I've only known him two months. I haven't seen him more than six times.'

'Oh,' her mother said. She brought her hands down flat and hard on the table. 'It's so *unsuitable*. Why are you throwing yourself away like this?'

'It's happened,' Merrion said. 'And I wouldn't stop it for the world.'

'But think of the pain you'll cause! His poor wife. His sons. What'll his sons say?'

Merrion took a swallow of her coffee. 'I don't know.'

'When I've wished things for you,' her mother said, 'and I've wished for a lot of things for you, I'd have wished for *anything* but this.'

'I didn't wish it. It happened. I wasn't looking for it. It happened. And now it's happened, it scares me to think it might not have happened.'

Merrion's mother got up. She went over to the sink and held on to the edge of it and stared out of the window at the bird feeder where three blue tits were hanging upside-down and helping themselves to peanuts.

'I don't want you to make a mess of things. Like I did.'

'Dad dying wasn't a mess. That wasn't your fault.'

'But after. After Dad died. That was a mess. I never could seem to get the hang of things again. I want you to have a future. I don't want you to get to my age and not have a *future*.'

Merrion got up, too, and went to stand by her mother. 'What's a future, Mum?'

Her mother said, almost angrily, staring at the blue tits jostling each other for the best position, 'A good relationship. A good companionship. Children. Grandchildren. Knowing you're leaving something behind you, knowing you've done what we're here to do.' She looked at Merrion. There were tears in her eyes. 'All the things in fact that this man of yours has got. He's got it all, and now he wants more. He wants extra. But you're the one who's got to pay for that extra.'

'I want him, Mum,' Merrion said.

'He's your father's age—'

'Yes. I expect that has everything to do with it. I'm not hiding from anything. It's very complicated and it'll get worse. But I've never felt like this about anybody, not remotely, not ever, in my whole life. He's called—'

'Don't tell me. I don't want to know any more about him.'

Merrion said, on a rising note of anger, 'How will that help?'

Her mother put her hands over her eyes. 'If I don't believe, maybe in time you'll see that you can't believe either.'

'And if you're wrong? If it turns out to be the real thing?'

'I'll cross that bridge when I come to it,' her mother said.

CHAPTER THREE

'TURN THAT *DOWN*!' Carrie Stockdale screamed up the stairs.

For several seconds nothing happened, and then a door opened onto the landing, releasing a yet more deafening blast of music, and a girl of about fourteen peered down.

'What?' she said sweetly.

'Turn that music *down*!'

Rachel shook her head and smiled. 'Can't hear you,' she mouthed.

Carrie started up the stairs. Rachel straightened up and removed the smile. 'OK, OK—'

'I have told you and *told* you. No music until you have finished your homework and no music *ever* that is antisocial in either type or volume.'

Rachel leaned back against the landing banisters as Carrie pushed past her daughter into her bedroom. It was quite dark apart from the greenish glow from the CD player and a small spotlight lamp on Rachel's desk. Rachel's books were open, neatly arranged and looked entirely unattended to.

'Mum,' Rachel said, suddenly loud, 'don't you touch anything. You touch *one thing*—'

Carrie stooped behind the CD player and pulled the electric plug out of the socket in the wall.

'How *dare* you,' Rachel hissed.

Carrie stood up. The silence seemed almost as loud as the music had been. 'Very easily,' she said.

Rachel wailed, 'I can't work if it's quiet!'

'You'll have to learn.'

'I'll get headphones,' Rachel said. 'Jack has headphones. Then I can have it as loud as I like.'

'Rachel,' Carrie said, going over to her desk and peering at the open books, 'try not to be so infantile. Is this your maths?'

'I hate it—'

'I'm sure you do. I used to hate it, too. You won't have to do it after the exams except if you fail.'

'Sadist,' Rachel said. She kicked a cushion lying on the floor. 'You really enjoy giving me a hard time.'

'Oh, I love it,' Carrie said. 'I'd no idea what fun being the mother of three adolescents was going to be. I'd no conception of how I was going to enjoy myself living with three perfectly intelligent people who choose to behave as if they were entirely subhuman.'

'OK, OK,' Rachel said again. She sidled past her mother and sat down in front of her maths books. 'Keep your hair on.'

Downstairs, the front door slammed and someone threw a rattling bunch of keys onto a hard surface.

'There's Dad,' Rachel said. She sounded relieved. 'You can go and take a pop at him now, can't you?'

Simon Stockdale, still in his crumpled mackintosh over a business suit, was in the kitchen riffling irritably through his mail.

'Hi,' Carrie said.

She went across the room and kissed his cheek. He made a simultaneous kissing sound, but didn't turn towards her.

She said, 'I was upstairs, yelling at Rachel.'

'Music?'

'If you can call it that.'

Simon took off his raincoat and dropped it over a chair back. 'When the kids were little,' he said, 'they'd come rushing downstairs to meet me when I came home. Remember?'

Carrie pulled a chair out from the table and sat down. 'That wouldn't be cool, now.'

He looked at her for the first time. 'Did we have them too early?'

She yawned. 'Yes.'

'You got pregnant though.'

'Hardly by myself. Are you suggesting we wouldn't be married if I hadn't been pregnant with Jack?'

'No,' Simon said. He rubbed his hands over his face. 'But here we are, not yet forty, and all we've done is work and have the kids.'

'Simon,' Carrie said, 'what is the *matter*?'

'Would you like a drink?'

'Not really.'

'Sure? I've got something to tell you.'

She sighed. She spread her hands out on the kitchen table and noticed that her nails and cuticles definitely needed attention. 'OK then. You're leaving me.'

Simon went over to a cupboard on the far side of the room and took out two wineglasses. Carrie looked at him. His shirt had come untucked from his trousers and a tail of blue cotton hung below his suit jacket. He had a good figure, like his father's, and his mother's dark hair.

'Nope,' Simon said, 'but close.'

Carrie sat up. 'Close!'

Simon put the glasses down on the table and retrieved a half-empty bottle of wine from the refrigerator. 'Mum called me in the office,' he said. He poured the wine. His hand, Carrie noticed, was not at all steady. 'Dad's leaving her.'

'Oh my *God*,' Carrie said. She put her hands over her face. From behind them she said, 'Say that again. Slowly.'

Simon pushed one glass of wine across the table towards her and sat down in a chair opposite. He said flatly, 'My father is leaving my mother. He has been having an affair for seven years and now he wants out.'

'Simon,' Carrie said from behind her hands, 'this isn't happening. Did she know? I mean, had she known about this woman?'

'She'd suspected. She said she'd always dreaded him having an affair.'

'This sounds more than an affair—'

'Yes,' Simon said. 'He wants to marry her.'

'Wow.' Carrie picked up her glass and put it down again. 'Who is she?'

'Some girl, some barrister—'

'A *girl*!'

'She's thirty-one,' Simon said. He bent his head suddenly, his tie flopping onto the table. 'Oh, God, Carrie, help me—'

She got up and went round the table. She put an arm round his shoulders and held him awkwardly against her.

'I can't *stand* this,' Simon said, 'I want to *kill* him.'

Carrie stroked his hair with her free hand. 'We'll have to look after your mother.'

'It's not that,' Simon said. He drummed his clenched fists on the table. 'It's *him*. It's always bloody been him.'

'Hey,' someone said from the doorway. 'What's going on?'

Carrie looked up. Jack, who was sixteen, stood easily there dressed in a T-shirt and sweatpants with his heavy, bobbed, centrally parted hair hanging over his face.

She said, 'We've had a bit of a shock.'

Jack came into the room, lunged across the table and picked up Carrie's wineglass. He took a swallow. 'Someone died?'

'No,' Carrie said. 'Nothing as simple as that.'

Jack looked at his slumped father, his mother stooped protectively over him. 'Is Dad ill?'

Simon raised his head. 'No,' he said crossly.

Jack flicked his hair back. He grinned. 'That's OK then.'

'No,' Simon said, 'it isn't OK. What has happened is extremely upsetting and will cause appalling pain.'

Jack looked interested. He slid into the chair his mother had been occupying. He gestured to his father. 'Shoot,' he said.

'Jack,' Simon said, 'there's no point in not telling you. You have to know. The girls have to know. Your Uncle Alan has to know. Shortly the whole bloody world will have to know. Your grandfather is proposing to leave your grandmother to whom he has been married for forty years and marry a woman with whom he has been having an affair for seven years.'

Jack was quite still. He stared at his father. 'Grando?' he said. 'Grando wants out and to start again?'

'Yes,' Simon said.

'This woman, how old's she?'

'Thirty-one,' Simon said with emphasis.

Jack grinned. 'And Grando's over sixty, isn't he? Old, anyway.'

'Too old,' Simon said with venom, 'for *this*.'

Jack picked up Carrie's wineglass again and threw the remainder of the contents down his throat. Then he gave the tabletop a kind of delighted slap, a gesture of approval, of abandon. 'Hey!' he said, 'thirty-one! That's cool.'

Simon lay looking at the familiar night-time blocks of shadow in the bedroom: window, table piled with books and clutter, door, wardrobe, chest of drawers, old sofa piled with clothes. He supposed Carrie was asleep. She was turned away from him, anyhow, her bony shoulder protruding from the duvet, and she was very still. Even if she wasn't asleep, there really wasn't much more to say at the moment, no new version of the shock and amazement and—in his case, anyway—anger that had preoccupied the evening and half the night already.

He turned his head. Carrie's fair hair lay tousled on the pillow close to his face. He liked it loose, always had. She had to pin it up or tie it back for her job as manager of a local medical practice, but at home she wore it down. He remembered that long ago he used to brush it. He liked brushing it. He hadn't brushed it in years. Mind you, Carrie wasn't a great one for brushing it herself.

He wanted her to be awake. He put a hand on her hip. She gave a small grunt, and didn't move. He had wanted her to be as angry with his father as he was but she said she couldn't be.

'It's this blood thing. If it was my dad I'd probably be incoherent with rage, but I feel more impersonal about yours. I mean, I like him, but I don't feel betrayed by him.'

'I do,' Simon said.

'Yes,' she said. She was putting supper plates in the dishwasher. 'And you always have.'

He took his hand off her hip and moved himself gingerly to the edge of the bed, trying to stay flat so as not to let a draught of cold air in, down her back. Then he slid out onto the floor and padded out of the room.

He went downstairs to the kitchen, switched on the low lights that illuminated the counter tops, and plugged in the kettle. Above the kettle hung a small mirror, which Carrie used for putting in her pierced earrings—'I can never remember where the holes are.' He peered into it now. He saw a tired man with bags under his eyes and sleep-rumpled hair. Do I look thirty-eight, Simon thought, or forty-eight? Or seventy-eight? Anyway, what does thirty-eight look like? And does thirty-eight with three children and a mortgage inevitably look quite different from thirty-eight with no commitments and a Porsche?

He made himself a mug of tea and carried it through to the little room they optimistically called the office. The house, like most of its identical Edwardian neighbours in this South London road, had an extension built out at the back. Some people had made kitchens out of their extensions, or sitting rooms with doors to the garden. Others had just left them as the warren of sculleries that they had originally been. Simon and Carrie had started out with the former intention and then, running out of money and enthusiasm, had allowed the extension to lapse into the latter category. The office, small and damp, had the feel of an Edwardian back kitchen. It housed the computer, the household files—approximately kept by Carrie—and Simon's law books.

Simon sat down in front of the computer. He had spent hours in this room, hours in front of this computer, setting up the free legal-advice clinics which he seemed to feel driven to do, working out strategies for people who couldn't cope, couldn't understand how they had gone wrong, how to get redress, how to survive an apparent injustice. He knew his father felt he had always spent too much time and energy this way, too much of his own resources in trying to help people whose cases—lives often—seemed futile, incapable of advancement.

'I need to,' Simon said, 'I have to. You live in an articulate world, where people have to explain themselves. But I don't. I can't, not while there are people who don't have a hope, ever, of explaining themselves to anybody.'

There had always been the assumption that Simon would follow Guy into the law. It wasn't Simon's assumption: it was Guy's. The law was what Guy knew, what Guy understood, what Guy was good at, and when Guy produced a clever son, the future of that son seemed to him a given, obvious. And it wasn't that Simon was averse to the idea of the law, it was only that he wanted his own approach, his own version.

'I don't want to be a barrister,' he'd said to his father when he was sixteen. 'I don't want to be all mentally ingenious and clever-clever, leaving people tied up in knots. I want to help people, I want them to know that I'm on their *side*.'

Rather later, when Simon was twenty-eight and Guy became a judge, and explained to Simon, with what he believed to be both courage and honesty, that he thought Simon's teenage accusations had had some truth in them, Simon wouldn't listen.

'Now he's on the Bench,' he said to Carrie, 'he thinks all advocates are just there to prove their own points, and only he can save the day. I can't *believe* it.'

Carrie was bent over Emma's high chair. Emma was two, then, and had discovered, a year before, the delicious tyranny of either eating at her own pace—interminable—or not eating at all. She had picked all the peas out of her dish, and was eating a single pea in her fingers alternately with dropping every second pea on the floor.

'Give him a break,' Carrie said. 'He can't get anything right, ever, can he? He's wrong for being a barrister, now he's wrong for being a judge. Emma, I am going to leave you to starve.'

Emma closed her eyes.

'He only wanted the Bench,' Simon said, 'for the status.'

'He didn't,' Carrie said. She turned her back on Emma. 'He did it because your mother wanted it.'

'He has never done anything my mother wanted in his *life*—'

'Simon,' Carrie said, 'don't be so bloody unfair. She's endured him working all the hours there are, all these years, and now she wants a *normal* husband, with regular working hours and a pension and health insurance.'

'Look at me!' Emma shouted imperiously. Carrie took no notice.

Simon stood up. 'Why are you on his side?'

'I'm not. I'm not on anyone's side. Your father may not be an angel but he's not the selfish monster you make him out to be.'

'You didn't grow up with him,' Simon said. 'You didn't see what he did to my mother—'

'*Look* at me!' Emma yelled. She flung her dish to the floor, scattering carrot and potato and slices of sausage.

'Go away,' Carrie said to Simon, 'just go away. I've got enough children to deal with, as it is.'

She had always been good for him, Simon reflected now, always balancing, always refusing to let him get too worked up about things, too emotional. He appreciated that, he really did. But what she couldn't see, what she would never be able to see because she hadn't been there, was the pain his mother suffered, had always suffered, on account of her quiet, unhappy realisation that she had taken a wrong turning, made a choice she couldn't—or wouldn't—escape from. Carrie had asked, more than once, why Laura didn't go, just leave, if things were really that bad, and Simon said she couldn't, she was of the wrong generation, the wrong temperament, the wrong upbringing, she was held by a sense of obligation—call it old-fashioned if you like— to lie on a bed she had chosen and then made.

'Well, don't let her exploit *you*,' Carrie said. 'It's not *your* fault she's in a twitch about your father.'

Sitting in front of the computer now, cradling his mug of tea, Simon thought about that. He *did* feel responsible for his mother somehow, always had, always had known that he gave her a strength she didn't seem able to find anywhere else, even from his brother Alan. He remembered playing cricket with her in Battersea Park when he was tiny, watched by Alan from his pushchair. She would bowl to him for hours, patiently and encouragingly.

'Now watch the ball,' she'd call to him, preparing to bowl again. 'Watch it all the way on to your bat.'

He'd adored her. He could recall the feeling still of a room being incomplete if she wasn't in it. Carrie had once asked him if he had been jealous when Alan came, resentful of this new and needy person in their lives, but he hadn't been. He'd always known he was safe, exclusive.

But it had been a relief to get away from his mother, later. He thought he'd probably been pretty unpleasant as a teenager, chilly and distanced, to punish her for having made her his whole universe when he was little. In any case, there was a certain perverse satisfaction in being tough with both parents when he was adolescent; it gave him a sense, however illusory, of his own separate stature. Sometimes he looked at Jack and wondered if that was precisely what Jack was now doing himself—removing himself crudely and visibly from the intimacy of the family circle to reassure himself of a separate and distinct identity.

Simon got up. What tea remained in his mug was cold, so he went back into the kitchen and put the mug down in the sink and ran water into it. It occurred to him suddenly and with guilty force that one of the strongest elements in his anger at this new situation was apprehension that his mother, alone now, abandoned, might want him back, might somehow feel she could retrieve that little boy in Battersea Park and ask him to give her the unconditional love he had been so eager, so willing, so *anxious* to give her then.

He gazed down at the cloudy water in his tea mug. I couldn't do it, he thought, I simply couldn't. It had been such a relief to fall in love with Carrie, such a heady release to find he had made a choice with his own heart, a choice that had nothing to do with duty or pity and everything to do with enthusiasm and independence and change. It had taken Laura a long time to accept Carrie; she had always been kind and civil, but a spark was missing, the spark of true warmth and sympathy. Carrie had noticed, but hadn't minded.

'Mothers-in-law are like that, aren't they?' she'd said. 'Especially the mothers of sons.'

Perhaps that was why Carrie and Alan got on so well, perhaps they shared the freedom—and exclusion—of not being Laura's chosen one, the apple of her eye. Alan! Simon banged the flat of his hand against his forehead. He'd forgotten Alan, quite forgotten in the turmoil of his own feelings, to call Alan as he had promised his mother that he would. He glanced up at the kitchen clock. It read twenty-past four. He couldn't do anything for the moment, except go back to bed and derive what comfort he could from Carrie's presence, her warm body not always wholly sympathetic, but real.

He went slowly up the stairs to the bedroom and slid gratefully in under the duvet. Carrie stirred, but didn't turn over.

'Ow,' she said. 'You're *cold*.'

The garden at Hill Cottage was Laura's creation. The house was, too, but Guy, who had an aptitude for seeing where walls should be taken out or put in, or furniture placed, had had a considerable part in the house. But the garden was Laura's. She'd thought about it, planned it, worked on it. Out of a couple of acres of derelict farmyard and run-down paddock, she'd made a garden and an orchard.

As the boys grew up, the garden sidled quietly into that part of her psyche and personality that had nurtured her young children. She told herself that Englishwomen of her age and type did succumb to gardening, and allowed it to dominate their lives as little children had once done. When Guy offered to take her to law conferences in Europe, or even the Far East, her first reaction—even above that of a small pleased excitement at the prospect of Paris or Tokyo—was whether the garden could manage without her for five or ten days. Suppose there was a late hard frost? Suppose the weather was unseasonably warm and dry and extra watering was required? Once, Guy had insisted she come with him, to Stockholm, and there had been a freak hailstorm in their absence and all the early roses collapsed into sodden brown lumps of blighted petals. She'd been distraught.

'But even if you'd *been* here,' Guy said, in exasperation, 'what could you possibly have done to save anything?'

Nothing, she knew. She pictured the hailstorm battering the rose heads with icy pellets. Of course she couldn't have done anything. She'd have been out there, miserable and impotent in the storm, but at least she'd have been there. It seemed impossible to explain to Guy that she had a sense of having let the garden down, failed it by not being there when it needed her.

Just now she needed the garden. It was where she had fled when Guy had told her he wanted a divorce so that he could marry someone called Merrion Palmer, but instead of receiving and consoling her, the garden had lain around her quite inert, almost indifferent. She'd begun to dig—a vegetable bed, ready for her precise rows of carrot and parsnip and beetroot—in the hope that strenuous physical activity would not only distract her but restore to her a feeling that the world was still, after all, recognisable. But all she'd felt after half an hour was that it was utterly pointless, that there was something deliberately masochistic about planting food for someone who had neither the desire nor intention of being there to eat it. She flung the spade away from her and it skidded into a leaning pile of glass panes she used for cloches over early lettuce, sending out a shower of green-white splinters. She sank to her knees, where she was, and let herself howl like a toddler having a tantrum in a supermarket. When it began to rain, she didn't move: it was almost a comfort to have something, however slight, happening.

The dogs, she could see, were watching her from the dining room, their paws up on the low windowsill. They were eager for walks, but considered gardening an incomprehensibly dull activity, best regarded as a spectator sport unless the sun was out. They were also anxious about her at the moment, anxious about Guy, about the atmosphere, about the suitcases on the landing ready for Guy to collect and take to his rented rooms in Stanborough, about the disruption of routine. Their anxiety took the form of following her about, even to the lavatory, lying down outside and breathing heavily under the door. When she wept, they came and camped on her feet, leaning against her legs. When she gardened, habit kept them inside, but worry drove them from their baskets to watch her through the window, straining to be reassured that everything was all right, in order again, normal.

'Get down!' she shouted at them. 'You're worse than *children*.'

They gazed at her, not moving. Poor dogs, she thought. They should have been a comfort just now, she should be grateful for their loyal, loving agitation, but instead all she could feel was that she hadn't a scrap of comfort to give them because she had less than a scrap to give herself.

She got up out of the muddy spring earth, banged at the clotted patches on the knees of her trousers, and went slowly into the house.

'**D**o we need to go at this speed?' Alan said.

Simon glanced in the driving mirror, moved the gear shift into fifth and pulled out into the outside lane to overtake an immense curtain-sided truck with French number plates.

'Yes.'

'Mum isn't expecting us till four.'

'I need to get there,' Simon said. He glanced in his driving mirror again. 'And then I need to get away again.'

Alan looked out of the car window at the cold, empty-seeming landscape, not yet free of the deadness of winter. It made him feel slightly hopeless, looking at it, or at least compounded the hopelessness he'd felt last night when the prospective owner of the bar in Fulham that Alan had been going to redesign, redecorate, had rung to say that the whole project was off: he couldn't get the financing. He sighed now, remembering, staring at the dead fields.

'I might stay the night,' he said. 'I'll see how she is.'

Simon said, 'We know how she is.'

'Yes, but I expect she varies. I mean there's probably even a bit of *relief*, but being Mum, she'll be managing to feel guilty about that, not thankful.'

'*Relief*?'

Alan yawned. 'It hasn't exactly all been wonderful, has it?'

'But she's stuck to it,' Simon said. 'She's made it her life, she's shaped everything round it—'

Alan shrugged. 'Her choice, boy.'

Simon beat lightly on the steering wheel with his free hand. 'No, it isn't. That's the point. She hasn't had a choice.'

'We all have choices. That's what Dad's doing now, choosing.'

'It drives me mad,' Simon said, 'to hear you saying things like that, as if it was perfectly OK just to duck out on four decades of a relationship because you're bored—'

'He's not bored.'

'Isn't he? Well, if he isn't bored, what the hell is he?'

'He's worn out,' Alan said, 'with never knowing what she wants, what makes her happy, what he's doing wrong.'

'Dad has done exactly what he wants always. He doesn't know what Mum wants because he's never *asked* her.'

'D'you ask Carrie?'

'She tells me,' Simon said. 'Mum isn't like that. Mum's never insisted upon anything for herself, ever.'

'Then she's colluded with being made a victim.'

'Alan,' Simon said furiously. 'What's got *into* you? Where's your loyalty to Mum?'

'I just see both sides,' Alan said. 'I'm sorry for Mum but I'm sorry for Dad, too. I can see what's happened. A bit, anyway.'

'And if he marries this girl and she has a baby and he alters his will in her favour, cutting us out, you'll feel just as calm and objective and bloody superior?'

'I expect so,' Alan said.

Simon changed gear at the wrong speed and the gears grated loudly. 'Hell,' he said. 'You and your moral high ground. You and your bloody smug refusal to be judgmental, as you put it. It must,' Simon said savagely, 'be such a comfort to know better than the rest of us. It must be such a *solace* to be gay.'

There was a small silence. Alan looked out of the window. He said, his head averted from his brother, 'Actually, it's the precise opposite, but at least it stops you expecting the impossible from anyone else.'

Simon swallowed. 'Sorry.'

'That's OK.'

'I'm just a bit apprehensive—'

'I know. That she'll want you to take Dad's place. Well, you don't have to collude with that either.'

Laura was waiting for them at the back door. She looked as she always did, composed inside conventional clothes—a shirt collar sitting neatly at the neck of a good sweater above well-tailored trousers and brushed suede loafers.

She said, kissing them both in turn as if the meeting was profoundly unexceptional, 'There's no etiquette for this, is there? I really don't know what to say to either of you.'

They followed her inside. The dogs raced madly about the kitchen and Alan crouched so that the dogs could wag and lick ecstatically all over his shoulders and face.

Laura said apologetically, 'I'm afraid they're hysterical with worry—'

'I don't mind.'

'And you, Mum?' Simon said. 'Are you hysterical with worry?'

'On and off,' she said. She began collecting a teapot and mugs and a bottle of milk.

'Could I have coffee?' Alan said.

His mother held up a jar of instant-coffee granules. She said, 'I so don't want to be a burden, a problem—'

Simon put his hands in his pockets and rattled his keys and his change. Carrie was always asking him not to. She said it was an exasperating habit, the male equivalent of the girls' endless fiddling with and tossing of their hair, and equally exasperating. Simon had a sudden longing for Carrie, to have her there in this well-ordered kitchen where nobody was behaving like themselves except the dogs. Carrie would help them to be practical, not emotional. Carrie would remind Simon, by her very presence, that his first obligation was to her and the children, and not to his mother. She would take away his guilt.

Simon said, 'Mum, you need help, though. Your future needs sorting.'

Laura turned her back on them to unplug the kettle. Her back was eloquent of someone who doesn't believe they have a future. She said, 'I'll manage.'

Alan rose to his feet. 'Shhh,' he mouthed at Simon.

Simon said, 'We have to do nuts and bolts, Mum. Money, housing, that sort of stuff.'

'Oh, I know.' She turned and poured water into the teapot and into Alan's coffee mug. 'But do we have to do that today? Shouldn't we talk about what's happened? How I feel? How—how I'm to cope?'

Simon moved across the kitchen and put an arm round her shoulders. 'Oh, Mum—'

She turned and put her face against his jacket. He put his arms round her. Her shoulders were shaking. 'Suppose I can't cope—'

'Hey, you can. You're shocked now. It's an awful shock.'

Alan came round the table. He stood close to his mother and brother. He said, 'In a way, you've been coping for years. If you think about it.'

Laura felt in her trouser pocket for a handkerchief. It was white cotton, nicely laundered. She blew her nose. She said, not looking at either of them, 'Have you seen your father?'

Simon snorted. 'Not bloody likely.'

Alan said, 'I'm seeing him on Sunday.'

'With—with—'

'I don't know. I don't think so. But she exists, Mum. She's part of the pattern now.'

'Of the *problem*,' Simon said.

They moved to the kitchen table and sat down.

'I always thought,' Laura said, to the tabletop, 'that I'd turn out not to be good enough, not exciting enough. I always thought he'd have an affair with one of his pupils. But he said he never did. He said there'd never been anyone—until, well, this one.'

Alan picked up the teapot and poured tea into mugs for his mother and brother. He put one mug in front of Laura. 'You don't need to analyse, Mum. You don't need to tell yourself you're not this or not enough that—'

'I *do*,' Laura said, raising her face. 'Why else would he go?'

Simon said tensely, 'Because he is who he is.'

'Si—' Alan said warningly.

'I'm not having Mum sitting here,' Simon said, too loudly, 'thinking it's her fault.'

Laura turned to look at him. She gave him a faint smile.

'What I can't get used to,' she said, 'is finding that something I've been afraid of happening for forty years actually is happening.'

Simon shut his eyes and wrapped his hands hard round his tea mug. 'Oh, Mum—'

'He wanted me to be like him, to be sure of who I was and where I was going. And I couldn't. I never have.'

Simon and Alan said nothing.

'You don't want to hear this,' Laura said. 'Do you?'

Alan made a face. 'It's not that—'

'Isn't it?'

'Mum,' Alan said. He put his forearms on the table and loosely clasped his hands together. 'Mum, it's not that we aren't sympathetic. But there's no *point*, Mum, in talking like this.'

Laura said tensely, 'What do you mean?'

Alan avoided Simon's eye. He said, 'What I mean is that we have to deal with what *is*, not what might have been.'

Laura half rose, shoving her chair back with a clatter on the tiled floor. She said, her voice rising, 'Are you taking your father's side? Are you *condoning* what he's done?'

'No,' Alan said. He didn't look up and his voice was deliberately steady. 'No. That's not what I said. I said—'

Simon stood up. Laura glared at him.

'Are you going to tell me just to get on with the wreck of my life, too?'

'Mum, he didn't say that, he didn't—'

'He did!' Laura screamed. Her face was flushed. 'He did!' And then she turned and fled from the room, slamming the door behind her. The dogs, back in their baskets for a temporary cessation of tension, looked as if they had been kicked.

'Oh my *God*,' Simon said. 'What the hell did you have to do *that* for?'

'She has to hear it—'

'Maybe, but not *now*. Not while all she can think of is that she's been rejected because she didn't make the grade.'

'The sooner she stops blaming Dad for every bloody thing, the better for her, for her recovery—'

Simon started round the table. 'I'd better go and find her.'

'Leave her,' Alan said.

'Al—'

'Simon,' Alan said. 'Leave her. For your own sake as well as hers.'

Simon paused. He put his hands in his pockets and shook up his change. He looked at Alan. 'I can't,' he said unhappily, and went out of the room.

CHAPTER FOUR

'I'M SORRY, GUY,' Merrion said. 'But I simply can't come.'

She was sitting on the edge of the sofa in her flat, nursing a gone-cold mug of herbal tea.

'He's a gentle soul,' Guy said. 'Very tolerant, very—well, whatever the opposite of volatile is. He isn't, perhaps, quite as clever as Simon but he's much less difficult.'

Merrion looked into her mug. The herbal tea was pale brownish yellow and smelt faintly and disagreeably of compost. 'But he's still your son—'

'Who knows about you and what you mean to me. He knows the *score*, my darling.'

Merrion put the mug down on the floor by her feet. 'What I hate is that the prospect of meeting a son of yours makes me feel *guilty*. I don't know why, but it does. I feel as if I'd have to say sorry for upsetting his mother—'

'Not much logic in that. His mother is the same person as my wife, and you very properly haven't been consumed by guilt there.'

'She's a different generation. Alan's my generation—'

'Merrion, what on earth has that got to do with anything?'

'I can't explain,' Merrion said, 'but it has.'

'Look,' Guy said. He came across the small sitting room and sat down beside her. 'Look, come and say hello very quickly, maybe even have a drink with us, and then go.'

She sat up straight and pushed her hair behind her shoulders. 'Would I be doing this,' she said, 'for you, or for me?'

'For us both. Even for Alan probably. He's going to love you.'

Merrion looked at Guy. 'Are you trying to show me off?'

'Of course.'

'And give us credibility?'

'That, too.'

'I tell you,' Merrion said, 'I do not like this stage at all.'

'I seem to remember—'

'Oh, I did,' Merrion said, standing up, 'I did want you to leave Laura and all that. I do want it. But you never know how the dynamics will change when you get what you want, do you?'

She stooped and picked up the mug from the floor. He caught her free hand.

'Are you losing your nerve?'

'No,' she said. 'But I just feel socially inadequate at the prospect of meeting your son.'

He gave her hand a little shake. 'Five minutes and it'll be over and that's another dragon slain.'

She sighed. 'Give me a wet Monday morning,' she said, 'in court with the most useless, truculent client to defend and a judge who can't stand women advocates, rather than this.'

'That's easy. That's professional. This is personal.'

'Too right,' she said. She took her hand out of his. 'OK. I'll come. For five minutes.'

Alan leaned against the pub bar and ordered a mineral water. He rather wanted something stronger, but thought he would wait for that until his father came and they could use the ritual of deciding and ordering and paying to get them over the first few minutes. It wasn't that Alan felt nervous about meeting his father, it was more that he felt anxious about conveying satisfactorily the important fact that he was going to stand by both his parents without getting heavy about any of it.

He didn't know this pub. He didn't actually know Bayswater at all well, it wasn't his bit of London, but his father had suggested it because it was close to Merrion's flat and he was spending the weekend with Merrion. Guy had said they'd meet for a drink in the pub and then go round the corner to a good Italian, a plan that made Alan think his father intended to include Merrion in the pub part, but not the Italian. He felt, in advance, a little sorry for Merrion. It would be an ordeal for her, however they played it.

Alan took a mouthful of his mineral water. He'd tried, during the long and distressing evening with his mother, to explain that neither Guy nor Merrion had planned the pain they were causing—to themselves as well as to anyone else—and that things happened in life, some good, more bad, and you had to just accept them without screwing yourself up apportioning blame and finding reasons. She'd got very angry with him, angry enough to ring Simon at home, twice, in order, Alan supposed, to get the kind of furiously sympathetic response she felt she was entitled to. Alan had tried to prevent her, but he couldn't. She felt he was no substitute for Simon, never had been, and she blamed him for, as she put it, making Simon go home instead of staying the night, as she'd wanted him to. Simon had needed a bit of urging, admittedly, but Alan could see that both Simon and Laura would be in pieces if Simon stayed. He'd have convinced her that she was utterly wronged and she'd have convinced him that only he could save her. So Alan had put Simon's car keys into his hand and told him to go, almost pushed him out of the door. Then he'd poured Laura a gin and tonic and she said she never drank gin and tipped it down the sink.

Alan hadn't minded. In his world, in his life, people got awkward when they got upset, it was part of the situation, part of the result of losing control. Alan had learned very early on, when he realised that there was something deep in him that made him an outsider to his upbringing, that there weren't patterns. There were consequences, sure, often as random as the behaviour that caused them, but there wasn't order, there wasn't symmetry and tidy sequence. There hadn't been much future in trying to explain this to his mother, who interpreted his efforts as a peculiarly unkind form of detachment from her suffering, and in the end he'd had to give up and simply sit there, holding her hand, and hoping that his silence and his touch conveyed at least something of what she wanted from him.

The double doors from the pavement swung inwards and Alan's father came in, holding one door open for a tall girl with a mane of hair, wearing a dark overcoat that came almost to the floor. Alan straightened up a little and turned towards them, but didn't move. His father looked—well, how did he look? Familiar, Alan thought, handsome, friendly. And tense. Distinctly tense. He took a couple of steps forward and put his arms round his father.

'Hi, Dad.'

'Alan,' Guy said. He held Alan hard for a second. 'I don't know whether to say thank you for coming.' He gave a brief laugh and curved an arm out to include the girl in the long overcoat. 'This is Merrion.'

'I had to be,' the girl said. 'Didn't I?'

She didn't hold her hand out. Alan smiled at her.

'Glass of wine?'

'No, thanks. I couldn't swallow anything right now.'

'She nearly didn't come,' Guy said.

Alan said, 'A drink would give you something to do.'

She shook her head.

Guy said, 'She won't ever do anything that makes life easier for herself. She was born in a hair shirt.'

'What d'you want, Dad, beer, wine—?'

Guy moved towards the bar. 'I'll get it—'

'No,' Alan said. 'You can give me lunch. I'm doing this.' He looked at Merrion. 'I'm going to order you a glass of wine. You can ignore it if you want to.'

She gave a fleeting smile. 'I wouldn't be that churlish.'

Alan turned back to the bar. Guy put out a hand and took Merrion's nearest one and squeezed it. He wanted to tell her that she didn't have to do anything, say anything, that she didn't have to perform, for him; any way she wanted to be was fine by him.

She took her hand carefully out of his and opened her coat. She was wearing jeans underneath, and a pale grey sweater with a polo collar. Alan turned back from the bar and handed her a glass of white wine.

'Thanks,' she said.

He held out a half-pint beer tankard to his father, then picked up his mineral water. 'No toast,' he said. 'We wouldn't know what to drink to.'

'I do,' Merrion said. She lifted her glass.

'You do?'

'Peace of mind,' she said. She lowered her glass and took a sip. 'I've never not had it before.'

In the sitting room of the house in Tooting, Simon lay asleep on the sofa in a drift of Sunday newspapers. Jack had extracted the sports sections earlier in the day, and Carrie had taken the arts and review supplements to read on the kitchen table, leaving Simon with news. He thought briefly, before he fell asleep, that these sorts of age and gender divisions about newsprint were probably happening along precisely these lines, all over the world. Women only wanted news if it concerned the humanity of human beings and men only wanted reviews of things they were going to see. Teenagers didn't want either. Culture smacked of school and news couldn't hold a candle to the gloomy drama of their own lives. Jack was very gloomy just now. Carrie thought he must be in love. Simon thought it was because he'd been left out of the long-jump team. Whatever the reason, Jack was fighting his demons with silence and an expression like doom.

Carrie had wanted Simon to go to bed after lunch, properly to bed with outer clothes off and the curtains pulled across. 'You look exhausted—'

He yawned. 'I ate too much lunch—'

'You know it wasn't that,' Carrie said. 'You know what this week's been like.'

She'd answered the telephone to Laura several times in the last few days and on a couple of occasions had not only said Simon was out when he wasn't but had also not told Simon of the calls.

'I want you to sleep *properly*.'

'Then I won't sleep tonight.'

They'd compromised in the end and Simon had settled down along the length of the sitting-room sofa. He declined a rug and blew her a kiss as she went out of the room. She closed the door behind her with something perfectly adjusted between a slam and a click.

In the kitchen, Rachel and Emma had cleared up approximately, doing the simple stuff like putting plates in the dishwasher and leaving anything that required application and conscientiousness, such as scouring out the roasting tin that had held the chicken. Carrie dug in the cupboard under the sink to find her yellow rubber gloves. Behind her, the back door that led to the garden, and to the path that ran along the side of the house from the road, opened.

'Hello,' Alan said.

Carrie turned. 'How very nice.'

He came in and closed the door behind him. He was holding a small bunch of creamy narcissi, which he laid on the table among the unused spoons and forks. He came to give Carrie a kiss, saying, almost conspiratorially, 'I met her.'

Carrie looked at him intently. 'And?'

'Tall. Very striking. Nervous as a kitten—'

'And?'

'Nice,' Alan said. 'Very. Not—' He paused.

'Not what?'

'Not after Dad for anything except Dad. As far as I could see.' He looked round the kitchen. 'Where's Si?'

'Passed out under the papers.'

'What's the score here?' he said, filling the kettle.

'In a nutshell,' Carrie said, her yellow-gloved hands deep in the sink, 'Simon is worn out with confusion and being pressured, Jack thinks it's really cool to fall for someone half your age, Rachel thinks it's weird and Emma is worrying about Gran's dogs.'

'And you?'

Carrie put the last saucepan upside-down on the draining board, and took her gloves off with a snap. She looked straight at her brother-in-law. 'I don't blame him.'

Alan said thoughtfully, 'You've never liked her much, have you?'

'Let's put it another way,' Carrie said. 'Let's say that she's never liked me much.'

'Oh, come—'

'Alan,' Carrie said, 'I don't even think it's personal. I don't think she'd have liked anyone who married Simon.'

'Does it get between you and Si?'

'Sometimes. Depends on how I'm feeling. He forgets sometimes, that since Mum died I haven't a mother myself to counter her with. She forgets that, too.' She went over to the table and picked the narcissi up, inhaling their astonishingly strong scent. 'These are lovely.'

'Would you like coffee?'

'No, thank you.'

'Dad is so happy,' Alan said. 'I do this laid-back stuff but I can't always carry it off to myself. I liked seeing him like that, I liked him being, well, appreciated.'

'Does she flirt with him?'

'No. Not the type. She's a professional woman, she's got a kind of detachment. And a Welsh accent.'

'Welsh!'

'Not very. Just a lilt. It's lovely.'

'Do you,' Carrie said, sitting down by the cluttered table, still holding the narcissi, 'feel disloyal?'

'No,' Alan said.

'Strict truth, please.'

'Yes,' Alan said. 'You should see her, Carrie. My mother's sitting in that house with every cushion plumped and the garden all perfect and you know she's trying not to ask herself what it's all for. For years she could kid herself it was for Dad, or Dad and her, but now that veil's been torn away, too. She's made something Dad's told her he doesn't want.'

Carrie began to unwrap her flowers. 'She didn't do it for him. She did it to show him he hadn't left any space for her, in his life.'

'Come on—'

'True,' Carrie said. 'Don't confuse independence and defiance.' She got up and began to search in a cupboard for a vase. 'When did she last earn a penny piece?'

'It's different for that generation—'

'No, it isn't,' Carrie said. 'My mother worked, my aunts do. Your mother stopped. She chose to stop.' She ran water into a narrow glass vase and put the narcissi in unarranged.

Alan held his hand out for the vase. 'Oh, *Carrie*. Let me—'

She passed it to him. The door to the hall opened and Simon came in. 'I feel awful. I shouldn't have slept. Hi, Al.'

Alan said, concentrating on the narcissi, 'I saw Dad.'

Simon sighed. He came forward a little and leaned on the back of the nearest chair. 'Well?'

'He's fine,' Alan said. 'He looks well and happy.'

Simon grunted.

'And she—'

Simon straightened. 'She!'

'She was there. Just briefly. And given briefly and first impressions and all of us jumpy, she's great.'

Simon closed his eyes. 'Give me strength.'

'It's no good, Simon,' Alan said. He put the broken-off pieces of narcissus stem into a neat pile. 'You can't write her off as a gold-digger or a marriage-wrecker or a legal groupie or a sex bomb. You can't write Dad off, either, as a classic male menopause victim wanting to reassure himself he could still double the world's population if he wanted to. She's the real thing. She's a proper person.'

'I think,' Simon said, taking his hands off the chair back, 'I've heard quite enough for the moment.'

'One more thing,' Carrie said.

'What?' Simon said, his voice full of weary distaste.

'I want to meet her,' Carrie said.

In her parents' bedroom, twelve-year-old Emma was sitting on the sofa experimenting with Carrie's make-up. Emma had make-up of her own, but that was for using, not for playing with. Carrie didn't have much make-up—not like Rachel's friend Trudy's mother, who had drawers and drawers of it—but she had enough to offer an intriguing alternative to the geography project (The Nature of Oceans) that she was supposed to be doing.

The telephone beside the bed rang. In a single swift movement, Emma was off the sofa and had the receiver in her hand. Even if the call was not for her, it was imperative for her to know who the caller was, and whom they wished to speak to. She crouched on the floor. 'Hello?'

'Hello, dear,' Laura said. 'Is that Rachel?'

Emma made a face at the telephone. 'No, it's Emma.'

'Emma dear, it's Granny.'

'I know,' Emma said.

'How are you?'

'Bored,' Emma said. 'How are the dogs?'

'Well,' Laura said, 'they're not very happy, of course.'

'Did they see Grando?' Emma said.

'No. I thought it would upset them. I put them in the garden room.'

'Did they bark?'

'Yes, I'm afraid they—'

'They wanted to see Grando,' Emma said. 'Poor them.'

'Emma,' Laura said, in a different voice, 'is your father there?'

'He's asleep.'

'Could you go down,' Laura said, 'and tell him Granny's on the phone?'

Emma thought about the dogs. 'I'll tell him when he wakes up,' she said.

'Dear—'

'He was really grumpy at lunch,' Emma said. 'He needed to sleep. I'll tell him when he wakes up. Have the dogs had their walk yet?'

'Of course. Emma—'

'Give them my love,' Emma said. She held the receiver a little way from her ear. She remembered a phrase Carrie and her friends used to each other at the end of calls. 'Bye, Granny,' she said. 'Take care,' and then she put the receiver down.

From down the landing, Rachel shouted, 'Who was that?'

'No one,' Emma called.

'Was it—?'

'No,' Emma said, 'it was Granny.'

Rachel said nothing. The volume of her music went up again. Emma got up from the floor. When she had dogs, when she was older, she'd never shut them up against their wills and she'd never do things to worry them. The telephone began to ring again. Emma turned her back and walked out of the room, leaving it to it.

Above the desk in Carrie's office, a notice board hung. It had a huge at-a-glance year-long calendar pinned to it, which recorded the hours worked by part-time staff, the doctors' days off and everybody's holidays. Round the edge, Carrie had pinned other things: notes to herself, photographs of Simon and the children, cartoons cut out from newspapers, and a postcard from her Aunt Cath on which Cath had scribbled *Try not to be perfect.* Cath had come to stay a year ago and surveyed Carrie's life and work and home with an astonished and slightly sardonic eye, and had sent the postcard as her thank-you letter.

Work, Carrie often thought, was the only area of her life where something even a quarter way to perfection seemed attainable. She had hours within which she worked, timetables that were comfortingly inflexible, and if the human element remained arbitrary, it almost always had to come to heel in the end. Doctors could throw tantrums, she had discovered, about not having the weekends off that they wanted, but if there was no one else available to be on duty, on duty they had to be.

'Sorry,' she'd say, staring straight at the doctor in question, picturing him telling his wife they couldn't have the weekend break he'd promised her. 'It isn't my fault and there isn't any alternative.'

'You enjoy this!' the doctor would yell.

'That's exactly what my children say,' Carrie would say, and then she'd go back to her office.

That was work for you. That was why work was such a pleasure. You took it on and off, like an overcoat, and you only took it home with you on very rare occasions. Above all, it allowed you to concentrate. At work, Carrie could give it her full, capable, impersonal attention. At home she usually felt as if someone had seized her attention, torn it into a hundred small pieces and tossed them into the air.

'I never finish anything,' she'd said to Simon, over and over. 'I'm never *allowed* to.'

Today, however, this Monday morning with all its demands built up from crises not being dealt with at the weekend, felt not like the finishing of things but more like their beginning. Or at least, their developing. Alan had stayed for supper the night before and when he was leaving had said in Carrie's ear, 'Do you want her number?'

She'd stepped a little away from him. 'Are you plotting?'

'The reverse. This girl exists. Dad loves her. Demonising her helps no one.'

'I do want to meet her,' Carrie said. 'It's just that Simon—'

'Does it really help Simon if you side with Simon?'

Carrie made a face. Alan gave her nearest cheek a quick kiss.

'I'll ring you at work. You don't have to do anything after that if you don't want to.'

She looked down at her desk now. Alan had left a message. Maureen, one of the district nurses, had taken it down while in Carrie's office looking, she said, for the list of babies born at the weekend and due for their first postnatal visit. Maureen liked taking messages.

Carrie, she'd written on a yellow sticker note, *Alan called 9.07 Monday. He said the number you want is as follows*. She'd signed the note *Maureen*, with a smiley face after her name.

Carrie looked at the telephone number. It was Central London. If she rang it now, she would get an answering machine and would have to leave a composed message. If she rang this evening, not only would she have to do it in some secrecy but also her father-in-law might answer, and she had an aversion to speaking to him just now, for reasons she couldn't explain. She looked at her watch. Ten twenty. Ten minutes before the weekly administrative practice meeting, which she chaired with tremendous briskness. She put her hand on the telephone receiver and dialled rapidly. Then she shut her eyes. The telephone rang out four times and then a woman's voice said, rather distantly, 'If you wish to leave a message for Merrion Palmer, please do so, after the tone.'

'Hello,' Carrie said, and stopped. Merrion's answering machine waited, in faintly humming silence. She opened her eyes. 'This is Carrie Stockdale. I'm Guy's daughter-in-law. Could you ring me at work sometime? Between nine and four thirty? Thank you.'

She put the phone down. She thought, suddenly and with unexpected guilt, of Simon.

Jack Stockdale leaned against the blank wall at the back of the science block. It was the place he and Rich and Marco came for a smoke usually, but he didn't somehow feel like a smoke today, and certainly not with Rich and Marco. Marco, blazing with unconcealed triumph, had taken Moll to the cinema on Friday night and had hinted at a night of clubbing together on Saturday. Jack had never breathed a word of his secret and intense interest in Moll to either Rich or Marco, but discovered that he felt brutally let down and betrayed all the same.

Moll was in the year below Jack at school, and therefore a year above Rachel. Moll was very athletic, with a strong, supple dancer's body and extremely straight brown hair which fell plumb down her back like a curtain. It was her hair that Jack had first noticed, walking by chance behind her down the main school corridor between physics and social studies, and seeing this long, calm, smooth sheet of brown hair. She didn't fiddle with it. She must have been the only girl in the whole school who didn't. She seemed to take it for granted, like she took her body for granted, the body that was so effortlessly proficient at gym and dancing and track sports. She'd only been in the school a term and already there was a buzz about her capabilities. In Jack's year, among Jack's mates, there was also a buzz about her sex appeal.

Usually, Jack joined in. He liked sex talk. He liked the jovial buddy stuff of boys talking dirty together; it gave him a feeling that he didn't have to go on this rather alarming journey alone. But now he didn't want to talk to anybody. When Adam said to him, 'What've you got the hump about, mate?' he'd shrugged and gone off to mooch about by himself.

The trouble was, he might not have said anything, but Marco knew, all the same. Marco glowed with the knowledge that he had somehow succeeded where Jack had failed. Marco had his Italian father's colouring and his Italian father's physical assurance, and beside him Jack felt suddenly raw and hopeless, physically and emotionally, pitifully unfinished. He knew he was being pathetic, but he couldn't see, right now, how to feel any other way. His father had put his finger on the problem, quite by chance, the other night. They'd all been hanging about the kitchen, wanting supper hours before it was ready, and Simon was chopping carrots on the table, very slowly, and Jack was watching him and waiting for Carrie to notice how thickly he was chopping them and say she wanted them cut much thinner than that.

'You know something?' Simon said.

Carrie was making a casserole. She was dipping a big spoon in and out of the pot while she added things out of bottles and jars. 'No,' she said. 'What?'

'You can handle anything in life,' Simon said. 'You can get anything sorted, can't you, as long as your emotions aren't involved. That's why work works and life mostly doesn't.'

Carrie turned round. 'Weird,' she said, 'I was thinking almost exactly that earlier today. Could you cut those a bit thinner?'

Jack had leaned across and picked up a piece of carrot. He'd rather wanted to ask his father more about what he'd said, more about this emotion stuff and how it made you suddenly want things you'd never wanted before. But he felt shy. Rachel was sitting at the table, too, supposedly slicing cabbage and learning a poem for English but actually doing neither, and she had ears like a lynx and a mind like an Exocet. Mention emotion in front of Rachel and she'd say, clear as a bell, 'You fancy Moll Saunders, don't you?'

He squared his shoulders against the science-block wall. He did fancy her, it was true. He was, in fact, spellbound by the way she looked and moved, by the way her hair fell. But there was more than that. He wanted to know her. He wanted to hear her say things to him. He wanted to do things for her. He put his hands flat against the wall and pushed himself away from it. He didn't want a cigarette and he didn't want two periods of physics followed by one of current affairs and he didn't want to go home after that and have Rachel watching him and knowing she knew what was the matter. He began to move slowly along the asphalt path that connected the science block to the main school building. He felt he could summon up no interest in anything because the one thing he was interested in wasn't interested back.

On the path, just out of sight of the back of the science block, a girl was waiting.

'Hi,' Moll Saunders said.

Jack stared at her, speechless.

'Did I scare you?'

'No. No, but I—'

'I've got a bit of a down on smoking,' Moll Saunders said. 'My aunt died of lung cancer.'

'Oh God,' Jack said. 'I wasn't smoking, in fact I—' His head was spinning. He put his hand into his trouser pocket and tugged out his cigarettes. He held them out to her. 'Here.'

'You don't have to do that—'

'I do,' Jack said.

'We'll put them in the bin.'

'OK.'

'Jack,' Moll said, 'I really like your painting, the black one, the one Mr Finlay's put up.'

He looked down at his feet. His ears felt the size of dinner plates. 'Wow—'

'I do,' she said. 'It's cool.'

When Laura brought the dogs back from their afternoon walk, their bellies and legs and paws were dark with mud. She tied them up to a ring set into the wall of the potting shed, and went to unravel the hose. They began to leap about and squeal. The hose was a horror worse than the vacuum cleaner. They hated the hose.

Laura held each dog's collar in turn and hosed it down methodically, despite the yelps; she did this in winter, she reflected, twice a day usually, twice a day seven days a week. When Guy was there, he'd walked the dogs perhaps once or twice at a weekend, but he never washed them properly. He never seemed to see the need, nor the need to walk them so regularly. Dogs, he said, ought to accommodate to people's lives, not the other way about. She'd talked about her obligation to the dogs, to the garden, to the house, to the servicing of their joint lives.

'Laura,' he'd said tiredly. 'Laura, don't mistake a tyranny for an obligation.'

She turned the tap off and untied the dogs. They shook themselves vigorously, then leaped away from her, chasing and tumbling over each other in their exaggerated relief that the ordeal was over. She watched them and felt like crying. They could, in their blithe doggy way, forget pain so easily, so cruelly easily.

There was a car in the back drive, an estate car with a jumble of flower-arranging paraphernalia in the back. In the driver's seat sat a middle-aged woman in spectacles writing absorbedly in a notebook. When she heard the sound of Laura's feet on the gravel, she wound the car window down. 'Thought that's what you'd be doing, walking the dogs—'

'Wendy,' Laura said.

'I was perfectly happy, sitting here. Gave me a chance to do the hospital-volunteer transport rota. How are you?'

'I don't know,' Laura said. 'Come and have a cup of tea.'

Wendy got out of the car. She was looking at the dogs waiting by the back door. 'It's probably good for you, having to cope with them. Domestic routine has its uses.'

Laura unlocked the back door and the dogs shot inside.

'It's kind of you to come,' Laura said.

Wendy looked at her sharply through her spectacles. They had blue frames and gilt side-pieces. 'My dear Laura,' she said, 'there, but for the grace of God, go *any* of us. Forty years of marriage. *Forty*. Do you think any of us went up that aisle forty years ago and thought about where we'd be forty years later? I didn't, for one. I'd have died of fright.'

Laura went ahead into the kitchen and filled the kettle. 'I was very nervous about marrying Guy,' she said. 'But I thought that was normal.'

'Roger fainted,' Wendy said, 'in the vestry when we were supposed to be signing the register. Not a wonderful omen, if you think about it. He's never fainted since.'

'And you still have him—'

'I do,' Wendy said, 'but only after some close shaves.'

Laura put tea bags in a teapot. 'Would you marry him again?'

'Given half a chance,' Wendy said, 'I wouldn't marry anybody. Except to have children.' She glanced at Laura. 'How are the boys taking this?'

Laura took mugs out of the cupboard and put them on the table. 'As you would expect. Simon perfectly sweet and sympathetic, and Alan making me feel that as this sort of thing happens all the time I shouldn't make a fuss but should just get on with the consequences.'

'Oh, Laura,' Wendy said, taking her spectacles off and buffing the lenses up against her cardigan, 'he doesn't mean that. Alan's a sweetie'

Laura put the teapot on the table and sat down. 'He makes me feel he thinks Guy has a point.'

'Laura dear, Guy is his father.'

'Who has been betraying me for the last seven years and has now walked out.'

Wendy put her glasses back on. 'You know, I have rather wondered what I'd do if Roger walked out.'

'And?'

'I think I'd go and live in Cornwall and run a bed-and-breakfast.'

'You only think that because you don't have to do it.'

'Laura,' Wendy said, 'are you very, very sure you weren't actually rather *tired* of being married to Guy?'

Laura stopped pouring tea. 'What do you mean?'

'That it's insulting and upsetting and frightening to be left like this, but that it just *might* be a chance to start again on your own terms?'

'At sixty-one?'

'At eighty-one, if needs be. No milk, thank you.'

Laura bent over her mug. 'I don't think you understand at all.'

'Ah,' Wendy said.

'I have never been able quite to live up to Guy, you see. I've never been able to be what he wanted me to be. The things I'm good at are the things he can't see the point of. I feel cast aside,' Laura said. 'Not good enough. Rejected.'

Wendy put her mug down. 'I have to say, except for very superficially, that isn't how it *looks*.'

'Oh?' Laura said sharply.

'It looks,' Wendy said, 'as if you'd just grown miles and miles apart. Simple as that. Nothing left but the formalities.'

'And if he'd never met this girl?'

'He'd probably have met another one.'

Laura got up to refill the teapot. 'Simon doesn't think that. Simon thinks it's all part of Guy's need to be centre stage.'

'Guy and Simon,' Wendy said, 'are very different people. How's that nice wife of his?'

'I haven't heard from her,' Laura said. 'Sympathy has never been Carrie's forte.'

'She probably doesn't know what to say—'

'Wendy,' Laura said, 'Carrie has never been lost for words in her life.'

She held the teapot up. Wendy shook her head.

'Will you be all right for money?' Wendy asked.

'Simon will see to that.'

'Will he? Should he?'

'Who else is there?' Laura said.

'You and your lawyer.'

'I hate all this. I hate all this exposure. I hate the loss of all I've known, the *status* of marriage—'

Wendy stood up. She looked down at Laura's smooth hair, at her face hidden in her two small, pale hands. 'My dear girl,' she said, 'do wake up. There really isn't much status *left* in marriage in this day and age.'

Because it was a Friday, Guy came up from Stanborough on the five o'clock train, and let himself into Merrion's flat. It was a relief to do that, not least because he felt it was one of the few things he could do openly, one of the few things he had, because of at last coming clean about Merrion, given himself proper permission to do.

During the week, in Stanborough, he lived a life he knew was—in a quite different way to his previous life—duplicitous. He had said nothing about his changed circumstances to anybody. If anyone knew, they hadn't confronted him with the knowledge and hadn't yet caught up with the fact that the town's Resident Judge had left his wife and was living, during the week, in rented rooms above an electrical shop in a small shopping parade.

Guy was grateful for his anonymity. They were unwelcoming rooms, bleakly decorated and furnished, but they fitted his sense of what was due to him just now, and he had no need, really, to tell anyone even his name. He had taken them for three months and moved into them just a minimum of clothes and books. Merrion—whom he refused to allow to see them—said they sounded like *his* hair shirt.

To Guy, they felt more like his limbo, his no-man's-land. When he left them in the mornings, they left no mark on his mind all day beyond giving him, when in his colleagues' company, a weird sense of rooflessness. At lunch, in the judges' dining room, he would listen to the usual banter, over gooseberry crumble served with custard, and find himself furtively wondering about everyone else's home lives, about the situations the others were going home to and how many of them, for various reasons, would try to spin out their days beyond the closure of the courts at four thirty, delaying the moment of climbing into their cars and heading back to resume whatever it was.

What haunted him was that his colleagues assumed something about him that was no longer the case. They assumed he'd be going home to Laura. Only a few of them had ever met Laura, but nonetheless she would be there, in the vague mental sketch they carried of Guy in their heads, along with the fact that he lived in the country, that he had sons, not daughters, that he wasn't much of a fishing man but had been a good cricketer in his day. It would have electrified them to have that sketch come sharply into focus and reveal the presence of Merrion in it, and not only in it, but right in the foreground. Some of them might remember Merrion, too.

Guy could not quite visualise the moment when he could reveal how his life was now, what had happened, how he had broken with the custom of forty years and taken a radical step into emotional territory he was very, very certain he had never even glimpsed before; and how he lived now, in a quiet and suspended state during the week—bringing home meals to microwave, taking his shirts to the laundry, changing the sheets punctiliously on his bed—and then on Fridays, taking the train towards truth and enrichment.

Merrion lived at the very top of a tall, white-painted house that had been converted into flats in the seventies. The flat was small, but very light, with views between the buildings opposite, to the tops of trees in Hyde Park. Her taste was spare; the floors were wooden, there were blinds rather than curtains and her make-up lived in a black wire-mesh basket in the bathroom. Guy had been shy about putting his shaving things next to it, anxious not to burden her, not to make demands, not to—well, not to seem too *husbandly*.

On Fridays, when he came to London, he always bought flowers. He bought them at the station and put them in water when he got to the flat, throwing away the dead ones from the week before, which she seemed never to have got round to. He turned some music on, checked the fridge for a bottle of wine, washed and changed out of his court suit, admired the Hyde Park trees from the window. And then he waited. He didn't mind how long he waited. She might be coming back from court in the Midlands, even the northwest, and while she did, he waited, his heart quietly lifting and lifting, until he heard the small crunch of her key in the door, and stood up to greet her.

CHAPTER FIVE

ON THE TRAIN back to London from Croydon Crown Court, Merrion managed to find a seat in a different carriage from the defending counsel she'd been against in court that day. She'd won—not really to her satisfaction, not well—and he hadn't liked it and had wanted his solicitor to complain to hers about inadequate instructions. Merrion's solicitor had refused, and the defending counsel had said that he'd have to have it out with Miss Palmer.

'I'd hop it,' Merrion's solicitor said to her, 'if I were you.'

She'd run, literally, to the railway station. As she hurried out of the court building, she'd seen her client—a thin-faced divorced woman in her forties with three wayward children—in a sulky huddle with her boyfriend. Merrion had won financial support, backdated for two years, from her ex-husband—who had briefly worked for an oil company in the Gulf and, while there, had made a half-hearted attempt to take his children with him—but her client didn't think it was enough. She'd wanted £200 a week. Her ex-husband was earning £310 a week. She didn't care, she said, she wanted what she wanted. What did it matter if the bugger starved? Merrion had won a payment of £80 a week, and the backdate. Her client had glared. She wouldn't speak to Merrion after the judgment.

'Bloody shower,' she'd said, audibly, to her boyfriend.

A train for central London was just pulling out as Merrion ran on to the platform. It didn't matter; the timing of her meeting with Guy's daughter-in-law in a wine bar near Victoria Station had been left deliberately vague.

Merrion bought a copy of the evening newspaper and retreated to the back of the railway platform. She saw the defending counsel, a solid man in his early forties, confident-looking, with a black velvet collar to his overcoat, come onto the platform and look about him. If he was looking for Merrion, he wasn't looking very hard. She held the newspaper up, opened out, in front of her face, and waited until he had passed her on his way to the station bar.

When the train came in, she allowed the barrister to board it ahead of her and chose a carriage well away from his. She found a seat next to a man engrossed in his laptop, opposite a girl in a leather jacket and red lipstick asleep with her mouth open.

'I think,' Guy said at the weekend, 'that you will like Carrie. I certainly do.'

'It was nice of her to ring me,' Merrion said. She was lying along her sofa, her head in Guy's lap, and he was reading a Sunday newspaper above her, with his arms held high, to keep the newsprint off her face.

'She's slightly acerbic in manner, but don't let that put you off.'

'I can be acerbic too—'

'I know.'

'Three kids,' Merrion said. 'Think of it. How old is she?'

'Forty-ish. Maybe less.'

'Wow. Three kids.'

'But not a promising career at the Bar.'

'Why did you say that?'

'To stop you making pointless comparisons.'

'It doesn't, however.'

'Carrie's father is a doctor. A GP in East Anglia. Her mother died quite a long time ago. That's hard. Carrie loved her.'

'Lucky her.'

Guy had bent over to look at her. 'Why do you insist on regarding your mother in this way?'

'Because it's how it is.'

'I never expected to be close to my mother,' Guy said.

Merrion reared up from the sofa and kissed him. 'But that's because things were different in your day—'

'Long, *long* ago?'

'Right,' she said. She grinned.

He smiled back. 'And now I can't talk to my own children, either.'

Merrion swung her feet to the floor and felt about for her shoes. 'Can you talk to Carrie?'

He put a hand out and took hold of a handful of her thick hair. 'I've never tried. It hasn't seemed, well—'

'Proper?'

'Perhaps. She's Simon's—'

'But with a mind of her own?'

'Oh, yes,' Guy said. 'You'll see that. At once.'

Merrion thought it must be Carrie, sitting at a corner table with a glass of red wine in front of her, scowling at the crossword in the newspaper, tapping her teeth with a pen. She had fair hair held up here and there with combs, and she wore a grey overcoat slung across her shoulders. Merrion made her way among the tables, holding her heavy briefcase up high out of people's way. She stopped in front of Carrie's table and rested her briefcase on the edge of it.

Carrie looked up. 'Merrion?' she said.

'Yes—'

'You're taller than I thought.'

'Five eleven,' Merrion said.

Carrie gave a faint smile. 'Lucky you. All my children will be taller than me any minute and then the last possibility of discipline will vanish.'

Merrion pulled a chair out and sat down. She put her briefcase on the chair next to her and shrugged out of her coat.

'Wine?' Carrie said. 'I'm afraid you have to go and get it.'

Merrion stood up again. Carrie watched her weave her way to the bar. She wore a black suit, the jacket quite fitted, the skirt narrow. She looked good in it, Carrie decided, good figure, good carriage, interesting hair. She imagined Guy looking at Merrion. Very exciting. Very—well, unexpected, fresh, energetic. She thought of Simon looking at her, too, confronting the fact that she was distinctive, almost dramatic, but not vampish, not obvious, not in any way easily dismissable. Simon would be in a terrible confusion. So would she, for that matter, watching him watching Merrion. She took a big swallow of her red wine. Thirty-one! When she, Carrie, was thirty-one, she'd had three young children and no money and no ambition much beyond getting to the end of each day without spinning off into a vortex. She glanced at Merrion's briefcase. She certainly hadn't had a career.

Merrion put a glass of white wine down beside her briefcase. Carrie looked at her hands. No ring.

'No ring,' Merrion said, smiling. 'Guy wants one. I don't. So, no ring.'

'Will you have a wedding ring?' Carrie said.

Merrion slid into her chair. 'Shouldn't think so.' She took a sip of her wine. She said, 'Did you just want to have a look at me?'

'Yes,' Carrie said. She took a comb out of her hair, and stuck it back in again, in exactly the same place. 'I wanted to see the reality. When someone's just a name in a situation like this, they can become a sort of bogy.'

'I wouldn't know,' Merrion said, 'I've never been in anything remotely like this in my life before.'

'There's a lot of drama. And things get distorted. People get angry.'

Merrion looked down into her wineglass. 'Like your husband.'

'Like Simon.'

Merrion said hesitantly, 'He has his mother to protect—'

'We'll talk about that,' Carrie said, 'when we're further down the line. If we get that far.'

Merrion picked her wineglass up and put it down again. 'Presumably you have an agenda.'

'No,' Carrie said, 'I told you. I just wanted to see the reality. It's odd when a crisis happens in your partner's family—you are at once absolutely involved and not involved at all. You spend a lot of time grappling with emotions on someone else's behalf. I just felt I could cope with what Simon's coping with if I met you.'

Merrion gave her a quick glance. 'Guy likes you.'

'I like him,' Carrie said.

'He'd like to talk to—to your husband.'

'Yes.'

'I don't know much about how men in families work together,' Merrion said. 'My father died when I was three. I have no brothers or sisters.'

Carrie picked up her wineglass. 'They're different. They interpret each other's actions instead of talking.'

'Are they competitive?'

Carrie gave her a sharp look. 'Yes.'

Merrion drank some wine. 'I see.' She flicked a glance at Carrie. 'So you have your own position to defend?'

'Don't go so fast,' Carrie said.

'I'm learning,' Merrion said. 'I'm learning all the time.'

'You've had seven *years*—'

'A secret love affair,' Merrion said, 'is a piece of cake compared to this.'

'Preferable?'

'In a way. I'm not particularly possessive,' Merrion said, rolling her glass between her hands, 'but I've been taken aback by the degree to which people belong to other people. Or believe they do. Not feeling free to act is one thing entirely. But not feeling free to even *decide* is quite another.'

'Perhaps you never gave much thought to Guy's life outside yours before.'

'And perhaps nobody in Guy's life outside mine gave much thought to *Guy*, before.'

'Whoops,' Carrie said. She emptied her glass and began to put her arms into her coat. 'I ought to go. I told a lie about where I'd gone so I'd better not make it a very long lie.'

'Why did you lie?'

'My daughters would be insatiably curious and Simon would be hurt.'

'He'd think you disloyal?'

Carrie said nothing. She stood up and stuffed her newspaper into her bag. Merrion stood, too. She moved the table so that Carrie could get out.

'Can I ask you one more thing?'

Carrie paused, but she didn't look at her. 'What?'

'Did I pass the test?'

'What test?'

'You know,' Merrion said, 'the real reason we're here. Which am I? Friend or foe?'

Simon drove down to Stanborough alone. He had told Carrie he was going, but not Alan. Alan would have offered to come, too, and Carrie would have encouraged him to. Both of them, Simon knew, wanted to save him from Laura and, at the same time, neither of them understood the precise nature of his obligation to her. Carrie said, in fact, that the precise nature didn't trouble her much: it was the *strength* she found so hard to contend with.

'We'd never have married!' she'd screamed long ago during one particular row (the children had been lined up on the landing, horrified and spellbound), 'if I hadn't been pregnant! Your mother would have seen to that!'

Laura had, admittedly, told Simon he was far too young to think of marrying. Twenty-one was absurdly young, especially for a man, especially for a man not yet qualified. And twenty-one was too young for Carrie, too, particularly as, having abandoned medicine for no good reason Laura could see, she hadn't decided what else to do. Of *course* she got pregnant! What else was there for her to do *but* get pregnant and have all subsequent decisions taken out of her hands? Vainly, Simon had tried to explain that Carrie didn't want to be pregnant, hadn't meant to be, was only going to go through with it because the baby was Simon's, Simon's and hers. Laura saw Simon as trapped. Simon saw Carrie as trapped. Carrie saw Simon as trapped, twice over.

'Her. And now me.'

'I *want* you.'

'I hope you do.'

He did. Seventeen years later, he still did. Carrie was the one decision—if, indeed, she'd ever been anything so crisp and deliberate—of Simon's life that he had never doubted.

Carrie had asked Laura to come and stay for a few days.

'I won't, thank you. It's sweet of you, but the dogs—'

'Can't they go into kennels?' Carrie said.

'I don't like to send them, at the moment.'

'Bring them, then—'

'Oh, I couldn't do that. It really is good of you, but I'm better here, really I am. Perhaps Simon—'

'It's maddening,' Carrie said, after she put the phone down. 'All that pure obstinacy masquerading as the poor victim.'

Rachel was leaning against the wall by the telephone, waiting for Trudy's line not to be engaged. 'D'you mean Gran?'

'I do, as it happens. But you shouldn't have been listening.'

'You shouldn't shout then.'

'I'm afraid,' Carrie said, sweeping past with an armful of laundry, 'that your grandmother is enough to make anybody shout.'

Rachel looked at her father. 'Wow!'

'Sometimes,' Simon said stiffly, 'it's a bit hard for one generation to understand the problems of another generation.'

Rachel grinned. 'Tell me about it.'

'Very funny.'

'C'mon, Dad. Gran's never been very nice to Mum. Has she?'

'I don't really want to talk about it. Not now,' he said.

Rachel turned her back and began dialling her friend Trudy's number. 'Or ever,' she said.

She was right, of course. He didn't want to talk about it. He didn't want to have to say out loud that he agreed with Carrie's view and Rachel's view—even if he did—because of the implications and consequences of such a confession as far as Laura was concerned. In fact, this Thursday afternoon, driving westward, he felt fairly irritated by Laura himself, not just because of her attitude and current conduct but also because it was so fiendishly difficult to get time away from the office, and his partners were beginning to complain.

'C'mon, Simon,' his partner Ted Freeman had said, 'your father hasn't *died*, has he?'

Sometimes recently, Simon thought, it might have been a lot easier if he *had*. If Guy were dead, there'd be none of these recriminations and resentments and endless conversations about what went wrong.

Laura was stooping in the garden, pulling the dead heads off daffodils when the car turned down the lane. She crossed the rough orchard grass to the drive, so that she was standing, waiting, when Simon pulled up.

'You are so sweet to come.'

He bent to be kissed.

'You look tired,' she said. She touched his forehead.

'Probably because I am.'

'Did you have any lunch?'

'I had a Twix bar,' Simon said. 'I bought it when I stopped for petrol.'

'Why didn't you buy a sandwich? Something sensible?'

'Because, Mum, I wanted a Twix bar.'

Laura put her hand inside his arm. 'I'm going to make you a sandwich.'

'Thank you,' Simon said. He glanced down at her. She looked small and pale and neat. She had her pearl earrings on. When she took off her gardening gloves and put a hand out to calm the dogs bounding round them, he noticed that she was no longer wearing her wedding ring.

'No ring,' he said.

She disengaged her arm and took a step ahead and opened the back door. She said, over her shoulder, 'Well, it's over, isn't it?'

Simon said, 'I haven't seen him—'

'Haven't you?'

'No. I spoke to him once on the phone.'

'And?'

'It lasted three minutes,' Simon said. 'My fault. I lost my temper.'

Laura said, her voice warmed with pleasure, 'I don't blame you.' She pulled a chair out from the table. 'Sit down.'

He sat, awkwardly. She took a banana out of the fruit bowl and put it down in front of him. 'Eat that while I make you a sandwich.'

He looked at the banana. He said, 'I'm not ill, Mum. I'm not a child, either. I'm just a father of three with rather more on his plate than is quite manageable just now, who, as I do most of the time, missed lunch.'

Laura was slicing bread. She said brightly, 'How's work?'

'There's an endless amount of it and seemingly no time to do it in.'

'But you have partners—'

'Yes, I do. But we have more work than we have people to do it.'

'Why don't you hire someone else?'

Simon pushed the banana away from him. 'Because the figures don't quite permit that yet.'

Laura put a plate down in front of him. It bore a thick brown-bread cheese sandwich. His mouth watered.

'Then we're going to have to come to some arrangement.'

He looked at her. She had turned away and was rummaging in the cupboard.

'What?'

'Well, I can't expect you to do everything for nothing. Not with Carrie and the children to support. Here we are. Apple and walnut chutney. I made it last September.'

'Mum,' Simon said, 'what are you going on about?'

Laura went past him, putting the chutney jar on the table, and plugged in the kettle. Then she turned back to Simon. Her expression was bright and slightly detached, as if she'd been rehearsing what she was about to say.

'I told you,' she said, 'it's over.'

'I know that—'

'And I don't want to have anything more to do with it. Or him. I telephoned him this morning and told him so. I want—I want to *erase* him.'

Simon pushed the sandwich plate away. 'But, Mum, nothing's sorted. Not the house, nor money, nor Dad's will or pension, not the divorce, *nothing*. We haven't even started.'

'I'm not starting anything,' Laura said. She spooned tea into a teapot. 'You are.'

Simon put his head in his hands. 'I came down today,' he said with resolute steadiness, 'at immense personal and professional inconvenience, to talk to you about finding the right person to represent you and to discuss what sort of deal you wanted. I came, Mum, to get the ball rolling. You agreed. Alan agreed. We all agreed.'

'Sorry,' Laura said. 'But I'm not instructing solicitors, I'm not planning strategies, I'm not—most emphatically not—having one more single thing to do with your father.'

He leaned across the table towards her. He said incredulously, 'But you want a settlement, don't you? You want a fair share of the assets, don't you?'

'Of course I do. I want that very much. It's the least I'm owed.'

'Then you have to have a lawyer. You have to have *some* communication with Dad.'

Laura began to pour the tea into blue-and-white-flowered cups. 'No, I don't. You are going to do it for me.'

Gwen Palmer had brought her own sandwiches with her, to eat on the train. Merrion would have laughed at her, she knew, would have told her she was turning into an old thing on an awayday pensioner's excursion ten years before she needed to. But for Gwen, the journey to London was quite enough by itself without worrying about buffet cars and being ignored by the bartender in favour of big men buying spirits.

It had dawned upon Gwen, during Merrion's last visit, that their lives were now so far apart in thought, word and deed, that it was sometimes difficult to believe that Merrion's childhood and adolescence had actually happened the way they had. Of course Gwen was proud of Merrion. Who wouldn't be proud of a daughter with such professional accomplishments. And yet there lurked in Gwen's mind an apprehension that Merrion had, for all the glory and shine of her life in London, taken some kind of wrong turning, set off down some path that seemed, almost inevitably, to lead away from all the things that Gwen believed contributed to womanly fulfilment. If she tried to intimate this to Merrion, Merrion told her angrily that she didn't understand, that she didn't know anything.

'I do,' Gwen said. She was angry, too. 'I do, so. I've been married twice and I'm a mother, which is more than you can say for yourself.'

'I'm joining you,' Merrion said, her voice suddenly quiet. 'I'm getting married. I'm going to get married, too.'

Gwen had burst into tears. She hadn't meant to, but they had rushed up her throat and out of her eyes before she could stop them.

'Don't,' Merrion said.

'It's you that needs don't!' Gwen had shrieked. 'It's you that needs stopping from throwing your life away!'

Merrion had said nothing. She had risen from where she had been sitting at the kitchen table, collected her coat and her bag and her briefcase, and had walked out of the house. She didn't look back. Not once.

That had been three weeks ago. Gwen had done a great deal of thinking in those three weeks. She catalogued, in her mind, all the things that in her view Merrion was doing wrong. And everything that was wrong came back to this man, with his voice and his education and his legal position and his wife and children and grandchildren. Gwen could hardly believe Merrion's stubbornness about Guy Stockdale. Seven years! Seven years out of a young woman's life already thrown away, and now she was blithely proposing to throw away the rest. *Marry* him! Sleeping with him had been hard enough for Gwen to contend with—but *marriage*. She had conducted long diatribes to Merrion on the walk to her—now part-time—job. She had found that, without Merrion there in the flesh, the words came easily, flowing furiously out of her mind. On these walks, Gwen told Merrion, angrily and silently, about everything that had ever happened to her, about how she'd felt, how she'd coped and how all that gave her both a right and a duty to try to prevent Merrion just wasting herself. Sometimes she dissolved into tears, so keenly did she feel what she was mutely describing.

She considered telephoning, but then she thought of Merrion's answering machine; she thought of the chance of Guy answering the telephone. She was suddenly struck, instead, by a bold plan. She would just go to London. She would choose a day when she wasn't working the day after and go to see Merrion. In her flat. She would simply *do* it. If Merrion was out, she would write a note and put it through Merrion's door. That would be almost as effective as actually seeing her. Whatever, Gwen told herself, it was a journey worth making.

She found a taxi at Paddington with no trouble. It was dusk and a light rain was falling, blurring the air and the car headlights and the lights in houses and shops. If Merrion wasn't in she could wait two hours, she had calculated, before she had to find another taxi and go back to Paddington for her train home. The taxi stopped in a wide street of huge white terraced houses, flat-fronted except for pillared porches over broad flights of steps.

Gwen paid the driver and went up the steps. There was a panel of entryphone buttons beside the door, each with a dimly illuminated name beside it.

PALMER. M., the top one said. FLAT 6.

Gwen took a deep breath and pressed the bell. There was a crackle and a hum and then a further crackle and a man's voice said, 'Darling? Did you forget your keys?'

Gwen froze. She gazed in horror at the entryphone panel.

'Merrion?' the man's voice said. 'Merrion?'

Gwen took a step back.

'Who's there?' the man said. 'Who is it?'

Gwen said nothing. She retreated to the edge of the porch and stood gazing at the entryphone. There was a clicking sound, as if a telephone receiver had been put down, and then silence. Gwen leaned against one of the huge pillars that held up the porch. It had been *him*.

She felt, suddenly, rather peculiar, almost faint. She took several deep breaths, leaning against the pillar, her eyes closed. Then she opened her eyes again. 'He's up there,' she said to herself. 'He's in her flat, and she isn't home yet. Gwen, you wouldn't *dare*. Would you?'

She stood upright for a moment. Then she adjusted her bag and holdall and transferred them to her left hand, stepped quickly across the porch and pressed the bell again.

The crackle came once more, then the hum and then the man's voice said, 'Either tell me what you want, or go away.'

Gwen stood up straight. She put her mouth close to the entryphone grille. 'It's Mrs Palmer,' she said.

There was a silence, a small, intense, complicated silence and then a buzzer sounded and the man said, 'Come in.'

Gwen pushed. The door swung open, still buzzing, and Gwen found herself in a long high hallway with a staircase at the far end. She went cautiously forward. She reached the foot of the staircase and put her hand on the rail. Someone was coming down the stairs, fast. She got six steps up, almost to the first half-turn, and a man in a dark suit appeared.

'Mrs Palmer—'

Gwen said nothing. She held the handrail, hard. He came down until he was on the same step as she was. He leaned to take her bags.

'Let me take those. I'm so sorry, but the lift is broken.'

Gwen opened her mouth to say it didn't matter, and nothing happened. He was good-looking. Merrion hadn't said he was good-looking. But then, she, Gwen, hadn't let her say such things, had she? She hadn't let her tell her anything about Guy Stockdale, in case knowing about him turned him into a reality, instead of some kind of unpleasant, improbable notion that might never come to anything.

They began to climb the stairs together. He was half turned towards her as they climbed, her bags in his right hand and his left partly outstretched as if to steady her, help her. 'I expect,' he said, 'you were hoping to find Merrion. Not me.'

She nodded.

'I don't usually come up to London on Wednesdays, but I'd had rather a tough day, so I indulged myself.'

She nodded again, her eyes on the fleur-de-lis in the carpet ahead of her, step after red step.

'She should be home any minute. She was in Peterborough today. She will be so pleased to see you.'

Gwen said, 'I don't think so.' Her voice came out in little gasps. It was the first thing she'd said to him.

He took her elbow. 'One more flight. Think of getting furniture up here.'

Or a baby, Gwen thought, without wanting to. She tried to remove her arm from his grasp, but he was holding her firmly. A skylight swung into view, and then at last they were on a small landing with a weeping fig tree in a terracotta pot and a cream-painted front door.

Guy put a key in the lock and turned it, then stood aside so that Gwen could go in ahead of him. She stepped in, slowly, turning her head this way and that, taking it in. It was all very light, very pale, like something in a magazine.

Guy put her bags down beside a long, cream-coloured sofa.

'Can I make you a cup of tea? Or get you a glass of wine?'

'Tea, please,' Gwen said.

He indicated the sofa. 'Do sit down.' He hesitated, and then he said, 'The bathroom is over there. Through the bedroom.'

The bedroom! Gwen swallowed. She sat on the edge of one end of the cream sofa. There was a low table in front of her, foreign-looking, with carved legs, covered with books and magazines. There was a vase of flowers on it, those Peruvian lily things that lasted well, deep rusty red.

Guy came out of what Gwen supposed was a little kitchen and put a tray on the table in front of her. There was a small white teapot on it and a white cup and saucer and milk in a white jug.

'Shall I leave you to pour out for yourself?'

She nodded.

He sat opposite her and said uncertainly, 'I am—pleased to meet you.'

Gwen poured her tea. She added milk and one sugar lump. She had come to London and found Merrion's flat and got herself up here. With him. She mustn't waste it. 'I want to say something to you,' she said.

He waited. He had leaned forward a little, his elbows on his knees. He was watching her.

'You are ruining my daughter's life,' Gwen said.

He bowed his head. She picked up her teacup—her hand wasn't at all steady—and took a sip.

'It's not that I think you don't love her. I know she loves you. But what's a man your age doing with a girl of thirty-one?'

Guy looked up at her. His eyes were veiled. Sad-looking.

'It's greedy,' Gwen said. She put her teacup down. 'I didn't mean to say this. I didn't intend to see you, after all. But now we're here, I've got to. I couldn't forgive myself if I didn't. You've got everything she'll never have because you're too old to let her have it. Suppose she wants a baby?'

He put his hands briefly over his eyes.

'If she has a baby,' Gwen said, 'you'll be dead before it's grown up. Have you thought of that?'

'Yes,' Guy said.

'And she'll be on her own for years and years. All that proper family life you've had, children and grandchildren, she'll never have that. Or not in the way you've had it.'

He said, steadily, 'I've said this to her.'

'Have you?'

'And her reply is that she would prefer to have the unorthodoxy of her relationship with me than—than any alternative.'

Gwen took another sip of tea. 'But she's never known anything but you. You haven't given her a chance.'

'I haven't kept her against her will—'

'But you haven't taken yourself off, either, have you? You didn't say to her, sorry, Merrion, I have a wife and family responsibilities and they are my first priority, did you?'

'No—'

'You might have broken her heart,' Gwen said, amazed at the words lining up in her head all ready to march out of her mouth just as they did during those silent, one-sided conversations with Merrion. 'At the beginning. You might have broken it then, for a while, if you'd walked away. But you'll break it anyway, now, won't you, sooner or later?'

Guy stood up. He looked very tall, in that small light room, tall and imposing. 'Don't think you're saying anything I haven't already thought or said. I know. Anything I say—' He stopped.

'Well?'

'Anything I say to you about the human heart will sound so feeble, so self-indulgent, so unrealistic . . . But she is my ideal companion. And I am hers. There's a feeling of—of *belonging* together. No—no, not a feeling. A knowledge. It was there from the beginning. I wasn't looking for it. Nor was she.'

Gwen said sharply, 'Anybody can do that.'

He gave a little sigh. She looked up at him.

'I know,' he said. He went across the room to a tray of bottles and poured himself some whisky. He said, his back still turned, 'We may be a living cliché, but that doesn't make us any less *true*.'

Gwen drained her teacup. 'You're a stubborn man.'

He said, his voice suddenly louder, 'That's the *last* thing I am!'

Gwen looked at the floor.

'I am trying to be patient,' Guy said. He came back to his chair, holding his whisky glass. 'I acknowledge the justice, for you at least, of what you say. Don't forget, I have children of the sort of age Merrion is, children—sons—of whom I still feel extremely protective. I know why you're saying what you're saying. I've let you call me greedy and selfish and unfeeling. But I will *not* be labelled stubborn.'

Gwen began to tremble slightly. The feeling of strange exhilaration that had buoyed her up so far was beginning to leak away, leaving her feeling—as she had so often felt, all her life—that she had bitten off more than she could chew.

She said, 'I ought to go.'

'Mrs Palmer—'

She waited.

'Mrs Palmer, we ought to be on the same side. We both love Merrion better than anyone else.'

'Better?'

'Yes,' he said, 'even me. I love her more than I love my children. I didn't know it was possible to love anyone this much.'

Gwen stood up. She was suddenly extremely tired and longing, childishly, for the train to take her back to everything that was unremarkable and familiar.

Gwen took a breath. 'If you love her—' She paused.

He stood, too. He looked enormous, suddenly, formal, authoritative. Gwen took a breath.

'If you love her that much,' she said clearly, 'then you know what you ought to do for her. Don't you?'

When Merrion put her key in the door, she knew immediately that something was wrong. The smell of it came out of the flat like a vapour, cold and raw. Guy usually put all the lights on, had music playing, supper started, sometimes even a bath run for her full of bubbles with a glass of wine sitting on one of the broad corners beside the taps. But tonight the flat was silent. And almost dark. Merrion stepped into the gloom and anxiety in a single stride.

'Guy?'

'I'm here,' he said. His voice sounded strained, as if it was difficult to speak, as if he'd been crying.

She moved into the sitting room. Guy was lying along the sofa, his jacket off, his arm flung across his face.

'Darling,' Merrion said, rushing forward. 'Darling, are you OK?'

He took his arm away, and held it out to her. 'Physically fine.'

She took his hand. It felt the same as ever, big and warm. She glanced down at the table beside him, at the tea tray on it, a proper tea tray laid for one with a pot and milk jug and a cup and saucer.

'Guy?'

He let her hand go abruptly and swung himself upright. 'I made it for your mother.'

'My *mother*?'

'Yes,' he said. 'Your mother's been.'

CHAPTER SIX

JACK AND MOLL spent the afternoon locked in the bathroom. At least, Carrie had supposed that the door was locked, but when she went up to shout that, whatever they were doing, could they please stop because other people might need the shower, Moll called—disconcertingly pleasantly—'Oh, come in!'

Jack was sitting in the middle of the room on a chair taken from Carrie's bedroom, draped in a hideous, fish-patterned swimming towel Carrie had bought in a street market. His hair—or at least the front of it—was intersected with neat little aluminium foil packets. Moll was wearing latex surgical gloves and her hair was tied back smoothly behind her head with a red bandanna.

'Hi,' Moll said. 'I'm putting highlights in Jack's hair.'

'Highlights—'

'Greyish blond,' Moll said. 'Ashy.'

Jack, under his frill of little silver packets, looked smug. He said, 'It'd cost forty quid at a hairdresser—'

'Perhaps you'd do mine,' Carrie said. Her tone of voice was somehow not quite what she'd intended.

Moll flicked her a glance. 'Sure. Any time.'

Carrie looked at the girl's deftly moving hands. She had a proper hairdressing colourist's comb, with fine teeth and a spiked metal handle.

'I was thinking of having a shower—'

'We can move,' Moll said. 'Any time.'

Jack looked briefly at his mother. 'Why now?'

'Because I've had a long day at work, I'm having a drink with your Uncle Alan and then I'm collecting Emma from drama club and I wish to do the latter activities showered.'

There was a tiny pause. Jack and Moll caught each other's eyes, for a fraction of a second, in the bathroom mirror. Jack said, 'Where's Rach?'

'Gone to the movies with Trudy. Then she's staying the night.'

'Uh-huh.' He sounded nonchalant.

'And Dad's working late,' Carrie said. 'What's new. So such supper as there is won't be until about nine.'

'We'll get supper,' Moll said.

Carrie stared at her. 'Will you?'

'Of course. We'll finish this off in the kitchen,' Moll said. 'And then you can shower. Just tell us what you want us to cook before you go.'

'Yes,' Carrie said weakly. Nobody had ever offered to get a meal before. 'Thank you. Heavens.'

Jack stood up, his silver frill glittering, the towel swinging round him like a cloak. He looked entirely unselfconscious, in fact, almost the reverse: pleased and proud. He picked up the chair he had been sitting on and went out onto the landing with it. Moll gathered up her bowls and brushes and comb and followed him. When they got to the bottom, Jack leaned sideways and gave Moll a quick kiss.

'Bingo,' he said.

Alan had already ordered for her. He was sitting with a glass of white wine in front of him and another glass, untouched, sat in front of the chair beside him. He was wearing a collarless white linen shirt under a black leather waistcoat. Carrie sketched a little gesture of approval as she sat down.

'Nice—'

He grinned. 'I've got a date.'

'You haven't!'

'A doctor. Nice car.'

'*Alan*!' she said. 'His car is the *last* thing that matters.'

Alan made a face. He looked very happy, almost mischievous.

Carrie said, 'There's a lot of love about at the moment, isn't there? Even Jack—'

'Jack?'

'At this precise moment Jack is having highlights put in his hair by a sleek little number called Moll.'

'Good for Jack.'

'I suppose so—'

'Carrie,' Alan said warningly.

'What?'

'Don't use that nobody's-good-enough-for-my-boy tone of voice about Jack's girlfriend.'

'Was I?'

'Yes,' Alan said, 'you were.' He raised his glass. 'Cheers.'

'You, too. I hope you have a lovely evening.'

'I'd rather have a wild one—'

'I don't want to know about that,' Carrie said.

He grinned again. 'I wouldn't tell you anyway.'

She looked at him. 'You *are* cheerful.'

'I know. Isn't it a relief?'

'Yes,' she said, 'it really is. I'm getting so used to gloom and doom I'm in danger of forgetting there's an alternative.' She took a mouthful of wine. She said, looking at the tabletop, 'I met Merrion.'

'And?'

'As you said, she's nice. And certainly determined to fight her corner.'

'Shouldn't she?'

'Of course she should,' Carrie said crossly. 'It's just that if she does I get torn in two.'

'Why?'

'Your mother,' Carrie said, her gaze back on the tabletop, 'has decided that although she wants what she sees as her fair share of your parents' assets, she is not going to soil her hands securing them. She has decided she is going to have nothing further to do with your father. You can guess the rest.'

'Oh God,' Alan said. 'And Simon agreed?'

'He doesn't seem to think he has any option.'

Alan took a gulp of wine. 'When did this happen?'

'This week. He didn't mean to tell me about it, but when he got back from Hill Cottage in such a state, I could *see* she'd asked for several pounds of flesh.'

Alan said, between his teeth, into his wineglass, 'I *told* him.'

'I know.'

'Has he spoken to Dad?'

'I don't know. I think Guy left a message. The thing is that almost leaving Merrion aside I can't help feeling your father has a point. I'm now facing the prospect of having to fight *your* mother for *my* husband.'

'Nonsense.'

'It isn't nonsense,' Carrie said. 'It's a fact. It's always been there, sort of latent, but she's never taken the gloves off before, never quite had to. Shall I tell you something?'

He nodded, waiting.

'It's not Guy's fault that Laura's always felt—lost. I bet he really tried to give her what made her happy, what gave her a greater sense of security and purpose, and all she did in return was make him feel he'd wrong-footed her deliberately, that he'd somehow made a career out of carefully removing life from her grasp. I'm probably out of order telling you this, but in my opinion Laura is one of the most self-absorbed, self-pitying women I have *ever* met.'

Alan gave a little shrug.

'I had to worm everything out of Simon the other night,' Carrie said. She was breathing fast. 'He didn't want to tell me anything, he didn't want me to have proof of how unfair and exploitative Laura is. He didn't want me, did he, to tell him how pathetic I think he's being—'

'Do you think he's being pathetic?' Alan said.

'Oh,' she said miserably, 'not really. I just think she's got him cornered. She was just biding her time.'

'So you bawled him out—'

Carrie's gaze dropped. 'Yes.'

'Carrie—'

'Don't tell me I'm jealous,' Carrie said, 'I *know* I am. But he is mine, you know. Mine *first*.'

'He knows that.'

'But you can't always have what you want if someone persuades you that you *owe* them first instead, can you?'

'I don't know,' Alan said. 'Look, I *want* to help, Carrie. But the two of them have been playing this game since before I was born.'

Carrie's shoulders slumped. 'I know.'

'What are you afraid of?'

She made a little face. 'I suppose—that we'll never be free of her. That she'll always be a consideration and, over time, the first consideration. That Simon will never be able to see her for what she is'

'Could you say that to her?'

'Oh, Alan, can't you see? I don't want to say all this stuff to Laura. It ought to be said, but if I say it she'll just stop listening before I even start. I want *Simon* to say it! I want Simon to open his eyes and see this whole situation for what it is and tell his mother that he is her loving and supportive son and that he is *not* a bloody substitute husband! That's what I want!'

Alan put out a hand and lightly touched her nearest one.

'Oh dear,' he said.

Simon let himself into the house quietly. Carrie had said she was seeing someone and then she was picking Emma up from something so she wouldn't be home until around nine. Rachel was out somewhere. And Jack—Carrie hadn't mentioned Jack. The thought of an empty house was oddly soothing. Usually, it was necessary to announce his return home by banging the door and flinging his keys onto the chest in the hall so that they would all know. They mightn't react, they certainly wouldn't all come skidding down the stairs to meet him, but at least they'd all *know*, and the human chemistry in the house could shift a little, to accommodate him, to acknowledge that he, Simon, husband, father, chief breadwinner, was home.

He put his keys softly on the hall chest beside a scatter of unopened mail and went into the kitchen. The room looked strangely tidy and smelt of something slightly chemical, like bleach. By the cooker was a pile of vegetables, tomatoes and peppers and aubergines and onions heaped up like a still life, on a wooden board. There was also a supermarket pack of pathetic little pink chicken strips confined under plastic film and looking as if they had never had the smallest association with anything living and breathing. Carrie, in a fit of forward planning, was evidently going to make supper when she got back.

He went out of the kitchen, hanging his suit jacket on the newel post at the foot of the stairs, and climbed upwards, loosening his tie and unbuttoning his shirt as he went. He felt, in a way he couldn't in the least account for, happier than he had felt for ages, oddly released, in the empty house with the late spring light fading outside and with the prospect of a long bath with Ella Fitzgerald playing or maybe some Gershwin. He went lightly along the landing, sliding his tie out from under his shirt collar, and opened his bedroom door.

The curtains were half pulled across, so that the room was dim. There was a peculiar silence in it, the silence you get with tension, or a terrific social awkwardness. Simon looked around. Carrie was in the bed, humped up as she was when she got one of her migraines. Poor Carrie.

He went softly towards the bed. He couldn't see her hair, only something dark and unfamiliar on the pillow. He said, whispering in case she was asleep, 'Carrie? You OK?'

There was a slow movement in the bed. The hump of Carrie stirred and flattened out into two shapes. Looking down, his tie still in his hand and his shirt unbuttoned to the waist, Simon found himself regarding Jack and Moll, their faces side by side and close together, looking up.

'Were you cross?' Carrie said. She was sitting on the bathroom floor, wrapped in a towel, clipping her toenails.

'No,' Simon said. He gazed down the length of the bath at his feet, arranged neatly either side of the taps.

'Why not?'

'Because I didn't feel it.'

'Jack expected you to be furious. He kept shooting you glances, like someone waiting for the big firework to go off.'

'It was very peculiar,' Simon said, 'but I didn't want to shout. I kept waiting for myself to say, "How dare you and in our bed," and stuff, but I never did. I felt . . .'

'What?'

'Rather envious.'

'*Envious*? Of Jack? Having Moll?'

'No,' Simon said crossly. He sat up and began to rub soap into a face flannel. 'No. Of them. Of, well, their freedom.'

There was a pause and then Carrie said, very shortly, 'Yes.'

Simon began soaping his face and neck and chest. 'They weren't really very embarrassed. Jack was a bit, I suppose.'

Carrie said, 'D'you think it was his first time?'

'I haven't the first idea.'

Simon put a wet arm out of the bath and pulled at the back of Carrie's towel.

'Don't,' she said. 'You'll make me jerk and I'll cut my toes not my toenails.'

'I'll suck them for you.'

'Simon!' Carrie said. 'What has got into you?'

'I don't know,' he said. He leaned back and floated the flannel in the water above a rising erection. 'I just feel better. I don't know why. I grasped a small nettle today. Maybe—'

'What nettle?'

'I rang Dad.'

'And?'

'I didn't speak to him, but I left a message.'

'Very brave.'

'Carrie.'

'What?'

'Come here.'

She got up and came to half crouch by the bath. Simon smiled at her. She had her hair held up in a tangle with one of Rachel's silly pink plastic spring-clip things. He loved it like that. She looked about sixteen.

'Get in the bath with me,' he said and reached out for her nearest hand. 'Come on.'

'Si,' Carrie said, 'you may have had a good day and think the Jack and Moll episode is just a jolly jape, but I haven't. And I don't.'

Simon twitched her towel off. 'Forget all that now.'

She pulled her hand out of his grasp and bent for her towel. He saw her breasts swing briefly, little pale globes. 'A mouthful,' he used to say to her. 'Just right.'

She stepped back. 'Sorry,' she said.

He looked at her. 'Even if I said please?'

She shook her head.

'When did we last have sex?' he said.

Carrie was struggling into her old cotton kimono. 'Oh, some time last century, I should think. And what happened to the phrase "making love"?'

Simon grasped the edge of the bath. He leaned towards her. 'Carrie,' he said, 'I really, really want to make love to you. Now. Please. *Please*.'

She put her hand on the bathroom door knob. 'It has to be for real.'

'It *is*. My God, it is!'

She opened the door. She had tied the kimono sash tightly round her waist. She looked as fragile as a porcelain doll.

'Nothing's real just now,' she said, and went out.

The valuer from the estate agent's in Stanborough turned out to be a woman. Laura had been expecting a man, one of those predictable estate-agent men in a dark suit and a white shirt and a slightly too loud tie with a silly motif all over it: cartoon pigs, or elephants, or camels under palm trees. Laura knew how to deal with those kinds of men, knew how to answer their questions. The valuer woman looked rather different. She was almost Laura's age, for one thing, and she had a quiet, firm manner that made Laura feel she was only interested in figures, and not in the least in Laura and Laura's plight.

Laura had made coffee but she declined it, and asked for a glass of water instead. She took two sips and then said, 'Perhaps you would show me round. And then I'd be most grateful to be left alone to measure up. Usually I have an assistant, but he has an exam today.'

Laura said, without intending to, 'Would you like me to help?'

The valuer looked at her. She gave a very small smile.

'No, thank you,' she said.

Laura walked ahead of her through the house. She had put flowers in the hall and polished the front windows where the wind always blew dust up from the gravel outside. She had told Simon she wasn't going to bother, that it was both heartbreaking and pointless to show off something you'd given so much time and thought and energy to and that you were now forced to lose.

Simon said, 'Just think of the money.'

'I wish it was that simple.'

'It is. It has to be.'

He had sounded exasperated, almost cross. Laura could imagine how little help Carrie was being, how unsympathetic she'd be about any part of Simon's life that didn't concern herself or their children.

When Simon had fallen in love with Carrie, Laura had said to Guy, 'Don't you think she's hard?'

'No,' he said. 'She's just very candid.'

'But does she see how sensitive he is?'

'Yes,' Guy said, 'and she's candid about that, too.'

'You've always wanted to toughen him up—'

'Not toughen. Teach to defend. Defend himself.'

'Toughen,' Laura had said again, very quietly.

After a few years, when Simon had actually married Carrie—his wedding day had been a hard day for Laura, hard in a way she saw nobody could perceive but herself—he used to say to her, when she called him in the office, 'Mum. Why don't you ring Carrie? Why don't you just ring her?'

She'd always let a little silence fall. In that silence she let Simon know—she had to let him know—that it wasn't Carrie she needed to speak to, it wasn't Carrie who knew her history, spoke her quiet, understated, meaningful language. After the silence had gone on for a little while, she'd say, 'I will. Of course I will,' and they'd both know she wouldn't. Only once had Simon said, 'Please, Mum, for my sake—' and she had said in reply, wanting him to know he was breaking their private rules, 'Simon. That isn't fair.'

'OK,' he'd said. 'OK. Forget it.'

He sounded weary. Next day, she rang to apologise.

'It's so difficult—'

'Don't,' he said. 'Don't explain. You don't have to.'

She'd smiled. 'No, I don't, do I? I never have to, with you.'

Now, she pushed the sitting-room door wide. The sun was coming in through the southeast-facing windows and lying optimistically across the sofa and chairs whose covers she'd made herself, across the pale-green carpet and the rug with its Tree of Life pattern that Guy had bought at an auction along with a chicken coop—never used—and a pair of Versailles tubs she'd stripped of their flaking varnish and painted dark green and planted with bay trees.

'Pleasant room, Mrs Stockdale,' the valuer said, surveying the room with an assessing eye. 'Good dimensions.'

'It was three little rooms,' Laura said, 'when we came. One was full of potatoes, all sprouting. You can imagine the smell.'

The valuer looked at her properly for the first time. 'How long have you been here, Mrs Stockdale?'

Laura moved to hold the back of the nearest armchair. She leaned on it. She wished that she could just stay plain angry all the time. Angry was fine. When she was angry she had purpose and energy, she could even sometimes glimpse a new self emerging from all this muddle and emotional squalor. It was the times when the anger died that she dreaded. Without anger, she fell prey to desolation, to a feeling of disorientation so deep she wondered if she actually had fallen right through the web of the life she had always—even in her darkest moments—taken for granted. Desolation meant grief, grief for the loss of so many huge and so many tiny things that it was quite beyond her to try to number them.

'Are you all right, Mrs Stockdale?'

Laura nodded. She made an immense effort and looked up. 'We came here thirty years ago. My boys were eight and five. Younger than my grandchildren are now.'

In a different tone of voice to the one she'd used earlier, the valuer said, 'It's a wrench, isn't it—'

Laura put her hands over her face. From behind them she cried, 'I don't want this to happen! I don't want to leave!'

'I'm so sorry—'

Laura took her hands away from her face. She said, almost gasping, 'Sometimes I think this is all I've done, all I've achieved. When I think of myself, Hill Cottage and the garden is *how* I think of myself. It's—it's my sort of landscape, my background. If I go—'

The valuer waited. She had put down her measure and her notebook and was simply standing there, almost as if she was braced to catch Laura should she fall.

'I'll vanish,' Laura whispered. 'There—there won't be any need for me, any more. Will there?'

The valuer bent and picked up her measure again. She held it out to Laura. 'I wonder, Mrs Stockdale, if you would be very kind and help me with this? After all?'

'Sorry,' Carrie said the next morning.

Simon was balanced astride the sink trying to fix the kitchen blind which had unrolled itself quietly in the night and was now declining to roll itself up again, and stay rolled. He gave a little grunt.

'About last night,' she said.

'I know.'

'It isn't very easy to explain—'

'Nothing is, right now,' Simon said. 'That's why twenty minutes of happy, uncomplicated sex would have been so great.'

'I know,' Carrie said. She poured cereal into two bowls. She said, rather hesitantly, 'Your—your mother—'

'What the hell has she got to do with our sex life?'

The blind, having hung limply above the sink, suddenly became galvanised with activity and rushed up into a tight roll, taking the tips of Simon's fingers with it.

'*Shit*,' Simon said, jumping lightly to the floor. He shook his fingers. 'My cheque-signing hand.'

She held her own hand out. 'Let me look. Are you hurt?'

He put his hand in hers. She bent and kissed his fingertips.

'Oh, Carrie—'

'I'm jealous,' she whispered into his hand. 'I want you back.'

'I haven't gone anywhere—'

'But you might.'

Simon took his hand back. 'I *have* to help her. There's no one else.'

'But you can't be held responsible for that. It isn't your fault that she's never made friends, that she hardly speaks to her sister, that she thinks Alan isn't a fully operational adult.'

Simon poured milk on to one bowl of cereal and held it out to her. 'What do you want to do?' he said.

'What do *I* want to do?'

'Yes.'

She looked down at the cereal. She seemed to be struggling either to say something or not to say it.

'It's not me—' she said finally.

Simon picked up the second cereal bowl, and a spoon.

'Let's not start on what Simon is doing wrong again. Please.'

Carrie took a breath. She put her cereal bowl down. 'OK,' she said.

He took a mouthful, and crunched it. Through it, he said, 'OK what?'

'I do want to do something.'

The kitchen door opened. Rachel, in her school uniform with the addition of a small blue glitter butterfly stuck to her cheek, came in, yawning cavernously.

'Morning, darling,' Carrie said.

Simon ignored his daughter. He said, his eyes on his cereal, 'What? What do you want to do?'

'I want to ask Merrion Palmer here. For supper. Or Sunday lunch.'

Rachel stopped yawning. 'Wow,' she said.

Simon looked up from his cereal and stared at Carrie. 'Merrion Palmer?'

'Yes,' Carrie said. 'Her.'

'With or without my father?'

Rachel leaned across the table and drew Carrie's cereal bowl towards her. 'Without,' she said.

Carrie glanced at her. Then she stood a little straighter and looked at Simon. 'Yes,' she said, 'Rachel's right. Without.'

Merrion lay on her sofa. She had taken off her work clothes and put on the dark blue bathrobe she had bought for Guy. It was new but he had worn it enough to have left it faintly impregnated, besides the smell of newness, with the smell of him.

She had made herself a mug of tea and a honey sandwich and had the telephone balanced on her stomach. In five minutes, she would ring Guy. He would be back in his flat then, in this flat he wouldn't talk about and wouldn't let her see.

'It doesn't matter,' he said. 'It's just a space, a passing practicality. I'm going to rub it out of memory when it's gone.'

Because he wouldn't tell her about it, she pictured it. She imagined it worse than it probably was. She saw a rickety shower and a dank little kitchen smelling of drains and his suits hanging in a plywood wardrobe with fancy plastic handles and doors that wouldn't shut. She couldn't imagine him in bed. She'd tried, and the picture that had swum into her mind, the bleakness and the loneliness of those nights, had been too much to bear. It was worse—weirdly worse—than all those months and years of knowing he was in bed at Hill Cottage with Laura. There'd been envy in that, but also a small thrill because of the private, certain—oh, so certain—knowledge of where he'd rather be, where he was thinking of being. But his nights in the nameless rented flat were different. There was no secrecy to them, no illicit, gorgeous longing.

She put her mug down on the coffee table and sat up sufficiently to be able to see the dialling buttons. She pressed the relevant ones rapidly, and lay back on the sofa cushions, the receiver to her ear.

'Hello, darling,' Guy said.

She smiled into the telephone. 'Good, bad or indifferent?'

'Patchy,' he said. 'Word has got out that Hill Cottage is on the market. They seem to know Laura and I have parted. I don't know if they know about you.'

'Course they do.'

'Really?'

'You know what gossips people are.'

'Well,' Guy said, 'everyone is treating me as if I was an invalid. Martin, the court manager, opened two doors for me today. He'll be giving me his arm up steps next.'

Merrion shifted her position a little. 'I've got something to tell you.'

'Something I'll like?'

'Yes,' she said. 'Carrie and Simon have asked me to supper. At least, Carrie has.'

'Oh!' he said. She could hear his voice warming, imagine him smiling. 'Oh, I *am* glad!'

'I am, too, in a slightly alarmed way.'

'Because of Simon—'

'Yes.'

'Merrion—'

'It's just very hard to be disapproved of for what you represent rather than what you are.'

There was a little pause and then Guy said, 'I know.'

'Guy. You're not still thinking about my mother, are you?'

'Dearest, it isn't something I can pretend didn't happen.'

She said earnestly, 'But you don't have to *heed* her. What she says and thinks is for *her* life, *her* personality, *her* circumstances. It's not for yours and it's certainly not for mine.'

'What I couldn't bear,' Guy said, 'is to do anything to impede your progress, clip your wings—'

'You don't. I've told you. Over and over, I've told you.'

'In ten years—'

'Stop it. Guy, *stop* it.'

'Things are changing,' Guy said. 'You take a step forward and all the landscape round you changes, the perspective is different—'

Merrion sat up. She wound the coiled telephone cable round her fingers and pulled it tight. 'Guy,' she said, 'I'm not having any more of this conversation over the telephone. We shouldn't talk like this when we can't get at each other.'

She heard him catch his breath, and then he said, in a stronger, more impersonal tone, 'When are you having supper with Carrie and Simon?'

'Tomorrow. I'm in chambers all day. Conferences and paperwork. So—well, that's good.'

'It is.'

'What's on the menu tonight? Chicken Korma and *Little Dorrit*?'

He laughed. 'Pretty nearly.'

She blew a kiss into the telephone. 'Miss you,' she said. 'Miss you all the time.'

She untangled the cable from her fingers and set the telephone down on the coffee table. Her tea was cold and her sandwich looked as if it might be an effort and not a pleasure to eat. She rolled back onto the sofa and faced the cushions along the back of it, running her forefinger along the bumpy lines of weaving in the nearest one.

Guy had been very shaken by Gwen's visit. In all their years together, Merrion had never seen him thrown to this degree, so disconcerted. And it was perfectly plain that he was still unable to shake off the effect of the visit, unable to get various ingenious little phrases out of his mind. Merrion knew that feeling, could probably even, after years of teaching herself to come to terms with the uneasiness of the relationship between her mother and herself, recall in precise detail various little barbs of Gwen's—and the extraordinary, enduring stabs of pain that went with them. Protecting herself had, over time, become one thing, but protecting Guy required something more proactive, and if it meant a stand-up screaming match—so familiar still, from her late adolescence—then so be it.

Merrion sat up, tightened the sash of Guy's bathrobe and pushed her hair firmly off her face and behind her shoulders. Then she picked up the telephone, put it on her knees, and dialled her mother's number.

'It's only pasta,' Carrie said.

Merrion was leaning against the kitchen cupboards on the opposite side of the room, holding a glass of wine. 'I like pasta.'

'So do I. But sometimes I get tired of it being such a staple. We eat it all the time, *all* the time, because I don't have to think about it and I know everybody will eat it.'

'When I was doing my Bar finals,' Merrion said, 'I ate baked potatoes like that. Every day.'

Carrie put a pan of boiling water on the stove.

'Can I help?' Merrion said. 'Can I chop something?'

'It's all done, really,' Carrie said. 'Rachel even made a sauce—'

'Rachel—'

'My fourteen-year-old.'

'Does she cook?'

'No. Never. But she made a carbonara sauce because you were coming.'

Merrion looked down. 'I don't know how to take that.'

'I wouldn't take it any way,' Carrie said. 'I'd just be prepared for it to taste a little strange.'

In the hall beyond the kitchen, the front door slammed and someone threw their keys on to a hard surface.

'Simon,' Carrie said.

Merrion put her wineglass down on the counter behind her.

Carrie gave her a quick smile. 'Deep breath.'

Merrion nodded. 'Yes—'

A man appeared in the kitchen doorway. Merrion had the impression of quite a tall man, a dark man, a man in a rumpled business suit and a blue shirt.

'Hi,' the man said to Carrie, in Guy's voice. He bent a little and kissed her. 'OK?'

'Simon,' Carrie said, 'this is Merrion.'

He turned towards her. The light from the window was behind him so she couldn't see him very well, only enough to establish that the outline was Guy's and the face was not.

'Hello,' he said.

She tried to smile. 'Hello.'

He put a hand up to his collar, to loosen his tie. 'Has Carrie given you a drink?'

'Oh, yes,' she said and then, as steadily as she could, 'I'm glad to be here.'

He nodded. 'Good,' he said.

'It was brave of Carrie—'

'No, it wasn't,' Carrie said.

'To invite me.'

'She is brave,' Simon said. 'Reckless sometimes.'

'I like that,' Merrion said.

There was the sudden sound of feet on the stairs, running feet, and then the thud of a jumped landing in the hall. A girl stood in the kitchen doorway, a big child girl in cargo pants and a tiny black top that showed a strip of pale, soft, very young midriff.

'Merrion,' Carrie said, 'this is Emma.'

'Hello, Emma,' Merrion said.

'When's supper?' Emma said to Carrie.

'Say hello to Merrion,' Carrie said.

Emma looked quickly at Merrion. Then she looked at the floor in front of Merrion's feet. 'Hi.'

'It's OK,' Merrion said, 'none of us knows what to do.'

'We will, though,' Carrie said. 'We'll get used to it.'

Simon took off his jacket and hung it on the back of the nearest chair. 'Come and sit down,' he said to Merrion. He pulled another chair out slightly from the kitchen table and patted the back of it.

'Thank you,' she said. She moved towards the chair.

'Bring your wine—'

'Oh—'

'I'll get it,' Emma said.

She put the wineglass down in front of Merrion.

'Thank you.'

Simon went over to the fridge and took out a wine bottle. He waved it at Carrie. 'Got some?'

She nodded, then turned to her daughter. 'Ems. Lay the table, would you?'

'I can do that,' Merrion said.

Simon put the bottle and a glass on the table opposite Merrion. 'Next time.'

She looked at him. He wasn't smiling, but he was looking back, straight at her.

'Oh—'

He poured the wine. Then he raised his glass.

'Cheers.'

Emma dumped a handful of knives and forks on the table. 'Rach's door is shut.'

'Maybe,' Carrie said, 'she's doing her biology.'

Emma snorted. 'Where's Jack?' she said.

'Out,' Carrie said.

Emma snorted again.

'Jack,' Simon said to Merrion, 'has a girlfriend.'

'It's pathetic,' Emma said. 'Pitiful.'

Merrion smiled at her. 'You wait,' she said.

Emma tossed her tuft of hair. 'I won't be pathetic, like Jack.'

'Maybe,' Simon said, 'you won't be able to help it.'

Merrion began to pick individual forks out of the pile of cutlery. 'How many places?'

The telephone rang. Emma said immediately, 'I'll go.'

'It rings all the time,' Simon said. 'All the time.'

'And never for us,' Carrie said.

'Hello?' Emma said, her back to the room. 'Oh. Oh—hi, Granny.' She swivelled round, gesturing. 'Yes,' she said, 'OK. No, no, he's here, I'll get him, I'll—hang on, Granny—'

She put her free hand over the telephone mouthpiece. Simon was on his feet already.

'Quick, Dad, it's Gran. She's crying. It's awful.'

There was a tiny pause. Then Simon said to Carrie, 'I'll take it in the office.'

'OK—'

'Tell her I'm coming, Ems. Tell her I've just gone to another phone.' He ran from the room. Emma took her hand away from the mouthpiece. She exchanged a glance with her mother.

Then she said into the telephone, 'It's OK, Gran. Hold on. Dad's just gone to another phone. He's coming, OK?'

CHAPTER SEVEN

SIMON WAS STANDING behind his desk when his father arrived. He'd been about to go round it and meet Guy in the doorway of his office, at least, but Guy was too quick for him.

He shut Simon's office door carefully behind him. 'Hello,' he said.

Simon swallowed. 'Hello, Dad.'

Guy seemed to hesitate for a second, and then he came determinedly forward, and took Simon in his arms.

Simon just stood there. He felt the bulk of his father; he smelt the smell of the old-fashioned citrus-based men's cologne he had always used, the smell that had pervaded the laundry basket at Hill Cottage, Guy's wardrobe, his shirt drawers.

'Relax,' Guy said.

'Please—'

'What?'

'Let go,' Simon said.

Guy stepped back a short pace. He held Simon still by his upper arms. Simon could feel the warmth of Guy's hands through the cotton of his shirt sleeves.

'Don't take it out on me,' Guy said.

'What—'

'The fact that you have been put in an impossible position.'

'She's afraid. She can't face anything she doesn't know.'

Guy gave Simon's arms a little squeeze and dropped his hands. He went back round Simon's desk and pulled up a chair. 'It won't help her, then, only communicating through you; it won't help her see that she might manage, that there is a future—'

Simon said shortly. 'I can only do what she wants. What she's able to want.'

'But surely a lawyer you know, someone you introduced her to—'

'No.'

'Have you tried?'

'That's none of your business,' Simon said politely. He sat down opposite Guy.

'I haven't seen you for so long,' Guy said.

'No.'

'Nearly three months.'

'Dad—'

'I'm not blaming you,' Guy said. 'I'm not blaming anybody. Except myself, probably. I could have come to find you any time. I could have told you any time. But I didn't. I didn't tell anyone. I told myself, instead, that a way would be made plain to me.'

'And it was.'

A look of intense and happy privacy passed briefly across Guy's face. 'It was.'

'Have *you* got a lawyer?' Simon asked.

'Yes,' Guy said.

'A friend of—Merrion's?'

'Yes.'

'So I will be negotiating with a friend of Merrion's. To whom you will make full financial disclosure.'

'Yes.'

'Dad—'

Guy leaned forward. He said, 'Shall we make a pact?'

'What?'

'Nothing but the facts? Only the facts? No opinions—'

'If we can stick to it,' Simon said. 'But there are things I have to tell you.'

'Like?'

'Mum is completely shattered about the house going. I mean devastated. Unhinged.'

'If I could afford to let her stay there, I would.'

Simon uncapped a ballpoint and began to scribble on the margin of a printed paper in front of him. 'It's worth three hundred and twenty-five thousand.'

Guy let out a breath. 'I paid six for it. Six thousand one hundred. Thirty years ago.'

'Half Mum's life.'

'Half mine, too.'

'But you're going *on* to something,' Simon said. 'You're moving *on*.'

Guy said quietly, 'Maybe I'd have done that anyway.'

'And she never would?'

'I did not say that—'

'But you meant it.'

'Yes,' Guy said, 'I meant it.' He looked at Simon again. 'Can you cope? You look tired—'

'I always look tired, for the simple reason that I am.'

'And angry,' Guy said.

Simon said nothing.

'Simon,' Guy said, 'you're my son as well as your mother's. You're my child, too.'

Simon said, his head bent, 'So what do *you* feel entitled to, then?'

'It's not that. It's just that because I'm your father I can't be indifferent to you, to your opinions, your actions, your attitudes.'

Between gritted teeth Simon said, 'Works both ways—'

'I'm glad to hear it—'

'Glad?'

'Glad that you do have a heart.'

Simon pulled a blank piece of paper towards him. He said, 'What is the name of your solicitor?'

'Susan Dewar.'

'I know Susan Dewar.'

'Good.'

'To whom you and I will both reveal statements of assets we both know already and then argue about them. What a bloody farce.'

'I won't argue,' Guy said. 'I'm not *fighting* your mother, Simon.'

Simon said, without thinking, 'She's fighting *you*.'

Guy stood up. 'It doesn't follow that *you* have to fight me.'

Simon said unhappily, 'I don't know—'

'Don't you?' Guy said. His voice was sharper. 'Don't you even know your *own* mind?'

Simon got up and said, 'You'd better go.'

Guy moved towards the door. With his hand on the handle, he turned to look at Simon. 'If we were Americans, we could tell each other we loved each other at this point.'

'Would that help?'

'I think it might—bridge a gap.'

'Would we have to mean it?'

'Oh, Simon,' Guy said. He turned the door handle. Simon looked away.

'Bye,' Guy said briefly, and went out.

Rachel stood in front of the mirror on Carrie's wardrobe door. She was trying on clothes. She'd put on her new baggy jeans—they sat on her hips most satisfactorily—and then over that a black lace mini dress she'd found in a secondhand shop for two pounds and over that a grey wool V-knecked sweater of her father's. Emma was out—drama club was rehearsing *Joseph and the Amazing Technicolor Dreamcoat*—so Rachel had borrowed Emma's new dark blue wedge-soled rubber mules. The effect was good. Rachel turned and looked at herself sideways. Her bosom—it was going to be really small, like Carrie's—hardly showed at all. Her tummy (her obsession) didn't show either, but she could see it all the same, pushing obscenely, roundly, at the denim and the black lace. She'd eaten nothing that day but two carrots, a bag of barbecue-flavour crisps and two handfuls of raspberry crunch cereal dry, straight out of the packet. She wouldn't eat any supper. Or at least, she'd pick out the low-calorie bits of supper and leave the rest. Carrie wouldn't notice. She was preoccupied at the moment and not as observant as usual. If she'd been observant, she'd have noticed that Emma had had her belly button pierced by a friend at school using a needle and a cork and some ice cubes, that Rachel was hardly eating and that Jack had enough condoms in his bedroom to kit out the British Army.

Jack had discovered sex. Rachel was half intrigued and half repelled. The word at school was that Moll Saunders knew what she was doing, and although not exactly promiscuous—she didn't go in for one-night stands—she was pretty experienced. And whatever experience she had, she was plainly imparting it to Jack, session by absorbing session, to the point where it was plain to Rachel—and probably to half the school, too—that it was absolutely all he could think about. When Rachel had had a good illicit snoop around Jack's bedroom, she had expected to find a lot of pornographic stuff about, magazines and videos. But, apart from the condoms, there was nothing, no sign of fantasy or solitary dreaming. Rachel had thought she felt disappointed; she expected, she knew, to find more: cruder evidence of Jack's unavoidable adolescent-boy preoccupation. But when she got back to her bedroom and lay on the bed in the dark listening to Brandy, she realised that she wasn't so much disappointed as jealous. She was jealous of Jack's intensity of feeling. She was jealous of Moll for having someone *that* interested in her, that obsessed. Rachel and Trudy scoffed at boys, scoffed together about them. But faced with Jack and Moll, Rachel knew she'd sell her soul to have someone—someone attractive, that is—so keen on her that he couldn't see straight.

There was a movement outside Carrie's bedroom door.

'Rach?' Carrie said.

'Yeah—'

The door opened. Rachel held one foot up, shod in Emma's mule. 'Don't tell me, I'm going to put them back.'

Carrie looked at her. 'I like the dress and the sweater, but why the jeans?'

'It's cool. It's the layered look.'

'But doesn't it matter what the layers are?'

'Jeans are OK, Mum.'

'If you say so.'

Carrie went past Rachel and opened her wardrobe door. She took off her suit jacket—rather tiredly, Rachel thought—and put it crookedly on a hanger. When she lifted it to hang it inside the wardrobe, it immediately fell off.

'Damn.'

Rachel bent and picked it up. It was still warm, from being on Carrie.

'Where's Dad?'

'Guess,' Carrie said. She took the jacket and hung it up again, her face averted so that Rachel couldn't really see it.

Rachel hesitated, then she said, 'I forgot he'd gone to Granny's. He—he asked me to go with him.'

Carrie stared at her. 'What did you *say*?'

'Well, I couldn't, could I? There's school.'

'It's half term,' Carrie said, looking confused.

Rachel squirmed faintly. 'I forgot.'

Carrie didn't say anything. She unzipped her work skirt and let it fall to the floor. She was wearing black tights underneath, and one leg had a narrow white ladder in it, running up Carrie's thigh from the knee. She stepped out of her skirt and picked her jeans up from the muddle of clothes on the couch. 'Poor Dad,' she said as she pulled her jeans on, struggling unsteadily on one leg.

Rachel watched her. Something about her new-found discovery of jealousy made her think Carrie looked sad, really sad, and not stupid or inept or typical-Mum-ish as she would have expected herself to think. She said awkwardly, turning up the long, baggy sleeves of Simon's sweater, 'Poor you.'

Carrie stopped pulling her zip up. Her hair was falling everywhere. 'Is that why you didn't go?' she said.

Rachel shrugged.

Carrie said, a little unsteadily, 'I don't want you to have to take sides.'

Rachel muttered, her head bent, 'I'll decide that.'

'It isn't that I don't understand,' Carrie said. 'It isn't that I don't see how difficult it is for him.' She finished pulling up her zip and reached for a red sweatshirt. 'I wouldn't like you to think—'

'I don't,' Rachel said. She took both feet out of Emma's mules and bent to pick them up. 'I'd better put these back—'

'Yes,' Carrie said. She ran a hand through her hair then came quickly over to Rachel and gave her a kiss on her cheek. 'Thank you,' she said.

Rachel couldn't look at her. There was a sudden lump of misery in her throat, hard and tight, like a hazelnut.

'That's OK,' she said, and went out.

Merrion's room in chambers looked down onto a narrow walk that led into New Square. People went up and down the walk all day, lawyers and ordinary pedestrians, and Merrion often wondered if they really felt as animated, as purposeful, as they looked.

Nobody in her personal life had ever seen her room, not even Guy, certainly not Gwen. Gwen would have thought it very impersonal, cold even, with its white-painted shelves of law books, its framed Hogarth prints of the Law Courts, its complete absence of photographs or flowers. It was how Merrion liked it, however: it was where she could think.

And at that precise moment she was thinking about her phone conversation with her mother. 'You had no business to attack Guy like you did,' Merrion had said. 'Me, well, OK if you simply have to, though I could probably write your speech for you. But you had absolutely no right to go for him. You took advantage of his good manners. He should have thrown you out.'

Gwen said, with a small note of triumph, 'He didn't think it was none of my business. He said—'

'I don't want to know what he said. It's happened, it's caused great misery and complication, but it's over. I'm just ringing to tell you it won't happen again. Ever. You will mind your own business in future.'

'I won't be patronised,' Gwen said. 'I won't be told.'

Merrion gripped the receiver. 'Too right,' she said. 'You won't be told *any*thing.'

Gwen had written to her, after that. She had written a letter ostentatiously addressed to Merrion in chambers, marked *Strictly private and personal*. It was a good letter, Merrion had to admit that. It was calm and dignified and made the point that Merrion's welfare could not possibly be a matter of indifference to Gwen, and that Gwen's standards and opinions, even if very much less sophisticated than Merrion's, did not on that account lack their own validity. It was not Guy as a *person* she objected to, but the consequences of his age in relation to Merrion's and the strength of his emotional desires which, even if they coincided with Merrion's, were nevertheless forcing a pace whose long-term outcome nobody seemed to be prepared to face squarely and openly.

Merrion did not show the letter to Guy. She was aware that this was not like her, that her instinct and habit had always been to tell him everything, not least because he was so wonderfully able to restore her sense of proportion. But in the past, her feelings about him had not been particularly protective. Merrion was aware from the beginning—rapturously aware—of Guy's delight in being able to talk to her, being free to talk to her, but she had never, until recently, felt the need to defend him, and, in the process of that defence, not only curb her own tongue but also refrain from asking too many questions. What had been so clear between them had become less definable. A veil had appeared, a series of veils, which made the business of loving no less ardent but much less simple.

It came down in the end, Merrion thought, to all these *people*. These people who had been names and images before, but no more. For years Simon and Carrie and Alan and even Laura had been in Merrion's consciousness, at one remove, the wife and the sons and the daughter-in-law. They belonged in a mental in-tray marked 'one day'. Merrion got very used to having that in-tray there, very used to thinking that the future was something like Christmas, undeniably there, not particularly threatening, which would quietly arrive in its own good time with an accompanying set of rituals and instructions.

But it hadn't been like that. It hadn't been like that, at all. One day, the future was where it had always been, comfortably upon some fairly remote horizon, and the next day, it had arrived. It arrived without warning and within hours Merrion had gone from an acceptance of how things were to a real, profound and painful longing for something more.

'I can't bear this,' Guy had said. 'I can't bear living this part-life with you any more. I can't bear the waste of it.'

And almost before the words were out of his mouth, she had realised that she had been desperate for him to say them, that she had had enough of not minding—not minding Christmas, not minding weekends, not minding Laura's birthday—and that (most extraordinary of all) what had for seven years seemed thrilling and potent and truly essential had come, in moments, to feel contrived and furtive and distasteful. In the space of a day her sheer pride in being Guy's *mistress* turned into something, at a stroke, whose glamour she could scarcely remember.

And then the people came in. The names were fleshed out, the personalities grew from little lists of adjectives into palpable beings, beings to be reckoned with. Guy—no less loving, no less attentive—seemed all the same to retreat into the landscape of these people. Whatever he did or didn't do, these people reclaimed him, recalled him, reminded him of what they felt he owed them. And, as a result, a kind of helplessness had descended upon Guy and Merrion; she saw the two of them, in her mind's eye, like two figures in German Romantic painting, clinging together on a clifftop while a huge, bruise-coloured storm rolled inexorably towards them.

She looked at her watch. It was two o'clock. She had a conference at three that would, with luck, be over by four thirty. Then she would telephone Guy.

'Come up to London,' she'd say.

'What? How lovely. A not-Friday—'

He never said no. He'd come up, on the five o'clock train, and be in the flat by six thirty, where she'd already be, with supper bought and wine in the fridge and her black suit exchanged for trousers and a jersey, and her announcement. She would announce that she was tired of taking what came, being paced and checked by other people. Whether he was divorced or not, whether Laura was dragging her heels or not, whether Simon and Susan Dewar were in agreement or not, she was going to announce a wedding day. Had he heard her? She wanted to decide a date to be married.

'Three offers?' Wendy said. 'That's wonderful.'

Laura said, 'One of them is quite a bit above the asking price—'

Wendy gave the garden table in front of her a little slap. 'Well, now that's something to rejoice over!'

'I'd have to share it with Guy,' Laura said primly.

'You said Simon was making him give you the lion's share.'

'Oh, yes.'

'Then if you get more money for this, *you'll* have more.'

Laura looked down the garden. The herbaceous border was full of bright clumps of new leaves, the first stirrings of lupins, aquilegia, delphiniums, foxgloves. She said, 'It isn't about that.'

Wendy looked at her coffee mug. Then she looked at the almost empty coffee pot. Then she looked at the tubs of huge blue pansies beside her and at the aubrietia and the iberis spilling over a low wall, and then she looked at Laura. 'You could do this garden again,' she said.

'What for?'

'For exactly the same reason as you did this. Because you're good at it. Because you like it.'

'But there would be no point to it . . .'

'Don't kid yourself.'

'About what?'

'That there was any point beyond your own pleasure in making *this* garden. Guy isn't a garden man. Never has been.'

Laura said to her lap, 'I wanted him to be.'

Wendy poured herself some cold coffee. 'Laura—'

'Yes.'

'You'll have to stop this.'

'Stop what?'

'All this pretending. All this being sorry for yourself. It's not fair on anyone, particularly not on your children.'

'Simon doesn't mind. Simon—'

'You aren't *allowing* Simon to mind,' Wendy said. 'You're treating Simon just like you treated Guy, taking the bits you want. I wonder sometimes—did you ever love Guy, or did you just want him to love you?'

Laura grasped the arms of her green plastic garden chair. 'How dare you,' she said. 'Why would I want him to love me if I didn't love him?'

Wendy leaned back and looked up at a trio of ducks flying in neat triangular formation overhead. 'You tell me,' she said.

'Oh!' Laura cried, and covered her face with her hands.

Wendy stood up. 'Tell you what—'

Laura waited, her hands over her face.

'I think you could do with a little therapy.'

Laura snatched her hands away. '*Therapy?*'

'Yes.'

'I'm not mad!' Laura shrieked. 'I'm not out of my mind!'

'I didn't say that. But some therapy could help you reconcile yourself to what's happened, to the future.'

Laura glared at her. She stood up abruptly. She seemed to be simmering with things she wanted to say and somehow couldn't.

Wendy stood up, too, and slung her bag on to her shoulder. 'Unless, of course,' she said, 'you really have no intention of ever being reconciled to anything.'

The senior clerk looked at his watch. Then he looked at Alan. He said, 'I'm expecting Miss Palmer back from court in about fifteen minutes, sir.'

Alan said, 'Can I wait?'

'Certainly, sir. Do you have an appointment?'

'No,' Alan said, 'I'm family.' He paused. The senior clerk had gold-rimmed spectacles and the air of someone who expects to be informed and, subsequently, to decide.

'I'll wait in her room,' Alan said. This was all an impulse, finding himself walking through New Square after a prolonged and happy lunch with Charlie, and deciding just to drop in on Merrion. It might be the Chianti—they'd shared a bottle and been hugely tempted by a second except Charlie had a four o'clock surgery—but Alan didn't feel inclined to be intimidated by Gold Spectacles. He put a hand on the counter separating the clerks from the outside world. 'If you'll just tell me where it is?'

The senior clerk hesitated for a second. 'Your name, sir?'

'Alan Stockdale. My father—'

'Exactly, sir,' the clerk said, and directed Alan to Merrion's room. 'I'll tell her you're here, Mr Stockdale.'

'Thank you,' Alan said. He gave Gold Spectacles a grin and went across the reception to the staircase.

Merrion's room was oddly quiet with a sealed-in feeling. Her mackintosh hung behind the door, and her barrister's wig hung on the knob of an upright chair back. Alan peered at it. Weird thing, bizarre, all those neat little horsehair rolls and rows. He picked it up and put it on his own head. There was a little mirror hanging behind the door. He leaned forward to see himself, see the crisp grey-white wig perched on his own dark hair, and made a face at himself. The wig might be too small but it was also strangely becoming. It made him look slightly authoritative in a distinctly attractive way. He thought, briefly, delightedly, of wearing *only* the wig.

The door opened. Alan snatched the wig off.

'Sorry—'

'Feel free,' Merrion said. 'It's a peculiar bit of kit, isn't it?'

She went past him, sliding her bag off her shoulder, and an armful of papers onto her desk. She was in a black suit and her hair was in a trim, fat pigtail with a black ribbon. She glanced at him. 'To what do I owe—'

'Nothing,' Alan said. 'Just an idea, a spur of the moment idea. I was walking back from lunch.'

Merrion said, smiling, 'Don't you work?'

He shrugged. 'In bursts.'

'Would you like some tea?'

'Is that—'

'A nuisance? No.' She gave him another quick glance. 'I'm glad to see you.'

He beamed. 'Oh good.'

'Sit down,' she said. 'I won't be a moment.'

She went out of the room. Alan sat in a green leather chair, opposite her desk. This was presumably where Merrion's clients sat, and looked at her across her desk top and thought: This is my lawyer who is going to save me, and who is going to cost me x pounds an hour at the same time. What did Merrion cost people? Eighty pounds an hour? A hundred and twenty pounds an hour? How were these things calculated, anyway?

Merrion came back into the room carrying a small tin tray with two mugs on it and a pint carton of milk. 'Do you have sugar?'

'No.'

'Just as well.'

He got up and took the tray from her. He said, 'I hear you had supper with Simon and Carrie.'

She made a space on her desk for him to put the tray down. 'I can't get used to the way news travels round families. I don't have a family really, just my mother, so I expect things I do to stay private and of course they don't.'

'I talk to Carrie a lot,' Alan said. 'We have a kind of unspoken pact.'

Merrion poured milk into their teas and pushed a mug towards Alan. 'I like her.'

He said, smiling, 'I expect she likes you.'

Merrion sat down in the high-backed chair behind her desk. 'Nobody can really come clean, though, can they?'

'What do you mean?'

'I mean,' Merrion said, 'that we can't, any of us, express our real opinions. We have to edit what we say, all the time.'

He leaned back in his chair. 'What would you like to say?'

She looked at him. 'Ready?'

'Ready.'

'Right,' she said. 'Well, it seems to me that the person who is creating the most difficulties right now, the person who is setting people most successfully against one another, the person who is being supremely unreasonable—is your mother.'

Alan looked down into his tea. 'Simon would say she is the most justified because she is the most injured.'

'Simon isn't here,' Merrion said. 'Anyway, from what I gather, she isn't exactly fair to Simon either.'

'Has Carrie said anything?'

Merrion drank some tea. 'She doesn't need to. While I was there for supper your mother rang in hysterics about the house sale. Nobody *said* anything, of course.'

Alan said thoughtfully, 'My parents have been married longer than I've been alive.'

'And me.'

'Does longevity give a situation precedence?'

'Not legally—'

'Morally?'

'I don't know,' Merrion said. 'All I do know is that your father wouldn't have fallen in love with me and stayed in love all this time if he and your mother had everything it takes to keep a marriage going.'

'Why didn't he leave her before?'

She said calmly, 'I didn't ask him to.'

'Did you now?'

'Not really. It sort of coincided with his offering to. It got to a point.'

'Between you?' Alan said. 'Or between him and my mother?'

'Both, I should think. But we'll never know precisely.'

'It just happened.'

'Yes.'

'And now you're kind of fighting her for my father.'

'Am I?'

'I think so,' Alan said. 'And Carrie is fighting her for Simon.'

Merrion said nothing. She got up and leaned against the window. 'I've decided to take a bit of a stand,' she said, to the window glass.

'Oh?'

'We're going to get married in October.'

'October?'

'Yes. Some time close to my birthday.'

'Six months. Suppose the divorce isn't through by then?'

'It will be.'

'How can you be sure?'

'I can't. But I can be confident.'

'Dad's being advised by a friend of yours.'

'Not a friend. Just a solicitor I know who I have confidence in. It's a tricky situation because of Simon representing your mother. It wouldn't stand up in court, a son representing his mother. We have to just hope it doesn't come to that.'

'You sound very crisp,' Alan said.

Merrion turned from the window. She said, in quite a different voice, almost a whisper, 'I want to rescue him—'

'Dad?'

'Yes,' Merrion said. She put the back of one hand up briefly against her eyes. 'I want him to see how it can be, how it's supposed to be. I want him to see that he's got it right, he's had it right, all the time, by just being the person he is—'

She stopped. She sat down in her chair again abruptly and put her elbows on the desk in front of her. Alan leaned forward and put his mug down on a pile of pamphlets and then he stretched an arm out and touched her very lightly.

'Good luck,' he said.

Guy was late, arriving at the court building. He wasn't very late—a mere ten minutes—but he disliked being anything other than early, always had. The morning train from London was slightly delayed at Reading—some signalling problem—and it was raining, which always meant a dearth of taxis at Stanborough Station. Eventually he found one, and it dropped him at the main entrance. He hurried through the public lobby and up the staircase to the courtroom floor. Two security guards were standing by the doors to Court Two, jingling their keys the way most men jingle their change.

'I've got three down there this morning,' one of them was saying. 'Straight off Planet Lager and it isn't even Friday. Morning, Judge.'

'Morning,' Guy said.

'Martin's looking for you,' the guard said.

Guy pushed open the door to the judge's corridor. It was quiet there, as it always was. Outside the door to Guy's own chambers, Martin was standing. The court manager was jacketless, as was his custom, and his shirt cuffs were rolled up above his wrists.

'Martin,' Guy said. 'Have I kept you waiting?'

'No,' Martin said. He opened the door to Guy's room and held it for Guy to pass through. 'I didn't have an appointment, did I?'

'I'm always in by eight forty-five—'

'Except when the trains are late,' Martin said.

Guy hesitated. He put his briefcase down on his desk. 'Yes,' he said.

'I'm not prying, Judge—'

'No,' Guy said. 'Of course you're not. It's rather difficult to get the timing right.'

Martin put a hand up and adjusted the knot of his tie. 'That's why I thought I'd come and see you.'

Guy made a gesture towards a chair. 'Do sit down.'

Martin sat. He linked his fingers together in his lap.

Guy leaned against his desk. He said, with a shyness he didn't seem able to control, 'I imagine—you have a good idea—'

Martin waited. He had noticed for some time that the judge had looked like a man with something on his mind, that he didn't look happy.

'My wife and I are separated,' Guy said. He leaned his hands on the desk edge, either side of him, and stared at his shoes. 'We are to be divorced. When we are divorced, I shall be marrying again.'

Martin said, 'Miss Palmer?'

Guy nodded. 'When I am in London, I am staying at Miss Palmer's flat. When I am in Stanborough, I have a flat out at Pinns Green. Usually, I confine my visits to London to the weekends. If you need those contact numbers as well as my mobile-telephone number, of course you shall have them.'

'Thank you, Judge.'

Guy transferred his gaze from his own feet to Martin's. 'Is that what you needed to see me for?'

'I just needed the fact,' Martin said. 'On account of the rumours.'

'Are—there many?'

Martin said steadily, 'You know how it is, Judge.'

'Well, I don't, you see,' Guy said. 'That's half the trouble. There's no rehearsal, is there, for something like this.'

Martin leaned forward. He put his elbows on his knees. 'I was divorced eight years ago.'

'I had no idea—'

'It was before I took this job, I was working in London then.' He glanced up at Guy. 'It's never easy.'

'Thank you, Martin. Do you have children?'

Martin stood up and moved towards the door. 'Three, Judge. Thank you for your time and for your confidence.'

'And do you see them?' Guy said.

Martin opened the door. As he went out he said, 'Like you, Judge, I spend my weekends in London.' Then he closed the door behind him.

Guy stood up. He went round his desk to the window and looked down at the car park. Poor Martin, poor man, probably living, as Guy lived now, in a strange homeless no-man's-land, where the sense of belonging that characterised so much family life was torn away, leaving a feeling of acute disorientation behind it.

'It's so odd,' Guy had said to Merrion not long ago, 'but sometimes, when I'm not with you, when I'm not in court, I have a feeling that I've become invisible. That I've vanished.'

She had been puzzled. To her, his status, his professional achievement, was more than enough to give him an inescapable identity. He saw that she couldn't understand—because she had never really known them—those subtler, quieter marks of self conferred by being tied by blood to other people. Guy had taken them for granted as the natural backdrop to everything he might accomplish. That human landscape was accepted, a given. And now it wasn't there. He thought of Hill Cottage; he thought of the steep field behind it and the well-known idiosyncrasies of both places—dark corners and sudden steps and uneven paths. It wasn't, he thought, staring unseeingly down on the dusty car roofs below him, so much that he longed for the place, but that he felt a painful space where his simple sense of domestic and family belonging had once been.

The door of his room opened at the same time as somebody tapped lightly on it. Penny put her head round.

'Five minutes, Judge,' she said. 'Court One.'

Laura was weeding. She was a meticulous weeder, on her knees hand-weeding with a small, light aluminium fork Guy had given her two Christmases ago. He nearly always gave her something for the garden. In the early days, he gave her books and jewellery, but the books were seldom to her taste and the jewellery was invariably too bold. There were boxes of it lying in the drawers of her dressing table, complete with the cards Guy had written to go with them. Laura had looked at some of those cards only the other night. *To my darling Laura*, they said, year after year. *All my love, Guy*. It was, now she came to think of it, seven or eight years since the jewellery stopped and the garden forks took over. About the length of time, in fact, that he had been having his affair with Merrion Palmer.

A car was coming down the lane. The engine note was familiar. Laura sat back on her heels as the elderly grey Volvo turned into the drive.

Laura stayed where she was, sitting on her heels, holding her aluminium fork. The car was Guy's, and Guy was driving. He went up the drive and stopped just out of sight, where he had always stopped, by the back door. Laura heard the dogs barking and squealing. She heard Guy's car door slam. She looked down at the patch she had weeded, at the moist, crumbly, dark earth that resembled chocolate-cake crumbs. She waited.

'Laura!' Guy shouted.

'Here,' she said, in a whisper.

She heard his voice going shouting round the far side of the house, and then the dogs came racing round to find her and tell her the joyful news that Guy was home. They bounded around her, trampling across her lap, licking and wagging.

'Don't,' she said, shielding her face. 'Don't.'

'There you are,' Guy said, following the dogs.

Laura looked down at the earth. He came over the grass towards her and crouched down two feet away from her.

'Laura,' he said.

She didn't look at him. 'What are you doing here?'

'I came to see you,' he said. 'I came to see Hill Cottage.'

'Why?'

'For some simple reasons and some rather more obscure ones.'

'Typical,' Laura said. She leaned forward and stuck her fork into the earth, under a flourishing clump of groundsel.

'Laura,' Guy said, 'could we talk, do you think?'

'You know what I said about that. I *told* you.'

'Yes. You did. But it doesn't work. It just makes things harder.'

Laura shrugged. She shook the groundsel roots free of earth.

'And it is extremely unfair to Simon,' Guy said.

'Please leave Simon out of it.'

'I can't,' Guy said. 'Like it or not, he is my son as well as yours. You can't appropriate him like this, and if you are going to instruct him as you have then he is automatically involved.'

Laura said nothing. Guy knelt on the grass to get closer to her. She could see the creases on the knees of his dark suit. She could smell, very faintly, the scent of his cologne, the scent that lurked so unkindly in the linen cupboard, in the little room off their bathroom where Guy had kept his clothes.

'Look,' Guy said, 'I will let you have as much of everything as I can. I will just leave myself enough to manage on.'

'Will that make you feel better?'

'I hope it will make *you* feel better,' he said.

'Please go,' Laura said bitterly.

'I will, but I have to ask you first if you will please, *please* release Simon. Please let him find you a solicitor to represent you whom he recommends?'

Laura took her fork out of the earth, and rubbed the tines clean on the grass beside her.

'This isn't the right kind of control,' Guy said. 'The control you need is the power to lead your own life, not manipulate other people's.'

'Why did you come?' Laura said again.

'I told you. I wanted to see Hill Cottage. I wanted to see you and ask you to reconsider this course of action. I wanted—I wanted to see if you were OK.'

Laura put the fork into the pocket of her gardening apron. Then she stood up, awkwardly and stiffly. Guy rose, too, and put a hand out to steady her. She ignored it.

'Go away,' she said.

'Laura,' he said. 'For your own sake if not for anyone else's, *please*.'

She looked at him, for the first time. Then she looked away. 'If you're homesick,' she said, 'then you'll just have to bear it, like I shall have to. And don't mention Simon to me again. I'm not making Simon do anything he doesn't want to do, is *glad* to do. If you're lonely, then you know who you have to blame.'

And then she turned and began to step deliberately towards the house, and away from him.

CHAPTER EIGHT

CARRIE LOOKED at the piece of lamb in the roasting tin. It didn't look big enough. It looked big enough for five people, perhaps, but not for seven, which is what they were going to be at lunchtime since she had invited Guy and Merrion. She'd done it on impulse, she hadn't even told Simon she was going to. Something about her funny little broken conversation with Rachel had made her feel more confident, less powerless. That she could strike some small blow for herself. So she had rung Merrion and left a message on her answering machine.

'Come to lunch,' she'd said. 'On Sunday. Just family. Just you and Guy and us.'

It was Guy who'd rung back to say they'd love to. He sounded pleased but tired. 'It's a lovely thought.'

When she told Simon, he had simply nodded. 'OK.'

'You're not going to bite my head off?'

'I haven't the energy.'

'No need to be so self-pitying. Sometimes I—' She stopped.

He looked at her. 'Sometimes you think I am just like my mother?'

'Yes,' Carrie said.

He'd shrugged. She heard him go upstairs and then the sound of running water and then he'd come down again before going out to one of the free legal-advice clinics he ran.

'Do you have to?'

He kissed her. 'Yes,' he'd said.

Now, looking at the undersized piece of lamb, she thought she'd better wake him. She'd let him sleep in—heavens, she'd let them all sleep in—but Guy and Merrion were due in an hour and a half and, in any case, her feelings of self-sacrifice for the family were running dry. Lay table and cook lunch, fine. Tidy up sitting room, find wine, clear hall of school clutter, check downstairs lavatory, too, not fine at all. Carrie put the roasting tin back into the oven and closed the door.

She climbed the stairs. Rachel's bedroom door was shut and music was coming from Emma's, although the curtains were still pulled. She glanced up the second-floor stairs towards Jack's room. There was a black T-shirt lying on them, and a single high-top trainer and a crumpled magazine. Carrie sighed. She'd tackle Jack later. She went on towards her own bedroom and opened the door. Simon was asleep on her side of the bed, clutching the pillow against him as if it were a person.

She went across the room and pulled the curtains back. Then she went to the bed and sat down on the edge, next to Simon. 'Si,' she said. 'It's getting-up time.'

'Mm,' he said.

'Getting-up and helping-good-patient-wife time.'

He smiled faintly, without opening his eyes. 'You're wonderful,' he said.

'I know. And about to be wonderfully cross.'

He yawned. 'Where are the kids?'

'Guess.'

He flung back the covers with sudden energy, and opened his eyes. 'OK,' he said. 'Sprint to bathroom before they do.'

From the floor above, Jack heard the groan and shudder of the water pipes as the shower was turned on. He'd been thinking about a shower, on and off, for some time. He felt tired. He hadn't felt so tired in ages, quite the reverse: he'd been full of an enormous, brilliant energy, a feeling of wanting to run everywhere and take stairs and steps three at a time. And then yesterday, out of nowhere as far as he could see, Moll had said she was busy on Saturday night.

'You mean I can't see you?' he said.

She smiled right at him. 'Yes.'

'What are you doing?'

'Something my mum wants me to do,' Moll said.

'Your mum—'

'We always do a lot together,' Moll said. She was still smiling. 'I just haven't lately. Because of you.'

'Oh.'

She gave him a quick kiss on the side of his neck, a Moll special which involved a flick of her tongue. 'One Saturday,' she said.

'But it's a *Saturday*—'

'That's why Mum wants to go out with me.'

Of course he'd smiled. Of course he'd said yes. She'd given him one of her long steady looks, right up close, and then she'd gone swinging off and he sat where she'd left him watching her bottom and her hair and the way she carried her bag over her shoulder as if it weighed nothing at all. He was so used to seeing her every day, so used to the assumption of seeing her, that he felt quite displaced. He beat his fists lightly on the seat of the bench he was sitting on.

'Get a grip,' he told himself. It was something Carrie often said to them. 'Get a *grip*.'

He went out for a beer, instead, on Saturday, with Adam and Rich. Marco had a date somewhere. The three of them went to two pubs and then tried to get into a club and were turned away for being too young by a doorman so stupendously bored with having to deal with anyone so juvenile that it rather put a damper on the evening.

When he got home, he went straight to the telephone in case she'd rung. She hadn't promised, but she'd sort of indicated she might. There were three messages there, two for Simon and one from Emma's friend, Sonia, about drama club. Jack trailed out of the kitchen and up the stairs. It was almost midnight. He felt almost too tired, he'd thought, to get as far as his bedroom.

The shower was turned off. He heard the pipes grumble into silence. Then he heard his mother call, 'Jack!'

She was at the foot of his staircase. He could picture her, face turned up towards the darkness of his floor.

'Jack!' she shouted again. 'Jack, will you please get *up*?'

'What'll we talk about?' Simon said. He was pulling a cork out of a wine bottle. He'd put on a blue denim shirt and his hair was still damp from his shower. Carrie rather wanted to go over and lean against him, but she sliced apples into a pie dish instead.

'We could start with the sale of Hill Cottage and the consequences of extra-marital affairs.'

'Very funny.'

'Well, really,' Carrie said, 'what d'you think? We'll get by. The kids will be there. Emma and Rachel have been in the bathroom for hours.'

Simon pulled the cork out with a jerk. 'Because of *her*?'

'It didn't escape Rachel's notice,' Carrie said, 'that Merrion was wearing an agnès b sweater when she came to supper.'

Simon ran a piece of kitchen paper round the inside of the wine bottle's neck. 'Who is agnès b?'

'Clothes,' Carrie said. 'Classic but cool.'

Simon shook his head. 'Just think, if Mum finds out—'

'She won't. Unless *you* choose to tell her.'

'I feel awful.'

'Ill? Or disloyal?'

'Disloyal.'

'Oh, Simon—'

He said, 'She's so vulnerable—'

'Is she?'

'You haven't seen her.'

'I've tried to. I've asked her here. I've asked your father here. The difference is that he said yes and she said no.'

'It isn't at all comparable.'

'No,' Carrie said. 'It isn't.' She was slicing the apples very fast. 'The other difference is that your father has always been very nice to me and your mother never has.'

'Carrie—'

'I'm sick of it,' Carrie said. She put the paring knife down and held her hands over her face. 'I'm sick of you leaping to attention every time she so much as raises an eyebrow. I'm sick of her polite but determined refusal to acknowledge that I'm your *wife*. I'm sick of you refusing to see what your priorities are. I am sick, sick, *sick* of coming second.'

Silence. She picked up the paring knife again.

'Aren't you exaggerating a bit?' Simon said.

She said nothing.

'Why be angry with me?' Simon said. 'Why aren't you angry with my father?'

'Increasingly,' Carrie said through clenched teeth, 'I have every sympathy with your father.'

'In that case—'

'Shut up!' Carrie shrieked.

He looked at her. 'Carrie—'

'I've had enough! I've had enough of your cowardice and your self-absorption and your bloody, fucking *mother*!'

Simon looked pained. '*Please*—'

She shook her head violently. Tears of frustration were beginning to leak out of her eyes. 'You're so *obtuse*.'

'Yes,' he said, 'I expect I am. Along with all my other failings. It's a wonder you stay.'

She glared at him. She'd put her hair up quite carefully earlier but now she could feel a lock or two sliding down her neck. 'Think about it,' she hissed. '*Think* why I stay.'

He looked at the floor. Carrie jabbed the point of the paring knife into her chopping board.

'*Think* about it, Simon. I'm not the sort of person who'd stay just for the children. If I was going, I'd take them with me. But I don't. I stay. Why, stupid, stupid Simon Stockdale do you *think* I stay?'

He gave her a quick glance and looked down at the wine bottle in his hand. 'I suppose—' he said, and stopped.

The doorbell rang. They looked at each other in horror.

'Oh my God,' Carrie said. 'It's them.'

During lunch, Jack watched his grandfather. His sisters, he noticed, were watching Merrion, albeit covertly. Her hair was all loose today and he could see Rachel wondering how you got hair to do that. Rachel's hair was like Carrie's, slippery and straight, with a tendency to divide over her ears. Merrion's hair was very thick. It curved behind her ears and looked quite content to do so. Jack had never really looked at girls' hair before. Before Moll, that is.

When you first looked at Grando, Jack thought, he seemed fine: normal, ordinary. But after a while you could see he was a bit on edge, that he was holding himself in a deliberately relaxed way, rather than being truly relaxed. He had a checked shirt on, open-necked, under a dark-green sweater. He was sitting next to Carrie. She was telling him about her job. 'You're amazing,' he said, and smiled at her. 'I don't know how you stand it.' Sometimes, when he reached to pick up his water glass, he gave Merrion the quickest of glances across the table and Jack felt a little jerk when he did that, a little twist of recognition and pain. He'd expected to think Grando pathetic; he'd told himself he was probably just a sad old bloke who'd made a fool of himself. But that wasn't how he seemed at all. He might be tense, but he wasn't apologetic, he wasn't pitiful, he was instead indicating—quietly but unmistakably—that the reason he was so happy to be in this room was because Merrion was in it, too. It filled Jack with awe and misery.

His father, he noticed, was talking law to Merrion. He wasn't looking at her, he was looking at the table just in front of her plate. There was a smile on his lips that didn't manage to look very smiling. For her part, Merrion seemed able to look at Simon quite steadily. Jack wondered what she was thinking, whether it was odd to look at a son and see something of the father you were really in love with. In love. Jack swallowed. He picked up his knife and traced patterns with it in the gravy left on his plate. Moll had said she'd call. 'Call you Sunday if I don't Saturday night, OK?' she'd said. The telephone had been quite silent, all morning; not even Trudy or Sonia had called. He pushed his chair back.

'Jack?' Carrie said.

He didn't look at her. 'I've got to do something—'

'Could you do it in a minute? After you've cleared the plates?'

Jack hesitated. He stood up. Grando was looking at him with an expression that oddly gave him courage.

'In a sec,' he said. 'I've just got to make a phone call.'

'Is Jack all right?' Guy said.

He and Simon were standing in the garden, their hands in their pockets. The garden was remarkably untidy, but neither he nor Simon had commented on it for the simple reason that neither of them had really noticed it.

'Never better,' Simon said. 'He's got a girlfriend. The first serious one. He's really star-struck.'

Guy looked at the grass. He jabbed at a dandelion with the toe of his shoe. 'He didn't look star-struck at lunch,' he said. 'He looked miserable. Everything else going all right? School and so on?'

'I think so,' Simon said. 'You'd better ask Carrie.'

'Why can't I ask you?' Guy said. 'You're his parent, too, aren't you?'

'Look,' Simon said with some heat, 'don't get at *me*. Anyway, who are you to talk? Who knew anything much about my schooldays but Mum?'

'Exactly,' Guy said. 'And I regret it.'

'So you'll salve your conscience by tearing me off a strip?'

Guy kicked at the dandelion again. 'Carrie's not happy,' he said. 'You're not happy. Jack's not happy. And don't tell me it's all my fault because that's neither fair nor accurate.'

'Did you come here to give me a lecture?'

'I'm not giving you a lecture.'

'Dad,' Simon said, 'we got through lunch all right. Don't start on me now.'

Guy said, 'I tried to see your mother.'

'I know.'

'I am advised,' Guy said, 'by my own experience *and* by Susan Dewar, to beg you both to find your mother an independent legal adviser.'

Simon looked at the sky. 'We've been through all that.'

Guy put a hand on Simon's arm. 'But you're *suffering*, Simon. And you're making Carrie suffer.'

Simon lowered his arm so that Guy's hand slipped from it. 'We're talking conscience here. 'Not just emotion. It's dictates of conscience, a sense of what is *right* to do.'

'So you are choosing to do right by just one person at the expense of everybody else?' He had dislodged the dandelion and bent to pull it and its root out of the lawn.

'Dad,' Simon said. 'That's the whole point. I'm not choosing. I haven't *got* a choice. In fact, I shouldn't be here with you. I should only be talking to you through Susan Dewar.'

Guy said crossly, 'Don't be so *idiotic*.'

Simon shrugged.

'I've got something to tell you,' Guy said.

Simon looked at him. 'Merrion's pregnant,' he said.

'No. Merrion is not pregnant. But we have fixed a date to be married.'

'You can't.' Simon said. 'We haven't even got full statements of assets yet. It'll take weeks, months even.'

'Your job,' Guy said.

'What?'

'I intend to marry Merrion on October the 20th. I intend to be divorced and thus free to marry her well in advance of that date.'

'But you can't, it isn't practical—'

Guy took a step away. 'That's up to you.'

'Dad—'

'You insist that you have no choice,' Guy said. 'These are the consequences. We can all be amazingly unreasonable if pushed hard enough.

It's your job, Simon, to get this divorce as fast as you can. You say you have no choice about your mother. In this instance you have no choice with me, either.' He looked at the dandelion in his hand and then hurled it into the bushes. 'And now I'm going to find the girls.'

'OK, mate?' Adam said.

It was the third time he'd said it that morning. The first time he'd said it, he'd put an arm across Jack's shoulders. Jack had shrugged it off. 'Get off me.'

'Sorry,' Adam said. He didn't seem offended. He kept looking at Jack, as if he was waiting for something. Rich did, too, although he didn't say anything, but then Rich never did say anything.

'I'm fine,' Jack said. He broke off a piece of the hot dog he was eating and pulled a strand of limp fried onion out of it with his teeth. 'I'm *fine*.'

'Good weekend?' Adam said.

Jack stopped chewing and stared at him. 'You what?'

Adam grinned. He was eating corn chips out of a bag. 'I said did you have a good weekend—'

'What kind of a question is that?' Jack said. 'You suddenly turned into my mother or something?' He looked at the rest of his hot dog. It suddenly seemed gross; greasy and rubbery and fake. He got up from the bench where they were sitting and dropped the remainder of his hot dog into a wire litter bin.

'Hey,' Rich said, 'I'd have had that.'

Jack didn't turn round. 'Too late,' he said.

He pulled his cigarettes out of his trouser pocket, the first cigarettes he'd bought since that incredible moment he and Moll had thrown his last packet away together and she'd kissed him for the first time. He felt seized by a sudden yearning, thinking about that kiss. He took a cigarette out of his new packet and lit it. Then he drew a deep mouthful of smoke. It tasted great, but not as great as he'd hoped it would. He turned back to the others. 'Ought to make a move.'

Adam was tipping the last crumbs out of the corn-chip bag down his throat. 'Hey! What's the hurry—'

'Double physics.' Jack dropped his cigarette on the ground and screwed the heel of his shoe into it.

'It was your idea to come out,' Adam said.

'I wanted some fags—'

'And you got them,' Rich said. 'And we came with you—'

Jack looked at him. 'Why?'

'To see if you were OK,' Adam said.

'Why shouldn't I be OK?'

Adam screwed his chip bag into a ball and chucked it at the litter bin. It hit the rim and fell on the ground.

'You—just didn't seem OK,' Adam said.

'There was a lot of family stuff at the weekend,' Jack said. 'I got tired.'

Adam said, 'The weekend's three days ago.'

Jack gave Adam's chip bag a flying kick. 'I know.'

Adam stood up. 'C'mon, then.'

Jack eyed him. 'What do you know that I don't know?'

'Nothing much—'

'I'm not asking for much,' Jack said. 'I'm asking for anything.'

Rich stood, too. 'It's probably not anything—'

'Tell me,' Jack said, putting his hands on Rich's shoulders. 'Is it Moll?'

Rich nodded.

Jack gave him a little shake. 'What? *What*?'

Rich ducked his head. He stared at the mid-point of Jack's school tie. 'Marco,' he said.

Jack took his hands off Rich's shoulders. He looked at Adam. 'Moll went out with Marco? On Saturday?'

Adam nodded.

'Sunday?' Jack said.

'Dunno—'

'Monday and Tuesday? Wednesday? Never there to answer the phone because she's out with fucking *Marco*?'

'Dunno,' Adam said.

'You knew.'

'Yeah.'

'You knew on Saturday?'

'Sort of,' Rich said.

Jack shook his head. He said dully, 'She said she was with her mum.'

'Yeah. Well—'

'She said she'd ring.'

Adam put a hand out and tried to take Jack's arm. 'C'mon, mate. Double physics.'

'Fuck off!' Jack shouted. He pulled his arm free.

'Cool it, mate—'

He glared at them. 'Fuck off, I said.'

'OK, OK—'

They took a step away from him. Rich's eyes looked odd, as if he was squinting or something.

'You *knew*—'

They said nothing. Jack wanted to rush at them, hurl himself at them and shove them back against the wall and really give their heads a banging, skull against brick, thud, thud, thud. He put his hands in his pockets. They weren't worth it.

'Fuck you,' Jack said. His voice was hoarse. 'Fuck you both,' and then he pushed past them and began to tear up the pavement among the Thursday-lunchtime shoppers.

Emma had a headache. She'd had a headache for two days now, but when she told Carrie about it, Carrie had given her a paracetamol tablet and told her to drink lots of water.

Emma had looked at the paracetamol. 'I hate these.'

'Swallow it,' Carrie said. She had her work suit on. 'Swallow it and go to school. You'll be late.'

The paracetamol blunted Emma's headache but didn't take it away. She felt herself watching it come back, creeping back, until her whole skull seemed to be full of black tendrils, all pressing on something until they hurt it. Emma endured the black tendrils through maths and French and religious studies. Then, at break, she made her friend Sonia come with her to find the school nurse.

'I've had a headache since yesterday.'

The school nurse was filling in forms. She hardly looked at Emma. 'Are you having your period?'

Emma looked at Sonia. She'd only had two. Sonia had started when she was eleven. She was really regular now.

'No,' Sonia said.

'Have you had your eyes tested?'

'Yes,' Sonia said.

Emma wanted to giggle. She looked at the school nurse's hair which was stuffed into an elasticated band, in a crooked lump.

'Is your mother at home?'

Sonia nudged Emma.

'Yes,' Emma said.

The school nurse reached for a pad. 'I'll write a note for your form teacher,' she said, scribbling rapidly. 'Then go home and tell your mother that if the headache isn't gone by tomorrow you should see your doctor.' She tore the form off the pad and handed it to Sonia. 'There you are.'

Sonia tried to walk Emma home. 'I better. Your mum's not there.'

'I'll be OK.'

'C'mon, Emma. Then I can bunk off second English.'

'I don't want you to,' Emma said. 'I don't want to talk.' She gave

Sonia's hand, still holding the sick note, a little slap. 'You hand that in for me.'

'OK,' Sonia said. She always gave in, Emma had discovered; she'd put up a little fight and then she'd give in. It was one of the things about her that Emma liked.

Emma let herself into the house. It felt weird—not quite empty but more as if it was waiting. She put her house keys in the zipped pocket of her school bag and went into the kitchen. Breakfast was still partly on the table, as it always was if Carrie wasn't the last to leave the house: smeary bowls and spoons and a cereal box with the inner packet still standing up so the air could get in and turn the contents soft.

She went across to the fridge and opened it. She wasn't exactly hungry but she felt she'd like to look and see what was in there all the same. She helped herself to a yoghurt and a cheese portion wrapped in plastic, then found a can of Coca-Cola, a packet of crisps and a banana, and went slowly upstairs to bed.

She'd made her bed, that morning, headache or not. She always made her bed, not because Carrie told her to, but because it felt dirty to get into, at night, if she hadn't made it. If you pulled the bottom sheet tight, Emma had discovered, it felt cleaner, newer. She put the food items on the bed, kicked off her shoes, pulled her socks off, unzipped her skirt and dropped it on the floor, and then her school cardigan. Her cardigan had been Rachel's, and the elbows were thin and shiny and the cuffs had frilled out and had ragged edges. Emma had fought very hard for new school uniform, but had only won a skirt. Carrie was adamant about the rest, absolutely adamant.

Emma got into bed in her knickers and her school shirt. She lay down on her pillow, feeling the food items tumbling about on her duvet as she pushed her legs down the bed. Her headache, she decided, was still there, but it wasn't worse. If she lay very still and ate very slowly, it might go away. She reached down for the cheese portion.

Below her, on the ground floor, the front door opened and shut with a slam. Emma froze. There was the thud of a bag being dropped and a clatter of keys. Then somebody went into the kitchen. Emma sat up. She put the cheese on the bedside table. Then she slid out of bed and went out onto the landing so that she could see down into the hall. It was Jack's bag in the hall and his keys were on the floor beside it. Emma went back into her room and found the mauve-and-white-striped pedal-pushers that Sonia had lent her and pulled them on under her school shirt. Then she went down the stairs in her bare feet and crossed the hall to the kitchen.

Jack was standing by the kitchen table eating sliced white bread out of its packet.

'What are you doing here?' Emma said.

He gave a little start. He said, round the bread in his mouth, 'You, too.'

'I've got a headache,' Emma said. 'I've got a sick note.'

Jack grunted. 'I didn't think there'd be anybody here—'

'Me either,' Emma said. She looked at him. He looked awful, sort of greyish and lifeless. 'Did you get sent home?'

'No.'

She advanced towards the table and snatched the bread bag away. Carrie hated them eating things straight out of packets and cartons. 'What're you doing here then?'

Jack lunged forward and whipped the bread bag back out of Emma's hand. 'Going somewhere—'

'Don't eat out of the packet,' Emma said. 'Mum doesn't like it. 'She leaned on the table. 'Where're you going, anyway?'

Jack finished the slice of bread. 'Doesn't matter.'

'It does. You've got to tell Mum. Tell me and I'll tell Mum.'

'Look,' Jack said. 'It's none of your business where I go and what I do.'

'It is,' Emma said. 'I'm your sister. I need to know stuff.'

Jack went past her without replying. She heard him go across the hall and into the downstairs cloakroom. She heard him pee, and then she heard the sound of water flushing. Jack came back across the hall. She heard a brief scrape as he picked up his keys from the tiled floor. Then he appeared in the kitchen doorway.

'See you,' he said.

She said, 'Aren't you going to change out of your uniform?'

He shook his head. 'No.'

'When will you be back?' Emma said.

'Dunno—'

'What'll I say to Mum?'

'Tell her I'll be back.'

'When?'

'Sometime,' Jack said. He looked down, jingling his keys, and then he turned went back across the hall to the front door. Emma heard the door slam again. He'd looked, she thought, like someone who'd been really told off, like people did when the exam results were put up and they discovered, despite saying they didn't care what their marks were, that they'd done really badly. Emma went round the kitchen table and put the bread back in the big plastic bread box. Her headache, she discovered, had quite gone.

'All stand!' the court usher said.

Guy rose from his seat on the small dais of Court One, and went out. It had been a long, trivial afternoon, full of applications by bailiffs for this and that.

Martin was waiting outside the court. 'Could I have a word, Judge?'

Guy paused. 'Of course—'

Martin reached up a little so that his face was close to Guy's. 'Your grandson's here,' Martin said.

'My grandson!'

'Yes, Judge. I've put him in your chambers. Penny found him in the lobby about half an hour ago.'

He walked up the corridor to his office. Jack was sitting at his desk. When the door opened the boy sat up.

'Jack,' Guy said. 'Dear fellow—'

Jack got up and shuffled sideways, away from the desk. 'You haven't got your wig on—'

'I didn't need it this afternoon. It was just a string of little civil cases.' He put the file down on the nearest grey plastic desk. 'Are you all right?'

Jack nodded. Guy walked over and put his arm firmly round his grandson's shoulder.

'Are you in trouble?'

Jack shook his head.

Guy said, 'Something has happened, though.'

'I wanted to go somewhere—'

'Look,' Guy said, 'I think you'd better sit down.'

He pulled Jack gently sideways. 'Sit here.'

'It's your chair—'

'It doesn't matter. Sit here.'

Jack sat. He couldn't look up. He felt worse than ever. He'd thought, when he got here, when he got to Grando, it would get easier. But it hadn't. Nothing had changed.

He said, to his knees, 'I don't know why I came. I don't—I'm sorry.'

Guy had pulled another chair up, the other side of the desk. He said, 'I'm pleased you did. Though I'm sorry you needed to.'

'It was after Sunday—'

'What was?'

'When I saw you, when you came, when—'

'Jack,' Guy said, leaning forward towards him across the desk. 'Jack, is it your girlfriend?'

Jack said nothing. He stared at his knees.

'Has she left you?'

Jack shrugged.

'Did she tell you she didn't want to see you any more?'

Jack raised his head a fraction. 'She didn't *tell* me . . . she said she was going out with her mother on Saturday. But she didn't. She went out with Marco.'

'And she left you to find out?'

'Yes,' Jack said.

Guy sighed. 'Poor boy,' he said. 'I could tell you the first time is always the worst, but it wouldn't be true. It's dreadful, every time. There's no pain like betrayal.'

Jack said, without thinking, 'Dad says—' He stopped.

'Your father says that that's what I've inflicted on Granny?'

'I didn't mean—'

'I know you didn't. But your father's right. Jack—'

'Yes?'

'Why didn't you go to your parents? Why didn't you tell them?'

Jack made a face. 'It doesn't matter to them.'

'Your happiness does.'

'You can't talk to them now. You can't tell them anything.'

Guy was silent. He looked down at his hands lying in front of him on the desk. After a while he said, 'We must tell them where you are.'

'Are you sending me back—'

'In the morning,' Guy said. He stood up. 'I must just make a call, and then you must ring home.'

Jack stood, too. He said, 'Do you want me to go out?'

'No,' Guy said. 'No. I won't be long. You can stay.'

Jack moved away from Guy's desk and picked up a legal book from Guy's shelves. It seemed, well, polite not to do nothing, not to watch.

Guy dialled a number on the telephone. He sat balanced against the edge of his desk, his back to Jack, his shoulders square against the light from the window.

'Hello?' he said. 'Hello, my love, it's me.'

Jack fixed his eyes on a page without seeing anything.

'Look,' Guy said, 'I won't be coming up tonight . . . Yes, I know I did, but something's happened . . . No, no, not Laura. It's Jack. He's had a bit of a crisis and turned up here. I'm going to give him some supper and take him back to the flat with me. He can get an early train back in the morning.' There was a pause. Jack glanced at Guy's back. His head was bent, as if he were listening very hard. 'Darling,' Guy said, 'I wouldn't be upsetting our plans if it *wasn't* important.' There was another pause. Very quietly Jack closed the book and slid it back onto the shelf among the other books. 'I'll ring you later,' Guy said, 'I'll tell you more then. No, not now, I'll ring you from the flat,' and then there was a tiny break and he said, 'Goodbye, darling,' and put the phone down. He sat there, quite still, his back to Jack.

Jack cleared his throat. 'Sorry,' he said.

'Don't be,' Guy said. 'You've done nothing to be sorry for.' He turned to look at Jack.

'You're supposed to be in London—'

'I can go tomorrow,' Guy said.

'Thanks,' Jack said. Somewhere, obscurely, a small light was breaking, a tiny beacon of relief. 'Thanks, Grando.'

'There's nothing to thank me for. Now. Ring your parents. With luck, you'll get them before they start to worry.'

CHAPTER NINE

MIRIAM HAD, AS USUAL, spilt Simon's coffee. He picked up his mug and blotted the wet ring under it with a piece of junk mail that had come in that morning's post. It was proving difficult to concentrate this morning. He hadn't slept very well, of course. Nor had Carrie. They'd lain side by side in bed and had silent and separate mental tussles about why Jack, upset by Moll's defection, should have gone to find his grandfather rather than one of them.

Carrie, Simon knew, blamed him. After Jack had rung from Stanborough and said he was staying the night and would be back in the morning, Carrie had looked at Simon for a long time. She hadn't said anything, she'd just looked.

After several minutes, Simon said, 'Will he be back in time for school?'

'Yes,' Carrie said. She was still staring at Simon. 'Guy's putting him on the seven fifteen.'

'Will you meet him?'

Carrie said, 'I rather thought you would.'

He made a face. He said, 'I've got an eight o'clock meeting—'

'I see.'

'He can surely get himself across London—'

'It isn't really about that,' Carrie said. 'Is it?'

Simon made one hand into a fist and folded the other round it. He said, 'I can't quite see why this little episode is my fault, too.'

'Doesn't it strike you that he might have chosen to go to his grandfather because he thought he had a chance of a sympathetic reception?'

'Oh, come *on*,' Simon said. 'When did Jack and my father ever have much to say to one another?'

'Things have changed,' Carrie said angrily. 'When something like this whole family crisis happens, everything changes, all the dynamics. It's only you that won't see that.'

She went out of the room then. She was hurt, he could see, badly hurt that Jack, in pain, had chosen a confidant other than her. But what Simon couldn't work out was why she was still angry with him, and not with his father. She seemed to feel that he had somehow made home impossible as a refuge for Jack when he needed one.

After his eight o'clock meeting, Simon had rung Jack's school to see if he had arrived. He had, and was about to go into a double period of business studies. Simon said, 'Give him my—' to the school secretary, and then stopped. What could he possibly send Jack in these circumstances, via Mrs Pritchard in the school office? 'Tell him I'll see him later,' Simon said. 'Tell him—I'm glad he's OK.'

He took a mouthful of coffee. It was lukewarm and thin-tasting. He put the mug back down on the damp junk-mail mat and pushed the whole thing away from him. A steady misery was settling on him, and with it a definite and rather tremulous desire to see Jack. He looked at the telephone. Perhaps he would ring Carrie and tell her he'd go to meet Jack from school this afternoon. He put a hand out towards the telephone and it immediately rang. He picked it up.

'Simon Stockdale.'

'Simon,' Laura said.

He shut his eyes. 'Hello, Mum.'

'Simon,' Laura said. 'What on earth do you mean by this horrible, formal letter advising me to accept the offer on the house.'

He took a breath and opened his eyes. 'It has to be formal, Mother. You have asked me to act for you legally. I have to deal with your affairs in a proper, professional way.'

'I accept that,' Laura said, in a voice that belied her acceptance of any such thing, 'but why write to me in such language?'

'I have to demonstrate that I am acting for you properly—'

'But you *still* don't have to write to me as if you hardly *know* me! There is a difference between clear legal language and plain cold indifference.'

Simon took the telephone away from his ear and laid it on his desk. He counted to ten and then he picked it up again.

Laura was crying. 'It just gets worse, every day gets worse. This place is the last thing I've got, it's all I am, it's—'

'*Please*,' Simon said.

There was a small, uneven silence at the other end of the telephone. Then Laura said, with difficulty, 'I am so *afraid*.'

'I know.'

'I can't imagine how I'll live, how I'll be.'

Simon wound a pencil into the coil of the telephone wire. 'Mum, look. I'm sorry about the tone of the letter, but I *have* to demonstrate that I have given you the best legal advice I can. And the best advice I can give you, as your lawyer and as your son, is to accept this offer on the house. It's an excellent offer. More than the asking price.'

There was a pause. Then Laura said, 'I see,' almost in a whisper.

'It'll mean you can buy another house. A nice house, with a garden.'

'Simon—' Laura said.

'What?'

'Can you come?'

'What, now?'

'Yes,' Laura said. 'Please. I know I'll be able to cope if you just come and talk to me about it. I'll feel differently if you're here. I know I will.'

'Mum,' Simon said, 'it's a working day, a weekday.'

'Surely someone else can cover for you?'

'It isn't work. It's Jack. He's been upset by something.'

'What thing?' Her voice was rising. 'What is it? *Drugs*?'

'No,' Simon said, too loudly. 'No, it's nothing like that. But his first—well, he's just been jilted. He's very cut up.'

'Do you mean to tell me,' Laura said, almost shouting, 'that you won't come to see me because Jack has had some—some little romantic *tiff*?'

'It's more complicated than that, Mum, more emotional—'

'More *important*!' Laura shrieked. Simon took a huge breath.

'Yes,' he said, and put the telephone down.

Merrion's case had been cancelled. The clerks had failed to reach her before she left home for chambers, and she had forgotten to turn her mobile phone on, so she arrived to find a blank diary.

'My apologies, Miss Palmer,' the senior clerk said.

She looked at him with irritation. Why couldn't he just say, 'I'm sorry,' like anybody else?

'It doesn't matter, Michael,' she said, walking through the double doors. 'I have plenty to do.'

Her room was inevitably just as she had left it, the file for the cancelled case lying ready on her desk, her wig on its chair knob. She dropped her briefcase on the floor and went over to the window. It was a sunny day, a bright, heartless, all-seeing, sunny day. Merrion sighed and drummed a little rhythm on the double glazing with her fingers. It would have suited her mood better if it had been raining.

She turned and went across to her desk. There were no messages. Guy had rung her that morning in the flat to say he would like to take her out to dinner to compensate for the night before. She had nearly said, 'Don't bother.' Only in the nick of time had she checked herself and said, 'Lovely,' but not in quite the voice she would have wished.

'Darling,' Guy said. His voice was slightly teasing. 'Darling, don't have a sense-of-humour failure. It *was* only dinner.'

'Yes,' she said. She wanted to say, 'No, it wasn't *only* anything.' Nothing, it seemed, was 'only anything' now; everything had come to have significance and echoes and implications. She found herself wanting to go *out* with Guy, to be *seen* with Guy. That was what last night's dinner had been about, an expedition to a restaurant where not only did it not matter if they were seen together, but where she secretly hoped they *would* be seen.

She sat down at her desk and pushed the file aside. She was ashamed of herself for feeling as she did, for behaving as she was, for being unable to feel genuine pity for poor, gawky, heartbroken Jack. She liked Jack. She found him appealing almost *because* he was so unfinished and because he couldn't help a certain softness in his nature showing through the cultivated nonchalance of his manner. But last night, she had been jealous of him. Plain, angry jealous. When Guy rang the second time—Jack was in the shower—she had wanted him to sound really disappointed at not seeing her. He'd sounded regretful, certainly, but his main preoccupation had been with Jack and their evening together and the unexpected success their conversation had been. It was really easy, Guy said, talking to Jack, whose outlook must, by virtue alone of a forty-five-year age difference, be completely poles apart from his own. But it wasn't. It had been a revelation.

'He doesn't seem to disapprove of me, either,' Guy said. 'You can imagine the relief *that* is?'

'Oh yes,' Merrion said.

'He's thought about more than you'd think. I suppose that's boys, really. Girls seem to do their thinking while talking. Boys do one and then some of them do the other, later. He isn't, oddly enough, very like Simon.'

'Oh.'

'I must get him out of that shower and into bed. The flat looks as if a bomb has hit it.'

Merrion looked down at her blotter. It was covered with doodles, the peculiar, asymmetric angular shapes she'd always idly drawn on scraps and in margins since she was little. And there were the letters. She liked forming and illuminating letters. At the bottom of the blotter there was a row of letters in pairs, linked together by a scribbled chain: 'MS, MS, MS. Merrion Stockdale.' She looked at it. Did she really want to be part of this Stockdale thing? Might it be surrendering, rather than joining? If she became Stockdale, what might happen to Merrion Palmer? Might she become just a lawyer, an earner, an expert in the abrupt procedures of abduction, and might the woman who had been Guy's cherished lover for seven years just blur and blend into Merrion Stockdale until she was as if she had never been? Merrion sat very still at her desk. Think, she said to herself. Think it through. *Think*.

When Charlie had asked Alan if he could cook, Alan had thought he'd meant just that, 'Can you cook?'

'Course I can.'

'Oh, good,' Charlie said, 'because I can't.' He'd been grinning at Alan, as if he could see a joke Alan couldn't see. 'And iron?'

'So-so. What *is* this?'

'I just wanted to be sure—'

'Sure of what?'

'Sure of your domestic skills before you move in with me.'

Alan had gaped. 'Charlie—'

'Will you? Will you move in with me?'

He remembered a little ecstasy. He'd known Charlie was in love with him, known he wanted to spend time with him, but there was something so carefree about Charlie that he, Alan, had never quite dared to hope that Charlie would suggest what he was longing for him to suggest. He could only nod, he remembered, like some daft mechanical toy.

And now here he was, early evening in Charlie's kitchen, throwing out all the rubbish in Charlie's cupboards, all the packets and tins and tubes and bottles long past their sell-by dates. It was hugely pleasurable. It felt as if he was getting rid of all the stuff that didn't count any more, all the stuff that was over, in order to make way for something not just new but lasting. It was this sense of its being lasting that filled Alan with a kind of awe, a sense that he had stumbled upon exactly what he had been looking for, for years, exactly the person who could give a point to everything.

From the sitting room, his mobile phone began its shrill squeal. He hurried through, smiling, ready to be tough and teasing to Charlie for saying his surgery had overrun again.

'Hel*lo*,' he said, with the special emphasis he reserved for Charlie.

'Alan,' Laura said.

His face changed. 'Hi, Mum—'

'Are you busy?'

'Not especially—'

'Oh.'

'What's the matter, Mum?'

Laura said tightly, 'Simon put the telephone down on me today. I rang to ask him why he had taken to writing to me with such hideous formality and he said he was too busy with some family crisis and put the telephone down.'

Alan moved across the sitting room and sat down on the sofa. He pulled one of Charlie's sweatshirts across his knees and patted it, as if it were a cat. 'What crisis?' he said.

'Some storm in a teacup between Jack and a girl,' Laura said irritably

'I think it was quite serious, Mum. For Jack at any rate. The first time he'd—'

'But not comparable in any way to what I am faced with!'

Alan said nothing. He smoothed a sleeve of the sweatshirt and folded it up neatly.

'Are you there?' Laura said.

'Yes.'

'Simon wants me to accept this offer on the house. He has *instructed* me to accept the offer.'

'It's a good price, Mum. And you did ask him to be your lawyer.'

'Because I believed he understood. Because he *cared*. I needed someone to turn to, Alan, someone to take my part. Can you really not see?'

Alan moved the sweatshirt to one side and lay down along the sofa so that he could pillow his cheek on it. 'You've asked for his advice, Mum. He gives you the best advice he can. Then you refuse to take it.'

'Yes, I do,' Laura said. 'I am not selling Hill Cottage.'

Alan sat up abruptly. 'Mum, you *have* to.'

'Why do I?'

'Because it represents the largest chunk of equity you and Dad have, and it has to be divided.'

'That,' Laura said, 'is your father's problem.'

Alan said patiently, 'It doesn't work like that. You can delay things, perhaps, but you can't prevent them.'

There was a small scrape of a key in the lock. The front door opened and then slammed.

'Home!' Charlie shouted.

'Who is that?' Laura said.

Charlie appeared in the doorway. His hair was tousled and his tie was at half mast. Alan's heart rose like a bird.

'A friend—'

'I want you to do something,' Laura said.

Charlie tiptoed over to the sofa and sat down beside Alan.

'What?' Alan said.

'I want you to tell Simon that I'm refusing the offer on Hill Cottage. I am not going to be treated like this. By *any* of you.'

Charlie picked up Alan's free hand and bit gently on his fingers.

'OK, Mum—'

'Are you listening?'

'Yes,' Alan said faintly, his eyes on Charlie's face.

'Then ring Simon,' Laura said. 'Ring him and then ring me back.'

'OK. Mum, I've got to—'

'What?'

'I've got to go,' Alan said.

Charlie took the phone out of his hand and switched it off. He winked at Alan. 'Unless she'd like to join in?'

When Jack saw Simon on the pavement outside the school gates, he had an immediate panic. Simon had never come to meet him from school, and the sight of him hanging about rather apprehensively on the edge of the pavement made Jack think immediately that there'd been a disaster. He forgot Adam and Rich, dawdling along beside him, and sprinted forward.

'What's happened?'

'Nothing,' Simon said. He was trying to smile.

'Where's Mum?'

'At work,' Simon said. He put a hand out to touch Jack and it hovered, uncertain where to land.

'Is she OK?'

'Yes, of course—'

'And Rach and Ems?'

Simon's hand brushed Jack's shoulder and slid off. 'Everyone's OK,

Jack. I'm not here with bad news. I promise.'

Jack peered at his father. 'Why're you here then?'

Simon shrugged a little. He said with difficulty, 'I felt bad. I felt—well, I felt I'd let you down—'

Jack glanced over his shoulder to where Adam and Rich were standing. He jerked his head in their direction. 'See you,' he said to them.

Adam glanced up, and Jack willed him not to say 'You OK?'

'You OK?' Adam said.

Jack nodded.

Rich pulled at Adam's sleeve. 'See you,' he said.

Jack nodded again and ran to catch up with Simon, who had begun to walk along the road.

'I didn't mean to embarrass you in front of your friends—'

'You didn't.'

'I just wanted to see you, to tell you I was sorry.'

Jack put his head down. He began to walk faster. 'You did. It's OK.'

'Can I ask you,' Simon said, dodging other people on the road edge to keep up with Jack. 'Can I ask you something?'

Jack nodded.

'When—when you found out—' He stopped.

Jack stopped walking. 'What?'

'When you found out,' Simon said, stopping, too, and facing him, 'why didn't you come and tell me or Mum?'

Jack sighed. He shifted his school bag from one shoulder to the other. 'I couldn't.'

'Why not? We'd met Moll, we'd seen what she meant to you—'

'Dad,' Jack said, interrupting. 'There wasn't any point.' He began to walk again.

'Can you tell me—'

'There hasn't been any point for ages. Ever since this Grando thing. You're always too tired or too busy or out or something.'

Simon said, 'And Mum?'

'Same,' Jack said briefly.

They stopped to cross the road by some traffic lights. The lights changed and they went across together.

'So you went to Grando.'

'Yes.'

'Can you tell me why?'

Jack screwed his face up. 'He's OK.'

'Could you try a bit harder?'

Jack stopped walking again. He said, staring past Simon rather than at him, 'He listened. He made time for me.' He looked quickly at Simon. He said, quite slowly, 'He didn't make me feel I was just a bloody messy teenage pest.'

Simon's face twitched. 'I see.'

'He's in this grotty flat,' Jack said. 'He's only got his clothes and some books there. But he never asked me to be sorry for him. He was just sorry for me.'

'Yes.'

'Because he knew,' Jack said loudly. 'He *knows*.'

Simon said tentatively, 'And I don't?'

Jack's gaze dropped. He kicked at the edge of a pavement slab.

'I don't know what you know,' he said. 'How can I? You never say.'

CHAPTER TEN

RACHEL HAD LEFT her bedroom door slightly open. The landing light was on as usual so that Rachel could see across the stairwell and notice that Emma's door was still shut. Emma had gone to bed halfway through supper, saying she had a headache.

'The same headache?' Carrie said. Carrie looked as if she had a headache herself.

'I don't know,' Emma said.

Carrie had found a packet of paracetamol in a kitchen drawer and made Emma swallow one. Then she'd taken Emma upstairs and put her to bed as if she was six.

When she came down, she said to Rachel, 'I wonder why she keeps having headaches?'

Rachel was reading the weekly colour supplement of the evening newspaper. There was an article in it on how stress made some girls into sticks and some into balloons.

'Stress,' she said.

'Why should Emma be stressed?' Carrie said.

Rachel shrugged. If Carrie didn't think the whole evening hadn't been stressed, with Simon first playing superdad all over Jack and then insisting on taking him out for a drink, then she wasn't going to point it out.

Jack looked as if he hadn't a clue as to what was expected of him. He hadn't eaten his spaghetti, either; he'd just picked some bits of ham out of the sauce and left the rest in a tomato-y mess, like Emma had. Rachel had eaten hers. She wished she hadn't, but she had. She tried not to think of how her tummy would look in the shower. She pushed the colour supplement away from her.

'I'll clear up,' she said to Carrie, and stood up.

Carrie was nursing a mug of herbal tea. Her hair was all over her shoulders. It needed a wash, Rachel thought.

'Don't bother, Rach. It's very kind of you, but I'll do it. I need something mindless to do while I wait for Dad and Jack to get back.'

'OK. See you later.'

Carrie lifted her face. 'Give me a kiss.'

'You never want a kiss.'

'I do now.'

Rachel bent and kissed Carrie's cheek. It felt dry and a little rough. Trudy thought Carrie was pretty but didn't make the best of herself. 'What d'you mean, the best?' Rachel said. 'She doesn't make *anything*.'

Once upstairs, Rachel lay on her bed. She raised her legs into the air, first left, then right, then both together, and felt the satisfactory pull in her abdomen. You ought really, she knew, to do these exercises on the floor, but it was too much to do at night, too much to ask of somebody with all the preoccupations Rachel had.

Downstairs, the telephone rang. Rachel became alert.

'Hello?' she heard Carrie say. 'Hello?' and then, in a different voice, 'Oh, hello, Laura.'

Rachel rolled quietly off her bed and onto the floor. Then she crawled out onto the landing and lay against the banisters, peering down towards the hall and the open kitchen door.

'No,' Carrie was saying. 'No, he isn't.'

Rachel heard the scrape of furniture on the kitchen floor as if Carrie was pulling a stool over towards the counter where the telephone was.

'He's out, Laura,' Carrie said. Her voice was quite loud, louder, Rachel thought, than it needed to be for an ordinary conversation. 'He's out with Jack. They've gone out together . . . No. No, I don't know when they'll be back, I didn't ask, Laura. I did not *ask*.'

There was a pause. Rachel pictured Carrie perched on a stool, her elbows on the counter.

'I'm not sure,' Carrie said, 'that that is any of your business, is it, Laura? Yes, Jack has been upset this week, but that's a family matter, a family affair—'

She stopped. Rachel raised her head a little. Emma's bedroom door opened a few inches and revealed Emma, in her pink pyjama bottoms and a white T-shirt with a diamanté heart on the front.

'Granny?' Emma mouthed.

Rachel nodded.

'No!' Carrie said with vehemence from the kitchen.

Emma opened her door a little wider and sat down in the doorway. 'Is she—?' Emma whispered.

'Shhh!' Rachel said.

'Yes, you did hear me,' Carrie said. 'I said no. No, I will not get Simon to ring you when he comes in. I may not even tell him you rang.'

The stool scraped on the kitchen floor. Carrie must be gesturing.

'Because he has had enough!' Carrie shouted. 'I have had enough. We have all had enough of your demands and your complaints. You are making our life intolerable, you are putting so much pressure on Simon and then he takes it out on us and we *all* suffer!'

She stopped again, abruptly. Emma crept forward until she was leaning against the next banister to Rachel.

'I don't care!' Carrie yelled. 'I don't bloody *care* any more! You can cry your eyes out but I've utterly run out of any sympathy I've ever had for you. And I'll tell you something else, Laura. If you fight me for Simon, I'll not only fight you back, tooth and nail, but I'll win. Do you hear me? I'll *win*!'

Then the telephone was crashed down. Rachel and Emma sat up.

'Wow,' Emma whispered. Rachel didn't answer. She crawled to the top of the staircase and crouched there, as if she was wondering whether to go down. They heard Carrie get off the stool and pad across the kitchen, then the soft rip of paper being torn off a roll of kitchen towel. Then they heard something else, a small, jerky, piteous sound, like a little animal in pain.

'Oh God,' Emma whispered. 'Rach, she's crying.'

Guy was possessed by a huge restlessness. Unable to sleep, he got up, gingerly, and went out to the kitchen, not turning any lights on in case he woke Merrion up.

He slid the kitchen door shut and turned on the lamp that stood in the angle of the tiny kitchen counter and threw such interesting angles of light and shadow. Guy had never considered light as an aesthetic form before. But Merrion thought about light. Her blinds and lamps and spotlights let light fall in certain pools and patterns so that moods and atmospheres were altered. Like so much about Merrion, her way of looking at things had made such a difference to him, such an intriguing, illuminating difference.

He filled the kettle and plugged it in. He wasn't sure he really wanted anything to drink, but he had a feeling that to go through the ritual of making a drink would be reassuring.

He made himself a mug of tea, turned off the lamp and slid the door to the sitting room back again. It was a clear night and the glow from the sky and the street filled the room with itself, and with big, soft shadows. Guy sat down on the sofa and put his mug down on the table. He leaned back and looked at the ceiling, at the narrow track of minute, brilliant spotlights that ran across it and which, when switched on, created such extraordinary effects. It was, he thought, like being with Merrion or being without her, like bumbling along in the half-light or suddenly seeing things with freshness and novelty. If only it were possible to prevent that novelty from colliding with other things, refusing to coexist.

'I could not bear,' he'd said at dinner, 'to feel I was in any way limiting you.'

She was eating a complicated salad with a fork. She didn't look up at him, instead endeavouring to fold a long leaf of rocket in two. 'We've had this conversation.'

'That doesn't deal with it,' Guy said. 'Looking at Jack the other night brought home to me how *young* you are. You're far closer in age to him than to me. *Far*.'

She put the rocket into her mouth, pushing the stalk in after the leaf, with her fork. 'Are we talking about babies again?'

'I suppose it's part of it—'

'Maybe I don't want a baby.'

Guy said gently, 'Don't be childish.'

'I'm so tired,' Merrion said, 'of you bringing up difficulties. You never used to.'

'And you always said they'd be there.'

'They *are*. But they don't need talking up a storm all the time.'

'Or ignoring.'

She speared a piece of red pepper, inspected it, and put it on the side of her plate. 'I'm not ignoring anything,' she said. 'I'm just finding it very difficult to cope with your preoccupations. I know you're having a hard time, I know Laura is being impossible and the flat is horrible and dealing with your children is at best difficult, but it seems to me—I have to say this—that you are drawn towards all that, almost that you're returning to something you knew long before me. It's almost as if you've found your family again.'

Guy said, 'But I want you to be part of that family—'

She said sharply, more sharply than she meant to, 'And is that a good thing?'

He raised his head. 'A good thing?'

'For me,' Merrion said. 'Is it a good thing for me to be sort of *subsumed* into your family? Is that what you and I are all about? Is that what we've been aiming at, all these years?'

He shook his head. He said, almost inaudibly, 'No.' And then he said, 'We didn't know, did we? We didn't know what was coming—'

'No,' she said. She pushed her plate away. 'I don't want to talk any more. I don't want to have to say things. I'm not ready for saying things yet. Not some things, anyhow.'

He opened his eyes now and reached for his tea. It didn't taste of anything much: he hadn't let the tea bag soak long enough. What he had wanted to say at dinner and been unable to bring himself to say had been that he couldn't, for reasons he couldn't explain, visualise how their life together was going to be in the future. In the past, he'd always had a clear picture of it in his mind, in equally clear contrast to the half-life he lived with Laura. He'd seen an urban flat, a big flat, full of his books and her objects. He'd seen a house somewhere, maybe even a town house, with doors opening to a small summer garden and music playing. Sometimes, they'd even played the luxurious game of imagining how things could be if they were free to make them so. And now that freedom was slowly advancing towards him, it seemed to be blurring his vision of the future. What was even more disconcerting was that he suspected it was blurring Merrion's vision, too, that vision that had always been so unclouded, that had always sustained him.

He stood up. The light was getting stronger, dawn triumphing over street lamps. He went quietly across the sitting room and opened the door to the bedroom.

'You've been ages,' Merrion said.

'Have I? I thought you were asleep.'

She turned towards him. He could see the dark mass of her hair on the pillow as he got back under the bedclothes.

'Guy,' she said. 'What is it?'

He looked at the ceiling. He said, 'I can't seem to see the way ahead. I always could, but at the moment, I can't.'

She felt for his hand, under the covers, and held it in both hers. 'Keep saying "at the moment",' she said. 'Just keep saying that.'

Her voice was apprehensive, almost frightened. He put his second hand over hers and they held on to each other, under the covers, hard.

It was almost nine thirty before Rachel heard Carrie go downstairs. On Sunday mornings, it used to be Simon who went down first, and he'd put a track suit on and go out for the newspapers and then he'd bring them upstairs, with a cup of tea, for Carrie. But the last few months, Sundays had been the other way about. It was Carrie who went downstairs first and made tea. She didn't go and get the newspapers until she was properly dressed, and she made the tea wearing the old kimono with blue cranes and flowers printed on it which Rachel could remember all her life. Simon had once bought Carrie a new dressing gown, a white one made of thick waffle-woven cotton, but Rachel knew it was still in its plastic bag on top of Carrie's cupboard.

Rachel got slowly out of bed and pulled on Simon's old sweater over the outsize T-shirt she'd slept in.

It was silent on the landing. Emma's door was shut and so was Simon and Carrie's and there was no sound from the little staircase up to Jack's room. Rachel padded downstairs. Carrie was standing in the kitchen, dressed in jeans and a checked shirt and a fleece jacket, with her hand on the kettle as if that would help it to boil faster.

'Hi,' Rachel said.

Carrie turned round. 'Morning, darling.'

Rachel went to lean against the counter near the kettle. 'You going to get the papers?'

'Yes,' Carrie said. 'Why d'you ask?'

'No reason.'

Rachel yawned. She said, 'Is that for Dad's tea?'

'Yes,' Carrie said.

'I'll do it.'

'Will you? Thank you,' Carrie said. She took her hand off the kettle. 'I'll go and get the papers then.'

She picked up her handbag and went out of the kitchen. Rachel heard the front door shut, not slam. She went across the kitchen and took a mug out of the cupboard.

Two minutes later she carried the mug of tea upstairs. Emma's door was still closed. Rachel paused by her parents' bedroom door, transferred the mug from her right hand to her left, and turned the door handle. The room was half dark with the curtains still pulled across. Simon was just a long hump in the bed.

Rachel put the mug down on the chest of drawers and pulled the curtains back with great energy.

'I know, I know,' Simon said from the pillows, his voice muffled.

'It's me,' Rachel said.

She went back to the chest of drawers and picked up the tea mug. Simon lifted his head from the pillow and stared at her.

'How very kind.'

'Yes,' Rachel said. She held the mug out. 'Here.'

He sat up slowly. He was wearing his pitiful dark-blue pyjamas and his hair was tousled. At least he wasn't going bald. He held a hand out and she put the mug into it.

'What have I done now?' Simon said.

Rachel thought about sitting on the edge of the bed and decided against it. She pulled at the hem of her T-shirt so that it came well below the hem of Simon's sweater. She said, 'You need a shave.'

Simon took a swallow of tea. 'I need one every morning and sometimes in the evenings, too. Rachel, can you say what you've come to say?'

Rachel inspected the cuticles of her right hand carefully. 'It's Mum.'

'What's Mum?'

'She's upset,' Rachel said.

Simon took another mouthful of tea and leaned away from Rachel to put the mug down on the cluttered table beside the bed.

'Of course she is. Jack being so unhappy upsets everyone.'

'It isn't that,' Rachel said. She peered at a hangnail and put her finger between her teeth. 'I mean she is upset about Jack, but it isn't the worst thing. It's you.'

Simon flung himself across the bed, tossing the duvet aside, and put his feet on the floor. 'Oh, I *know* it's me—'

'Not like that,' Rachel said, chewing at her hangnail. 'She's not upset because you're such a pain. She's upset because of Granny.'

Simon said steadily, 'I have to help Granny.'

Rachel started on her other hand. 'She was crying the other day.'

Simon turned to look at Rachel. 'Crying?'

'She said if Granny made her fight for you, she'd win. Then she was crying.'

Simon stood up. 'She said this to you?'

'No,' Rachel said. 'She was on the phone. I was listening.'

'Did she know you'd heard her?'

Rachel put both hands by her sides and held them there. If she chewed any more, she'd make herself bleed. 'No.'

'Why didn't you say?'

'There was no point,' Rachel said. 'I know what she thinks. I know what she's feeling. It's *you* that needs to know.'

Simon gave a hitch to his pyjama bottoms. 'I see,' he said.

'You don't,' Rachel said rudely.

Simon looked at her. Rachel could suddenly, for a fleeting moment, see what he must have looked like at Jack's age. He said uncertainly, 'What don't I see?'

Rachel put her hands on her hips. She said, almost contemptuously, 'That she likes you.'

Laura had bought two dozen new delphinium plants. They were excellent specimens, leafy and robust. She was going to make a new border along the wall where the old cow shed had been, a blue border edged with French lavender which could spill over onto the brick path she had laid herself seven years ago when Guy was at a legal conference in Kuala Lumpur. And when she had planted her blue border, she thought she might change the dining-room curtains to echo it, since the dining-room windows faced across a small lawn to the old cow-shed wall.

She placed the delphiniums carefully on the dug—and fed—border and stood back to see if they would be in the right relation to one another for size and colour. She was good at that. Even Wendy conceded that, and Wendy had a distinct pride in her own garden and was, in any case, like many people with multiple competences, not very good, in Laura's opinion, at dishing out the praise. You had to confront her to get any, stand up for yourself. It had happened the other day when Wendy had arrived with a bottle of wine and banged it down on the kitchen table.

'We're drinking *that*. I'm not having any more cups of tea and accompanying fiddle-faddle.'

Laura had decided to be dignified. She put the bottle and two glasses on a tray with the corkscrew and a little dish of enamelled-looking Japanese rice crackers and carried it into the sitting room. She said, with her back to Wendy, 'I suppose you have come to tick me off again.'

'Of course I have,' Wendy said. She flung herself back into an armchair and took off her spectacles. 'What on earth else do you expect? You get offered twenty thousand pounds over the asking price for this house and you turn it down!'

Laura put the corkscrew very precisely into the neck of the wine bottle. 'How do you know?'

'For God's sake, Laura, *everybody* knows! Everybody thinks you are completely insane! It's only me that knows you practically *invented* obstinacy.'

Laura poured neat half-glasses of wine. She arranged a tiny smile on her face and carried the glass over to Wendy's armchair. There was a little polished table beside it bearing a coaster with a camellia printed on it. Laura put the wineglass down carefully on the centre of the camellia. 'Suppose we don't talk about that?'

Wendy was breathing heavily on her spectacle lenses before polishing them. She stopped, mid-breath. 'What?'

'Suppose,' Laura said, putting the disk of rice crackers beside Wendy's glass, 'we don't start all over again on all the things you think I'm not doing right and concentrate on the things you think I *am* doing right.'

'Heavens,' Wendy said. She took a gulp of wine.

Laura sat down in the opposite armchair. She put her knees and feet together and smiled at Wendy. 'What am I doing right?'

Wendy gestured wildly with her hand holding her spectacles. 'Well, you haven't gone to pieces—'

'No.'

'You look, well, neat as a pin as you always have, so does the garden and the house—'

'Yes.'

'And you haven't slagged Guy off in public, I suppose. You may have to me, privately, but in in public—"

'Yes,' Laura said.

Wendy put her spectacles back on. 'So, well done for that.'

'Thank you,' Laura said.

Wendy heaved herself forward in the armchair. 'But that doesn't mean you get good marks for everything.'

Laura stiffened. 'Here we go again—'

'Yes,' Wendy said, 'we do. You can't take a unilateral decision. Half of this house belongs to Guy. Legally. It belongs to him.'

Laura looked straight ahead. She held her chin up defiantly. 'I've made my position quite plain,' she said. 'And I'm not discussing it any further. They can all come to me when they have everything sorted, but I'm not involving myself any more. I am going to get on with my new life instead.'

'Your new life?'

'Living here,' Laura said. 'Living here alone and making something of it.' She took a sip of wine. 'I may take in bed-and-breakfast guests. I read that you can charge guests up to twenty-five pounds a night each.'

Wendy had left soon after that. She had left in a slightly clumsy, flurried way, not even finishing her wine. Laura put the cork back in the bottle and stored it in the refrigerator. Perhaps Simon would like it, when he next came. *When* he next came.

Now, regarding the delphiniums and wondering whether to grade the blues from dark to light, or to mix them, Laura reflected that her conversation with Wendy had been something of a small triumph. It was extraordinary how, when you could take charge of your life again after a profound shock, you found you had the power to choose again, to decide, to arrange things in a way both satisfactory and suitable to yourself. There had been that terrible time when she thought she would *have* to leave Hill Cottage, when she saw her whole identity being somehow melted out of her and poured away by people who simply could not see where the core, the mainspring, of her being lay. She had been terrified then, almost desperate. But then something amazing had happened, some weird new strength had come to her, and it had come to her most inexplicably after Simon had written her that dreadful letter that really ordered her to sell Hill Cottage. It was as if a voice had said inside her head, 'Don't. Don't give in. Don't move.'

'I needn't,' she said aloud to the dogs, almost in wonder. 'I *needn't*! I don't have to move!'

After that, nothing seemed to hurt so much, nothing seemed to touch her with quite the exquisite painfulness that everything had touched her with previously.

From inside the house, the telephone began to ring. Seconds later, the dogs began barking, a maddening habit they had developed lately in order to tell her that the telephone was ringing. She pulled off her gardening gloves, dropped them beside the tools on the path, and ran in.

'Hello?' she said. 'Hello?'

'Mum,' Simon said.

She smiled broadly into the receiver. 'Darling!'

'You sound out of breath.'

'I was in the garden. Planting a new blue border. It'll be lovely.'

There was a silence and then Simon said, 'I was wondering. Could I come and see you?'

'Of course!' Laura said delightedly. 'When?'

'Tomorrow?' he said.

'Perfect. Lovely. For lunch?'

'I really don't need lunch,' Simon said. 'I just need to see you for half an hour—'

'Lunch,' Laura said firmly. 'Twelve thirty.' She smiled, and put up a hand to touch her hair to smooth it back. 'Drive carefully.'

This is the last time,' Ted said to Simon.

Simon nodded.

'It isn't that I'm not sympathetic, but we can't just go on with you so preoccupied with your family troubles that you're only half with us.'

Simon nodded again. Ted was eight years older than Simon, and when he wanted to make a point behaved as if the age difference was almost a generation, as if he were a father reprimanding a son. Mostly, Simon bore it. In the first place he liked Ted, and in the second Ted did all the personal-injury work in this office. If you did personal-injury work, you got paid by the insurance companies at about £120 an hour. If, however, like Simon and Philip, you did mostly employment and immigration and housing, you got paid at the legal-aid rate, which was only about a quarter of that. Ted never said, overtly, that he was the one who paid most of the bills, but the implication was there, in his attitude.

Simon picked up his jacket. 'I'll be back at four.'

'Four! It's only half-ten now—'

'I can't concentrate,' Simon said. 'I'm no use here this morning.'

'I'm fond of my mother,' Ted said. 'But basically she does what I tell her.'

Simon went past him to the door. 'Lucky you.'

He drove out of the derelict yard behind the office where they parked their cars, and headed west. It was a warm day, humid, and the car's fan system blew tired, gritty air into the car. At least only Ted knew where he was going; it was better that Carrie didn't know he was going to see Laura, better that no one knew anything until the deed was done.

Laura looked better. She greeted him without any of the heavy, needy dependency she had greeted him with for months, and and led him round the house to the place where she was making her new border. She looked almost happy, almost girlish. There were delphiniums planted all along the back, in the painstakingly turned earth, and a neat regiment of lavender plants sat on the path in pots, ready to go in.

'Lovely,' Simon said. He put his sunglasses on.

'I knew you'd like it,' Laura said. 'You've always been interested in my garden.'

Simon squinted at the sky. He wasn't sure he'd ever been very interested in any garden. His own garden was a shambles. Ask Carrie.

Laura led Simon round to the terrace and sat him in a garden chair. 'I'm going to get you a glass of wine,' she said.

Simon gave her a quick smile. 'No thanks, Mum. I'm driving.'

'Just one glass—'

'Mum, no, thank you.' Simon took his glasses off. He said awkwardly, 'I'm glad—really glad—to see you looking so much better.'

'I am!' Laura said. She smiled at him. 'Of course I am! I just couldn't bear not knowing what was going to happen to me. But once I knew I was staying, everything fell into place.'

Simon leaned forward. He put his elbows on his knees. He said, staring out across the grass and the borders and the greenhouse to the field that rose steeply behind the house, 'I'm not sure you can assume that.'

Laura said sharply, 'Simon, I hope you're not going to start ordering me about again as if I had no mind of my own.'

Simon said slowly, 'I am not advising you about one more single thing.'

'Excellent,' Laura said. 'Now let me get you something to drink.'

'No,' Simon said. 'No. I'm not staying.'

'But you said you were coming for lunch!'

'I didn't,' Simon said. '*You* did.' He sat up straight and turned towards her. 'Mum, I can't be your lawyer any more,' he said.

'What?'

Simon looked straight at her. 'I can't cope with you any longer. I shouldn't ever have agreed to be your lawyer in the first place, but I did and now I have to get out before any more damage is done.'

Laura put her hands to her face. 'I'm not quite sure—'

'I was sorry for you. I *am* sorry for you, but you've exploited me and played games with me and set me against my own family, and I'm afraid I've come to the end. I'm not your lawyer any more and I can't compensate you for anything Dad has or hasn't done.'

Laura said unsteadily, 'I can't quite believe I am hearing this from you, of all people. Are you telling me that you are abandoning me but you still care?'

'Yes,' Simon said.

'Oh, Simon,' Laura said, 'who has made you so heartless?'

'You have. You've pushed me to the limits, and beyond.'

'Don't speak like this to me, don't—'

'Mother,' Simon said, 'I love you. As my mother. I always will. I'll stand by you as much as I can. But you are not first with me. You were, I'm sure, when I was little. All mothers are like that, to their little children. But you aren't now. You haven't been, since I married.'

'I *knew* Carrie came into it!'

'Not because of anything she's said,' Simon said. 'Not because of any pressure she's brought to bear on me. She doesn't even know I'm here.'

'What am I supposed to do?' Laura said.

Simon put his sunglasses on again and stood up. 'Find a new lawyer,' he said. 'I'll send you a list.'

'Don't go,' Laura cried. 'Simon, don't go! I'll do anything—'

'Sorry,' Simon said. He turned and blew a sketchy little kiss towards her with his right hand. 'Got to go.'

Laura cried, 'You can't leave me like this!'

He didn't look at her again. He said, 'Bye, Mum,' almost with his back to her, and then he went quickly across the terrace and out of her sight round the corner of the house towards his car.

Rachel was standing by the kitchen table, eating crispbreads out of the packet. There were scattered crumbs all across the table. She glanced up when Simon came in. 'What are you doing here?'

He dropped his jacket over the nearest chair back and tugged his tie loose. 'Thanks, darling, for the welcome—'

'It's ten past four,' Rachel said. 'Why aren't you in the office?'

'I have been in the office.'

'Why're you home now? You never come home early.'

'Then today's different, isn't it? Can I have one of those? I'm starving.'

'They're pretty boring.'

He bit into it and crunched. She watched him.

'Where've you been?'

'I'll tell you in due course. Where's Mum?'

'She isn't back yet.'

Simon reached across the table for the crispbread packet and took two more biscuits out. 'I'm going to have a shower. Will you tell Mum I'm here when she gets back?'

'OK.'

'Thank you,' he said.

She watched him go out of the room and heard his feet go up the stairs, quite fast, as if he was running. Then she heard various doors open and shut and the thud of his feet across the floor above and then the unmistakable groan and shudder of the shower being turned on. Rachel never used the shower. She preferred baths. She liked lying in the bath with the door locked and her music on, very loudly, so that, if anyone banged on the door and told her to hurry up, she genuinely wasn't able to hear them.

She put the crispbread packet in a cupboard and took a tired apple out of the fruit bowl—Carrie would never buy new fruit until the old fruit was eaten—and sat at the table, chewing at the apple. Simon had looked, well, sort of OK. Not exactly happy, but not tired and grumpy either. She heard the shower being turned off. He'd wind a towel round himself and pad into his bedroom before drying, leaving blotches of wet on the carpet. Jack did that, too. Perhaps it was men. Rachel sighed. Thinking about men made her think about women, too, and she didn't want to do that at the moment. She'd thought about love for years, it seemed, years and years. But now—or for now—she discovered she didn't want to think about it. It didn't seem an adventure, if her family were anything to go by, it just seemed to be a mess.

A key turned in the front-door lock and the door opened.

'Hi!' Carrie called.

'Hi,' Rachel said, nibbling tiny last pieces out of her apple core.

Carrie appeared in the kitchen doorway. She was carrying her bag and her briefcase and jacket. 'Hi, Rach. Whew, it's hot.'

Rachel put the apple core down on the table. 'Dad's back.'

'What, home? Is he ill?'

'No,' Rachel said. 'He's having a shower. He said to tell you.'

Simon was standing in the bedroom, dressed only in his boxer shorts, towelling his hair. Carrie stood in the doorway, leaning against the frame. She took one shoe off and flexed her toes.

'Hello,' Simon said.

Carrie stepped out of her other shoe. 'You're early.'

'I couldn't concentrate. I went back to the office but I was just too restless.'

'Back?'

'Yes,' Simon said. 'I went to Stanborough to see Mum today.'

'Oh,' Carrie said. She bent and picked up her shoes. In a careful voice she said, 'And how was she?'

'Devastated,' Simon said.

Carrie didn't look at him. She went past him slowly in her stockinged feet and sat on the sofa. 'What about, this time?'

'Me,' Simon said. He stopped drying his hair and threw the towel onto the bed. 'I went to tell her something.'

Carrie bent forward to massage one foot.

'I went to tell her that I'm not acting as her lawyer any more.'

Carrie stopped massaging and stared at the piece of carpet immediately beyond her foot. It had a stain on it, a small greyish stain the size of a fifty-pence piece.

'I told her that she was on her own now,' Simon said. 'That I'd always be her son but I couldn't be anything more than that. And that I'd had enough of being manipulated. I had quite a lot of things planned to say about the nature of love, too, about generosity in love, but there wasn't a chance really. Rather a waste. I'd done a lot of rehearsing in the car.'

Carrie stared at the stain. There seemed to be two or three of them. The harder she stared, the more they seemed to multiply. She felt Simon come and sit down next to her. He was damp and warm.

'Carrie,' he said.

She turned her head and put her face down on her knee, sideways on, so that she was looking away from him.

'I'm sorry,' Simon said, 'I am so, so sorry.'

She felt his hand on her back through the cotton of her shirt.

'I went to tell her that you come first,' Simon said.

She sat up and he put his arms round her. She laid her face against his shoulder. He lifted one hand and pressed her head into his shoulder.

'I should have done it years ago,' Simon said.

He kissed the back of her head. She lifted her hands and put them tentatively on his sides. Then she slid them round his back and held him.

'I don't know if I couldn't see or I wouldn't see,' Simon said. 'But the thing is, I do now.'

Carrie nodded. She thought: I'm going to cry. I don't want to cry, I *hate* crying. Simon loosened his hold on her, disengaging her arms, and then put one arm under her thighs and one around her back and lifted her across his lap. He said, right into her face, 'All yours now. All yours. If you'll still have me.'

She shut her eyes. She felt him lick along under them, where the tears were. She nodded again. 'OK,' she said. Her voice sounded tiny, as if it came from far away. 'OK.'

CHAPTER ELEVEN

PENNY HAD LEFT the customary pile of folders in Guy's chambers. He had asked her not to leave them without at least forewarning him of the court order of any day, but as she was incapable of ever doing exactly as she was asked, she left them stickered with yellow adhesive notes instead, covered with her small, sloping, unformed script.

He sat down at his desk. He had risen at six that morning, in order to catch a train to Stanborough that would have him in his chambers by eight thirty. Because he had woken, Merrion had woken, too, and they had showered and dressed around each other, silent with the knowledge that it was better to say nothing much than to court even the smallest danger of saying too much when there was neither time nor atmosphere to say it in. He had left the flat before her. She'd kissed him. Neither had said anything significant, even then, just, 'Speak later.' He had gone down those long flights of red-carpeted stairs very slowly, a weight upon him, silent and muffling.

He shuffled the folders. Mr Weaverbrook of the animal sanctuary was again among them. Mrs Weaverbrook would be back, more exhausted than ever with the effort of finding more excuses for Mr Weaverbrook's non-appearance in court, and simultaneous steady acquisition of farm machinery whose provenance he could not account for. Guy did not feel like Mr Weaverbrook, or anything that reminded him of the intractability and persistence of human things. He put his fingers into his waistcoat pocket and took out his father's watch. Ten past nine. It was unlikely, Guy thought, that his father had ever looked at that watch and confessed to himself that he did not feel like dealing with the working day ahead. 'I don't mind if you don't want to do it,' Guy's father would say, only half-humorously, to his sons, 'I only mind if you don't do it.'

The telephone rang. It might be Merrion. She had a conference at nine thirty. He picked the receiver up and waited, half smiling.

'Dad?'

'Simon!'

'Hello,' Simon said. He sounded shy.

'Hello to you, too. This is a very nice surprise. How is Jack?'

'A bit better. At least he ate something over the weekend.'

'No sign of the girl?'

'No,' Simon said. 'I rather think even Jack doesn't want to see her.'

'I wonder.'

'Dad—' Simon said.

Guy looked at the ceiling. There was a plume of discarded cobweb hanging from the light fitting.

'Has Mum spoken to you?' Simon said.

'Silly question.'

'It's just—well, I went to see her at the end of last week.'

'Yes,' Guy said levelly.

'No,' Simon said. 'Not like that. I told her that I can't act for her any more. Legally, I mean. It's caused so much trouble, it's—' He stopped, and then he said, 'I should never have agreed in the first place.'

Guy looked down at his blotter. With his free hand, he picked up a pen and wrote *Simon* on his blotter. 'Good for you,' he said.

'I thought,' Simon said, hesitantly, 'that you ought to know.'

'Thank you. That was brave of you, telling your mother.'

'She—' Simon said, and stopped again.

'I can guess. But you've survived.'

'Yes!' Simon said. His voice rose a little. 'Yes, I have. In fact, I—well, it seems to have sorted out quite a lot of things.'

'I'm so glad.'

'Dad,' Simon said, 'are you busy at the weekend?'

'I don't know,' Guy said. He was conscious that his voice sounded surprised. 'I don't know yet. Why—'

'Well—would you like to come over? Sunday supper, or something?'

'That's very sweet of Carrie—'

'It wasn't Carrie,' Simon said. 'I mean, I know she'd like to see you, but it's me asking. Me asking you.'

Guy suddenly felt rather unsteady. He held the receiver, hard, gripping it. 'Thank you—'

'And Merrion, too, of course.'

'Thank you.'

'Give me a call,' Simon said. 'A bit later in the week?'

Guy nodded. 'I will. Thank you. Thank you for ringing.'

'That's OK,' Simon said. There was a small pause, and then he said, 'Take care, Dad,' and put the telephone down.

Jack could see her, all the way down the main corridor. She was standing by the notice board, with a group of other girls, reading the end-of-term arrangements. She had pulled the long side-pieces of her hair back tightly and secured them with a band at the back of her head. Jack didn't like it. It made her look hard.

Adam thought Jack should just ignore her. 'Make like you can't see her. Like you've never heard of her.'

'That won't finish it,' Jack said.

'But it *is* finished,' Adam said.

'It isn't finished for *me*. I never said anything. I just got dumped.'

Jack looked down the length of the corridor, considering. She had her back to him now. Her school-uniform skirt fitted sleekly over her bottom and her legs looked as he remembered them, smooth and pale brown. Jack took a breath. He shifted his bag to his right shoulder and set off down the corridor.

The girls round her saw him coming before she did. He saw their eyes widen. One of them, a heavy girl with thick black curls, put a hand out and touched Moll's arm. Jack saw her say something, too. Moll turned and saw him coming.

Jack stopped in front of her. 'Hi,' he said.

She gave the heavy girl a sideways glance, then Jack an even more fleeting one. 'Hi.'

'Got a minute?' Jack said.

She put her chin up. 'I've got nothing to say—'

'I have,' Jack said.

'I don't want to hear anything you've got to say.'

The girls giggled faintly.

'I'll tell everyone else then,' Jack said. 'I'm not fussy.'

Moll gave a small, private smile. She glanced down at herself and brushed an imaginary piece of lint off her skirt.

'It wasn't being dumped I minded,' Jack said.

The girls stared at him. He hitched his bag a bit higher.

'I mean,' Jack said, 'nobody wants to be dumped, but it happens. You go off people like you go on them. It happens.'

Moll shrugged. She looked at Jack's feet.

'What got me,' Jack said, 'was not being told. You couldn't even *tell* me, could you? You just did it.'

'Nothing to tell,' Moll said.

'Oh really?'

She shook her head.

Jack leaned forward a little. 'Well,' he said, 'when you dump Marco, try to remember to tell him, will you? Try just to have enough guts for that, OK?'

'Fuck off,' Moll said.

Jack took a step back. 'Oh, I'm going,' he said. 'I've said what I came to say.'

They watched him go. He went down the corridor, the way he had come, with long, loping strides.

'He looks like Steve from Boyzone,' one of the girls said. 'Doesn't he?'

Moll turned back to the notice board. She lifted her hair with both hands and dropped it smoothly down her back again.

'Dream on,' she said.

Alan had made a curry, a careful, hot, Bengali curry. He'd done it properly; shopped at an Indian grocer, ground his own spices, everything. It looked wonderful when he'd done it, shining and exotic. It had taken all afternoon to make, but that was a good thing because it had taken his mind off Laura. She had left four messages on his mobile, and now she had written. She had written a letter to his old address and he'd picked it up there and brought it back to read in Charlie's flat.

It lay where he had left it, on the couch in Charlie's sitting room. Every so often, in the course of his chopping and pounding and grinding, he thought about the letter lying there, on the squashed cushions.

In the letter, she said that Alan was the only ally she had left in the world. Alan didn't want her to say things like that. In Alan's book, human beings shouldn't put that kind of pressure on one another, shouldn't try to hand the burden of themselves to someone else to carry. It distorted things, ruined things.

The letter had made Alan think a good deal about Simon. Splitting the stiff little grey-green pods of cardamom seed with a sharp knife, Alan had wondered if this was the kind of thing Simon had had, one way or another, all his life, with Laura. When he was little, maybe the surrender had naturally been his, and then he'd grown up and found Carrie and gradually tried to withdraw his submission, and then, bit by bit over the years, Laura had taken the dependency over, as if she were calling in the dues of the past, the dues of Simon's childhood. The thought made Alan shiver. And that was followed by a sudden and blinding flash of sympathy for Simon, a pang of knowing, of the emotional marsh Simon had waded through all his life, a marsh of obligations owed and demanded and expected, rather than of anything given out of the sheer desire to give.

And then there was Carrie. Alan didn't feel very comfortable about Carrie, either. They'd always talked about Laura, sure, they'd talked about most things, but it had been easier—for Alan anyway—to keep Carrie and Laura's relationship as a joke: a tired clichéd joke, but a joke all the same and therefore manageable. But perhaps it had all gone deeper for Carrie, really deep, to a level where an irritant became a threat, a menace against which she seemed to have no weapons. Of course he'd listened to Carrie, he'd listened to her recently when she got quite vehement about Laura, but his reaction had been along the non-committal lines of, 'There, there.' He felt ashamed of himself; he'd been no real support to her at all.

'Hey there!' Charlie shouted from the front door.

'Kitchen,' Alan called.

'I can smell,' Charlie said. 'Boy, can I *smell*. What have you been doing?'

'Curry,' Alan said. He didn't look up.

Charlie put an arm round Alan's neck. 'What's the matter?'

'I had a letter,' Alan said. 'It just got to me a bit—'

Charlie looked at him. 'What's the yellow on your face?'

Alan put a hand up and brushed at his cheek. 'Turmeric—'

'Where's the letter?'

'Over there,' Alan said. 'On the sofa.'

Charlie let go of Alan's neck. He went through into the sitting room and picked up the letter. He stood reading it, his back to Alan, legs apart. Alan watched him.

'Well,' Charlie said, finishing the letter. 'Who's a poor wee me then?'

'My brother's had it for years,' Alan said. 'All his life.'

'The favourite?'

'Always.'

'And do I gather your brother has now thrown her over?'

'Yes.'

'Oops. So you're next in line.'

'Yes,' Alan said. 'But I can't. I can't do it.'

'You don't have to,' Charlie said. He dipped a forefinger into a bowl and licked it. 'What's that?'

'Lassi.'

'As in dog?'

'As in yoghurt. I just don't even want to be pursued. I don't even want to be *asked*.'

'She's on her own,' Charlie said. 'She doesn't know how to cope. Lots of women her age don't. Men, too.'

'Whose side are you on? You can't want me to take her on, can you?'

'No,' Charlie said. He peered into another bowl. 'We'll take her on together. I'm good at mothers. Ask mine.'

'But you don't know her—'

'All the better.'

'And,' Alan said, 'she doesn't know about you.'

Charlie came round the kitchen table. He put his arms round Alan. 'She soon will.'

'I don't want you dragged into this, Charlie. I don't want you mixed up in it.'

'If it gets nasty, I'll get out. Taking you with me.'

'Are you sure?'

'Course I am. We do everything together, right? No exploitation permissable or indeed possible.' He gave Alan's back a thump and shifted his arms to hold him by the shoulders. 'Right?'

Alan grinned. 'Right.'

'Now then,' Charlie said, 'why don't you make a phone call? Tell your mother that you'll see her on Sunday. And that you're bringing a friend.'

'**I** think we should go for a walk,' Guy said.

Merrion moved slightly under the crackling mound of Sunday newspapers. 'I thought,' she said, 'that you were going to see Simon and co.'

'That's later.'

'Oh.'

'I do wish,' Guy said, 'that you'd come with me.'

She shut her eyes. She said, 'I'm not being unfriendly, I like them all, I really do, but I can't get my head round it.'

He reached for the nearest section of newspaper and folded it up. 'It isn't a big deal, dearest. It's just supper.'

'So you go. I'll come another time.'

Guy stood up. 'Come on. Walk.'

She stretched. 'Can't.'

He bent and took her hands and pulled her up. 'Got to.'

'Bully,' she said. She took her hands out of his and moved towards the bedroom. 'I'll just get some shoes.'

Guy bent and picked the newspapers up, section by section, and folded them in a pile on the table. Then he shook the cushions out.

Merrion appeared in the bedroom doorway. She had put trainers on. 'Ready,' she said.

He smiled and held his hand out to her.

'Got the key?' she asked.

They went down the long flights of stairs in silence. In the entrance hall, someone had left a double baby buggy chained to the bottom of the banisters with a plastic-covered cycle chain. There was a green plush frog in one seat of the buggy. Merrion glanced at it when she went past. It had huge yellow plastic eyes and a wide red felt mouth. Why give a child anything so gratuitously ugly to play with?

'Hideous,' Guy said, glancing at it, too.

She nodded. He went past her and opened the huge front door to the street and held it.

'Thank you,' she said.

They went down the pavement together, towards the park. He took her hand, as he always did, and held it with their fingers interlaced. It was warm and clear and there were bright soft leaves on the trees and drifts of spent blossom in the gutters. People were out, everywhere, couples and families, and people with dogs and people lying on the grass and sitting on the benches. The sight of all these little figures, running and cycling and walking made Merrion feel intensely lonely. She thought of her hand lying in Guy's hand and it felt as if it didn't belong to her.

They took a meandering route through the park, moving along the crowded paths with weekend aimlessness until Guy led Merrion away from the water and the people and the darting children, towards the nearest trees.

'Sit down,' he said.

She looked at the grass. 'Here?'

'I think here will do.'

She released her hand and sat down on the grass, holding her knees. He sat beside her, turned towards her. Even without looking, she could see how he looked, how he had arranged himself.

He said, 'I didn't plan to have this conversation this afternoon. I just knew I had to say it sometime.' He put a hand out and laid it on hers. 'I think—oh, my dearest, I *know*, that I shouldn't marry you.'

She stared straight ahead. She said softly, 'Here it comes.'

'It's not your age,' Guy said. 'It's mine.'

'And suppose I not only don't mind your age, but I like it?'

'Now,' he said, 'now you do. But not later. In eight years I shall be seventy and you won't even be forty still.'

She unclasped her hands and swung her knees to the grass so that she was facing him. Her hands were shaking terribly. She tucked them under her thighs.

'Are you going back to Laura?' she said.

'Absolutely not. I never could.'

She said, her eyes on the grass beside her bent knees, 'I always knew it would be hard. I always knew it would get complicated and painful—but I never knew it would get like *this*.' She inched forward and laid her head against him. 'I'm not—sure if I can bear it.'

He put a hand round her head, round her thick, strong hair. 'Nor me.'

'Guy—'

'Yes?'

'Please—'

He said desperately, 'My darling, if there *was* a way to do our future, don't you think we'd have thought of it by now?'

She nodded.

'Imagine it,' he said, 'you going deservedly up the scale, me retiring soon, all those impossible checks and balances, all those things you might not say or do because of me, all the things I might feel but could not say because of you. We've seen what it's like confronting all the elements we couldn't allow for, already. There'd be more.'

She lifted both her hands and took his away from her face and held them. 'I'd still risk it.'

He looked away for a moment. 'I can't,' he said, 'I can't risk *you*.'

'But all this love—'

'Not wasted,' he said. He looked down at the grass. He said, round incipient tears, 'Nothing lovely ever is—'

She said wildly, 'I just think I'm going to break up!'

'I know.'

'I can't bear it, I can't stand it, I can't—'

He twisted and put his arms round her and held her tightly against him. 'You can. You will.'

'I've been so vile,' she whispered, 'these last few months. Awful to live with.'

'No, you haven't.'

'I was frightened—'

'Rightly so,' he said sadly.

She pulled away a little, and said childishly, 'I don't *want* to live life without you. I'll be walking wounded, I'll be half alive—'

'Not for ever.'

'And you?'

'I don't know,' he said. 'I really don't know anything at the moment except what I've got to do. I don't know how I'll do it, any more than you do.'

He got to his feet, slowly and stiffly. Then he bent and held a hand out to her. 'Come on,' he said. 'Up you get.'

She took his hand and let him pull her up. He held her for a moment and then he took her left hand as usual, interlacing the fingers with his, and began to lead her back across the park towards the flat.

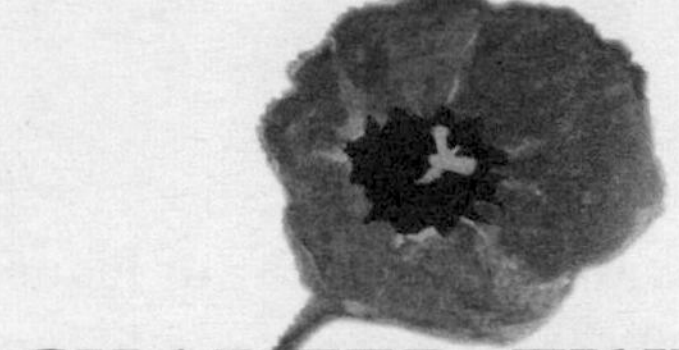

CHAPTER TWELVE

IT HAD BEEN, Gwen calculated, two months since she had spoken to Merrion; two months and three days. It was exactly two months and one day since she had posted her letter. Merrion hadn't replied to the letter, but Gwen hadn't really expected it. She wasn't sorry she had sent it. She had said things that needed to be said, that she had needed to say, and she had tried to say them in a way that Merrion couldn't take exception to because of being unable to avoid seeing that Gwen loved her and was anxious for her welfare.

It had been a long two months. There had been times when Gwen had had her hand literally on the telephone, ready to dial Merrion's number. There had been moments when she thought she might send a postcard and just write simply *Thinking of you. Love, Mum* on the back. But she hadn't done either. She had, instead, like a girl waiting for a boy to make the first move, felt that the right thing to do was to wait for Merrion. She had to let Merrion feel she was making the moves, dictating the pace.

She had tried to keep herself busy. She had filled in at work with extra hours, while people went on holiday. At home she washed all the curtains and starched the nets and planted her hanging baskets with petunias and trailing lobelia. She went up into the attic and sorted boxes and suitcases and found a whole lot of photographs, taken in France all those years ago, with Ray and Merrion. Merrion was scowling in a lot of the pictures, scowling into the sun or into the camera lens.

How could I? Gwen thought, looking at Merrion's scowl. How could I ever have put her through all that?

She brought the box down to the kitchen. Left to herself, she'd have thrown them away. But she felt she ought to show them to Merrion before she did that, and suggest, by showing them, that she, Gwen, didn't think she'd got life right, either. Not by miles. But, of course, she couldn't show anything to Merrion until she saw Merrion again. She couldn't do more than make plans of what she'd do when the lines of communication were open again. When Merrion chose to open them.

She put the box on the kitchen table. Perhaps she would at least sort them, throw out the views she had taken, all the hills and valleys and little town squares she had photographed as if they'd had significance. She took the lid off the box—an old shoe box, it was, brown Start-Rite sandals of Merrion's, size eight with a daisy pattern, she remembered, stamped out of the toe—and tipped the photographs out onto the plastic tablecloth.

The telephone rang. Gwen jumped. She dropped the box and hurried round the table to the telephone.

'Hello?'

'Mrs Palmer?'

'Yes—'

'Mrs Palmer,' Guy said. 'This is Guy Stockdale. Am I interrupting you?'

'No, no, I was just—'

'Mrs Palmer, I wonder if I could come and see you? There's something I'd like to tell you—'

'Tell me now,' she said. 'Tell me over the telephone.'

'I'd rather see you. I'd rather see you face to face.'

'Is it Merrion? Is Merrion ill?'

'No,' he said, 'Merrion isn't ill. Merrion is fine.'

'Why isn't *she* ringing me?'

'Because I said I would. Because I asked her if I could.'

'Very well,' she said. She'd heard that at the office. 'Very well,' her boss said, several times a day, on the telephone, 'Very well.' It sounded dignified, a slight put-down.

'Thank you,' Guy said.

Gwen looked round her kitchen with its washable wallpaper printed with grapevines growing through trellises. She tried to imagine Guy, in his suit, sitting at her plastic-covered table, staring out of her kitchen window at her bird feeders.

'I'll meet you in Cardiff,' she said.

'Of course—'

'I'll meet you on Friday. At the Angel Hotel. About four o'clock.'

'Thank you.'

She put the receiver quietly back into its cradle and went back towards the kitchen table. The photographs lay there where she had spilled them, the views and scenes of provincial France, Ray in the Hawaiian print shirts she'd so detested, Merrion in her sundresses with her hair in fat bunches and her scowl. Gwen bent over and began to scoop the photographs together into a rough pile. The sight of them suddenly made her want to cry.

Laura had all the sitting-room windows open. She had opened them the minute Alan and Charlie had gone, to try and get rid of the smell of cigarette smoke. Of course she'd always known Alan smoked, but when he had come to Hill Cottage in the past he had never smoked in her presence. Now, however, he seemed to have a new confidence, almost an assertiveness. He came into the house with something like a swagger, laughing, a lit cigarette in his hand. With Charlie.

Laura had in no way been prepared for Charlie. Like the smoking, she knew, without admitting she knew, that there was a reason for Alan's not being married, for Alan's never having had a girlfriend. But she'd never been confronted with evidence of Alan's sexual orientation before.

'Hello,' Charlie had said, perfectly at ease. He had his hand out. He was smiling.

Laura had put her hand in his, hesitantly. His hands were huge, huge hands on this tall, gangling red-haired man with jug ears and a wide smile.

'I'm Charlie,' he said. 'I'm a doctor. I expect Alan told you.'

She looked at Alan, who was perched on the edge of the table. 'Nope,' he said cheerfully, 'I haven't told her anything.'

Laura tried to extract her hand. Charlie held it.

'Plenty to say then,' Charlie said.

He'd brought her a bottle of wine and a book. Not flowers, or chocolates, or something conventional, but a *book*.

'It's about a woman restoring a house in Tuscany,' Charlie said. 'An American woman. My mother loved it.'

'Thank you,' Laura said faintly.

They uncorked the wine and poured out huge glasses. Laura watched them. Alan didn't take her pretty, modest-sized cut-glass wineglasses out of the cupboard but the big rough green Spanish ones that Guy had bought once, on holiday. Then he almost filled them.

'I couldn't drink all that,' Laura said.

Charlie smiled. 'Yes, you could,' he said. 'Good for you. Trust me.'

They went out into the garden with their glasses. The dogs thought that Charlie was wonderful and he threw sticks for them and they lay panting at his feet and slavered worshipfully. He told Laura about growing up in Devon, and how he missed the sea and sailing and walking on Exmoor. His father built boats, he said, and his mother ran art courses for people wanting to make pottery and jewellery.

Alan held out his wrist. There was a thin black bangle on it, threaded with a single red bead. 'She sent me that.'

Laura stared. 'His—his mother?'

'Yes.'

'Have you—have you met her?'

'No,' Alan said. 'But when Charlie told her about me, she made me that.'

Charlie leaned forward. 'Drink up,' he said to Laura.

She felt slightly dizzy when she went into the kitchen to dish up lunch, dizzy and disorientated. As she drained the chicken fat out of the roasting tin she could hear them laughing, all the way from the terrace, laughing and sort of *shouting*.

The men ate lunch with relish. Feeding Charlie was like feeding an enormous adolescent. He ate everything: two, three, four of everything. After lunch, they put Laura in a chair in the garden and brought her coffee, in a mug. It seemed churlish to say she would have preferred her coffee in a cup, but she said it, all the same.

'Too late,' Charlie said cheerfully. He winked at her and went back inside to help Alan wash up, leaving her with the mug.

She must have gone to sleep. When she was conscious again, the coffee was cold and the dogs had gone. She got up and went into the house. They'd washed up, certainly, and the kitchen table was strewn with the results, haphazard piles of plates, and damp tea towels draped across chair backs. In the sink, a dirty ashtray sat under a dripping tap.

'Good, but not good enough?' Alan said from the doorway.

She turned from the sink. 'I was just—'

'We took the dogs out,' Alan said. 'Up the hill.'

Charlie appeared behind him in the doorway. 'Lovely place,' he said. He had his hand on Alan's shoulder, not just resting it there, but holding, holding on. 'Lovely view of it, from above like that. I'm so glad, that you've had such a good offer for it.'

Laura opened her mouth. They moved into the kitchen and stood on the other side of the table, looking across at her, and smiling.

'I—'

'It's awful to have to leave somewhere like this,' Charlie said. 'Somewhere you've made. But it must be amazingly satisfying to know what you've made it *worth*, over the years.'

Laura said, 'I don't think you quite understand—'

'He does,' Alan said, glancing at Charlie. 'He understands completely.'

Charlie put his huge hands down on the kitchen table and said comfortably, 'We're here to help you, you know.'

'We?'

'Oh yes,' Charlie said. 'We.'

Alan took his cigarette packet out of his pocket. 'We'll help you find something else, Mum,' he said. 'Help you move.'

Laura looked at Alan. He was lighting a cigarette.

'Alan, I'm not sure—'

He took a breath of smoke and blew it out. Through the faint blue cloud he looked at her. 'We are. We're quite sure, Mum,' he said.

Guy reached the Angel Hotel twenty minutes before his appointed time for meeting Gwen. He chose a corner sofa in the lounge, a sofa with an armchair opposite it and a low table between them. After he had ordered tea for two, he took out his new, and disliked, reading spectacles and a legal journal that he felt obliged to take each month and seldom read. He crossed his legs and balanced the journal on his knee. A boy arrived with a huge metal tea tray and began to unload its burden of cups and plates and pots and jugs with immense laboriousness.

'Will that be all, sir?'

'Yes,' Guy said. 'Yes. Thank you, it will.'

He took his reading glasses off. The boy went back across the lounge, holding the metal tray in front of him like a shield. In the doorway he paused, then retreated a step and turned sideways to allow a woman to come in. Gwen entered very falteringly, and paused, looking about her.

She was wearing a printed summer dress with a pale jacket.

Guy got up and went across the lounge towards her. 'Mrs Palmer—'

She looked up at him. She said in a small voice, 'Oh, yes.'

He gestured towards the corner where he had been sitting. 'I ordered us some tea.'

'Oh, yes,' Gwen said again, as he guided her across the room.

'Would you like the armchair?'

'Thank you,' she said.

He went round the low table burdened with tea things and sat down again on the sofa. 'I'm very grateful to you for coming.'

He poured her a cup of tea. It rattled in its saucer as she took it.

'That's all right,' Gwen said.

Guy poured his own tea. 'I want to reassure you that Merrion is fine. I'm not here because there is anything—' He paused and then he said, 'Anything the matter with Merrion. Nothing for you to worry about.'

'I wouldn't have come,' Gwen said, 'I wouldn't have agreed to meet you, if I wasn't worried. Would I?'

He looked down at his cup. She was such a disconcerting mixture of sharpness and shyness. 'No,' he said. He leaned his elbows on his knees and linked his fingers. 'Mrs Palmer—you remember when we last met—'

'Oh, yes,' she said. 'I remember *that*.'

'And you remember what you said to me? That I was greedy and selfish. That by persisting in my relationship with your daughter, I was depriving her of all the natural human joys of a traditional family life because, at my age, I already had all those things and would not want more of them.'

Gwen stirred her tea. 'I'm sure I didn't put it like *that*.'

'No,' Guy said. 'But I think that is what you meant.'

Gwen gave her head a tiny toss. 'I may have done—'

Guy leaned forward. He said, looking straight at her, 'Mrs Palmer, you were probably right. You probably *are* right. There are other factors, of course, but I never forgot what you said, I never wanted, never meant—' He stopped, and bent his head. It was suddenly, physically, impossible to go on. He looked hard at his linked hands and fought with the obstruction in his throat.

Gwen was watching him intently. 'What are you trying to say?' she said.

He shook his head. He could not trust himself to speak.

'Mr Stockdale,' Gwen said, 'what are you trying to tell me?'

Guy swallowed hard. He made himself look up. 'I am not going to marry her,' Guy said indistinctly.

'What?'

'It isn't fair, I shouldn't— I can't ask her to—'

Gwen gave a little scream. 'Oh no,' she said. 'Oh *no*!'

Guy put out a hand towards her, almost involuntarily. 'Mrs Palmer, I thought—'

'Oh!' she said, putting her hands up to her face, holding her cheeks, staring at him now with eyes like saucers. 'Oh!' she cried in anguish. 'What *have* you gone and done now?'

Simon went round his desk in order to open the door for Mrs Akimbi, who was his last appointment of the day. He had just agreed to act for her in her case against the local council. Mrs Akimbi had worked for the council for fifteen years, through all the problems of being abandoned by her husband and bringing up their three children alone, and it had suddenly dawned upon her that, in all those fifteen years, she had never been promoted. She felt she had been discriminated against on grounds of race and sex, and Simon was taking the cast to the Employment Tribunal.

'Don't get stressed out about it,' Simon said. 'It'll only take a day.'

'Stressed!' Mrs Akimbi said. 'Stressed! You have no idea. I am altogether stressed out already.'

As Simon opened the door, he saw that someone was standing there, waiting outside his office, someone in a black suit with long hair tied back behind her head.

'Merrion!' Simon said.

She said, 'I don't want to interrupt.'

'You aren't,' Simon said. 'My client was just going.'

'We are finished,' Mrs Akimbi said. She hardly looked at Merrion. 'For now.'

'Goodbye,' Simon said, and held out his hand.

Mrs Akimbi took his hand but said nothing. She went past them down the short corridor to the reception area.

'I should have rung,' Merrion said.

'It doesn't matter.' He held the door. 'Come in.'

She went and sat in the chair Mrs Akimbi had occupied.

'Are you all right?' Simon said.

She looked at her lap. 'Not very.'

He propped himself on the desk edge, close to her. He said, 'I'm quite surprised to see you, I have to say.'

She glanced up at him. She said, with a faint smile, 'I just felt I ought to come. In person, I mean. There are some things you have to say face to face.'

'Oh God,' Simon said, trying to sound facetious. 'What's coming now?'

'It would have been easier to go and see Carrie, I suppose,' Merrion said, looking away from him. 'Which is probably why I didn't do it. As Guy would say, typical hair shirt. He thinks I was born in one.' She stopped.

Simon looked at her partly averted profile. She didn't look very well, very happy. He said gently, 'What's going on?'

She turned her head. She said, looking up at him, 'We aren't going to get married.'

He said nothing. He felt an extraordinary stillness settle on his mind, freezing it.

'It's sort of mutual,' she said. 'I mean, it wasn't a great scene with one of us begging and pleading for a change of heart. We both sort of knew. I suppose we'd known for ages.'

'What had you known?' Simon said, almost in a whisper.

'That—that what we had, what we felt, might not survive being married. That—that the change would kill it. And we couldn't bear what that—might do to us.'

'Oh, my God,' Simon said.

'We couldn't,' Merrion said, 'bear to hurt each other. We couldn't risk it. Not hurt like that.' She looked down again and said in a voice so low he could hardly hear her, 'Though at the moment I can't imagine hurt worse than this. He's been my whole life, my—' She stopped again.

Simon moved a little against the desk. He looked down at her bent head, at her bowed shoulders.

'So it's over?' he said.

She nodded.

'Are you sure?'

'Yes,' she said, 'it has to be. You can't go back ever, can you?'

'No.'

'Only on,' Merrion said hardly audibly. Her shoulders shook a little.

'Come here,' Simon said.

She lifted her head. 'What?'

'Come here.'

She stood, uncertainly. He held his arms out.

'Here,' Simon said. He pulled her towards him and then held her in his arms, his face against hers. 'Poor girl,' he said. 'Poor, poor girl.'

He felt her lean against him; he felt her beginning to shake slightly, her body loosening. He gave her cheek a brief kiss.

'You cry,' Simon said. His own voice was far from steady. 'If you want to, you cry.' He moved his head so that his cheek was against her hair. 'This is the place to do it, Merrion. This is the place. If you want to.'

CHAPTER THIRTEEN

THE SHADOWS, Jack noticed, were getting longer. The most extensive one, belonging to the chimney pots on the roof, had now reached three-quarters of the way across the lawn. Soon he would get out of his deckchair and go in and find someone. Anyone, really.

When Jack had said, that Saturday lunchtime, that he'd tidy up the garden a bit, Simon had stopped doing what he was doing (putting a new fuse in the vacuum-cleaner plug) and said, incredulously, 'What?'

Jack shifted from one foot to the other. 'I don't mind. I'll do a bit out there if you want.'

'In the *garden*?' Simon said.

'It's a right mess—'

'I know,' Simon said. He put down the plug and the screwdriver. He said, a little awkwardly, 'Thank you. Thank you, Jack.'

They'd gone out into the garden together and looked at the border. It was, to Jack's eye, just a huge green tangle.

'Start with the weeding,' Simon said. 'Take out things you don't like the look of. Make a pile.'

'OK.' Jack looked at a huge lilac bush still bearing the rusty bunches of its spent blossoms. 'Can I cut stuff?'

'I don't see why not.'

'Will Mum mind?'

'Mum will be ecstatic.'

'OK,' Jack said.

He went across the grass to the shed where the tools were kept and where he'd once kept his bike, too, before he'd decided it was juvenile to ride a bike and sold it, for far too little, to Rich's kid brother.

The garden tools lay in a heap against the shed wall where they had been thrown, tangled up with stray lengths of wire and wood. Jack didn't know much about garden tools. He turned the pile over gingerly and selected a spade and a fork and various blades and large scissor-like things and carried them out onto the grass. He picked up a pair of secateurs and released the safety catch. Maybe he'd start with a bit of cutting.

He wasn't at all sure why he'd made this offer of gardening. He hadn't really planned to, he had just found himself offering, and then, after he'd offered, being sort of glad he had. Maybe it was something to do with the way things felt around the house now, the way the girls didn't have their bedroom doors shut all the time and Carrie didn't bang meals down on the table as if she was so fed up with getting them that she didn't really care if anyone ate them or not. She'd had her hair streaked, too, and it made a big difference. There were a few new clothes, as well; nothing major but definitely some new tops and a pair of sandals he'd seen Emma trying out, along the landing.

And then Simon had said that they were going on this holiday. They'd all been completely amazed, stunned.

'A *holiday*?' Rachel said, as if she hardly understood the word.

'Yes,' Simon said, grinning. 'I thought we'd go to Majorca.'

Jack wrenched off another branch of the lilac bush and threw it behind him on the lawn. They'd never had holidays. They'd had school trips, sometimes, and once in a blue moon Simon and Carrie went away for a night at a weekend, but Simon always said there wasn't any money for holidays. And then he dropped this bombshell. It was such a bombshell that Jack wasn't even sure he wanted to go at first.

'Course you bloody do,' Adam said.

'With my kid sisters? With my parents?'

'Forget them,' Adam said. 'Think of the other things.'

'Like?'

'Sun,' Adam said. 'Booze.'

'Girls,' Rich said.

'Girls!'

'You can go out on the pull every night,' Adam said. He closed his eyes. 'Think of it. Sun and booze and scoring. All day, all night. What are you bloody waiting for?'

Jack stood back and looked at the lilac. There was much less of it, certainly, but rather unevenly less. It looked a bit naked and pathetic, like somebody caught half-dressed. Jack chucked the secateurs onto the grass and picked up the garden fork. As he stuck it into the earth, he thought of Majorca, and what Adam had said. He didn't want to score every night, indiscriminately, after a skinful. But he'd like to score once, maybe, with somebody nice, somebody he liked.

'Jack,' Guy said, from behind him.

Jack turned. 'Hi, Grando.'

Guy came close and put his hand on Jack's shoulder. He looked at the lilac bush. 'Do you know what you're doing?'

'Not a clue,' Jack said.

'Would you like some help?'

'OK.'

'We could level that up a bit.'

'OK.' Jack stooped for the secateurs and handed them to Guy.

Guy gave him a quick glance. 'How are you?'

Jack looked down. 'All right—'

'Better?'

'Yup,' Jack said. 'I did what you said. I went and told her.'

'Good for you,' Guy said. He stepped into the border and began to even up the lilac bush. Jack looked at his back. He was wearing one of his usual check shirts, with the sleeves rolled up. From the back, he looked just as he always did, always had. It was from the front that he looked different. Jack couldn't quite define why, but it was as if something behind his face had fallen in, leaving hollows and shadows. Perhaps it was that he looked old, now. Jack wasn't sure. He *was* old, of course he was, but Jack knew now that just because you were young—or old—you couldn't make assumptions about age, about looks or feelings or anything. Look at Carrie. Some days, just now, Rachel looked older than Carrie.

'Grando,' Jack said.

Guy turned and came out of the border with an armful of branches. 'Is that better?'

'What's happening?' Jack said.

Guy dropped the branches on the grass, then reached out and took the fork from Jack's hand. 'I'm moving to the north.'

'Why?'

'There's a judge up there, a Crown Court judge like me, who has cancer, poor fellow. So he has to retire early and I'm being transferred up there, to take over. Resident Judge. Just like Stanborough.'

He turned away and began to push the fork into the matted earth round the lilac tree.

'Don't go,' Jack said. He hadn't meant to. He felt a fool the moment he had spoken.

Guy paused long enough to give him a quick look. 'I have to, old boy.'

Jack sat down on the grass. He felt, suddenly, like a little kid, like a little lost kid. 'Why d'you have to?'

Guy stopped digging. He turned round completely. 'Because I'm divorcing Granny so I shouldn't stay in Stanborough. Because I'm not marrying Merrion so I shouldn't stay in London.'

Jack swallowed hard. He began to rip at tufts of grass round his knees.

'I'll recover,' Guy said. 'Like you have. It'll take me a bit longer and I may never get over it completely, but I tell you one thing.'

'What—'

'I couldn't have borne it not to have happened. I couldn't have borne not to know Merrion. I couldn't have borne not to have loved her.'

Jack got up and picked up a hand fork. 'What'll Merrion do?'

'She'll go on to be an extremely successful family law barrister and probably take silk in about ten years' time, become a QC. And I hope she will marry and have children, too.'

'Do you?'

'I'm training myself,' Guy said. 'Now look. Can I show you how to do that?'

Jack surrendered his fork. Guy knelt beside him.

'Doors close in your life,' Guy said, 'doors open. They don't always do it together and they don't always do it when you want them to. But they keep doing it. Now watch. You have to sift the earth through the fork as you dig to break up the lumps and let the air get in.'

'Air?'

'Yes, you chump. Air.'

Jack stretched now and felt the unyielding bars of the deckchair behind his head and his thighs. They'd done the whole border after that, foot after unyielding foot, and at the end Guy had made him cut the grass at the edge of the border with the shears, to give it a finish. He'd done that with great care, really paid it attention, and then Simon had come out and admired what they'd done and taken Guy off to have a drink somewhere, before supper. After that, Carrie had come out, bringing Jack a glass of lemonade, and said the kind of things Jack didn't associate with Carrie at all. He'd looked at the new stripes in her hair and the way they made her hair look thicker, somehow, and shinier, and it occurred to him that maybe she'd actually brushed it, too, because it looked smooth and almost curtain-like, the way he now knew he liked girls' hair to look. When she'd finished talking and he'd finished the lemonade, she took the empty glass back inside and Jack lay down in the old deckchair he'd found in the shed, and looked at his handiwork. He felt it was pretty sad to want to look at a border, a garden border, but there was no one to see how sad it was, after all, no one to spoil this bizarre and perverse pleasure.

He looked up at the sky. It was clear and pale blue and the sunlight was getting lower and more golden. He thought of Carrie in the kitchen, probably opening and shutting cupboards with her striped hair swinging. He thought of Majorca and the sea and a girl in the sea with hair like that, only wet, plastered to her shoulders. He thought of Simon and

Guy in a pub somewhere, maybe sitting on a pavement on metal chairs next to a little round metal table, with their glasses of beer, sort of circling round each other like dogs who know they're going to play together but have getting-to-know-you stuff to do first. He thought of Adam and Rich and Marco and Moll, of Moll reduced to saying, 'Fuck off,' pathetically, because she couldn't think how to reply to him, how to concede that she hadn't, as she thought she had, called the last shot. He thought of what Guy had said about doors: doors closing and opening in a ceaseless, irregular movement all down those corridors of life, those long corridors that were sometimes terrifying to think about. He leaned forward and eased himself slowly and stiffly out of the deckchair. He liked the idea of looking through those doors, seeing what was there. He put his arms above his head and stretched as high as he could, and then, giving the border one last glance, he sauntered across the grass towards the house to see what, if anything, was going on.

JOANNA TROLLOPE

Since her separation in July 1998 from her second husband, the playwright Ian Curteis, Joanna Trollope has slowly discovered a new independence and strength. Speaking about the experience, Joanna Trollope says, 'The end of a long relationship is very disorientating: suddenly it comes to an end and you just vanish, because you are so used to thinking of yourself in a relative way. And then suddenly you feel fine, you have returned to your own skin and you pick up your own name again. But during that acute period of disorientation, you have lost a handrail. I don't see Ian now and I don't know what he's doing, though I wish him well. But I see his two sons: they and my two daughters, who are all grown up, are devoted to each other and are clinging on to each other for dear life,' says Joanna.

When Joanna Trollope moved out of the family's medieval manor house, she rented what she calls her 'little Georgian doll's house' fifteen miles away. She began to write *Marrying the Mistress*, but it proved to be 'much the hardest book I've ever written. With all the other books,' she says, 'people would always be sweeping back into the house at any minute. In the case of *Marrying the Mistress*, though there was no one else around, so I couldn't seek another human gauge. I had to discipline myself to sit at that kitchen table by nine each morning, and just stay there until one o'clock, with no nice little breaks.'

The author firmly believes that the mistress is still very evident in modern life, although she has subtly changed over the decades. She may no longer be the financially dependent woman who is given a cosy flat somewhere and an allowance: now she is a career woman in her thirties or forties, a woman who knows what she wants out of life, where a married lover fits the bill very well. 'In *Marrying the Mistress* I was interested in how the dynamics change when the unorthodox or "forbidden" relationship becomes orthodox,' Trollope explains. 'A mistress has an exclusive hold on the person who is her lover, and the secrecy of the relationship can be very important. People in this situation sometimes want the secret relationship to become acknowledged and visible, without then being able to take on the consequences of that visibility.'

Joanna Trollope is now living on her own for the first time in thirty-three years and has recently bought a two-bedroom flat in London, an ambition she has had since she was seventeen. At weekends, to escape from work, she heads for her London bolthole while most people are fleeing to the tranquillity of the countryside. 'I feel freed at last to be who I really am,' she says. 'I know what my next two books are going to be about. It has always been that way—stacked aeroplanes waiting to land. As for feeling fulfilled, I hope never to feel completely fulfilled because then the point of the journey would be destroyed. You've got to have curiosity, hunger and a slight anxiety. But I can ride out storms better now and I'm less afraid of things going wrong. And, you know, other things come to be far more beguiling than happiness.'

Beans

The House Husband

Owen Whittaker

My life's dream of being a rock star, playing Wembley Stadium with under-age groupies falling at my feet is about to take a serious tumble into reality. My last chance of recognition as a brilliant songwriter and a bass player of distinction is slowly slipping through fingers already greased with zinc and castor oil and cleaned with baby wipes. Move over fame and fortune. For destiny—and a severe lack of money—has proclaimed that I become a house husband instead.

'THANK YOU, NEW YORK! *You've been a wonderful audience!'* I'm announcing this as I leave the stage, having just played my last encore.

A girl has climbed up from among the vast crowd and has rushed at me. My minders are closing ranks around me, but it's all right, she's not carrying a gun.

'I love you!' she's screaming at me.

Someone's taken my guitar for me and I'm being swept past the crowd of well-wishers into my dressing room.

Tonight's the night I've finally made it. I look at the sea of well-known faces in front of me, all offering their congratulations. Paul McCartney, Stevie Wonder, Sporty Spice and others too numerous to mention, but I'm not concentrating. In a corner of the room there is someone I've wanted to meet for a long time. She's smiling at me.

'Hi,' I'm saying, crossing to her.

'Hello. Good to meet you at last,' she's replying.

I can't believe it. I'm actually talking to Kate Bush. She looks as sexy and as beautiful as she used to on the poster above my bed.

'Car's ready, guv'nor,' someone's whispering in my ear.

I've grabbed Kate's hand and I'm dragging her behind me as we're ushered out of a back exit and into the rear of a waiting limousine.

'Sorry,' I'm apologising to Kate, 'I suppose this is a bit of a liberty. But I couldn't let you go now that I've met you.'

'That's OK,' she's saying to me, 'I'm glad we're alone.'

I've fantasised about this woman since I was eighteen.

I think I'm about to pass out from the excitement. Kate is unbuttoning her dress. She's looking directly into my eyes and she's saying ...

'UGH! NO! I've just trodden in some poo-poo!'

Actually Kate Bush isn't saying this. My daughter is. She's in the garden somewhere, with her mother. Another daydream ruined, a fantasy foiled.

I'm looking out of the window. There are about two acres of land in front of me, most of it consisting of field. Coarse, rough grass of a deep, lush green. Definitely ride-on mower territory here, except for us poor buggers who can't afford such luxuries.

Our fields slope downwards towards the road, on the other side of which is, you guessed it, another field. A large gathering of motherly looking cows chew so lazily that half the grass falls back out of their mouths in soggy clumps, to be skidded in by some welly-booted farmer later in the day.

And at the bottom of that field sits the Atlantic Ocean. It's late October, nineteen ninety . . . what is it? Ninety-six, and today, miraculously enough, the sun is shining. The ocean looks as blue and enticing as any in the world.

I'm supposed to be trying to write a song, here in my music room, in our house.

Well, that's a lie for a start.

It's the building society's house. We just plummet ever closer to bankruptcy trying to renovate the sodding thing, let alone trying to pay a mortgage, the size of which borders on the criminal.

Still. Cracking view. When the sun is out. Which is about ten times per year.

Odd that I have a feeling of space, because my music room could only be regarded as spacious if it were a toilet. Once I'd filled it with my guitars, keyboard, amplifiers, desk and sofa bed, movement became a bit of a problem.

Yet I sense space.

Bit of a paradox, that, really . . . Ooh, 'paradox'! That's a clever word. Must see if I can work it into one of my songs, establish a cult following: the thinking man's rock'n'roller.

Better fantasy: thinking woman's rock'n'roller.

I digress.

No, the feeling of space is one of the real bonuses of life since we moved here from London to west Cork, Ireland, a couple of years ago.

Ah, the space, the countryside, the ocean, all so inspiring! My writing must surely have become more prolific since I moved here? Songs materialising faster than Barbara Cartland novels?

No. Afraid not. Quite the opposite, actually.

But surely the people of west Cork are awash with friendliness and character. Each with a fascinating tale to tell, true or otherwise. They must have provided a vaultful of material to write songs about.

I cannot argue. All the above is true.

Trouble is, I spend all my time in the pub getting langers (Cork for falling-over drunk) with them and enjoying their company so much I never seem quite able to drag myself back here to write.

As for the beauty of the place, it lulls you into a dangerous and indigenous philosophy, which is . . .

Feck it! I'll do it tomorrow.

Out there in the garden, beyond the window, I can see two female figures climbing the sloping grass back to the house. The bigger of the two is my wife, Gina. Driving, intelligent, independent Gina. She's gorgeous! Shoulder-length blonde hair, high cheekbones with the sort of doleful eyes and petite body that make you want to protect her and shag her senseless at the same time.

Leading the charge is Sophie, our daughter, who's just turned four years old. Big blue eyes like her mother, long, flaxen, curly hair flopping round a face filled with mischief. A two-and-a-half-foot fireball of energy, coupled with an extraordinary eccentric personality.

Nicola isn't with them. That's our other daughter: three months old and gluttony personified.

She who never sleeps. In fact, I seem to be the only member of our family who isn't hyperactive.

They're wrestling now, Gina and Sophie, on the grass. Gina's making the most of it before she returns to work.

Work.

Shit! Trouble is, it's hard to get motivated, because there's no recording contract.

You see, the problem is —

'Andy! There's been a disaster! The washing machine is having a fit, so it is. There's water everywhere. Sorry, did I startle you?'

Perhaps it's the fact I'm clutching my heart that made her form that opinion. She did burst through the door like an SAS soldier who'd forgotten his balaclava and boot polish.

'It's all right, Noreen, I'm coming.'

I'm following her out of the door, through the lounge and into the kitchen. Noreen's in her early twenties and she's been with us for six months or so. Bit of cleaning, bit of cooking, bit of baby-minding. A little treasure.

I'm paddling into the kitchen now. It's like Niagara Falls. Water is spewing out all over Gina's precious newly laid quarry tiles.

'Bloody hell! You weren't kidding, were you?' I'm staring at the washing machine. 'What shall we do?'

'What if we turn off the water at the mains, Andy? Will that help?'

'Good thinking, Noreen.'

'Where's your stopcock?'

'I don't fucking know! What are you asking me for?'

'Sorry, Andy. It's just in our house, now, my dad would be the one who knows where it is.'

'Sorry, sorry, Noreen. I'm panicking. Don't take it personally. You know what a useless git I am when it comes to this sort of thing.'

Gina and Sophie have just walked into the kitchen and Gina has just turned off the washing machine and unplugged it.

Brilliant. Why didn't I think of that?

'Andy. Where's the stopcock?' Gina's asking.

'I don't know! Why's everyone asking me, like it's some secret I've been entrusted with? I haven't got a clue.'

'Well, you should know!'

Oops, she's shouting at me now.

'Look at the water, Daddy. Whee!'

Sophie's kicking it up into the air, soaking the kitchen cupboards.

'Don't do that, Sophie. You'll make Mummy cross.'

'Why?'

'Andy.'

'Yes, Gina?'

'Don't just stand there like a wet fish. Phone a plumber.'

'Daddy? Shall we get our swimsuits on and have a splash?'

'Andy! Phone! Now!'

'Yes, yes. I'll use the one in the music room.'

'Dad? If I got my sandbox, we could have our very own beach, couldn't we?'

'Not a good idea, Sophie. Right, phone the plumber.'

I'm back in the music room. I've climbed over the amp to get to the desk where the phone is.

Quick flick through the *Golden Pages*. They may be yellow in England, but here they are golden.

I'm dialling . . . no reply.

'Have you contacted anyone yet, Andy?'

Gina's peering through the door.

'There's no answer.'

'That's just typical. If we were in England we could just call Dyno-Rod and have someone here within twenty minutes. In Ireland they don't even *answer* the bloody phone for three days.'

'Relax, Gina. What does it matter if it takes a few days?'

'It matters because I've got three linen baskets full of dirty clothes upstairs. Try another number.'

I'm dialling the next one on the page.

'I dread to think what this will cost us,' Gina's saying as she shakes her head. 'I just hope we don't need a new machine. We can't afford one.'

'We'll have to pick one up, secondhand.'

'Andy! The one we've got *is* secondhand and it's the third time it's gone wrong.'

'Well, how much is a new one?'

'About four hundred pounds.'

'*How much?* Strewth, that's a lot of money just to wash a few socks, isn't it?'

'Don't be ridiculous, Andy! There are four of us to wash clothes for, one of whom is a new baby. You just don't think, do you?'

'All right, all right.'

She turns to close the door, then stops in afterthought. 'By the way, I've asked Noreen to baby-sit for us. We're going out tonight.'

'That'd be nice.'

'We need to talk, Andy.'

She's gone.

I was wrong. I can't see 'nice' being on the agenda tonight. I've seen that look before, the one on Gina's face. Brow furrowed, eyes set. It means trouble.

Suddenly, the feeling of spaciousness has evaporated.

Why are we here? And who in their right mind would choose an Irish pub in which to have a private conversation?

I'm thinking this as Gina stands at the bar. She's buying the drinks. A pint and a glass of Murphy's.

I've suddenly noticed she's wearing sheer stockings. Nothing unusual in a woman wearing suspenders you might think, but the point is, the only time I'm treated to a bit of nylon-inspired excitement these days is when there's trouble afoot.

Then, at the end of the evening, after a massive tear-inducing, glass-breaking, soul-baring argument, there is sometimes a bout of frantic, passionate, overexcited and quick sex.

But only if I've given the right answers. If I fail, the suspender belt is tucked pointedly back in the drawer and we sleep with our backs to one another.

So, Regina, this is serious.

My wife's full name is Regina. Pronounced Ree-gee-na. At school, apparently, it was purposely mispronounced to rhyme with vagina.

Regina the Vagina, she was known as.

'I promise you, Andy, my nickname had nothing to do with me being promiscuous.'

Makes you wonder, though, doesn't it?

Andy, that's *my* name. Andy Lawrence.

Actually, it's an abbreviation, because my full name is also a bit of an embarrassment. Having said that, I suppose I've half given it away now and, yes, all right, it's Andreas. Hideous.

The fact that Gina and I had both shortened our Christian names to avoid flak was one of the things that drew us together in the early days.

She's walking back towards me now—drinks in hand. Her stern face is still fixed in place. It's a professional expression. To help her survive as a journalist. Underneath the mask there lurks a complete softie.

We are in O'Leary's. It's an old pub, a muso's pub, slap in the centre of Ballinkilty, which is our nearest town. There's a folk club at the back. I play bass guitar there for a local band on Sunday nights.

'Well?' Gina's saying as she puts the drinks on the table.

'Well what, sweetheart?'

'Andy. Have you any idea what I want to talk about?'

'No.' At least I'm honest.

She's chewing her lip. Frustration, I presume.

'Come on, think for a change, Andy. This is important.'

Silence.

'Well, say something!'

'What? I'm thinking like you told me to! Look, can't you just tell me, Gina? You're making me a bag of bloody nerves.'

'I've mentioned the subject constantly since Nicola was born. You just chose not to listen, as usual.'

In fairness, she is probably right.

'Sorry. But then, we have been married nine years. You are well aware by now that if you wish to make a point to me you do not spend weeks dropping subtle hints. YOU FLASH IT IN FRONT OF MY EYES IN HUGE FUCKING NEON LIGHTS!'

'All right, keep your voice down, Andy.'

'I said you were making me nervous. I always shout when I'm tense.'

'OK, I'll tell you. Simply and plainly. Now, Andy darling, you've got to listen. Concentrate. I don't want you drifting off into your own space. Understand? How much do you know about our financial situation?'

'Oh, God!'

I'm now diving for my pint. Our finances have a tendency to make me want to do that.

'Don't bring Him into it. He is not our accountant. Do you know the state of our finances or not?'

Shit. She's just produced a notepad from her handbag.

'Enough to know we're skint. That we shouldn't really be here drinking away the money for the phone bill.'

'But you couldn't tell me facts and figures?'

'You know I couldn't.'

'I see.'

She's taking another sip. I'm taking a ruddy great gulp and signalling 'Same again' to the barman.

'Do you know why we are short of money?'

'Gina! What is this? Sodding *Mastermind*? Your specialist subject "The Causes of the Lawrence Family's Poverty, 1987 to 1996"?'

She looks guilty and pained simultaneously.

'I'm not trying to be difficult, Andy, I promise you. I hate talking about this. It's just I need to know how aware you are yourself before I fill in the gaps.'

'Right. Fine.' I'm nodding as I light a cigarette. 'Let's start with the house. We can't afford it. The estate agent's details said it needed work. Roughly translated that meant it was a case for euthanasia, Gina, not life support.'

'It was a sound investment at the time, Andy.'

'Was it really? Take our time. Do it slowly. That was the theory, wasn't it? We've done it slowly, all right. Two years, and by my reckoning there are just three rooms completed. Every time we attempt to start a new one we uncover another major problem.'

'Yes,' Gina agrees. 'However, the fact that your DIY skills are limited to putting up the odd shelf at a jaunty angle only for it to collapse three weeks later hasn't helped. Come on, Andy, even you must admit you're useless.'

She teases me light-heartedly, trying to make me smile.

I say nothing, but begin my second pint.

'OK,' she sighs. 'What else?'

'We overspend. Fail to live within our means. I pop to the pub for too many swifties. You are prone to whipping out your credit card, purely on reflex, when you're within a hundred yards of a clothes shop. You come home loaded down with bags crying, "It's all right, Andy, I only brought them home to try them on." Then three weeks later when you've worn them a couple of times and spilt red wine all over them we get a thumping great bloody bill.'

Gina is blushing. 'All right, accepted, but a woman has to have a new outfit occasionally. Anything else?' she's asking, changing the subject.

'Your change of job?'

'Not the factor I'm looking for, but you're right. What about my change of job?'

'We came to Ireland because you had the opportunity of a superb job editing a new magazine. Ireland's answer to *Tatler*. It went arse up within six months. Unable to find anyone insane enough to buy our house and then scarper back to London, you were forced to take the editorship of another magazine here. Infinitely inferior, with a salary drop to match. Ireland's answer to *Just 17*. All photo-stories and teenage angst. Although, this being a good Catholic country, the problem page is somewhat tamer, if not positively limp.'

She's smiling. 'Very accurately summed up.'

'Thank you. Can we talk about something else now?'

'No, we bloody can't!' she says, playfully slapping my arm. 'You're missing out the biggest single contributory factor, Andy.'

I'm beginning to sulk.

'I'm fed up with this game, Gina. It's not fair. You know the rules and I don't. So can we cut to the chase, please? What *is* the missing link?'

I watch as Gina takes a deep breath, as if to give herself courage.

'*You*! Andy Lawrence. *You*'re the missing link!'

'Gina . . .' I'm instinctively fumbling for another cigarette.

'Oh, now, surely I'm not after interrupting a lovers' tiff, am I? You two feckers are far too old for all that, so you are.'

Belly O'Hea.

That's all I need. Belly barging in, completely devoid of tact and sensitivity. An earthquake couldn't shift Belly O'Hea once he's got his backside sat down.

'Now, tell me something, Gina. You live with this feller, so you do. Have yer ever seen him without a drink in his hand, now be honest?'

Brilliant, Belly. Just fucking great.

'How are you, Belly?' she's asking.

'I'm grand altogether, but then when you're as handsome and talented as me, you're always fierce happy, isn't that right, Andy?'

'If you say so, Belly.'

Gina's somehow smiling and gritting her teeth at the same time. Any man in the world, other than Belly O'Hea, could read the words 'Piss Off' stamped all over her face.

He's an old rock'n'roller, is Belly. The wrong side of sixty years old, I would guess. Huge fun, in small doses.

Very small doses.

Oh, shit. He's sat down.

'Now then, Andy. Are yer any nearer to superstardom than when I last gazed upon yer fascinating features?'

'Afraid not.'

'Are yer still playing with that bunch of losers?'

'I am.'

Two members of my band, Michael and Bridget, left to form another group about six months after I started playing with them. Belly manages Mix and Match, the breakaway group.

'Would there not be any joy with those demo tapes of yours?'

'Record companies are not exactly beating a path to my door, Belly.'

'You can't just send them into a slush pile, unsolicited.'

'What should Andy do, then?' Gina asks, surprisingly.

'He should find a manager with style, sophistication and, above all, contacts. But sure, he wouldn't be after recognising one even if he were sat right under his fecking nose, now would yer, Andy?'

Belly has put his face flush up to mine as he speaks.

'I take your point,' I'm replying, although his face is so close that by moving my mouth I'm in danger of kissing him.

'I tell yer what now, Andy,' he's saying, leaning back in his chair, thank God. 'Why don't yer give me those tapes of yours and I'll see if I can do anything with them?'

'How much is it going to cost me?'

'Ah, now, Andy. Do yer have to introduce so vulgar a subject as money into such an artistic discussion?'

'How much?'

'If you get some sort of deal, I'll take ten per cent. It'll be up to yerself if you decide to keep me on as yer manager or employ someone less gifted with a cockney accent. Fair enough?'

'Oh, go on, then. I'll drop them in to you over the next day or so.'

He's shaking my hand. 'Right I'm off.' He's spotted Michael from Mix and Match walking into the bar, and Belly's gone without saying goodbye.

'Well, that's something, isn't it?' Gina's asking.

'Belly O'Hea? Managing my career? I can't see him playing Colonel Parker to my Elvis, can you?'

'No. I can't. However, he has given us further evidence as to the cause of our financial ruin.'

Oh, well, time to come clean. I confess I've known for some little time where this conversation was heading.

'OK. Another reason we're so broke is because I haven't been very . . . lucky. With, my career, I mean.'

'I'm not blaming you, darling, and I can't tell you how dreadful I feel raising it. But you've earned virtually nothing, Andy, for the nine years we've been married.'

'No. You're right. I haven't.'

Painful things, home truths.

'I go back to work next week. The magazine have been very good letting me have three months' maternity leave, considering the short time I've been there. I don't want to go back, Andy. I'd much rather stay at home and look after baby Nicola and Sophie. But I can't. If I don't work, we starve.'

'Yes,' I agree, meekly.

She's running her hands through her hair. Tugging at it.

'What did you think would happen when I went back to work?'

'How do you mean?'

'The children. Concentrate on the children.'

'Oh, well . . . I sort of presumed . . . that Noreen would, sort of, you know . . . take over. Up her hours or something.'

Gina has reached for a cigarette. This must be serious: she only smokes when things are desperate.

'Andy, darling. I don't earn half the salary I used to. When Sophie was born it was different. We could afford help then. I adore you, but we are in serious shit. Noreen has got to go altogether. We have to economise if we're going to survive. Everything that costs money is under review. Including the one pound fifty you slip the young lad at the garage to wash the car, before bringing it home and claiming your back's in pieces from all that graft?'

How did she know about that?

'What will we do without Noreen? You're at work. Who's going to run the house? Look after the kids?'

She's staring at me, not speaking.

I'm looking at her and . . .

No!

A horrible thought is penetrating the mist in front of my eyes. Does she mean . . .? No! It's almost too ludicrous to consider.

I haven't spoken. I don't have to.

'Yes, Andy, you're right. Who's going to look after our kids and the house while I'm out at work? *You* are.'

She's gone to the bar.

The ramifications are making me dizzy.

My face is red, my jaw is dropped widely open. If I don't move soon someone will call an ambulance.

Gina's back. She knows I'm in shock because there's a whiskey chaser to go with the Murphy's.

'Well, darling?' she's asking.

'There must be some way round it.'

'Must there? I don't think so. Andy, darling, I love you with all my heart. I've been happy to support your dreams all the time I've been in the position to do so. But, I'm sorry, I just can't do it any more.'

'I'll get a job,' I say, with enough enthusiasm to try to buy me some time.

'Andy, my love, I hate to disillusion you, but even if U2's bass-player died tomorrow they're unlikely to ring you and beg you to replace him.'

'No,' say I, feigning hurt at being misconstrued, 'I mean a *proper* job.'

'Be serious, Andy. You tried that before, remember? In the early days. Brilliant at the interviews, sacked within three weeks of taking the bloody job.'

'But, Gina, it just doesn't seem right somehow.'

As she's stubbing out her cigarette, her eyes are narrowing.

'Right? I'll tell you what's right, you whinging bastard. There's no money to pay for any other fucker to do this. You have a duty to look after your two beautiful children. That's what's right. Andy, please don't think this is easy for me either. I could spend my days arranging afternoon teas with other stay-at-home mums. Good grief, the only deadline I'd have to worry about was whether I could finish the ironing before the baby woke up. Bliss!'

'Hold on a minute, Gina, you love your job. You've spent your life trying to claw your way to the top. You've always wanted the big career.'

Gina's eyes are beginning to fill with tears.

'I do . . . I mean I did, oh, I don't know. Being a mother . . . changes you. How you feel. All I'm saying is we *both* have to make sacrifices.'

'I suppose you're right.'

'You'll do it?'

'Do I have to wear an apron?'

'You can wear a French maid's outfit, if you like. I've no problem with cross-dressing as long as the kids are fed and the house is tidy.' Her face relaxes and she puts her hand on mine. 'However, I do insist you buy your own knickers. I don't want mine falling round my ankles halfway through an editorial meeting just because you've stretched them.'

Her eyes are kind, warm, as she squeezes my hand.

'We'll see how it goes, then, shall we?'

'Thanks, Andy. I know what I'm asking, but life's been cruel and there is just no other way. Look, I'll get another round,' she says, before disappearing back to the bar.

'Saints preserve us, would yer be after looking at that? Andy, yer have a face like a smacked arse. Why are yer so fierce feckin' miserable?'

It's Belly O'Hea.

'Don't tell me. That fine woman of yours has finally rejected yer blatant and clearly perverse sexual requests, so she has.'

'Something like that.'

'Well! I'm fecked if I'm going to sit around here trying to cheer you up. Yer clearly a lost cause. Don't forget to drop those tapes off, now.'

'If I have time.'

'Time is it now? Tell me, Andy. What the feck else have yer got to do with yer time?'

Good question.

I'm a bit confused, a bit steamrollered.

Have I got this wrong?

Because the fact is, as I see it . . .

I have just agreed to become a House Husband.

OUR GEORGIAN SLUM is on the border of a village called Ardfield, about four miles outside Ballinkilty, a picturesque town, painted in cheerful Mediterranean pastel colours. You fall over it as you drive down the N71 from Cork. The N71 is the major road in west Cork, although I use the term 'road' loosely. It's more a cross between a ploughed field and a roller-coaster track.

So Gina and I are back home now. Our home.

I'm in the kitchen, one of the rooms we've actually managed to complete, give or take a few finishing touches.

Like a cooker, for example.

We're saving up, in theory, for the obligatory Aga. In the meantime, we're making do with a microwave and a hob, run off a Calor gas bottle. You know the type. The sort that makes you update your will before lighting it with a match at arm's length.

Gina's in the lounge.

It's the second of the three rooms we have finished. All pinks and yellows and checked curtains. It's been finished less than three months and already the combined efforts of our two children are beginning to make it look seedy.

Deirdre has just entered the kitchen with Gina.

Noreen was too busy to baby-sit. Deirdre is our only back-up. If she can't do it, it's a takeaway and falling asleep in front of the telly. Deirdre is clearly pissed off that we returned an hour later than we promised. That's why I've stayed in the kitchen while Gina pays her off and apologises profusely.

I'm a coward, on top of all my other faults.

'Take care and we'll see you soon,' Gina's shouting after Deirdre, as she scuttles out of the door and heads for home.

'Thanks for the back-up, Andy.'

'I was covering your rear.'

'Well, sweetheart,' she nibbles my ear, 'if you want to uncover it, you'd better fix us a nightcap while I check the kids.'

Gina goes upstairs to look at our daughters.

Both the kids were accidents. I confess I felt cheated. Selfishly, the idea of trying for a baby for six months or a year appealed to my libido enormously. I had always fantasised about Gina screaming, 'Now! It has got to be now!' and me unzipping my flies and saying, 'Not again, surely?'

But no, both children were great big 'whoops!', two glorious, adorable, lovable little shysters. Literally the greatest mistakes of my life.

I've poured us both a Bailey's. Ice in Gina's, none in mine.

Gina has reappeared. She's wearing her towelling robe. I've taken a quick glance underneath. The stockings are still on.

She's taken the Bailey's from me and downed it in one. Then she's given me a big hug.

'I know how hard this is for you, Andy. If there was any other way . . .'

'I know,' I say, returning her hug.

'You'd better lock up quickly. You don't want me to fall asleep on you, do you?' she's saying, smiling as she heads out of the room.

I've drunk the Bailey's and I'm turning the key in the door.

I don't know. I feel as if . . . in some way . . . I just sold out.

It is now five o'clock in the morning and I am freezing. Nicola, our baby, is lying on the floor at my feet. She is underneath what I believe is called a baby frame. A cheap, overpriced piece of plastic, from which hangs a mirror and a couple of rubber squeezy toys, in this case Pooh, Piglet and Eeyore.

I'm cold because I'm naked.

I must have said the right things to Gina last night because, after both of us had checked the sprogs once more, we were thrashing around the king-size with more enthusiasm and invention than I can remember in ages. At least, as far as Gina is concerned. I tend to be consistent in my zest for such matters. Gina is a different matter.

When we first met, we'd rip each other's clothes off morning, noon and night. Then we got married . . . then we had kids . . . then we ran out of money . . .

For some reason, all this seems to have affected Gina's libido.

I, on the other hand, see it as a reminder of why we put ourselves through all this.

Anyway, the nightmare scenario inevitably clicked in. As I'm thrusting my way towards crescendo, Nicola decides to join in the chorus from her cot in the room next door. Funny how the tiniest of murmurs from one so young can be heard above all the grunts and moans and cries that accompany intercourse. To be fair, I can't have been doing a bad job because Gina was pretending she hadn't heard it as well.

But three seconds after a copious climax on both our parts, Gina suddenly decides she can hear little Nicola now and, rather breathlessly says, 'Baby's awake.' She says this in a way that implies, 'You've had your oats. Now get your arse out of bed and feed the baby for a sodding change.'

I may not exactly have earned the title 'new man', but I have *occasionally* dragged my carcass out of bed at silly hours of the morning with both our kids. I'm perfectly capable of staggering downstairs, retrieving a bottle of baby milk from the fridge and warming it in the microwave. But now I am shivering. I did not have time to slip on a dressing gown and Nicola insists on screaming every time I try to sneak up the stairs to grab some protective clothing.

So I'm now debating whether or not to put the heating on.

Trouble is, our system was bought secondhand from a chap called Noah and ripped out from a sort of overgrown houseboat. If I take the brave decision to flick the thermostatic control to ON, this will result in several loud clunks followed by a sort of Shostakovian symphony played on bass panpipes and didgeridoos, which continues for about an hour.

Oh dear. Gina will be awake in a couple of hours and she will want to discuss my My New Career in detail. She likes pinning things down.

Gina is a born leader. In the Great War, she would have been the sort of officer to lead from the front, climbing out of the trenches, charging up over the top calling, 'Come on, men, let's sort these buggers out!' whereas I would be ferreting around in the mud trying to find where I'd put my rifle and helmet shouting, 'Two secs, be with you in a minute.'

A marriage of opposites. She needs me to calm her down, stop her burning herself out. I need her to kick my arse into gear.

A couple of hours. Not very long to come up with a strong argument against role reversal.

Maybe, under the circumstances, there isn't one.

It is now 5.49am and I'm about to creep back up the stairs with a sleeping baby.

I can never remember which stairs creak. Shit! That's one of them. Phew! Got away with it. I left the nursery door open wide enough to get through as that creaks as well. One baby flung as gracefully as I can manage into her cot, one toy giraffe placed in little arms, one duvet tucked into sides of cot, one father now exiting as fast as he can. YES, SUCCESS!

'Good morning, Daddy.'

There is no more deflating feeling in the whole world than getting one child off to bed, only to be greeted on the landing by the other.

'Daddy.'

'*Ssssh*. I've just got the baby off.'

'Dad . . .' she begins, just as loudly as before.

Why do four-year-olds find it physically impossible to whisper, for crying out loud?

'Dad, let's have a cuddle on the sofa and watch cartoons,' Sophie suggests, as she clumps her way downstairs like a pocket storm trooper.

I follow her down and switch on the television. For some reason it's stuck on some German-language channel, selling the latest rip-off for tightening your abdominal muscles. I flick through the channels until I see the familiar face of Scooby-Doo and sit next to Sophie resignedly.

'Dad?'

'Yes, daughter.'

'You used to watch Scooby-Doo when you were little, didn't you?'

'Yes, Sophie.'

'Dad?'

'Yes, Sophie?'

'Was I there?'

'No, of course not.'

'I was, you know,' she says, winking, as if she's just let me in on a secret.

'How could you have been, Sophie? I hadn't even met Mummy yet.'

'Ah, but you see, Dad,' she begins, in a slightly patronising tone, 'I was behind you.'

'Oh, well, that explains it,' I reply, too tired to argue.

'Dad?'

'Yes, daughter?'

'You see, Dad, usually, you see, I have my breakfast when Scooby-Doo's on.'

'What? Even if it's lunchtime?' I argue facetiously, trying to stall.

'Don't be silly, Daddy,' Sophie replies seriously.

'Right. OK, what do you want?'

'Er . . . er . . .'

'Yes?' I wait, as her eyebrows knit together in thought.

'Not Coco-Pops.'

'Right.'

'Not Weetos.'

'OK.'

'Not fruit.'

'Yes, look, Sophie, we've established what you *don't* want, how about a little clue as to what exactly may tickle your taste buds?'

Damn. I was a little short-tempered there. I didn't mean to be, but I'm tired and cold and there's an African rhythm section playing in my head and . . . oh, I don't know. How does Gina cope with all this? Perhaps, and more poignantly, this will be a compulsory and regular part of my new job spec. If so, how the hell am I going to deal with it?

'Toast.'

'Pardon?'

'Toast, Daddy.'

'Toast, right, yeah, breakfast, I'm with you. Just as it comes or . . .'

'Er . . . not jam . . .'

'Don't start that again. Do you want anything on it or not?'

Short-tempered again.

'Marmite.'

'I see. Well, I'll do my best.'

'Daddy,' Sophie sighs, and raises her hands again, 'it's easy. You just put the bread in the toaster thingy and spread the Marmite . . .'

'Well, if you're so clever, little madam, you make the breakfast!'

'Dad?'

'What?'

'Why have you got no clothes on?'

'Sorry? Oh! Er . . . Well, you see . . . Crikey, I don't know, ask your mother!'

'Ask me what?'

As if by magic, like the cavalry appearing over the hill, Mummy is there. Resplendent in bright blue towelling robe and red bedsocks.

'You're up early, Gina.'

'I know.' She kisses me. 'I couldn't sleep. I've been thinking.'

Oh fuck. That spells more trouble.

'Mum?' interrupts first-born.

'Yes, Sophie, darling?'

'Er . . . Mummy?'

'Yes, sweetheart,' Gina replies, with sickening and enviable patience.

'Er . . . Mum, why is Daddy not wearing any clothes?'

'Well, you see, it's all baby Nicola's fault,' Gina replies smoothly.

'That dratted baby,' says Sophie, smiling, shaking her head knowingly, completely satisfied with the flimsiest of explanations.

Brilliant. Why didn't I think of that?

'What time did Baby go back to sleep?' Gina asks me.

'Half an hour ago.'

'Did she have her bottle?'

'Yep.'

'Did you change her nappy?'

'Er . . . no.'

'Oh, Andy Lawrence!' she chides me affectionately.

'Gina, you know I've got a weak stomach. I can't help it. I get instantaneously nauseous.'

'Well, you're going to have to get used to it, in the light of our little conversation last night,' she whispers.

Bugger! She hasn't forgotten, then.

'Mum?' Sophie choruses.

'Yes, Sophie?'

'Mum . . . Mummy, you said Daddy was going to be looking after me and he can't even make Mummy's Special Toast!'

'Don't worry. Mummy will just have to show Daddy *how* to make it, sweetheart.'

As my wife leaves the room, I'm left feeling outraged that she has discussed this with our four-year-old child before she'd even finished closing the deal on me.

SUNDAY, 10.00PM.

I've spent the day trailing Gina round the house, like the Sorcerer's Apprentice receiving exact instructions from his master. I never realised what a little miracle-worker Gina is. Well, apparently from now on, the loaves-and-fishes routine is down to me. She's even written things down, compiling them into a sort of House Husband's Manual.

God, I needed a drink. So now I'm in O'Leary's with Connor. He is probably the best friend I have here. He's also my drinking partner and I've been bending his ear all night about my sorry state of affairs.

He's at the bar getting in a round. He's chatting to some young girl. They all adore our Connor. Women, that is. His wife died in a freak car accident a year or so before Gina and I came to west Cork. He still hasn't recovered from her loss.

Michelle, Gina's best friend here in west Cork, is determined to find him a new woman. She seems to have a production line of no-hopers, which usually last no longer than a date or two. They exit screaming that they cannot compete with the memory of Connor's dead wife.

Maybe that's what attracts the ladies to him: the air of unavailability. Extremely tall, with Liam Neeson-type looks, all soft blue eyes and rippling muscles. Plus a lilting baritone voice of the liquid honey variety. If his hair wasn't thinning I think I'd be seriously jealous.

'Calm down now, Andy,' he's saying, as he places the Murphy's on the table. 'You were saying you told Gina you'd get a proper job, but your track record in that department is not good, is that right?'

'To put it mildly,' I confess, as I grasp my pint.

He's shaking his head. 'You really are a useless article, aren't you? What about your musical talent? Is there not some down-market use to which you could put those skills to earn a punt or two?'

I'm gulping more stout before my next confession.

'I've tried that. I played "mood music" as part of a trio in a hotel bar managed by a closet gay. Drove me up the wall. I got the sack from there as well.'

'What did you do?'

'I dedicated a tune to the manager on his birthday.'

'What tune was that, exactly now?'

'"Nobody Loves A Fairy When She's Forty".'

He's laughing.

'What do I do, Connor?' I sigh.

'Andy, you have to see it from Gina's point of view. The poor woman has steadfastly kept you for nine years without complaint. But money, or the lack of it, has reared its ugly head and belts have to be tightened. Be fair now. You have a beautiful wife and she's given you two lovely children. It won't kill you to look after them for a bit.'

'I suppose you're right. Listen, speaking of Gina, can you spin her to and from Cork? We've only the one car and I need it to chauffeur the kids, apparently.'

'Of course,' he's replying, before draining his pint glass.

'Thanks. I'm very grateful.'

'Right, I'll buy the poor condemned fecker a large whiskey to go with his pint.'

Monday, 11.30pm, and I'm in the kitchen, finishing a ciggie.

I've always hated Mondays, and this has been a particularly crappy Monday by anyone's standards.

We had to fire the staff today. Hark at me sounding like something out of *Upstairs, Downstairs*. What I meant was, today was the day we tossed a coin to see which poor sod had to tell Noreen that her services were no longer required.

I lost the toss.

Truth is, if it were a decision based purely on Noreen's abilities as a cleaner, neither of us would have minded telling her. It has never occurred to Noreen, for instance, to go as far as moving the furniture in order to Hoover underneath it. Why bother when you can dance the vacuum gleefully round it?

But, of course, it's not that simple.

Overall, Noreen is kind, helpful, and very, very likable. Both the kids love her, and she's very good with them.

As I explained the situation to Noreen, I was grateful that Sophie was at playschool.

She started crying on me. Genuine tears of loss and sadness. I explained the reasons for her dismissal truthfully and she nodded and said she understands and says she thinks it's very sad but not to worry . . .

Then Gina, who had been listening from behind the lounge door, finds this is all too much for her and bursts into the kitchen.

So now there are two of them in tears.

I left them opening a bottle of wine while I went to pick up Sophie from playschool, and by the time we got back, that had been drunk and severe headway had been made into a very nice Australian Shiraz I'd been saving for a special occasion.

Sophie wanted to know why everyone was crying, and when we told her it was Noreen's last day . . . you guessed it, she immediately joined the waterworks club.

Sophie now definitely sees Noreen's departure as my fault, subsequently refusing to speak to me apart from the occasional news bulletin.

Example: 'I'm going up to my room, Daddy, to play by my *own*', or 'Daddy, I need to go for a wee-wee. If Mummy needs me, that's where I am.'

So tomorrow I'm looking after a four-year-old who sees me as the moral equivalent to Stalin.

The rest of the day was spent being brainwashed by Gina in the Dos and Don'ts of House Husbandry.

Every hour on the hour there was another A4 page of notes, descriptions and diagrams, until it began to resemble an unbound car-owner's manual. It was also full of mother-and-baby speak, and about as clear as the average MFI instruction leaflet. Apparently, a soother is a dummy is a suckie is a yum-yum. Ruskie-Puskie is not a nickname for a tramp from Moscow, but a type of cereal biscuit. By the end of the day, I was just nodding and smiling. It was all too much.

Then, just to round off a perfect day nicely, I came downstairs after reading Sophie a bedtime story to find Gina curled foetus-like on the sofa in floods of tears.

'What's the matter, Gina?'

'Nothing,' she sobbed, 'I'm fine.'

One of her contradictory little idiosyncrasies. It's like interpreting a foreign language. Roughly translated, 'I'm fine', means, 'I'm a mess', so I immediately joined her on the sofa and gave her a cuddle.

'Want to tell me about it?'

'Oh, I don't know, Andy. Maybe we made a horrible mistake coming to Ireland. I dragged you here under protest for a stupid job and now . . . I DON'T WANT TO WORK!' she screamed, suddenly. 'I don't want to leave my babies,' she said, as the corners of her mouth slowly turned downwards and the sobs returned once more.

I didn't know what to say, really. I could hardly tell her I didn't want her to go back to work either, so how the hell did she think *I* was feeling about this arrangement, could I?

'I'm sorry, Andy. I really wish things were different. I don't want you to have to be a house husband, for pity's sake! I feel so horribly guilty.'

Howls of hysteria.

'No, Gina, no, it's not your fault,' I said, but I'm not sure I meant it. Maybe there is a small, selfish part of me that does blame Gina for my fate. But that's probably because it's too painful to face up to my own shortcomings.

That is why I am still wide awake while Gina snores in the slumber of the emotionally drained.

I am so wound up that when I move I look as if I'm giving a very bad impression of Captain Scarlet.

I need some help to calm down.

It is now 12.10 on Tuesday morning and I've raided the teapot with the missing handle. This does not mean that I have stolen the electricity money, but rather that I have indulged in the traditional vice of musos everywhere. I've had a little smoke. Not as in Benson and Hedges, as in joint—but not as in roast beef. I'm much more relaxed now. Much more in touch with who I am.

I'm Andy Lawrence. I'm thirty-seven. I'm tallish, brightish, and while I may not give Jon Bon Jovi sleepless nights, I'm reasonably good-looking. I must be. You do not land a woman as gorgeous as Gina unless you have something.

Gina. Youthful-looking, slender, are-you-sure-she's-had-two-kids? Gina.

I love her. So very much.

It bothers me that I may have let her down. I'm useless when it comes to reality. I can't cope with bills, with DIY, with illness, *et al*.

Am I a good father? I ask myself.

Probably. I'm here, for a start. I'm not disappearing before they get up and coming home ten minutes before they're tucked up in bed. I mean I give them constant attention, total love. Sophie never goes short of a story or a wrestle. Nicola gets regular raspberries blown on her tummy to make her laugh, and silly songs sung to her in front of the mirror to calm her down.

All right, I don't change nappies that often, or feed, or clothe, or bathe or—oh, shit! Now I'm saying this I'm thinking, What the bloody hell *do* you do, you useless great prat? I suppose most of it comes under the heading 'entertainment', instead of 'practical'.

Gina's right.

Financially, we have no choice.

I love my wife, I worship my kids, it's just, phew, twenty-four hours a day and all that that entails.

Am I up to this?

I honestly don't know.

It's 1.30am and I can't believe what I'm doing now.

I'm cuddling my bass guitar. Yep, embracing it, like an old, familiar, if somewhat frigid, lover. What a sad bastard I am. Get a grip, Andy. You love your kids, and all you're being asked to do is look after them.

So why am I lying on my sofa with my arms wrapped round a piece of metal with four strings? Am I touching my instrument for luck? Or am I saying goodbye?

How did it all go wrong? What caused the transition from Andy Lawrence, brilliant bass-player, talented vocalist, writer of definitive rock songs and just waiting for that lucky break, to Andy Lawrence, the little woman at home who is going to cook bangers and mash and wipe his baby's arse?

I'm trying to think how it all began . . .

I first met Gina when her boyfriend—I understate—her *fiancé*, brought her round to my flat at 11.30 one summer's night.

Must be ten years or so ago.

Her intended was called Max and he was a talent scout for a major record label. I was playing in a band called Don't Ask and we were hot. People were talking deals, and Max was at the head of the queue.

Having said that, I was not expecting him to turn up at my flat with a woman in tow. Consequently, I opened the door wearing my Tintin T-shirt and a pair of Rupert Bear boxer shorts, given to me by a previous girlfriend. This was not the outfit in which I would have chosen to meet the man who held my future in his grubby hands *or* the most beautiful woman I had ever seen.

Gina looked just sensational—a ringer for a young Mia Farrow. I instantly wanted her to adopt me. She stood in my doorway smiling and I was transfixed. I didn't even notice Max was there until he sang out, 'Hi yuh, Andy!'

'Hello, Max.'

'Listen, man. This is a bit awkward, yuh, but is Arnold in?'

'No, he isn't. If it's him you've come to see, you're out of luck. He's spending the next couple of days with his girlfriend.'

'Phew, yuh! Arnie baby! Right. Listen, Andy, this is a bit . . . uh . . . listen, Andy, can we come in for a minute?' Max requested.

This was a man who might be about to offer me a recording contract. Of course he could come in.

'Take a seat, angel face,' he said to Gina, who reclined stylishly on my MFI sofa. 'That's it, babe, mellow out while I put my man here in the picture, in the frame. You take a seat as well, Andy.'

'Thanks,' I replied.

He began to walk backwards and forwards, shakily.

The man was very, very pissed. Or stoned. Or tripping. Or all three.

Gina, on the other hand, seemed perfectly sober.

'Right, yuh, now, the thing is right, you know . . . it's like . . . kinda . . . yuh, yuh . . . where was I?'

'Something about "Arnie baby"?' I suggested.

'Right, yuh, right, that's it, good old Arnold, right. Yuh, bit of a problem there.'

'Is there?'

'Yup, yup, fraid so. Sorry and all that, man. But, hey! That's life, man.'

'Has this got something to do with the recording contract, Max?' I enquired, trying to cut a few corners.

'Right, yuh, absolutely, you've pinned it . . . you know . . . hit that ol' nail . . . got it in one, man.'

Gina was beginning to shift uncomfortably on the sofa. This could have been due to Max's drunken ramblings or the fact that my MFI sofa was so hard. It would turn the average-sized bottom completely numb within fifteen minutes. Either way, it drew attention to her perfect legs, so that even I began to lose concentration.

'Max,' I said, tearing my eyes away from Gina's thighs, 'is there a problem with the contract offer?'

'No, man, it's solid, you know, and I mean, it's a cool offer, it's going to be big. But, uh, you see . . . Arnold, no. *Comprende*?'

Eventually my brain made a rough, if relatively accurate, translation. 'Are you saying the record company want Arnold out?'

'Uh . . . yuh.'

'Why?'

'Oh, right, well . . . it's, well . . . he's so *pig ugly* man!'

Poor guy.

Max had a point. Arnold had all the sex appeal of a freshly dug whelk. But he could play guitar and his lyrics were sharp and incisive. He was also my friend and my flatmate.

I glanced at Gina. Her face was red with embarrassment.

'Max, I don't know about this. Arnold is not a handsome boy, I admit. But he's good. Very good.'

'Hey! Andy! This is business, right? We're talking major investment here. You follow me, man?'

I did follow him. Max's eyes had taken on a look of steel, and I began to see through the slur and appreciate how he earned his money.

'I'll give you ten minutes to decide, Andy. You're the leader,' he said, flopping down clumsily onto the sofa, his head landing in Gina's lap.

I looked at her again. I could not figure out why she was engaged to marry such an arsehole. Then again, Gina looked so sad. She did not look comfortable with Max lolling all over her.

I stood up wondering what to do, when the room was filled with the guttural sound of one comatose talent scout, snoring like a geriatric.

Then a voice said, 'Oh, God! Please, Max, don't do this to me!'

My heart melted.

'Look, don't worry . . . er? I'm sorry, I don't think Max introduced us. Unless your name's Babe.'

She smiled.

'My name's Gina,' she said.

'Nice to meet you, Gina. Tell you what, I'll call a cab. I'll ask them to send a strong driver, then we can throw Sleeping Beauty here in the back of the car.'

'You won't shift him. He's very heavy.'

Max wasn't the tallest, but he was all muscle.

I tried to wake him. I slapped his face, a little harder than necessary. Partly for Arnold, and partly because I couldn't forgive him for having such a gorgeous woman.

'You won't wake him,' Gina said, somehow extricating herself from under his dead weight.

'Shall I order *you* a taxi?' I asked.

'I live in deepest Surrey. It's a hell of a trek. We were supposed to be staying in a hotel tonight, but I've no idea which one.'

Gina looked so forlorn, rather like a child who had lost her mother in a large supermarket. I somehow resisted the temptation to throw my arms round her and hug her. I had the strangest feeling that we'd known each other for much longer than the past fifteen minutes.

'Tell you what? Let's do what Brits do in times of crisis and have a cup of tea. Give Rip Van Winkle a chance to wake up.'

'OK.' She nodded and followed me into my shamefully filthy kitchen.

Moving a couple of pairs of Arnold's underpants, a bra, which certainly wasn't Arnold's, and a pile of newspapers from a black vinyl-covered chair, I shifted it back from the table and Gina sat down gingerly, while I switched the kettle on. Gina leant her elbows on the table as I brought the tea across and sat down. 'Max is a pretentious prat, isn't he?'

I nearly choked on my cuppa. This was the woman who was just about to sign a contract to spend the rest of her life with him and have his babies.

'I—'

'Come on, Andy. Just because he's going to offer you fame and fortune, it doesn't mean you have to like him.'

'I think you're wrong there,' I said, with feeling. 'I could learn to like Colonel Gaddafi if he was offering me similar. I mean, it's not as if I have to sleep with him or anyth—'

The words fell out of my mouth before I could stop them.

'Sorry,' I muttered, blushing.

Gina blushed too. 'It's OK. You're right, of course.' She sighed, deep and long. 'I'm getting married in six weeks' time. Three hundred guests and a huge reception at a hotel in Surrey and . . . and . . .' her eyes filled with tears '. . . I don't like him, let alone love him. I'm sorry, I shouldn't be telling you all this. It's just that I looked at him, passed out on your sofa, and finally knew that I'm about to make the biggest mistake of my life. Max needs a woman who is prepared to live in his nice big house in Kent, issue the cleaning lady with instructions and tolerate his revolting habits for the sake of financial security, and for a wardrobe full of designer clothes and a holiday in the Bahamas twice a year.'

I gazed at her in silence, wondering whether I could facilitate an immediate sex change and become his fiancée as soon as the post had been vacated.

'I thought I could do it. I mean, Max is most girls' dream man. And my mother thought . . . *thinks* he's wonderful. She's thrilled I'm going to marry him. But . . . oh, Andy, I can't, I just can't!'

She sobbed some more. I placed an arm ineffectually round her shoulder.

'You see, I have a job, too. I know Max decries it, because it's not as high-flying as his own, but I like it. I enjoy being a working woman, earning my own way, making my own decisions.'

'What do you do?'

'I'm a journalist. I work for a female glossy, test face creams, compare penis sizes, you know the kind of thing.' She smiled at me through her tears.

I didn't, actually. *Melody Maker* and the *Guardian* were more my scene but, to be sure, I was going to pick up a glossy the next time I stepped into a newsagent. After all, even though I'd never had a female actually complain, it would be interesting to compare . . .

'Max never bothers to ask my opinion. He even orders my food for me in restaurants! God! Now I think about it, I've been such a fool!' The anger in Gina's eyes made her even sexier. 'Do you know, Andy, that I got a first in English at Exeter? Max, on the other hand, was kicked out of Harrow for smoking pot. He's only got where he has cos his uncle owns the bloody label! The point is, intellectually, I can beat him hands down, but he's not interested in my brain, oh, no.' She shook her head violently. 'I first knew I was in trouble when we tried to compile our wedding list. I wanted nice, normal things like a good dinner service and some Waterford crystal. Max insisted on adding a leopard-skin bedspread, a ceiling mirror and a remote-control camcorder!'

I giggled, and suddenly so did she.

It was *great*.

'God knows what my mother will say, but I have to do something before it's too late. It's partly my fault. But it was almost like Max and my mother conspired to waltz me down the aisle and I just got taken along with them.'

I was just boiling the kettle for another couple of mugs of tea and further revelations when a figure appeared at the door of the kitchen.

'Hey, babe! What's goin' down, huh? Can I join in?'

Gina's expression changed immediately. 'We were just talking, Max, while you took a nap.'

'Yeah, uh, right. Well, time to go, yuh.'

'Of course, Max.' Gina stood up and moved towards him. She went through the door and Max slapped her bum.

I could have killed him. Honest.

I followed them to the front door and opened it.

'Right, uh, well, Andy. Thanks.'

'Bye, Andy.' Gina reached forward and kissed my cheek. 'And thanks.'

'Bye, Gina, bye, Max!'

The door had closed behind them and I stood there forlornly, knowing I was In Love. I had just met My Perfect Woman. Gina had intelligence, opinions, articulate conversation, a sense of humour *and* tight buttocks. She was . . . *everything* I'd ever dreamed of.

But there wasn't a hope in hell of it ever progressing. Even if Gina did cancel the wedding, she was hardly likely to settle for a penniless musician.

Two weeks later, having attempted to claim back my emotions and my brain from a misty, faraway, rose-coloured land, I received a letter.

From Gina.

To tell me that the wedding was off and 'thank you for being so sweet and understanding'. Could she take me out to dinner to repay me?

I left it an appropriate amount of time—three minutes—before I called her at her glossy magazine. And we arranged to meet at a restaurant in Belsize Park.

And the rest . . .

The rest is history.

Max took it very well, considering, leaving aside the recording contract, which he took great pleasure in tearing into tiny pieces in front of my wonky, bleeding nose.

Marrying Gina did not do a lot for my career . . .

TUESDAY. Today is the big day.

As it *is* my first day I have been allowed the luxury of a shit, shave and shower. I have been assured that this will not usually be the case and I will have to work these things into my new routine when I can.

What do I do exactly? Do I lay Nicola on the bottom of the bath while I shower above her? Do I shave while doing an impression of Santa Claus with my white foam beard, as Sophie and Nicola play with my spare razor blades to keep them quiet?

Sophie comes into the kitchen already dressed, fed and watered, and I shudder at the thought that tomorrow I'll be responsible for this as well. She still hasn't forgiven me for Noreen's departure, so I'm hoping a morning at playschool will help her forget what a ruthless pig her father is.

Nicola is in the lounge playing under her baby frame. She's being PB, Perfect Baby, but the day is still frighteningly young.

'So, what do you have to do when Sophie and I leave?' asks Gina. Oh, God, yesterday was the lesson, today she's asking questions.

'Er . . . breakfast.'

'Very good,' Gina says, a tad patronisingly. 'Now,' she continues, 'I've left the box of baby porridge and written instructions by the kettle for you. Just do what it says and you can't go wrong. OK?'

I nod. I didn't like to tell her I'd been thinking about my own stomach. You know, more bacon and eggs than prepacked slop.

'Right, then. I'm taking Sophie to playschool. Remember, today she's staying to lunch there, along with Michelle's little Richard.'

'Oh, what are they eating? Tutti-Frutti?'

'Pardon?'

'You know, is Long Tall Sally joining them?' I try again.

'Who's she?' Gina asks me.

I shrug in despair. 'No one. Muso's gag.'

'Concentrate, Andy! You'll need to cook her a proper meal for tea. Bangers and mash, or something equally simple.'

Bangers and mash are not something 'simple' to me. Bangers and mash are grey, watery spuds, grill on fire, belated cremations of bits of pig, to me.

'Michelle will bring Sophie home when she picks up Richard, so you don't have to worry about that today.'

Gina had crossed to Nicola. 'Bye-bye, my angel,' she says, as she kisses her, before turning away, tears in her eyes.

'Now, kiss Daddy goodbye, Sophie,' Gina says, snivelling as she leads the way out of the house towards the car.

I'm offered a cheek by my daughter. I suppose, the way she feels about me today, I'm lucky it's the one on her face.

'Bub-bye. I'll see you later. Have a good morning, Stinks.'

That's my nickname for Sophie. It's a hangover from the first few weeks of her life. She didn't seem to be here for five minutes before she permeated the flat with noxious smells.

Gina has just thrown her arms around me and given me the sort of kiss she hasn't often blessed me with in the morning since our courting days. 'Look after them for me, won't you? You'll be just brilliant, I know you will. I love you.'

I've just closed the door. This very second. Simultaneously Nicola starts crying at full volume.

I've swooped her up in my arms, but it's no use. She's at full throttle. I've been alone with her for three minutes and already the sheer intensity of her screaming has frayed my nerves into a thousand fragments.

Breakfast.

I'm jigging her around with her back to me and we're looking at each other in the mirror. Finally I get a smile. I tell her she's beautiful in one of those silly voices you automatically adopt when you're a parent and, yes, the smile develops into a chuckle, and OK, I admit it, there's nothing like the sight and sound of your baby laughing to make you feel good.

That's enough of the gooey stuff. Back to business. She'll be going red in the face with anger if I don't feed her soon.

So, I'm putting her in her highchair with cushions stuffed down the side to stop her leaning like the tower of Pisa. I boil the kettle and read my idiot-proof instructions. According to Gina, I need to mix some pure fruit in with the mush to make it more appetising, and there's a jar in the fridge. So there is. Right, pour flakes in . . . add water . . . mix . . . make a paste . . . more water . . . add fruit . . . test . . . not too hot . . . shove in baby's gob. Right, super.

Except it's not. Why does my baby's porridge look like the sort of gruel they fed Oliver in the workhouse, with half a dozen suet balls thrown into the middle for good measure?

Nicola's complaining of hunger so there's no time to make some more. It'll have to do. That's it, open wide and . . .

Aren't babies' faces expressive?

A smile tells you she's having a good time and to continue. A rubbing of the eyes and a yawn tell you she's tired. And a screwing up of the face, gagging and the clenching of teeth to avoid a second spoonful tell you you're a shit cook.

OK, no need to panic. A quick trip to the fridge reveals some *fromage frais*. All right, this was supposed to be lunch but we can worry about that later.

There is a sense of sheer relief from Nicola as she recovers from the trauma of having her mouth prised open with a spoon to discover the taste of something she enjoys.

She'd better get used to this. Nicola could be eating bucketfuls of *fromage frais* in the future.

Disaster. I forgot to remove the porridge, such as it was, from the tray on the highchair. Nicola may not have been prepared to eat it, but she had positively no objection to wearing it as make-up and body lotion. I've whipped her into the lounge, laid her on her changing mat and set about her with baby wipes, scraping her clean, or sort of.

She's just turned very red in the face.

Oh, Lordy. It's here. The moment I've been dreading. She's done a packet. A steamer by the smell of it.

I peel off her Babygro and vest as, according to my manual for house husbands with a brain the size of a pomegranate seed, it's time to get her dressed. I've unfolded a new nappy, on which I congratulate myself for being quite forward-thinking. I'm undoing the dirty nappy, while holding my breath.

Hellfire and bloody flame! It's everywhere. I'm setting to work with the wipes, dumping them in the old nappy.

I now have a dilemma. It would have been different if I had produced a son. I would have no hesitation in wiping off any residual waste that had become glued to his little testicles. I could have said, 'Sorry about this, son,' and could have heard him reply in my head, 'Hey, Dad, no problem, it's gotta be done.'

But with a girl it's different. I mean, these sort of organs are more what you might call . . . internal. We're talking invasion here. I'm sure this is a major reason for my reluctance in nappy-changing . . . I'm looking at her little . . . *folds*, shall we say? And I'm thinking, am I out of my jurisdiction here? On the other hand, to have any orifice clogged up with poo can't be that healthy, can it?

I take an executive decision and wipe it away, apologising to her profusely as I do so.

Oh, yuck! That's disgusting. While I was distracted, Nicola has located the old nappy, which I foolishly left open, and is now using her left foot to paddle in her own poo!

More wipes.

It's now time to find the girl some clothes.

Back to the manual for house husbands with the imagination of a professional potato peeler. Sure enough, I find a page or two on clothes, and, for day one, the exact dress she is to wear.

Fine, so I'm up the stairs rummaging about in the nursery, clean vest, top, tights . . . Where is the sodding frock? Bingo! Back down the stairs. Talk to Baby as I put on her vest, top, tights. Shite, these things are tricky. Nicola is not playing ball. Every time I get one foot in, she wriggles out of it before I can put the other in place.

The thing is, as a man, you spend most of your adult life trying to pull tights down, not up, so I'm having to think in reverse here. Probably just as well you don't have to put tights on before sex. Even I would have lost interest by the time I'd got the gusset into position.

Now the frock. Oh, Gina, you git! Look at all these buttons! I could grow a beard before I get this frock on her.

There. I've succeeded. Oh, and that's a yawn. My manual for house husbands who can barely dress themselves, let alone a child, says it may be time for sleepsy. So bottle and cuddle in front of MTV, methinks.

Nicola is in her cot, asleep.

I can't settle. I keep running up and down the stairs, listening at the nursery door.

Something useful? I know, I'll go and peel the spuds for Sophie's mash. Wah-ho-ho! Forward thinking again. I may just prove better at this than I thought.

Cancel that last statement. The rest of the day has been a catastrophe.

The first thing that went wrong was that, having taken the trouble to peel the potatoes early, they happened to catch my eye as I was waltzing Nicola round the kitchen while singing 'Edelweiss'. (If any of my muso friends discover I was singing 'Edelweiss', I'm dead.)

So the potatoes catch my eye and they've turned brown. Why? I consult the house-husband manual for the culinarily challenged and there it is. *Remember to put the potatoes in water if you peel them early, otherwise they will turn a funny colour.*

I don't find brown particularly humorous.

So I have to peel a whole new bunch. Bloody nightmare.

The one moment of light relief was when Michelle, Gina's friend, brought Sophie home from school.

I like Michelle. She's tall and athletically built, and quite a live wire. Very toned body. Quite fanciable, actually.

We have a good rapport, consisting of mock-flirtatious banter, largely based on sexual innuendo. I can't remember how that started but I've kept it up, if you'll pardon the expression, because she has such a wonderfully dirty laugh. It's infectious.

She's married to Norman. Solicitor. Successful. Very.

Man, oh, man, what a boring bastard he is.

Anyway, I was clearing banana and milk from the floor when she walked in with Sophie.

'My God, Andy! You're going to make someone a beautiful wife.'

'Fuck off, Michelle.'

'Daddy, don't swear,' my four-year-old reprimands me.

'You're quite right, poppet. How's my bestest girl?'

'Fine.'

'What did you do today?'

Big sigh. 'You know, Dad, I can't remember. Can I watch cartoons?'

'Yes, of course you can. Go on, I'll ask you about your day later.'

'Cup of coffee?' I ask Michelle, desperate for an adult interlude.

'I'd love to stay and talk to you but I can't today. I'll call in at the end of the week to see how you're getting on. I'll bring a bottle of wine, sit on your knee and mop your furrowed brow while you tell me how unappreciated you are.'

'I'll look forward to that.'

The rest of the day has been kids, kids, kids.

Sophie's tea was a flop. The sausages were well tanned, to say the least, and the mashed potato was 'lumpy, dumpy', apparently.

It's now six o'clock and Sophie's still watching television. I feel bad about that. I want to wrestle with Sophie. I want to pretend to be Fireman Sam, or Big Ears, or whoever. But Nicola won't let me do anything else.

Funny thing is, Sophie hasn't asked. Odd. Maybe she knows I'm struggling to cope.

Ten past six and Gina has just walked through the door.

Do I hug her? Ask how her first day back at work has been?

Do I bugger!

I pass Nicola to her at the sort of speed one might pass a grenade that has just had the pin pulled.

'Hello, Sweetums, Mummy missed you, yes, she did,' she says, giving Nicola a big hug. 'Well, then, Baby, how did Daddy get on?'

Am I invisible? 'Fine, fine, fine.'

OK. I'm lying.

'Daddy could have tidied the kitchen a bit now, couldn't he, little one?' She's still speaking to Nicola as she sits down at the table.

'Give us a break, Gina,' I groan.

'Why is Mummy's darling's dress on back to front?'

She'd get a shock if Nicola answered, wouldn't she?

'Is it?' I ask, between clenched teeth.

'Yes. Daddy didn't realise the buttons go at the back, did he, darling?'

'And where's Mummy's other girl?' Gina asks, still talking to me through Nicola, as if the baby is some kind of interpreter.

'In the lounge. Watching cartoons.'

'You've not been letting her do that since she got home, have you?' Gina's enquiring, deciding she can talk directly to me now.

'Well, I've been a bit busy,' I tell her, trying to keep my temper.

'You'll have to play with Sophie as well. You can't let this little madam take up all of your time.'

'Oh, don't worry. Tomorrow I'll put on my clown's costume and throw a few custard pies.'

'My, my, Daddy is a little testy, isn't he?' Gina observes, while bouncing Nicola on her knee. 'What's for dinner, Daddy?'

'Sorry? Dinner? That's part of my job spec as well, is it? I'm supposed to turn into Keith bloody Floyd now, too, am I?'

'Well, you can drink like him. Let's see if you can cook like him,' Gina says bitchily, as she stands up and walks with Nicola into the lounge.

At half past eleven at night. Gina and I are sat on opposite ends of the sofa, blearing at some action picture on the movie channel. We haven't spoken. I haven't forgiven her for not congratulating me on my efforts and she hasn't forgiven me for making her feel guilty for asking me to be a house husband.

So we don't talk.

I want to. I'd like to talk about why I made such a mess of things today. But I guess it would just sound like a series of excuses.

So I say nothing.

Neither does she.

It's 12.15 on Wednesday morning, and I'm watching Gina undress for bed. I'll say one thing for her: she certainly has the kind of body that makes you want to forgive her very quickly.

Same morning. One thirty. We are lying in bed with our backs to each other.

As I saw it, I may have had an error-strewn day, but I made a heroic bloody effort worthy of some reward in the way of rumpty-tumpty.

Gina, though, was having none of it.

So here I am with my back to my wife, sulking.

And I can't sleep because I've got the car tomorrow. Connor's giving Gina a spin to work. I'm worrying about how I'm going to get the baby fed, and Sophie to playschool and wash and shave with Nicola in tow and give Sophie more attention and . . .

How do I feel at the end of my first day?

Don't know.

Except, and this is worrying as it's only been one day . . . I'm not sure I feel like *me* . . . really.

Wednesday morning, 4.30.

I'm having a cup of tea as I can't get back to sleep.

I've been having some funny dreams. All about my past. Some of it was quite nice. Apart from the scenes when Sylvia, Gina's mother, or my father appeared. That was sodding nightmare territory.

On the train down to Surrey to meet her mother, Gina had told me that her father had been Irish and had left home when Gina was eight. She never saw him again and Sylvia had remarried, purely for money. She drove her second husband so hard that the poor man died of nervous exhaustion.

As we'd walked up the drive, Gina had suddenly stopped and grabbed my arm. 'Just remember, I love you, darling.'

A sentence delivered with all the urgency and passion of a woman whose lover was about to go off to the battle of Ypres.

As it transpired, Ypres was not a bad analogy.

My first impression of Sylvia was that she looked very young. I also noticed that her clothes were so crease-free you would think they were sewn on, like a second skin. But, admittedly, she was very attractive.

Gina did not look unlike her. It's the only thing I've ever been grateful to Sylvia for; that she passed on her pretty face and slim figure to her daughter and kept her sour personality to herself. If Gina was love-at-first-sight, then meeting Sylvia was the exact opposite.

'Mother, this is Andy.'

'Pleasure to meet you, Mrs Wilson.'

'Well!' Sylvia replied, before sitting down on the chesterfield, leaving my outstretched hand clutching at thin air. 'I wish I could say the same about you, dear. You're the loser my daughter has thrown everything out of the window for, are you?'

I'll say one thing for her, there was no attempt at diplomacy. Open hostility, right from the start.

'Erm . . . yes . . .' I responded feebly, looking to Gina for guidance.

'Mother, for goodness' sake! I love Andy. And we're going to get married, whatever you say. So you might as well get used to the idea.'

'Love, yes, of course,' Sylvia mused, slowly. 'You're quite right, Gina dear. I was forgetting. Why don't you make us all a cup of tea? Give Andy and me a chance to start again.'

Gina looked at her mother in a way that warned her to behave.

I looked at Gina in a way I hoped conveyed, 'Don't leave me alone with this witch,' but I must have failed dismally in the subtle-exchange-of-glances stakes, because Gina headed off to the kitchen.

'Well, Andy, I will not sit back and let you destroy my daughter's future happiness. Gina was just weeks from a lifetime of security and you come along and ruin it all. I will do everything in my power to ensure that this . . . fling, is as short-lived as it deserves to be.'

I was speechless. I just gawped at her like a goldfish with lockjaw.

'*Mother!*'

'Gina?'

She had appeared from nowhere, like the rabbit out of a hat.

'Gina, darling, it's you I'm thinking of.'

'No, it isn't, it's you! What *you* think is right, what makes *you* happy, not me. I don't want a cold marriage with pots of money and no love, I don't care how many houses or cars or trinkets Max could have bought me, because I don't want to be bought by *any* man. I'm going back home with Andy now. Think about what I've said.'

With that, Gina headed for the door.

'Right, then, looks like we're off,' I said, rather feebly, and followed.

It actually took ten minutes into the journey back to London before I could speak again.

'Gina . . .'

'I want to thank you, Andy,' Gina interjected cleverly. 'That's the first time I've stood up to my mother since I was a brattish four-year-old.'

'I don't think she liked me very much,' I stuttered, as always, the master of understatement.

'Oh, she's just scared that I might have to live how she did when my father left—we had some dreadful years before she remarried. It's left her very bitter. Don't be too hard on her.'

Gina reached for my hand and tucked it into hers. 'Anyway, I couldn't give a fuck what she thinks. I love you and that's all that matters.'

So I held her close.

I've never really wanted to let go ever since.

In retrospect, I've realised that, in the early days, Sylvia's opposition drew Gina and me closer together. There's nothing like a bit of parental disapproval to make someone more attractive.

Apart from embarrassing Christian names, Gina and I had something else in common. My father left home as well. The difference is that he kept coming back. Periodically. A jazz musician of moderate success, he'd just piss off on tour at the drop of a hat, leaving my mother and me to fend for ourselves. One tour lasted three years, the whole time I was at university. He came back to find he was divorced, so he just buggered off on the road again for another six months. My mother married and emigrated to Australia, and I graduated and moved into a flat in Balham.

My father has only given me two things of any worth. One: taught me how to play the guitar. Two: turned up unexpectedly at the register office for my wedding, accompanied by a small troupe of fellow musicians to play at his son's meagre reception.

Nice touch.

That was our wedding, then. Sylvia sulked and my father got stoned, played guitar brilliantly and sang appallingly.

For the next few years Gina and I were blissfully happy. Gina was rising steadily up the ranks in the world of problem pages and articles about the G-spot, and I had formed another band that was beginning to do well. With a bit of juggling of figures we got a mortgage and bought a small flat in Crouch End. I'd never seen Gina so happy.

Then one cosily drunken night, Gina got her dates confused and one year after she had reached the dizzy heights of assistant editor we stood speechless, staring at the glowingly cerise pink of 'Positive'.

Sophie was on her way.

OWEN WHITTAKER

WEDNESDAY MORNING, 8.20.

Gina has gone to work. Connor has taken her.

The baby is half-dressed. She's had her breakfast.

Sophie has had a bowl of Coco-Pops. According to the manual for house husbands who are brain dead, she should also have had a chopped apple and sliced banana. But I didn't have the energy for the fight this morning.

I've abandoned dressing Nicola halfway through because I've panicked. I have to get Sophie's clothes on her ready for playschool and I know from bitter experience that trying to get Sophie dressed is a harrowing ordeal. A five-minute job is expanded, due to the eccentricity of my daughter, to anything up to three-quarters of an hour. Between each article of clothing, she has either to run round the room, or stand on your thighs and pinch your face, or throw herself over the back of the sofa. On an average day, when the world is drifting on around you, and somebody else, namely Gina, is in charge of the task, this can be endearing, even amusing. When it's day two and you're in a big hurry, it drives you up the effing wall.

Currently, she is lying on the floor next to Nicola.

'Come on, get on your feet. No, Sophie, don't stand on my thighs. Ouch! Sophie, don't pull my hair. It hurts Daddy.'

'Yer Jessie!' she shouts disrespectfully, if entirely accurately.

OK, vest on. Shirt on and I lay her down for the dungarees. I hate these things. Why does Gina keep leaving out clothes that are like the mental puzzles on the *Krypton Factor*?

'Ugh! Ugh! Daddy! Daddy!' says Sophie, suddenly agitated. 'Nicola's done a poo!'

She's right. Unquestionably.

'Oh, Daddy, Daddy, I can't stand it. The smell makes me feel sick,' Sophie declares dramatically, and is off chasing round the room again.

'I hate to be the one to tell you this, Sophie, but yours does not exactly have the scent of Calvin Klein's Obsession either.'

'Ooh, Daddy, *ooh, Daddy*!'

'Sophie, come here and get your dungarees on.'

This is getting bloody ridiculous. I'm now chasing my daughter round the sofa, up and down the lounge, in and out of doors, like a scene reminiscent of a silent movie.

Caught her. Tickled her. Wrestled on the dungarees.

Change Nicola's bum. Put her in an all-in-one snowsuit, which makes her look like she's been swallowed down the throat of a polar bear with stunted growth, and time to load them both into the car.

It is the briefest of drives to the playschool, along a winding country road, then another, even narrower country road that after a few more twists and turns leads to the tiny building that houses Sophie's playschool. An idyllic setting in which to learn.

Inside the door and pleasantries exchanged with the teacher, I'm getting flustered as Sophie insists I take off her shoes and put on the obligatory slippers for her. She's perfectly capable of doing this for herself, but has decided this is part of the routine.

Objective achieved, Sophie is giving me a big hug goodbye.

I should be pushing her away and running back to Nicola, asleep in the car, but I'm not.

This hug tells me I'm forgiven for Noreen's dismissal.

I'm running back now and, sure enough, Nicola is awake and howling blue bloody murder.

I'm now panicking as I see a woman leaning into the window of my car. That would look good, wouldn't it? My baby snatched on the second day I'm in charge of her.

It's OK. It's only Michelle.

'Sorry, Michelle. I should have taken her with me. Where's the bloody soother?'

'Surely you don't need that, Andy? I would have thought a man of your experience knew lots more interesting ways to help a girl relax,' she says, winking.

'I do. I just need them to be a little older and preferably not a blood relative.'

I'm diving into the back of the car to search frantically for the ejected soother, dummy, suckie, yum-yum.

'How's the legal eagle?' I'm referring to Norman, her husband.

'Oh, you know. Busying about with his briefs.'

'Really? Didn't he give that up when he discovered girls?'

She's laughing, huskily. 'Anyway, Andy, must dash. I'll pop in later with that bottle of wine.'

'Do, and make it a fucking big one, will you?'

'Bye.'

Now where is that soother? Nicola's still bawling.

It's a recent discovery this. Not only can she take the soother out of her mouth with her hand, but she can now spit it over great distances. When she's older and it's time to play Let's Lean Out of a High Window and Flob on the People Below, Nicola is going to win high praise from her peers for her power and accuracy.

Can't find it. Mental note to take a spare next time. She'll just have to scream until she falls asleep or I crash the car.

Whichever comes first.

How do you keep two children amused at the same time?

I am finding this desperately difficult. At the moment we are all three on the bed. Mummy and Daddy's big bed. We are playing spaceships.

Number one daughter is enjoying herself immensely. I'm happy about this. I'm trying my best to include Nicola in this game, but if it wasn't for Sophie diving periodically under the duvet to make her laugh, I'd think she'd be in floods of tears by now.

Oh, balls, what did I tell you? The floodgates have opened. Time to get the baby bouncer.

It's 4.00pm. A moment or two of sanctuary.

Nicola's asleep, though probably not for much longer.

Michelle's here, which means Sophie's playing with Richard in the lounge while we consume a large bottle of particularly acidic Cabernet Sauvignon in the kitchen.

'You're far too tense, Andy Lawrence. You must get Gina to help you to unwind,' she says, in a loaded manner.

'There's wishful thinking.'

'Oh dear. Gina not fulfilling her conjugal duties, then?'

'It's not her fault, Michelle. She was knackered after her first day back at work. Mind you, if it keeps on like this I'm going to hand her a pipe and slippers as she walks through the door.'

'Ooh! Cross-dressing. Now there's a game I'd like to try.'

'Norman objects to putting on a bra and French knickers, does he?'

She's giggling. 'I'm afraid that Norman is a jump-on-jump-off, straight-up-and-down man.'

'Should you be telling me this?' I ask.

'I'm surprised Gina hasn't already. We do discuss our husbands, you know. Apparently,' she looks up at me from under hooded eyes, 'you're a bit of an animal in the sack.'

'Daddy, the baby's screaming,' Sophie tells me, as she and Richard fall through the kitchen door.

Michelle is draining her glass. 'I must be off, anyway. Tell Gina I'll phone her later, OK?'

'I will. See you soon, then. Bye!'

Shit, Nicola's probably turned purple with rage by now.

At 5.54pm, before Gina's imminent return, I tried making a game of dusting with Sophie and Nicola. Big mistake. I smashed a piece of Lladro china. I've sworn Sophie to secrecy, explaining that it would only upset Mummy if she knew and, after all, we were only trying to help.

To make matters worse, Sophie spilt a glass of Coke over the sofa.

Still. I tried.

Gina has just arrived home. I didn't hear her coming because Connor dropped her at the end of the drive.

So here I stand. Fag in mouth, gin and tonic in hand and not a child in sight.

Bollocks, bollocks, bollocks!

So unfair. It's creating such a false impression.

'Hello, sweetheart.'

'Hi, Andy.' She kisses me. 'Where are the kids?'

'In the lounge. Nicola's under her baby frame and Sophie's chatting to her for five minutes.'

'And what, might I ask, are you doing?' Gina takes the gin and the fag and has a slug of both.

Sophie comes rushing in from the lounge and Gina guiltily stubs out the cigarette.

'Hello, my little darling, Mummy missed you.'

'Mummy, Mummy, Daddy smashed the Lladro!'

The little shit! Snitch! Grass! Tale-teller!

'It was an accident. We were dusting,' I tell Gina, with the emphasis on the *we*.

'Never mind now. I'm sure Daddy tried to do his best. Did Daddy Hoover as well, Sophie?'

I'm invisible again. I'm biting my tongue.

'No. *Daddy* didn't. *Daddy* tried, didn't he, Sophie? But the Hoover wouldn't work.'

'Did Daddy try emptying it, we wonder?' Gina has just winked at Sophie conspiratorially.

'Yes,' I spit.

I'm lying again.

'But *Daddy* couldn't find the Hoover bags, could he, Sophie?'

'Mum, Daddy says he—'

'Blind as a bat, your daddy. Try under the sink next time, Andy.'

'Sorry, it wasn't in the manual,' I say pointedly. 'Anyway, how come it's my job to Hoover as well?'

Gina sighs. 'How come it was my job for the last God knows how many years, eh? Anyway, we'll discuss this later, shall we?' She shoots me a not-in-front-of-the-children type of glare.

So I'm exiting into the lounge, where Nicola's playing happily under the baby frame, looking as if butter wouldn't melt.

It's really pissing me off, that Gina walks through the door and, instead of saying well done, nitpicks on the things I haven't managed to get to.

Baby's pooed. Right, Mummy can have this one.

Midnight.

I'm writing myself a list of things I've got to do tomorrow. I've found looking after children erodes your memory.

I bathed the kids and put them to bed, and when I came down I discovered Gina had cooked us both a nice meal.

Over pudding, Gina glanced at me. 'Why exactly are you sulking, Andy?'

I shrugged.

'I suppose I just feel my efforts are a little unappreciated, that's all.'

Gina went off into peals of laughter.

'A couple of days as a house husband and you're muttering the war cry of stay-at-home women everywhere. Honestly, Andy.'

'The point is,' I whinged, 'I'd like some encouragement.'

'Well, you don't inspire me to drag my arse into Cork every day. You haven't once said, "Did you have a nice day at the office, dear?" Shall I tell you how I spent my day?' she asked rhetorically.

I did not try to interrupt.

'The first thing I discover is that a commissioned article has still failed to materialise, ten days past its deadline, so I have to ghost-write a two-thousand-word article on a subject about which I know nothing.'

'Which was?' I asked.

'"Is the reason teenagers are no longer becoming nuns because the modern Irish girl refuses to give up her love life?"'

'I can see the title now: "When Giving Up Sex Becomes a Bad Habit!"'

'Don't be flippant, I'm not in the mood,' she rebuked me. 'Then I discover our one remaining staff photographer has broken his wrist, and on top of that, I have to sack one of my junior reporters, and do you know why?'

'Tell me.'

'Because she is pregnant. That's why. My staff budget is cut and we do not have the money to pay her maternity leave. To make matters worse, it is illegal to fire someone because they are with child. Which means I have to pretend I am sacking her for incompetence. So, Mr Lawrence, you're not the only one who's had it tough,' she said, slamming her wine glass down on the table.

Long pause.

I took her hands across the table.

'I'm sorry, I had no idea. It must have been awful for you.'

Gina sighed and drank the last dregs of her wine. 'No, I'm sorry too. I'm finding it harder to adjust this time, compared to when I returned after Sophie.'

'Hold on a minute, Gina. I've just realised. You've turned this around. This is my whinge. I bagsy it. I started first.'

She chuckled. 'Let's call it quits. Come on, Andy, we'll take our coffee into the sitting room and I'll smooth your furrowed brow.'

We snuggled on the sofa and indulged in a passionate kiss. Then, just as things looked as if they were going to become excitingly rude, Gina complained of a soggy bum. Consequently, she discovered the spillage on the sofa.

She was not best pleased.

IT'S FRIDAY. Nearly 9.30am. The end of the first week, and we've just arrived at playschool.

'Come on, Sophie, pick those feet up.'

'I can't. I'd fall over, Daddy,' she replies, in a rather literal manner.

'It's an expression.'

'No, silly, this is an expression.' And she pokes her tongue out and screws up her eyes.

'Very funny, Sophie. No, by expression I mean—'

'Hi, Andy, how's the happy homestead running? Like clockwork, I presume?'

It's Michelle.

'Of course. I'm taking Nicola into town for a coffee to celebrate surviving the first week. Fancy joining us?'

'Sorry, Andy. I'd love a date with you, but Sorcha's got an appointment with her gynaecologist.'

'Who's Sorcha?'

'Fionnuala's mother.'

'Oh, right.' I'm none the wiser. 'So you've got to hold her hand while Doctor gropes around in her naughty bits, have you?'

'Don't be disgusting. Her husband's doing that.'

'What? Groping around in her?'

'No, holding her hand while she's examined. I'm looking after Fionnuala for an hour or two. Anyway. I didn't think husbands did grope around with their wives any more, only with their mistresses,' Michelle informs me, adopting a French accent and looking into my eyes.

'Daddy,' Sophie interjects, perhaps not before time, 'Dad, what's a gyna-ger-opa-miss?' she asks.

'Er, it's a type of doctor, darling.'

'Like a vet, Daddy?'

'Very similar, Sophie. They go in up to their elbows on occasions as well.'

This joke has brought Michelle's rude laugh to the fore.

'Listen, sorry about coffee, but you and Gina must come to dinner tomorrow night. Tell you what, I'll give Connor a ring. I've found him a new woman, did I tell you?'

'No, I don't think you did.'

'She's a friend of Norman's, actually.'

'Oh dear,' I say, before thinking.

'Now, don't be like that. She's . . . interesting.'

'Blimey, she must be ugly if she's . . . interesting.'

'Oh, Andy, you're an awful man,' she tells me, giggling.

'I'll get Gina to call you. Come on, Sophie, let's get you into school.'

'Is it like one of those doctors what fixes your teeth, Daddy?'

'What, darling?'

'You know, one of them like what you said . . .'

I've just come out of the playschool and I'm making a mental note to stop sexual-innuendo jokes with Michelle as they're getting a bit out of hand.

Actually, Michelle is still here. Her legs are dangling out of the driver's door of her Mercedes and she's flicking her shoe on and off her heel. I wonder if women know men find that sexy?

'You waiting for someone?'

'Yes, I'm waiting for you, how would you like me to take Nicola off your hands for an hour or two this afternoon, Andy?'

Would I!

'You serious?'

'Yes. I've got a houseful and one more won't make any difference. Bring a goodie bag to playschool at lunchtime. Nappies, wipes, bum cream, baby food, bottles, that kind of thing. Then you can pick her up at, say . . . three o'clock? I'll have a large gin poured to toast your successful week,' she tells me, as she swings her legs back into the car.

'Great.'

'Go down the pub, Andy. The boys are beginning to wonder whether you're still alive. Take Sophie and buy her a Coke and some crisps.'

Three hours later, it's 12.35pm and I've already handed Nicola over to Michelle. I noticed she'd changed her dress. Bit flimsy, I thought, for this kind of weather. It's turned into a filthy day. When it rains here you can feel it pouring down the back of your shirt and filling your boots.

Right. Car parked, miles from the pub, needless to say, off we go. I can taste that pint of Murphy's already. I'm running Sophie down the street, then pushing her through the pub door to get her out of the rain and me to my pint.

It's O'Leary's. The same pub where Gina bullied me into submission, the one with the folk club at the back. All the local bands play here and most of them drink in it as well.

We enter the pub drenched, like the survivors of a shipwreck.

What's that noise?

Oh, shit.

That noise is three blokes standing at the bar singing to me. '*MAMMY*, HOW I LOVE YER, HOW I LOVE YER, MY DEAR OLD *MAMMY*!'

All waving their hands like Al Jolson.

I think this big mammy is going to have the urine extracted from him pretty heavily this lunchtime. Fifteen minutes of flak, at least.

'I saw a lovely set of saucepans for sale in Cork the other day and I immediately thought of you.'

'Don't you just get pissed off when you've slaved away looking after the kids and your husband walks through the door and demands sex?'

Still, they let me off reasonably lightly, I suppose.

Let me explain who *they* are. The *they* in question are the Blow-ins. That's the name of the band I fart-arse around with while I'm waiting for the Beatles to re-form and ask me to replace John Lennon.

We do cover versions, and occasionally I'm allowed to slip in the latest song I have penned.

We're called the Blow-ins, because that's the expression used in west Cork to describe us immigrants.

Back to the group.

Matt: American, thirty-three, talented guitar-player, decent singer (we share lead vocals), loud, brash, tactless, married to a very weird girl, who gives classes in homeopathy and reflexology.

Johan: Dutch, forty-two, drummer. Been there, seen it, done it and failed at it in just about every other country in Europe, so it was time to give Ireland a try.

Fozzie: nickname, obviously. Fozzie, as in Bear. No need for a physical description, then. Rhythm guitar. Harmonises well, but voice a little thin for lead vocals. Married, four kids, English, nice guy.

Andy: the sex symbol of the group. Not difficult if you see the others. Best songwriter, great bass-player.

So there you are. Ladies and gentleman, I give you . . . the Blow-ins.

Well, here I am, halfway down my second pint of Murphy's, my reputation as one of the last great bohemian eccentrics in tatters and my four-year-old running riot round the bar.

'Andy, what are we going to do about Thursday afternoon rehearsals? Is the game still on, or are we busy changing diapers instead of key signatures?' Matt's asking me.

Bit of friction between Matt and me. We're the ambitious ones. We both think we're too good for this group.

'Change it to Thursday nights.'

'No-can-do, boiz. Luf to, but Thursday nights I haf to wurk at the restaurant.' Johan is apologising, again. It's what he does best.

'I don't know, guys. Christ, does it matter? I mean, all we do is run through the same bloody numbers we play every week. We do that on Tuesday nights anyway. Do we need Thursday afternoons too? Maybe it might be worthwhile if we were going to throw in a few more originals.'

I'm pitching for my own material now. I can't resist it.

'Scuse me, buddy boy, but I hardly feel you're in a position to blackmail your songs into the act any more,' replies Matt, the jealous bastard.

'What do you mean, "blackmail"? Look, guys, if you're trying to tell me you want to replace me just because I'm going to find it difficult to rehearse on Thursday afternoons . . .'

Silence.

'Daddy, that little boy over there says I'm beautiful.'

This is more than I can cope with. While I'm arguing the toss with the band, my daughter's pulling blokes in pubs.

I take a good look at her. She has tomato ketchup round her mouth, her dress is black from romping on the floor, and her hair looks like a backcombed wig. I have respect for the young man in question. If he thinks this is beautiful, it must be love.

'Look at the state of you, Sophie. Your mother's going to kill me. Come on, let's pick up Nicola and get the two of you home.'

To tell the truth, I'm happy for the excuse to get out of the pub. I'm feeling uncomfortable.

Sophie is ignoring me. There are none so deaf as children if they do not like the gist of what they are supposed to be hearing.

'Sophie, come on, now, we've got to go.'

I hate being ignored, it always makes me tense and short-tempered.

'*Sophie!*'

'No, I won't.'

'You'll do as you're told, young lady. Come and put your coat on.'

She's sat down on the floor. Slap in the middle of the pub.

'Sophie, you're getting in people's way.'

'Don't care.'

That's it. I've snapped.

'*Sophie! Get off your backside this instant. Come and put your coat on before I really lose my temper with you!*'

'You bad Daddy,' she's spat at me. She's pushing all her body weight into the ground and I can't lift her up.

I'm sliding my child across the pub floor like a human mop. I look like a lion dragging an unsuccessful kill back to my lair.

'*Nahhh!* Bad Daddy, bad Daddy!'

It's show time for the entire bar.

The band are exchanging unnerving glances between them.

I want to die.

'NAHH! I WANT MUMMY! I WANT MUMMY!'

'I don't think Mummy would want you if she saw how you were behaving,' I tell her, as I throw her across my lap and force her arms into her coat.

'Listen,' I'm saying to the band, 'I'll see you Sunday for the gig, unless I hear otherwise, OK?'

There's a variety of mutterings to this, at varying levels of enthusiasm.

'Bye-bye, pumpkin.' Matt's bidding farewell to Sophie. Ever the charmer. He enjoyed the floor show. I'm certain of that.

'Do you know, Matt? Daddy's my new mummy. He's not very good.'

I'm stunned. Why did she say that? I swear I'll kill her when I get her home. We're out of that door as fast as I can get us there.

I'm not sure which makes me more angry, the shame of Sophie's outburst or the Blow-ins' intolerant attitude.

I actually think they might want to kick me out of their little tinpot band because I can't rehearse on Thursday afternoons.

But what's really bugging me is that *I'm* the pro. I shout, 'Amateur!' when one of the others can't make a practice session. Now *I'm* the one saying I have other priorities.

As Sophie would say, her new mummy is too busy looking after *her* to come out to play.

Damn! Why did she call me that?

We've arrived in Glandore. This is *the* place to live if you have a bit of cash. It's a small harbour as beautiful as the Bay of Naples about four miles or so from our house. Norman and Michelle live on top of a hill with a panoramic view of the bay.

Am I jealous? I'm luminous ruddy green.

Maybe this is an uncool feeling for a wannabe rock star. I should be all left-wing youth culture and balls to the Establishment.

Tosh! Name me a rock icon who doesn't own at least four houses.

I rest my case, as Norman would say.

I pull into the long drive of Michelle's house. A small, pale yellow mansion would be an accurate description.

Time to collect my baby.

'You stay in the car, Sophie. I won't be long,' I bark at her, in a way that tells her not to argue.

I knock on the back door, basically because front-door bells are a rarity here. In fact, not that many people bother to knock, they just stroll into your house.

Michelle opens the door. 'Come in, Andy. Richard's playing and Nicola is having a little sleep.'

'Oh, Gawd! She'll keep me up all night, now.'

'Your kind of woman, eh, Andy?'

She laughs suggestively.

'Come through to the sitting room. I've got a fire going and a bottle of wine open.'

'I'd better not. I've just come from the pub, thanks to your kindness, and I'd better be careful. Anyway, it's a fair drive to my house from yours and if I don't get a move on I'll be all behind schedule.'

'You disappoint me, Andy. You sure I can't persuade you to stay for a bit?' Michelle's asking, her eyes twinkling with mischief.

'No. Sorry.' She's sighing.

'Oh, OK. I'll fetch Nicola.'

I follow her into the hall and watch her ascend the opulent staircase. I'm trying not to look up her skirt.

I feel a bit uncomfortable, somehow.

'You load her in the car, Andy, and I'll bring her kitbag.' Michelle is saying, as she comes back down the stairs and hands Nicola to me.

I've bimbled across to my battered Ford Sierra and I'm placing Nicola in her car chair.

'Here we are,' Michelle's saying, as she hands me Nicola's bag. 'Cheerio, then.'

She's thrown her arms round my shoulders and is giving me a big hug. I was right, that dress is flimsy. No Wonderbra there. I can feel . . . Put it this way: it must be colder than I thought.

'Bye, then, and thanks,' I say as she releases her grip and walks back towards her house.

I do feel unnerved, for some reason. Must be the pressure of looking after the kids. Psychiatrist's couch within a month, I reckon.

It's 6.15pm and Gina's on the phone. I didn't hear her come in as I have the CD on full blast. The phone must have rung and she picked it up just as she walked through the door.

I've got Nicola in my arms. We've been dancing round the lounge to Kate Bush's 'Rubber Band Girl'. It's Sophie's favourite song and she's shaking her bum in time with the rhythm.

We've forgiven each other, Sophie and I.

When we arrived home she said to me, 'Dad? I'm sorry about that, Dad. I probably just need some Oasis.'

'Some what?' I enquired, perplexed.

'Oasis, Dad. You know, the drink. It gets you back to your old self.'

She watches far too much telly. Particularly commercials.

But I had to laugh.

I know. As a disciplinarian, I suck.

Gina has just walked into the room, her eyebrows tied at the centre in a reef knot.

'Everything OK?' I ask.

'Fine.'

Liar.

'Connor's popped in for a sundowner. Do you want to fix us all a drink?' she says, taking Nicola from me.

'Yeah, OK. Back in a minute, Stinks,' I tell Sophie.

I'm following Gina into the kitchen. What's eating her?

'Hi, Connor. Come to raid my booze cabinet again, have you?'

'Now, don't be like that. Am I after mentioning a word about the vast fortune in petrol I'm spending taking your wife to her place of employment? You wouldn't begrudge me a small gin now, would you?'

'Probably cheaper to pay for the petrol,' I tell him.

'Not at all. Gin is cheaper than petrol.'

'Not the amount you drink, it isn't.'

Gina is pacing back and forth with the baby slung under her arm. She's rattled about something.

'Who was that on the phone?' I'm asking her as I fix the drinks.

'Michelle. I hear she took Nicola for a couple of hours this afternoon while you went for a pint.'

'Yes, she did. That's all right, isn't it?'

'Well, it's just . . . I feel a bit . . . funny about you dumping the kids on somebody else while you swan off down the pub.'

Connor looks embarrassed. We don't usually air our dirty linen in public. Especially not Gina.

'I didn't *dump* them. I took Sophie with me for a start, and I left Nicola with Michelle. Your best friend. You know, the one *you* leave her with in emergencies, like when you just have to go shopping for a new pair of shoes.'

'I know it's . . . oh, you're probably right. Listen, I'm going to get the kids in the bath. Excuse me, Connor, but if I don't do it now we'll get all behind.'

'That's fine, Gina. You work away, now.'

She's gone. I can hear Sophie complaining about bath-time from the lounge. She must think it's hair-washing night again.

'Honestly, Connor, what is it with that woman? I can't do a bloody thing right these days.' I sigh as I pour us both a stiff Cork Dry Gin, and ferret around in the cupboards for tonic water that still has some fizz.

'Don't take it so seriously, Andy. Look at it from your Gina's point of view. She's relinquished the care of her beloved babies to you. She's their mother. Mothers like to be in control of their children. It's only natural. She's bound to worry.'

Another reason for his attraction to the opposite sex. He sees their point of view so clearly. I look at Connor now. He's got it all in some ways. He's good-looking, wealthy. Yet he's lonely. I suspect he'd give it all up if it would bring his wife back. I still have Gina and the kids. So far. Maybe I'm luckier than I think.

'Yes, you're right.' I nod balefully. 'I'd better go and apologise.'

'There's something more important you have to do first.'

'Oh, is there?'

'Yes. Will you finish fixing my gin?'

I'm reaching for the tonic bottle, laughing.

'Speaking of alcohol, I saw Michelle today. She's inviting us round for a drunken dinner party tomorrow. Says I just *have* to meet your latest paramour.' I smile at him.

'So you do, Andy.'

'What's she like, then?' I ask, as I pour the tonic water.

'I'll let you judge for yourself,' he's saying, sighing heavily.

'Funny, that's what Michelle said. Right, there's your gin, I'll go and grovel to Gina. Back in a mo.'

'Daddy!'

Sophie's just run into the kitchen dripping and thrown her arms round my waist.

That's the first time since our new arrangement began that she hasn't disappeared up her mother's skirt for the entire evening.

So, ironically, I must have got something right today.

WE'RE OFF TO DINNER at Norman and Michelle's tonight. Gina has taken an eternity to decide what to wear before going back to the first dress she had on, of course, so I have five minutes to make myself presentable.

I've been thinking about Gina and her tetchy behaviour. Trying to figure it out. It got me into nostalgia again.

Things became difficult for Gina with the birth of Sophie. Understandably Gina became confused. Part of her wanted to pursue the career she had worked so hard to build, and part of her wanted to do nothing more than stay home and look after the baby.

To make matters worse, my second group disbanded, so money became even tighter. Gina had to go back to work soon after Sophie's birth, and any pitiful amount I earned went on paying someone to help with Sophie.

Sylvia moved to Highgate to give a hand which, needless to say, put more strain on our marriage than all the rest put together.

This went on for two and a half years, until one day my spouse walked through the door with a smile on her face and announced she'd been offered a job in Ireland and how did I feel about it?

I wasn't exactly what you might call . . . keen.

London is where it's at. It's the only place to be if you want to be 'discovered'. Ireland seemed like professional suicide.

Yet, living in the capital, my luck had begun to seem genuinely poxed. And Gina . . . well, Gina wanted to move *so* badly.

I still occasionally miss the pace, the action, the anything-could-happen-tomorrowness of London.

But the compensations are fantastic. Especially for the children. Clean air and open space and, above all, safety. It's a dodgy thing to say, in this neck of the woods, but I'm a convert.

At 10.30 or thereabouts, then, on a Saturday night, we're sat round Norman and Michelle's dining table, having recently devoured something green and spicy and distinctly vegetarian.

Maybe that was in deference to the latest girlfriend Michelle has drummed up for Connor. She's English. Terribly. She has large, come-to-bed eyes and full lips, but her face, hairstyle, demeanour . . . everything about her screams, 'Save the sodding whale!'

Norman is on top form tonight.

It's partly Gina's fault. She made the mistake of asking him how things were at work.

You see, as I may have mentioned, Norman is a solicitor in west Cork. He deals with conveyancing, land disputes and insurance claims.

He is not Rumpole of the Bailey.

So, we've had a riveting half-hour of courtroom drama about the exact positioning of somebody's fence posts.

What does an attractive woman like Michelle see in Norman? Dollar signs? Can it be as simple as that? I don't know.

Talking of Michelle, she's opposite me in a little black number so tight you can hear it rustle when she breathes. She's winked at me so many times tonight I've begun to think she has a nervous tic.

I wonder if anyone else has noticed.

'Tell me, Norman . . .' Elisa is saying—that's Mrs Greenpeace, Connor's woman.

She's very taken with Norman. Good luck to her.

'. . . if you were to win the lottery tomorrow, what would you spend the money on?'

'Now, Elisa. That's a very tricky question.'

Oh, please! Methinks it's time to top up the old wineglass.

'What would you use it for, Elisa?'

Make a good politician, Norman. He follows the maxim 'Answer a question with another question.'

'I think I'd reforest Ireland. I mean, there are no trees any more. Ecologically, it's a disaster.'

Oh, for fuck's sake! More wine.

'Yes . . .' Norman is oozing sincerity. 'Yes, I might be tempted to agree with you there, Elisa. What about you, Andy?'

'Well, if you two are reforesting Ireland, I think I'll build a papermill.'

Connor is forced to spit his wine back into his glass or choke with laughter.

'Andy!' Gina is rebuking me. Under the table she is clattering my shin with her heel.

'Sorry, only joking.'

'Anyway, Andy?'

'Yes, Norman?'

'How's your new . . . employment going?'

Here we bloody go. I'm surprised it's taken this long. He smirks as well. Another slug of wine, Andy. I think you're going to need it.

'I'm adjusting.'

'Adjusting,' Norman repeats, thoughtfully. 'Adjusting, yes, good choice of word.'

What? Wanker!

'I mean . . . '

'Yes, go on Norman.'

'You know . . . adjusting . . . to not being the traditional breadwinner.'

'Gina's always been the breadwinner, I've just never been the bread-*maker* before.'

'Well, I think it's fantastic, what Andy is doing,' Michelle has suddenly put in.

'Well said, now, Michelle,' Connor adds, 'and Gina is doing wonders holding that magazine together. They're a fine partnership.'

'It's fantastic that you can do it,' Michelle continues her praise, licking her lips. 'You're brilliant with your kids, Andy. I could even grow to love you for it. I mean, Norman would be useless.'

I can believe that.

'I've only been doing it, for a week.'

Did I hear the word *love* mentioned?

'You see . . .'

Oops, Norman's woken up again.

'. . . I'm afraid I was raised to believe that the wife stayed at home and the man went out and earned the money.'

'On the other hand there is something very sexy about a big strong man with a baby in his arms.' Michelle is eyeing me, dipping her finger in her wine then putting it in her mouth.

I've just caught Connor's face out of the corner of my eye.

He's raising a suspicious eyebrow at me.

'Now, some may say that's old-fashioned of me,' continues Norman.

Lord! This man is insensitive. More wine, Andy, definitely more wine.

'Norman, you're not with me here. Supposing, perish the thought, in a few years' time your practice decided to make you redundant in favour of a younger man. Let's say when this happens, because of your age, you can't get another job. But Michelle can get decent employment . . . I don't know—running an escort agency or something.'

Shit! Why did I say that?

'Thanks, Andy. You can be my first customer.'

'That's OK, Michelle. Now, Norman, under those circumstances, would you be happy to stay at home and look after young Richard?'

'But I'm a partner, Andy. That's what makes this so silly. I am a great solicitor.'

Jeez! That's it, I've lost it.

'You sanctimonious bastard, Norman. You sit there, completely fucking oblivious to real life, smugly thinking nothing can ever go wrong in your little world, and do you know what really pisses me off? You're probably right.'

Norman's face has frozen solid. He may even have stopped breathing.

You're up to your neck in trouble now, Andy.

'It's like this, Norman. Andy is doing a difficult job in tricky circumstances, and he's doing it very well. Because, you see, it's not as easy as most men think.'

That from Gina. High praise indeed. I'm quite touched.

'Well, I'd marry you tomorrow, if you were free,' says Connor. 'What do you say now, Andy? Will you have me?'

'I *have* had you, Connor, and you were rubbish.'

General laughter.

He knew what he was doing. Connor, I mean.

Bailed me out there. Someone remind me to thank him.

It's 1.30 on Sunday morning and Michelle is saying good night at the door. Norman's inside, recovering, and helping Elisa on with her back-pack, for all I know. I'd better apologise.

'Good night, Michelle, and listen, sorry . . .'

'Forget it, Andy. You're right. He is a sanctimonious bastard.'

She's kissing me lightly on the mouth.

Either I'm very drunk or I just felt the faintest sliver of tongue slide between my lips.

Alarm bells are ringing like fucking Notre Dame in my head.

Gina always says I have no idea when a woman is flirting with me. Well, even I can't have got this one wrong, surely?

Gina has just given Connor a good night kiss as he stands in front of his passenger door. As I approach she turns and walks towards our own little rust-bucket.

'Good night, Connor,' I say, as I reach him. 'Drive carefully, now.'

'Andy,' he's whispering to me, 'watch yourself with young Michelle, now. She's lusting after you, I swear.'

'Oh, behave yourself. She was just a bit langers, that's all. She won't remember in the morning.'

'Have it your own way, but you be careful. You have a lovely wife, and her best friend behaving like this just isn't on, now.'

'You're beginning to sound like a priest.'

'I'm only trying to warn you. Listen, your wife is a vision of loveliness tonight, so she is. Take her home and look after her, if you know what I mean,' he tells me, accompanied by a suggestive wink.

'Nice idea, but I think I might have blotted my copybook a little too much for that to happen.'

He's laughing as Elisa clomps across the drive, struggling to keep her feet encased in her wooden mules.

I'd better join Gina in our car. She's driving.

I'm getting in, bracing myself for thirty-nine lashes.

'Before you say anything, I know. I was out of order, Gina. I'm sorry.'

'No. It's OK. I understand.'

She's starting the engine.

I have the feeling that's all she's going to say.

Why?

It's something about the look on her face that's worrying me.

Sunday, 8.00pm.

I've enjoyed today. Gina's been round and she's taken charge of the kids. I had my customary wrestles with Sophie and cuddles with Nicola.

We popped to the pub, all four of us, then came home, lit a fire and had tea and cakes in front of it.

Both children behaved perfectly. Maybe they just liked having things back to their old routine. Maybe everyone relaxes when the responsibility is shared.

And now I'm going out to do what I do best. Make music.

Gina seems happy as there is a soppy film she can curl up in front of on Sky Movies.

A toot of a horn means my spin is here. I'll load my stuff into the van, kiss Gina goodbye and be off.

But I've just had a nasty shock.

I opened the door to the back of the van in order to load my gear into it and there, buried amongst the drum kit, is Belly O'Hea.

'What the bloody hell are you doing there?'

'What a lovely man yer are, Andy. Sure now, you're awash with English charm. I was after thinking, if Muhammad won't go to the mountain, then the mountain will have to get off his arse and go chase up the lazy little prophet.'

'Very good, Belly. Very cryptic. Don't know what it means, but it sounds impressive.'

'I've come to collect the tapes. The demo tapes. You know, the ones you were promising to spin round to me a couple of decades ago?'

'Oh, shit! Yes. Hang on, I'll go and get them,' I say to him, as I slide my bass guitar between a set of cymbals and Belly's left leg.

'Will it be taking long now? Only yer wouldn't believe the angles and directions I've had to stretch my fine figure of a body into in order to fit in the back of this feckin' van. You may not believe it to look at me, but I was not born a natural contortionist.'

'No, no. Two secs.'

Poor Belly.

It's a pointless exercise giving him my demos.

But at least he's enthusiastic. Which is more than anyone else is. Including me, these days.

It's now 10.45pm and the band is taking a break. Wow! I'm on a real buzz. I've been let out of the madhouse and allowed to behave as I want.

Even Matt, ballsing about with his riffs and making snide comments, can't bring me down. I'm cooking tonight. This is my show and he knows it.

People keep coming up to me and telling me what a great gig it is. Women mostly. I feel sexy again. It's ruddy hard to feel attractive when you're spending your days wiping your baby's vomit from off your shirt or crawling about on all fours pretending to be Baloo the Bear.

But tonight I'll have them dancing on the tables.

'Hi, Andy!'

'Michelle! What are you doing here?'

She's sidled up to me and put her arm through mine.

'I came to watch you play. Join me when you've finished. I'll have a pint waiting for you,' she says, planting a kiss on my cheek.

'Sorry, Michelle, no-can-do. I've got to discuss future gigs with the boys, I'm afraid.'

The smile is fading from Michelle's face as she turns away and heads for the bar.

Oh dear.

Monday, 1.35am. I'm in the back of the Transit van being driven home, which is just as well as I'm a bit drunk. I spent the money I earned tonight on booze, trying to make the performance high last longer. So I'm skint again. As bloody usual.

Oh, feck it! Who cares?

I was on top form.

I'm even tempted to see if I can make Gina feel a bit frisky.

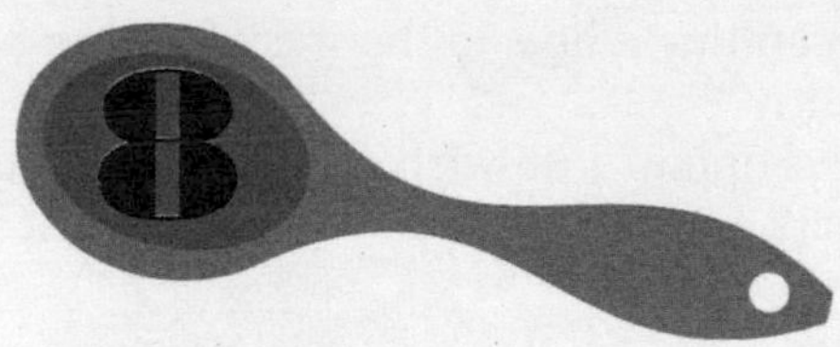

DECEMBER 11.

Ding dong merrily on bleeding high. Yippee, it's Christmas. Well, not quite, it's the second week of December.

We've got the tree up. Decorations festoon the house.

I like Christmas, usually. Gina adores it. But not so much this year. Mr and Mrs Festive we ain't.

But, then, money is tight and Gina and I . . . well, you know how it can be. Can't be sparks and fireworks all the time, but the odd banger would be nice.

Ho, ho, ho, eh? It's two o'clock in the afternoon and Sophie has just bowled me a googly.

The nativity play. She's an angel.

What's the problem? Costume. Apparently it's a DIY job.

I should have been informed of this three weeks ago.

Yes, that's right, there is a dress rehearsal . . . tomorrow.

At least the baby's having a nap. Let's hope it's a long one. I need as much time as I can muster. I have never been the type of person who would have stood a cat-in-hell's chance of passing a *Blue Peter* audition.

OK, I have an array of goodies strewn on the floor before us and I have my model ready and waiting.

Where to begin?

Sheet.

'Daddy?'

'Yes, Sophie.'

'That sheet's not white, is it, Daddy?'

'Isn't it? It is . . . sort of. It's cream, ivory or something.'

'Angels dress in white, don't they, Daddy?'

'That's stereotyping.'

'They do, don't they, Daddy? They dress in white, don't they?'

I hate it when she looks at me like that.

'Sophie, darling, don't worry, it'll look white under the lights.'

'Ooh, are we having lights at playschool, Daddy?'

'I'm sure you are, and dry ice as well, now . . .'

She's gone quiet. She's thinking. It unnerves me.

'What are you doing, Daddy?'

'I'm cutting a hole in the sheet for your head.'

'Daddy?'

'Yes, Sophie.' I do wish she'd shut up and let me concentrate.

'That's one of Mummy's best sheets, isn't it, Daddy?'

'Yes.'

'Ooh, Daddy!'

'"Ooh, Daddy" what? Unless you wanted to be dressed in pink, I don't see what choice we have. Try this.'

It fits over her head all right, but she now has a train behind her roughly three times the length of the *Flying Scotsman*.

Bit more chopping to be done, methinks.

My daughter will be the first angel in history to wear a minidress.

'Right, that's that, then. Now for the halo.'

It's now 6.10pm, same Wednesday, and we're done. It took a little longer than I thought, but it wasn't helped by interruptions from Nicola and all that that entails.

Sophie is modelling for us, spinning like a top. Then she reminds me that angels have wings. Of course they do!

So my daughter, the angel, stands before me. Her dress barely covers her knickers. The halo is a pair of Deely Boppers. I've cut the antennae off them and attached one of Gina's Alice bands to the top.

The wings were made by attaching two coat hangers together, then glueing them to bits of sheet I had already cut trying to make the dress.

She looks . . . hideous. She looks like a tacky monster from a particularly low-budget episode of *Doctor Who*. If this angel descended from on high to bring peace on earth, the shepherds would not so much be sore afraid as shitting fucking bricks.

Gina has just walked into the lounge.

'Mummy, Mummy, I'm an angel, I'm an angel. Daddy made it, Daddy made it!'

Gina's pausing.

'Well, that's lovely, Mummy's girl. In fact, you look *so lovely*, Mummy's going to get the camera and take a picture.'

There's something in Gina's eyes, but I can't recognise what.

I'm following her into the kitchen and closing the door behind me.

She's crying, I think. Her shoulders are visibly shaking. She's stood up now and I see tears are streaming down her cheeks. She's putting a finger to her lips and gesturing to the lounge with the other hand.

Blimey! If Gina keeps on like this she'll have a seizure.

Good to see, though.

That's what it was I didn't recognise in her eyes: laughter.

Thursday afternoon. Ballinkilty. 2.43pm, to be precise.

I hate shopping. Granted, shopping for food isn't as bad as shopping for clothes, or cookers, or houses, but it's still shopping and I hate it. Loathsome. Especially when it's food-shopping for Christmas, with two kids in tow.

I didn't do it when Sophie was in playschool rehearsing for her starring role, because Michelle popped in.

I used to enjoy our chats. You know, adult conversation. Saves your sanity. Now it's different.

This morning when Michelle popped in she gave me a Christmas present and told me to open it. It was a pair of black silk boxer shorts. 'I hope they're big enough,' she said. 'Why don't you try them on, Andy?'

After that I made some excuse about having to pick up a prescription for Gina, before collecting Sophie, and ushered her out of the house as quickly as I could.

I dumped the boxer shorts in a hedgerow *en route*. Don't want to have to start explaining *those* away to Gina.

Anyway, that's the reason why I'm shopping in Ballinkilty now.

My immediate problem is this: I have one of those special baby trolleys, and, because Nicola is riding in the baby seat, Sophie has to ride in the trolley too. In the main compartment. So where am I supposed to put the bloody shopping?

I have a list, longer than the Gettysburg Address, so I have had to take a second trolley. In a feat that would test your average pentathlete, I'm wheeling these buggers in a straight line up and down the aisles, cornering included.

'Daddy, I want a bread roll.'

'You can't have one, Sophie.'

'I *always* have one when Mummy wheels me round the supermarket.'

'No, Sophie.'

'Daddy! It *is* Christmas.'

She's got me there. Cute little bugger. Accuse someone of Scrooge-like tendencies at Christmas and it nails them every time.

Dickens has a lot to answer for.

'Having fun there, Andy?'

It's Connor.

'Hello, there. What are you doing here?'

'Sure, the same as you, Andy. Suffering.'

'Why didn't you do it in the city?'

'I did. I liked it so much I thought I'd come out to Ballinkilty and do it all again, so I took a half day off.'

'Pardon?'

'Finishing off, Andy. The bits I was after forgetting.'

'What about Gina?'

'She's at home. Dropped her there meself.'

'Oh, right. Shit. I wish I'd known. She could have joined me.'

Connor's sighing. He's taken the list out of my hand and torn it in half.

'There. I can't stand to see a grown man despair. You work away on that half of the list, I'll take this trolley and sort the other. Last one to the checkout is a pillock.'

Good man, Connor.

At 4.40pm, I'm home at last.

'Hi!' Gina appears to have been diligently wrapping presents at the kitchen table. 'And where have you been?'

'Shopping.'

'All this time?'

'You should have seen it. It was heaving. Chaos, absolute chaos.'

I've neglected to mention the quick detour to the pub with Connor. I paid. I was last to the checkout.

'I got home early,' Gina says, putting Nicola in her high chair.

'I know. Connor just told me.'

'Oh, you've seen Connor? That's why you're late. You've been to the pub.'

Rumbled.

'Well, he did collect half the shopping for me. I couldn't really refuse, could I?' I ask rhetorically, as Gina heads for the washing machine.

'Did you put on a wash today?'

'Yes. Oh, damn! I forgot to take it out.' I'm remembering this as Gina is pulling it out of the machine.

'Oh, for crying out loud, Andy! What did you put in it?'

She is holding up a blue sweater. 'This is hand wash only. I hope you like the colour blue, Andy Lawrence, because thanks to you, that's the only colour any bugger in this house is going to be wearing for the rest of the month.'

Oops.

'Oh, no, Jeez!' Gina has clapped her hand to her mouth in horror.

'What is it?' I say, nervously.

'Sophie's angel dress was in there.'

'Is it . . .?'

'Blue? Oh, yes,' she tells me, firmly. 'It's ruined, Andy. What are we going to do? We could bleach it, I suppose. You try it tomorrow. When she's not here to see or there'll be hell to pay.'

'OK, leave it with me. Right, I'll get the shopping in from the car.'

I look at the vast array of shopping bags in the boot of the car. At least we'll be able to eat and drink ourselves into oblivion this Christmas.

There are worse ways to go.

Then again, I can think of better.

Friday morning, 12.30.

Backs to each other again. We're not exactly running the full gamut of the *Kama Sutra* from A to Z these days.

There's a cruel irony here. On the one hand, I'm certain I have a woman waiting for the slightest encouragement from me before tossing her knickers gleefully in my direction, while my wife, the woman I love, is treating me like a sexual leper.

It has to be said that having financial pressures isn't conducive to nice, relaxed nookie.

But it's more than that.

It seems difficult to ask for certain things, or take charge, when your partner is holding the purse strings.

You feel guilty about hassling your old lady for sex.

Add *this* to the equation: *you* are now the little woman indoors. Not only are you financially inferior to your wife, but you have now swapped roles totally to complete your emasculation.

I can't talk it through with her because I'm a man and that's all we're interested in, right?

Fuck it, I'll get up and make a cup of tea.

Saturday morning.

There are certain phrases, expressions and clichés in the English language which should never be used. They are a curse.

Only this morning I used the phrase, 'Things might be difficult, but we can still have a good time,' in reference to Christmas.

Prat. You'd think I'd know better.

I nipped down to the shops with Nicola this morning to buy a newspaper, and when I returned Gina gave me a big hug. She expressed concern that I was looking so tired. She suggested I have a bath and then two minutes after I climbed into the hot water, she fetched me a gin and tonic to 'help me relax'. By this time I was suspicious. It was only a quarter past eleven.

Just as she reached the door—no, correction, as she was halfway out of the door, her hand poised to close it behind her—she said, 'Oh, by the way, I forgot to mention, Mother's coming for Christmas.'

Then she was gone. Vanished. I could hear her running downstairs.

So here I lie. Nuked. The gin has disappeared down my throat in one desperate gulp.

Sylvia is coming for Christmas.

Today I watched Sophie in her nativity play.

Gina couldn't make it. She was devastated, so I filmed every precious second with the camcorder.

Sophie was just gorgeous.

Come on, let's hear it for the proud parent!

We are all watching the video, including Nicola, thirty seconds after poor Mummy has walked through the door.

The costume, by the way, barely resembles its original design. It fell apart when I bleached it, so Gina stayed up into the small hours and started from scratch.

She's preening, is Sophie. She's a star and she knows it.

'You were just the best, Sophie.'

'Was I, Daddy?' she says, with the casual air of a film star.

'Yes, Mummy and Daddy are so proud of their girl,' Gina's adding.

We've all laughed and Gina's just hugged me in a way she's neglected to do for some time. A sort of we-made-her-that-little-girl kind of hug.

It's 12.45am and we've just made love. Sort of.

I don't know why it happened tonight after so long.

It could be that the video of Sophie brought out the romantics in us. Reminded us of the love that made her. And the passion.

Wasn't perfect. Very tense. Very by numbers.

But better than nothing.

The Saturday before Christmas, lunchtime, and my father's just turned up. He does that. No prior warning. Just appears.

No need to panic as he's not stopping. Passing through, as usual, on the way to some gig or other. Jazz musician, I think I told you.

He wants me to go for a drink in town, which has not pleased Gina.

I'll suffer the consequences later.

Four o'clock, and I'm still here. In the pub, with my dad. Not one of the usual pubs I prop up. And there are a few of those. I've done my best to help keep them afloat, especially in the winter when the tourist trade drops off. But I don't take my father to one of my favourites. He's too . . . unpredictable.

He plonks another round on the table.

'What exactly are you up to these days, son?'

'Not a lot. Few demo tapes on a few desks, but I'm not holding my breath.'

'Why don't you come and play jazz with me?'

'Because I hate jazz. Anyway, I can't go dragging my carcass round Europe with you, I've a wife and family to think about.'

'So?'

'So not everyone can just bugger off and leave their emotional ties behind them, the way you did.'

He shrugs, unaffected by my criticism. 'So get a proper job, then, if you're settling down.'

'I've got one. I'm looking after the kids while Gina works.'

'Eh?'

'I'm a house husband. The "other half". I'm a "new man".'

'You're a fucking poof!'

'What?'

'House husband! My son. *My* son, looking after the kids, doing the shopping, washing the nappies?'

'You don't wash nappies any more, they're disposable.'

'Oh, well, that's all right then, as long as the bleedin' nappies are disposable. Is this Andy I'm hearing? The best bass-player to emerge in the last twenty years. He's washing dishes and sterilising dummies? What's happened to you, boy?'

'Life, Dad, life.'

'Don't give me that. It's that woman of yours. Look how well you were doing until she came on the scene. Everyone was after you, everyone. You were going places, Andy lad.'

'But they were blind alleys, all of them. I want big-time or nothing. I don't want to be over sixty and scrubbing about doing sad little gigs, talking about the old days like some sad, pathetic . . .'

'Like me, son.'

'Yes, Dad. Like you.'

He's standing up, gathering his things together.

'I'll be off, now.'

'Where you heading?'

'Schull.'

And he's walking out of the door.

Funny, I just found myself arguing the house husband's corner.

But he's just walked out of the door, backpack and guitar, and part of me is jealous. Envious.

And he knows it.

December 22, 11.30pm.

I've just got back from the pub to find Lucretia Borgia sitting at our kitchen table. 'Good evening, Andy. I was about to put the kettle on. You look as if you could use a coffee, dear.'

It's started already. Fifteen-love to Sylvia.

Gina has entered the kitchen. 'Hi, Andy. How was Connor?'

'Fine. I've invited him for Christmas Day as usual. No point in him being by himself.'

'No, of course not,' says Gina, looking a little awkward. She generally does feel uncomfortable when her mother and I are in the same room.

Sylvia stands up. 'Well, if you'll excuse me for a moment, I'll just get ready for bed. Finish making the coffee, would you, Andy? There's a good boy.'

I resist the temptation to bark and wag my tail.

'What do you take in your coffee these days, Sylvia? Milk? Sugar? Strychnine?' I add, when she's out of earshot.

'Oh, Andy!' Gina reprimands me. 'Promise me you'll get along with her this Christmas.'

'I'll try.'

'Thanks, darling, it is appreciated,' and she gives me a hug.

'That's better,' Sylvia says, as she re-enters the kitchen. 'Oh, Andy, you haven't finished making the coffee.'

She is resplendent in red velvet dressing gown with matching hood. I bite my lip to prevent myself from telling her that she has left her beard and sack back in Lapland. For Gina's sake.

There's a knock at the back door.

'I'll get it,' Sylvia insists, taking over as usual.

She has opened the door and somebody has fallen through it, landing right on top of her. Sylvia is pinned to the ground.

'Hello, son. My gigs got cancelled. So I thought I'd spend Christmas with my favourite boy.'

He's suddenly noticed that Sylvia is underneath him.

'Ironically enough, it looks like I've finally landed on my feet, so to speak,' my father says, grinning. 'Hello, sweetheart. Give us a kiss,' and he swoops his lips down to meet hers.

'Dad . . .'

Sylvia is screaming, as Gina and I just grip each other's hands in sheer horror.

Christmas Eve, 7.10pm and I've just walked through the door.

I'm soaking wet, and I've just driven halfway round west Cork.

But I'm happy.

Why? Because I've got Texas Tessie!

It's not a porn video, it's a toy. Correction it's *the* toy, at least as far as this Yuletide is concerned.

No store in Ireland has Texas Tessie, except a little feller called Sean, who lives in a village the other side of Cork, who had a few that had toppled off the back of a lorry. So, in the light of this, he was willing to sell me one at roughly two and a half times the manufacturer's recommended retail price.

I didn't care. I tracked Sean down, I tracked down Texas Tessie.

Tomorrow, when my little girl rips off the wrapping paper and sees the doll of the year in her sweaty little paws, I'll be there.

I've got the toy hidden inside my coat while Sophie's in the kitchen, sitting on the floor, drawing another picture of Santa.

Gina's looking at me as if to say, 'Did you get it?'

I'm winking and giving a little nod.

She's smiling at me and I'm smiling back.

It's the first joy we've shared since the gruesome twosome arrived.

Christmas Eve, 10.00pm.

I'm only just putting a very overexcited Sophie to bed.

'Dad?'

'Yes, Sophie.'

'How does Father Christmas manage to fit down the chimney?'

'With great difficulty, I should imagine.'

'Cos he's quite fat, Dad, isn't he?'

'I suppose so. But he's also magic. Now get to sleep.'

'OK, Dad. Good night. Merry Christmas.'

'Merry Christmas. Sweet dreams, Daddy's girl.'

'Dad?' a little voice sings out as I reach the bedroom door.

'Yes, Sophie.'

'Is Father Christmas really on his way?'

'Of course he is.'

'Then d'you think it would be a good idea to put the fire out? We don't want him to go to hospital with three-degreeve burns, do we, Dad?'

'The word's degree, Sophie. Don't worry, I'll get right onto it,' I'm saying as I exit, laughing.

The rest of the evening resembles peace negotiations in the Middle East: tense, with war likely to resume at any moment.

We're all a bit drunk, so we're playing the obligatory charades.

'Are you sure this is a television programme?' my father enquires.

'Yes, Edward,' Sylvia replies.

Dad hates being called Edward and she knows it.

'How many words is it?' asks Gina.

'Three, dear, three, but I'm doing the whole thing.'

'Well, what are you doing? *War and* bloody *Peace*?' my father asks.

'I'm doing *The South Bank Show*, you ignorant little man!'

Stunned silence, which I break. 'You were doing the *whole* of *The South Bank Show*?'

'Of course. I did a bit of music, a bit of painting, sculpting, acting, dancing. I even pinched my nose and mimed talking through it.'

'You should have seen the faces you were pulling,' my father says, shaking his head. 'It was more like *Some Mothers Do 'Ave 'Em*.'

'And so do some fathers,' Sylvia replied, bitchily.

'What do you mean by that?' My father is leaping to his feet. Sylvia joins him and they stand toe to toe, their noses almost touching.

'I mean, what sort of a man would let his wife work all the hours in the day while he loafs about writing songs that nobody will buy?'

Well done, Sylvia. Great. Here we go.

'The same sort of man who will let a woman destroy a promising career just because she has a nice arse,' my father retaliates.

'Mother!'

'Dad!'

Gina has followed her mother upstairs, needless to say.

I'm turning to my father. 'Dad, you're such a—such—such a wanker!'

I've stormed into the kitchen in search of another beer and he's trotted behind me.

'I'm sorry, son, but I just can't stand by and see you . . . emasculated like this.' Dad sighs. 'I've never been a better than average musician, but you, son, you're different. You have real talent, and am I supposed to stand by and let you piss it away in the back of beyond?'

'Oh, fuck, I don't know. Dad. I'm all confused.'

There's a brief silence, during which I sink into one of the kitchen chairs.

Eventually Dad says, 'It's gone awfully quiet upstairs, Andy. Maybe you'd better tiptoe on up there and see if things have calmed down.'

'Yeah, I suppose I'd better,' I say as I put down my beer and head for the stairs.

Now I'm hovering on the landing, just outside our bedroom door because I can hear Gina and Sylvia talking.

'Believe me, Gina, I know what it costs to love a man like Andy. How long can you keep him? Pay the bills, organise your finances, wipe his backside along with your children's.'

'Mother, Andy is doing a wonderful job . . .'

'. . . looking after the children, I know. Meantime they're growing up, changing, developing, and you're missing it all. If Andy had any sense of decency he'd forget about becoming a pop star, or whatever he wants to be, and get himself a proper job. One that pays a decent wage. Look after his wife and children.'

There was an unnerving silence for a while. Then Gina: 'In so many ways Andy is the perfect husband. He's a kind man, he's funny, intelligent, a good father. That's the man I love.'

'But you don't love the man who daydreams and never earns a penny, do you, Gina?'

The pause is agonising from where I'm standing.

'No . . . yes . . . I don't know, Mother. It's all so difficult.'

'Leave Andy now, Gina. Before you lose all respect for him. Before you begin to resent him. Before you make the children resent him.'

I've heard enough.

I've come downstairs to the kitchen and rescued my beer. The house feels suddenly cold. I've noticed the back door is ajar. I've found the note on the table: CATCH YOU SOMETIME. HAPPY NEW YEAR TO YOU ALL.

Seems he's run out at the first sign of trouble once again.

JANUARY 27, 1997, 11.30AM.

Christmas passed in a flash, to be replaced by the soggy grey realities of a west Cork winter. It just hasn't stopped pouring down and the rain has become our jailer. Children make the most hysterical of cellmates, believe me.

Texas Tessie has been buried alive at the bottom of Sophie's toy box. Gina and I are left with a collection of letters from credit-card companies threatening public execution.

The month has been miserable. Broken nights, shopping, pissing rain, money worries, back-to-back sleeping, runny noses, etc.

Oh, and returned demo tapes with complimentary rejection letters, just to add to the general gaiety.

I'm in the pub. Not O'Leary's. The next one along. Sophie's in playschool. I'm here with Nicola, who is sleeping peacefully in her buggy.

So I'm having a pint with Norman.

Why? That's what I'm wondering. I just bumped into him in the street. That's odd in itself. Especially in the daytime. He's usually in court on some life and death matter. Like an argument over land boundaries.

He suggested we went for a swift one, and now he's teetering across the pub floor towards me now, spilling the drinks as he walks. By the time he gets here my pint will be a half.

'There you are, my friend.'

My friend!

'We haven't had a chat, just the two of us, you know, for ages. Man to man, as it were.'

Man to man? Is he thinking of telling me the facts of life?

'No,' I'm replying sceptically, 'I don't think we have.'

Bit of a hiatus now.

He's not saying anything. He's just sat opposite me smiling. Falsely. Down to me, then.

'So . . . Norm, what exactly did you want to talk to me about . . . man to man?'

'Ah, yes, I'm glad you brought that up, because it's a bit delicate, actually. A bit tricky.'

Oh, Gawd, is it? 'Just give me the general drift, Norman.'

'Sex, Andy.'

If there was one word I never thought I'd hear Norman say it was 'sex'.

'I see. Er . . . having trouble with the construction business, are you?' I ask, tactfully, I thought.

'Pardon?'

'Struggling to erect the old scaffold?'

'No!' he replies, looking wounded. 'Well, not exactly. It's not me, you see. Actually, it's Michelle.'

I'm beginning to feel very uncomfortable about this.

'Michelle's all right, isn't she?'

'Yes, yes, she's fine. It's just that she's always had a healthy appetite in the bedroom department, as it were. But lately, she's . . . she's . . .'

'Gone on a strict diet?' I suggest.

'No! No, quite the opposite. She's uncontrollable! She won't let me work, she won't let me sleep. It's intolerable. Really, I mean it,' he adds, probably in response to a half-grin I failed to suppress.

'She's stripping off at the drop of a hat. I come home from work, she's lying naked on the sitting-room sofa. I try to work, she's crawling under my study table and fiddling with my flies. I just don't know what to do.'

'Have you tried satisfying her demands?'

'No, I can't. I mean I could, there's nothing wrong . . . technically. It's just that it's . . . putting me off. It's just not what I'm used to, you see.'

'Yes, quite,' I say, half envious that Gina isn't crawling under my study table and grappling with my 501s. If I had a study table. Or a pair of 501s, come to that.

'The thing is, Andy, and this is where I think you may be able to help, there has to be some reason for this increase in desire. I've heard somewhere that sex actually increases at home if your partner is playing away. I mean, do you think Michelle is having an affair?'

Oh, shit, shit, *shit*! Alarm bells are ringing again.

'Surely that's just an old wives' tale, isn't it?' I reply, trying to defuse the situation.

'No, no, no. I'm certain I'm right. If a partner is having . . .'

'Sex,' I help out.

'. . . an affair, then they often up the rations at home. Sort of all part of the deception, if you understand me.'

'If you say so, Norman. But we're talking about Michelle here. She loves you. She's always telling me how . . . exciting she finds you.'

What else can I say? 'Well, actually, Norman, I can't say for certain she's shagging someone else, but I have a sneaking suspicion she's set her heart on a length or two of my dick.'

'Is she? Of course, that could be part of the pretence as well. Tell me, Andy, you know Michelle as well as any of our friends. If she was going to stray, who do you think she would choose as a lover?'

Aghhh! Does he know? Is this a warning? Know what, for fuck's sake? Nothing's happened.

'What about Connor?'

Phew! 'Connor? God, no, he's still in love with his dear departed. Even if he was over it all, I can't see him taking another man's wife.'

'No, you're probably right. Who, then?'

'Norman, aren't you rushing ahead of yourself here? You're a legal man. Have you discovered any other evidence? Any love letters? Diary entries? Condoms blocking up your U-bends?'

'She's sterilised.'

'Pardon?'

'Michelle. After giving birth to Richard. Said she wasn't going to go through that pain again for all the tea in China.'

'Really? Never mind, you're missing the point. Maybe she just fancies the socks off you and is frustrated because work takes up so much of your time.'

'Possibly,' he acknowledges, without much conviction.

'Why don't you try giving in gracefully occasionally?'

'Because—because she's an animal, Andy. It just turns me off.'

'Well, then . . .' I'm searching frantically for the right key here '. . . then fantasise. Who have you secretly thought about having it off with? Claudia Schiffer? Elizabeth Hurley?' Wait a minute, this is Norman. 'Delia Smith? Angela Rippon? Clare Short? There must be somebody.'

He's grinning ruefully.

'There is someone, actually. Do you think it will help?'

'I'm convinced.'

'Yes, yes.' Norman's nodding in agreement. 'Gosh, look at the time. Must dash. Thank you, Andy,' he says, 'you're a real friend.'

'Any time. Glad to help,' I say, as he heads for the pub door.

Nicola is awake in her buggy, just staring up at me.

If I didn't know better, I'd swear that look said: 'You hypocritical old basket, Dad.'

February 3, 1.45pm. My nerves are too frayed to be accurate.

Nicola is asleep in the back of the car. Sophie is in her car chair next to me. She's unusually quiet and I'm not surprised.

I've just had an awful shock.

I arrived at playschool this lunchtime to find Sophie was nowhere to be seen.

'Sophie just left. Michelle said that that was the arrangement. That was all right, wasn't it, Andy?' the teacher asked.

'Yes, sure, no problem. Must have slipped my mind.'

I hotfooted it immediately to Michelle's house, to be greeted by incredulity at my fear.

'I'm not trying to kidnap your children, Andy. Gina asked me to collect Sophie. Something about you taking Nicola off somewhere?'

'The doctor's, but that's tomorrow morning.'

'Maybe I got it wrong, then. Sorry. Anyway, no harm done. Sophie's playing quite happily upstairs with Richard. You look tired, Andy. Has Nicola been keeping you up at nights?'

'Yes, yes, she has.'

I admit I was thrown off track by this show of concern.

She appraised me again. 'You're obviously not eating properly, Andy, I'm worried about you.'

'Really, I'm fine, Michelle.'

'Anyway come through into the dining room. I've fixed us a light lunch.'

She headed off, obliging me to follow.

The dining-room table was fully set. A bottle of white wine stood in a bucket of ice. Two candles stood burning in a silver centrepiece.

It was then that I took time to notice what she was wearing. It was a black blouse of see-through chiffon. A matching lace bra was visible underneath. Her long skirt was slit to the thigh.

It looked wonderful, but not the sort of thing one wears for a casual lunch with an old mate.

'Michelle, look, you really shouldn't have gone to all this trouble.'

'It's no trouble, Andy. You're working so hard looking after your children, and no one is looking after your . . . needs.'

She crossed her legs as she said this.

I felt very . . . threatened.

'Sit yourself down, Andy. We haven't chatted for ages. I was beginning to think you were avoiding me,' she said, as she took the wine from the bucket and filled two glasses.

At this point, Sophie came down the stairs and ran into the dining room. Clearly she was not playing happily with Richard.

There were tears in her eyes. 'Daddy, you didn't tell me you weren't picking me up today.'

Sobs. Floods of tears.

I cuddled her. 'I'm very sorry, Stinks. There must have been some misunderstanding.'

'Can—we—go—home, now?'

'Yes, of course we can.'

I could have kissed her.

So that was that. I made a hasty exit, apologising as I went.

I hadn't taken the sleeping Nicola out of the car.

I'd had a suspicion we would need to make a fast exit.

That evening I casually asked Gina if she had asked Michelle to pick Sophie up from school that day.

'No. Why?' she replied.

'Oh, there was a bit of confusion. Sophie got a bit upset. Anyway, all sorted. No harm done.'

I don't like this one little bit.

I'm in Ross Carbery. It's a beautiful village, like so many others in west Cork, and it's full of nice pubs and restaurants and cheerful people.

But I do not want to come to Ross Carbery today. That's because our doctor also resides here, and it's vaccination time for Nicola.

That's why I'm sitting outside the surgery, ready to take the poor little mite in to be tortured.

I'm looking at Nicola now.

I can't do this. I shouldn't have to do this. She trusts me. What is she going to think when I goo and gah at her and cuddle her and introduce her to the nice nursey and nice doctor man, and two seconds later they're shoving ruddy great knitting needles up her jacksie?

She's smiling at me. A big, gummy smile.

Oh, well, here goes.

So far, so good. Nicola's lying on the bed in the surgery. She's playing with my car keys. I've had to strip her down to her vest and take her nappy off. She's been weighed. She's suitably fat for her age, even though my earliest culinary attempts forced her into a starvation diet.

The nurse is going to take her temperature and then we'll see the doctor.

'Right, Daddy. If you can amuse Baby for me for a second.'

'Eh, Daddy's girl. Now open wide for the nice nursey.'

'Don't be silly, Daddy. We can't expect Baby to hold a thermometer in her mouth, now, can we?'

Oh, jeez, shit, bugger, hellfire and flame!

She's just shoved the thermometer up Nicola's bum.

'Is that really necessary?'

'Trust us, Daddy, it's the best way. It's no trouble.'

Maybe not to you, I'm thinking, but what about poor Nicola? How would Nursey like someone to shove something solid up her anus five minutes after meeting them? Though by the look of her . . .

'It's all right, darling, Daddy's here.'

I'm looking at Nicola . . . and she's not bothered.

'All done, Daddy. Temperature's fine. Doctor will be with you in a moment. You can put a nappy on her now.'

I'm putting a Pampers Premium protectively round her little botty. Before she comes here again, I think I'll have a miniature-size suit of armour made especially for her.

We're back in the car now and she's laughing again.

It was awful. It went from bad to worse. A pipette full of heaven-knows-what squirted down her throat, one needle jammed in her leg, another in her arm.

She screamed. Floods of tears. I felt such a bastard. I wanted to punch the doctor for hurting my girl.

Gina can take a sodding day off work next time.

I AM NEVER DOING THAT AGAIN!

The next morning, 3.10.

It never rains but it pours, isn't that what they say?

Well, here it hurricanes, tornadoes and monsoons. Indoors and out.

We're all up. Gina, Sophie, Nicola and yours truly.

Sophie started the ball rolling. A cry from the bedroom, a sprint to watch her puke majestically onto her mattress.

Why do four-year-olds never stand still when they're being ill?

Twenty minutes after she began, her room looks as if it were the venue for a rave. You would never believe it was all the work of one small child.

'What have you been feeding her?' was Gina's one line of criticism.

'Nothing,' I replied, defensively, and there's an element of truth in that. She's been off her food lately. I mention this to Gina and she looks horrified.

'Why haven't you mentioned this to me before?'

'I'm sorry, Gina. Look, she hasn't been *ill* as such, until tonight. I just thought it was a . . . a phase or something.'

'Just tell me next time, OK?'

'I will, I promise.'

At this point, Nicola woke up screaming due to the noise the rest of us were making. She's a bit off as well. It could be teething or it could be a reaction to the injections.

Gina is seeing to her.

I'm cuddling Sophie on the sofa. She doesn't seem to have a temperature so no need for immediate panic.

Aghhh! Kids!

It's 4.02am. Nicola's back in her cot and Gina's back in Mummy and Daddy's big bed. I insisted she went, she looked exhausted and she has a heavy day at work tomorrow. I'm in the single bed with Sophie.

This is more uncomfortable than it sounds. There may not be much of her, but when she gets into bed she sort of . . . swells to ten times her size and spreads herself across the entire mattress. I'm left balancing precariously on about two inches like a Russian gymnast on the beam.

She had finally drifted off, leaving me wide awake and hovering over her like a mother hen. Maybe I should have kept a closer eye on her.

Is Sophie ill because I haven't looked after her properly?

Anyway, she's sleeping now.

What a dreadful, dreadful day.

February 14, Valentine's Day. Embarrassing when the most you can afford to show how much you love your spouse is a pathetically small bunch of flowers.

Equally depressing is that you cannot afford to go out to a nice restaurant, just the two of you, so, in order to make some effort, you have to have friends round to dinner.

This is particularly morale-shattering, when one of those friends has to be Norman.

I subtly found a quiet moment to ask if he'd sorted out his little problem, *re* Michelle. He looked momentarily flustered, and said, 'Yes, yes, everything's fine,' and went back to being his irritating self.

So, no more man-to-man chats with his big pal Andy, then.

Tonight he's enthralling us with a tale of bitterness and revenge, envy and despair.

Apparently a friend looks after her neighbour's toucan while they're away on holiday. Needless to say dear old Beaky croaks while neighbour is swanning around the Seychelles.

'So what happened then?' Gina's asking.

'Well, the poor friend was mortified,' Norman's informing us in deadly earnest, 'so she purchased another toucan at great expense and gave it to her neighbour with a sincere apology. The neighbour accepted the toucan and told her friend to drop dead.'

I've just felt a stockinged foot creeping up the inside of my leg to my crotch. I've looked across the table at Gina who is smiling.

Things are looking up.

'Who are you representing, Norman?' Gina asks, her foot continuing to tease me mercilessly under the table.

'I'm defending the friend, of course.'

Gina has started to gather dishes.

'It's OK, I'll do that,' I'm saying, giving her a suggestive wink.

'No need,' she says, still smiling and, sadly, removing her foot.

I've just noticed.

Gina isn't wearing stockings or tights but . . . socks. You know, the sort that used to be the prerogative of men until Top Shop or some such decided they were trendy for women to wear, thus killing off foreplay up and down the country.

Gina isn't wearing stockings.

But Michelle is.

Now I'm the one being winked at suggestively.

Shit! Shit! Shit!

I'd better have a word with Michelle as soon as possible.

I feel a disaster looming.

It's 3.17am and I've just been refused sex.

I mean, it's Valentine's Day for heaven's sake! A time for lovers. Maybe she just doesn't fancy me any more.

February 16.

My birthday. I'm thirty-eight.

Ugh!

We've no money, so celebrations have been somewhat muted. A chicken tikka masala that Gina brought back from Cork, and a bottle of sparkling vinegar.

A few cheap, though admittedly thoughtful, gifts, and I was let off the washing-up.

No birthday treats in the bedroom department either, surprise, surprise.

Perhaps I should fuck Michelle. At least she wants me.

Middle of March. I haven't spoken to Michelle since Valentine's Day. Norman whisked her off to Sri Lanka or somewhere. Came back without her. Apparently she decided to stay on.

It's a Tuesday night, the Blow-ins have finished rehearsing and Matt and I are opposite each other in O'Leary's.

'Listen up, boy, because have I got some news for you, my friend. We've been offered a tour.'

'A tour?'

'Yes, sir. You know, where you travel around playing lots of different venues. Like, a tour, man.'

'Really? Where do we play? Limerick? Galway? Dublin?'

'No, sirree. Frankfurt, Hamburg, Essen, Cologne, and one or two other places I can't pronounce,' he quips at me.

'Correct me if I'm wrong, but that's Germany, isn't it?'

'Woah! Way to go, Andy. Top marks for geography. And there's more. We get a chance to cut a record, too.'

'You're pulling my plonker. Why would they want us to record?'

'It works like this: we record the CD at the start and sell it at the gigs. The people play the CD, then a few months later we go back and do the same tour again, hopefully with a bigger following.'

He's buzzing. I've never seen him so animated.

'A second tour?' I'm asking, trying to grasp all this.

'That's what I said. So. Are you in or not?' he's asking, slugging back his lager while he awaits my answer.

I'm nodding cagily. Don't want to seem too eager at this stage. Though the adrenaline is pumping round my body.

'It sounds fun. What's the money like?'

'So-so. Two fifty a week. But listen, man, wowee, the venues! These are big cities, loaded with possibilities eh, boy! Course if you've got other priorities now . . .'

I'm placing my pint down on the table and I'm staring at him.

'What's that supposed to mean?'

'You know what I'm getting at, man. Since you took over the family bra, you haven't shown the same commitment and you know it.'

I'm furious. 'Bullshit!'

'No, it's not, Andy. You're here, and yet you're not here, man. If you catch my drift. I don't know where your head's been.'

I'm sighing heavily. 'When is this tour?'

'Ten days. We hit the road in ten days.'

'Jeez!'

'So are you in or out? 'Cos if you're out, man, we have to move real fast to replace you.'

He doesn't want me in.

'Look, you'll have to give me a couple of days.'

'Andy, we don't *have* a couple of days.'

'Fuck you, Matt! I've worked hard for this band and I've covered everyone else's back countless times. *I want two fucking days*! You owe me that much at least.'

'All right, Andy, you got it. Two days, but no longer.'

'Leave it with me. I'll ring you Saturday night.'

'OK. Do your best, you hear?'

I've driven home. I'm sat inside the car, just outside the house, practising what I'm going to say.

I've got to mention it tonight. I haven't the time to wait.

You see, the thing is, they're playing some big cities and I could probably argue for using more of my new material, which will probably be recorded and . . . well . . . I'm running out of last chances.

This is the biggest opportunity to present itself to me in years.

So it's got to be tonight.

Here goes.

Gina is standing in the kitchen.

I've closed the door behind me.

'Hiya, Andy. Good rehearsal?'

'Yes. Gina?'

Bugger! She's walked into the lounge. Freshly made cup of tea in hand. Just as I'd screwed my courage to the sticky place, or however the quote goes.

I've taken off my jacket, and now I've joined Gina on the sofa.

She looks odd. Something's wrong.

'You OK, Gina?'

'Fine.'

'Sure?'

'It's just . . . I'm late.'

'What for?'

She's sighing. Usually a sign that I'm being thick.

'*Guess.*'

'All right, all right. So, what for? A deadline?'

'No.'

'An appointment?'

'No.'

'A very important date?'

'*No*!'

'What then?'

'My period.'

'Therefore . . .?'

'You got there, well done. I might be pregnant, yes.'

'I see.'

Outwardly, I'm nodding calmly.

Inwardly, I'm screaming in blind panic.

'You need to go to the chemist for me tomorrow. Pick up a home pregnancy test.'

'Right. Leave it with me.'

'*Oh, Andy*! We can't have another baby now, we can't. I can't get maternity leave—the magazine's struggling as it is. If I left, I wouldn't have a job to go back to. And you've got your hands full enough. What are we going to do?'

Good question.

Pity I can't find a worthy answer.

I can't even remember having sex. Maybe we did, once. Must have, under the circumstances.

Gina is physically shaking.

Maybe tonight is not the right time to mention the tour.

Following evening, 6.30.

I don't know what day it is. I don't know whether I'm on my head or my arse at present. I've been climbing walls waiting for Gina to come home and do the test. I still haven't mentioned the tour. I can't.

She's just read the instructions and apparently I purchased one of the few kits you have to use first thing in the morning.

Just what I wanted to hear.

I'm running out of time if I'm going to get on that tour.

What am I going to do?

Following morning, 6.00.

Gina's just emerged from the bathroom and the test is negative—after all that.

Apparently it means nothing. The home kit said negative last time, and a few months later out pops Nicola.

Gina's too distraught for me to begin to mention anything else.

It was a two-test packet. We'll double check tomorrow.

Next day, 6.30am.

Negative again. Yet still no sign of blood.

So that means she's pregnant, doesn't it? Plum duff, up the spout, bun in the oven, one on the way, pregnant.

It's all very well Gina freaking over this, but it's me that will have to look after the sodding thing.

I can't cope!

Fuck it! I'm past caring. I won't be trapped. I'm just going to pick up my bass guitar and get on that bloody plane to Hamburg.

Ten days later. Back end of March, I think. I'm not sure.

It's morning. I know that much because Sophie's at playschool. I'm walking round the lounge with Nicola in my arms.

This morning was surreal. Weird.

Blood.

Gina doing cartwheels of joy round the lounge, screaming. *'Yes! Yes! Yes!'*

Ten days. Ten long days of mental torture.

It's 11.30am.

The plane is taking off for Hamburg and I'm not on it.

I didn't discuss the tour with Gina.

Like the baby, the timing wasn't right.

I'm crying.

I am crying because we're not going to have another nipper and I'm actually happy about that.

Or am I weeping because I'm not on that bloody plane?

Do I feel I've not so much missed the plane as the boat?

Is that it?

Who knows how long I'll have to wait for another opportunity?

All I know is I'm holding my baby daughter close. Hugging her.

I'm holding a baby and crying like one.

All I know is . . .

I'm fucked up.

10

IT'S EASTER. Well, just after. The last day of Sophie's school holidays and, for a change, the sun is out.

Gina's at home with Nicola. She took Easter Week off.

So I've brought Sophie to the beach.

There are lots of beautiful beaches round here. We've come to Inchydoney today, the biggest in the area. It's the kind of picture-perfect bay everyone seems to remember from their childhood. We're waiting for the waves to sweep towards us and then we're rushing towards them, trying to jump up out of their way at the last minute. So, I'm getting my gonads tickled by freezing cold water and Sophie's getting drowned from head to foot and adoring every second of it.

I love seeing her like this. It makes up for all the days when she's a complete pain to look after. All those times when she's awkward, difficult, demanding and obtuse. It's all forgotten. We've made sandcastles. Dug up half the beach and had an ice cream.

There's a tug on my arm.

'Daddy?'

'Yes, Sophie?'

'Daddy. Can I whisper?'

'Of course.' I'm bending down so she can reach my ear.

'Can I have a secret wee-wee?'

'No, Sophie, not now.'

'But, Dad, I'm desperate.'

'Go on, then. Be discreet.'

I can't believe it. She's just flung down her knickers, opened her legs and piddled where she's stood. In full view of everyone.

Howls of laughter, hysterical cackling from the dozen or so people close enough to witness the show.

She's looking up at me now. Smiling.

'Daddy?'

'Yes, Sophie?'

'What's discreet?'

Time to go, I think.

Following morning, 11.00.

I've been shaking for the last ten minutes.

It's Sophie's first day back at playschool and Gina's back at work.

Just an ordinary day in the life of a house husband. Nothing to give me the slightest clue as to what was about to unfold.

About half an hour after I've put Nicola in her cot, Michelle turns up. So I try not to panic. I've been waiting for an opportunity to let Michelle know it's no-go and here it is.

I make a couple of cups of coffee and we go into the lounge.

My mind was whirring as I tried to think exactly what to say. How to phrase it so we can both walk away with our dignity and remain friends.

Michelle sat on the sofa and I sat on the chair opposite.

'So how was Sri Lanka?' I asked, stalling for time while I tried to give my courage a good plucking.

'Wonderful! I rediscovered the joy of painting. I found it helped me to relax,' she informed me, slipping her high heels off her feet. 'How have things been for you?'

'Oh, you know. Same as ever, really.'

'Mmmm, for me too, since I came home. It gets so repetitive, routine. There's no . . . excitement.'

She kept tucking her legs up under her bum then stretching them out again and I kept getting a flash of her knickers.

'Don't you ever wish for something amazing to happen, Andy?'

'Yes, if I'm honest. I suppose I do. Little fantasies, you know.'

'Ooh, Andy, tell me more.'

First mistake.

'No, not that sort of fantasy. I'm talking about record deals, telephone calls from the Gallagher twins, that sort of thing.'

'I have those sort of fantasies.'

'What? You dream of getting a record deal as well, do you?'

I knew what she meant. I was just desperately trying to defuse the situation with a feeble attempt at humour.

'No, sexual fantasies. Well, Norman and I haven't had it for months and that makes a girl's mind wander.'

'I'm sure it does.'

'Sometimes I fantasise about someone from the telly or a film star. But my favourite is when I fantasise about a friend. Someone I know, really quite well.'

I tell you, by this time my heart was beating a drum solo.

I couldn't speak. I just stared at her.

'Do you like my tan?' she asked, suddenly, changing the subject.

'Yes, you look wonderful,' I said, and immediately wished I hadn't.

'I usually sunbathe topless, but I didn't this time.'

'Really?' I managed to splutter, my voice breaking like a choirboy's.

'No. If you ask me nicely, I'll let you see my white bits.'

'Listen . . . Michelle . . . before we go . . . any further . . . I . . .'

At that moment she missed the edge of the coffee table with her cup and spilled the contents down the bottom half of her dress.

It was timed to perfection. It looked like an accident.

'I'll get a cloth,' I said, and I ran into the kitchen.

I fished a clean J-cloth out from under the sink and walked back into the lounge.

And there she stood.

Naked.

'Sorry, Andy, I was soaked through,' she explained, as she placed her dress and knickers on the nearest available radiator.

She turned to me and smiled.

'So, Andy. Was I right to keep my bikini on?'

I didn't reply. I just stood there, still holding out the J-cloth I had brought for her to use.

'Which bit of me are you going to dab first?' she asked, laughing, before crossing to the chair behind her.

She sat down, arching her back slightly to accentuate her breasts, which stood full and beckoning before me.

'You can fuck me if you like, Andy. Here, now. No strings, no emotions, no ramifications, no repercussions. Just sex.'

'I . . . I . . . I . . .'

In the days when I was young, free, single and gigging in London, I'd have leapt upon Michelle with all the enthusiasm of a lapsed hunger-striker at a running buffet. But now, with Gina and the kids . . .

'Michelle, this isn't . . .'

'I know you want me,' she said, standing up from the chair and crossing towards me.

'I can see you do,' she said, as she stroked my erection through my jeans.

OK, I admit it. It doesn't matter what signals of panic or alarm bells my brain was sending down to my groin, *he* wasn't listening.

At this point I was tempted.

'Gina and I, we haven't . . . we don't . . . Well, she doesn't seem to want to . . .' and here was Michelle, naked, falling to her knees, undoing my trousers.

'What have we here?' she said, as she her mouth moved towards—

Finally I came to my senses.

'No!'

I stepped away from her. As I did this I tripped over my jeans, which by this time were residing around my ankles, and went arse over tit, landing my full body weight on my swollen member. I let out a scream of bloody agony.

'I'm sorry, but I love Gina,' I panted out, amid whimpers of pain.

'Bastard!' Michelle screamed, before sweeping her clothes off the radiator and heading in the direction of the downstairs loo.

By the time she came back into the lounge we were both dressed.

'I'm sorry, Andy.' Her eyes were red, but she spoke softly and appeared to have calmed down. 'It's just, I need to feel attractive.'

'You are, Michelle. You're a very beautiful woman, with a lovely body and—'

'How can you say that? I just stripped naked and you turned me down.'

'Not because you're not sexy. But because I love Gina and—'

'Oh, Andy! You're such a sap! You fucking deserve to get hurt.'

And with that she stormed out.

So that's why I'm here drinking a huge Scotch, hoping Nicola doesn't start screaming for me before I've steadied my nerves.

I've ballsed up here. We were good mates, Michelle and I.

True, we've become closer since I started looking after the house and the children. We may have joked a bit about sex but we always have.

Did I encourage this? Maybe I just enjoyed the attention. I must admit, since Gina and I have stopped making love so frequently I have been more . . . aware of other women.

Fucking hell! Is this my fault?

I still can't believe it was offered to me on a plate and I refused the meal. Ironic, isn't it? I'm gagging for Gina. Aching for her. Then along comes a very good-looking woman, with a lovely body, and says yes, please, and I freeze with fear.

I don't think I'm going to tell Gina. I can't.

I need advice.

I'll ring Connor.

I'm on the phone and I've just given Connor chapter and verse.

'Fucking hellfire! Oh, Andy, didn't I warn you this would be after happening?'

'I know, I know. I suppose you think I should tell Gina?'

'Are you barking mad? You tell *any* female that another of her sex threw off her clothes and begged you for it, there's not a woman in the world would believe you didn't grasp the opportunity. Not even your Gina.'

'But I *didn't*.'

'It's beside the point. Most other men would have taken full advantage. Just lay it to rest now, why don't you?'

'What if Michelle says something to Gina?'

'She won't. She'll start off being too busy to see Gina until she's gathered her nerves, and then she'll act like nothing's happened.'

'Well, if you're sure.'

'I am.'

'Oh, God, Connor! It's such a mess. How did I ever let it get to this?'

'Ah, come on now, Andy. Don't be too hard on yourself. Listen, if it makes you feel any better, you're not the only man in the world who's recently made a mistake with a woman.'

'What's-her-name giving you trouble, is she? You know, Ms Save the World and Eat Vegetarian?'

'Correct. Sadly Elisa is no more.'

'Oh. What happened?'

'She ditched me after catching me kicking the cat's backside.'

'You're joking!'

'No. It was dragging a piece of chicken I thought was safely hidden across the kitchen floor, so I sort of double-faulted really.'

He's a good lad, is Connor. Always cheers me up, just in time.

'Listen, now, I have to be getting some work done. Go away and just be thankful the women still fancy an old git like you, OK?'

'OK.'

MIDDLE OF JUNE, 12.30pm.

Things have been calmer of late. A lull after the storm.

A bit of peace. Well, what passes as peace when you have children.

Nicola is in her highchair, finally sated after a large bowl of baby rice and Pure Fruit, two *fromage frais*, three Nice biscuits, topped off with a half-bottle of milk. Still can't get her to eat much in the way of savoury.

She's saying, 'Mama!' and 'Dada!' in turn. Sophie is at the table eating frankfurters, mashed potatoes and carrots, under sufferance.

She's so eccentric. All these things have to be served to her on different dishes. Why? It's all ending up in the same stomach, isn't it?

Sophie broke up from school last Friday, so this is the first day of an agonisingly long summer holiday, during which I have to look after *both* the fruit of my loins from the crack of dawn onwards.

Fortunately, we're actually having a heatwave.

It should make an enormous difference. The garden will become accessible, the kids and I can take a picnic to the beach, and Sophie can burn off as much steam as she needs to in the wide open spaces.

Anyway, I have had my two little darlings for less than a day and I am already screaming '*Submit!*' at the top of my voice. They have been tortuous this morning. I never realised how much energy Sophie must work off at playschool until now.

Today she's been trying to re-create her morning session at home. That's meant we have had to read stories, sing songs and paint pictures.

Actually the last statement is not quite true. She's painted the kitchen table, the walls, the floor, the front of the fridge, the portable telly and, oh . . . Nicola. I've shouted, '*Sophie, no!*' so many times I'm thinking of using it as a refrain for one of my songs.

Nicola is clearly pissed off that Sophie has encroached on her quality time with Daddy. So she has whinged and shouted, 'Dada!' all morning. Which is clever, because as soon as I hear her call, 'Dada!' I go all soppy and give her my attention.

'Daddy?'

'Yes, Sophie?'

'I don't want this.'

'Really? That's sad because you've got to eat it. You don't want another tummy bug, do you? A girl can't live by sweets, crisps and Mini-Rolls alone. Now eat.'

'Wish Mummy was here.' She sulks as she pounds her mashed potatoes with a teaspoon.

'She'd tell you exactly the same, Sophie.'

'Dada!'

'Yes, darling, what is it?'

I'm turning to demanding daughter number two.

'Maybe Nicola would like some frankfurter?'

'No, Sophie. Nicola isn't going to bail you out either. Get back in your chair and eat.'

I'm ageing. Fast.

It's 6.15pm and I'm knackered.

Part of my list of written duties was to take Sophie for a haircut.

Disaster.

Sophie was hysterical, writhing round the floor, screaming, 'Please, Daddy, no, Daddy!'

Frankie, the hairdresser, did his best, but was obviously worried about his trade. If someone walks by a hairdresser's and the screams emanating from within are louder than those from the average dentist's, they're likely to go elsewhere.

So, consequently, Sophie's hair is not a millimetre shorter than when we left.

Mine is. Quite considerably.

I sat in the chair and let nice Frankie run riot with full creative freedom in order to show my darling daughter that it didn't hurt.

Consequently I look like a Latin American rent-boy, and to add insult to injury, Sophie now wants to play hairdressers.

I'm lying on the grass in the garden and blowing raspberries at Nicola. I'm also making 'snip-snip' noises to Sophie at the same time.

Gina has just walked into the garden.

I'm rolling Sophie off my stomach, taking my hair from Nicola's clenched little fist, and shouting, '*I surrender!*' at the top of my voice.

Gina is laughing at me.

'Nice haircut,' she says.

It's about a week later, last week of June? Who cares. I'm a broken man, physically wrecked.

A week flying solo with my two demolition-derby experts and anyone would need a month at a health farm, coupled with intensive psychiatric treatment.

Pin back your ears for this one. Listen up, now. This defies belief.

It is 12.15am and I have just refused sex.

Well! You see, Gina, yes, *Gina*, came in a bit frisky. I don't know if it's the hot weather, or what, but she was definitely in the mood.

And I . . . wasn't.

I'm too tired. My kids have already left me feeling completely fucked. I just couldn't get it up tonight.

Gina has taken it personally. Tonight she is positively sulking.

Next night. About the same time.

It's all right. I haven't become impotent. It still works.

Gina rose to the challenge.

She's lying with her head in my lap at the moment.

'We don't do this often enough, Andy.'

'You're telling me, girl!'

'Not just sex,' she says, playfully slapping my thigh, 'I mean, spend time together. Alone, free from the kids.'

'You're right. I can't remember the last time you and I were by ourselves,' I confess.

'It's just I think we need to make more of an effort with each other. The past few months have been difficult for us both. We seem to be growing apart, Andy.'

At least she recognises this too.

'And I don't think I want that to happen. Not to us.'

She doesn't *think* she wants that to happen?

'I do still love you, you know,' she says, before closing her mouth around me.

Twenty minutes later and my wife is asleep in my arms.

There is not a more beautiful woman or a more sexy body in the whole world. Trust me. I love Gina.

I just wish I could more often.

It's the middle of August.

The sun's shining, but for once I'm not on the beach with my brood, I'm in town.

I've just put Nicola in the pram-stroke-buggy thingy, and I can tell you that is no mean feat in itself—it's like an overgrown puzzle. Anyway, car's parked, pram's up, baby's loaded, Sophie's holding onto said pram and we're off to do bit of shopping.

'Look, Daddy! Look, it's Fozzie.'

So it is. I suppose I'd better have a word.

'Hello, Fozzie, how was Germany?'

'Oh, hi, Andy, good to see you. Yeah, yeah, it was really good, you know, really great, really . . . successful.'

Embarrassed or what?

'How long have you been back?'

'Er, about a week or so, now. Yeah, about that long,' his slightly nasal voice and Essex accent somehow exaggerated by nerves.

Now, Ballinkilty is a small town. Everyone knows everything. I know full well the band has been back for at least a fortnight.

'Oh? Only nobody's rung me.'

'Sorry about that, Andy. Meant to give you a bell. Got a bit sidetracked. You know how it is.'

I wasn't sure, but I'm beginning to get the picture.

'So, Fozzie . . .' I'm not letting him off the hook. I sort of know already, but I just want to hear it. '. . . what's happening about the Sunday-night gigs?'

'Look the thing is, Andy, it's like this. Gerry came in . . .'

'Gerry?'

'A Dubliner. Plays with the Farmer's Boys.'

'Oh, I know, go on.'

'Well,' Fozzie's continuing, 'like I say, Gerry did well on the tour and the lads all like him and that. So . . . the thing is, Andy, it went really well. Germany, I mean. We're going back. But they want the same line-up, you see.'

This isn't Fozzie talking. It's Matt.

'Fozzie, cut to the chase, will you?'

'Yeah, well, right. Look, Matt was supposed to do all this.'

'I bet he was.'

'The thing is, Andy. You're out, man. Sorry, it's nothing personal. Look, I'm really sorry, Andy. I didn't like the idea . . .'

'Fozzie?'

'Yeah?'

'It doesn't matter. Don't upset yourself. It really doesn't matter.'

But it does.

'Yeah. Well, I'd best be off. Catch you around.'

I never knew he could move so fast.

'Aren't you going to be in the group no more, Daddy?'

Ears like radar, Sophie. Even when you think she's not listening.

'No.'

'Ooh, Daddy! What are you going to do?'

It's a good question. Punch Matt? Go to the next gig and heckle?

I have to do something. It's all slipping away. It's just children, housework, children, washing, children, gardening, children.

'I'll tell you what I'm going to do, Sophie. I'm going to buy you a Coke and a packet of crisps and Daddy a pint of Murphy's with a whiskey chaser, and slip a brandy in Nicola's bottle.'

'But, Daddy . . .' She's looking at me earnestly. It unnerves me when she does this.

'. . . I don't think that's very . . . erm? What's the word, Daddy?'

'I shudder to think.'

'Responsible. That's the one, Daddy. It's not very responsible, is it?' she's announcing to me, looking very pleased with herself. 'I might have to phone that woman and tell her.'

'Might you? What woman?'

'Esther. The one from Childline.'

'Childline! Childline, for fuck's sake! Where did you hear about Childline?'

'I'd better have a word with her about your swearing too, Daddy,' she's sighing at me.

'I'll give you Childline, you little horror! Come on.'

'Where are we going, Daddy?'

'I told you. To the pub. We're going to find a payphone and I'm going to ring Esther, then I'm going to beat the crap out of you and hand you the phone so you can complain live on air.'

I'm pretending to strangle her now and she's giggling.

Boy, do I need a drink.

It's about 5.00am.

Nicola's crawling under her baby frame. I'm perched on the edge of the sofa looking at her laughing.

She has a lovely chuckle. So natural. Babies don't look for laughter, search for it frantically, the way an adult does. They don't have to. Joy just comes to them. Little, daft, simple things give them such pleasure.

We lose that, us grown-ups.

By 6.15am, Nicola's nodded off, so I've put her back in her cot.

I should go back to bed, really. I could get another hour maybe before Sophie comes bounding down the stairs.

No point. I wouldn't sleep, so I'm smoking a joint.

I know. It is shameless behaviour at this time of the morning, but I don't get much chance to be shameless any more.

My job now is to be respectable, sensible, the voice of authority and reason for my children. Now my last dabblings at being an artist have disappeared with my sacking from the Blow-ins. It hurts. I feel desolate.

I look at Nicola, and I think. Yes, she loves me now because I'm funny and I feed her and I love her and look after her. But what happens when she's in the playground and everybody's comparing their daddies' jobs? What will she say? Will she be proud of Daddy then?

Sophie could face that pretty soon.

I feel so depressed. Time has all but run out.

You could count the grains in the top half of the hourglass on one tiny hand.

Saturday, back end of August, 3.00pm.

I'm changing Nicola's scutty bottom on the floor in the lounge. Gina is hovering over me, nit-picking.

The attempt at rekindling our love lasted for about a day. Then it was back to sniping at each other.

'Oh, Andy, look at Nicola's little bottom. It's red-raw. Have you been changing her regularly?'

'Like clockwork, Gina. She's teething. You know she gets a little sore when she's teething.'

'That nappy rash will never dry up if you don't let her run about without a nappy for a bit. Get some air to it.'

She says this in a you-don't-have-a-clue-how-to-look-after-a-baby-like-I-do way.

She's thinking this. Needless to say, she does not say it.

'Couldn't you be a little gentler putting on her little tights?'

I'm biting my lip.

'Wouldn't it be easier to slip that little suit over her head than hauling it up over her hips like that, Andy?'

'She hates having her face covered. It's best to avoid it.'

'She's never going to learn that way. She won't be able to pull all her clothes on over her hips when she gets older, will she?'

I'm gritting my teeth.

'Well, you fucking dress her, then. Do something constructive instead of sitting on your arse criticising.'

'Sorry, Andy, I didn't mean—'

'Didn't you? It's the weekend. I spend all week doing this. Why don't you take over for a change?'

'I will. Happily. I am her mother, after all.'

'Oh, really? There was me thinking I was.'

'That's not fair. If you earned any bloody money then I'd be happy to stay at home and look after my children.'

'I haven't noticed you barging me out of the way, nappy in hand. You haven't moved from in front of your bloody computer today.'

'I can't help it. I've got work to do.'

'Why have you? Shit! You spend enough hours working overtime.'

'Because the magazine's struggling, and if I don't pull it round it'll go under, just like the first one. Then we're really fucked, Andy.'

'Really fucked? Interesting choice of phrase. I can't remember what it feels like to be *really fucked*.'

'Oh, that's just typical. Why do you have to talk about sex every time we argue?'

'Because it's the only type of oral sex I get to indulge in, these days.'

'And if you had a bloody job, earning decent money, I might not be working myself to death and I could find the energy for sex.'

'Well, I work my arse off all day and I still—'

Silence.

I think we both realised simultaneously.

Sophie is standing in the doorway.

'Mummy? What's all the noise about?'

'Nothing, darling, nothing at all.'

'But I heard you shouting. It was *very* loud.'

'Oh, that was just Daddy getting carried away.'

Thanks, Gina.

'Yes. Just silly Daddy, Sophie. I was telling Mummy about the goal my footie team scored and I got a bit excited. I'm a twit, aren't I?'

I hate lying to my kids.

Sophie looks calmer for the explanation.

'You are a twit, Daddy. Football's boring, isn't it, Mummy?'

'Yes, darling, it is. Now, how about some tea and biscuits?' she's saying, as she steers Sophie back into the kitchen, pausing to shoot me a concerned look over her shoulder.

Damn! I wonder how much she heard?

It's 11.00pm. I'm in bed. Alone.

Gina is downstairs talking to her mother, my number one fan, on the telephone.

I know what's being said. Within a little.

Sylvia's slagging me off and the brainwashing usually takes its toll, especially in the current Cold War climate of our relationship.

Only one thing can stop it. Success. I need my music to bring some success.

I have to find some time for me. Otherwise all this time spent being the little woman at home, trying to keep the marriage together, will have been academic. Because I'll lose them all anyway.

I can feel it.

Not much longer now.

Following Tuesday, 6.00pm.

Gina's just telephoned. She's got to work late again. This is the second night on the trot.

It's such a pisser!

Now I've got to get everyone's supper, bathe the little buggers all by myself, make bottles, pyjama Sophie, Babygro Nicola, put them to bed, read stories . . .

God, this is bringing me down.

Wednesday, 7.30am.

Nicola's recently back in her cot.

Sophie is still asleep.

Gina's up, though. She's just brought us a couple of mugs of tea into the lounge. She looks pale and stressed.

'So what exactly did you have to do last night?' I'm asking as she hands me a mug and sits on the sofa next to me.

'Eileen was sick. I had to stand in. I was interviewing a girl who's just had her first book published at the age of sixteen.'

'It seems to be happening rather a lot lately.'

'You're telling me! I'm the one who is having to do three hundred jobs at once to hold together a magazine that has a smaller circulation than your average pamphlet. You think I'm enjoying this, Andy? You think I like working in a shit job just so I can provide this family with a living wage?'

'That's all it is now, isn't it? Work, kids and money worries,' I say, shaking my head in frustration.

She takes my hand. 'Neither of us is happy with our lot, Andy. I feel guilty and depressed because I'm not looking after my kids, and you feel terrible because you're not the one earning the money. I want my old Andy back. The proud, funny, talented, unique man I married.'

'I don't know where he is. If you find him, let me know.'

'Andy, darling. I didn't mean—'

I feel my head exploding with sudden, uncontrollable rage. 'Well, Gina, of course I've changed. I mean, look at me. The old Andy was not a man in a vinyl bloody pinny. He was a musician, and a bloody good one at that. He had hopes and dreams and ambition and . . . and I'll tell you something else. The old Andy would not have sat around staring at bits of bloody litmus paper waiting to see if they turned pink. He would have been on that plane with the rest of his band grasping probably the last chance he'll ever get to salvage some fucking pride!'

She looks confused.

'You mean the tour?'

'Yes, of course I mean the tour.'

'But you told me the rest of the band didn't want you to go. You said they never gave you the choice.'

'Yeah, well, I lied. They kicked me out when I turned the tour down. I put you and the kids first, Gina. It's what I do. Only you seem to have conveniently forgotten that.'

Gina is sobbing now and I feel like a total and utter bastard. Why didn't I keep my big mouth shut about the tour? I should never have mentioned it.

The fact is, I've hurt her.

And I've never wanted to do that.

It's all getting out of hand.

SUNNY SEPTEMBER. We're talking Indian summer here. Often the case in this neck of the woods, according to local legend. The minute the kids go back to school you can guarantee the sun will shine. I've started a petition suggesting we send the little buggers back on August 1.

It's about 10.30am. Sophie started back at playschool today and I can almost hear the sigh of relief from my weary body.

We're having a cup of coffee in the little teashop that's attached to the local supermarket. Well, obviously Nicola isn't having a cup of coffee. She is, however, getting into an extraordinary mess with a chocolate éclair I bought for her. I probably shouldn't have, but she grabbed it off the plate on the top of the counter. Once she had her grubby paws on it I felt obliged to pay for the ruddy thing.

Actually, I'm completely overexcited.

Stanley Clarke is coming to Ballinkilty. I couldn't believe it when I saw the poster, but it's true.

I mentioned this to Connor last night and he said, 'Who the fuck is Stanley Clarke?'

Dear, dear, what gaps we have in our education today.

Stanley Clarke is recognised as one of the greatest bass-guitar players in the world. I'm tingling with anticipation.

I keep looking at Nicola, burying her face in the cream and saying, 'Ooh, Nicola, can you believe Stanley Clarke is coming to westie Corkie? Isn't it exciting? Are you excited, Daddy's girl? Are you?'

She's clearly not heard of him either.

Connor also said, 'So, Andy, if he's the bee's bollocks, like you say he is, what's he doing playing a folk club in Ballinkilty, now?'

A fair question. A favour, I would guess. Unless he's on one of those hey-I-want-to-get-back-to-basics-playing-to-small-audiences-to-get-back-on-track kind of trips. They do that, don't they? Successful musicians. I won't. When I get there it'll be Shea Stadium or you can sod off. I want to be a pinprick in the distance to someone who's forked out a week's wages just to see me play live.

Trouble is, he's playing tonight. One night only.

That means, when Gina walks through the door, moaning and groaning and bitching on about how tired she is, I'm going to have some serious grovelling to do.

It's 6.30pm. I've been in a state of exuberance all day.

Neither Sophie nor Nicola can understand the sunny-natured man that has taken care of them. Sophie even went as far as asking, 'Are you all right, Daddy?' Makes you wonder if I'm that awful on a normal day, doesn't it?

One problem: no sign of Gina.

I'm running out of time to be charming, understanding and helpful before appealing to her generous nature.

Nicola's in bed, Sophie's in her pyjamas and still no sign of Mummy, although it's 7.20pm. I've checked the answering machine, in case I was in the bathroom or bringing the coal in, or something, when the phone rang.

Nothing.

Phone's ringing. I have a bad feeling about this.

Sophie's answered the phone in the kitchen.

'Oh! It's Mummy, Daddy.'

I'll have to wait. If I rush Sophie off the telephone now, she'll have a major tantrum.

'Yes, yes. Fine. That's OK, Mummy. Yes, bye!'

She's just blown a kiss and put the bloody receiver down.

'Sophie! What are you doing?'

'It's OK, Daddy. I've finished speaking to Mummy now.'

It's ringing again.

There's no sodding justice in the world. Tonight of all nights.

The telephone conversation went like this:

'Hello?'

'Andy. It's me. What happened?'

'Sophie hung up.'

'Little devil.'

'Why aren't you home?'

'I've got to work late again.'

'You can't. Not tonight, Gina.'

'I've no choice, Andy.'

'But, Gina, you see there's this gig—'

'Take the photos across to the opera house. They've asked for approval before we can print.'

'*What?* Gina, what are you going on about?'

'Sorry, darling. I wasn't talking to you.'

'Well, I'm trying to tell you something.'

'What's that, then? No, *now,* Katrina. Straight away.'

'Gina!'

'Sorry, Andy. You were saying?'

'Look, there's this bass-player—'

'Katrina, don't go without taking this!'

'Gina. Stanley Clarke is playing in Ballinkilty tonight. It's a one-off—'

'I'm sorry, Andy, I've got to go. I'm really busy.'

'Oh fuck it! I'll see you later.'

Then I followed my daughter's example and I hung up.

It's just not bloody fair.

I tried ringing Deirdre to baby sit, but she's studying for mock exams. I gave Noreen a call, apparently she's in Limerick visiting her aunt. I even gave Connor a buzz. Well, the kids know him and he wouldn't have had to do much.

No answer—wouldn't you have guessed?

I really want to see this gig.

I'm in charge, am I not?

'Sophie. How do you fancy coming out to listen to some live music with your old daddy?'

'But I'm in my PJs, Daddy.'

'I'll pull some clothes on over the top.'

'Erm . . . OK.'

That's settled it, then.

It's 9.00pm, and I think I may be responsible for causing something of a stir.

I've just walked into the pub with a four-year-old hanging onto my shirt-tails and my arms full of baby.

To add to the equation, I have a Pooh Bear changing-bag slung over my shoulder like a badly chosen accessory.

It is perfectly common, in a child-orientated society such as the one we have in west Cork, for parents to take their children into the boozer at lunchtime. Ditto early evening. It is not exactly unheard-of for those same children still to be trying to drag their mater and pater away from the bar at nine o'clock at night. It is unusual, however, for someone to *arrive* at the pub with sprogs in tow at this hour.

The landlord is giving me black looks.

Tough. In the past, I've worked hard entertaining his punters for peanuts while his bar takings double, so he can't lodge a complaint now.

I'm moving through to the folk club. I've just commandeered a couple of seats at the back.

Matt and Fozzie are in the front row, I see.

Johan's not here. He must be waiting on tables to get a bit of spending money together for the tour.

Unless they've given him the boot as well.

It's 11.30pm and I'm trying to make a fast exit. Two reasons. First, I'm in a real rush to get home to Gina. When you're on Death Row with no hope of a reprieve, you want them to break the gas pellet as fast as possible. Second, my children have no social graces whatsoever.

Maybe it's my fault. Partly, at least. After all, it's my job to teach them things. Basically, they're the sort of people who are likely to keep Club 18–30 holidays in existence well into the next century.

I'll begin with Nicola.

The first number began and Nicola shot up. Bolt upright.

Boy, did she scream!

First number and I had to take her out.

I asked a young, spotty pseudo-hippie to keep an eye on Sophie for me and I took Nicola out into the main bar.

Then I'm panicking because I've left Sophie in there and I have visions of her being kidnapped or something.

I calm Nicola down by walking round the bar singing 'Bare Necessities' to her, I take her back in and Sophie is fine. Not only oblivious to my absence, but she's standing on the chair, shaking her bum in time with the music. This, much to the annoyance of the punters behind her who can't see a thing but Sophie's *derrière*.

I persuade her to sit and just as things seemed to have settled down, Nicola decided she had another trick up her sleeve.

Or, should I say, up her nappy?

I was cradling her in my arms listening to a great bass riff when Nicola decided to play one of her own. Moments later, people all over the place were sniffing disgustedly and looking for the feckin' dog in order to give it a good kicking.

She began complaining bitterly about this, so I begged assistance from the pseudo-hippie once more and ran out with my Pooh Bear bag to change her.

The pub is not exactly packed with facilities for such things. Consequently, I had to change her on my lap in the gents, while my own posterior rested on the only toilet.

Murphy's Law said somebody would bang on the door, urgently requiring somewhere to lodge his deposit, and sure enough, they did.

The technicalities of changing a bum while sitting on the loo are difficult enough. If someone is banging on the door enquiring what is going on, suggesting scenarios as diverse as masturbation to a *ménage à trois*, the pressure is frightening. Fingers and thumbs cease to function.

Therefore, by the time I staggered past the aggressor, apologising profusely, Nicola may have been clean, but my jeans were not.

The pong may have lessened, but it had certainly not disappeared. Upon our return, even the hippie had the gall to move his chair a few significant inches away from my own.

And that was just number two daughter's contribution.

Here are a few edited highlights, from my first-born:

'Daddy, I can't understand what they're saying.'

'Daddy, why does that man pull such funny faces when he's singing?'

'Daddy, why does that man tell boring stories between all them songs?'

And, the most cringe-making of all:

'DADDY, THAT MAN'S BLACK, ISN'T HE, DADDY?'

Oh, God!

Now let's get one thing straight. Neither Gina nor I have a single racist bone in our bodies. The simple truth is, west Cork has extremely few people of African or Asian descent.

As Sophie pointed out, in an incredibly booming voice for one so young, 'YOU DON'T SEE MANY OF THEM ROUND HERE, DO YOU, DADDY?'

So there you have it. In one evening my children have destroyed any respect, reputation and love I may have enjoyed in Ballinkilty.

'Daddy, can we go home, now?' Sophie's asking me, unsteady on her feet through sheer exhaustion.

'Of course we can, Stinks. Right away.'

We're in the car park at 11.40pm.

I'm holding Nicola under one arm and dragging poor Sophie to our car with the other hand.

'Daddy?'

'Yes, Stinks?'

'Daddy, why is the car next to ours moving up and down like that?'

She's right. It's a Nissan of some kind. I half recognise it from somewhere. It's bouncing up and down as though it were epileptic.

'I don't know.'

Yes, I do. My memory is flashing me a mental picture of a car or two of mine rocking and rolling like that.

'Daddy, there's people in there. What are they doing, Daddy?'

No! I don't want her to see this.

'Never mind, Sophie. We're in a rush,' I say, as I bundle her into her car chair, then strap Nicola in the back.

I'm walking round to the driver's door and I can't resist taking a closer look.

They're using the back seat. The woman is crumpled up against the door closest to me.

Blimey! He's giving it some stick! If he's not careful—

OH, LORDY! What did I tell you? The door nearest me has opened and the woman's tumbled backwards. She's stopped herself falling, putting her hands on the ground, her very impressive breasts tumbling towards her chin.

'Sorry, don't mind me,' I'm saying, stifling a laugh.

Shit. I recognise those breasts.

'Michelle.'

'Hello, Andy,' she's replying, as she disengages herself from the man, pulls down her top and clambers out of the car.

The man has not moved. I can now see his face.

I thought I recognised the car.

'Johan?'

'Oh, fok! Hello, Andy. Sorry about this. Luffly to see you again.'

No wonder he wasn't at the bloody gig.

'I suppose you'll tell Norman,' Michelle snaps at me.

'No, I won't. But you have to admit it's not very fair to him. I mean, in a car park! You know what this town's like for gossip.'

'So, if I'd been discreet, like some others I could mention, that would have been all right, would it?'

'I didn't say that.'

'Oh, piss off, and don't look so bloody smug. I'm not the only wife fucking another man behind her husband's back, dear!'

'What do you mean by that?!'

'Daddy, I can see Johan's bum!'

Shit! Sophie. She's round the other side of Johan's car, having escaped from her car chair.

'Come away, Sophie.'

Michelle's face has changed. The aggression has gone. What's replaced it? Is that shame?

'I'm sorry, Andy,' she's saying, as she gets into Johan's car.

'But, Dad?' Sophie's saying as she reaches me. 'Why *is* Johan's bum hanging out of his trousers?'

'I don't know, Sophie,' I'm saying, as I load her into the car, strapping her in this time.

'Don't they fit properly, Dad?'

'Erm . . .'

'Perhaps a bee stung him on his botty,' she says, giggling, 'and Michelle had to suck the poison out. Yuck!'

'That's exactly right,' I'm agreeing as I start the car.

I'm racing home. Both daughters have passed out, thankfully.

'I'm not the only wife fucking another man behind her husband's back.'

That's what Michelle said, wasn't it?

What did she say on the day I rejected her advances?

'You deserve to get hurt.'

Am I putting two and two together and making five?

My mind is racing, searching for clues.

Is Gina . . .?

I must get home. I've got to find out.

It's 12.10am, and I've just driven down our lane and have rather unusually passed a car coming the other way. I half thought, for the second time this evening, that I recognised the car. For one daft minute I thought Johan had sprinted home ahead of me on his rounds, servicing the frustrated wives of . . .

But that's just me being paranoid. It's probably Gina's taxi.

Suppose I'd better pop my head round the door and hope it stays on my shoulders long enough to get the children out of the car.

Besides, I've a question or two of my own to ask.

It's 12.25am. I've just unwrapped Nicola and put her to bed. Gina is currently doing the same with Sophie.

'I'm going to bed,' she says.

'Gina, don't go . . .'

'I just want to say that I can't believe you did that, Andy. You can't justify this. It's outrageous.'

'Tosh! Overreaction. The children came to no harm. They were well looked after. Sophie had a good time.'

'This wasn't about Sophie having a good time. It was about Andy Lawrence doing what he wanted to do.'

'And where the fuck were you, Gina? Tell me that?'

'I was—no, hold on a minute. You're not turning this one round and making me feel guilty.'

'Look, I've spent the last ten months doing nothing but putting the kids' needs before my own. This was *one* night, Gina, and they're fine. Unharmed. So where's the fire?'

She's sighing. 'I'm not going to argue with you, Andy. Whatever you say, you'll never convince me you weren't way out of line tonight.'

Door slammed.

I've just been completely sidetracked.

Perhaps that's not a bad thing. I mean, what if I'm wrong? Michelle could be just be making mischief. If that's the case I could open up a whole set of wounds we just don't need right now.

I'm sat up in bed at 1.25am.

It's been a backs-to-each-other night, you'll not be surprised to hear.

That's not why I am now sat upright.

I've just realised something.

The car that brought Gina home.

That wasn't a taxi. I recognised that motor.

It was Connor's.

It was Connor's car that brought Gina home, after midnight, tonight.

I HAVE TO ASK.

I've been awake all night thinking about it, my imagination running riot. Is my suspicious mind warping the perfectly innocent?

Gina's stood in the kitchen, looking extraordinarily beautiful.

I have a strong feeling that I am on dangerous territory. I may hear things I do not wish to.

Well, here goes:

'Gina? I want to ask you something.'

'If it's a favour, Andy, I'd advise you not to.'

'No, it isn't.'

'Go on, then, out with it,' she's urging me, as she puts her cup down on the work surface.

'How come Connor brought you home last night?'

'What makes you think he did?'

'Are you saying he didn't?'

She looks flushed.

'No. He called me to say he was going out for a drink after work and couldn't take me home. I told him I was working late. So he said he'd swing by the office when he'd finished partying and see if I was still there.'

'And?'

'And I was. I told him I had a taxi booked, but you know how insistent he is. I've never been so petrified in all my life. He's not the safest driver *before* he's had a few. We were all over the road. That's why I was so tense when I arrived home last night, if I'm honest.'

But she's not being honest. I know this woman very well.

'I know you're lying to me, Gina. You're having an affair with Connor, aren't you?'

Time has slowed down. I seem to be waiting hours for Gina to reply, yet I know by the time she speaks only seconds will have passed.

I hear the clock ticking, the fridge-freezer whirring, the heating clanking. But these are silent compared to the sound of my own blood, rushing round my veins and gathering weight in my temples.

I look at her. There are the beginnings of tears in her eyes.

Perhaps I'd rather not have hit this particular nail on the head. I think I would happily have missed and struck myself across the wrist. The pain would have been considerably easier to live with.

'I . . .' she's wringing her hands. 'Andy. It's not quite as bad as it seems.'

Howling from the bedroom above.

'Baby's awake,' Gina's saying, wiping her eyes with the back of her hands. 'You get her up. I'll make a couple of fast calls and we'll go somewhere and talk. Away from the kids.'

I'm cradling Nicola in my arms. I don't want to let her go. I'm not sure how long I'll be doing this. Not here, anyway.

I'm back in the lounge now with Nicola, and Sophie's up now, cuddling Gina.

'Mummy's been crying, Daddy. She banged her toe. But it's all right now 'cos I kissed it better.'

'Thank you, Sophie. Good girl.'

Gina's stroking Sophie's hair.

'I know what will cheer you up, Mummy.'

'What's that, darling?' Gina's asking.

'Daddy and I can tell you all about the concert we watched last night. It was dead good, wasn't it, Daddy?'

'It was.'

'Yes, Mummy. It was real, live music. You could see them sweating and everything, couldn't you, Dad?'

'You could, Sophie.'

'Thing is, though, they didn't play any tunes I knew, did they, Dad? The men didn't play no Boyzone or Spice Girls or Smurfs or anything. So, you see, that bit wasn't so good.'

'Well, still sounds fantastic. Mummy's sorry she missed it.'

'And then, when we got to the car park . . .'

'Sophie! You can tell Mummy the rest later.'

'But, Dad—'

'Listen, Sophie,' Gina interrupts her, 'Mummy has a surprise for you.'

'A surprise!'

'Calm down! It's not that exciting. Noreen is coming round to see you in an hour or so.'

'Is she going to look after me again?'

A painful exchange of glances between Gina and me.

'I don't know about that, she's just going to play with you for a few hours while Daddy and I pop into Ballinkilty to have a chat.'

'Why can't you just chat to Daddy here? Silly.'

'Well, we've a bit of business to sort out. We won't be long. Then I'll come home and play with you, darling. I've taken the day off.'

'Oh. OK.'

A bit of business to sort out.

Yes indeed.

Must be a bit after nine o'clock. Approximately.

Duneen beach.

Not a massive beach, but big enough. Very beautiful and, when virtually empty as it is now, very serene and peaceful.

Gina and I are sat next to each other on my coat, retrieved from the boot of the car where it's spent the summer in hibernation.

We haven't spoken yet.

Gina has lit two cigarettes and passed one to me and we've smoked in silence.

'How long have you known?' she's asking me.

'I didn't know. I just suspected. Then we bumped into Michelle last night. We caught her humping Johan in the back of his car—'

'What?'

'I know. It seems infidelity is catching, doesn't it? That's what Sophie was about to tell you this morning.' I'm pausing as I stub out my cigarette on a rock. 'In her embarrassment yesterday, your friend hinted she was not alone in seeking satisfaction elsewhere.'

'Bitch!'

'Yes. You can't trust anyone these days, can you?' I say pointedly. 'Even then I was tempted to dismiss it as shit-stirring. Then on the drive home I began to think. Little nigglings: the way Connor continually told me how beautiful and wonderful you were, the fact he always saw your side of the argument, not mine. Then I've rung him a few times when you've been working late, just to see if he fancied popping round for a chat or to watch a football match. He's never been there, of course. And when I suddenly realised it was his car last night . . .'

She's silent.

'It's over. I finished it last night.'

'What does it matter? The damage is done. You fucked him, didn't you?'

'Andy, please . . .'

'Didn't you?'

'Yes, all right. I admit it. I fucked Connor. There. Happy now?'

This hurts, it really hurts! There can be no greater physical pain. No disease can rampage through you like this.

'How many times?'

'Shit, Andy. I wasn't keeping count. What difference does it make?'

'It does to me. Because I'm humiliated, Gina. All those times you've found it so easy to say no to me, all those nights of sexual rejection and then Mr Sensitive comes along and your knickers hit the ground faster than a dropped crystal glass. So I want to know. I want all the gory details. When did it begin? Where were you when you did it the first time? Did he go down on you? Is he a better screw than me? Is that why you let him have you?'

'STOP! STOP! STOP!'

She's crying.

'I'm sorry, Andy. I really am.'

'That's it, is it? I'm supposed to peck you on the cheek and say, "Never mind, all's well that ends well", am I?'

'No, of course not.'

'Gina, there is not a worse scenario than your wife and one of your best friends. It's such a sodding cliché. Like one of those photo-stories in that tacky little magazine you edit.'

I know. I can't help being vicious. Not now. I want to hurt her. I want revenge for the way she's making me feel.

'It's a standard, isn't it? The boss and the secretary. The teacher and the pupil. I know, I'll go home and give Noreen a seeing-to, and we can have the husband and the nanny as well.'

'Look, Andy, I have had an affair with Connor. I've admitted it. But what's more important is why I did it and what *we* are going to do now?'

'So why did you, Gina? Why did you cheat on me? Why did you find Connor so irresistible? You tell me.'

She's lighting another cigarette. She looks tired, suddenly. Weary.

'Because he's so capable! So . . . in control. It's difficult to explain. Well, it goes back a long way, really. You're not the man I married now, Andy. You're not fun any more. You've lost your . . . charisma. You've become bitter, Andy. Depressed. Maybe looking after the children . . . maybe it's taken you even lower.'

'So that's why you slept with Connor?'

'Yes, in a way. Because Connor is what you *used* to be. He's a poorer version, but he's witty and charming and bright and attentive and—'

'And rich and successful and powerful—'

'Oh,' she shrugs, 'maybe.'

I'm lighting another cigarette. I'm feeling empty, drained.

Gina continues. 'I love you, Andy—'

'Oh, that's fucking obvious.'

'—and I know you love me—'

'Do you now?'

'—but I'm not sure if we're *in* love with each other any more.'

Slam!

My guts are torn.

People are starting to arrive on the beach.

We stay quiet until the last of them are out of earshot.

'Maybe we both need a bit of space,' she's saying. 'It's probably easier to see things clearly if we're apart. Maybe I should go back to England.'

'It doesn't matter, Gina. Problems do not disappear just because you move house. They travel on the van with you, along with the fridge, and the telly and the bathroom bloody mirror.'

'I know, I know,' she says, tugging at her hair, 'but I still think we need thinking-time apart. I'll move out,' she's announcing, 'take the kids.'

'Wait a minute, those are my children too!'

'I know, Andy. I promise you, I don't ever want to take your children away from you.'

'You can't take them away from the house, Gina. It's their home. Look, I accept we need some time to sort out this mess. So maybe I'm the one who should go. We'll have to talk some more tonight. I can't talk any more now.'

I've stood up and I'm making my way back to the car, leaving Gina to follow me . . . at least, I presume she's following me.

I'm not stopping to check.

I'm parked just round the corner from my house.

I've dropped Gina off.

I couldn't go in. Not just yet.

I won't let my children see me cry.

My world has just folded.

I have nothing left now.

Except . . .

There's somebody I want to visit.

My wrist hurts.

I've practically broken it hammering on Connor's door.

He's not in. Unless he's cowering in a corner somewhere.

It's a nice house. A big house right on the water at Ross Carbery. No leaking roofs or dodgy heating systems here.

Maybe he's at work.

No point in hanging about outside. I'll go back to the car.

'Is it Connor you're after?'

A man in wellies clutching a pair of hedge-clippers has appeared from goodness knows where.

'It is.'

'You'll have a bit of a wait, I'm thinking. He's off abroad. Business. He'll be gone a couple of months or more.'

'I see. Thanks anyway.'

'No problem.'

Out of the country. How bloody convenient.

It's Friday. It's been two days now since I found out.

We've talked a little, Gina and I, but I keep walking out in the middle of the conversation. I get upset, or angry, or frightened.

I'm finding it difficult to think of a life without . . .

Oh, well, early days.

It's Saturday lunchtime.

Three days since the earth was pulled from under my feet.

I'm still scratching about trying to find a foothold.

We're in a pub garden having a drink.

Gina's idea. She's inside getting another round.

The sun is still shining. Nicola is in her buggy, parked in the shade. She's chuckling and waving her arms while watching the chaos Sophie and half-a-dozen newfound friends are making, desperate to join in.

They're playing on the boards still in place after the last ceilidh. Sophie's attempts at Irish dancing have to be seen to be believed. Doesn't stop her bowing stupendously. She's such an actress.

Gina's just returned with the drinks.

'Andy, I know you find it hard to talk, but we have to come to a decision. I think we definitely need some time apart.'

'Yes, I know, I've said already. I'll go.'

'Have you thought what you'll do for money?'

'No. Get a job. Sign on.'

'We'd probably have to legally separate straight away in order for you to receive enough benefit to live on.'

I hadn't thought of that. Shit! The ramifications just go on and on.

She's pausing, thinking, before she continues. 'Unless?'

'Unless what?'

'I've had a thought. You're going to need somewhere to live right? And you're going to have to pay for that. It could get awkward. There's not much employment in this town, and you don't have transport.'

She's right. This just gets worse and worse.

'Can I run an idea past you, Andy? Just to see how it sounds?' Gina's asking me, as Nicola's patience runs out and I lift her out of the buggy.

'Go on, then.'

'What if you carried on looking after the children in our house. You find a flat or something in Ballinkilty and I'll pay you a wage to look after the kids.'

'I can't take money for looking after my own children!'

'I know, but if you don't look after them I'm still going to have to pay somebody else to do the job. And you know what Sophie's like. She loves her daddy. It's going to be hard for her to deal with someone else.'

'You're emotionally blackmailing me, Gina.'

'I don't mean to. But you must see the sense of it? The money I give you will pay for the flat and your keep, just about. Then we wouldn't have to involve anyone else. Not until we're certain what we're going to do. Say yes, Andy. Please. Not for me. For the kids.'

What choice do I have? If you look at the cold facts. I said I'll do it.

'Daddy! Look, Daddy! Look at Nicola!'

I'm looking at Nicola and she's walking . . . teetering towards her older sister.

Her first steps.

I'm turning to Gina.

And she's crying as she watches.

Back at the house, it's 3.15pm.

Not sure if it's even *my* house any more.

In front of the children it's as if Gina and I were in a play. We pretend to be the perfect couple, behaving as if everything was just fine. Then when the kids have gone to bed it's like living in a library.

Silence. Afraid to speak in case it breaks the rules.

I'm supposed to be sleeping in the spare room. But I spend most nights pacing about . . . thinking.

Today, however, I've thrown myself a lifeline.

I've just been to see Dan, who owns O'Leary's.

I bought him drinks and I argued with him. I bullied him, blackmailed him, until I came out with what I wanted.

A Monday night's residency. Trial period for a month. Starting at the end of October. Just me and a guitar. It'll be tough. Monday night is the graveyard shift, but I have complete autonomy. I decide what I play.

It's a golden chance to air some of my songs.

It'll help fill the time.

Stop me thinking.

Strange. I don't actually have to clear it with Gina, do I?

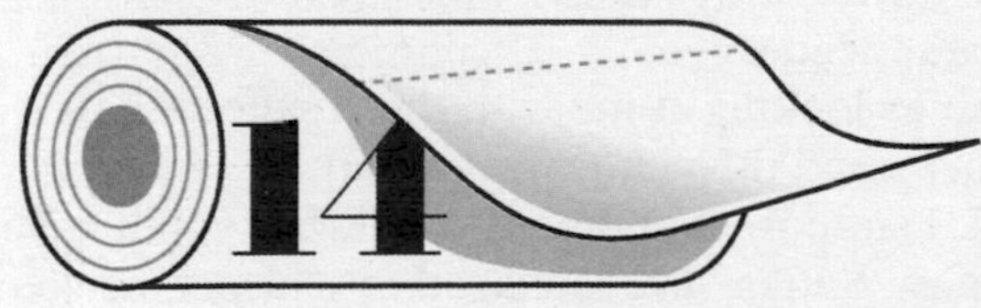

IT'S 10.30AM, Tuesday, October the something or other. Mid-ish in the month.

I've found a box to live in. Nearly thirty-nine years old and I'm moving into a sodding bedsit.

It's nicely situated, though. Slap-bang in the middle of town, a few doors away from O'Leary's where I'm going to be playing. Big window overlooking the street. A minimalist's dream residence.

Shit! Who am I kidding? It's so depressing, you'd still want to weep even if the room were filled with laughing gas.

I've negotiated a reasonable out-of-season rent, although my landlord informs me he will want me out of here by next May because he can get double the money from some poor, unsuspecting tourist. I haven't got the strength to argue. It's taken me weeks to find this.

The landlord's given me the key and left me here to make a decision.

7.15pm.

Nicola's tucked up in her cot. The rest of us are in the lounge. Sophie is standing in front of Gina and me, scratching her head. Mummy and Daddy are at opposite ends of the sofa. Like oversized bookends.

'Why can't you do your work *here,* Daddy? Like you always do?'

'I have to concentrate really hard, Sophie. If I'm here in the evenings I'll just flop in front of the television, as usual.'

'But when will you come back, Daddy?'

'Well, in some ways, Sophie, I won't really be going away. I'll be here before Mummy goes to work and won't leave until Mummy gets home. So I'll still spend the days with you and Nicola.'

'But, Dad! When will you see *Mummy*?'

Oh, God! I'd hoped she wouldn't ask that. Why do we adults continually underestimate our children? A child instinctively knows when something is wrong. They sense it.

'It's going to be difficult for Mummy and Daddy, Sophie,' Gina's chipping in. 'But it probably won't take long. Nobody's saying it will be for ever.'

Oh, really, Gina?

'Just until Daddy's finished his work?'

'That's the idea.'

Sophie's looking at me with those saucer-shaped eyes.

I can't stand this. It's tearing me apart.

'OK. I suppose it will be all right. But you'll have to be quick, Dad.'

'I know, Stinks,' I've managed to whisper, brokenly.

'Can I watch a video?'

'Yes, go on.'

I've noticed something.

Sophie often wants to watch a video when things are not quite right.

If she's unsettled, she likes to drift off into another world, handed to her on a plate by the screen in the corner of the room.

11.30pm.

I'm in my little garret in town. I've been here three days. Well, nights, really.

I haven't settled.

Maybe I *should* move back to London.

No. I can't.

I'd still be a failure, you see.

I'd have to be somebody, achieve something big before I moved back.

Plus the fact my children are here.

I miss them at night.

I'm still bawling my eyes out pathetically as I go home every evening. Everything feels empty. I can't get used to not running up and down the stairs to check that the babies are OK.

Then I try to sleep.

Trouble is, I'm soaked in the habit of keeping one ear cocked in case Nicola wakes.

Night shifts. They're going to kill Gina. Still, I suppose that's her problem. I've got to try to stop caring. After all, she's stopped caring about me.

My work isn't really happening either.

I was used to writing in an atmosphere of natural chaos. Interruptions from Sophie or the baby, Gina or the telephone have become part of the creative process. I've spent years thinking how wonderful it would be if I had the time and solitude to concentrate on my compositions and now all this silence is driving me up the wall.

Find yourself with an unexpectedly large amount of time to think and you start to brood.

Trust me.

11.45am.

Day four of my part-time exile.

I'm in the car with the children. I'm to have the car during the week. Gina has found another spin to Cork, a woman this time. So, unless she fancies seeing how the other half live, we should be safe from any more scandal.

Not that it matters any more.

Day four and the word is definitely out.

Gossip. A major drawback of living in a town this size. Everyone knows your business. I had not been installed in my broom cupboard five minutes before I was the recipient of sympathetic stares and concerned enquiries.

I have never been so embarrassed.

Today they started treating my kids like the children of Chernobyl—over-friendly, over-concerned, over-the-top.

Sophie's never had so many free lollipops and punt coins pressed into her sweaty paws in all her life. If this keeps up, Gina and I could retire and become her managers. She's completely bemused.

We're driving home. To my *old* home. Sophie's eyebrows are furrowing in exactly the same way her mother's do.

There's a question coming. I know it.

'Daddy, why does everybody keep talking in that funny way to me? Why did that woman keep saying, "Are you all right, Sophie?" '

'I don't know. I expect she was concerned about you.'

'Why? Do I look a bit sick, Dad?'

'Not to me.'

A thinking pause.

'Dada, Dada, DADA!'

'Yes, Nicola darling, Daddy's here.'

'Why did that woman call Nicola a big brave girl, Daddy?'

'Search me, Sophie.'

'I mean, she hasn't *rescued* anybody, has she Daddy?' She's shaking her head.

'No.'

'She's not had any nasty medicine or put a fire out, has she, Daddy?'

'Not that I'm aware.'

'So she's not brave, then, is she, Daddy?'

'No.'

She's looking out of the window now.

I'm not convinced the interrogation is over.

'Dad?'

Told yer.

'Yes, Stinks.'

'Er . . . Dad? What does dee-force mean?'

'Sounds like something out of *Star Wars*. I don't know, what does it mean?'

'I don't know, that's why I'm asking you, silly! When I told Richard you were living in Ballinkilty he said Mummy and you were going to buy a dee-force.'

Oh, fuck, fuck, FUCK!

'So you must know what it is if Mummy and you are going to buy one.'

'I don't think we are, Sophie. We probably couldn't afford it anyway.

Shall we pop into the sweet shop by the supermarket?'

I'm swinging into the car park off the roundabout.

I know I'm avoiding the issue, but I just can't handle this.

Not now.

It's too soon.

6.15pm.

Gina's home.

Sophie's just leapt off my lap to go and hug her.

Nicola's on the floor tearing today's newspaper to shreds.

'How've they been?' she's asking me.

'Fine. But I fear word has spread around town,' I say cryptically, above Sophie's head.

'Oh, God.'

'Keep a close eye on madam, from now on,' I'm advising her, gesturing to Sophie, whose face is buried in her mother's skirt.

'Yes, OK. Come on, Sophie, get your coat on. We're giving Daddy a lift.'

Of course. It's Friday. Gina has the car.

I'm not looking forward to the weekend.

Gina will have the children to herself on Saturday and most of Sunday too.

We'll just meet up for Sunday lunch, for the kids' sake. Somewhere cheap.

Long couple of days ahead. I must get down to some work.

It'll help.

IT'S 7.30AM.

Monday, I think. December.

Soon be Christmas again. Lord knows what we're going to do about that. The weekends are bad enough.

I've written some new songs. Lots of lyrics about loss and separation and loneliness and failure.

I'm feeding Nicola her breakfast as she sits in her highchair shouting, 'MORE!'

This child shows no sign of losing her appetite with age, and a career as a supermodel seems increasingly unlikely.

I arrived to find Gina drinking coffee in a state of half-readiness.

Beautiful as ever.

For one brief moment I wanted her again.

Then a mental picture of Connor undressing her and making love to her flashed before my eyes.

I was immediately overwhelmed by pain and bitterness.

I stopped *wanting* her . . . I didn't say I'd stopped *loving* her.

Then she went upstairs to finish dressing.

'Good morning, Daddy.'

Sophie has finally appeared in the kitchen just as Nicola has regretfully resigned herself to the fact there is no more room in her stomach.

Next shift.

'Morning, Stinks. What do you fancy for breakfast?'

'Honey Nut Loops.'

Gina's just returned. Fully suited.

'Sophie's complaining of tummy ache again. Keep an eye on her for me and make sure she eats properly, could you?'

'Of course.'

'Oh! Nearly forgot. Belly O'Hea was on the phone for you last night. Just said he had some news for you.'

'Why didn't you send him round to the bedsit?'

She's looking at the floor suddenly.

'I didn't know if he knew. I thought if I mentioned the flat he might start asking questions and I might find that . . . difficult.'

'I see what you mean.'

I'm well aware that Belly would have found out weeks ago, along with the rest of Ballinkilty. But I'm not going to say anything.

A thought's occurred.

'I wonder if he's managed to do something with my demo tapes?'

'Oh, yes. I'd forgotten you'd given him those. Perhaps he's got some good news for you. That would be nice, wouldn't it?'

She's looking at me with the faintest trace of something in her eyes.

Hope, possibly?

'Daddy! Where are my Honey Nut Loops?'

'Sorry, petal. The bees are just fetching the honey as we speak and I'm busy punching the holes to make the loops.'

'Well, hurry up, I'm starving!'

'Yes, ma'am.'

'Dad? When are you coming home again?'

'I don't know yet, Stinks. Now eat your breakfast.'

10.15pm. O'Leary's.

I'm just about to start the second set of my gig and the place is beginning to kick a bit.

I have played eight or nine of my own songs so far this evening, all well received.

I met Belly O'Hea as soon as I arrived. He was full of smiles beneath his whiskery face, said he just had to pop out but not to worry he'd be back soon.

In the interval I caught him at the bar, but he said he couldn't talk because he was just about to pull a German tourist with, quote, 'the biggest pair of knockers you were ever after seeing in all your Godforsaken feckin' life, Andy boy', unquote. He said he'd talk to me after the gig.

So, I'm just about to begin the second set and I'm none the wiser. I still don't know what this 'news' is.

I know one thing, though. Judging by the way Belly's pissing me about, winding me up . . . *he* thinks it's big shakes.

I'm sat at a table opposite a grinning Belly O'Hea.

He still hasn't said anything, apart from mentioning that the German tourist was obviously frigid, as she had hastily departed.

I'm glad. I want Belly's complete attention, which is inclined to wander at the best of times.

Belly has insisted we wait for our pints to arrive before he imparts his news. Why is he milking this so much? This is excessive even by his standards.

The barman has very kindly brought our drinks across and Belly has paid him.

'You've had long enough, Belly. Come on, out with it.'

'Ah, don't be so hard, Andy. You know how I like to cherish these moments.'

He's putting his glass down. Now he's wiping the edge of the table, his hands going in opposite directions, as if smoothing out an imaginary tablecloth.

'You remember those demo tapes you gave me?'

'Belly . . .'

'Well, dear old Uncle Belly O'Hea, that washed-up old has-been of a rock'n'roller, the finest blues voice never to make a million—'

'BELLY!'

'—has managed to get a result. Well, to be fair now, half a result.'

Half a result. I knew it. I was certain it was never going to be worth this much of a song and dance.

'Go on.'

'Well, I realised there was one tape I had shamefully neglected to send out, so I did.'

'Oh, which one?'

'You remember those little ditties you recorded on Michael's eight-track? Three songs you recorded with Bridget singing lead vocals, just before the two of them left your band to form Mix and Match?'

'Oh, yes, I'd almost forgotten about that. I hadn't been here that long. I was going through my Irish-musical-influence stage, mixing traditional Irish sounds with modern rock.'

I'm laughing at the memory.

'It's all coming back to me. What was that first song I'd knocked off? You know, the sort of Riverdance-meets-Deff-Leppard track? All thrashing guitars mixed with jiggidy violins, Celtic harps and bloody panpipes. Probably *the* most awful song I've ever written. What did I call it? Celtic Saxon or something equally pretentious.'

'"When Cultures Clash", actually. I'm telling you it grows on you.'

'It was OK. It just didn't fuse, Belly. It sounded like three musos locked in a room having a barnstorming argument. The other two songs were sort of OK, as I remember. Tell you the truth, I'm surprised I gave it to you.'

Belly's signalled for another round of drinks.

'Well, Andy. God moves in mysterious ways, so he does.'

'Does he now? Care to explain that?'

Why am I suddenly suspicious?

'I decided to try a different tack with this tape. The recording was after being a bit rough, so to speak, so I didn't see the point in sending it to a recording company, so I entered it for a competition.'

'Competition? What sort of a competition? Oh, is this that Best Band thing—you know, with all the regional finals and stuff?'

'No, it would be too late for that. No, this would be . . .'

Why's he pausing?

'. . . more of a song-writing competition, so it would.'

'Interesting,' I'm saying, having finally finished my first pint. 'So what happens then?'

'Well, in September, songs are submitted from all over the country and gradually whittled down to a small selection of what is after being considered to be the best. Then those chosen few are given an airing on *Kenny Live.*'

'On what, sorry?'

'*Kenny Live,* man! For feck's sake, Andy! How long have you been in the country now and you don't even know what *Kenny Live* is? You be telling me next yer think Gay Byrne is a sexually depraved act, performed by cigar-smoking homosexuals!'

'Oh, it's on the *telly*. Irish telly. RTE. Yes, I have heard of it, of course I have.'

'"Heard of it" he says! Do you never watch it?'

'No. I just can't get a decent picture. Something to do with the wind that's constantly trying to blow my house down. That's why we had to buy a dish. Consequently I'm an expert on seventies television reruns and bugger all else. So remind me, *Kenny Live* is a bit like *The Gay Byrne Show,* only a bit more trendy. Am I right?'

'Ah, well, it's near enough, I suppose, for the purposes of this discussion. Anyway, as you've probably guessed by now, unless you have the intelligence of a lemming, I sent in yer tape.'

'And?'

'They liked one of the songs. It's been chosen to enter the final stages and Mix and Match will play it live on the *Kenny* show, with your permission, o' course.'

I'm staggered.

'You're joking.'

'I am not.'

'Well, who'd have believed it? That's excellent. I think. One of my songs on the telly. Amazing. Thanks, Belly.'

'My pleasure. My fees are minimal.'

'Just a minute. Which song did they like? Not . . .'

'"When Cultures Clash". Yes, I'm afraid that was the tune that turned them on.'

Oh, bugger! I finally get a song on national television and it has to be that one.

'I wonder what made them choose that one? I'm sure the other two were better songs.'

'Well, it suits the competition very well, so it does. The sort of mix of Irish and British. The lyrics helped too, now. All that stuff about us all being cousins and having respect for each other and working together, and understanding each other. It's very topical, what with the peace process going on, an' all.'

'Really? So what sort of a competition is this? Some kind of Save the Planet sort of thing?'

'In a manner of speaking.'

'Sounds more like Miss World.'

'I wouldn't go as far as saying that, now. Though it's usually fierce overflowing with gorgeous women in outrageous frocks.'

'Well, what is it, then? What do you win? It's not a recording contract, is it?'

'Well, now, some of the winners of the ultimate final have been given recording contracts, so they have.'

'Ultimate final? Is there another stage after the *Kenny Live* bit?'

'Oh, that's when it really hots up.'

'Well, what is it, then? What exactly are we talking about here?'

He's taken a deep breath. Why do I get the impression he doesn't *really* want to tell me?

'It's the Song for Europe, Andy.'

'Song for Europe ? What's that? Er . . . Euro . . . Euro-ver—something?'

Splash.

'THE FUCKING EUROVISION SONG CONTEST!'

'Ah, come on. Calm down, now, Andy. It's not as bad as all that.'

I'm about to have a seizure.

'The *Eurovision Song Contest* is the kiss of death to any street cred any artist might have had, Belly. You know that. What do most people think of when they hear the word Eurovision? Eh? Johnny bloody Logan! Bucks Fizz! Dana! Heaven help us, the Brotherhood of fucking Man!'

No wonder he didn't want to tell me! I cannot believe Belly is sitting here trying to persuade me that it's a cool thing to do.

'Why don't you be the one to change all that, Andy? It's a way in. Lord knows, you've been trying to find a door for long enough. Yer can't just slam the first one shut that's been left ajar.'

'Can't I? Watch me. I want out, Belly.'

'Will yer stop being such a selfish bastard for five seconds and listen to me? What about Mix and Match? They're going to be delighted when I tell them. What about sweet little Bridget? Shite, she's gonna be after thinking this is going to make her a star. Yer can't take that away from the girl. Can yer? Now come on, can yer?'

Must everybody in my life take it in turns to emotionally blackmail me? This has nothing to do with the fact Belly manages Mix and Match, of course.

'That's unfair, Belly. Why didn't you tell me you were going to do this?'

'I only did it as an afterthought. I didn't think it would get this far.

Listen to me now, Andy. Have yer any idea how many hundreds of songs are entered every year for this little shindig? Ten grand nobs from the music business, an' the top executives from RTE have to love yer little ditty as well, before it can reach the last eight. Those are some odds to have stacked against you.'

'Belly, my friend, I'm a rock'n'roller! I've spent years looking down on this kind of thing. Everyone will laugh at me.'

'There'll be those that'll take the piss, right enough. But, let me tell you, there's an awful lot of them as have tried to get a song selected themselves and failed, miserably. Listen, there's a press launch fer the eight songs that have reached the final. It's in a week's time.'

What! I have a twinge of pain. I think it's because someone has just grabbed me by the short and curlies.

'I don't know whether to laugh or cry.'

'Do neither. Get yer equipment together and come back to me house. I've a fine bottle of whiskey, just made for drinking while poring over a dilemma like this. Come on, now, let's be having yer.'

What do I do?

I know. Drink the fucking whiskey.

I can't see me doing much sleeping tonight.

6.45am, Tuesday. Next day.

I arrived at my old house extra early today. I must look like death. I haven't slept, I haven't shaved, I'm hung over and still partially stoned.

Gina's looking at me now as if her home has just been invaded by an escaped convict.

'You look as if you could use a cup of coffee.'

'If you're making one.'

'Heavy night last night?' she's asking.

'In more ways than one. I finally caught up with Belly O'Hea.'

'Oh! That's why you're looking so rough this morning.'

'Well, I've found out what all the fuss was about.'

'What?' She's smiling.

'One of my songs is to be aired live on *Kenny Live*.'

'That's wonderful, Andy!'

'There's a drawback. It's competing to be the Irish entry for the *Eurovision Song Contest*.'

She looks confused.

'But you're English.'

Not exactly the response I was expecting.

'I know. You remember that session I did with Bridget and Michael before they formed Mix and Match? The one where I sort of got carried away with all things Irish?'

'Yes, I do remember.'

'Well, it's one of those songs. The worst one, I think. But, lyrically, it's all about building bridges between the two nations and that's what has appealed. It sort of fits the present attempts at *détente.*'

'Fantastic! Congratulations.'

I can't believe it. She's giving me a beaming smile.

'Gina, it's the *Eurovision Song Contest*. You know, that comedy programme hosted by Terry Wogan back in England. A sort of glorified travel show advertising whatever country it's held in, interrupted by middle-of-the-road artists singing dreadful songs. It's got sod all to do with rock'n'roll.'

She's shaking her head, firmly.

'No. I'm sorry, but I think it's brilliant. Hundreds of people try to get their work chosen for this and you just have. "When Cultures Clash". That's the song, isn't it?'

'Yes, it is,' I'm replying, somewhat stunned that she remembered.

'Good song. I always liked it. Weird mix. Works, though. It may well win. Let's face it, Andy, Ireland usually does. In fact, they won last year so they're the host nation yet again.'

'Oh, but, Gina, how can I hold my head up high over this? It's hardly bloody Woodstock is it?'

'Well, then, don't play with the band on it. Just be the songwriter. That way you can say you couldn't deny the band their chance. If it all falls flat, you can hold up your hands and plead a certain amount of innocence.'

Gina's good at this. Seeing logical options. She did this all the time we were married. We're *still* married, though, aren't we?

'It's an idea, I suppose.'

'Don't look so fed up, Andy. Darling, this is good news. Don't throw away the chance for a bit of joy, a bit of excitement at last. Please?'

'I've got to decide soon. There's a press launch next week.'

'Good morning, Daddy. Baby's awake.'

Sophie wades through our conversation, as always.

'Oh, Lord, I'll go,' says Gina, before rushing out of the kitchen.

'Morning, Sophie. Sleep well?'

'I never sleep—remember Dad?'

'Of course. Silly me. What's for breakfast, then? Honey Nut Loops?'

'Toast and a banana.'

'Coming up.'

Gina has just walked in with a grizzling Nicola in her arms. She's teething. Her Babygro is soaked with dribble. Shit! A bad-tempered baby is not what a man with a hangover and an important decision to make needs in his day.

Gina hands her to me.

'So you think I should let all this go ahead?' I'm asking Gina.

'Definitely. Your daddy's going to be a star, Sophie. Tell her, Andy.'

Gina's disappearing out of the room to get dressed.

'What do you want to tell me, Dad?' she says to me, in that way that sometimes makes me think she was born middle-aged.

'Oh, don't worry, Stinks. It's a bit complicated.'

'Daddy! Stop treating me like a little girl.'

'OK, I'll keep it simple. Should Daddy let one of his songs be entered for the *Eurovision Song Contest*?'

'Ooh, yes, Dad. I think you should.'

Why not take my daughter's advice? I may as well.

Remember what they say about children's instincts.

3.15pm.

Pearse Street, Ballinkilty. Just for a change, it's pissing down.

I've just emerged from the Credit Union where I've been begging for another loan. Nicola behaved, but Sophie kept sitting in the wastepaper bin, for some reason.

Anyway we've just made an ungainly sprint for the car, and bumped straight into Bridget from Mix and Match.

She's a sort of pocket sex-symbol, really. Very short, yet curvaceous with blonde, spiky hair.

'ANDY!' she's screamed, with her usual youthful subtlety.

'Bridget! How the devil are you?' I say through the torrent, as I park myself and my brood in the doorway of the dry cleaner's.

'Oh, now, I'm so excited by the news, Andy, I cannot begin to tell yer. The boys are all thrilled as well. Michael's trying to pretend he's all cool about it, but he's desperate for the big day.'

Michael and Bridget are an item, as they say.

'Just a minute, Bridget. I got the impression from Belly that he hadn't even told you yet. I mean, he only told me last night. I still haven't agreed to let the song be used. What is going on?'

She looks suitably embarrassed at this.

'I'm sorry, I had no idea. I swear. You know what Belly's like, Andy.'

'I'm beginning to find out. I think I'd better give him a ring. Liberties have been taken.'

'Ah, Andy! You're not going to pull the plug on all of this, are yer? It's such an opportunity for us, and they don't come along too often in this country, so they don't. Please, Andy?'

I seem to have been presented with the final piece in the *fait accompli*.

'No, you're all right. Of course we'll go ahead. But don't tell Belly that just yet. I want to see him sweat a bit for being a naughty boy.'

'You're wicked, so yer are. Listen, we're rehearsing tomorrow night up at Michael's. Can yer come along?'

'What time?'

'Eightish.'

Translated into Irish time, that means closer to nine.

'Yeah, OK. I'll be there.'

She's given me a bear hug that has taken my breath away.

'See you tomorrow night.'

She's sprinting down the street.

Time to go home and feed Nicola. Again. Then I'll give Mr Belly O'Hea a call.

'Who was that lady, Dad?'

'Don't you remember Bridget? She used to sing in the first band Daddy played in here. She's going to sing my song in the competition I told you about.'

'She's very pretty, isn't she, Daddy?'

'Is she? Sort of, I suppose.'

'I think she's beautiful.'

'I'll tell her. I'm sure she'll be very pleased to hear it.'

'Do you fancy her, Dad?'

'Where did you pick up an expression like that?'

'Are you going to leave Mummy and marry that lady, Dad?'

I'm stunned.

'What makes you think that?'

'At playschool, Richard said that's what his daddy is going to do.'

I'm going to strangle Richard . . . wait a minute, Richard's daddy? *Norman?*

'Are you sure that's what Richard said, Sophie?'

'Yes. He's going to marry someone called Lisa. Richard says she doesn't eat no meat. Wish I didn't have to eat no meat either.'

Lisa . . . Lisa . . . Oh, Christ! Not *Elisa*, surely? Not Mrs Save the Frigging Whale?

Poor Michelle. Beaten at her own game. I'd never have believed old Norman had it in him. I want to ask Sophie more, but I see she needs to be reassured.

'No, I'm not going to marry that lady, I promise you, Sophie.'

'Dad?'

'Yes, darling.'

'Nicola's been sick.'

She has as well. A fair chuck down the front of her anorak.

I'm wiping the residue off Nicola with a baby wipe.

'Dad?'

'Yes, Sophie.'

'I've got a tummy ache too.'

'That'll teach you to eat your meals and not to scoff sweets all day, won't it? Is it really bad?'

She's nodding.

'Shall we pop to see the doctor?'

'No. It's OK. Come on, Dad, let's go home and watch a video.'

She can't be that bad, then.

MIDNIGHT. First week of February.

I'm in bed. Thinking. Here in my cheery little cell.

Tomorrow we're off to Dublin for the first stage of the competition. All eight songs are aired on *Kenny Live* week by week. Then there's a grand final in early March. That's when the winner is chosen.

To be honest, I'm a bit jealous. You see, after much thought, I had decided I was *definitely* going to play 'When Cultures Clash' with the band. But when we discussed this it was not difficult to gather that they would be happier if I didn't. Ungrateful gits. If it wasn't for my song they wouldn't have got a sniff of national television.

Still, I've quite enjoyed the little bit of local fame that has come my way as a result of the press launch in the national newspapers. Everybody keeps smiling at me and wishing me 'all the luck'. On the other hand, I've hated the sniggers from the snobbish local musicians I've bumped into in the pubs.

The Blow-ins are back in Germany. It will be interesting to hear their response upon their return.

I've mixed feelings about tomorrow. I still think the song is rather weak, but I've rejigged it with the band and it's much more palatable now. And, OK, I admit it, buried secretly in the back of my mind is the thought we may just have a chance of winning the bloody thing.

12.30am.

There's a knock on the door of my *pied à terre.*

Who the hell can it be? Who do I know goes visiting at this time of night?

Well, logic says, if its an axe murderer, he's unlikely to knock politely and apologise for disturbing me. I'd better pull on a robe to cover my nakedness and answer the door.

12.40am.

A bottle of whiskey has been opened.

I'm sat on the floor, cross-legged in towelling robe and nothing else, like a particularly laid-back disciple of meditation. Bridget is sat on the bed. Tears were flowing from her eyes when she came in. It seems she has telly fright, if there is such a thing.

'I can't go through with it, Andy. I just can't do it.'

This is just what I needed to hear.

'Why?'

More sobs.

'Look, singing in the back of O'Leary's is one thing. But this is television, Andy. There's millions after watching this thing. I know I'm going to fuck up under the pressure, I just know it.'

'Don't be daft, Bridget. Of course you won't.'

I'm giving her a big hug. Not an entirely unpleasant experience.

'Listen, Bridget. You have a wonderful voice and you're a fine interpreter of songs. On top of which, you're pretty, full of personality and very sexy. This is a great opportunity. You could go far.'

'Oh, Andy! Do yer really think so, now?'

This time she hugs me. I could get used to this.

'Listen, tomorrow isn't too important. Treat this as a dress rehearsal. Then when the final comes along in March you'll have worked on live television once and you won't be half as nervous about it.'

'Yer right. I hadn't thought of it like that. Thanks, Andy,' she says, releasing me from her grip and flopping onto my duvet.

So, I've exaggerated a little but what else was I supposed to do? In fact, she does have a decent singing voice. But is she sexy, though? Well, let me put it this way. You wouldn't kick her out of bed on a cold night.

She's a sort of poor man's Gina, really. With bigger breasts and shorter, chunkier legs. If I were not still besotted with Gina, I would have tried to jump Bridget's bones by now.

I'm staring at her now. Gina did it. So why not?

Oh, fucking behave yourself, man! You've got enough trouble sorting out your emotions without clouding the issue any further.

1.30am.

We've been psychoanalysing Bridget's fear while drinking heavily. I've decided against seduction. Now, how can I get shot of her, for crying out loud?

There's another knock on my door.

Hell's bells! This is turning into a party!

I'd better answer it.

It's Gina. She's standing in the door holding Sophie in her arms.

'Sorry, Andy. I didn't know what else to do.'

'No, it's fine, come in. Hello, Stinks, what are you doing awake at this hour?'

Sophie's not answering me. She's too busy sobbing her little heart out.

'Hello, Bridget. Not interrupting anything, am I?' Gina's asking.

'No, of course not,' I interject. 'What's the matter with Sophie?'

'My tummy, Daddy. It really hurts bad.'

'How long has this been going on, Gina?'

'She said she didn't feel well just before she went to bed. Then she woke up about an hour and a half ago and she's got steadily worse. She's got a temperature. I've given her Calpol but it's not coming down.'

'Better get her to the doctor.'

'No, Daddy! Please don't make me see the doctor.'

'Come on, Sophie darling. We've got to get you better. That's what doctors do. They make people better. It's their job. If the car was broken you'd make me take it to the garage, wouldn't you?'

'Yes,' she snivels, before wincing with pain.

'Well, I've got to take you to the *doctor's* to get *you* fixed. Speaking of cars, Gina, how did you get down here?'

'I rang Deirdre from the farm. She gave me a lift. Listen, Andy, will you come to the doctor with us? Sophie wants you.'

'Of course. You try and keep me away.'

I'm picking the car keys off the bedside cabinet and handing them to Gina.

'Car's parked right in front. Get in. I'll be right down.'

'DADDY!'

'Daddy's coming, Sophie. I'll be two minutes.'

Gina's taken her downstairs.

'Sorry, Bridget.'

'Not at all. Is there anything I can do?'

'Yes. You can warn everybody I might not make it to Dublin tomorrow.'

'I will,' she says as she leaves, pausing to give me a supportive hug.

Right.

Clothes and wallet.

I've climbed in the driver's seat. Gina is in the back cuddling Sophie, who appears to have calmed down a little.

'Have you rung the doctor?'

'Yes, she's expecting us.'

I'm starting the engine and heading off to Ross Carbery, to the surgery.

'Should we stop off for Nicola?' I'm asking Gina.

'No. She's fine with Deirdre.'

'Right then.'

'Bridget's a pretty girl, don't you think?' Gina's asking, out of the blue.

'Pardon? I don't know. Sophie said that the other day.'

Now I realise how it must have looked. Shit!

'She's petrified. She's got stage fright about the show tomorrow. She got me out of bed to tell me she wasn't going to sing.'

'And you were . . . comforting her, I suppose?'

'Oh, Daddy, my tummy!'

'Nearly there now, sweetheart. We'll soon have you put right. Can we clear up that other matter a little later, please, Gina?'

'Nothing to clear up, I can hardly complain, can I? What's good for the goose and all that,' Gina's replying on a monotone.

'It wasn't—oh, never mind, we'll talk later.'

I wish Sophie would stop crying. I can't stand to see her in pain.

1.45am.

Doctor's surgery in Ross Carbery.

Sophie's screaming in agony.

Gina's in floods of tears.

Why do doctors insist on poking and prodding the area that causes you pain until you feel ten times worse?

I must calm down and stop being stupid. It's not the doctor's fault.

'I can't be certain. She could have a virus but on the other hand it could be appendicitis and I think, all things considered, it's best to have her admitted to hospital.'

'NO, DADDY! NO, DADDY! NOT TO HOSPITAL!'

'Sophie, darling, calm down, sweetheart. We've got to get you better. Mummy and I will be with you. You'll be all right, I promise.'

'Do you have a preference for any hospital?' the doctor's asking.

'The Bons Secour,' Gina has replied.

It's where Nicola was born.

'I'll see if they've got a bed.'

It's in Cork. It's at least an hour's drive.

Shit, shit, shit.

We're back in the car and I'm starting the engine.

I've stuffed the letter for the hospital in the glove compartment.

'Damn! Gina, we've got nothing for her.'

'It's all right. I've a bag packed. It's in the boot. My instincts told me we might need it.'

I hope there's not much traffic on the roads. The appendix can perforate, can't it? That's dangerous, isn't it? Life-threatening.

I hope it's a clear road. The way I'll be driving I won't be taking prisoners.

It must be about 3.30am at least, but I've lost all track of time.

We're at the hospital. Sophie is screaming and crying again.

She's frightened.

I'm fucking terrified.

But I can't let my Sophie see that. Or Gina, who is not handling this well.

They're taking blood. Sophie's on a trolley bed and Gina and I are on either side of her.

'NO! NO! NO! Help, Daddy, HELP! NO!'

It's over, thank goodness.

I'm cuddling her.

'Who's Daddy's big brave girl? It's not fair, poppet. Poor Sophie.'

'Oh, Daddy, it's terrible.'

'Never mind. Soon be over.'

'We're going to send her for an X-ray.'

'NO, DADDY, NO, MUMMY!'

'It's all right, Sophie. It won't hurt, Mummy promises. It's just like having your picture taken, that's all.'

'Yes,' I'm adding, 'except they photograph what's inside you. Yuck, can you imagine what's floating around your stomach?'

She's giggling. Half-heartedly. Still, that's a relief.

'We'll wheel her down now, Mr Lawrence.'

'NO, DADDY! *I don't want to go on the trolley*!'

'It's all right, Sophie,' Gina reassuring her. 'Daddy will carry you.'

'Oh, if I must. Come on, you great oaf!'

She's in my arms.

'Blimey. I thought you hadn't been eating much lately. You are *such* a lump. You weigh a ton. I hope it's not far. Poor Daddy.'

She's giggling. 'Poor Daddy. Poor Daddy.'

One of the advantages of going to a private hospital in the middle of the night is that there is not the customary four-mile queue to have your insides photographed. A radiologist appeared as if from nowhere.

'Right, which one of you would like to come in with Sophie? I should mention, Mrs Lawrence, if there's any chance you may be pregnant, you'd be advised to let Mr Lawrence bring Sophie in.'

We're looking at each other. I realise that for the first time in our relationship I cannot answer that question.

'No. There's no chance,' she's saying to me, and not the radiologist.

'In which case . . .?'

'Sophie? Shall Mummy or Daddy come in with you?' Gina's asking.

'Daddy.'

Gina's not offended. She'd be the first to admit that hospitals make her uneasy.

I'm probably the right choice.

Back in the cubicle. X-rays all finished with.

Sophie panicked, yet again. It was only by complaining about how ridiculous I looked in the solid apron I had to wear for protection that I was able to rescue the situation.

The surgeon has signalled he wants a word with me.

I'm following him out of the cubicle.

'I think we'd like to keep her in over what remains of the night, Mr Lawrence. We'll see how she is and take a decision in the morning about operating. We'll keep a close eye on her, try not to worry.'

'Can we stay with her?'

'One of you, certainly. Though it won't be very comfortable.'

'That doesn't matter. Thanks for your help, Doctor.'

'Not at all.'

Better go back and break the news.

We're in a ward with four beds. One other occupant. A small boy. There's a chair next to Sophie's bed for one of us to sleep in.

Sophie's much calmer.

I've explained we have to be quiet because the other little boy is sleeping.

I'm ferreting through the bag Gina packed.

'Oh, look, Sophie. Mummy's brought the book we were reading. You try to find the page we were on. I just need to have a quick chat with Mummy.'

I'm leading Gina out into the corridor.

'Listen, Gina, why don't you go home? Nicola needs her mummy too.'

'It's not fair to leave you here alone.'

'Gina, we've two kids and we have to take care of both of them.'

'Oh, Andy. Supposing something goes wrong?'

'I'm sure it won't . . .'

Am I? Am I really?

'It's probably just a virus. She looks better now. Go home and snatch some sleep before Nicola decides it's time to play.'

'You will ring me if . . .'

'As soon as there's any news, I promise.'

'OK. If you're sure. I suppose it's only fair to Nicola. Andy?'

'Yes?'

'I'm sorry about earlier. About you and Bridget. . . . I mean, I suppose it's none of my business anyway. I couldn't blame you if you did . . .'

I'm holding up my hand to stop her.

'Don't worry about it. It must have looked dreadful. I just hope she holds her nerve and sings well tomorrow. What am I saying? *Today.* Look, could you phone Belly for me? Tell him I can't make it to Dublin.'

'Oh, Andy, you must!'

'Ssh. My place is with Sophie. Anything else can wait.'

'Andy?'

'Yes?'

'Thanks for being here tonight. I needed you. I can't tell you how badly. You promise you'll ring?'

'I promise, Gina.'

She's just kissed me lightly on the lips, before departing.

I stand watching her walk down the corridor.

She needed me. Was that what she said?

Was she jealous of Bridget and, if so, what does that mean?

I'd better get back to Sophie.

Being brave for Gina's sake is all very well. Truth is, I'm shit scared.

She's going to be fine. Of course she is.

I'm walking into the ward.

Sophie has fallen asleep, thank heavens.
She looks so tiny in that big bed.
So bloody vulnerable.
Time to sort out my sleeping arrangements.

I've just phoned Gina and I'm walking back to the ward. It's 9.30am.
No sleep in that bloody chair, which I'm sure had been designed to keep the hospital osteopaths in employment. I ache all over.
After some consultation, Sophie was allowed breakfast, which meant an operation was clearly off the agenda, and a virus was pronounced as the most probable reason for her illness.
Something else was also suggested. The doctor asked me, rather pointedly, if there had been any trauma in Sophie's life of late. I was honest with him. After shaking his head he hinted there was a chance Sophie's problem had been brought on by stress.
Could Gina and I be responsible for this?
The doctor has made me wonder. I must talk to Gina about it.
Anyway, the good news is she can come home after lunch as long as there's no change.
Yippee!
Gina's on her way up now, and Deirdre is looking after Nicola until we get back.
Children's powers of recovery are remarkable. Sophie is a completely different child this morning.
We have to try to keep her quiet as the virus could stay in her system for up to a fortnight or more, apparently.
I've just turned into the ward and you won't believe what I'm seeing.
'Sophie! What are you doing?'
'I'm having a bounce, Daddy.'
'I can see that. Will you stop it? This is a hospital. I thought you were supposed to be sick. Sit down and finish off that toast.'
'Oh, *Dad!*'
'Come on, monster. We're not out yet. They want to see you eating first. I want to get you home today. So come on, munch.'
I've just jammed the toast between her teeth to the accompanying sound of muffled laughter.

2.30pm.
We've just got home and Sophie's bounded in, happy to be back on her patch.
Deirdre's in the kitchen. Nicola is in her arms.

'My, my, aren't you looking better than the last time I saw you?' Deirdre's smiling at Sophie. 'How are you?'

'Fine. Dad? Can I watch a cartoon?'

'Yes, and sit on the sofa quietly. No more charging about.'

She's off.

'Seriously, how is she, now?' Deirdre is asking Gina.

'OK. The doctors think it's a virus. We've got to watch her for a week or two, though.'

'Could have been worse, then.'

'Much.'

'Well, I must be off,' Deirdre's saying, perhaps sensing our need to be alone. She's handing Nicola to Gina.

'Bye, Deirdre. Thanks ever so much.'

'No problem. Bye!'

She closes the door behind her. There's an awkward silence between us. Automatically I go to the kettle and switch it on.

'Something I ought to mention, Gina. The doctor hinted that Sophie's tummy problem may have something to do with the effect you and I breaking up has had on her.'

'Oh, really?' she replies, and looks at the floor. I don't blame her. We don't need to discuss it any further. Just be aware.

'Pop in and see her, Andy. Nicola and I will bring you a cup of tea.'

'OK.'

I've walked into the lounge and Sophie is sprawled on the sofa watching *The Flintstones.*

'Oh, yes! Good old Barney Rubble. Make room for me, Stinks.'

I'm sitting on the sofa, giving my daughter a cuddle.

I'm exhausted from lack of sleep.

My head's a mess because of the state of my marriage.

My career, such as it is, is happening elsewhere in the hands of people I don't altogether trust.

I don't give a flying fuck.

My little girl is all right.

That's all that matters.

It's latish.

I'm too knackered to be precise. We've just watched my song on *Kenny Live*. Mix and Match played very well, a lively performance, and Bridget was fine.

Sophie, who was allowed to stay up and watch it with us, said my song was 'Terrific, Daddy'.

Gina squeezed my hand.

'Right, little girl,' I'm saying, as I ruffle Sophie's hair, 'you've had an exhausting twenty-four hours and you need your sleep.'

'I don't sleep, remember, Dad?'

'Whatever, it's time to go to bed and then Daddy must be off.'

'NO, DADDY!' She's howling. 'I don't want you to go.'

'Daddy's not going anywhere, are you? He's going to stay here and look after his girl.'

Gina.

I'm looking at her.

She's smiling.

'Of course I am. Come on let's go upstairs.'

It's past midnight. I'm in the spare room.

Anyway, Sophie will be fine in a few days and then it's back to my bunker.

Though now I'm back here it has crossed my mind . . .

I don't think so . . . somehow.

9.30pm.

Location?

O'Leary's.

Date?

February 16.

The occasion?

My thirty-ninth birthday.

It's been a funny day. I was really depressed when I woke up. You know, the big Four-O just round the corner and no further on et cetera, until Sophie came storming into the spare room carrying a little fistful of presents. Gina and Nicola followed her in and so we had a little present-opening. A compact disc from Nicola, a jumper from Sophie and a watch from Gina. Well, they're all from Gina, really.

So I decided to banish my usual oh-my-God-I'm-so-old-and-still-a-failure birthday blues and I have had a lovely day. And tonight Gina gave me a spin into town and I'm having a bit of a session in the bar.

Belly's here, plus Mix and Match, plus sundry bodies we have picked up along the way.

Belly's going to give me a lift home, which if I was sober would frighten me witless because he's drunk twice as much as I have.

'Hello, Andy. Happy birthday to you.'

It's Matt.

'Matt! Long time no see. Back from conquering Bavaria, then?'

'That's right, boy. And have *you* been busy while we've been away. Eurovision, Andy? I mean, come on, you'll be offering to write for Julio Iglesias next.'

'I don't know why you're being such a snob, Matt. A little bird told my you've submitted at least two songs for Eurovision and got fuck nowhere.'

I wish someone would photograph Matt's face right now, and frame the picture for me.

'Who told you?'

Bingo!

'Nobody, Matt. I just took a lucky guess. Aren't you going to buy your old mate a drink for his birthday?'

'Sure,' he's muttered at me, before heading for the bar.

Hoots of laughter all round.

Little victories, man. Little victories.

Ssh!

It's late and I'm struggling to get in the house without waking everybody up. I'm still there, in the spare room. It's been over a week now. I'm trying to go in the back door, and I'm so pissed I can't find the ruddy keyhole.

There we go. Gotcha!

Right. Where's the door out of here?

Ouch! Ooh, bugger, I've fallen over now.

It didn't hurt, but I bet I don't find it this funny in the morning.

Hello?

That's a pair of feet, isn't it?

Someone's helping me up.

It's Gina.

'HELLO, GINA!'

'*Sssh!* You'll wake the babies.'

She's steering me through the lounge and towards the spare room that lies off it. Thankfully we don't have to negotiate the stairs.

She's thrown me on the bed for the first time in all our years of marriage.

Hello! She's undressing me.

Off comes the shirt, now the shoes and socks, jeans.

'I don't usually do this on the first date, you know.'

'Be quiet!' But she's laughing.

Boxer shorts as well, ooh-er, Mrs Lawrence.

Something's just landed on my face.
No need to panic, it's the duvet.
'Go to sleep, you drunken sod.'
Now, focus: the room is not moving . . . it is not moving . . .

Something's happening. I can feel it.
Familiar.
A sensation.
A *lurvely* sensation.
Where am I?
Someone has got my cock in their mouth.
Shit, Michelle!
I've half opened one eye. *No*.
It's Gina.
I don't know what to do.
I'm not talking sexual ignorance but, it's just . . . I'm so confused.
She's mounting me now . . . moaning . . . whimpering.
Oh, fuck! She's riding me hard.
She's taken my hands and placed them on her breasts.
I'm caressing them instinctively.

Part of me wants to throw her off. This is not mine any more, it's Connor's. Yet I can't help feeling . . . desire . . . lust . . . warmth . . .

Love.
What . . . do I . . . do . . . ?

I'm alone again.

After we climaxed—and I'm fairly sure we both climaxed—Gina slid off me and gave me a long, deep kiss.

Then she left the bedroom.
She never spoke, not a word.

I'm replaying it all in my mind. My most lasting impression was the noise of it all. In all the years that Gina and I have been making love, I have never heard her cry out like that. It somehow made it more . . . special, the way she was really giving herself to me.

The trouble is, she gave herself to Connor as well.
I'm just not sure I'm a big enough man to deal with that.

UGH! What time is it? What day is it?
And why does my brain feel as if it has recently haemorrhaged?

I'm giggling now, internally, because speaking of recent strokes, Gina has just entered the spare room.

Oh, God! The morning after the night before.

And what a night!

'Morning,' I've managed to mutter. 'What time is it?'

'About a quarter to twelve.'

'Shit! Sorry.'

She's laughing at me.

'That's all right. I figured you could probably use a lie-in.'

'Aren't you going to work?'

'No, not today. I've phoned in and told them I still can't leave Sophie. Bugger them. Coffee?'

'Please.'

'I've some filter already made. Back in a sec.'

Gina's back.

She's sat on the edge of the bed and handed me my coffee.

I've sat up, gingerly.

'Listen, Andy. About last night.'

'You took advantage of me, Gina.'

'Yes. I know I did. That's what I want to say.'

She's running her hand nervously through her hair.

'I'm sorry, Andy. I didn't mean it to happen, I just couldn't control myself.' She stands. 'I made a mistake and I know I have to pay for it. But I can't bear being apart from you. I hate it. I love you, Andy, and it was . . . other things getting in the way. Not how I felt for you.'

She's pacing backwards and forwards as she speaks.

'When we . . . look . . . What I mean is . . . this isn't easy to say . . . When we were together at the hospital I realised just how much I needed you. How much I loved you. I knew I wanted you back.'

She's stopped pacing and she's staring at me.

'Oh, come on, Andy, help me here. You must have noticed. Sophie's been fine since she first got home, really. I haven't exactly been rushing you out the door, have I? Sophie needs you too. She's been so much happier since Daddy came back. Nicola as well, we all have. You're such a kind man, Andy. A good man. I was a bloody fool.'

'Gina, have you thought this—'

'And when I saw you with that, Bridget—'

'Hang on! She's a nice enough girl.'

'I'm sorry, but I was so jealous. I don't want anyone else to have you. You're mine. The children want you back. I want you back, for all our sakes, please come home.'

She's crying.

I've always hated it when she cries.

'Gina. I'm not sure . . .'

'I'll do anything you want. I'll never deny you sex again—'

'Yes, you will!'

'Oh, Andy, do you still love me?'

'Yes, Gina.'

'Can you forgive me?'

Decision time. Now it's my turn to search for the right phrases to explain how I feel.

'I'm not sure how strong I am. I can't promise Connor's face won't leap into my mind and twist it. I can try, Gina. I can't promise any more than that. But I do love you and I do want to see if we can . . . get it back together.'

She's put her arms round me. 'Thank God,' she's whispering.

We're holding very tight.

Fear? Love? Both?

There's a third pair of arms.

It's Sophie.

'Why are you being soppy?'

Gina's smiling at me. 'Because Daddy's coming home, Sophie. He's finished his work.'

'Oh, goody! About time, too!'

MARCH 3. It's the final of the *Song for Europe*. In an hour or two we'll know if 'When Cultures Clash' will be representing my adopted homeland in the *Eurovision Song Contest*.

We're at the RTE studios in Dublin. Gina's with me, and Deirdre and her family have the children up at the farm behind our house.

Right, this is the form then: songs played; break; phone vote.

Ten juries, comprising sixteen people of mixed ages, spread across the country. They've listened to the song during the day, tonight they watch the show, then phone in their points, live on air. Twelve points for the best, down to three points for the song they like least.

I was present at rehearsals this afternoon and they went well.

Bridget has changed out of all recognition. The shy, I-just-can't-do-this girl who sat on my bed has been replaced by a flirtatious *femme fatale* tarting her way around the studio, making Michael seethe with jealousy at the attention she was giving the producers and the crew. I had to tell her to calm it down. It was causing friction.

Anyway, now I'm here I want to win.

Entering *Eurovision* may have caused me some internal artistic debate, I confess. However, losing at this stage would want to make me keep a very low profile indeed.

I had a listen to the competition this afternoon—all seven, four of which are a pile of shite, in my humble opinion. The other three are serious threats. Here goes.

One rip-roaring ballad, *à la* Johnny Logan. Good, if you like that sort of thing. Sung by the composer. Female, very sophisticated. Thinking-man's crumpet territory.

Then there's a typical all-girl sexy group. Very 'pop', very catchy chorus, well-choreographed dance routine showing off their bits and pieces. The sort of thing the British usually toss into the Eurovision arena.

Last, but not least, the Irish-language entry. Very simple, very well written, very haunting. If I could understand the lyrics, I'd probably love it.

The lights dimming. We're live on air in ten seconds. Gina's squeezing my hand and kisses my left ear, before whispering, 'Good luck.'

Yer man Kenny's come on, and his mere presence has heightened the atmosphere. We have rapturous applause and we're under starter's orders.

Mix and Match are fourth in line to play.

The bottom has fallen out of my stomach.

I just hope the stomach doesn't fall out of my bottom before this evening is out.

All done bar the shouting.

All the songs have been heard. All the composers have been ushered backstage to see their performers and indulge in a little liquid hospitality. Steady the nerves before the voting.

This is nerve-racking.

Why? How can anyone take this seriously?

But you sort of get sucked into the whirlpool of it all.

Mix and Match were excellent. I've hugged them all. Even Michael, who's being sullen and moody as usual. Bridget has just leapt at me, squealing, 'Ah, Andy, didn't it go well? Didn't it?'

'It did, Bridget. Whatever the result, I couldn't have asked for any more from you.'

'We won't win,' says Michael. 'The girl'll win. They loved her.'

I fear he's right.

Wonder if it's too late to get a bet on?

'Mr Lawrence?' The floor manager's appeared beside me. 'Can you take your seat? They're after collecting the results from the juries.'

And I'm walking back out into the studio with Gina.

'I'll still be proud of you, win or lose,' she says.

'Thanks, Gina.'

She doesn't think we're going to win, either.

My face.

Everywhere.

On all the monitors around the studio.

Why?

'Stand up! You've won, you daft git.'

Gina's pushing me up out of my seat.

I've suddenly noticed Bridget going wild on the studio floor.

Yer man Kenny himself is shaking my hand. He's pointing the microphone at me. He's going to want me to speak.

I don't know what I'm going to say.

You see . . .

I'm not used to being a winner.

Saturday. April.

Down the pub. About a month or so after the *Song for Europe* final.

I'm a star!

Well, in Ballinkilty, at least. No, cancel that. In Ireland.

Is this, as Mr Warhol once suggested, my fifteen minutes of fame? Possibly. Though if I could stretch it to an hour it would be nice.

Am I enjoying it? You bet your life I am!

People in this town have been fantastic. Hugs, pats on the back, free drink, free meals and lots of well-wishing for the grand final.

I've been interviewed by the local and national press, where I've let it be known there's plenty more songs where 'When Cultures Clash' came from.

We've recorded the song and it's storming up the Irish charts.

Plus I'm £1,000 richer.

Sophie has been incredibly overexcited. She is acting just like my agent. She walks up to complete strangers and tells them, 'My daddy won the *Eurovision Song Contest*. He's ever so clever.'

I've tried to tell her I haven't yet, but she just says, 'You will, Daddy.'

Nicola is blissfully ignorant. A quick puke down my best shirt and my feet soon touch the ground.

Gina has thoroughly enjoyed it.

Boy, has she enjoyed it!

In the kitchen, in the lounge, in the bed, half dressed, naked, in stockings, in ankle socks . . . (So? I'm kinky). My success has turned her into a nymphomaniac.

I've even had a card from Matt, unbelievable—congratulating me on my success and saying we must meet up for a drink soon, 'old pal'.

Huh!

Still, the world's a wonderful place. My wife's beautiful, my children are wonderful and everyone's happy.

I'm on a roll. It seems things are looking up.

No more misery.

Me and my big mouth.

I've just taken a call.

It was Connor. He wants to see me. To explain.

So, I'm off to his house.

It probably isn't a good idea, just when things are going so well.

But I'm going. I have to.

As I drive, all the feelings of hate and anger and betrayal are welling up inside me again. Filling my head, sickening my stomach.

I should turn back, but I can't.

Things are fine now. I've almost exorcised the ghost of Gina's affair. But in a month, a year, five years, it might start to haunt me again.

So I have to face him.

I've rung the doorbell. I'm shaking with nerves, or anger.

Connor's answered it. Parting the lips that parted my wife's, he says, 'Hell, Andy. You'd best be after coming inside.'

I'm following him, I'm right behind him.

We're moving through the hall into the sitting room and he's turned to face me. 'Can I get you a drink at all?'

I've hit him.

I almost felt my fist passing through his head.

He's fallen back, groaning. The front of his sweater is covered in blood from his nose.

I may have broken it.

I may also have broken my hand.

It's a toss-up which of us is in the most pain.

'I never want to see your face again, Connor,' I tell him, as he picks himself off the floor. He staggers to a chair and slumps into it.

'You won't. I'll be gone in a fortnight. I'm moving the business to England. I've bought premises and a new house there.'

'Why, Connor? Were you following your dick?'

'Gina was just . . . so unhappy. I started out wanting to help her, as a friend. Then I fell in love with her, Andy. That, I think you will believe. The house in England? It was to be for the two of us, you see. She's a special woman.'

'I know.'

I've opened his front door. He follows me to it, cradling his nose.

'Gina was never really prepared to risk losing you. She's hurt you, Andy, but forgive her. I took advantage of her at a time when she was very vulnerable.'

'I'd get that nose looked at if I were you.'

I've slammed the door shut behind me.

I need some air.

A chance to think.

Duneen beach, the little cove, remember?

It's bloody freezing. The gusts of wind I'm swallowing are virtually ripping my lungs apart.

I feel better, though.

My head is clearer. My body becalmed.

I feel cleansed.

I've come home.

I've just walked into the lounge and my family are all here. Nicola is sitting on the floor, playing with an electronic cube with touch-sensitive controls.

Sophie and Gina are watching television.

'Mind the baby for two minutes, could you, Sophie?'

'Oh . . . OK.'

I've dragged Gina into the kitchen.

'What's all this about?'

'I've just been to see Connor.'

'Oh.' The colour has drained from her face.

'Did you know he was back?'

She's shaking her head.

'But you *do* know he's going to England?'

'I—wasn't sure . . .'

'If he'd still go, alone?'

'Yes.'

'Well, he is. Are you going with him?'

'NO!'

'Do you love him, Gina?'

'No! Andy, I love you. Honestly I do.'

She's crying.

Big breath, Andy. 'OK. It's over. I never want it mentioned again. Understand? It's you and me and the children from here on in. You and me, Gina. Always.'

She's crossed to me and she's in my arms.

With luck, that's where she'll stay.

IT'S SATURDAY, May 13, 1997.

Today is the big day!

We're at the Point in Dublin for the final of the *Eurovision Song Contest*.

When I say we, I mean Mix and Match, Belly O'Hea, Gina, Sophie and even little Nicola.

Noreen, has been roped in to come and help look after the two children while we're in Dublin.

Everybody is staying at Jury's Hotel in Ballsbridge. We have two rooms next to each other. Gina and I in one, Noreen stuck with the brood in the other. We'll see how it pans out.

We've already filmed our 'Postcards'. You know, the naff sequences that supposedly introduce the band and the composer but are really one big advert for the host country.

We filmed it around Ballinkilty.

It has taken us to megastardom in our home town. The local townspeople are ecstatic. The local businesses are awash with gratitude. I'm glad. It's nice to give a little back.

The BBC cottoned onto the fact that an Englishman had written the

Irish entry and they sent a film crew across. A short piece for Wogan's Euro preview. I was able to talk about myself and my career. Allowed to sing and play and generally show off.

So that was nice.

The band and I have been in Dublin for a week. It's been wild.

We were met at the airport by our guide, a woman called Mary West, who has basically organised and looked after us all week. There was a welcoming reception in the Royal Hospital, Kilmainham. I don't mean we were drinking and boogieing in Intensive Care: it's now a prestigious conference and banqueting centre. Very posh.

Then what they call 'The Euroclub' moves to different venues round Dublin each night. A variety of meals and piss-ups, culminating in a midnight cabaret on Thursday with Linda Martin, whose special guest was . . . you guessed it, JOHNNY LOGAN!

There were two dress rehearsals yesterday, the evening one in front of an invited audience and recorded as a production standby.

Right now, it's Saturday afternoon and the family are all in the auditorium watching the *final* dress rehearsal before the big event.

Mix and Match are a bag of nerves. Bridget is closer to the panic-stricken girl of the midnight visit. Even Michael has been seen to sweat.

Competition. That's what I hate about all this. It's sort of false.

Still, I suppose you get heard, and 300 million individuals will certainly hear my shitty song tonight.

I've sat down next to Sophie.

'Dad?'

'Yes, daughter?'

'This is boring, isn't it?'

'Do you think so?'

She's nodding.

'I think it's a bit crap, isn't it, Daddy?'

I'm laughing.

Out of the mouths of babes . . .

8.10pm.

It's finally here. We've kicked off.

We're in the green room, a large backstage area filled with circular tables. The first song is about to be performed.

Everyone is ready. As ready as they'll ever be.

Make-up is applied, voices are warmed, any alcoholic or illegal substances that were necessary to still the monster nerves that are so large as to be almost tangible have been consumed.

Now we wait. A considerable time, as a matter of fact.

Mix and Match go on about halfway through the running order. Not as beneficial as going on last out of the zillion-and-one entries, one feels, but at least we haven't had to open the ruddy show. That honour has befallen the Greeks, and bloody good luck to them, too.

It's just finished, actually.

'That was a funny song, wasn't it, Daddy? I don't think that will win, do you, Daddy?'

'Sssh, Sophie. Keep your voice down. All these people in the room with us are in the competition.'

'Can't I say what I think, then, Dad?'

'Sssh! Yes, but you'll have to whisper in my ear.'

'All right, Daddy.'

She's putting her mouth next to my ear.

'THAT WAS RUBBISH, WASN'T IT, DADDY?' she's shouted.

'Yes, Sophie,' I'm whispering, as I laugh.

I had to fight to bring Sophie in here with me. It's against the rules. Only those directly involved, musicians, composers, et cetera.

But Sophie wanted to come and . . . who am I kidding?

I wanted her here.

To keep me sane.

These little films shown between songs really are the living end.

Swiss bimbettes are taken fishing for mackerel, an Italian stallion is forced to drink Guinness after a trip to the brewery. His speech, in Italian, said it was nectar, while his face and stomach were clearly trying to determine who was trying to poison him.

The best 'Postcard' so far?

The French girl, Françoise.

Everything about her screams sophistication. A class act, sex on legs. So, what do they do with her?

They give her a touch of Irish culinary expertise. Boiled bacon, cabbage and potatoes.

They slap this slop down in front of her, the smell of salt and cabbage assaulting her cute little nose, which visibly wrinkled in displeasure. She tasted it and grimaced.

Got to admire her, though. At least she didn't pretend it was delicious, in the name of *détente*—or votes.

I've just watched her song and it was good. The audience loved her.

She's entered the room and is receiving congratulations from fellow performers as she makes her way to the French table.

I'm standing up as she's passing. I'm offering my congratulations. She has a gloriously deep husky voice and has bent down to talk to Sophie. I'm trying not to look down the front of her dress but it is requiring extraordinary will-power.

She's waving goodbye.

'That lady talks funny, doesn't she, Daddy?'

'Sounded pretty good to me, Sophie.'

'Dad?'

She's beckoning me.

It's time for her verdict.

'I THINK THAT WAS PRETTY COOL, DON'T YOU, DAD?'

My ear is ringing.

I just nod in agreement.

Music should be about notes. In other words, in a competition like this, melody should be all. Having said that, am I the only one who gets up and puts the kettle on when a song is sung in Croatian, or Hebrew or Dutch?

Unless it's being sung by a swarthy, good-looking hunk of a man, or a girl in the briefest of skirts, of course.

How does that affect the voting, I wonder.

We shall see.

They're on, Mix and Match.

I'm cuddling Sophie. She's riveted.

Shit, I feel sick.

I'm disappointed.

They were OK, don't get me wrong, but they've been better.

They were scared and the harmonies were a bit off, Bridget's voice a little strained.

Damn!

Oh, well, it doesn't matter. We've come this far.

'What did you think, Sophie?'

She's holding onto my ear now. 'I THINK WE WAS PRETTY GOOD, DAD.'

Oh, well, maybe it wasn't as bad as I thought.

The band have just shuffled back to join us at our table. I have champagne for all.

'Well bloody done! Everyone grab a glass. Sophie and I thank you, Ireland thanks you. Now, have a few drinks and relax. There's nothing to do now but panic and you might as well be comfortable while you do it.'

Bridget's beaming.

'Well, let's hope we have all the luck, then. Cheers.'

I don't think we have a prayer.

They're about to vote.

They're calling up the first jury now.

Greece, I think.

Sophie, who has been bored out of her box ever since Mix and Match finished playing, has fallen asleep across two chairs.

She tried to stay awake for the voting—'That's the exciting bit, isn't it, Daddy?'—but she didn't quite make it.

We've got a six. Not a winning start, but not bad.

The French girl got a whopping ten.

Clearly a male-dominated jury, the Greek panel.

About ten countries have voted.

We've had two tens and a few mid-scores.

The French appear to be romping home at the moment.

Cyprus and Greece have given each other top marks, surprise, surprise. Neither voted for Turkey. The politics involved is unbelievable.

YES! YES! YES!

We've just been given our first maximum score. Twelve lovely points from the Swedish jury.

When you get a maximum vote the camera pans your table. Bridget actually just gave a thumbs-up sign.

How bloody naff!

I can't believe someone I know did that.

I've warned everyone that if we get another twelve I'm going to moon.

Ireland have just given the United Kingdom *twelve* points.

How bloody ironical. Ireland never give the English any points!

OK, I confess, I may have watched this a few times. You know, when I've come home from the pub. In fact, when I first arrived in Ireland I remember joking about this with Michael. I can hear myself saying how annoyed I was that every year, without fail, we'd traditionally give Ireland ten or twelve points and in return the Irish jury gave us bugger all. 'That's because your songs are crap,' I think he said. 'That's beside the bloody point,' I replied. 'Since when has the voting in the *Eurovision*

Song Contest had anything to do with the songs?'

Judging by what I'm witnessing tonight, I had a point here.

A maximum score has brought the UK right into the reckoning. They're in second place now.

I'm superstitiously reticent to mention this, but we're third. Eight points off the lead.

The French are still in front.

I'm getting caught up in all this and I hate myself for it.

It's bloody exciting, though!

We've just scored another maximum.

THANK YOU, NORWAY!

Wonderful country. Won't have a word said against it.

A second little moment to cherish.

I wish I could see into the auditorium, just for Gina's reaction.

The English have just given us four points!! I ask you! Can you believe it? Four measly, stingy points. The miserable buggers! Now I know why I left. You just can't rely on the Brits any more.

Sophie's woken up.

Probably because of me leaping up and down and shouting expletives. I've got me a few frosty looks from round about as well.

I think some people thought it was not in keeping with the spirit of the competition.

There's just one vote to go and . . .

We're leading!!

My heart is pounding, my nerves are in sodding tatters.

The French have just had four zeros in a row and it led to a bit of a charge from behind. By my calculations, even allowing for the fact that my grasp of maths is elementary in the extreme, I think we would have to be given less than five points for anyone to catch us. If that happened, then any one of the three or four countries behind us could win.

They've gone to the last jury now. I'm hanging onto poor Sophie for dear life. She can't move, poor love. If she does, I might fall over.

It'll take three minutes and feel like thirty years.

One point to . . . Bosnia and Herzegovina!

For crying out loud, who can remember that song? The jury foreman just wanted to prove he could pronounce it, surely?

Four points to Germany, well, there's proof there's no accounting for taste.

Five to France, looked a winner earlier on—obviously fewer red-blooded males dominating the last juries.

We can't get less than five now.

Six to . . .

I can't listen. I can't watch.

I've put my head in my hands.

'Are you all right, Daddy?'

'Yes,' I'm reassuring her, if in somewhat muffled tones.

Seven to . . .

I can't believe it.

Too fantastic to believe.

A duck. A blank, balls-all, zero, zilch, nixie, strike, a big fat nothing!

Who did it? Which jury was it? What bastard gave us nothing?

And you want to know something worse?

The English have won it.

The fucking English have won!

Katrina and the Waves.

The same joker that gave us nothing gave them twelve.

We've come second, for what it's worth. Which is sod all.

Can you imagine the reaction!

The Irish entry written by an Englishman loses to his native country.

Oh, the bloody shame!

Why couldn't Switzerland have won it?

Bridget is in floods of tears and I don't blame her. We were so close. Michael's hugging her.

'We didn't win, did we, Daddy?'

Sophie's standing in front of me. The look of disappointment on her little face is ten times more painful than losing.

'No, darling, we didn't.'

'Doesn't matter, really, does it, Dad?'

'No.' I'm giving her a cuddle.

It does matter, a lot.

Who remembers who came second in the *Eurovision Song Contest*? No one rushes a contract under the nose of the runners up. Second prize means a ticket back to obscurity.

For me, it may just mean the end.

I'm finished.

It's finally brought it home to me, this night. My career was all over long before I came to Ireland. Tonight, my ambitions, my fantasies, my desires have all died.

I'm too old and too tired to keep them any more.

So what's left?

My children.

I'll return to my kids, whom I love.

There's a big thrash organised. Lots of bigwigs, a celebration of the event.

I don't want to go.

I can see the winners reprising their song on the monitor.

I want out of here. I need to find Gina and take Sophie back to the hotel. I want to knock on Noreen's door and go in and take a peek at my sleeping Nicola.

That's where I want to be. With my family. It's where I belong.

I want out of this shit. It's not real.

I accept it may have been different if I had won.

But I didn't.

END OF MAY 1998. A year on. 11.30am.

I suppose you could call this an epilogue.

The thing is . . . I've had a resurrection.

At the moment I'm in my music room, where I write my songs.

Songs I am now *paid* to write.

Briefly, it went like this:

The people of Ballinkilty were wonderful when we returned from Dublin after the competition. Big parties! Rivers of alcohol. You would never have believed we hadn't won.

And some guy from EMI Records saw the *Eurovision*, plus the preview interview with me on the BBC.

He liked me.

He also liked Bridget.

Alas, he hated Mix and Match.

He insisted they were ditched. Michael and she have parted. It's tough but it's the price of fame. She's left town and moved to London to be a star.

Anyway, the bigwig from EMI asked me to write a follow-up single for her. The record was banged out quickly to cash in on the relative success of 'When Cultures Clash' and it worked. A ballad this time, called 'You'. It got a lot of airplay and charted at number fifteen. I was then commissioned to write an album for her, which will be recorded in September at the Abbey Road Studios. John, Paul, George, Ringo and now Andy . . .

Bliss!

Next, I was flown over to London for a meeting with the bigwig and asked to write more songs on a freelance basis, for a variety of new artists in the EMI stable. I spent a whole week being introduced to groups, boy-bands and solo female artists. I left London completely dizzy with it all.

I'm now so busy I spend most of the time chasing my own tail and am in danger of disappearing up my own backside.

So officially I became a successful rock'n'roller just before I turned forty and, unofficially, became an old fart.

I can't tell you how important that was to me.

Financially things are ace! I'm now the main breadwinner. Lordy, lordy, who'd have believed it! Our house is being tarted up to within an inch of its life, as Gina relishes spending my money. I was even offered a bigger room to work in, on the back of my burgeoning success, but I've stuck with the old one. It feels sort of comfortable.

Speaking of my lovely wife, after years of fantasising about it, I've at last been able to make one of her dreams come true. My new-found income has enabled Gina to leave the magazine to look after her children. I've also paid for her to take a course in massage and aromatherapy. Twice a week strangers are to be found wandering round our house wearing a towel and sometimes nothing at all, which is a bonus, as her clients are mostly women. The place smells like an exotic knocking shop. Heaven knows what the town thinks is going on out here, but Gina is extraordinarily happy and that's fantastic.

Our relationship has never been better, apart from one slight problem: the kids.

I just can't stop being possessive about the children.

I've spent so long looking after them that every time I hear Nicola cry or Sophie shout I fly from my music room to find out what the problem is. I have become Gina's worst nightmare.

Trouble is, I'd like total control. I'd like to be able to have both my children and my career in just the right fractions to suit my needs.

Maybe I had a sort of mental sex-change when I became a house husband and I'll never be the same again.

So, I've booked us a holiday. Hired a villa in the sun for the whole of

August. Fuck the world! I'm going to spend a month making love to Gina, chucking Sophie in the sea, wrestling with Nicola and generally spoiling them rotten. After all . . .

'DADA!'

Two-year-old Nicola has just fallen through the door.

'I'm sorry, Andy. She's so quick. Are we disturbing you?' Gina asks, as she sweeps Nicola up into her arms.

'No, it's OK.'

The door swings open again.

'Er . . . Dad?'

'Yes, Sophie.'

'You know . . . er, Dad?'

I'm smiling.

She has no reason for barging in, other than perhaps she saw Gina and Nicola do the same.

She's walking towards me.

'What's this one, Dad?'

She's twanging my guitar.

'That's a G-string, Sophie, and I don't want you to have anything to do with those until you're much, much older.'

It's getting a bit too busy in here.

'Now, come on, everyone. Daddy's got to work.'

The telephone is ringing.

'I'll get it, Daddy.'

'No, Sophie.'

'Dada, DADA!' Nicola shouts as she launches herself out of Gina's arms towards me, forcing me to catch her.

'Hello, who is it?' Sophie's speaking into the receiver, amidst the general chaos.

'Will I take her off you?' Gina's asking.

'Yes, yes. Fine.' Sophie continues her conversation on the phone.

Nicola is howling in temper as I pass her back to Gina.

'OK,' Sophie says, finally putting the receiver down, though thankfully not on the hook for a change.

'Who is it, Sophie?'

'Er . . . I forgot.'

'Oh, Sophie!' I say, as I struggle by her towards the phone.

'She's gotta funny name, Dad. Hedge, or Shrub, or—'

'Hello!' I'm barking down the phone, unable to wait any longer.

I can feel the colour draining from my face as I hear the voice on the other end of the line.

'Thank you, that's very kind of you to say so.'

Gina is mouthing, 'Who is it?' silently.

I move my mouth equally quietly to form the words . . .

'Kate Bush!'

'*Fucking hell!*' she mouths back at me.

'Well, at the risk of sounding like a mutual admiration society, I'm a long-term fan of *your* work too, Kate,' I'm telling her, as coolly as I can.

'What's she saying?' Gina is whispering to me.

'She says she's heard some of my songs and she likes my work,' I mouth.

'Well, that sounds like a wonderful idea. I'm very flattered,' I'm trying to say calmly, while punching the air with my fist.

'What? WHAT?' Gina's asking, at stage-whisper levels.

'She's recording. She wants me to go and work on a song with her.'

Gina's hugging me with excitement.

'When would you need me, Kate?' I'm asking, straining to hear her above Gina's muffled squeals and Sophie singing 'Puff The Magic Dragon' out of tune.

'Oh, I see,' I say flinching.

'Yeah, those dates are a bit of problem.'

'What? No! Tell her you'll be there! Tell her you'll be there!' Gina's whispering anxiously at me.

NO.

I've looked round the room at my family and I've decided.

'Kate, I'm sorry, but I'm snowed under at the moment. Look, see how you go with it. I'm actually at Abbey Road on another project in September, so . . .'

Gina has put Nicola on the floor and she has immediately toddled over to Sophie. They're now fighting over my guitar.

'Thanks, Kate. Yes, I'll let you know if there's any change.'

I've put the phone down.

'What! What's the problem?' Gina's asking.

'She's having trouble with a particular song and she wants me to try working on it with her.'

'So?'

'The problem is the dates. I'd have to go in August.'

'Oh,' Gina says, her shoulders sinking. 'Look, Andy, you *must* go, of course you must. We can always take another holiday.'

I'm so tempted. I mean. Kate Bush! But . . .

'No,' I say pulling Gina into my arms. 'She might still be working there in September. I may be able to do it then. Anyway, I'm looking forward to our holiday too much to cancel. Besides, Sophie's been packing for the last two months.'

'I haven't finished packing yet, you know, Dad,' Sophie informs me, temporarily breaking off her fight with Nicola.

I'm holding Gina close. 'What's working with Kate Bush compared to a holiday with you? I'm looking forward to sun, sand, sea . . . and sex,' I whisper the last into her ear and she giggles.

'I love you, Andy,' she tells me, and I hug her.

Sophie has grabbed hold of our legs and she's giggling too, trying to tickle us.

And Nicola?

Nicola has just hit me across the arse with my guitar.

OWEN WHITTAKER

When I set out to meet Owen Whittaker I felt I had a very good idea of what he would be like. Even though *The House Husband* is fiction and not biography, I was sure no man could write such a book without having experienced at first hand what it is like to bring up two young children virtually single-handed. Indeed, I bet myself that Owen would be just like Andy: very amusing, but tousled, slightly scruffy, and totally disorganised.

We arranged to meet at the George Hotel, Stamford, one of England's greatest coaching inns, and near to where Owen lives. The confident and extremely good-looking man I met there almost exploded my preconceptions—until he started to talk and display all Andy's warmth and humour. Indeed, with a pint of Guinness in front of him, ('the Murphy's is just not as good in England as it was in west Cork') and a cigar in hand, as he has just given up cigarettes, ('five weeks, six days, but I'm not counting!') Owen might have been Andy.

Owen started out wanting to be an actor and after leaving the Bristol Old Vic Theatre School, he became, as he describes it, 'commercials king', appearing in adverts for Flora margarine and for Nat West bank. He also starred in two television sitcoms, *Home James*, with Jim Davidson and *Hillary*, playing the son of the late Marti Caine. He also appeared in repertory and played Brad in *The Rocky Horror Show*. 'But by the time Harry was born, in the early 1990s, the recession was upon us and acting work just dried up,' he says with a shrug. 'It was an absolute financial disaster.' At that time, his wife became a full-time author and to reduce their financial problems, they moved to west Cork, Ireland, where creative artists such as

writers pay no tax. It was then that Owen became a house husband looking after Harry and, later, daughter Isabella. 'It's not an experience I would have missed out on for the world,' he says in retrospect. 'Yes, I made mistakes like putting nappies on too tight so legs turned blue, putting Windowlene in the washing machine, stuff like that. But the hardest part, for me, was that people judge you by what you do, and then by what you earn and as a house husband nobody knew quite where to put me. When I went into the pub it was like that scene in *An American Werewolf in London* when everyone stops talking and stares at the newcomers. And then my friends would ask me if I wanted a pint or a Campari and soda? I wasn't even welcome at toddler groups as the women there wanted an hour or so to slag off their men. I was in limbo!'

In order to raise his self-esteem Owen opted to try his hand at writing a novel, the subject of which was never in doubt: the whole extraordinary experience of being a house husband. According to the author, the novel virtually wrote itself overnight.

Although Owen and his wife are now divorced, he still plays a very proactive role in his children's lives. As we sit chatting after lunch, he suddenly looks at his watch and says, 'Goodness, is that the time? I must go and pick the kids up from school.' No longer a full-time house husband but definitely a loving, dedicated father and a novelist to watch.

Jane Eastgate

PICTURE CREDITS: COVER: Gettyone Stone. Anna Maxted photograph: David Harrison. Joanna Trollope photograph: Paul Massey/Frank Spooner Pictures. GETTING OVER IT: pages 6 & 7: Gettyone Stone; page 175: David Harrison. MARRYING THE MISTRESS: pages 176 & 177: Jenny Wheatley; page 327: Paul Massey/Frank Spooner Pictures. THE HOUSE HUSBAND: pages 328 & 329 and decorations: Ingela Peterson/The Organisation.

Printed and bound by Maury Imprimeur SA, Malesherbes, France

601-007-2